HORSE
HEALER

THE
HORSE
HEALER

a novel

Gonzalo Giner

Translated by Adrian West

Grupo Planeta

Originally published in Spain as *El sanador de caballos*

Translated from Spanish by Adrian West

Copyright © 2008 by Grupo Planeta

English translation copyright © 2015 by Adrian West

Cover design by Mauricio Díaz

978-1-4976-9755-3

Grupo Planeta
Avenida Diagonal 662-664
08034 Barcelona
www.planeta.es

Distributed by Open Road Integrated Media, Inc.
345 Hudson Street
New York, NY 10014
www.openroadmedia.com

Dedicated to the love of my life, Pilar

THE
HORSE
HEALER

PART I

Borderlands

In 1195, in the vicinity of Alarcos, the troops of the Almohad caliph Abu Yusuf ben Yaqub al-Mansur had just faced off against those of Alfonso VIII of Castile. Defeated, the Christian monarch manages to flee Toledo in extremis. From that day forward, he will be tormented by this humiliation.

I.

They had been born and taught to kill.

They called them Imesebelen, the bridegrooms.

They were African warriors with black skin, fanatical and fierce assassins, chosen from childhood to become the guardians of the caliphate of Al-Andalus.

For them, there was no greater honor than to die in its defense.

In Alarcos that day, the earth shook beneath the gallop of their horses. There were more than a thousand of them, and they galloped as fast as wind. They were following the trail of their Christian enemy with a single object in mind: his extermination.

The orders given by their superior still rang out in their ears, that extraordinary person with the noble name, long allied to the king of Castile, and now become his vicious betrayer.

"Decapitate them all! Burn their fields and pillage their possessions. Take their women and destroy their houses. . . . But remember, above all, that not a single witness should be left alive."

"And, Father, if we do not win this war? We live too close to the border of Al-Andalus, and they could attack us. . . ." Young Diego, very astute, hastened to the bed where his father was recovering.

"That won't happen, son. The Order of Calatrava will protect us; remember that we are their vassals."

"And if they can't? What should we do then, Father?"

Don Marcelo remained silent and looked at him. He was as uneasy as his son, but he could not allow himself to burden the other with his worries. In the present situation, he tried to tell himself that when the time came, the knights of Calatrava would defend them, because if not . . . if not, he couldn't protect his own, and Diego, only fourteen years of age, was too young to defend the inn and all the family.

Don Marcelo could feel the charge of the Imesebelen. Terrifying words of the brutality of those African warriors had spread through the inn. His thoughts led him to shiver, but he did not want to buckle before his fears or convey the smallest bit of cowardice to his son. To the contrary, at that moment, he wished with all his might to inspire that young man with all the bravery and security he was going to need.

"Come closer to me."

Don Marcelo took the boy's hands and noted his disquiet.

"I trust you, son, and I know that if something happens, you will do what is right. Don't worry; everything will turn out fine. You'll push on ahead. You're intelligent, strong-willed, and a good son besides. But now, listen to me well because I have to ask you for something important." He breathed in and continued talking in a more solemn tone. "Swear to me you will do it, no matter what, even if you don't understand. . . . Will you?"

"As you wish, Father," Diego said, concentrating on his words, aware of their significance.

The man pulled the boy's hand to his heart.

"Nothing bad will happen to us, but if something does, if for some reason the Muslims attack and we are separated, if I cannot be at your side, I want you to know that, as the only male in the family, you will inherit this humble inn and the pact that binds us to the Order of Calatrava. But that is not my will."

Diego looked at him, confused.

"I don't want you to end up being a vassal like myself. . . . No. You will take your sisters and you will look for work far from here, in Toledo, perhaps, that's the nearest city. If you content yourself with following my example, you will never fully become a man. Dream high and fly like the eagles. That's what you should do, to reach life's highest peaks. Look for wise people, learn from them. Cleave to your ambitions, so long as you hurt no one. Always do your work well, never give anyone reason to rebuke you. And whatever the contest, play to win. Don't let anybody make you their vassal, and even if you were born into a humble home, don't think you're any less dignified for it. If you fight with valor, you will achieve whatever you go after. And last of all, take care of your sisters, protect them, your blood runs in their veins. . . . My son, never forget you had a father who loved you more than anything in the world, and who will one day look down on you from heaven full of pride."

"I don't want to leave your side, Father," Diego protested. "We could make improvements to the inn and the stables as well—"

Don Marcelo stopped him short.

"Swear to me that when the time comes, you will do what I have asked!"

The boy looked into his eyes and immediately understood what his answer had to be.

"You have my word, Father."

"Then it's done, and we needn't talk about it anymore." He stroked his son's chin. "Now go back to the stables and carry on with your chores."

"Father, when will I have to leave?"

"You'll know in due time, son. Don't ever forget what I've told you to do, and consider it a sacred duty." The boy nodded his head. "And never, ever forget your sisters."

"I promise to protect them."

II.

————————

Don Marcelo was lord of a very modest inn near the hamlet of Malagón, on the shores of the Great Lake, lying along the route that joined Toledo to Al-Andalus. Through its possession, he incurred a small tribute to the monks of Calatrava as a part of the terms of his vassalage, and yet he was always one or two months in arrears.

Before taking up that occupation, if that's what it could be called, he had been a pastor, blacksmith, day laborer, and farmhand. A long life of work and dedication that, in his case, could be portrayed in just two words: sweat and penury.

Three years back, he had watched his wife die in the inn, and he had been bedbound for the last two, victim of fevers that had left him paralyzed.

Since then, his four children had taken charge of the inn. Belinda, Blanca, and Estela shared the kitchen work, took care of the diners, and the cleaning up; Diego, the lone male, worked in the stables, in the smithy, and at the old mill. The boy had learned to make horseshoes with his father and also to care for the beasts. He adored them with such a passion that he said he could anticipate their reactions and always knew what they were thinking.

The three girls were red-haired like their mother. But Diego's hair was black and stiff like Don Marcelo's.

Estela, though she was a year younger than her brother, was his truest ally. With freckled skin and an upturned nose, she was always smiling and was the most cheerful of them all.

Belinda, on the other hand, was pure nervousness. She was easily intimidated and had the capacity to pass her anxiousness on to everyone in her vicinity. She lived obsessed by cleanliness and order, and as a consequence, suffered when her siblings did not do things as she wished. She was also a screamer and angered very easily. But all her severity vanished when you looked into those deep blue eyes, which she had inherited from her mother, that were incapable of transmitting anything but kindness. Then, no one could resist her will. Her gaze exercised an almost magical charm.

About Blanca, the middle daughter, her father said that she had inherited her mother's character and her sense of sacrifice, but especially her sweetness.

Business at the inn had never gone well. Not even in peacetime—when the way between Toledo and Calatrava was still open—did many travelers stop there to rest. They went to another inn, a few leagues away, which was famed for its cooking. In any case, since the first rumors of war had begun to be heard, they only received the occasional visit from a straggling soldier or some of the few neighbors who went on living in that small village. And to make their already desperate financial straits worse, the troops who had recently passed through the inn had left without paying, claiming they had a right to dine there for free.

Don Marcelo, who was in charge of the accounts, was used to seeing little money in the strongbox, though he never thought the situation could grow as bad as it had over the past few months.

On that hot day, in the middle of the afternoon, shortly after hearing the seven tolls of the bell from the neighboring church of Malagón, the tavern, which scarcely ever held more than a half-dozen patrons, was witness to a very grave occurrence.

Estela and Blanca were waiting on the guests, and Belinda was in the kitchen preparing supper. Outside the main building, in the stable, Diego was brushing Sabba, his sorrel-colored Arabian mare.

And it was then that he arrived.

A soldier, coated in dust and sweat, his eyes bulging from their sockets and his hair matted and filthy, entered the tavern in a rush. He bumped against a table, pushed two chairs out of his way, and nearly fainting, he gave out a strident cry. Everyone present looked at him in huddled silence. The man, badly injured and exhausted, fell over one of the tables with three arrows plunged in his back.

"Imesebelen!" he shouted, spent. "They're here. Flee!" As soon as he had finished his phrase, he gave a piercing cry.

No news could be worse. The presence of the Africans could only mean that their enemies, the Almohads, had won the battle. They were known for being ruthless murderers. A terrible fear gripped everyone, sinking down into their entrails. They understood that no one and nothing could free them from the danger and savagery. By now, their defenders, the Cala-travans, would be retreating or else dead.

As if chased by the devil, all the guests abandoned the posada in terror, leaving faces fraught with panic and frailty behind them.

Blanca ran to the stables to warn her brother of the danger. Estela stayed back with the wounded man. She didn't know what to do. Her family couldn't escape. Her father was infirm; it was nearly impossible to move him from the bed, let alone get him into a carriage to escape.

She went over to the man on the table and looked into his eyes. Death was marauding through his pupils.

"Tell us how close they are, please. . . . "

The man clutched at her arms as though trying to find the hope there of somehow clinging to a life that was draining away.

"There's no more time. . . . They attacked me," he answered her in a whisper. "They had black skin . . . and they rode on white coursers. I thought they were the sons of the devil himself. . . ."

Estela tried to break free, but the man's calloused hands seemed to have melted into her arms. The girl screamed as loud as she could.

Belinda heard Estela cry out and ran from the kitchen to defend her. She tried to snatch her from his arms, using the knife she carried in her hands.

"Let her go!" she said, showing him the blade of steel. "If you don't, we'll all die. You were very generous, coming here to warn us of the danger; now continue to be so, I beg you . . ."

The dying man focused on her eyes, and they seemed to him like the gates of heaven. He also looked at Estela and saw in her the living image of horror.

"Go with God, both of you!" In the agony of death, he let the girl free.

At that moment, the other two siblings ran in.

"I've just readied the horses for the cart," Diego calmly announced. "As soon as we bring Father down, we can leave."

A disturbing ringing of bells warned them that the danger was immi-nent. There was no more time. They went up to the second floor and into their father's bedroom. Without knowing what had happened, the man had glimpsed the gravity of the situation, and though they explained to him the cause of it and what they planned to do, he refused to come with them. He would only slow them down, and they would run a greater risk of being captured.

"I refuse to leave my house behind," Don Marcelo said, clutching the sheets with force. "I lived here with your mother, and I witnessed all of you being born here. You all run, save yourselves. I order you! I'm not going."

The three daughters prepared everything for their escape, trying to ignore their father's words. Belinda, Estela, and Blanca went from one end of the room to the other, picking up the few things they might need.

Don Marcelo shouted, and for a moment, everything stopped.

"I told you to get out, and to carry on without me!"

"But we can't do that, Father. Either we go together or we stay together," said Belinda, the oldest child, sternly.

The father pinned Diego with his eyes, and his son understood the message. It related to what they had talked about only a few hours before. From that moment, Diego felt that the responsibility of taking charge of the family's destiny had fallen on his shoulders.

The boy came over to his father, kissed his forehead respectfully and sorrowfully.

"Obey Father's will and come with me. We don't have more time. Fast! Let's go, now!"

Diego remained strong in spite of his sisters' refusal. He pressed the two younger ones, hoping to receive the support of the elder.

"It's fine, let's go," Belinda said, coming down from the bed and pulling at her two sisters. Though it hurt her to say these words, she knew it was the right decision.

With nearly no time to mourn, unable to react to all that was happening to them, the girls took leave of their father. They kissed his cheeks, his hands; they didn't know how to tell him good-bye. But he pushed them so they would leave as soon as possible.

Then they all fell quiet, hearing shouts and the sound of horses approaching the inn.

"Get out now!" the father screamed, enraged.

The four children went down the stairs tumbling one against the other, and when they'd made it out of the house, they rushed to the stables. A cart waited for them there, hitched to two nervous horses ready to set off quickly on their journey away. Diego helped his three sisters get in. Once he was in the coachman's seat, with Belinda at his side, the boy snapped the reins over the animals' flanks and they responded by setting off at a ferocious trot.

After they had gone only a few yards, amid the crack of the road against the horse's hooves, Diego heard a high-pitched whinnying behind him. He turned and saw his mare, Sabba. She ran behind them like a lightning bolt, slicing through the air. Her tensed body and her determined look made her the most beautiful animal in the world. That mare had come into his life shortly after his mother had died, to help him overcome his deep sadness. Don Marcelo had paid a great deal for her, and yet he never rued doing so once he had seen them together.

Diego shouted her name and Sabba sped up more until she came up alongside the cart. The mare snorted with pleasure when her master reached out to stroke her head. Her eyes showed loyalty, but also fear.

"Poor Sabba . . . I forgot you."

His words made him think of his father. With a wounded heart, he looked at his older sister, he begged her pardon, passed her the reins, and in one leap bounded onto Sabba's back.

"I have to help Father . . . !" he shouted while he watched them speed on. "Don't stop for anything until you get to Toledo. When I can, I'll come look for you. Go, don't turn back. We'll see each other again in Toledo."

III.

When he arrived at the inn, Diego tied Sabba up in the stable and ran toward the house. When he entered the bedroom, Don Marcelo broke into recriminations, accusing him of betraying his word.

He sat up, very angrily, trying to see his daughters through one of the windows, but his body was dead weight, and he couldn't reach it.

"Go back with them now! If they die, it will be your fault," the man yelled hotly, in a way Diego had never seen before.

Abashed by his mistake, the boy decided to go back and look for them, but he stopped when he heard voices outside and cast a questioning glance at his father.

"There's a crossbow in the trunk; bring it to me! You take the sword, and when you can, go back for them. Understand me: I don't need you. . . ."

When Diego went for the weapons, he was able to make out the carriage and the four horseman riding alongside it, on the verge of reaching it. They were far, very far, but he could see how one of them was trying to take the reins and how Belinda was striking back at him bravely. Then the girl struck the horses, to make them run faster, but her pursuers did the same and quickly covered the distance between them.

One of them was brandishing a terrifying sword and was very close to catching them. And it was then when he saw the glimmer of steel falling hellishly over his sister's arms and saw how the man hacked away at them.

Diego was breathless. He couldn't react. He listened to his father scream at him, but the sound was distant from him. His attention was hypnotized by the scene that his eyes could never again unsee. He never imagined he could witness something so terrible. But still, seconds later, he had to watch as the horseman stopped the two horses and brought the cart quickly to a halt. Diego felt his muscles stiffen and lose sensation. He felt the absence of air when his father asked him what was happening. He couldn't talk.

At that moment, more soldiers had reached the roadway and held down his two younger sisters, covering their mouths to silence their screams. Belinda was shoved brutally from the cart and lay there outstretched on the ground. One of the black-skinned horsemen grabbed her by her hair, so forcefully it twisted her neck, and screamed something at the other sisters that Diego couldn't make out. In a mere instant, Diego saw the shimmer of a dagger that sliced through the air and plunged into Belinda's body with devilish coldness. His sister, his beloved older sister, collapsed over the earth. She fell like a dead body while he could do nothing but look on.

The killer jumped into the driver's seat and took the reins. Blanca and Estela were thrown over the haunches of the two horses and landed at their captors' feet. They turned the cart around and headed toward the south. Just three-quarters of a league afterward, they overtook the hill, shrouded in a cloud of dust.

He was going to speak when he heard steps once again, this time on the stairs. He threw the crossbow to his father and hid, sword in hand, behind the door. He felt his heart pounding, and a cold sweat dripped down his neck. He asked himself if he would be brave enough to face them.

By the sound of the steps, it was clear there were two of them.

Diego nudged the door with his right arm to surprise the first person who came in with his sword. He squeezed it with all his might, preparing himself to pierce a coat of chain mail if necessary. He heard one of them breathing and poised for attack.

He looked at his father.

He had the crossbow aimed in the same direction. And when Diego saw the first shadow cross the door, and his sword began to travel through the air, a shout stopped him.

"Hold back, son! They're from our side."

Two knights of Calatrava appeared in the doorway bearing two heavy blades. The tension of the past few hours was legible on their faces.

"Are you the innkeeper?"

"Yes, I am."

"We've come with orders to help you flee, just as our brothers are doing in all the other villages. We have to get away immediately," he continued, his voice faltering. "They're close on our heels."

The one who looked older tried to help Don Marcelo get out of the bed, but he refused.

"You saw your sisters in danger, right, Diego?"

The boy nodded, full of anguish, without daring to recount what had happened.

The knights were watching but didn't understand what lay behind those words.

"Run and help my daughters," he said to the Calatravans. "Something has happened to them and they've tried to get away. They need you more than I do. Go fast, before it's too late."

The men looked at each other without being able to hide an expression of absolute disagreement. That was going to complicate their task. They were knights, and they couldn't abandon a defenseless man, but they also did not wish to leave women in danger.

They decided to split up and help both the father and the girls, but at that moment they heard a great rejoicing on the lower floor. They heard voices, crystal-clear, speaking in Arabic.

"They're already here!" One of the Calatravans looked out the window to see the location of the stables. He confirmed there was no danger in going to them. "We can hold off the first attack and maybe even the second, depending on the number of our enemies, but we won't hold out for much more."

"Tell me how I can help," Diego interrupted.

One of the knights gave him a severe look.

"When they get here, you jump out of this window," he said, pointing to it. "And then I want to see you run to the stables and get on a horse. Once you do it, ride off, and don't let it stop until you're far away from here. You should head north."

"I won't obey you!" he responded.

"My son . . ." Don Marcelo struggled, enraged amid the sheets, and pierced the boy with his gaze. "You've already made one mistake! Don't do it again."

"But, Father, how can I abandon you?" Diego ran up to the bed.

"You disobeyed me and now your three sisters are in danger. It's time you do what you're told for once! Listen to the man!"

"They're coming up!" The Calatravans stood one on each side of the door.

"Run, now!"

One last look full of pain, full of love, between the boy and his father before madness struck. Three men with black complexions, turbans, and flamboyant uniforms gave off loud cries, shaking Diego from his stupor. The first clashes of the swords, the enraged faces of the Christians, his father's entreaties—maybe all of it together filled him with confusion as he stood beside the window. He jumped and rolled over the earth. Then he ran and ran. The stables seemed farther away than normal. He found his mare, who was nervous and trying to tear herself loose. To save time, he jumped on her without saddling her and grabbed hold of her mane, weaving it between his fingers.

"Get me out of here, Sabba," he whispered in her ear. "Fly . . . and don't stop until I tell you."

The mare headed toward the wooden doorway and when she'd stepped out of the stable, she flew into a gallop, leaving behind twenty soldiers who were snooping around the area of the inn, looking for more Christian victims. Just as quickly, three of them hopped on their horses to pursue him. Diego, almost falling over his mare's neck, spoke to her gently, encouraging her to show the power her breed was known for, the strength of her noble blood. He needed her to outrun his enemies.

Going over a low promontory, in shock, he found his sister Belinda's body. He saw it from afar and felt the sting of powerlessness. He knew he couldn't stop. When he looked back, he saw a thirst for death that infused the faces of those who stalked him, the fury of their horses, and the danger in their intentions.

He came within a few feet of her. Her face showed a terrible, bottomless fear. Her body was covered in blood and her nails were digging into the earth, as though by holding on to it, she could hold on to life as well.

Still at a gallop, without ceasing to look at her, Diego understood what his obligation was, remembering the promises he'd made his father, and he decided to go help his other sisters. Sabba, disciplined, noticed the slight pressure of his knee in her left ribs and changed direction.

Hundreds of pebbles flew up from her hooves, even more so when she understood her master's wishes. In fact, he scarcely had to guide her; she herself chose the route. She stayed clear of the rockier areas that would slow her down and sped up over the smooth, sandy plains.

On reaching an elevation, Diego looked back, thinking he had put some distance between himself and his attackers. But it wasn't so. One of the men, perhaps with a stronger horse, was coming up on him with hellish speed.

Diego spoke to Sabba again, asking her to run harder, to give it everything she had. And she did it, without knowing where such energy came from. She galloped tirelessly southward, ignoring the strain of it, measuring neither time nor distance.

After making sure he'd been able to leave his attackers behind, he came up to a tortuous mountain pass. There, in the deepest part of a narrow gulch, he found the cart, but not his sisters.

A large group of soldiers, black skinned like the others, were seated on blankets, passing around a variety of objects. It seemed they had stopped to gloat over the spoils of war.

The camp consisted of a single, fairly small tent, round and vivid red in color.

Diego dismounted from Sabba, told her to keep quiet, and crouched behind an enormous boulder, studying how to make his approach.

He spied ten women tied together close to a fire. His sisters weren't there.

When twilight fell, white-faced men began to leave from the tent, dressed in their battle clothes with shields, turbans, and leather helmets. One of them was dragging Blanca by her hair while she kicked and screamed. Behind her, in the hands of a taller man, was her sister Estela. Her skirt was shredded and her shirt torn and hanging open. The scoundrel was dragging her by the wrist as if she were an animal he had hunted and killed.

Diego breathed rapidly, imagining with dread what must have happened to them. When he saw the man with Estela, he noticed an unmistakable particularity in his face. A scar ran across his forehead, from one end to the other. But something else called his attention as well: both in his dress and in other aspects, he seemed to be a Christian soldier and not a Saracen.

He sat up to see him better, and it was then that the man, turning his head and looking in the same direction, revealed his face in full. Diego memorized it. He saw how Estela hit him and how her captor, enraged, slapped her face. And suddenly the black guard looked up to where Diego was. There was no chance to hide. Had he seen him? Diego doubted it.

He heard horses approaching and realized he couldn't risk waiting if they were coming from those who had chased him before. Aware that alone, he could do nothing, he thought of the Calatravans; they could help him.

He mounted Sabba and decided to turn back toward the inn. At his orders, the mare flew off, pushed ahead by the fury of the deserts that coursed through her veins. The wind blew away her sweat and the earth seemed to press her ahead. The animal was compressing all the strength of her breed in that dazzling getaway. And in that way, they distanced themselves from the area, so much so that she began to gain confidence and to slow down to a soft trot. A little later, once again close to the inn, Diego studied the situation with extreme care, making sure that nobody was lurking around.

Soon he found Belinda's stretched-out body, but she was not alone.

Vultures were tearing at her clothing and her flesh. He prodded Sabba to frighten them off, holding back his urge to vomit. It took various attempts before he managed to run them off, and afterward, he got off the horse to embrace her. He squeezed her in his arms, telling her he loved her, screaming into the air so all the world would know of her misfortune. But he refused to look at her; what he held in his arms was not his sister anymore.

He raised up and hopped back onto Sabba's flanks. With Belinda's mutilated cadaver, he headed toward the inn with no idea of what else he would find there. When he arrived, he left the mare tied to a tree and looked for the entrance. He crossed through the dining room. Everything was quiet and disordered. Nothing indicated the presence of another soul. He climbed up to the second floor and found the two dead Calatravans. The bed was empty and the sheets scattered on the floor, blotched with blood. Diego looked for his father among the three other bodies lying on the floor, but none of them was him. Unsettled, he couldn't figure out what had happened.

He went downstairs to look for some clue but could find nothing inside the house. He went outside, and when he turned toward the stables, he stopped short.

There he was, in a horrendous pose. Diego's pulse began racing and he ran over to his father. They had thrown him out the window, and his head was cocked at an impossible angle.

Diego wept for him, bit his lips, felt a hate inside himself he'd never known before. And there, crouching down at the side of his father's body, he remained, without knowing how many hours might have passed. Drowning in agony and fear, his mind had fogged over, as though he was living in an all-encompassing nightmare with no exit.

The coolness of the afternoon finally pulled him from his delirium. He had to think of what to do with those dead bodies. He grabbed his father by the ankles and pulled, dragging him over the ground, unable to look at him and horrified by what he was doing.

He looked for Sabba. The mare recoiled nervously on seeing them appear and Belinda's body tumbled to the ground. Diego, panting, laid his father beside Belinda while he cried disconsolately. He thought of where to bury them and looked around. He remembered the two knights. He knew he couldn't dig four graves and he thought of burying them in the same pit. But when he saw the lake, another idea occurred to him.

With Sabba's help he took them all to the edge of the shore and tied heavy stones to them. Afterward, out in the water, he sank the two brave men, saying prayers for them.

When Diego saw his father's and sister's faces disappear in the cloudy water, his soul was torn in two. Only a few hours separated him from his previous happiness, normality, his life together with his family, the beings he loved more than anything. And now, his father and his sister were sunk in the lake and Blanca and Estela victims of a cruel destiny.

Everything he was—his family, his roots—everything had been devastated at the hands of those barbarians whom he now hated down to the very depths of his soul.

His father's final rebuke resounded in his mind. His disobedience had brought about his older sister's horrid death and the kidnapping of the other two.

"I made a mistake," he repeated over and over, crying without respite. "I beg the forgiveness of God, of the heavens, of everyone . . ."

With his feelings on edge as he traveled to Toledo where he would look for help in rescuing his sisters, Diego slowed Sabba down, almost stopping her. He turned back. It was almost night.

His gaze turned southward, toward nothing in particular.

At fourteen years of age, without family, without money, abandoned to an uncertain future, he felt lost. He had the feeling he had lost his past forever.

And there, trailed by a cool westerly breeze, surrounded by the aroma of broom and with his mare, Sabba, as a witness, he swore out loud he would avenge his people's deaths.

One day, he would defeat the Imesebelen.

IV.

Toledo didn't want them.

The doors to the city were closed by order of the bailiff, who was alarmed by the massive numbers of country people coming from the south.

An endless line of carts had blocked the bridges over the Tagus River as well as the other roads into the city and its outskirts.

The authorities had tried to convince people to set up camp in the royal gardens, the Huerta del Rey, to the north, over a broad field bordered by the river, which the king himself had placed at their disposal, but nobody obeyed. To the contrary, the embittered masses began to respond with sticks and stones, and they menacingly waved their rakes and pitchforks.

Thousands of throats shouted, indignant, complaining of their rejection. Voices of farm workers and commoners, men and women turned out of their houses by war, still terrified, thinking the enemy was at their back.

Never before had Toledo been witness to so much desperation in one place, nor to such a clamor.

Diego had arrived at dawn, protected by a large caravan, and now he found himself trapped between the entrance of the bridge of Alcántara, pushed by a furious sea of men and beasts, carriages and freight.

On the way, he found out that the caliph's troops had taken all the land stretching from Malagón to the Guadiana River. The place where his family's inn had stood no longer belonged to the kingdom of Castile. The situation was so dangerous there that to turn back could only be called suicide, not valor. Those he talked to assured him he would find no one willing to help him find his sisters and that he would die if he attempted to turn back.

With the memory of his disgrace still fresh before him, and the contagious nervousness all around, he sensed the proximity of disaster as he stood there on the bridge. Sabba did as well. She shook her head tensely and tried to find an opening amid the multitude. Diego began to scream at the people around him, pressuring them to step aside. Fearing they would be trampled, some let them through, glancing at Diego and Sabba with jealousy and rage.

And all of a sudden, a mounting racket drowned out the din of the people. Thousands of women, filled with tenacity and rage and weary of so much disdain, began beating their pots and pans and all sorts of other objects against the stones of the bridge. That penetrating noise became lodged in the stones of the city walls themselves, as well as in the consciousness of those who had barred the people entry, and began to echo in their ears.

Sabba, terrified, reared up angrily and lifted her forelegs, at last making an opening. Horse and rider managed to escape from the lunacy just in time to avoid the frightful wave of panic that swept through the crowd right afterward.

Someone shouted that the Saracens were coming and that word coursed through the procession of the displaced like a terrible wind. Such terror arose that the people made a mad dash for the city walls. Some, in despair, jumped from the bridge into the river. Others leapt over the crowd, until others pulled them down and, finally, they were trampled. The horses kicked and bucked around them. Many women, arduously carrying their children, fell to the ground and disappeared amid the hysterical multitude. Those who were closest to the gates were crushed against them, and even still, they weren't opened.

Luckily Diego had managed to make it onto a hill from which he could see the profusion of jagged stone that bore up the city of Toledo, three of its four sides protected by the jagged cliffs leading down to the river. From there he could also see the frightened multitude. The people massed together flowed over the bridges then pressed themselves into the gates of the city amid wails and howls. The air shattered before them and panic descended upon everyone.

When they figured out the warning had been false, a chorus of grief and sorrow shuddered through the scene before him. The carts were piled with bodies and the atmosphere was dense with an extraordinary grief. Little by little, as the hours passed, the refugees dwindled away and they began to be seen again at the Huerta del Rey.

Diego remained still, standing before the city with his soul in torment. The memories of his previous trip to Toledo made him forget the enormity of the experience he'd just lived through for a moment.

He had gone with his father three years ago, when Don Marcelo's terrible illness was only beginning. There had been a few severe but inconsistent fevers that would sometimes cause him to lose consciousness. Then there were the spasms, and immobility in his arms. The village barber declared it beyond his abilities and counseled Diego and his sisters to take their father to the offices of a famous surgeon in Toledo, a Hebrew of great fame and hands of gold.

As he gazed now at the city's profile, Diego had no problem making out the Jewish quarter, the *aljama*; it was an enclosed area, walled in on the eastern side. He remembered its tortuous alleys leading up to the house of Josef Alfakhar. He was a scrawny person of wizened aspect, old, with a cultured way of speaking, graceful manners, and a sharp gaze. Diego could still remember the intense aroma that infused everything there and the image of flasks of herbs and colored powders extending far and wide over the walls of his office.

When after a long examination the surgeon explained what Don Marcelo had and what the cause was, Diego had understood nothing. Nor, when they had returned to the inn, did his father seem to accept the explanation of an excessive concentration of black bile.

The strong impression that the bustling city had made on him, back then when the biggest place he'd been was the village of Malagón, resounded in Diego's memory as well. He remembered Toledo's huge churches, the richly scented quarter where thousands of Muslims, who were called *mudéjars* or "accepted ones," still lived. He was charmed by their markets, their many colors. He was astonished when he saw houses with more than two floors, magnificent palaces protected by armed guards, and especially when he saw the streets, lined with so many kinds of shops and businesses.

A neigh of warning brought Diego back to reality. A group of young people were coming toward them. There must have been ten. Diego sensed something strange and was on guard.

"That's a precious nag you have. . . ."

The one who spoke had an ugly scar on his forehead and was missing hair on part of his head.

"What do you want from me?"

Without answering, four of them surrounded him and the others charged with the idea of stealing the animal. Diego rammed Sabba against them, sure of winning. The mare responded energetically and with two strikes of her hooves, she had gotten free of them. Still, one managed to dodge her and grabbed onto her mane, while another took her by the tail.

"Now we've got her," they both shouted together.

At that moment, the others leapt on Sabba and tried to immobilize her, but the animal wouldn't allow it. She struck the ones who flanked her with her rump and kicked without mercy at those behind her. She got away from them one by one, kicking at their thighs or knees. And once out of danger, as soon as she could, she hurried downhill until she arrived at a leafy forest where she and Diego were out of view.

Shortly afterward, the pair found a large clearing thick with green grass. When she saw it, Sabba began to eat.

Seeing her so happy, Diego stroked her and realized she had eaten nothing for the past two days apart from a half-dozen bitter plums while they were traveling.

He didn't have money, nor anything that he could sell. He had fled so quickly, with so few resources, that he had not even a saddle or stirrups. There was nothing he could exchange for food. Just a bridle.

When Sabba was done feeding, they made off toward a group of houses toward the east in search of provisions. There was a garden there and a number of fruit trees.

When they hadn't yet passed the first, two crude-looking men came out onto the path.

"What do you want?" one of them, the fatter of the two, screamed. Diego saw him wave a wooden rod, but in spite of this violent gesture, he approached him.

"Answer the question!" the other one shrieked, a toothless man in his sixties. "Tell us what you're here after or you're going to have a big problem on your hands."

"I had to escape from the Imesebelen, and I just arrived in Toledo."

"And you're hungry . . . for sure," the first one interrupted him. "And when you passed by here you asked yourself if we'd have something to give you, maybe in exchange for work. Right?"

"Yes. You've got a good eye."

"Well, go back the way you came, and run if you don't want all your bones broken."

"But what did I do to you all?" Diego pulled Sabba back, letting her know of his intentions.

"You haven't done anything because we haven't let you. . . . Others have already come through with the same thing in mind and they've robbed us of all our fruit and vegetables."

Diego made Sabba turn around and squeezed his knees into her sides. The animal burst into a trot, taking them away from those men.

"We'll kill whoever steps onto our land! Tell everyone!"

Rather dispirited, Diego came across several groups of refugees, but none of them seemed ready to share their food. The women looked at him suspiciously and the men sent him away, some casting insults and stones.

After numerous leagues riding slowly around the outskirts of Toledo, when night had begun to fall, Diego realized that nobody was going to do anything for him. They had tried to rob him and fight him, and the reality was, he felt treated worse than a stray dog.

He passed that first night without being able to sleep, watching over Sabba, because he was afraid someone would steal her.

Nor did he eat anything the next day until night had nearly fallen. Every time they came across an encampment, he would look through the rubbish furtively, trying to find a little bit of cast-off food. Only in one did he find a few chicken bones, and in others, a few apple skins that he chewed slowly, savoring them, as though they were manna from heaven.

Increasingly desperate, he decided to try his luck on another farm. He found one isolated on a hill; it looked abandoned, but a delicious scent filtered from it.

The only thing he had to sell was Sabba's bridle. He would exchange it for dinner if they wouldn't accept his labor.

"You'll see how our luck is going to start to change. . . ." he told Sabba.

The mare responded with a neigh and a shake of her head, as though she understood.

The ramshackle dwelling had a small garden on one side and a neglected stable on the other. As he faced the door, Diego thought it would fall to pieces if he knocked too hard. He was bowed over, just like the walls in the humble adobe façade.

At that moment, a delicious aroma of stew reached him and his stomach burned with hunger.

The first two times he struck the wood, nobody responded; it was only with the third that a woman appeared, as filthy as she was indifferent, ugly, and haggard."We don't pass out alms here!"

She was going to shut the door in his face and yet something made her change her mind. She began to scrutinize him from head to toe, as though he reminded her of someone. Her eyes traveled over his face, his neck and ears, and then his skin, his height. . . . Seeing him so thin, for a moment she almost seemed to pity him, but then, without knowing why, she decided to carry on and sent him away.

"Wait, lady! If you help me, I'll pay you."

That worked wonders. All of a sudden her eyes began to sparkle, and a fake welcoming air came over her face.

"Well, come in then, boy!" She opened the door and stepped aside to let him through.

Diego took the bridle from Sabba and felt nauseated as he entered. A mixed scent of cats and urine impregnated the interior. He counted some twenty cats of different colors and ages scattered around the modest dwelling. Some stared at him, without showing much interest.

The woman walked toward the stove and began to stir a cauldron. Diego didn't manage to see what it was.

"Ma'am, I won't beat around the bush. I'm hungry, and when I smelled your stew . . ."

He took the bridle from his coat and showed it to her.

"I'll give you this piece of excellent leather. It's got fine embossing and it's barely been used. At the least it's worth ten denarii."

The woman grimaced—she'd imagined she would see cash—but in an instant, she had snatched the bridle away. She assayed its quality and, between her teeth, uttered the words: "It'll do."

She grabbed her skirt to wipe out an earthenware bowl and filled it with the contents of the pot, then she left it atop a table beside the fire. Diego pushed a stool over and sat down to eat eagerly.

"You're not eating?"

"I will later, when my son comes home."

Generous chunks of meat and lots of vegetables floated in the dense broth. Despite the bad impression the place had given him at first, this had convinced him: Finally, he had made a good decision.

"It's very tasty," he said, wetting a piece of black bread and gulping it down with delight. "What does your son do?"

The women grunted.

"You talk too much! I've never liked people who carry on asking one thing after another, I don't like that, not at all." She waved her arms to emphasize her point.

"Sorry. I wasn't trying to bother you."

Diego thought that perhaps she was mad, and he turned his attention to the meal he was savoring.

"My son is a menial," she announced.

Recalling her previous reaction, Diego doubted whether he should ask what exactly her son's job consisted of. She guessed what he was thinking and explained.

"He has a donkey that he loads with clay pots. He fills them with water in the river and then he sells it through the streets of the city." She waved her filthy rag demonstratively, as though it were a fine silken cloth. She covered her face with it, in imitation of a noblewoman. "The ladies he serves are so delicate, they can't even go down to the river to get their own water."

"That's better for your son's business."

In a flash, Diego had an idea that gave him hope.

"Where can someone buy those clay pots?" The job seemed simple and Sabba was far stronger than any donkey.

The woman leaned into his back so that he felt her breath on the nape of his neck. She was checking to see how much of his meal he had left. Her presence annoyed him, but Diego's hunger took priority over any discomfort, and he concentrated again on his stew, sopping up the very last drops with his bread.

"No one can sell water without permits, and it's been years since they've issued any. There's no room for any more commerce here!" With obvious rage, she spit into the fire.

Diego understood the woman's motives and decided to find out about purchasing pots elsewhere. He showed her his empty bowl in case she might fill it up again.

"You pay me with some filthy old leather and to top it off, you come back for seconds." She gave an exaggerated laugh. "Go on, get out, or you really will make me angry."

She cleared off the table, taking the empty bowl, and looked at him shamelessly, waiting for him to stand. Diego got up and left the house. He untied Sabba, secreting away a leather cord with which he could rig up another bridle.

When he was about to leave, with the aftertaste of the food still in his mouth, he turned back to her.

"One last question." The woman looked at him displeased. "Was that a rabbit stew?"

She smiled maliciously.

"Good lord, no. . . . It was cat." She drew her eyes together in a feline manner. "Tender, savory, homemade cat." She laughed immoderately.

Diego felt a jab of nausea. He pressed his knees into Sabba's ribs and they trotted away from that hellhole. He felt so ill that before they'd even covered half a league, he was overcome by the need to stop and vomit. He did it three times in total.

In the course of the next few hours, he wandered through the outskirts of the city, not knowing where to go. He felt a stirring in his entrails, almost a revolt, and every few minutes there came a sharp pain in his abdomen that hardly let him breathe.

When night fell, he approached the riverbanks in the Huerta del Rey. Many of the refugees had gathered there.

He chose a tree-lined bend, isolated from the meadow where hundreds of people had set fires and were sharing their misfortune.

There he stretched out at the feet of an old holly oak and drank fresh water. Sabba found abundant grass nearby and set to feeding tranquilly.

At midnight, Diego began to feel hot and to shake terribly. Worried and in pain, he crouched under the tree and his thoughts began to fly, like a fleeting mirage, to happier moments in his life.

The following hours were passed between dreams and convulsions. Once in a while, he would wake up in distress and when he opened his eyes, he would notice they were hot and swollen. It took a long time, but at last he fell into a deep sleep.

"How bad he smells! How disgusting!"

The shouts of children awakened him.

When he opened his eyes, he saw the face of a woman and two children who could not keep quiet. It was already day. The sun heated up his face. He asked himself how long he had been sleeping.

"Who are you? What's happened to me?" An acid odor filled his nostrils in a gust. He touched his tunic and notices it was wet and sticky.

"You've been throwing up all night. You were lucky my children found you. You were very sick . . ." The woman brought over a sage tea to help him recover. "Drink this; it will help with the nausea. It tastes bad, but it will do your body good."

That concoction was as bitter as it was sickening, but it worked its powers and soon he began to feel better. He looked for Sabba, but he didn't see her. He whistled twice to call her, but he heard nothing, neither footfalls nor a single neigh.

"Has someone seen my horse?" A black thought clouded his gaze.

The woman shook her head.

One of the boys remembered something.

"Last night we saw some men grappling with one; they dragged it away by force. It was cinnamon colored, with white spots on its head and breast. . . . It was a little before we found you."

Diego shivered with fear, because they had just described Sabba. She'd been stolen.

Queasy, with burning lips, he sat up and turned his back to them.

"I need to be alone, I beg you. . . ."

The woman took her children and looked at him with pity just before she left. He shook uncontrollably and seemed wounded and fragile. She felt miserable for him.

Hours later, he could be heard by many of the people camped out in the Huerta del Rey. A rending cry crossed the river and the treetops. It also pierced many of the people's hearts.

"Sabba!"

V.

They all wanted to be with the redheads.

Blanca and Estela were huddled in one of the five tents their captors had raised to shelter themselves from the terrible storm. It was night, and it wouldn't stop raining. They had been with those men for several days and they still didn't know what would happen to them. Estela, the youngest, was sure that they'd only been captured to intimidate the Christians and that sooner or later they'd be set free. Blanca, seeing what they'd done to Belinda and how they treated the other women who had been with them a long time, did not wish to make any prediction about their future and just stayed quiet and observed.

Suddenly, the sisters heard various voices on the other side of the canvas, a great uproar, as though they were arguing.

"What are they saying, Blanca? I can't see them, I don't understand." Estela started shaking and took shelter in her sister's arms.

"You have to be strong, Estela. . . . Don't think about them; remember the inn and think of something that used to make you happy there and try to go back to it now."

Blanca tried to comfort her sister, to soften the situation that they were living through, but even if she tried to show calm, in her face you could see a grimace of terror.

"What's going to happen to us, Blanca? What's going to happen to us?"

Blanca caressed Estela's hair and saw a deep worry in her eyes.

"I'll always stay by your side. I'll protect you."

Soon one of the warriors lifted the canvas and stumbled in. Another did the same behind him, slapped the nape of his neck, and took a number of playing cards from his hand. He made a half turn and pointed at them, smiling, before he left. In horror, Blanca deduced what they were playing for, and that the first man had won. She quickly jumped in front of Estela to hide her with her body.

The man came close to her, whispering in that language she didn't know. Blanca could understand nothing, and that made everything worse.

The soldier came right up to her face. She held his gaze coldly; she wanted to attract his eyes so that this animal would not even for a moment notice her sister, who was hidden behind her. Blanca could feel his respiration, his nauseating breath, his incomprehensible whispers . . . And then, she felt how a hand pulled her shirt open and stroked one of her breasts. Blanca shook, but she didn't say anything; she didn't even try to move, because she didn't want Estela to have any idea of what was happening. She raised her head, stiffened her body, and pushed out her breasts so he would choose her.

And he did. He chose Blanca. The girl felt enormous disgust when he kissed her on the lips. He smelled worse than an animal.

The soldier took off his sweat-soaked vest and undid Blanca's shirt with the intention of indulging his lascivious intentions. But to her misfortune, Estela let a hiccup escape her, and that was enough to attract his attention. He pushed Blanca aside in one go and found Estela hunched over, her face hidden between her knees.

Suddenly Blanca leapt on him like a madwoman, biting his back, clawing him all over. The man turned in self-defense and managed to get hold of her neck. He squeezed until she was choking and screamed at her. Blanca stopped kicking when she could no longer breathe and she felt herself dying. She remained still and looked at him pleadingly, making him see that she was on the verge of death and that she'd given up. An then he let her go, gasping from tension, her cheeks red with rage.

Blanca remained still, filled her lungs with air, and let herself be taken. Inflamed with passion, the man stripped her bare quickly and took possession of her body with great violence.

Meanwhile, Estela, frightened, moaned in a corner. In whispers, she began to pray, asking for God's assistance. She was trembling with panic. She remembered Belinda's horrifying murder. And she cried for her father, imagining an identical destiny for him. And she thought of Diego: What could have happened to him?

"Out of the tent!" That harsh voice drew everyone's attention. He spoke first in Romanic and then in Arabic. It was the man with the scar.

The warrior pulled away from Blanca and left the tent running; there was no need for him to hear a second time.

Blanca ran to her sister and covered her as much as she could. They looked at the man. He was tall and strong.

"My name is Pedro de Mora, and I'm Castilian, like all of you. . . ."

"I beg you then, don't let this go on." Blanca spoke to him as if she might be able to win him to her side.

"I'll try to make it so. . . . Don't worry."

The man, with a neatly trimmed beard and a cold gaze, kept silent as he paced around them, studying them. Blanca began to rub her hands into her face, trying to wipe away the scent or any other memory of that brutal individual. When he passed by Estela, he grabbed a lock of her curly hair and admired its softness. He also smelled it. He stroked her cheek slyly and looked into her eyes.

Blanca, afraid of his intentions, stood up, naked, to attract him.

"She's only thirteen."

Don Pedro paid her no attention and stretched his hand to Estela. In her language, and in a polite tone, he said: "Please come with me, little girl."

VI.

___

The first week was very hard for Diego.

He strolled, aimless and desperate, through the outskirts of Toledo and asked everyone he came across about Sabba. He explained to them that he couldn't go looking for his sisters without her and the locals looked at him with compassion; the lands he spoke of had passed into Muslim hands and to go there would take daring. Since it was an obligation, Diego focused on the search for Sabba until finding his mare became an obsession for him.

Diego looked closely at all the horses that came across his path. He would run after any cinnamon-colored mare, and when he reached her, he would look for the same white spots that his had on her breast and forehead.

He lived in great poverty, because he had decided hunger was not one of his most urgent necessities. Finding Sabba was more important.

At night, he slept in a rock grotto under the city walls. It wasn't very deep or comfortable, but it was dry and he could cry there without anyone bothering him. He had found it by chance one morning while he was chasing after a rat. Lacking anything else to eat, he found its meat fairly agreeable, though a little tough.

During those days, the authorities had arranged for a transport north of the multitude of refugees who were pounding on the gates of the city. With the promise of a tract of land, they had managed to convince everyone who was willing to start a new life elsewhere to move to the south of the Duero River, in what were known as the repopulation zones. Once the outskirts were cleared out, the gates of Toledo were reopened and the city's life resumed its accustomed rhythm.

Diego would spend the whole day seated at the gate of Alcántara, the most heavily trafficked one, observing every animal that entered or exited.

He was surprised by the immense quantity of people that passed through every day, and how different they all were. Friars in black habits and others in white; Jews with their pointed caps; noblemen and knights with their pages and beautiful consorts; vendors from all the Christian kingdoms, Frenchmen, Germans, and Normans. He never could have imagined so many people talking in so many languages!

The cobblestone trembled when a number of enormous carriages passed by, some pulled by as many as six oxen. They were transporting great blocks of granite or thick logs that would serve as beams in the roofs and walls. Others were bearing pigs, lambs, ducks. Still others carted wool and colored silks.

One morning, almost at dawn, Diego saw a rather old pastor appear with around a hundred sheep. Two dogs and his crook helped him to direct them to the gate that Diego watched over so jealously. But when they arrived, they stopped short, refusing to take even another step. The old man, exasperated, screamed and provoked his dogs. They barked and nipped at the sheep's heels, but the animals simply pressed together and none of them would dare to take the first step.

Diego stood up and raised his voice over the racket of their bleats.

"Can I help you?"

"Grab one by the foot and drag it through the gate. The others will follow," the man answered.

Diego managed to grab one with his first attempt. His strength overcame its resistance, and, pushing and shoving, he maneuvered it through the archway. Its companions in the flock observed nervously, perhaps afraid, but they bleated happily when it escaped from Diego's hands and trotted happily back to them.

With an irritated gesture, Diego lurched to grab another one. The animals were jittery, moving around him like a whirlpool, pushing him and kicking against him at every opportunity. Amid more bleating and protests he dragged a larger one up to the same point, and without letting her go, he waited until the others took an interest in what was happening. Some made a decision and the others followed in their wake. A wave of wool almost dragged him off, but he smiled happily. He had done it.

"Good job, son," the pastor said, clapping him on the back.

Diego accepted his praise thankfully.

"It's nothing," he said, shrugging it off.

"Why are you not at the big market?"

The old man looked aside at his flock, which had, however, come to a halt at a plaza near the gate.

"What market?"

"You don't know the Zocodover? It's the most important in all the Trasierra,[1] if not in all of Castile. It's happening today, just like every first Friday of every month. That's where I'm taking my sheep. I want to sell them."

"Do they sell horses, too?"

"Of course! The most beautiful specimens you can imagine, especially Arabian ones. You'll see the bidding going as high as two hundred *sueldos* for the best ones."

It could have been a sign from heaven or just a presentiment, but Diego decided to go to the market immediately.

"Can I come with you?"

Boy and pastor left the former palace of the caliphs and the Frankish quarter behind them. An enormous uproar animated the streets. People complained as they passed. Some scrubbed the caked-on dirt from their clothes onto the filthy animals' woolen coats, others screamed out profanities when they accidentally stepped in the excrement the sheep left behind them.

When they entered the market of Zocodover, Diego was mesmerized. Never before had he heard such a chorus, a mix of men and animals, nor had such aromas ever risen to his nose all at once. An immense cloud of dust engulfed that unique spectacle of fervid activity.

He took leave of the pastor once he found out he could see the horses on the eastern side of the plaza.

To make his way through that crowd he had to have sharp senses and pay extra attention. It was hard for him to stay the course, since the mass moved from one side to the other, deciding his steps for him. He was pushed until he finally ran into the hindquarters of an ox. Beside him, he heard two men arguing in Arabic, haggling over a leather moneybag full of coins. The language produced such displeasure for him that he ran away in dread. He turned back to look at them, full of rancor, about to fall on top of a small woman walking with a bent back and two small nanny goats under her arms. A few steps later, a man screamed at him, so close to his ear that he needed a moment to recover. With pushes, shoves, and more than one elbow, Diego opened a path leading to where the horses were bought and sold.

The animals were kept in a fenced-off area with makeshift pens. People crowded in to make deals, to find out prices, and to look at the beautiful

---

1   The Trasierra is an old term for the lands lying between the mountain ranges of the Sistema Central and Andalusia. [Author's Note]

examples on display, of course. The numerous interested people made it difficult for Diego to see more than ten or twelve horses, though there must have been five hundred or more there.

"I don't remember ever seeing as little movement as there is today," Diego heard an old man say to another in a conversation.

"It's because of the war," his companion remarked. "This week nothing's come in from Al-Andalus, and what's here isn't the best quality. They say a lot of the animals are from the refugees."

"Excuse me for interrupting," Diego said, and the two men turned toward him. One kicked, thinking he was a thief. Diego dodged as well as he could and then asked their pardon again, hoping to win their confidence.

"I just wanted to ask you something."

"Then be fast and don't bother us anymore."

"Do you know if any of these traders have Arabian horses as their specialty?"

Diego looked awful. His hair was dirty and matted. His clothing smelled and if his skin was already olive colored by nature, it was now so filthy it looked nearly black.

"Where are you from?"

"Malagón."

"We believe you, but if you had said Marrakesh, we might have believed that too." One of the old men grabbed his arm and saw how thin the boy was. Diego was used to hearing these kinds of comments in the inn.

"If you keep going along the fence, you'll find a guy from Jerez," the other interrupted. "You'll recognize him by his bald head, his long red goatee, and a gold ring he has in his nose. He's the best vendor of that type of horse, though not the only one. Try and talk to him, but the way you look, I doubt he'll pay you any mind."

Diego thanked them and followed the direction they had pointed out, not ceasing to observe all the other horses as he passed them. As much as he could, he sifted through the flood of animals and customers, and when at last he found the man, a mix of hope and despair made him hold his breath.

The man from Jerez was brushing a precious stud, black, with a pure Arabian profile. A girl came up to him with a wheelbarrow of oats that she wheeled along unsteadily. She arrived at the horse trader at the same time as the boy.

"I'm Diego," he said from behind the fence, hoping to get the older man's attention.

"I'm Kabirma. Allah be praised for all time," the man answered, without even turning his head.

He was Muslim, like the men who had killed Belinda and his father. Diego stayed there silent, staring at him. The girl observed him and said something in a low voice. Diego couldn't manage to hear her. He would need to overcome his impulse to reject this man and ask about his mare.

"Could you help me?"

"Sure. What?" The man still kept his back to Diego.

"If you had a completely unique mare, of an excellent breed, perfect, bursting with desert blood, who would you turn to?"

That seemed to interest the trader, who finally turned around. But when he saw the boy, his attitude changed straightaway.

"Get out of here, you dirty beggar!" He threw a wooden brush at Diego so forcefully it split his brow. He realized he'd been wounded when the blood began to drip down.

"Father! You hurt him. . . ."

"If he hadn't come around bothering people . . ." He spit at the ground with pure bitterness and without an ounce of remorse.

The girl's eyes looked at Diego with pity.

"A few days ago they stole my mare . . ."

"So you're accusing me of dealing in stolen animals?" The bald head and the face of that gigantic man grew red with rage. "If you don't get out of my sight, you'll have more than your eyebrow split open." Now he threatened him with an iron bar.

"Let him talk, Papa," the girl interrupted. This Kabirma turned back to the stud horse and brushed his forehead energetically. The animal responded by sniffing at his hand.

"She was a sorrel mare, a perfect example of her breed, four years old, cinnamon colored," Diego went on. "She has two white spots, one between her ears and one at the base of her breast."

The man cleared his throat three times in a row, and his daughter did not overlook it. Diego hushed in the vague hope that he had told the man enough.

"I've heard you and I don't have anything to say."

Diego had the sense he was hiding something.

"You haven't seen her?"

"Get out!" he growled, enraged.

Diego pulled away, afraid of getting hit again, and walked off with a bowed head.

He meandered through the rest of the stalls and asked at every one. The ones who didn't insult him sent him away disrespectfully. He wandered for hours through that madhouse. He looked everywhere but never saw anything. He stumbled between the people, running into them, pushed by one after the other until he fell on the ground a number of times. He looked like a drunk, but it wasn't wine, but rather the enormity of his despair that made him act that way. Almost at dusk, he looked at his feet. Several of his toes were poking out from his shoes and they hurt from so much walking. He had nowhere to go and no reason to live.

"Come with me." A hand grabbed his shirt and pulled on it. Turning around, he saw the girl's face, the daughter of the man from Jerez.

"Where?" Diego looked disconcerted. His chin and legs shook from pure weakness. His need to eat had grown to ravenous proportions.

"I'm taking you to Galib's house."

"Galib?"

"He's the most famous albéitar in the city," the girl explained. "He's the one who bought your horse."

Diego's face lit up, and his eyes, and his smile.

"Don't think ill of my father. He has a harsh character, but he's a good man. Some men sold him your horse a few days back, and of course he had no idea it was stolen."

"Does he know what you're doing now?"

"No."

"Why are you helping me?"

She didn't answer. A chance bump from an old woman helped her to avoid doing so. In fact she didn't have any logical reason to help him. Maybe she felt regret, she wasn't sure, or maybe she was just letting herself go, acting on impulse. Feeling his gaze upon her, she only shrugged her shoulders.

"An albéitar . . ."[2] Diego said, thinking out loud. "I thought they only had those in Al-Andalus."

"The profession of albéitar is an old one in this city. It was practiced when this was still a Muslim realm, before it was conquered by the Christians. I believe that Galib escaped from Seville fleeing from the mad Almohads, and he had to start here from nothing and almost without means. Now it's said there exist no hands better than his when it comes to treating a sick horse. He's so wise that many doctors are envious of his knowledge of science, even if they don't share the same kind of patients."

"Is he Muslim as well?"

---

2   *Albéitar* is a term coming from Arabic, roughly equivalent to the English *farrier*. However, since frequent reference is made in the book to its Arabic origins, it has been left in the original here. [Translator's Note]

"Like me," the girl answered while she decided which street to take. "Around here they call us mudéjars, tolerated Muslims."

Diego again felt a deep rage, having to be faced with more Moors, but above all, he needed to get Sabba back.

The two youngsters headed south, toward the Muslim quarter. Before leaving the market square, the girl stopped at a stand where they were selling a kind of sweet called marzipan. She bought a half dozen and offered them to him, taking pity on him for his extreme gauntness. Diego barely stopped for a breath as he ate them and she explained to him that they were made with a paste of ground almonds, glazed with egg yolk, and then baked.

They crossed through a number of side streets full of luxurious shops selling silks, jewels, and marble from the Orient, objects of silver, fine hand-worked cordovan leather, and many weapons, particularly swords. These were adorned with beautiful filigree in gold over blue steel.

"This neighborhood is called La Alcaicería. They sell very valuable wares here, and for that reason, it is closed every night and watched over by fearsome armed guards."

After passing over a few more streets, they reached the Great Mosque and a madrassa where the Koran was studied.

From this point, they entered into the Muslim quarter proper.

"Where are you from?"

"From Malagón, a village to the south of Toledo."

"If you find your horse, will you go back there?"

"I can't," he answered brusquely.

"Why?"

"All those lands are now in the hands of the Almohads. I have no family left there. My father was killed, my older sister, too. And I lost my other two sisters. I don't know how to find them or even if they are still alive."

The girl felt shamed, but it seemed absurd to her to ask for forgiveness for the savage conduct of others who had nothing to do with her, and she preferred to simply offer her hospitality to the boy.

"My family and I live on the outskirts, close to the river, between the gardens they call al-Hufra and the road that leads to Mérida. We have a little house there and some stables where we keep the horses before we sell them. I'm in charge of caring for them. When we buy them, they've normally been neglected, and often they're starving. We don't put them up for sale until I've gotten them in better shape. If you'd like to go some time, you'll find me there."

"Or in the Zocodover."

"Of course, or in the market." She looked thoughtfully at the ground. "We're almost there."

They passed alongside a potter's workshop, and at the end of a narrow street they came to an imposing wooden door with a hinged opening in its center.

The girl beat energetically at the wood with a heavy doorknocker shaped like a horse's head. Almost immediately they heard the turning of a lock and there appeared an old man's face in the window, pudgy and rather dark, with a nose that bent extremely to the right.

"What you want?" His voice was deep, almost raspy. He seemed to be a foreigner.

"We're looking for Master Galib," the girl answered with a generous smile.

"He busy. No time for snot-nose kids. Me Sajjad and no like kids. Sajjad no want see you."

The children looked at each other, stunned by the man's strange way of speaking, while he shut the wooden panel abruptly.

The girl didn't accept his no and beat at the door more energetically than before, but she didn't receive any answer. After numerous attempts, it still wouldn't open again. All they could hear, once, off in the distance, was the sour voice of that individual telling them to go to hell.

"What do we do now?" Diego asked in desperation.

"I have to go. My father will be worried. But you wait here until Galib comes out. Sooner or later he'll have to, to visit one of his patients. Nearly thirty thousand souls live in Toledo, and though they pray to different gods, almost all have in common that they own a horse or a pack mule, or a few, in the case of those who work the land. Galib isn't the only albéitar who attends to all those animals, but he's the best. Be patient."

The girl could see the abandonment in the eyes of that young man who looked at her, begging for compassion. She came close to him and caressed the wound her father had given him.

"Diego, I have to leave you now. My name is Fatima. If you need me, you know where to find me. Wait for Galib. I have to go."

Fatima went off down the street, but before taking the first corner, she turned and smiled at the boy. She felt good for helping him. When she had left the narrow street behind her, she sped up her step, fearful of her father's reaction.

For the next hour, the door only opened to let out two women bearing clothes to be washed. But a little later, Diego heard the locks opening again and saw a man on horseback emerge. He must have been around forty, with a dense beard, very dark brown except for two pale strips of gray hair on either side of his chin. He was wearing a dark blue turban and a simple tunic of white cotton. His flared pants were the same color as the fabric covering his head.

"Señor Galib?"

The man sat up in his saddle and grabbed his riding crop when he saw a filthy beggar hanging from his reins.

"What are you after?" he said. The horse lurched nervously and bucked, trying to escape from that stranger.

"I'm trying to find my mare. Some men sold her a few days back, but she was mine. She's an Arabian mare, cinnamon colored, with two spots, very calm and very sweet. I'm sure she misses me. . . . Please, Señor Galib." He grasped the leather even tighter, running alongside the albéitar.

Apart from his raggedy appearance, Diego looked mad. His eyes gave off a strange anxiousness and he didn't provoke a feeling of trust.

The man looked at him, preoccupied, afraid the boy wanted to attack him.

"Leave me in peace!" Galib raised his voice and beat at the air with his riding crop, threatening to bring it down on the boy's skin.

"I won't let you go!" Diego shouted, pulling on the bridle with all his might.

The man dug his heels into the horse's ribs and the animal broke into a trot, pulling away from Diego and leaving him behind.

When Galib came back that night, the boy was still there. He had to show him the riding crop again and make the horse rear up before the boy would let him enter his house.

And so it went, every time he left or entered, for the following days.

With infinite patience and determination, Diego had decided not to leave that house until he had reached his objective: seeing Sabba again.

VII.

And there Diego was.

Every time the albéitar crossed the doorway of his dwelling, he found the insistent beggar lying prostrate. For days now, his voice raised, he had clamored over and over after that mare.

The boy had been steadily losing strength and composure. He could scarcely stand on his feet, but he kept on. From the fifth day, Galib no longer saw him stand, but the boy just went on calling out with his gaze.

Galib realized the boy would die before he left his house. It seemed he had nothing to lose, and nothing else to do either. When the first week was up, he could no longer resist, and before returning to his dwellings after a long day at work, he came over to talk to the boy.

"What's your name?"

Diego reached for his last bit of strength and jumped to his feet. At last, the man was paying him attention.

"Diego. Diego from Malagón."

"And the mare?"

"Sabba."

"A pretty name. It means 'east wind' in my language."

Galib observed the boy, who seemed to have nothing else to say. He recognized his stubbornness and after a long silence, he risked letting him enter.

They crossed a broad courtyard that opened onto a large stable to the left. They passed through a storage room and after that were a dozen stalls where the horses were kept. When they came to the last one, Galib made a motion with his finger.

"There you have her."

Diego pulled open a large lever and pushed at a low door. At that moment, his heart beat frantically. Sabba sat up upon seeing him and snorted with joy.

"Sabba, my Sabba . . ."

Diego embraced her neck and began to squeeze the base of her mane. What emerged from his mouth seemed more like faint moans than words. Then he came close to her nostrils and blew on them. The animal responded with a neigh of absolute contentment. He looked at her eyes, stroked her head and ears. The mare seemed to whisper to him, her murmurs like echoes, as though the two of them shared a secret language. Diego felt the animal's fidelity, its warmth, which had accompanied him for years. Sabba was more than a horse; she was his faithful companion, the creature that had remained by his side ever since the death of his mother.

Holding his breath, Galib observed the scene with trepidation. That astonishing relationship told him everything, conveyed everything.

"She's had a fever, right?"

"Do you think she has one now?" Galib answered, to test him.

Diego shook his head. He knelt and felt around in an area where the straw seemed damp, then sniffed his hand afterward.

"Then what makes you think she did have one?"

"Her breathing," Diego said without hesitation. "It's a little faster than normal, and her gaze isn't as clear as it is normally."

"Anything else?"

"Her urine smells different and her ears aren't cold, though they aren't hot, either."

Throughout his career, Galib had seen affectionate reactions on the part of animals toward their owners, sometimes even heroic ones, but never a loyalty and commitment such as that boy had for his mare, his willingness to die of hunger at the gates, staying there for more than a week. Maybe it was for that reason he began to see him with different eyes. He didn't know his story, but two things were clear: the boy was telling the truth when he said the animal was his, and he wasn't just some beggar.

Not knowing the man's thoughts, Diego eyed him cautiously.

Galib breathed twice and thought a bit more. He was a steady person and rarely let himself be carried away by impulse, but on this occasion he was going to. He felt compassion for the boy and wanted to help him.

"Boy, what do you know how to do?"

"I grew up at an inn, far from here, and I've always been around horses. I know how to shoe them and care for them." He clicked his tongue and Sabba responded by sniffing at the palm of his hand.

"This mare cost me one hundred forty *sueldos*. A high price, but I knew she was worth it from the beginning." Galib stroked her head. "Her blood is excellent and she might be the finest horse I have in my stables at present, but until I can make that money back . . ."

Diego distrusted the Muslim. He was neither very tall nor strong, but he seemed distinguished. His skin had begun to show the ravages of time and his few gray hairs gave him an air of wisdom, of gentlemanliness and of kindness. Still, Diego couldn't trust any son of Allah. He didn't like any of them, though the man's words and his appearance left him wordless.

"You know I can't pay you . . ."

"Then work for me. I need another stable boy, and it's a job you're well suited for. If you're in agreement, you can make two *sueldos* a week, though I will keep half of that to pay for the mare. You'll have food but no bed, because you're Christian and here in Toledo we're not permitted to sleep beneath the same roof. . . . Do you agree?"

Diego took a moment to respond. What was proposed seemed the best way out of his situation, but if he accepted, he feared he would be betraying the memory of his dead family members. His misfortunes had come at the hand of Muslims, and Galib was a Muslim as well. He had never imagined himself living close to them, listening to their prayers, eating off their plates. The idea didn't appeal to Diego at all, but then he remembered the oath he'd made to his father, when he'd asked the boy to flee from poverty however possible and fight for a better destiny without being defeated by adversity. He asked himself if this might not be a situation he should run from and imagined what his father would have said.

"I am grateful to you, yes."

Galib clapped him on the back and made as if to look for someone.

"Sajjad?" He raised his voice.

To Diego's displeasure, that man with the twisted nose, acid temperament, and strange manner of speaking limped forth, the man he had first met that day with Fatima.

"He's my stable keeper; you take orders from him. He's a good man and he has been with me for I don't know how many years."

Sajjad pulled a dopey grin.

"Master good with me." He grabbed Diego's tunic and pulled on it. "Follow now Sajjad. Sajjad will teach you."

The old man tried to take Diego to the kitchen to offer him some food, but the boy wasn't prepared to leave his mare even for a moment, so Sajjad had to bring him a bit of bread and cheese right into the stall. Diego sat down by Sabba's side, felt her heat, felt the cold of night, but was happy.

It was then that he saw her for the first time.

Her beauty was uncommon. Her name was Benazir and she was Galib's wife. When Diego saw her pass in front of the stables, he thought he'd never seen anything as beautiful as her.

Benazir was a daughter of the desert, born in the faraway lands of Persia. With the nomad blood that flowed through her veins, she possessed a savage and unpredictable side, though she was also warm and vulnerable, like someone who had breathed the winds of the Orient.

She had met Galib in Seville ten years before. Benazir was the daughter of the Persian ambassador, and when she fell in love with Galib, her father was in charge of the grandest breeding stable in the world, the Yeguada de Las Marismas. As property of the caliph, his five thousand or more horses of pure Arabian blood trotted freely over those marshlands near the mouth of the Guadalquivir River, a region of extraordinary beauty.

While Galib lived in Seville, the capital of the caliphate, he enjoyed an invaluable social standing. One night, during the events organized by the ambassador to welcome two of his colleagues, Galib met Benazir, and from that moment they fell hopelessly in love.

With the passage of time, he came to the conclusion that Benazir carried passion in her veins. She was warm and sensual, but also dangerous and indomitable. Galib came to understand that to love her, he had to learn the laws of the desert, to recognize their changing nature, and to never try to conquer her completely.

When Diego saw Benazir again, the next morning, as he began working, he understood immediately how much Galib must love her. Her mere presence exuded sensuality, and she was incredibly beautiful besides. She moved like the wind; at times smooth, at other times with strength and seductively, like a perfume that overcomes the senses. He was afraid of her without knowing why.

Sajjad, to the extent he was able to express himself, had ordered Diego to saddle the woman's mare and told him where to wait for her in the courtyard. He did so, and while he was adjusting the seat, he saw her appear.

She was dressed in all black, with an open tunic. Her hair was pulled into a single braid running down her back, as dark as it was silken. Her eyes, the color of honey, had an exceptional brilliance.

When their gazes crossed, she took a large veil that hung down from her head and covered her face with it.

"Good day, ma'am." Diego positioned some wooden steps at the animal's side and held the mare until Benazir had taken the reins, and he wished her a happy journey.

Behind him, Sajjad dealt him a resounding slap on the nape of his neck. "Diego respect mistress. Diego no talk if no master here."

The old man ran, limping, to the wooden portal and opened it partway. Benazir made the mare turn and moved toward the exit, but before she left, she looked back at Diego.

"Welcome to this house."

VIII.

S ajjad was a strange and unpredictable creature.

He could be joyous and kind, and the next moment irascible and grumpy.

For the first three weeks, Diego worked hard to finish quickly all the tasks that were assigned to him; he worked with enthusiasm to make sure that all of them were done well and on time.

He washed down the floors, scraped the filth from the walls, scrubbed the tools. Soon he had to clean the enormous stables of the most famed albéitar in the city. The interior was divided into twelve stalls where the sick horses were housed. And in a wing off to the side, at an angle to the main structure, were another five where the owners' horses were kept. It was in one of these that Sabba stayed.

Sajjad showed up from time to time to look over his work. If Diego heard the words *Sajjad happy*, then the man approved of his labors, but it wasn't always so; at times there would be a chorus of grimaces, shrieking, and reproving phrases like "No obey Sajjad. Diego bad and Sajjad talk to Galib."

The man was strange even when he was praying. He had a spot in the middle of his forehead, a bruise, actually, like a signal of his fervent religious identity. He recited his prayers on his knees, beating himself against the floor with incredible severity, and maybe for this reason, his prayers came out curt, the way that he spoke.

Sometimes Galib needed his help on some visit and Sajjad would go along happily. On his return, he would smile and repeat the same phrase over and over: "Sajjad serve good, help much."

Even if his mind was rather limited, he didn't seem like a dangerous person; on the contrary, Galib appreciated his loyalty. The truth was that when he got to know him, Diego forgave him nearly everything. But Sajjad had two bad habits that Diego came to detest: hitting him with a cane every time he found the boy stalled or resting, and snooping into everything he did, all of which he was sure to repeat sooner or later to Galib.

When they finished their interminable workdays, Diego would sit by his mare and talk with her. In their particular form of communicating, both understood each other and though Sajjad couldn't understand what the boy and the horse were doing, Diego wanted nothing more than to caress Sabba and let time pass.

One night, Sajjad saw that Diego hadn't left the stables. He was watching him without the boy realizing it, and when he noticed that the boy was taking shelter in the warmth of his mare and getting ready to sleep, he entered the stall, fighting mad, and began to scream: "No, no. Sajjad no let . . . sleep here no." He raised his voice so much that he alarmed everyone. "Be dangerous for master. . . ."

"It'll only be for tonight," Diego begged him. "Until I find somewhere else."

"Sajjad say no."

"What's going on?" The figure of the albéitar was reflected ominously in the shadow of the night. While Sajjad and Diego were arguing, they hadn't recognized that he was there, posted at the entrance, listening to them.

When Sajjad saw him, he tried to explain in their strange language that Diego wanted to stay there to sleep, but Galib did not let him speak.

"Diego, quickly, I have an emergency, and this time I need you to come with me. Go saddle my horse and your mare and we will leave as soon as possible."

Although Galib thanked him for his watchfulness, that was a tough blow for Sajjad, for he understood from that moment on, he would have to begin to share his work obligations and his master's favor with that mendicant who had sat begging in front of the door to the house only a few weeks before.

"If it's colic, like they've said, I'll need help, someone resolute and strong. My old Sajjad can't make those kinds of efforts anymore," Galib said to Diego when they set off.

The narrow streets of Old Toledo followed one after the other, without any apparent order, along with the steps of the nocturnal visitors, amid mist and impenetrable shadow. To keep from getting lost, Diego made Sabba walk just beside the hindquarters of the other horse. They had to make it quickly to the edge of the Jewish quarter as the order had come from the estate of the *almojarife,* the treasurer in charge of the finances of King Alfonso VIII. They galloped along and were hardly able to talk, but Diego tried to beg pardon for what had happened back at the stables.

"I know I can't stay and sleep, but some men threw me out of the cave where I pass the nights, on the outskirts of the city, and I didn't know where to go."

"You don't have a home? You don't have anyone to turn to?"

"No, master. My family and I lived in Malagón, but after the Battle of Alarcos, the Imesebelen killed my father and my older sister." Diego lowered his head under the enormous weight of his memories. "And they kidnapped my two younger sisters, too."

"What?"

"I had to flee my home and I don't know how to go back. My father . . . my father ordered me to escape with them, but I disobeyed him; I wanted to rescue him and it was then when those men showed up. . . . They spoke your language but they painted everything in blood: my house, my life, everything. Then, in Toledo, no one would help me go back, everyone said it was madness." He looked at Galib and without a doubt saw an opportunity. "Maybe you could do something for me? I don't know how to find my sisters. . . . Maybe if some time you are traveling through those lands. . . . Could you find out what happened with them? I would be eternally thankful to you, I would work for you even if you paid me nothing."

"Diego, that is impossible. I'm sorry, I can't. I'm Muslim, but I'm not one of them. Even if it sounds strange to you, and you think we all worship the same God, we're not the same. I can't travel through those regions without serious problems; they could recognize me. And you could travel there even less. Believe me, you shouldn't even think of it. The Almohads are dangerous."

Diego felt lost; no one seemed to want to help him. Galib tried to explain his reasons better.

"I've never understood how someone could be pushed aside for their beliefs. It's precisely for that reason that I came to Toledo. Unlike what happens in the south, here the three religions live side by side. And if not, think of where we're going. . . . We don't have the same rights as Christians, that's true as well, but at least we can do business here, intermingle, and go to the religious festivals. Here I can pursue my trade and win a degree of prestige. For all that, I love this city."

Diego didn't say anything to him, out of respect, but he couldn't clear from his head the idea that this man's religion had been responsible for his misfortune. Galib loved Toledo; Diego hated Islam.

IX.

Aboumán Abenxuxen was a wealthy Jew. In addition to collecting money for the crown, he had loaned enormous sums of money to the monarchs to aid them in their costly campaigns against Al-Andalus. The shadow of his power was long and his political influence enormous.

"Do you know what colic is?" Galib asked Diego before they arrived at the fort, his voice clipped and hurried.

"I saw it a few years back, in one of our mares. I remember she had a swollen, painful belly and that she sweated a lot."

"What did you give her?"

"My father made a preparation of flowers, but it didn't work and the animal died."

"Typical of a blacksmith. . . ."

Angered, Diego wanted to tell him all the things a blacksmith could do for a horse, but Galib interrupted him.

"The truth should never be offensive, young Diego."

"What truth?"

"Blacksmiths can do some things, they can try to cure the animals, but they don't know the why and wherefore of their actions. Being a blacksmith doesn't give you wisdom. To be an albéitar, you have to read, to get hold of the books necessary to be able to cure the horse. There you find experiences based in centuries of close observations. That's why I am blaming the blacksmiths, for believing that they possess knowledge when in fact it's what I call luck. They have one remedy and it cures a certain illness and from that moment on, it becomes law. Then it's transmitted from father to son or from master to apprentice, like something unchanging, until someone else hits on another remedy with better results. And so the process goes, without anyone ever asking what the ultimate purpose of these things is. This is especially common in Christian lands, where my profession is reviled and very few practice it."

"Do there really exist reasons for illnesses?"

"Good question. I have to recognize that it's difficult, if not impossible, to answer. We know little, very little still, too little, in fact. There's a need for more study, more time, and for the mind and the heart to be opened to science."

They reached the gate of the Jewish quarter. It was closed. Without losing time, Galib called in a loud voice to the gatekeeper. The man, made aware of their arrival beforehand, rushed to let them through and guided them to the residence of Abenxuxen.

It was a beautiful palace. Two enormous torches illuminated the portico of the entryway. Their yellowish shadows danced on the wall and licked the polished copper of a doorknocker fashioned in the shape of the Star of David. Galib knocked only twice, for before the third time, the door opened and they passed into a majestic courtyard. There they dismounted and followed a rather old man.

They entered by a passageway that opened onto a large space where they found a well-lit stable. It seemed busy with people.

"The albéitar is here! Make way for him!" one shouted.

Galib identified the *almojarife* from among the group. His face showed enormous worry.

"Excuse me for passing over the customary courtesies with you, but I understand the situation requires the greatest urgency." Aboumán invited him to enter the stables. On the way, he explained the problem. "I need this horse. Not another. This one."

Galib's expression showed that he was utterly perplexed.

"I'll explain myself better; my apologies, I'm nervous. What I mean to say is that tomorrow, I have to make a long journey to Frías to resolve a matter of extreme importance for the king. And Andromedes is the only one I trust for this undertaking. There is no other as fast as him."

"They have mentioned colic."

"Since this afternoon . . . yes. It seems he's eaten more rye than permitted." With anger, he looked at one of his stable keepers, who reacted by blushing red.

"How much?"

"I don't know. . . . A lot."

They still hadn't finished talking when they heard an awful screech. They ran to see and found themselves faced with a wooden fence in wreckage. The animal had kicked against it in a rage.

"Let's see what's happening."

Galib nodded his head at Diego, beckoning him to follow.

When they peeked in, they saw the animal nervous, moving from side to side, agitated. Immediately he began to dig at the soil and turned his head toward his flanks over and over. One side of his abdomen was more swollen than the other, and he had some slight wounds on his flanks. While they watched him, he fell to the floor and began to roll around on the straw. He had sweated so much that even the air seemed thicker.

"Look, Diego, to have a proper diagnosis of colic, you have to observe the mucus in the mouth." Galib spoke to the boy patiently, wanting him to understand everything.

"And what am I looking for there?"

"Now he's too nervous, but if he sees we're calm, he won't hurt us. We have to go in and look at his gums, his upper incisors, and see what color they are."

From the door of the stables, they observed the animal, now on his feet again. He looked more agitated than before and seemed dangerous. Diego had never seen anything like it. He swallowed his saliva.

"Are you scared to go in?"

Diego said nothing, opened the small door, and walked in cautiously. Galib followed him, nodding. The horse observed them irritably. He neighed twice and took refuge in a corner. Diego came close to him decisively and repeated once more something Galib had seen him do with Sabba. He breathed on his nostrils and the animal responded in kind. Galib passed Diego the bridle and he tried to put it on very slowly. The horse, responding to a jab of pain, pulled fiercely, escaping from them, and began to trot about madly. Galib stood by Diego's side and instructed him on how to approach the horse from the side.

"Don't worry," Diego said. "I think I know how to calm him down."

The *almojarife* gave Galib a nervous look. If that was his helper, he couldn't understand how the albéitar would leave him to work alone. He trusted the Muslim, but it was a matter of an irreplaceable horse for him.

Galib calmed the man down with a wave of the hand and stepped farther away to get a better sense of the difference in the volume of the horse's abdomen and its way of walking. From a small bag he withdrew two pinches of mallow, three of poppy, one of viola, and he passed them to a stable boy to prepare him a tincture.

"Bring a bit of oil, salt, and a big handful of wheat bran."

Diego clicked his tongue a few times, making a sound that seemed to calm the animal, and approached the horse with caution. He managed to get a rope around its head and then tied it to a bar on the wall. He began to speak to it in whispers until he felt the horse was more relaxed, and without missing the opportunity, he pulled its lips apart to look inside.

"He has a kind of ring around his upper teeth, with an orange or almost red color."

"Perfect, Diego, that is the definitive sign of colic. Get out of there. We'll figure out now how to treat it."

"Will he be well by tomorrow?" The Jew was thinking about his journey.

"Impossible. Forget that idea."

The *almojarife* raised his hands to his head and looked for a kerchief to wipe off his sweat.

"This is a terrible setback for my plans." He looked for the stable master. "Can I take the black mare?"

"I fear not, master, she is too far pregnant."

"Well then?"

Galib sent for a bundle of esparto and a long pole of wood coated with oil. He had another of the stable boys come with straw to create an elevation on one part of the floor.

"If you don't have another fast horse, I can lend you one of mine. Sometimes I think it can run on air."

"Galib, I will accept it. You always know the solution to a problem. . . . I thank you for it."

Galib paid the matter no mind and turned to Diego.

"Are you all right, are you frightened?"

"No, but you have to be very careful with his mouth. He looks like he wants to bite."

"I hadn't noticed that, I'm surprised by your intuition. Tell me why you smell them and why you breathe on them."

Diego found the question strange and tried to respond.

"I noticed that they do it that way, especially when they meet for the first time. Maybe it's their way of saying hello, I'm not sure, or maybe it makes them trust you, like when we shake hands."

"I understand. . . . Did you detect any strange odor on his breath?"

"Maybe something acidic."

"That's logical. The stomach of a horse is very small and that means they have to eat frequently and very little at any one time. When they eat a great deal of grain, like in this case, their digestion stops and they swell, as though the grain was fermenting inside them. Then come the terrible pains. The wounds on the flank indicate where the problem lies. Often they look to that area and they pound against anything nearby as if trying to rid themselves of the source of their illness. There are many other causes for it, not only food."

At that moment, a girl entered with a large pot and the tincture Galib had asked for. Next he asked for a bottle with water and ordered Diego and another strong man to hold on to the horse for the treatment. He mixed the water with the brew to cool it down and refilled the first bottle. He ordered the horse to be positioned so that its back was against one of the walls, to avoid any kicking. He also had its rear legs placed over a pile of straw so they would be higher than the rest of its body and its bowels would lurch toward the front.

"You, Diego, keep him calm like you have shown you know how to do. I need to get him to drink two bottles."

They all did as Galib had asked and he confirmed that the position of the horse was correct. With the determination that comes from experience, he opened its mouth and inserted the bottle of curative liquid, repeating the same maneuver twice more.

Then he rolled up the sleeves of his tunic, he tightened his belt around his waist, and he asked Diego to take the other end of the greased pole. They passed it under the horse's stomach.

"Use all your strength. We have to push up and forward several times."

Diego clenched his teeth and held his breath to try and lift the animal with the pole. They rubbed the wood against him for a long time with the idea of softening him up and getting him to feel better. It seemed to help the horse. Galib's tunic was soaked in sweat, and sweat poured down his face, which was as red from the effort as Diego's.

"He shouldn't eat anything solid for one day, at most a little hay and even then, only if it's of excellent quality," he said to the stable boy.

They brought a basin with warm water and some cloths to clean off and afterward they stayed a while more with the owner observing the animal's behavior. They talked about legal matters, the political situation in Toledo, the Almohads. Diego listened without participating, surprised by the tight relations that Galib maintained with many of the persons whose names came up in the course of the conversation.

The horse was getting visibly better. Its expression was more serene. Little by little it began to pace around the yard without looking back at its flanks.

The *almojarife* observed the animal contentedly and made plans so that the horse Galib had promised him would be delivered that very night.

"You are incredible!" he proclaimed in a loud voice. "I don't want to bother you any more. Go home. . . . It's late. As you see, the horse is cured.

And by the way, I would like very much to have you and your lovely wife for dinner. My wife adores her. Will you come?"

"I thank you. I will tell her."

On the way home, Diego and Galib were so tired that they almost did not talk. For Diego, it had been a formidable experience, and he felt like he had participated in something important. It had been fascinating to see Galib in action He wanted to know everything that man knew, to accompany him everywhere, to learn, to read the hundreds of books he had read. He was lost in his own thoughts when he realized that they had arrived at Galib's house. The boy stopped and remained outside. He didn't know if Galib would let him spend the night in the stable or not.

Galib crossed the threshold without saying anything and the boy remained at the entrance. He felt as though again he had nothing but the sky over his head. He embraced Sabba and they set off, looking for somewhere to take shelter. He didn't know where, but they would find it. Suddenly, the creaking of the door of Galib's house made him turn around. There was his master. He had dismounted from his horse and was inviting him in.

"You can spend the night in the stable. You've earned it."

Diego spurred Sabba with his heels and entered triumphantly through the gate of that house which would become the school where he would embark on an exciting future.

X.

Science spoke in Arabic.

That language. Its sound was a torment for Diego, but he also knew that it harbored the secrets that Galib possessed. For many afternoons and many long late nights, he had watched Galib pass candlelit hours in silence amid books and writings. One day, he explained that he was reading the works of the wise Greeks, gathered and translated into Arabic by Persian scholars. Sometimes, when Diego was leaving from the stable to approach the house to share some bit of information with Galib, he would see him surrounded by books, reading, concentrating, taking pleasure. Galib whispered words that seemed like poetry to Diego, but when he least expected, his head would be filled with bloody, vicious thoughts.

The memory of his sisters was always horrible for him. Each time they popped into his mind, they always ended up lost in a cloudy mental labyrinth, where not even with his imagination could he come up with a way to help them.

Six months had passed since that first visit with Galib, and for Diego things had gone a bit better. With his first wages he had been able to rent a bed in a Frankish quarter, in a modest house where he shared a room with two other men.

Sajjad, besides living in his own world full of contradictions, had begun to show an alarming jealousy toward Diego. That was primarily because Diego had received his first important responsibility: taking charge of the workshop.

Galib, more impressed every day by his talent, began to give him some simple tasks, like making sure the horseshoes were of the same thickness or filing off their sharp edges. But given his skill, after a short while, he ended up tasking him with forging new ones.

At times, when Diego left early, he would leave off drawing whatever he wanted in a square of sand on the floor of the stable. More than once Diego found Sajjad erasing it with his canvas shoe, though afterward he would beg for forgiveness and insist on the purity of his intention.

"Sajjad good, Sajjad help Diego," he would repeat over and over.

Forging the horseshoes took up half the morning and the rest of the day Diego dedicated to the other chores, like carting hay, spreading straw out for the beds, or brushing and cleaning the animals.

After a year, Galib entrusted Diego with administering cures to those sick horses that were kept in the stables and that needed to be watched over closely.

Diego was meticulous in preparing their doses, paid careful attention to the progress of the animals, intuited their responses, and, moreover, could remember each one's treatment, although many included more than ten ingredients. He memorized with remarkable speed.

None of this escaped Galib, or Sajjad either.

One day, when he had passed more than a year working for Galib, something very serious happened.

"Someone must have fed her bad oats. . . ."

Galib, agitated and beside himself, tried to reanimate the animal. He had found it with a high fever and intense diarrhea. It had only spent a single night in his stables.

Diego and Sajjad huddled down, witnessing the disaster, without knowing what to do or say.

"And the mare of the justice of Toledo to boot," Galib blabbered in desperation.

He had no idea how to explain to the man that his best animal, one he had sent over for a small procedure on its hooves, was now suffering from extreme indigestion with acute pains and fetid excretions. And all this because she'd been fed damp grains.

He knelt down and looked at both of them in the eyes with rage.

"Was it you, Sajjad?"

Diego winced for the poor old man. His legs shook like a rabbit's and his teeth chattered uncontrollably. Tension racked his squalid body.

"Sajjad see Diego." With a trembling finger, he pointed at the boy. The boy's expression changed first to surprise and then to indignation. Galib's did as well, but in his case, the feelings were of fury and perplexity.

"Sajjad tell him no do, but Diego no obey Sajjad, and . . ." The young apprentice glared at him, wishing to strike him, to explode in protests. He held back, though, and swore he wasn't the one who'd done it.

Galib was disconcerted. He began to walk around them, his head down.

He seemed to be ruminating on a difficult decision while he seethed, infuriated. After a moment that seemed to them like an eternity, he sighed three times and at last spoke.

"Sajjad, make a ball of coal and clay to absorb the mold, and if the owner comes, don't let him in. Tell him that she will be ready tomorrow, but be careful he doesn't see her today.

"And you, Diego, come with me. I have to talk with you."

Diego followed him, frightened. For a moment, he imagined himself on the street, without work, without having learned almost anything.

They plunged into the narrow streets of the Muslim quarter, and without leaving the city, Galib informed him of his intentions.

"To be an albéitar means study, tenacity, effort, the cultivation of curiosity, and, above all, to read; to read the wise men and to learn from them. It is to live committed to the service of others."

Diego trotted along in silence and waited each moment for Galib's reprimand to come.

Galib maintained the tension, not slowing down and always looking ahead.

"You don't have anything to say?"

"I'm so sorry for what happened. . . ."

"I know Sajjad well and I know when he's lying. His face gives him away. . . . But perhaps you need to be more attentive to what is happening in the stables."

"Sometimes Sajjad . . ."

"Yes, I know. Sajjad doesn't let you. He's stubborn and jealous besides. He has never lied to me before, but he's old now and he's afraid. You have to understand him."

"I . . ."

"I will have to think of how to arrange things so he feels more important, maybe charging him with some task, I don't know. . . . He will need it, because from now on, Diego, I want you to be my assistant."

"Are you serious?" Diego said in a whisper.

"You've been with us for more than a year. You have the ability to learn and, of course, a great deal of talent with animals. If you put in effort aside from that and you have the willpower, you could learn the trade, little by little. If you want it and you commit yourself, you could be an albéitar one day."

Diego was stunned. Of course he wanted it. He had dreamed of that ever since he saw Galib cure the first horse. But not in his wildest dreams had he imagined it could become a reality. A whirlwind of emotions swallowed his tongue. He breathed in a mouthful of fresh air, conscious of the import of that moment, and felt an agreeable inner confusion as he answered.

"I won't let you down," the boy shouted, full of satisfaction.

"Well, if you want to be the best, we'll have to hurry. We're going to the castle of the most important man in Toledo, one from the Lara family, and if we don't arrive on time, neither you nor I will be able to go on working. So gallop!"

Galib sped up as fast as he could. Diego followed. The tears in his eyes did not let him see the road, but he looked into the sky and knew his father was guiding his steps.

Royal ensigns, butlers, herdsmen. The highest responsibilities of the government of Castile were and had been forever in the hands of the Laras.

Between their properties and the concessions the king had granted them, half of Castile was theirs. Galib and Diego had to visit one of them, Don Álvaro, the count of Lara. That was a title the king had only bestowed upon nine illustrious figures in Castile, and six of them belonged to that family.

Diego was astonished when he found himself crossing over the moat of a fabulous castle where he knew King Alfonso also lodged when he passed through Toledo.

"Do you know why I have brought you here?"

Diego was taken aback by the magnificent spire while he waited for the nobleman to arrive.

"The stables hold no fewer than two hundred horses and today we're going to bleed all of them. It's best to do it every season, for their health and to balance out their humors."

To both sides of an enormous and beautifully carved door at the base of the ponderous tower hung two banners with the family's arms. From the interior emerged two knights escorting a very young woman.

"Get down from your horse and salute them," Galib whispered to Diego.

The girl had very white skin, green eyes, and lips of an intense red.

"How happy I am to see you, Galib! And you have a new companion as well."

"I present you my new assistant, madame; his name is Diego and he is from Malagón."

To Diego's ears, that title sounded like the purest glory.

The woman, overrunning with spontaneity, grabbed the boy's arm, directing them to the fortress's stables.

"My name is Urraca." She lifted her hand as though excusing herself. "I know it's an ugly name, but that is how my father, Don Diego López de Haro, wanted it." She tried to pull Diego away from Galib. "I don't want him to hear me, but you must know you are at the side of the greatest albéitar in Toledo, though I also hear he pays very little."

"Well . . . no . . ." Diego felt disconcerted.

"We'll see if I'm telling the truth." She winked. "I've known him a long time and I know how he is. He asks for everything but you can't squeeze a single *maravedi* out of him."

"Don't take her too seriously, Diego. Madame Urraca likes to joke around."

"You're telling me." A man's voice sounded from behind Diego's back.

It was Don Álvaro Núñez de Lara. The woman patted her stomach, seemingly offended, and then threw her arms around him blissfully.

"We have very good news."

"Does such a thing exist in these turbulent times?" Galib was feeling around in his kit to be sure he had brought enough lancets for the bleeding.

"I'm pregnant." The woman's eyes reddened with emotion. Don Álvaro stroked her belly with pride.

"Congratulations."

Galib's felicitations sounded somewhat dry. He still had not been able to have children with Benazir and that was a real torment for them. For her, because she was afraid of being rejected, in accordance with Koranic law. For him, because he could not fulfill his great dream of having an heir. The situation was uncomfortable for him, and he tried to change the theme.

"What about your father?"

"Since the defeat at Alarcos, we haven't seen him again. We know that he has marched toward Aragon and Navarre to try and join forces with Castile. His position as the royal ensign makes him King Alfonso's right hand and counselor. Knowing him, he is trying to help, especially after the recent disgrace."

"It's understandable," Galib answered. "People are nervous. We're anxious to stop the onslaught of the Almohads. . . . They're too close."

"That's why we've called you. We need our cavalry at the ready at all times," Don Álvaro added.

When they arrived at the stable entrance, Galib made a number of signs to Diego. The boy had seen bleeding done before and it didn't seem especially difficult, but he changed his opinion when he saw it closer up. The animals facing them didn't seem like horses; they were enormous, gigantic, heavy steeds, strong enough to wear armor and carry horsemen and knock down fences and walls of men in battle. He had never seen a breed of warhorse as grand as these. Galib told him they were Bretons.

"From the biggest ones you'll draw three pints of blood, and even four from the ones that look the strongest and most vigorous. Only when you get to the coursers and the pack mules will you limit yourself to two."

To begin, they looked for the end of the stables and in front of the first animal, Galib began to give orders to the stable boys. Four of them got between the horses, pushing against their ribs to make room for the albéi-tar, so that he could reach their necks without being crushed. Others held the jars where the blood was collected and measured. And to the rest, he explained how to press the wound after the blood was drawn and where to clean the lancets with warm water between horses.

"Watch how I do it with the first and then you try with the next one."

Galib approached the animal's neck and he had to raise his arms to reach the vein. With one finger he felt its pulse, and then he stretched another hand up to press down on the vein.

"You have to insert the blade of the lancet so that the hole in the skin doesn't strike one of the blood vessels. That way we avoid a posterior hemorrhage, which can cause problems, or the appearance of an ugly hematoma." He did it, and immediately the first stream of blood surged forth.

Galib upbraided the stable boy at his side for not being fast enough with the jar, and he showed him how to hold the lancet and at the same time catch the blood.

He passed another lancet to Diego and pointed to the next horse. To Diego, this animal seemed even larger and taller than the previous one. He normally wasn't afraid of horses, but a mere stomp from one of those hooves could leave a person lame for the rest of his life. Galib stood at his side.

Diego felt the vein, but when the animal felt his hand, it turned its head back, showed its teeth, and snorted furiously. That hot breath let him know he couldn't waste time. A second warning would be much worse. . . .

He squeezed the vein with his hand and brought the lancet close to it. Galib corrected the angle. When he stuck it in, the animal's skin and muscles tensed, and that caught Diego by surprise; he hadn't taken care to hold on to the instrument well and that meant that the first stream of blood came out in a broad arc that soaked his face and his tunic.

Some of the stable boys laughed at Diego's inexperience. Galib turned to them angrily.

"The next person who laughs can volunteer to do it himself."

"Do you know the most recent news about the king of León?" Don Álvaro said, breaking the tension. He often confided details of state, since he appreciated Galib's wisdom and good sense.

"I can't imagine what ugly situation he has gotten himself wrapped up in, but knowing him . . ."

Once he had confirmed his assistant's technique with the next two horses, Galib directed his attention to Don Álvaro Núñez de Lara and his wife. While Galib bled the fifth horse, Diego had only managed one, but after a while, he began to pick up speed. They were so far apart that in the end, Diego couldn't hear what they were saying.

"After the loss at Alarcos," Don Álvaro carried on, "our king met his cousin Alfonso IX of León in this very castle. Stunned by the defeat, the Castilian reproached him for his absence from the battle, though the other one justified it as the consequence of a delay against his will. It seems it was then that the Leonese, seeing his cousin's weakness, took advantage to reclaim from him some castles on the frontier that have been disputed for years. Since our monarch denied him, and was moreover angry at his opportunism, we have heard that when he returned to his lands, the traitor signed a treaty to fight alongside the Almohad caliph against Castile."

Madame Urraca, moved by her husband's respect for her father and always loyal and faithful to her king, intervened.

"I can't manage to understand what filthy interests could make him join with that fanatical Muslim who has already spilled so much Christian blood. Castile has tried to unify the rest of the kingdoms to fight together against their ruthless invader. If we don't oppose them, they'll make us slaves to their faith, subjugating all of us without the least mercy. They are cold and wicked. I've heard dreadful stories from the siege before the loss at Alarcos. It seems impossible that Christian blood could flow through the veins of Alfonso IX. I only ask God that one day he be made to pay."

Diego had approached them to consult with Galib when he heard the words *siege* and *Alarcos*. Without being part of the conversation, he was moved, and he couldn't help but ask them: "My apologies, my lady; without wanting to, I have heard you speak of Alarcos, and . . ." He hesitated.

"Ask without fear, young man."

"On that day, two of my sisters were captured in Malagón by a group of dark-skinned Africans after they had murdered the third one, the older one. No one has known what might have happened to them or how I can find them. I wondered whether you might have heard of what happened afterward."

The answer came from Don Álvaro.

"The most likely thing is that they ended up in a harem, maybe belonging to the vizier of Seville, or one of the many governors in Al-Andalus."

Doña Urraca took pity on the boy and tried to soften her husband's crudity.

"I am sorry it sounds so terrible, but it is what usually happens with the female prisoners."

Diego lowered his head and went silent, swallowing back his tears and his pain, with his mouth dry from anguish.

He went back to finish his work and felt a jabbing pain in his stomach after taking in what he had just heard. While he pierced the vein of a giant Breton with his lancet, he imagined those men with dark skin and longed for their deaths.

The heat of the blood running between his hands stoked his desire for vengeance against those who used religion to frighten and cow the rest of humanity.

XI.

Diego's pain preferred silence and darkness.

In one of those magic nightfalls of Toledo, when the sun had given up its strength and was lost in the last colors of ocher, Galib found Diego leaning against a fence, pensive. He was watching a black mare, its glimmer intense and almost blue, with a very long mane. He watched her run the circular track where they normally trained the horses.

Galib respected his silence and for a while watched the magnificent stride of that lovely horse.

"One of our prophetic traditions affirms that the first horse created was a dark bay. And Allah, blessed and praised be his name, said: 'I have made you Arabian. I wanted you to have the most abundant sustenance from among all the animals; the sheep will follow at your back and you will have the finest pastures.'" He recited from memory. "Also there are those who say that the first man to mount a horse was Ishmael, the son of Abraham, who was also the first to speak in Arabic, the language that Allah used to reveal the sacred book to the Prophet. He had five horses, and he commanded us to take care of them, to be kind to them, to love them and admire them as you are doing right now."

Diego kept his gaze fixed on the spirited mare, drunk with feeling. The thin, calm air from the recently ended day combined with the soothing effect of Galib's words.

"The Prophet also said that there were three classes of horse: 'some dedicated to combat for God, which would deserve all grace in the Last Judgment; others dedicated to ornament, which deserved nothing; and others devoted to the vainglory of their owners, which would be disdained on the last days of this world.'"

Galib breathed deeply and opened his heart.

"These teachings led me to embrace the albéitar's task. I decided to dedicate myself to helping others by caring for horses, a good so beloved of Allah. Soon I learned to do it without any sort of training, but if wisdom is in my hands, my mind, or my perception, it is thanks to the will of Allah. He wanted it thus, just as now he wants you to have it."

Diego sighed and swallowed his saliva, plagued with doubts. To become an albéitar seemed as exciting as it was intimidating. He was suffering a difficult inner conflict. It was a profession of Arabian origin, and Galib was a believer in Islam, a servant to that God in whose name Diego had suffered such terrible torments.

"Other sons of Allah like you, undoubtedly invoking his name, killed my father and my older sister and took my other sisters away. . . . Since then I have hated your religion and everything related to it."

"Believe me, your pain hurts me as though it were my own." Galib did not look away when Diego stared at him imploringly, wanting answers that gave some reason for his pain. "Many have mistaken the words of Allah. In their filthy hearts they believe he is talking to them when in fact it is the devil."

Galib came over to the boy and sat down by his side. When he saw his young assistant's desperation, he wanted to confess his feelings.

"Your enemy is not Islam, Diego, it is the Almohads. They have interpreted the Koranic law in an absolute way, and since they entered Al-Andalus, they are trying to convert everyone to Islam by force. If they are not stopped, they will impose their values and their beliefs on all the world. They will not accept any other religion than that of Allah, the one, and they will say that the trinity of your God is the worst of heresies. That is why, in their eyes, they try to convert everyone by force, Christians and Jews. They tried with me when I lived in Seville and it was their fault I had to emigrate. . . ." He stopped and, after taking another deep breath, continued: "I was never a believer in their principles, they knew it. They couldn't accept that someone who wasn't one of their people could hold such an important position, and they ended up hunting me down with the sole end of ruining me professionally, ruining my reputation. They threatened me with death, and in the end I had to leave everything behind and escape, like you did, Diego." He looked into his eyes with determination. "They are the ones who carry out the devil's will, believe you me. They are wrong, their doctrine is mistaken. My religion is kind and does not support evil; it is based in love and charity, just like yours."

Diego turned to Galib, his eyes filled with tears.

"You speak beautiful words and the truth seems to lie beneath them. And yet I feel so much hate still. My heart bears so much pain, so much that it won't let me see clearly who are my enemies."

Galib did not doubt it and embraced the boy, taking in his grief. For a moment he felt strong emotion, as if he were playing the role of father. A shiver ran over his flesh.

"You have to learn Arabic, Diego. If you come close to our culture, you will learn to love it. To understand the language of horses, you have to understand the language of the desert, if Allah wills it. And when you have mastered it, you will think the way our greatest scholars did. You will understand why Allah used this language to reveal his laws to us. Its sound is beautiful and it will caress your tongue. Its echoes will soften your palate and you will recognize in it the language of love and the power of the wind."

She began by teaching him the numbers, then the letters and their sounds. She followed that with common expressions, making him repeat them countless times until he could memorize every aspect and reflect their depth or subtleties as she said. Further on they went into the verbs, and afterward, a copious vocabulary. Thousands of words, of complex but beautiful sounds, some whispering, others sharp, like a restrained sigh.

Diego was now almost sixteen and Benazir a bit over thirty. Except for his mother, whom he scarcely remembered, and his three sisters, he had never spent so much time close to a woman.

Every morning, when he finished his forging and shoeing and whatever other chores Sajjad had in store for him, Diego would enter the large house.

Until then he had hardly heard the voice of Benazir. It wasn't customary. But when Galib had given his blessing to that daily contact, it charmed him, above all its musicality. When she spoke, the words seemed to flow like silk until they struck against the veil that covered her face, almost ethereal, but then they would disperse in the air like a soft breeze.

Every day, Diego went to the dining room and he waited for her, going through everything he had learned the day before in his memory. Those waits became the most longed for and exciting moments of the day. To see Benazir appear was like a mystery. Every day she wore a different tunic, and if not, she would change her vest.

She had slippers of every color, and hundreds of sashes, adorned with gold, of the most distinct shapes, and more than a dozen bands she would wrap around her waist. There was only one thing that was always the same, her perfume. A blend of sandalwood and violet, an intoxicating aroma that rocked all the senses to sleep.

They would sit side by side atop comfortable cushions, over a gorgeous rug brought from her country of Persia. With her legs bent to one side, she would hold a chalkboard on which she would write out the different words. To Diego's surprise, she did so from left to right, the opposite of him. When she passed him the piece of chalk she would write with, sometimes she grazed his hand. Those subtle touches began casually, but as time went on, Diego tried to make them happen intentionally.

She was more than just another woman; she was the pure essence of woman. The smoothness and generosity of her body, which he could sometimes make out beneath her garments, began to shake Diego like a palm tree in the wind.

They awoke in him an infinity of feelings, first contained, but eventually becoming turbulent temptations.

One day, Benazir lifted her veil for the first time, to vocalize a difficult word.

"Pay close attention to my lips and try to put yours in an identical position."

Diego did so, immediately quivering as he saw the textured flesh of her own. He stuttered a few times until he finally tried to pronounce the word.

"No, no, no. You have to tense your upper lip and make an echo against the roof of your mouth. Look . . ."

She took one of his hands and drew his fingertips toward her lips. Then she repeated the word a number of times.

"Do you see the difference?"

Diego breathed three times until he had regained control of himself and drowned the desire to kiss her then and there. When he felt that sweet touch, he thought he had died. He tried to pronounce the word, though with little enthusiasm, so that he could repeat that caress. Benazir knew what he was thinking and put his fingers on her lips again.

"Try one more time."

In his solitude, Diego would savor that sensual memory, like others that would come over the following six months. But particularly that day, he smelled his hand and looked for the remains of Benazir's fragrance that lingered there. And again he wanted her, though with shame, because she was Galib's wife.

The force of instinct, of his unbridled youth, the sensuality that Benazir gave off from each of her pores, weighed more than his own sense of wrong.

XII.

Their naked bodies shook in the warm breeze.

It was the breath of the desert that came through the windows of the luxurious harem of Yusuf ben Yaqub al-Mansur in Marrakesh, over them, the two new slaves brought there expressly for his pleasure.

They had just emerged from a room saturated with steam. They were lying atop marble tables suffering the rasping of rough gloves. Women were cleaning their skin and seemed almost to be peeling it off. In compensation, they would receive an agreeable bath with hot water.

Blanca and Estela looked at each other. They had slept a whole day after the long and painful voyage, first in carriage for several weeks, then in a ship for two days, and at last on horse back for four days more.

That morning, from daybreak, a huddle of women had watched over them and the first thing they did was undress them. They looked at their intimate parts without concern, and amid laughter, they pointed incredulously at their orange hair. Blanca and Estela were defeated. They could scarcely put up any resistance.

"What will they do to us?" Estela looked with terror at her older sister.

"I don't know, but I'm afraid we'll find out soon."

Blanca turned to a high window that rose up from the floor. Through it could be seen a fantastic pond next to the building, full of calm blue waters. And in the distance, magnificent mountains raised their snow-capped summits against the horizon.

A tear slipped down her cheek when she imagined how much humiliation and suffering still awaited them, now inside a palace, perhaps to be enslaved by some man of high rank.

Estela tried to push aside a woman with a rotund body and a cold face who was feeling the firmness of her breasts, but the woman paid no attention and went on to her hips and buttocks. Blanca pretended to trip and fell against the woman to push her away from her sister, but in return she received a violent slap and a torrent of imprecations in Arabic. Angered, the woman began to push at their backs with the intention of moving to another room.

Holding hands, the two sisters were walking completely nude, but no one seemed to care.

The new room was completely lined in pink marble and had an enormous pool in the center. Blanca and Estela had to lie down so that their heads were just over the water. Two young women with dark eyes and olive skin, almost their same age, entered the pool and washed their hair from inside it. With their hands covered in a reddish mud, they scrubbed their heads, massaging them unhurriedly. Then they rinsed them, over and over, until their hair was loose and silky. Once it was dry, they scrubbed their feet with a rough stone until they were well polished, and then they left without saying anything.

Estela covered herself with a cloth and remembered the inn and her family.

"Every day I pray for Belinda, and I also remember Papa and Diego. . . . Something tells me we won't see them again. . . ."

"Don't say that!" Blanca said angrily.

The women who had washed their hair came back, now with trays and two steaming containers. Blanca and Estela immediately perceived a sweet scent of caramel with a touch of lemon.

They were told to lie down again and each woman grabbed a small wooden spade. With them, they spread that sticky brew and anointed the women's arms and legs, armpits, and sex. . . . All the hair on their bodies was covered with that unguent, which was then left to dry. When the women began to peel it off, especially in the more sensitive areas, Estela could not restrain her tears and shouted in pain.

Then the women opened some small jars and smeared their fingers with a whitish paste. To their surprise, the women inhaled it at one go. Then they took another small quantity and came closer. Though the sisters resisted, the women pressed it into their noses. Immediately they felt nauseated, but with a pleasant sense of well-being just afterward, as if they were floating. Half dazed, they hardly complained during the rest of the depilation, and not at all when they made contact with the warm water of the bath, where they were left to relieve their stinging skin.

Amid orange and almond trees, in the gardens surrounding the great pond of the palace, two men were talking.

One of them represented the maximum authority of an empire based in the north of Africa and Al-Andalus: the Almohad. He was the great caliph Yusuf ben Yaqub. The other, a Christian and a knight of noble birth, wanted nothing more than the defeat of the Castilian king, his worst enemy, though he also appreciated the gold he received from the caliph and the promise of great tracts of land in exchange for his service. An enormous scar spanned the width of his forehead. It felt tight in the dry air and reminded him of who had given it to him and when.

Five years had passed, but he still remembered the sword of King Alfonso running across his face in the duel that no one would attest to. The friendship that they professed since childhood had shattered into pieces when the king threw in his lot with the Lara clan in a plaint that they had levied against his family, the Moras, which represented a loss of enormous domains for them. Don Pedro had put all his effort into achieving the opposite result and, because of his influence, even though he knew they didn't belong to him, he pushed Alfonso to unbearable limits. He even threatened him with making public the adulterous relationship that the monarch himself carried on with a Jewess from Toledo, violating a debt of secrecy. That filthy ruse won him a challenge to a duel, a defeat at the hands of Alfonso VIII, and Mora's later eternal exile from Castile, to which he was sentenced by the king himself.

The caliph knew what he could get from Mora without ever forgetting his true nature as a traitor. The name Mora, as illustrious in Castile as that of Lara or Castro, had been tarnished for some reason he did not know, but so gravely that it had made him come to hate the king.

For Yusuf, the friendship of the Christian was useful, and for that reason he paid him with his generosity and favors. But he also took care and watched out for him.

"Our holy war bears a resemblance to that game, one that not all poets dare to engage in. Do you know it, Don Pedro?"

"No, sir. I have had little experience of poetry."

Yusuf II looked at him with disdain. He loved poetry. To cultivate the spirit through the different arts was the most precious gift a man could possess.

"It consists of improvising and continuing with a verse that another person has begun. Now do you remember it?"

"I believe I've seen such a thing before in Al-Andalus."

"Certainly. It is very popular there, even among the country people. The war we are engaged with against the Castilian king has taken a form up till now very similar to that game. In fact, I began the first stanza with my victory at Alarcos. Then, the kings of León and Portugal, by suing for peace, have gone on adding rhymes, and now you should help me finish my recital."

"How?"

Yusuf laughed at his confusion.

"You will leave to speak with Sancho of Navarre. You should convince him to sign a peace treaty with me as well. Make it happen however you must. Do what you think necessary. Buy his ambition, look for his weak point. Give him all the gold he wants, if that is what he longs for. If we do it, we will break apart the various kingdoms and that way, we can defeat Alfonso of Castile. My plan is to enter from the west, crossing the river Tagus and taking back Toledo. That way the poem will be finished and we will win the game."

"Excellent thinking, sir. . . . I admire you."

The caliph proudly breathed in the dry desert air mixed with the fragrance that transpired from an enormous jasmine. He believed in the success of his plan because the Christians always fell victim to the same mistakes: greed for widening their territories and an obsessive need to feel different from one another.

Very frightened, the two sisters entered into a round hall where a group of women were seated on the floor listening to another older woman. They were dressed in diaphanous garments, perfumed silks, and seemed lulled to sleep by the music of the words coming from her mouth.

A young woman with black skin came over to them and showed them where to sit. The two sisters looked at each other without knowing what lay in store. They observed the girl who was preparing a mixture of rice powder and egg white in a container and then came over to spread it on their faces. With a salve of incense and carbon she darkened their eyebrows and eyelashes, and then she painted their eyelids with a red cream.

The other women murmured, pointing at them and laughing. One of them, a redheaded one, with blue eyes and fine features, stood up and came over to them. She appeared to be a Christian.

"My name is Yasmin. You are now in the harem of Great Caliph Yusuf and I am his favorite wife. Behave well and you can live here tranquilly and according to your wishes."

To their surprise, the woman spoke Romanic, which relieved them to a degree. Blanca was going to speak, but the woman gestured for her to be silent. Without another explanation she pulled back Blanca's veil, looked at her mouth, and smelled her breath. She did the same with Estela. Afterward, she gave an order in Arabic to two girls who ran off.

"We were kidnapped," Estela whispered into her ear.

In her innocence she thought the woman would help them once she found out about their misfortune. But not only did she fail to demonstrate any kind of sensitivity, in fact she laughed back at her cruelly.

"I haven't heard anything so funny in a long time." She dried the tears from her eyes. "You are talking to the caliph's first wife and the mother of the heir to the throne. I was born a Christian in your lands, but then I was married to Yusuf and I owe myself to him and to Allah. I am in charge of this harem, where I live with the rest of the women. Two hundred concubines also live here, and other women who distract him with their dances, their songs, and their poetry."

The two girls who had left the chamber returned with something in their hands.

"Now we will whiten your teeth with ground eggshell. Then you will wait until you are ordered to enter."

"Enter where?" Blanca asked.

The woman delivered her a resounding slap.

"Don't talk to me again without my permission. Do you understand?"

Both girls responded by nodding their heads.

"I am made by Allah for the glory of my master, and I walk proud down my own path. I give power to my lover over my body and my kisses I offer to those who desire them," she recited without taking a breath. "These rhymes were written by a wise poetess from Córdoba, and you will live them out tonight. Offer them your kisses if they are desired."

Marrakesh had become the capital of the Almohad Empire and boasted its finest buildings and its artists, thinkers, and sages.

From a broad terrace of the palace, with the sun on the point of disappearing, the city began to live the night. The new mosque shone, proud, a lofty tower a copy of which had been built in Seville. When the sun had fallen, you could begin to see the first torches being lit.

"Shall we serve you your tea, Your Highness?"

Caliph Yusuf lifted a hand and shook it a few times. It was his particular way of saying yes.

Lying over soft cushions and among leopard skins, he contemplated the nightfall. A fantastic range of colors, ocher, copper, and orange, were splayed out over the houses, plazas, and alleyways of the beautiful city.

A smooth melody rose to his ears and provoked an immediate shiver of pleasure. He breathed in the night air, savored the warm notes floating through it, and felt all his senses sharpen. At a second clap of his hands, he had a servant kneeling at his side. He ordered him to bring dancers.

"Also, I have brought you a gift from my travels," Don Pedro said, as he continued his conversation with the Yusuf.

"I like surprises." The eyes of the caliph shone with feeling. "What could it be?" He stayed there pensive. "You know that I love literature . . . I know. You've come with some new writing salvaged from some library in Córdoba."

"No. I am sorry I cannot give you such a pleasure, but I trust this will be even sweeter to you. You will know soon," Don Pedro de Mora answered mysteriously.

Only a few moments later, two shivering women knelt in front of them pushed along by various servants. They looked at Don Pedro and were filled with fear. That wicked man had dishonored them numerous times in the course of the voyage.

"Here is my gift. Two beautiful Christians who are, moreover, sisters. Look at their bodies, at their hair." He pulled away the cloth that covered them. At once two orange manes unfurled.

Yusuf ordered them to come close so that he could see them better. They resisted, furious, but they were dragged to him. He took Blanca's chin and kissed her on the lips. Then he grabbed a handful of hair and brought it to his nose, absorbing its aroma, while he stroked one of her breasts.

She glared at him in disgust.

Then he touched Estela's thighs and was surprised by how smooth and firm they were. Her lips pleased him even more.

"Dear friend, you are always wise in your gift-giving. God willing, you will be as assiduous with my requests."

He clapped twice, calling his secretary and personal servant over.

"Take them to my chambers and make everything ready."

XIII.

Fatima had prepared an exuberant and succulent dinner.

Diego and Galib were moved by the way Kabirma and Fatima were regaling them. It was obvious that Fatima and her father were making great efforts to make the albéitar and his assistant feel at ease and enjoy the evening. Fatima had spent hours in the kitchen preparing dishes and spices to offer their guests an assortment of culinary delicacies.

"My dear Fatima, whether you believe me or not, I assure you I've never tried a cake like yours." Galib closed his eyes and savored it. "It's, it's . . . grand, subtle, but filling at the same time. . . . Excellent, in truth."

"You're very kind, but I don't believe it's so good." The girl, blushing slightly, tilted the tray to serve him a bit more.

"First you find me a dedicated helper and now you show your remarkable gifts in the kitchen." He turned to the father. "Kabirma, your daughter is a jewel."

"Fatima is like no other," her father answered. "Her mother couldn't teach her anything; she died when Fatima was scarcely a girl, and yet she has inherited her touch in the kitchen." He gave her a tender pinch on the cheek. "I have to admit that this plate may even be better than the ones I remember her mother making."

"Don't talk so much and get to eating. It will get cold."

The girl sat down at Diego's side. Though they hadn't seen each other again since the day they met, she was happy things had gone well for him and felt proud of having helped him in a moment of great desperation.

"To meet you that day was a stroke of luck," Diego confessed.

"Now you seem like someone else, in truth. You were so famished and sad. And as soon as my father met you, he hurt you. So in those circumstances, I had no choice but to take pity on you."

"I remember," Kabirma said. "I confused you with a rogue."

Diego ignored the comment and focused on the girl. Though they hadn't seen each other since their meeting, he liked Fatima a lot. She had a face covered in freckles and thin, expressive lips. Her deep, very dark eyes went well with her brown skin. Her body was thin, well formed, with attractive legs. With all those attributes, the girl could have anything she wanted, though she was not flirtatious, rather the opposite.

In her way, she was a little like Diego. Both had lost their mothers when they were young, they had both passed quickly from childhood to working, and they knew well the meaning of such words as *sacrifice*, *dedication*, and *sweat*.

Even if they hadn't seen each other in all that time, Diego saw Fatima as a loyal and open person whom he could talk to without fear. He regarded her as a friend.

Since he had begun to work for Galib, Diego had not gone back to Zocodover. He had so much work that he could hardly step away from the stables of his master except when he accompanied him on one of his visits.

The same was not true for Galib, whom Kabirma would call on at times to attest to the health of certain horses in transactions where a great deal of money was changing hands.

Kabirma, from Jerez, was undoubtedly the greatest trader of Arabian horses in all of Toledo, and he was known as such throughout Castile. No one looking for a good example of that breed could find one in any stall in the market except for his. All those who moved in his world respected him, and he attributed this to always working with the best breed at a reasonable price.

No one knew who brought him the horses. That was his greatest secret, since it was the source of a great deal of his success. But in just that regard he was having serious problems, or better yet, extremely grave problems. His best purveyor was falling short with alarming frequency and the most recent group of horses had been a complete disaster.

Together with the terrible shipment, to make the situation worse, he had received a letter in which his man in Al-Andalus explained that this would be the last consignment he could sell him, because he had lost his license to sell.

From that lot, Kabirma still had one stud horse that he'd been unable to sell due to the lamentable state of its hooves. It needed to have its hooves treated so that it could be put up for sale. At last, he thought of Galib, and an idea occurred to him. He called Fatima and asked her to organize a good dinner. He had business to take care of.

～

"These sweets are typical of Gadir."

Fatima put a tray on the table and sat down again next to Diego. She had just watched him heal a horse next to Galib and was surprised by his skill.

Neither father nor daughter had dared to approach that stud horse on account of his fiery attitude. He had reared at them various times for just peeping in. And yet Diego had entered the stable without showing any qualms, though the animal, when it saw him, started salivating with fury. The boy got behind it and began to beat at its flanks, fearlessly following its steps. A little while later they heard him make soothing sounds with his mouth that calmed the animal down until it was more peaceful than a lamb. Thus Galib was able to take care of each one of its hooves, putting them between his legs and trimming off the deformations. Then he made some padding for the hooves from a few molds filled with clay and had Diego put on some temporary horseshoes. The next day they made the real ones.

Fatima offered them anise tea and more cakes, this time of honey and almond.

Galib and her father were discussing the need to improve the Norman and Breton breeds, the classic ones among warhorses, mixing them with the Arabians for greater agility in combat.

"The Breton, which the Christians use, is an enormous animal. But the Arabian is pure nobility, nerve, and agility. It's flexible, in contrast to the others."

"If we cross them, we will inflame the veins of the Christian horses with the energy of those animals born among the dunes, under the punishing sun." Galib loved that breed almost as much as he loved his job.

"The Christian cavalry is conceived to vanquish, to destroy everything it encounters in its path," Kabirma argued. "If you reduce their weight and strength, they won't be able to support the armor or fulfill the work expected of them."

"I know, but their enemies attack fast, with quick retreats and changing offensives that end up wrecking the classic attack technique of the Christians. The Christians' military strategists should begin to think about how to improve the qualities of their horses or else they will have trouble."

Galib tries one of those almond cakes and moaned with pleasure from the touch of cinnamon and sesame that Fatima had given them. He was going to congratulate her, but Kabirma cut him short.

"If you were right, we would need a great number of studs."

"Who better than you to engage in such an enterprise?"

"I have to confess something to you . . ." Kabirma stood and began to walk around his guest.

"Something's happened with you." Galib was made nervous by the somber expression on his face.

"I remember once that you spoke to me of the Yeguada de Las Marismas and I need to know more about it."

"I remember that, too, but I don't see what your interest is."

"Well, I'll explain. But before that, I have to tell you a secret, and I beg you to be discreet."

"Of course."

"The truth is that I have a terrible problem with my supplier of Arabian horses. It seems he's fallen out of favor with the governors of Al-Andalus, and without them, he can't sell to me. Without him, I don't have material, and Toledo will not see a single example of that breed. That's how bad things are."

"To travel there is madness," Galib said, knowing what the man from Jerez was thinking. "The *yeguada* is a jewel for the caliph, a bequest from his ancestors, something incomparable. A caprice that he keeps his eye on and that nobody in their right mind would come close to, let alone steal a few from their number. . . . Besides, they would recognize me. Forget it, Kabirma, it's too dangerous."

Everyone turned to him confusedly, except for Kabirma, who knew what he was talking about.

"I know a route that's almost untraveled. You wouldn't run any risk. Don't think of it as so dangerous. I tell you, it can be done," the man from Jerez roundly affirmed.

Diego understood what they were talking about and thought that this could be the opportunity he had been waiting for.

"I could come with you! You can count on me."

Fatima looked at each of them without knowing what they were talking about.

Galib scratched his beard and his gaze seemed to wander to some indeterminate place, very far from there.

"Not a day passes that I don't dream of seeing the Yeguada de Las Marismas again, in that land blessed by Allah; so beautiful that nothing else like it exists. Amid its marshes, as fertile as they are warm, you find the finest examples of Arabian horse that have ever existed. You can see them running there and feeding in complete freedom."

It was the first time Diego had heard Galib talk with feeling about that place.

Suddenly, his mentor seemed to return from that daydream and turned back to them.

"More than two hundred years ago, the greatest of our greatest, our first caliph, Abd-ar-Rahman III, possessed the best herd of Arabian and Berber horses ever brought together. He housed them in a city that he had constructed solely from love for his wife Azahara; Medina Azahara, it is called. Decades later, Caliph Almanzor took it to the islands of Guadalquivir, a land that they called Al-Madain or Marismas. There they brought together three thousand females and more than a hundred studs. I know it well, as I was one of its last guards. I watched over it like the irreplaceable treasure that it was, protecting it and keeping it pure, for the future. But I had to abandon it when things worsened with the new rulers, the Almohads, and my political persecution began."

"How many were there when you left?"

"Five thousand mares and two hundred stallions."

"Let's go for those horses, in Allah's name," Kabirma added with great determination.

Galib returned to the danger that such a trip would imply and tried to refuse, but both Diego and Kabirma insisted on doing it, perhaps the upcoming summer.

"They say that a new treaty between Castile and Al-Andalus will be signed next year. Perhaps then we won't meet with the same risks as now," Kabirma said, trying to support the idea with the information he had.

Galib looked at their faces, half defeated against so much insistence, and in all of them he met with the same desire to embark on, see, and live that once-in-a-lifetime experience.

"We will see. . . . There's still almost a year."

"Why do you love that breed of horses so much?"

Diego always took advantage of his journeys with Galib to get to know him better. His wisdom and his goodness enraptured him. He admired the man from whom he learned so much. He felt proud to be at his side, beside someone whom everyone listened to and asked for advice. That's why, when he found himself alone with Galib, he always tried to get the most out of him.

That night, back at Galib's house, after the dinner with Kabirma and Fatima, Diego tried to figure out what it was he saw in that breed.

"Among us, there exists a legend concerning how the Arabian breed was created. According to Ali ibn Abi Talib, the cousin of Muhammad and wife of his daughter Fatima, he heard it from the lips of the Prophet himself. It goes thus:

"When Allah wished to create a horse, he said to the south wind:

"'From you I will produce a creature that will be the honor of my followers, the humiliation of my enemies, and my defense against those who attack me.'

"And the wind replied:

"'Lord, do it according to your will.'

"Then he took a fistful of wind and created the horse, saying:

"'Virtue will suffuse your mane and your haunches. You will be my favorite among all the animals because I have made you master and friend. I have conferred upon you the power to fly without wings, whether attacking or retreating. I will sit men upon your haunches and they shall pray, they shall honor me and sing alleluias to my name.

"'Now, go! And live in the desert for forty days and forty nights. Sacrifice yourself! And learn to resist the temptation of water, bronze the color of your body and make lithe your muscles, because of wind you came and wind you shall be as you run.'"

Diego felt taken aback before such beauty and couldn't say a word, even less when Galib spoke again, making reference to his mare.

"Your beloved Sabba, wind of the east in my language, will carry you through lands you've never dreamed of. And from now on, I tell you, it will be horses that will guide your path. They shall make you great, Diego. I swear it. You shall do good with them, a great good indeed."

XIV.

B eauty should never be hidden.
   That is what Diego thought when he found Benazir with a niqab that covered her face. Though he could hardly see her eyes through that narrow slit, when he watched her, he thought that even dressed like that she was lovely, and that black favored her.

Benazir and Diego walked through the backstreets of the city of Toledo. She had asked him to accompany her up to the workshop of a famous translator where she had to pick up a book for Galib.

Gerardo de Cremona, the owner, had just come into possession of the library of a powerful deceased Jew, and when he saw that treatise on botany, he thought immediately of the albéitar.

"Do you feel uncomfortable at my side?" Benazir asked Diego.

"I don't understand."

"A Christian and a Muslim together. You will see how some would think ill of it. Galib didn't want us to leave together, but I don't think anything will happen."

Her husband had prohibited her from going out into the street without him or Sajjad. But that afternoon, since no one else could leave, she had convinced him to let her leave with his assistant.

"Let them think. . . . I don't see anything strange about it," Diego answered.

Benazir looked at him obliquely without talking. Sometimes she didn't know how to act with that boy. In reality, she didn't know how to act with anyone.

Since she arrived in Toledo Benazir was convinced that everything had gotten worse, or almost everything. She felt deeply deceived. She lived jailed inside that house, hardly seeing anyone, a second-class citizen in a Christian society that looked down on her and even insulted her. But she felt even worse when she remembered the years she had passed in Seville as the daughter of the ambassador. There she had enjoyed an exciting social life, full of parties and many other diversions, knowing herself to be one of the most attractive and desired women in the capital. But with her marriage she had thrown away a great deal of her expectations and dreams, and some were torn away completely.

She loved Galib but not like at the beginning. When she met him, he was a man with prestige, class, one of the most important officials in the caliph's court, and therefore respected by everyone. She had fallen in love with the man, but also with his position. And that was only half of what it had once been. In Seville, Benazir could breathe like a woman; in Toledo, she was being asphyxiated.

That is why when Diego appeared, something began to change inside her. The boy needed her. He came daily to her Arabic classes as if it was the most important task of the day. Diego fought against his misfortune without looking back and put his vitality and his enthusiasm at the service of learning. The boy's intelligence and inner beauty amazed Benazir and gave her days a new meaning.

She recognized her own free spirit in Diego, as well as his enviable youth. But she also admired the surprising ease with which he learned. In only four months of work, he had managed to read fairly fluently and to participate in a conversation; he had even dared a poem or two. But the most remarkable was his powerful memory. Diego was capable of remembering a text after reading it just once, however long it was. Benazir could not help but be stunned every time he did it, and even if those virtues were notable, the boy possessed another that was even more important for his learning—he was tenacious. When something was put before him, he didn't give up until he'd conquered it.

For the past few months, he had been obsessed with that journey to Las Marismas. Following that dinner with Kabirma, Diego constantly asked Galib if they would go there the following summer, but Galib didn't want to talk about it. He had a lot of work and too many worries. As much as it bothered him, Diego had to accept the situation and carry on with his daily tasks until he could try again later.

"You're very quiet." Diego looked at Benazir sideways.

She excused herself with a smile but continued in silence. He tried to forget the disagreeable scene in the stables that had preceded her departure.

"Sajjad always be watching. Sajjad no like what he see. Madame not yours. . . . Not yours."

"Be quiet and don't talk like that! The master will hear you. You're saying stupidities."

"Sajjad not dumb. Madame pretty. No lie to Sajjad."

It seemed the old stable keeper had nominated himself guardian and protector of Benazir's virtue, and though he wasn't wrong in his impressions, Diego was bothered by his ever more frequent warnings. Besides, he didn't understand how he had noticed, when he only saw her for his classes and Sajjad was prohibited from being in the house.

When they entered the Christian neighborhood inhabited by the Franks, where Cremona had his translation workshop, Diego noticed gestures of disapproval on the part of numerous passersby whenever they walked past them.

"They're looking at us cruelly."

"It's not because of you," Benazir responded. "They don't like my garments. My mere presence bothers them. Many of them are what you call Ultramontanes, natives of the Pyrenees, and they would like a crusade like the ones that liberated Jerusalem to expel us or to exterminate us all."

When they entered an alley, a strong gust of wind blew against them, making walking difficult. Diego contemplated Benazir. The air pressed her dress into her body and revealed a lovely figure with generous contours. He felt guilty. How he wanted to run his hands over it. . . . And at the same time, he hated himself for it. He couldn't manage to express what was happening to him but he knew he shouldn't even be thinking of it. It wasn't right. Benazir was the wife of his master and, if Diego acted on his feelings, he would never be able to renew Galib's trust in him.

"Forget them, it's not worth it." She spoke to him in Arabic.

"They owe you respect," he replied, also in her language, with a defiant look. "And a man can't allow . . ."

Benazir pulled at him and sped up her step with the intention of getting away, proud at Diego's reaction. After they turned a corner, they took a narrow alley where the translator's workshop was located. A strong door was hidden in the center of a wall covered with marigolds and an enormous asparagus plant. To the left, a wooden shield indicated the owner.

They entered after calling twice at the door without receiving any reply. It seemed like any other shop, although slightly strange, since apart from having a large counter no one was waiting on anyone and there were no objects on the shelf.

They waited a moment, but not a soul appeared. There was just a door that seemed to lead to the interior. It was half closed. When they pushed it, it creaked resoundingly, and yet that didn't attract the interest of its owners either. Benazir peeked in and was astonished by what she saw. She stepped aside for Diego.

"Come in and see how marvelous . . ."

It was a rectangular room, not very large but with a special charm. A thick column of light fell from a high alabaster ceiling, coming to rest on two enormous tables that ran from one end to the other, leaving a narrow passage in the middle. Atop them reposed, tranquil, hundreds of beautiful books bound in fine cordovan leather. Their careful and sinuous Arabic script, embossed in gold on their covers and spines, shone beneath the reflection of the sun.

Looking more closely, Diego discovered among them the texts of such signal Muslim authors as Averroes and Abu Zakaria, whom Galib cited frequently. Others were unknown to him, like Aristotle, Heraclitus, or Hippocrates.

He ran a finger over their spines. Out of respect for their valuable contents, he didn't want to touch even one of those manuscripts, but he looked at all of them, one by one, until he reached the edge of the room, where another door awaited them, this one of exquisitely carved oak. When they came close, they heard a grave and raspy voice. It was pronouncing a long phrase in Latin.

Benazir opened it with purpose and entered into a smaller room. Inside there were three men who turned around immediately in curiosity.

"Is one of you Gerardo de Cremona?"

One, with abundant gray hair pulled back in a ponytail, weathered skin, and small, deep-set eyes, set down the book he had in his hands and smiled at her.

"So they call me. Gerardo de Cremona, translator. One of the many employed nowadays in this profession in Toledo."

With him was an unkempt-looking friar and a person with a wrinkled face topped with an enormous yellow turban.

"How can we help you?"

"I am Benazir, the wife of the albéitar Galib, and this is his assistant, Diego."

The face of the translator relaxed and he remembered the order.

"Ah! The albéitar Galib. Welcome. Come in, please. Make yourselves at home. I have your order in another room."

Gerardo de Cremona turned to the door that led to the next room but realized he hadn't introduced them to the people he was with.

"How rude I am! Excuse me. I don't suppose you know my companions.

Friar Benito, besides a Calatravan priest, is a great expert in the Latin language. He doesn't always work with us, only when his master charges him with some task." The person referred to stood and made a kindly face. "Now we are working on a treatise of Avicenna, *The Book of Healing*. We will translate it from Arabic to Romanic and then into Latin."

"Why wouldn't you do it directly into Latin?" Diego asked, interested by everything he saw and heard in the room.

"Arabic is a complex language. The vowels can sound different depending on how they are intoned, and their meaning changes as well. In our case, Habim bin Dussuf"—the person referred to bowed his head, the traditional form of salutation—"is responsible for reading the text in the original. He has two advantages; not only is it his own language, but he is a recognized theologian, and he thus knows the material well. While he reads the original, I make the translation into Romanic, your language, and Friar Benito translates that into Latin and writes it out."

Habim turned toward a corner where he picked up a bronze jar and offered them a cup of tea.

"Though it may strike you as too long or laborious a process," Gerardo de Cremona continued, "in practice, it isn't. Besides, it is more common nowadays to find someone who knows Arabic and Romanic, or Romanic and Latin. Very few people have mastered both Arabic and Latin. Do you understand?"

"What types of books do you translate?" Diego drank the tea, flavored with honey and scented with sandalwood, in one sip.

"It depends on the buyer. The church wants treatises of Muslim thought to better know who they're up against." Friar Benito nodded, completely in agreement with this mission. "Even so, the books of medicine and science remain the most popular, both the writing by the Greek philosophers and those coming from noted Arabic doctors, philosophers, and scholars."

He took up a thick volume from a shelf and caressed it as though he held a delicate treasure in his hands. Diego read the name Dioscorides on the cover.

"They come from all over Europe looking for them," Cremona continued. "Ancient wisdom disappeared from the West when Rome lost her empire. It was only preserved in Byzantium. Many Arabic scholars compiled them for the libraries in Baghdad, Damascus, or Egypt where they were translated. Some of those treatises were copied and wound up in the most famous libraries of Al-Andalus, where they were studied and preserved as authentic jewels of knowledge. But seventy years ago, as a result of the Almohad invasion, many wise Jews and Arabs were so threatened by the religious and cultural extremism that they had to flee. Toledo was an ideal destination, and for that reason many of them settled among us, and this is how there came to be created what some now call the School of Translators, an immense group of illustrious men dedicated to translate that ancient wisdom from Arabic into Latin or Romanic. King Alfonso of Castile is the greatest promoter of this enterprise. He has brought many scholars to Toledo who are fleeing from the one-sided vision of the Almohads."

"Who else buys your work?" Diego asked while he leafed through the book the man had treated so carefully.

"Our clients come from the most far-flung universities and cathedrals and they pay well. They normally look for the philosophical works of Arabic authors, like Avicenna, most recently, or of Jews like Maimonides of Córdoba."

"In the other room, I saw a beautiful collection of books and I was interested in one in particular, but I don't know what its value could be."

Galib had spoken to him numerous times of that treatise on the albéitar, the work of an anonymous author and the first written reference to the profession. Diego had found it on one of the tables.

"Boy, I regret to tell you that those books are far outside your reach. I hope I am not offending you. Do you understand?"

At that instant, Benazir made a discreet but portentous face. The translator understood and reacted immediately, inviting them to look at the books.

He stood between the two tables and ran his hands over their entire contents.

"Here you see my entire supply. They are all the books translated by my team and some in their original languages. When I sell one, I make a new copy, taking advantage of an identical copy I keep in another room. But tell me: Which were you interested in?"

Diego took it respectfully in his hands. At once he realized that however much it might interest him, it was possible that he could never pay for it in his entire life.

"This one."

"*Treatise on the Albéitar's Art*," the owner read its title out loud. "A book by an unknown author, who they say may have been a Castilian residing in Córdoba. Excellent choice, young man. It is believed to be the first book dealing with the illnesses of horses and their cures, very important for your future profession, of course." He opened it and suddenly remembered something. "Sadly, I have to tell you that I don't have it translated."

"He knows Arabic," Benazir interrupted.

"You really understand it?"

Diego opened to a page and began to translate the first paragraph. Gerardo de Cremona stood behind him, confirming the young man was right in almost everything he read.

"Really, you wouldn't have much difficulty in reading it."

"I don't think I could pay for it, but could I come some afternoons to consult it?"

"Diego, allow me to give it to you," Benazir exclaimed, proud of her student's progress. "You'll see, it will help us with our classes."

"I don't know if I should . . ." Diego hesitated.

"It's decided. I will take two books, my husband's and this one."

Once in the street, Benazir was happy to see the smile on the boy's face. He held on to the book as though it was his very soul, and his face reflected his overwhelming gladness. Benazir walked at his side, satisfied with what she had done. She felt comfortable beside a boy so full of nobility, simplicity, and talent.

She looked at him sideways and saw he was doing the same. She felt a strong temptation to embrace him, but they were in the middle of the street. It couldn't be. . . .

A few streets farther on, they came across the men from the tavern again and one of them recognized them.

"Mix with Moors," he said, "and you'll get contaminated with the evil they carry around inside."

Benazir kept Diego from looking at him.

"Don't get angry, I beg you." She lowered her head and asked him to keep walking.

"But . . ."

"That is how they see us; there is nothing we can do. They also call us the king's Moors, because we belong to him the way the Jews do. We are *mudajjan*, mudéjars, free Muslims, permitted to live, pray, and work in Christian lands, but in these turbulent times, it is very hard to find peace. That is the truth. That's how it is."

"Leave your slave with us and we'll send her back happier than she is with you," another insisted, making an obscene face.

Diego couldn't resist and leapt at the second man even though he was clearly twice his age. Perhaps because he caught him by surprise, Diego managed to knock the man down and hit his face with punches. But the same didn't happen with the rest. They responded in kind, without paying attention to Benazir's cries for help, falling on Diego and beating him so badly that blood soon stained his clothes and ran over the paving stones in the street. Fortunately, a knight arrived with various neighbors to stop the bloodbath, because otherwise, it could have proved fatal for Diego.

Hours later the boy rested in Galib's house at Benazir's firm request. His side hurt. A doctor had just examined him and had not found any fractures, but a few of his ribs were damaged and he had abundant scratches and bruising. He rubbed him down with a thick salve on the affected area, which relieved him a great deal, and then he bandaged Diego tightly.

From that moment, Benazir did not leave him even for a second. She relieved the burning of his wounds with a damp cloth. Where she saw a bit of inflammation, she rapidly covered it with a paste made from willow leaves. She had him drink a liquid she had boiled with the bark from the same tree to soothe his pains, and she gave him a piece of sugarcane to bite so it wouldn't be so bitter.

"I'm sorry, everything was my fault. I owe you a favor."

She pulled back her veil and took his hand, kissing it in gratitude for his reaction. And suddenly Diego saw how her eyes strayed over his nude torso, young and muscular. Benazir looked at it, feeling a strong urge to caress it, to kiss it, though she immediately rejected those thoughts. Startled, she stood up brusquely and turned toward a balcony to take in a bit of fresh air.

"Do you feel bad?" Diego asked, surprised by that abrupt action.

"Worse than I had even imagined. . . ."

XV.

————————

Even when she would leave, her perfume was still notable for hours in the room.

Diego smelled his hands and she was there. He tried with the sheets and recognized her as well. Benazir never left that room.

He had been staying in Galib's house for four days, forced to remain there until his wounds had completely healed. He felt well, but the doctor had the last word and he still hadn't given his approval.

At the beginning, Diego had offered innumerable objections to staying in the house, but soon he realized it would allow him to be near Benazir every day, and he stopped protesting.

She passed the hours at his side, sewing, reading him poetry, and above all, telling her stories. She gave him enough clues to understand her past, and with her tales, he found himself transported to Persia. As the days passed, the conversations became more intimate and Benazir began to share some of her dreams and feelings as well.

In that atmosphere of trust, Diego took interest in the most intimate aspects of her personality, and soon his doubts blossomed, the first indications that she was living in a deteriorating relationship.

Sometimes she would sit close to him on the bed, to care for his wounds, and then Diego would think he was dying. That became a ritual rife with sensuality. First, when he was turned around, she would take off the bandage from the day before and clean the wound with a cloth soaked in warm water, very slowly, washing him afterward with its other side. Her other hand almost always rested on his shoulder, or in different places on his back. Diego concentrated on feeling the tenuous warmth of her skin, its smooth touch. Then she would ask him to turn over so she could see the cut on his neck. It was then that he had her closest to him. He would focus on her eyes, on her sensual mouth and the tautness of her cheeks. When she tried to clear away the small bits of blood or scabs, her hair would fall freely over him, grazing his chest, his face.

Diego felt her so close sometimes that he had to grasp the sheets in his hands, almost tie himself to them, so he wouldn't wrap his arms behind the woman's back.

In the afternoons, by candlelight, Benazir would enjoy reciting him some poem of Arabic origin. And that was another of those moments of special emotion. Diego would close his eyes and concentrate on reciting the soft whisper of her words in his interior, the cadence of her tone, the pauses, the restrained breath; Diego absorbed every small detail that flowered from that woman, plunged into happiness and joy.

One of those afternoons, Diego decided to leave the bedroom to stretch his swollen legs. He felt impatient to take back up his normal life and he decided to force the doctor to give him a good bill of health the next day.

He didn't see anyone; he only heard his own footsteps. He thought that the servants must already be sleeping downstairs, and he only saw light emanating from Galib's bedroom. Between his own room and that of his master there was a glassed-in gallery that opened onto a lit yard. As he crossed it, he saw that the door of those rooms was open and he saw Benazir inside, next to Galib. The growing darkness that enveloped him made it so no one could realize he was there. He was curious and he stayed there quiet, observing them.

Benazir was wearing a white nightgown, very thin. She had just given Galib a tightly wrapped package. He was concentrating on opening it and with great emotion he took out the book he had chosen from the translator's workshop. With so much going on in the house, she hadn't had time to give it to him before. Diego heard him say thanks and then he immediately embraced her.

While she was being kissed, Benazir loosened the cord that held her gown to her neck and half of her body was revealed. When Diego saw her naked back, he felt a shiver of emotion, a strange anxiousness, a great inner heat. And in that moment, he wanted to be Galib, to receive her in his arms, undress her completely, try the taste of her skin.

And yet his master didn't seem to recognize the passionate intentions of his wife, and he pulled away from her to examine the book. He opened it and began to turn pages, lost in himself. Benazir turned her back to him in disappointment and walked to the door, with half her body exposed. And then she saw Diego. Her first reaction was to cover herself, but almost immediately she took her hands from the cloth that covered her and the fabric fell to the floor. Diego felt moved without knowing what to do. He did not know whether to stop looking, to leave, or to approach her.

Their gazes met and he read the frustration in her eyes, and he thought he saw pain, too, provoked by her husband's disdain. He, though, wanted her. . . .

He swallowed and his saliva tasted bitter. It wasn't right what he was doing. It was as if he was stealing an intimacy that didn't belong to him. For that reason, he turned and ran from the gallery. He needed to breathe, to get a bit of fresh air and meditate on what he had just seen.

He looked for Sabba in the stables, and without saddling her, he mounted her and left the house. His entire body hurt, but his pain transcended the physical.

He crossed the streets of Toledo perplexed. He still felt the palpitations in his heart and continued to see her before him, so lovely . . .

"Sabba, I have to tell you something. . . . That woman has me under a spell. Take me to our house. I can't go on here."

The mare reared her head back, caressing him with her mane, and neighed softly, as though trying to calm him with those warm sounds. Diego held on to her without directing, and closed his eyes, pensive and without thinking of what path they had taken.

To his surprise, Sabba didn't take him to their house, but rather to the outskirts of Toledo, to another place he found familiar, Fatima's home. The animal stopped close to her door and whinnied. The boy heard bells and counted to ten. He needed to speak to someone and Fatima was a woman, she was his age, and she would understand. He congratulated Sabba for her decision and dismounted.

"But what are you saying? Isn't that your master's wife?" Fatima was shocked by what she had just heard.

"I know. . . . It's absurd."

"Not just that, if he finds out, you are gambling with your life and a promising future."

Diego kicked a rock inside Kabirma's granary, where they had gone to be far from indiscreet ears.

"Your relationship with Galib requires trust and loyalty. I don't want to imagine what could happen if you don't control yourself. Besides, that woman is much older than you. I don't know . . ."

"But she is so beautiful. . . . You're completely right, Fatima. But I feel crazy when I see her. She possesses something around her that attracts me savagely, until I can't take it anymore. Do you understand me? Do you think it's normal what is happening?"

Fatima observed him. More than a year had passed, but he was no longer the boy she'd found weak in the middle of the market. His robust body, his hardened hands, his skin, his ever-warmer gaze, his face . . .

"It could be you're confusing her intentions."

"I don't think so, not anymore." He remembered her naked in front of him.

"Think about it, she feels attractive and desired by you, and she might do things she doesn't really want to do. It happens to me. When I see a man who attracts me, to get his attention I might act in a way that later seems absurd to me. But not in that moment, I don't know, it's like a force of nature makes you show all your seductive power, apart from other things, and that might happen with Benazir and you."

"You're explaining what happened as if everything was due to the influence of the instincts, and I have those too, believe me."

"No, it's not just that. Maybe that woman is passing through a difficult moment in her relationship with Galib; she feels discouraged and she sees the opposite of him in you. You just said to me you almost feel yourself dying at her side; she knows it, don't think she doesn't realize. She has seen the power of attraction she wields over you, and if in other circumstances she would have avoided it, now maybe she needs it and that is why she has opened a door for you."

"I have to get out of her house before temptation defeats me and I end up opening that door."

"I understand, Diego, but I don't think it's right for you. You still haven't learned enough with Galib; don't waste this opportunity. Be brave, resist temptation, avoid it. I know you can manage. There are many other women in Toledo, and much younger ones, too."

Diego rubbed his eyes to erase all the memory of what had happened in Galib's house.

"You are strong and intelligent. You should face up to the situation. You have no excuse not to show respect to your master. The consideration Galib has shown you is far from usual between master and apprentice. He loves you, he looks at you like a son. . . . You have to keep that in mind."

Diego and Fatima had raised their voices in the course of their conversation. They had gone far from the house to be able to speak without fear, but suddenly, Fatima heard a noise, someone wandering around close to the granary.

She put her hand over Diego's mouth and they hid in a corner. They waited a few seconds in silence.

Diego leaned on a pile of straw and curled up, defeated by the truth of Fatima's words and the weight of his guilt.

Fatima looked at him with pity and approached him to cheer him up. Amid whispers she offered him her confidence and all the support he needed. The girl embraced him to suffuse him with the strength she was capable of giving; then she felt Diego's tenderness, his warmth, his heartbeat, and the strength of his body. She separated from him and fixed her gaze on his lips. They were like that for several endless seconds. Diego felt uncomfortable with that silence.

"Maybe I should go, Fatima. . . . It's a little late."

XVI.

Sabba was in danger.

Diego woke up knowing it. He called for her.

He ran as fast as he could through the dark streets of Toledo toward Galib's house. In his rush to get there as soon as possible, he cut through the neighborhood of La Alcaicería, one of the most luxurious markets, and it was a bad decision. He wasn't a thief, but he must have seemed so to the eyes of the guards when they saw him pass through without stopping, even if they had let him through a number of times. They ran behind him though they couldn't catch him; Diego slipped and fell and hit his head very hard. Without losing time, he stood up agilely, filled his lungs with air, and took off even faster than before.

Two streets before he reached the alley where the door to Galib's house was, he could smell it. There was a fire somewhere close by, and he was afraid of where it might be. He clenched his teeth and closed the last few yards of distance without taking a breath. As he was about to arrive, he ran into two men fleeing in the opposite direction. In their eyes he saw hatred; they ran off, and then he saw the flames. They had reached Galib's stables, but not his house. He beat at the gate with all his might, and since no one responded, he leapt over the barrier and ran to the stables, screaming to wake everyone up.

With his shoulder, he knocked down the door to the stables, and when he entered, he was blown back by a gust of heat. Covering his face with his arm, he decided to enter. First he heard the nervous whinny of Sabba and other horses, but he did not hear Sajjad. He looked for him amid the thick smoke that came out between the stalls, near to his narrow quarters, but he didn't find him there, either. The flames began to graze a large pile of straw that divided him from that area. Without losing time, he grabbed an old blanket and threw it over his head. He crossed through the curtain of fire without breathing and kicked the door open. Sajjad woke up and saw him through sleepy eyes.

"Get out of here! The stable's burning! We have to get the animals out now."

"Sajjad no sleep. . . . Sajjad help. Run."

They crossed through the fire again, wrapped in the blanket, then separated to rescue the animals. Diego ran after Sabba. He found her huddled in a corner, with panic in her eyes. A roof beam was burning just next to her. From so much pulling at the rope to free herself, her neck was bleeding. The poor thing was sweating, terrified. They looked at each other. Sabba snorted with fright, though she felt better when she saw her master.

"Hold on. . . . I'm with you."

She whinnied loudly.

Diego threw the blanket over the flaming wood and ran over to untie her from the wall. Once she was free, she looked toward the exit, but an enormous column of flame began to rise over the walls and blinded her. Her muscles tensed, her nostrils expanded, and she looked for a way out. She seemed guided by her survival instinct to escape from that hell, but without pulling away completely, she looked at Diego, as though wishing to know first what her master would do. Since she was an animal, her reaction seemed absurd, given the danger they were in, but Diego understood her motivations with great feeling. They should flee, it was urgent, but still, they stayed there a moment, looking at each other. Diego understood was Sabba was thinking. She turned her head toward her flanks and Diego leapt on her back. Like a tightened spring, her hind legs took them from that oven through the fire until they arrived at the courtyard.

Galib and Benazir were there, desperate, moving from one side to the other incessantly. Sajjad was there too with the other animals, some badly burned and hysterical. They all relaxed when they saw him arrive mounted on Sabba, with fire still smoking on her mane. Diego put it out with his own hands and then put his hands around her neck, caressing her tenderly. Diego was crying from joy.

Galib ran up to them, and Benazir as well, and both saw, astonished, that Sabba was crying as well.

Without losing any time, they tried to put out the fire, but it was impossible. The flames spread and engulfed the stables without anyone being able to do anything but rescue the animals.

Galib knew it was useless to try and stave off the fire and simply prayed to Allah that it wouldn't reach the house. When they realized it was impossible to do anything against its devouring fury, Galib asked everyone to throw water onto the façade of the house so the fire wouldn't attack it. If the two structures had been closer, there would have been no use in the efforts they were making, but luckily, between the house and the stables there was a space that acted as a firebreak and kept the flames from following their path.

In the middle of the night, Galib, Benazir, Sajjad, and Diego watched powerless as the dreadful fire consumed the last remains of the stable. And there, exhausted, wearied, and stunned, they saw the effects of it without being able to do anything but think about all they had lost.

"So many years of work . . ." Galib mourned. "Since my arrival in Toledo I have given everything to be able to build these stables and make a name for myself."

"Why . . .?" Benazir embraced her husband. She wanted to console him, but she didn't know how. She felt defeated as well.

Diego remembered the two men he had come across and mentioned them without being able to give any other detail about their identities or intentions.

"What could we have done to them to end up like this?" Benazir asked impotently. "First they attack us in the streets, then they burn our possessions. Galib, don't you think perhaps we should leave?"

He looked at her and then at his helpers, lowered his head, and turned to the ruins of what had been his stables.

Diego left him alone and went to check on the horses that had survived the fire. Some bellowed from pain because of the severe burns they had received. Alarmed by their state, he knew he needed to act quickly. He would have preferred Galib's help, but he could see he was too deeply desolate.

Although he tried to take care of them, he was humiliated by his slow results, and knowing he couldn't take care of all of them, he decided to ask for help. He found Galib crying in the middle of the burned area.

"Galib, if we don't hurry, other horses will die." His master didn't answer. Diego came closer to him and put his hand on his back. "We will make it through this. . . . We will get past it. You can count on me."

With feverish eyes, the man looked at Diego. He saw serenity in the boy's face and became even more touched. Allah had wanted this boy to be at his side and he thanked him for it every night in his prayers. He had earned his post and now he was making a place in Galib's heart.

Galib rose from the floor, leaned on Diego, and walked to where the animals were. When he saw them, he was in agreement. They would have to act fast to save them all.

He left Diego calming down a furious mare and he went to look for a salve he had prepared for burns, a mix of quince and lily oil with an extract of almond bark. Luckily, he found it quickly and they began to spread that paste over the sores that looked the worst; apart from protecting the exposed tissue, it brought the horses relief almost immediately.

The aftermath of the fire was terrible. The stables were all turned into ash, and with them, the fruit of years of labor. Besides that, eight horses had died, five of which weren't Galib's and had only been there to be treated.

For days, Galib wandered around the ruins of the stables in anguish over the disaster, without imagining who could have done that terrible thing to him. In his heart, he preferred to think it hadn't been on purpose, but he knew that many people hated them for the simple fact that they were Muslims.

Galib could have asked for justice, he could have looked for the guilty parties if there were any, but he didn't want to bother anyone, and as always, he preferred to take refuge in his work and to push forward.

In addition to the problem of the lack of stables, there was another, almost worse: the enormous debt he now owed to the owners of the dead animals, which began to feel overwhelming. He owed them more than five hundred *sueldos*, and he had nowhere near that amount. He looked for credit with the Jewish moneylender but what he received wasn't enough to pay even half.

As soon as he heard what had happened, Kabirma came to see him.

"It isn't right what they've done to you!" The trader contemplated that scene of destruction while he walked over the ashes of what was left of the stables.

He and Diego helped Galib look for tools, hinges, horseshoes, anything that could be still useful. The strong burned scent had still not disappeared, and nothing was standing but the furnace and the two anvils for the forge.

Kabirma did not need his friend to give him too many details to deduce the serious economic difficulties Galib was passing through, but he felt incapable of helping pay for the five dead horses, let alone build new stables. He would need them for his profession and they would cost a fortune. In that situation, Kabirma thought once again of the longed-for voyage.

"What better opportunity to get hold of animals from Las Marismas? That way you could end up with better horses and better clients, and for the ones I take and manage to sell, I would give you half my profits." Galib's face was tense. He still considered the plan too complicated. Even if Kabirma was right, he couldn't see it as feasible.

"My situation right now is critical, Galib. I've gone for weeks without selling anything, since the Arabian horses even bring the attention of customers who end up buying something else. Without them, I'm losing my prestige, and people have started talking. . . . If I don't do anything, I may even have to close the stand in Zocodover; I can't pay the rent on it."

Galib listened to him with respect and understood the situation, but even then, he wasn't convinced. He lacked the strength, the will; everything scared him: to stay and not be able to get ahead, to flee and leave his wife alone, if they recognized him and arrested him. . . . When he said good-bye to Kabirma, his fear showed, although this time he did not give a firm negative.

A few days later, while Diego was examining the progress of the wounded animals, he saw Galib's desperation and couldn't help but relive what he had gone through at the inn.

Almost three years had passed since then, and in addition to his circumstances, he himself had changed. His body had left adolescence behind, and his mind had opened to knowledge, to science, and to his passion for the noblest of professions, that of albéitar.

Diego had also learned to love a culture that was not his and that he had once cursed and hated. Now he saw values and principles as admirable as those of his own religion in the Muslims. From that visceral rejection that had characterized his initial relations with Galib, there had grown inside him a certain understanding that finally became sincere respect. From Benazir and from his master, Diego had learned to distinguish between the goodness of their beliefs and the intolerance of the Almohads' doctrines.

Galib had taught him to recognize and treat the most common horse illnesses and had instilled in him a discipline to comment on and debate everything he read. Now Arabic was not difficult for Diego, and he even memorized what he read without the need to translate it. Between them they always spoke in that language, and he began to do so with Sajjad as well.

A little before the fire happened, Diego had felt a great satisfaction when he had finally paid for Sabba. Not only did he mean to repay a debt to his master, it was also for her, in gratitude for her eternal loyalty.

Throughout this time, he had gotten to know Galib quite well. At the beginning, he was overawed by his knowledge, but now he admired him more for his professional honesty and his humanity. He had never seen him downplay adversity, and when there was something he didn't know, he didn't hide that either. One thing that characterized him was the constant thirst to know everything, to know more every day. Constancy in work, an almost sacred respect for his clients, his invariable capacity for wonder, and an inexhaustible curiosity were only a few of the many virtues that Diego wanted for himself.

Galib pushed him and encouraged him to use his abilities, his exceptional ability to analyze and predict animal behaviors, because, he said, all that would help when he was making his diagnoses. Diego was tremendously intuitive and also possessed great manual dexterity. Galib reproached him for his impatience in making a diagnosis too quickly, without considering all the information, and told him that if he could overcome that defect, he could become an albéitar before the six years other apprentices needed were up.

Diego, the albéitar. Could it one day be a reality?

In the days that followed the disaster, Diego saw a transformation in Galib. A strange bitterness appeared in his character, though he wanted to give the impression of everything being normal. Diego thought his apparent good humor might be a smokescreen behind which lurked the rest of his problems.

Like Kabirma, Diego thought the best solution to all their ills was to take the trip to Las Marismas. On their return, they could resolve all their debts and start a new life.

Every time Diego brought it up, though, Galib would look away and think of simpler solutions that might free them from that situation.

XVII.

G alib and Diego worked night and day.

Busying himself with the animals, the albéitar wanted to think of nothing else. His wife was passing through a bad moment and his young assistant seemed always ill because he was so tired. Still, Galib had been sucked into a spiral of work and it didn't even permit him to see anyone else's problems.

Diego and Sajjad had proposed to Galib that he contract a builder to organize the new stables, but Galib either didn't want or couldn't permit himself a single expense except for returning the money for the animals that had died in the fire.

For that reason, Diego and Sajjad began to rebuild the stables themselves with the little they knew about construction. At the same time, Diego accompanied his master and gave remedies to the animals that had to stay with them regardless of the circumstances, but if they cured them during the day then they wouldn't have to sleep outside.

Galib lost his serenity. He paid visits during the day, helped to raise the new stables in the afternoon, at night, before dawn. He tried to get everything ready as soon as possible and all he managed was a ramshackle construction that collapsed after a few days and wounded Sajjad's already injured leg. Sajjad had to remain bedbound a few days and Galib felt responsible as well for what had happened to his old helper. For that reason, whenever he could, he went to see him to attend to whatever his needs were. To his misfortune, he had lost a worker and now had another task on his hands.

"This situation is madness!" Benazir shouted at him one day. "I can't do it anymore. You don't sleep, you don't eat, you don't leave anyone in peace. It was your small-mindedness that led to Sajjad's accident. You made him work on something he didn't know how to do. You should have paid someone to build the stables. . . . Our life has become a madhouse!"

"I can't do anything else. It will only be awhile, then it will be over."

"I can't do it anymore. I think you're losing your judgment. I see Diego working alone on the construction and he's going to get hurt, too, or else you will, I don't know . . . We can't go on like this."

That day, Galib left the house so he wouldn't argue with Benazir. He knew she was right, though he didn't want to admit it. He had put useless pressure on everyone, since getting back to his previous situation would take lots of time that he didn't have. He spent all the day away without anyone knowing where he had gone, and when he came back, well into the night, he told everyone his decision.

"I will go to Las Marismas with Kabirma and his daughter. I've already talked it over with him. He assures me there is a route that almost no one else knows. That's the one we will take. Getting through the guards who normally watch over the wetlands is another matter, but we'll figure that out when we get there. We'll leave in four days. I'm counting on you"—he looked at Diego—"to take care of Benazir and Sajjad in my absence. I can't risk your safety."

When he heard this, Diego felt crestfallen. He was going to be left in Toledo. For three years he had dreamed of only one thing, going to rescue his sisters, and his master knew that was what was most important for him.

"Don't ask that of me, I beg you." To stay looking after the house and Sajjad would mean being too close to Benazir, and many hours alone with her. And he didn't want to even imagine that torture.

"It's decided," Galib said. "I understand your disappointment and I can imagine the cause of it, but I cannot put my wife's life in danger, and besides, I will try to make the journey quickly, take what animals we can, and return. If we had to go looking for your family, we wouldn't even know where to start. You don't know Seville. It's a big city. Perhaps you think you would arrive and they would be there waiting for you. That is the furthest thing from reality. I don't know where they might be. Nobody does. It would complicate everything and it would leave me exposed. It can't be, no."

Diego clenched his fists with rage, angered by Galib's lack of sensitivity.

"I don't understand."

"What more can I tell you? Have I not been very clear?" Galib stared at him firmly.

Diego thought of a new argument, refusing to accept the situation.

"I don't understand how you can leave Benazir in Toledo after knowing the fire was set on purpose, maybe by someone who considers all Muslims his enemy. . . . Have a good time. Even if I try to take care of her, there will be many times when I will have to be away, and I remind you, I have to sleep in my house at night. Remember the prohibition?" Galib was affected by the reasonableness of what the boy said. "Imagine what could happen to Benazir if word gets out that she sleeps alone at night, her only help a cripple, which is what Sajjad is now."

"And what will we do with Sajjad?" Galib replied, clearly with less strength than before. "We can't take him with us, but I think he can take care of himself."

"Sajjad no give problem. . . . His leg better," the poor old man said.

"And how will we manage to convince them that you are not Christian?"

"Take me with another name. I will dress like you. I don't see the problem in it."

"If they find us out, they will kill us. This journey will not be easy."

"If Fatima is going," Benazir said, "I don't see what is wrong with all of us going. Diego is right, it's no less dangerous going than staying here."

"It's very risky, Benazir, and you know it. We live in very troubled times. I am especially worried about our entrance into Seville. Who doesn't know you there?"

"Diego can go to Seville with Kabirma. We can wait for them elsewhere, far from there."

Galib spent three days more preoccupied than normal, barely speaking, as if he still hadn't decided one way or another. But the next morning, Benazir found him setting clothing over a blanket and laying his surgical instruments in a small suitcase.

"Well?" his wife asked him.

"Get ready, I will go to speak with a friend who owes me a favor so that he comes to see Sajjad from time to time. Tell Diego as well, we are going. When you have everything ready, we will go look for Kabirma. He will be waiting for us."

Hours later, once they were together, they headed west and then south. They had decided against taking the route that united Toledo and Córdoba, the one everyone used. Their path would take them two days more, but it was scarcely populated when it wasn't completely empty. It passed far from the castles and fortresses, both the Arab and the Christian ones, and it was the one Kabirma always took when transporting his merchandise.

The man from Jerez had a prized safe-conduct paper signed by the vizier himself, which gave Kabirma freedom to roam and to buy and sell in Al-Andalus. Still, that pass did not render the travelers invulnerable, especially during the first four days of their travels, before and after they crossed the frontier. There, the tension was higher, given the numerous raids that took place among the different groups of bandits. In total, they calculated it would be fifteen days until they arrived at Las Marismas, as long as they didn't take too long in Seville. Diego promised he would lose little time there, even though he would try to figure out where his sisters had ended up. All of them had a spare horse and the utensils and rations they would need so that they would be able to make it through the whole trip. Fatima rode her handsome Asmerion, an Arabian stallion with an almost white coat and a mane so long it almost stretched to the spurs. Her small, lithe body seemed almost lost atop his enormous back.

A few leagues from Toledo, on the way to Pulgar, they came across a dozen Calatravan knights and their squires. They were coming back from an incursion into enemy territory, a place near where Kabirma's group was about to pass.

That first night, they camped on the banks of a creek and built a fire. A little after dinner they slept, barely speaking, in pain and tired from their many hours on the road, seated in the hard saddles. The next day, a long journey up to the most dangerous portion of the journey, the frontier, awaited them.

They woke up very early and headed south. At midday they stopped at the banks of a small river where Kabirma explained to them the next steps.

"For the next few days, we will follow a long ravine that was used by pastors looking for the cool pastureland of the north in the summers and those of the south in the wintertime."

Kabirma knew it well, since he had used it transporting horses in times when it was prohibited. That path, between low hills and mountainous ports, valleys, mountain paths, and plateaus, trailed along far from the important villages and was peopled only by jackdaws, thrushes, and many vultures. It was the perfect path to pass unperceived at least to the Sierra del Norte in Seville. From there, they would have to be more careful, because the later routes were more traveled.

When the afternoon was almost over and they were close to the frontier, they skirted a small town called Alcoba and then scaled a series of hills from which they could see the narrow valley and then beyond it, the Guadiana River. When they finally reached its edge, darkness enveloped everything, and they decided to stop on the outskirts and cross over the following day.

"If we light a fire, it will give us away," Kabirma said, stopping Galib. "It's better if we eat something cold."

The tension in the air was evident. They all knew that it was one of the most dangerous moments of the trip and Kabirma and Galib tried not to worry their companions, but it was clear that they felt rather nervous.

The man from Jerez decided to set up camp in a narrow clearing between a group of twenty or so hundred-year-old birches. While Benazir made something for dinner, Diego and Fatima took the horses over to the river to let them drink.

They descended down a sharp slope to a flat terrace at a bend in the river, with plenty of pasture and easy access to the shore. They let the horses loose and sat on a tree trunk while they observed their movements.

"It seems that your mare and Asmerion are becoming something more than just mere friends." The stallion sniffed at Sabba with interest and she did not appear to reject him.

Fatima loosened her ponytail and let her hair fall over her shoulders flirtatiously. She saw that Diego was very stiff. He looked around to see if anyone was spying on them. The girl tried to lower the tension and resumed the conversation they'd had several months back.

"Are you in love again?"

Diego swallowed and sighed uncomfortably without giving an answer. He felt incapable of expressing his sentiments and didn't know how to distinguish them. Love, attraction, he didn't know what he felt. Except for Fatima and Benazir, the only feminine references he'd known in his life were his sisters, and he'd never spoken to them about these matters. He looked at her askance and felt something like vertigo, as if he was pushing into an unknown world, rife with uncertainties.

Fatima didn't realize that Diego didn't enjoy talking about these topics and thought he was just on edge because of the danger that Kabirma and Galib had warned him of.

"I don't know if you've ever felt true love. But . . . the real thing," she stressed. "Do you know what I'm talking about?"

Fatima had been suffering from it for weeks. Since that fleeting visit in the stables, Diego's mere presence, or the very echo of his voice, woke up feelings that she had never known she could have. The past few nights, she had even fallen asleep imagining herself in his arms.

"I think so," the boy answered.

She imagined that Diego didn't share her feelings and that he was still enchanted by Benazir's maturity and beauty. In fact, she had caught him more than once glancing at her secretly. Fatima wanted to attract him but she didn't know how. She had tried during the journey, but for one reason or another, without rejecting her outright, he hadn't shown any interest.

"Let's go swimming in the river!" She stood up and pulled him so he would follow her to its banks. Before Diego could react, she removed her bodice and her skirt and jumped into the water in her petticoat. Her head emerged from the river and she looked at him, laughing.

"What are you waiting for?" She splashed him. "It's great!"

Diego felt pressured, so he ignored the caution he should have displayed and undressed with more speed than good fortune. He threw himself in the water, but he didn't find it as agreeable as his friend had told him.

When he came over to Fatima, she tricked him again, telling him to be careful not to trip over a large rock on the river's floor. Diego tried to walk slowly to keep from falling. When he got to her side, she pushed his head under and splashed away.

Diego lurched after her and managed to grab her ankle. She kicked and resisted, but at last he managed to grab hold of her and dunk her under as well. When her head emerged, a metallic crack came from the trees and caused her to prick up her ears. He turned toward that point. Some branches of broom were moving. It could be a man or an animal. There wasn't enough light to see it. The flowing of the river was the only sound, and Fatima, more and more frightened, grabbed hold of Diego's body, looking for protection. Almost without breathing, they followed the track of those movements through the darkness until they saw who was making them. It was a soldier with a turban, a sword in his hand, wearing a leather cuirass, and he walked out onto the rock terrace. He approached the horses and gazed around in search of their owners. Luckily for them, it didn't occur to him to look in the river, though it would have been hard for him to see them, since nothing was showing of them but their eyes and their noses. They made sure he was alone and waited without moving to see what he was going to do.

"If he sees us, he'll kill us." Blowing water out of her mouth, speaking very softly, Fatima conveyed her fear to Diego.

He covered her mouth and held her tighter. Their bodies were completely united.

When the soldier seemed relaxed, some voices coming from inside the forest made him pause. He hid his face with his own turban, took out his sword, and headed toward the place where Galib, Benazir, and Kabirma were.

"We have to do something," Fatima whispered to him.

"Let's see what he does first. . . ."

The Saracen climbed cautiously up to a plain limited to the north by a forest. He listened closely and heard voices again. His muscles tensed when he confirmed that they were Christians. He inspected the terrain up to the beginning of the tree line and decided to go to a grassy area where his steps would be softened.

Making use of all five senses, he hid among some trees until he arrived at the edge of a small clearing; there he found two men and one woman seated with their backs to him. He put his sword aside and crouched. He took out a dagger and crawled until he had made it less than ten feet from Galib.

XVIII.

A muscular arm surrounded Galib's neck and the point of sharp blade was pressed into his throat.

Everything happened so fast that no one could react.

The aggressor asked them in Arabic what they were doing there and who they were. His uniform led them to think he was a soldier from the frontier. He was filthy and he smelled of the swamp. His hair was disheveled and very long, but what stood out the most was his stare, cold and full of evil.

"We are just two humble tradesmen trying to return to our home in Seville," Galib answered. "And this is my wife."

The warrior cast a lascivious glance at Benazir.

"And where are you coming from?"

The man kept his eyes on the man with the red goatee; he looked to be the most dangerous. He felt in Galib's belt and found his knife. He gestured for Kabirma to take his out as well.

"From Toledo," Kabirma responded. "If you'll allow me, I'll show you our safe conduct . . ."

He tried to look for it in his clothes.

"If you keep moving . . ."

He ran the dagger along Galib's neck as a warning, but when he heard a noise behind his back, he turned and could just make out a large piece of wood moving toward his head. It was held by a young man he hadn't seen. The log hit the man and knocked him down. As he fell, the furious soldier jabbed at Galib's neck, opening a large gash. And then he observed in anguish that the stronger of the men was headed toward him.

Without thinking, he slashed his dagger through the air in all directions, screeching like a madman and trying to wound anyone who came close to him. It was thus that he managed to wound Diego in his thigh and

Kabirma in the belly. The soldier recovered his strength and tried to get to his knees, but Diego clasped his neck, stopping him. With them on the ground, Kabirma was able to step on his hand, and with it, his weapon, and without thinking twice, he sank his dagger to the hilt in the man's chest. He let loose a high-pitched cry, on the verge of death, but still had enough strength to bite down vengefully on the arm of the boy who held him.

Soon they noticed that his strength was draining from him and that his death would come soon. He began to cough up blood and to choke and soon after he was dead.

Benazir ran to her husband who was stretched out on the ground surrounded by a pool of blood. Kabirma and Diego did the same.

"Don't worry. . . ." Galib calmed them. "It was close, but he didn't hit the jugular." Benazir dried the wound with a strip of fabric she'd torn from her skirt. "Help Diego and Kabirma; they're wounded as well. . . ."

Benazir examined Diego's arm. The teeth had left a mark and there was some bleeding, but nothing that seemed serious. There was a deeper cut on his leg. She tore another strip from her dress and knotted it over the top to stop the bleeding. Kabirma's wound was hardly a scratch.

"All in all, we were lucky," her husband remarked, relieved. "No one has been gravely injured."

"We've just entered enemy territory," said Kabirma, more worried than the rest of them. "We should get out of here as soon as possible. . . . There could be more like him." He dragged the body to the base of a tree and began to throw leaves over it. "Go find the horses. . . ." He pointed to Diego and to Fatima, who had hidden during the assault.

"We didn't see anyone else."

"That's good, but we can't risk it. If they find us now and see what we've done, we're dead."

Shortly afterward, they crossed the river at a bend where the current was slow, and from there they drove their horses onward at a mad clip. Galloping intensely, Kabirma's words echoed in their ears: This was enemy territory. Fear made them look over at everything that moved, staring into the shadows, imagining that in any moment more soldiers or more dangers could step out into their path. The five riders were conscious they were crossing one of the riskiest areas, the border. They grabbed onto the necks of their horses to make a single body with them and thereby gain speed.

In the dead of night, they reached a plain where they could speed up the pace of the horses. The animals sweated and seemed exhausted, but their owners' panic did not allow them any rest.

Benazir saw how Fatima shook, suffering from cold. The wind turned her soaked clothes into a coat of pure pain. With their hasty escape, no one had asked why she showed up wet in her underwear with Diego. The girl saw Benazir's glance and understood the meaning of her coldness.

Many leagues later, when the day had dawned, they reached the bank of the river that Kabirma recognized as the Zújar. If they followed its course, the water would mark their route almost all the way to the Sierra Norte.

They stopped a moment to let the horses drink and Kabirma spoke alone with Galib.

"We have to follow the direction of the river until we arrive at the bottom of the mountains. Once there, we'll look for a town called Castella, and there, I'm hoping we can take refuge in the house of a friend. But before that, we have to cross a ravine that leads to a populous village, around a day and a half from here, where we might well come across some armed patrols. If we keep this same rhythm, we'll get there at night, which will help us avoid them. Now we have to push our horses a little more so they don't stop until we're well into the night."

Galib scratched his beard nervously.

"Why do you want to stop in Castella? It seems less risky if we don't let ourselves be seen, don't you think?"

"We've been traveling too many days and we're all showing signs of weariness. I think we would all appreciate being able to stop one night under a roof and sleep in a bed. It could also help us, being able to talk with our contact; he's an influential man and can tell us how to enter Seville without running more risks than necessary. But until that moment comes, we can't let down our guard. We still have to cross through that village that I mentioned before. Once that's done, I have faith that everything will be easier."

"And why are you so afraid of that territory?"

"It's full of Turks."

"Turks? Here?" Galib couldn't help but show the dread on his face. He knew the kind of excesses they were accustomed to.

"The caliph ceded them a few towns and those lands for cultivation, in return for some favor in war, I assume. We have to be careful, believe me; those troops are very violent. They're crazy."

In the middle of the night, without resting the entire day, Kabirma headed toward a leafy forest that they would have to cross. One by one, he explained to them very quietly what they needed to know.

"Don't talk and try to keep your animal as quiet as possible. If it makes a noise, quiet it down fast. We are going to enter into a high-risk area."

They went on in the darkness under the cover of the trees, nearly unable to see anything. The horses, exhausted, walked heavily, sniffing everything in search of a little grass they could eat.

Along with the strong scent of wood and rotten leaves, with the silence of the night as their only company, they passed through the grim forest in silence until they arrived at a clearing free of vegetation and illuminated by the moon. But as soon as they entered . . .

"Turks!" Kabirma was the first to see them. "On the other end of the plain!"

They assumed there was nothing they could do, since the Turks had seen them too.

Kabirma quickly said, "Let me talk and stay quiet. . . . It's important that they see us relaxed at all times. I imagine they'll want to see my safe-conduct paper. When they find out it's signed by the vizier, I don't think they'll give us too many problems, and they'll let us go on our way."

"I hope you're right." Galib swallowed and looked at his wife. Benazir and Fatima covered their faces, and Diego found his dagger and moved it to where it was easier to grab.

A half-dozen men soon surrounded them and glared at them mistrustfully. One of them was first to speak. He turned to Galib.

"Where are you going tonight? I don't know you. . . . Show me your pass."

Kabirma answered.

"We are relatives of Altair ibn Ghazi. Do you know him?" He took out his safe conduct from his tunic and passed it to them. "He governs in Castella. That's our destination."

The man held up the parchment and read it thoroughly. When he reached the vizier's seal, he paid special attention, noting something strange in the signature.

"Who gave you this?" He shook the parchment with an irritated expression. The rest of his soldiers, their eyes squeezed like slits and their skin dark brown, took out their swords and lost no time in coming over.

"What do you mean, who? It was the vizier himself who gave it to me. . . . And that can't have been more than a few months back. You have his signature right there." He pointed with his finger. "And here above it my name, the person this was written for: Kabirma from Jerez. I'm a horse trader and I've taken this same route many other times. I don't know why we haven't met before, but I do know others of your companions. . . . Today

I'm traveling in the company of my family." He remained calm. "These are my children. . ."—he pointed at Fatima and Diego—"and this is my brother, with his wife." Galib and Benazir saluted respectfully.

The Turk looked back at the document, trying to confirm the truth of the signature. Two weeks before, he had been with the vizier and he remembered how his sign was. He turned the safe conduct in various directions to better catch the reflection of the moon, but the darkness of night didn't allow him to be completely sure.

"I think you're lying!" he suddenly shouted.

"Don't think that. . . . It's not true."

"You are going to come with me into town; I need to confirm something. The rest can wait here. We won't take long."

He made a sign to two of the soldiers to stay back with them.

Kabirma obeyed him, but before doing so, he had his horse approach Galib so he could speak with him. No one noticed but the albéitar.

"Flee without me. . . ." he thought he heard. "It's false. . . . I'll meet back up with you."

Galib was paralyzed with fear when he understood the gravity of the situation before them. While he watched Kabirma go, surrounded by four of the soldiers, he was afraid, for him and for everyone else as well.

Calmly, he told everyone to dismount and asked Benazir to make some food to eat during the wait. The two Turks got down as well, without looking away from them even for a moment, though they had begun to think those people presented little danger.

Fatima helped Benazir make everything. They looked for some rolls that they had kept wrapped in cotton cloth and opened them to fill them with cheese and quince. From time to time, they looked over at Galib without knowing what his intentions were, attentive to his every movement. Little by little, Diego came closer to his master and was able to ask him in a low voice what was happening. Galib answered, almost without moving his lips.

"Look in my medicines and find one of the bottles of poppy extract. And when you can, give it to me."

"What are you talking about?" One of the Turks approached. "Until they come back, I want to see you all calm and silent. Understood?"

They accepted his orders and stood right in front of them. Diego asked permission to look for a waterskin; meanwhile, Benazir prepared the rolls so that everyone could eat. The soldiers were hungry and watched them enviously, but without speaking.

Diego found the flask that Galib wanted and hid it up his sleeve. The soldier at his side did not see it, even though he was watching the whole time. Diego sat back down between Benazir and Galib and listened to what he should do next.

"Soak a few of the rolls in that liquid."

Benazir heard her husband and understood what he was trying to do. She stood in front of Diego when the moment came to soak the bread and when that was done, she took one and held it up.

"We haven't offered you anything. Would you like to try a bit?"

The Turks looked at each other without knowing what to do. In their orders it was laid out that they should never accept anything from an enemy, but in this case, it couldn't be said that these people wished any ill on them. They looked at the bread doubtfully. It looked tasty . . .

"Bring it." One stood up and snatched it from her hand. He broke it in half and passed some to his compatriot. Before they bit into it, they watched the others eating without any fear, and they decided.

"Take another, we have too many. I imagine it's been hours since you've eaten." Benazir approached them, giving them the bread and a captivating smile.

They ate it as fast as lightning, and two more that Diego prepared in the same way. Afterward they helped themselves to a long swig of water that they had Galib bring them.

Shortly afterward, they were sleeping tranquilly, one leaning against the other. The effect of the narcotic had fulfilled its mission, and now Galib and Diego helped the women mount as quickly as possible.

"Let's get out of here fast."

"And my father?" Fatima looked nervously in the same direction they had taken him. "We are going to leave him alone? I can't go, no. I'm staying to wait for him."

"Are you mad?" Diego interrupted. "Do you want to see how they'll react when they wake up and see you here?"

"Your father will find us on the way. Relax. He told me that when they were taking him away." As Galib reassured Fatima, he made a sign to Diego to tell him to grab her reins.

They spurred the animals on with encouraging words, trying to reach the path at top speed. It was urgent to make it out of the clearing as quickly as possible.

Galib directed, trying to find the path in the darkness. Once they had made it out of the dense forest, they found an enormous plain, completely empty. Galib didn't know which was the best way to pass unseen, but finally, he decided the best thing was to follow the riverbed to his left.

"Follow along the banks!" He pointed out the direction.

They made a break and went down a steep hillside where there was a narrow tree-lined path that would help them to hide. Fatima, back in charge of her own reins, was the first to make it onto that green pathway, so dense that soon they had lost sight of her. Following in the rear was Diego. In that mass of vegetation, the darkness was almost complete. Sabba followed on the haunches of Benazir's horse, and she followed that of her husband.

Diego thought he heard noise behind his back. He couldn't tell what it was. It could be some animal, but he warned those ahead of him and immediately they picked up the pace as much as they could without fear of being whipped in the face by the hundreds of branches that came out from every side of their path. They seemed not to care, and each knew what had to be done in that moment. The desire to get out of there was a sufficient motive for crossing through that dense area without any fear.

After two days, once they had arrived in the foothills of the Sierra and were free from any more danger from the Turks, Diego and Galib decided to wait for Kabirma there.

"He'll come . . ." Benazir enveloped Fatima in her arms and looked northward with her. They had been doing it every once in a while for many leagues now.

"We were able to trick our captors, but maybe my father wasn't. . . ."

"We won't leave until he appears. . . . And he will," Galib said. "Your father is a man of many resources; he'll have made it, you'll see." He got off his horse and climbed onto a large boulder. He invited Fatima to come with him. From that height, you could see more than five leagues into the distance.

The girl was suffering the unspeakable. With all her might, she wished things wouldn't end in that way. Could something have happened to her father? she thought timidly. And if they had taken him prisoner, or worse, had hurt him? She shook from anguish. Galib guessed what she was feeling and tried to console her with a long embrace.

He thought the same and was deeply sorry for all that was happening to them. He had warned them all. Their journey was dangerous. . . . Why hadn't they listened to him at the time? If they had stayed in Toledo, none of this would have happened, and Kabirma would be safe.

In midafternoon, when the sun had begun to descend and they were filled with despair, Fatima thought she saw a small shadow moving in the distance. She squinted her eyes and shouted to everyone. She thought she saw him. Yes. It was her father!

After Kabirma had made his way to them, he embraced his daughter, enchanted to be back together with her. He hadn't know whether they had managed to escape the men guarding them or not either. He admitted he had been tormented by doubt as much as or more than they had, especially since he was alone. He explained how he had managed to escape unharmed as the reunited group got back on the trail, because he wished to leave those wastelands behind him and take the road farther into the Sierra.

He had, in fact, falsified the signature, he admitted, but the Turk had taken too much time trying to verify it.

"I passed through some tough moments. But like always, I was able to use a solution that has never failed me, I swear."

"How much did it cost you then?"

"You're an old dog like me, Galib, my friend. You know what I'm talking about, right?"

"It's true I've met a few Turks in my time."

"His silence cost me a hundred *maravedíes*, everything I had, but I consider it a deal."

"Father . . ." Fatima grabbed his arm and covered it with kisses. "For a moment . . . I thought I'd lost you."

"I'm not afraid of weapons or of tricks, I know they'll never defeat me, but I confess that just one look from you can do it every time." He stroked his daughter's cheek.

From then on they looked for the cool hillsides of the Sierra and climbed less nervously, their spirits renewed, feeling somewhat closer to their desired destination. Diego only thought of Seville, of being able to find out something about his sisters.

"We should make it to Castella before night falls. . . . I don't want any more scares, and I know we'll find protection there. Altair is a friend."

XIX.

The walled city of Castella, or Cazalla de la Sierra as it was also known, opened its doors to them when they announced whom they had come to visit.

Altair was a curious person with an appearance that surprised people from the first glance. His extreme obesity seemed out of proportion with his tiny head. It was the same with his face, where he had an enormous mouth with fat lips that jutted out and an almost nonexistent nose.

When they arrived at his home, as soon as he saw his friend Kabirma, the man flew into a fit of joy. But only a minute later, without any sort of segue, he entered into a state of hysteria. He shouted a string of orders to his people to prepare milk and dates to welcome his guests, a dinner for afterward, and then beds and baths for his newly arrived friends.

The house was also occupied by some family members who had shown up not long before, fleeing from Castilian territories. Even so, Altair held Kabirma in such esteem that he tried to offer them the best rooms. Soon everyone had lodgings, everyone but Diego. Altair begged pardon and suggested that the young man sleep in the hayloft.

"I'm sorry I can't offer you anything better." He seemed distraught.

"Relax, Altair, for days we've been sleeping out in the open. I'm sure he'll sleep better there than on the grass."

"Of course, don't worry about me."

After quickly washing up, they met for dinner. The table was set for the invitees and Altair's family in a courtyard with flower beds and a melodious fountain at its center.

They sat atop cushions and admired the elegance of the gathering. On a tabletop of leather, they had placed plates and bowls of crockery lined with decorative glass, olivewood spoons, candles and aromatic lamps in the center, and rose petals all about.

First they served them meat pastries fried in olive oil, as delicious as they were filling, and then followed savory grilled pigeons with an eggplant soup.

Apart from his hospitality, Altair was also an excellent conversationalist. He spoke to them of his ancestors, Andalusians as far back as anyone could remember. He also recollected to them his earlier pledge to breed the finest race of horses that Allah had ever created: the African Berber. It was for that reason that he had met Kabirma.

"After my active participation in numerous wars against the Christians, they gave me a public office in the town. Now I am the zalmedina, responsible for governance and administration. Not a well-paid job, but an easy one. Castella is a calm place where almost nothing ever happens, though that changed a few days ago. The mood has changed and the people are living anxiously. All because of some terrible news. . . ."

Galib and Kabirma made faces that indicated their ignorance.

"You must be the only ones who don't know what happened with the fortress Salvatierra. . . ."

The man's cheeks reddened to the point of exploding.

"A few days back, my brother-in-law Ahmed and my sister Layla had to flee from there, just like all the other brothers of the faith who were defending it. The most beautiful fortress, the greatest, was attacked and captured by that order of friars and soldiers from Castile, the Calatravans." He shook his head in disgust and asked Allah for advice, yelling.

They all stopped eating, alarmed by his expression.

"Salvatierra!" He began to wave his arms like a man possessed. "Doom is near!" he screamed again, now beating his chest with both hands, as if trying to expel his pain. "With this conquest, the infidels have shot an arrow into the heart of Al-Andalus. Now they are much closer to our homes, our women, and they will fight to destroy our faith; the faith revealed to our Prophet Muhammad."

His reference to the Calatravans and their invasions provoked Diego to ask a question: "Excuse me, sir, did you see the Battle of Alarcos?"

Galib and Kabirma looked at him, immediately disapproving of his insolence.

"By Allah the Magnificent, of course I was there. That was already three years back. I remember a great deal about it but more than anything, the humiliating and harried retreat of that ambitious and petulant Castilian king. Yes, sir, a victory, unprecedented, on the open field!"

With those words, his face lit up with a broad smile.

"Do you know what happened to the Christians captured over the following days?"

Diego's question sounded as bad as it was inopportune, but there was nothing to be done. Altair sat there staring at him, not knowing quite what he was after.

Kabirma came to his aid.

"Our friend Fadil . . ."—that was the name they had decided to call Diego so that no one would discover his Christian origins—"has had the idea of getting hold of a couple of slaves for some time. He heard people say that was one of the biggest hauls in terms of quantity and quality that has ever been conquered."

"Now that you say it, it's true. Many, and some very pretty. In fact, I myself still have two very beautiful ones." He slapped the boy's back on being informed of his carnal intentions.

"They're sisters, now that I think of it, they must be very thankful to me, since I've kept them together."

Diego couldn't contain himself and Benazir saw it. He seemed to be close to asking after them without any restraint. If he did, his interest could seem excessive and it might compromise the security of the rest of them. To avoid that, she intervened.

"I object!" she raised her voice.

Everyone looked at her, perplexed.

"To speak of the beauty of Christian women offends both Allah and his daughters, and I am proud to count myself one of those. Does the Prophet not say we were created the most beautiful, the best, the most fertile?"

Altair was embarrassed. He begged pardon, full of praise for the most perfect of all creations, and tried to justify himself.

"You are right, ma'am. Besides, mine are not so pretty. . . . If you have paid attention, they are the ones who have served the dinner."

Immediately, things grew calmer in the courtyard. Diego looked at Benazir thankfully. She returned his expression with a sly wink.

"The best among those women, and all those younger than twenty," Altair continued, "were sent to Marrakesh, to the court of the caliph, to form part of his great harem."

"All?"

"That's what they say. The caliph prefers them young."

Full of rage, Diego held back his tears and continued talking as though none of this had affected him.

When dinner was over, in the darkness of the stable and over a rough bed of dry straw, Diego cried like a child while he remembered his sisters' faces.

To imagine them in that place was almost worse than to imagine them dead.

Though it was hard for him to sleep, a little noise awoke him as soon as he did. When he opened his eyes, he saw Fatima's sweet smile. She lay down next to him and curled up to his body.

"You're crazy! If your father finds out, he'll kill us."

"I couldn't sleep. I imagined you were feeling bad because of your sisters, and I felt bad that you were alone."

She stroked his cheek.

"When they took them, Estela was only thirteen and Blanca a year older than me, fifteen. I can't think of how much suffering they must be going though if what that man said is true. I feel so guilty."

His tears flowed again.

"I didn't do what I should have. . . . I left them alone."

"Diego, don't torture yourself more. You'll find them."

"I won't find them, Fatima. They are too far. . . . How am I going to get to Marrakesh?"

"And if they aren't in Marrakesh?"

"They're there. They were young and Altair told us himself. They must be there. I don't know what to do."

Diego stayed quiet. Fatima didn't know what to say to him or how to console him. Maybe he was right. She didn't know of any slave who had been rescued from the territories of Al-Andalus, and even if Diego proposed it, it seemed like an almost impossible task.

The girl searched for him with her lips. She wanted to erase his tears, for him not to be sad. She kissed his eyelids and stroked his hair. He wanted to say something, but she stopped him, pressing her lips against his. Diego savored them, and again felt her body rub against his, as in the river before. Her hair fell over his face and with it, he breathed in the aroma of her desire, at once contained and intense.

"Fatima, listen . . . I don't know if this . . ." He pushed her from him and they looked in each other's eyes. He needed to be sincere with himself and with her especially, but once again he felt awkward and incapable of expressing what he really thought. He knew he didn't love her, but he wanted her passionately in that moment.

"Don't speak, don't think, don't breathe, and don't plan, either; just enjoy." She went for his mouth again and offered him her breasts.

They didn't know it, but someone was watching them in the darkness, nearly suffocating. It was Benazir. Like Fatima, she too had come up with the same idea of consoling him, never imagining what she would find.

She watched them, stunned and confused.

She felt a pang of remorse.

Galib was her reality and she loved him, but if she thought of Diego, the idea of making him hers was almost overwhelming. When he was by her side, she felt more alive. If she thought about him, her imagination would travel through worlds much more exciting than those where she passed her anodyne day-to-day life.

That night, Benazir felt the complicity of the two adolescents. Every one of their kisses was a distressing reality, a shattering of her hopes.

But her martyrdom didn't last long.

She heard Diego ask Fatima to leave and she saw the girl take leave of him with one last kiss.

There, hidden behind a thick door, Benazir felt, as though pierced with a dagger, the flicker of joy that Fatima bore on passing so close by her.

When they left Cazalla the next day, they had dismissed the thought of taking the route through Seville, convinced that it would be pointless for Diego's purposes, and decided on another that would lead directly to the valley of the Guadalquivir River, passing over the basin of the Guadiamar.

Galib directed the group, since he was more familiar with the territory than Kabirma, because the latter's business had never taken him this far south.

Diego was at his side, freighted with worries.

Undoubtedly he had his concerns, but Galib felt more at ease. Seville would have put him at grave personal risk. In any case, he felt sorry for Diego, he understood his disappointment and wanted to give him hope.

"I would do whatever it took to help you, to take away that pain you're carrying around inside. I can see you are happy in your work, and I think in our company as well, but at the same time, I understand that you won't reach true peace until you're reunited with them. . . . It's logical."

"Galib, you've given me much, everything, but . . . my father . . ."

"I know, Diego. One day, I don't know when, your moment will come, you'll see. Then you'll be ready to do what your father asked. You shouldn't go on blaming yourself for what happened. You have to look ahead with your head high. You are intelligent, intuitive, and tenacious. I'm sure that one day you will reunite them at your side."

Diego embraced Galib. He felt comforted by his words and also knew he was right. In life, things came when they were supposed to. He would wait until his time arrived.

Without hearing what they were talking about, Benazir was pensive beneath her veil. She felt bad for her attitude the night before, but it also hurt her to see how her fidelity to Galib was crumbling away bit by bit.

As they left behind the last hill of the Sierra, she looked for Diego and gazed at his lips, dreaming of them. Far from her intentions, Diego still remembered Fatima's kisses, without knowing what to think. The sweetness of his friend caused him to speed up, and yet something inside him told him that it wasn't good to lead her on, since he didn't love her.

The dawn of the next day surprised everyone half asleep, still on their horses' backs. After resting one night in the house of Altair, they had passed another night riding, taking advantage of the energy they had gained in that brief respite to push on ahead.

The first ray of sun that appeared over the horizon called the attention of the group. They looked toward it and Galib, with immense satisfaction, was the first one who saw them.

"There they are!" he shouted.

The light reflected in thousands of points along the immense wetlands. For mid-May, the heat was more like that of summer. And yet the abundance of flowers, millions of them, extended in multicolored sheets amid the earthen walls that separated one pond from another, told of the presence of spring.

From the beginning, Galib made them go in single file so they wouldn't get lost in one of the bogs where the horses could encounter serious problems. His face showed pure joy; they had arrived in a corner of the world, the most beautiful of all, that had to be the garden promised by Allah to all his believers, Galib thought, absorbing in his memory for all time every corner that came into his view.

The rest went on, overwhelmed by that extraordinary beauty, grand and also aromatic. The silence of that region seemed to reject their very voices; it only allowed for the soft click of the hooves against the earth, or the crackling of some tree, and perhaps, the breathing of the horses.

They plunged into a pine forest scattered with gentle hills of sand. Without stopping, they reached a summit free of trees. On the opposite edge, there awaited them an incredible spectacle as hard to imagine as it was grandiose. They made out an extensive plain sprinkled with thousands of lakes of the most varied colors, spanning green and blue. And throughout, stopped, grazing, galloping, lying down, or splashing about in the water, in groups or alone, there were thousands of beautiful horses.

There was the herd of the former Caliph Abderrahman III, the famed Yeguada de Las Marismas.

XX.

_____

All of her body was one beautiful tattoo.

Her name was Najla, "she of the large and lovely eyes," and she was the daughter of Caliph Yusuf.

For ten years, Najla had lived in Seville to receive the best education at the feet of the best professors, artists, and poets of Andalusia.

Normally, once a year, she would go back to Marrakesh, but it had been three years that she hadn't done so, the same years that Estela and Blanca had spent in the harem. And now that she had come back to set foot in her palace, she heard of them, found out they were her same age, Castilian, and with red hair, and she wanted to meet them without delay.

Princess Najla was prohibited from speaking with the concubines, from entering their chambers, asking questions, showing her face, walking alone, singing, looking at men, letting them look at her, choosing what to talk about . . . In reality, she suffered from a never-ending list of limitations that made her life one long restriction. For that reason, tired of being imprisoned, she decided to trick her guard, one of those severe Imesebelen, one night, and after hiding, she ran down those interminable hallways toward the chambers where the Castilian women stayed. Ardah, her servant, came with her, though she reproached her continuously for her craziness from the moment they left her rooms.

"Wake up."

A soft and quiet voice interrupted Blanca's sleep.

When she opened her eyes, she saw a girl with dark hair, a bluish gaze, and a kindly smile, with her face painted all over, so much so that it was hard to tell her true skin color. Reflexively, Blanca hid herself beneath the sheets. She was afraid of some new abuse, or to have to repeat the experience of lying with that repugnant man, which she'd already done too many times.

"Don't be afraid. I won't do anything to you. I'm Princess Najla." Her generous smile exuded trustworthiness. "Get up quietly and follow me. We'll go to a secret room on the other side of the sewing room. There I'll explain to you."

Blanca didn't understand what all that meant, but she felt she was in danger and woke Estela. Together, the three of them left the small room where twenty women normally slept, some on top of others.

Najla seemed very sure of herself, but at the same time very nervous. She spoke perfect Romanic although too fast, and she changed from one theme to another, almost without reason.

"The painting that's covering up my pale skin is called henna. The pigment comes from a plant that is very common in these parts. Ardah, my slave. . ."—the coppery woman bent forward respectfully, concealing the profound contempt in which she held her mistress, because she treated her indifferently and punished her terribly—"is my nekasha. She is a little lazy but she tattoos much better than the rest. She drew this for me."

She showed them her hands. There was a large sun in the center of each palm, and rays like fingers emerged from it, twisting into volutes and flowers on her fingertips.

"You have precious but strange hair; it seems like the color of clay." She came close to study it. Estela's interested her more because it was curly.

"Do you like poetry?" She didn't wait for an answer. "I do. I have been able to listen to the best poets in Córdoba. And bazaars? I love them, but they don't usually let me go. When I manage to escape my guardians I look at everything, I search, dig around, ask questions . . . They really excite me."

She stayed there pensive for a moment, without resting long, and then leapt into another topic.

"I like perfumes, especially the ones with rose essence. I hate the scent of mosques, and I love horses. When I ride them, I feel so free."

The two sisters stayed sitting there on comfortable cushions without understanding what was happening there. Since they'd entered she hadn't stopped talking as if they were old friends.

"Can you tell us why you've had us come here this early in the morning?"

The princess was frozen by the words and her face turned sad.

"I just returned from Seville, far from the court and my family, but still, I feel captive."

"You're not the only one," Estela immediately remarked.

"My confinement is different. I've always had permission to go out, to talk. I'm respected in the court because I'm the caliph's daughter, but I hardly know him or my mother. When I'm allowed to laugh, I have to do it carefully, and if I need to cry, I have to do it alone. I've never decided what I eat or when I go to sleep. They choose my clothes and dress me. Someone else decides how often I need to bathe. . . . And you would still have done all this without asking anyone, right? You must even know what love consists of. . . . I don't. I've only lived the little I've been allowed."

Ardah insisted that she talk more softly, because too much could be heard.

"I want to know your religion. I want to hear what Castile is like, understand the people there. I need you to tell me. Half my blood comes from your land, because my mother was Castilian, but she's never talked to me about it. I need to know. . . . I'm itching to know all that has been hidden from me since my birth." Her eyes expressed sincerity. "What I want from you, the reason I've gotten you up, is just . . ." Najla slowed down her waterfall of words and looked elsewhere. She felt overwhelmed. "What I'm trying is . . . I'm just trying to be friends with you."

"Are you kidding?" Blanca was indignant. "Do you think you make friends by ordering people around? The same way they do with our bodies? Do I have to remind you that we are here as slaves and concubines? Or do you not know who it is that abuses us day after day?"

"Don't get angry, please. You live in a harem. You shouldn't be surprised when that happens." Her expression was natural. "My father feeds and protects you, he dresses you and takes care of you. He also enjoys you. Can that be evil?"

"That's a strange way to look at it," Estela said.

"Does the same not happen in Castile? Are there not harems there?"

"In our land, a man has only one wife," she answered.

"They don't buy slaves there?"

"No . . . Well, yes . . . Some do."

"And they don't make use of them?" Najla couldn't believe what they were saying.

"Maybe, but it's not the right thing to do."

"Then they do the same thing as we do, but they lie about it. Our laws and codes say that the woman is at the man's service and only lives for him. She gives him pleasure whenever he wants it and she receives it as well in exchange. It doesn't bother us if our husbands enjoy other bodies so long as they respect the order of the women and protect the privileges of the favorites, the ones who provide heirs. The rest, the same as with you two right now, owe him for his hospitality. I just see it as him taking payment the best way he can."

"How can you say that? It's our bodies that he's violating. And do you think it's right that your brother Muhammad does it with me, for example?" Estela had met him the night before.

"Of course! You should be proud of it! When our father dies, he will be the next caliph. Imagine the honor if you could become one of his first concubines. Many women would like to have the same luck as you," she assured with utter conviction.

The sisters looked at each other in shock. They couldn't understand how Najla could think that way, now matter how different her vision and her personal situation were. Still, Blanca thought that the relation with Najla could be helpful to them.

"Will you be my friends then?" she asked again with an expression full of hope and innocence.

"It would be an honor," Blanca answered for both of them.

Pedro de Mora reached the capital of the kingdom of Navarre, Tudela, after two weeks navigating from Marrakesh to the port of Fuenterrabía, and two more on horseback.

He had chosen that route, longer and more complicated, to avoid crossing Castile, where he could be identified. As the ambassador of Caliph Yusuf his purpose was to convince King Sancho to sign for peace with them, as he had already done with the king of Portugal and the monarch in León.

"Don't insult me again!" the Navarrese king shouted, enraged. "Did you not hear me say that I just signed an accord with Alfonso of Castile and another with the king of Aragon to fight together against your caliph? It is something that's been made public; at this point your leaders must know this as well."

Sancho stood up and walked toward him decisively.

"I haven't finished speaking," Pedro de Mora replied without being intimidated. The king looked at him disdainfully.

"You should turn yourself in to Alfonso of Castile. . . . Aren't you the one he hates so much and is looking for?" While he talked, Sancho walked around Pedro, taking advantage of the intimidating effect his height usually produced when he spoke. The ambassador touched the long scar that ran across his forehead without showing the least worry.

"I am. It is true. He accuses me of being a traitor after usurping lands that belong to me, after insulting my name and smirching my honor, the same as he's doing with you, though you don't recognize it."

"Be more explicit and don't talk in circles. Tell me why now you're trying to include me in your plaint."

"According to what you've just told me, you have decided to unite the three kingdoms, to make a single court by means of marriage arrangements. Is it so?" Sancho confirmed it. "How should one understand then that your cousin Alfonso of Castile does not want to return first the lands of Logroño, Cameros, and Nájera, which once belonged to Navarre? If, in this hypothetical kingdom, everything belongs to everyone . . . what problem would he have in ceding them to you now?"

That comment deeply affected the Navarrese monarch, and he turned, furious. The crafty Pedro de Mora still had a second and even more effective strategy in reserve. He knew that Sancho had just repudiated his wife, Constanza de Tolosa, because she hadn't given him descendants. And it was clear that his marriage with one of the daughters of the other kings would never be accepted by the pope since their bloodlines were too close. He waited to see the king's mood worsen before he remarked on this straight out. After, he studied the effect of his words.

The monarch looked for a glass, filled it with wine, and without waiting, drank it in one gulp. Then he looked at the ambassador with justifiable suspicion and sat back on his throne with apparent defeat.

"You're not ill-informed. . . . The possession of those lands has led to many a long argument, and many times, moreover. . . . Disgracefully, we haven't gotten anywhere, it is true, and the same goes for the marriage arrangements."

"Believe me, the shadow of my lord reaches unsuspected places, and his ear has heard more than anyone can imagine. He knows, for example, that your finances are not in the best of states . . . if not, indeed, in the poorest."

King Sancho arched his brows and bit his lip at the cruelty of that comment, although it was true.

"I suppose he aims to better them?"

"Something much better than that, Your Majesty. He invites you to visit Marrakesh. There a surprise awaits you."

"Marrakesh?"

XXI.

In those lakes, somewhere, maybe already observing them, always ready to kill, there were Imesebelen.

Galib warned them of it as soon as they stepped into the waters, even if he was intoxicated by the beauty of the surroundings. The others studied the area nervously, confirming no one was at their backs, and scanned the horizon. They didn't see them, but they knew they were there.

"The marshes are enormous. We would need a day to take them all in," Galib warned. "In my time, the guardians normally kept watch over the great wetlands closer to the south, where most of the herd can be found. These first pools are less closely watched, but take every precaution and don't relax. It will be necessary to react with extraordinary speed."

Galib felt the caress of the warm wind, the intense scent of the prairies, and felt deeply intoxicated.

"But I need . . . before . . . I have to fulfill an obligation." He sucked air into his lungs and watched the frolicking of a dozen mares. With them he absorbed the peacefulness of the place, the tranquility of a scene full of sensations and life.

Despite his own recommendations, he galloped off to greet them, feeling how his tears dampened the air around him. And he ran to meet a lost love, swallowed by emotion. He reunited with those memories and was absorbed in them, feeling himself at home there.

Diego, like the others, was conscious that he was witnessing a unique and irreplaceable ceremony. And yet no one could avoid the nerve-racking dread, feeling the proximity of those black-skinned assassins, who for Diego personified the memory of his worst misfortunes. Every time someone mentioned them, it loosed a chain of emotions in his interior: vengeance, rancor, panic, interest . . .

Kabirma lived in his own dream in those moments. He looked all around, impressed. He had never seen horses as impressive as these, descendants of those who had one day crossed the strait, four hundred years before, coming from Arabia, from the desert or the mountains of North Africa.

Fatima and Benazir approached a group of mares that were tranquilly feeding. They were vigorous, elegant, and delicate animals, with fine heads, small in relation to their large bodies, small muzzles, dark, expressive eyes, and their tails always raised. Three of them were almost white and their coats were so fine that you could observe the veins beneath their skin.

"Look at that black stallion," Kabirma said, pointing at a handsome male. "There doesn't exist a more beautiful profile than his: arched neck, open, fierce nostrils. What an elegant step he has. You can see he's proud of the noble blood he carries in his veins."

"Father, how many are we going to take?"

"Since there's five of us, and each of our harnesses can take another five, calculate. We will try to get mostly females, not all twenty-five, but at least twenty."

Galib, who had strayed from the group, galloped along the edge of a broad pond, startling the horses he passed. He disappeared for a while among them, though you could tell where he was by the movements of the horses around him.

A strange anxiousness overcame Benazir; she intuited that something could change, and that the beauty around them could work against her. She looked at her husband nervously and asked for Kabirma's help.

"I'm afraid for him. We can't let him go so far away from us. I know him, and I know he can get lost in this paradise. If he keeps letting their sensuality get the best of him, he will soon forget the dangers all around us."

They looked for him fearfully, without making noise, careful not to frighten the animals and call the attention of those soldiers with the brutal reputation, whom they didn't see, but whose proximity they could feel. When they found him, he was passing over a hill. He seemed self-absorbed, with red eyes, leaning on the neck of his chestnut-colored mare. His gaze searched out an undefined place on the horizon.

"Master Galib . . ." Diego was the only one who dared to break his trance. Not even Benazir considered it. "If you don't mind, we should get started with the horses."

"Of course, yes. Look at those females, they seem to be waiting on us." Galib indicated a hundred mares feeding without fear, a few steps away from them. "They are noble beings even though they were raised wild. Back when I had to tattoo them or capture one for some other reason, I found a way to approach them without frightening them. It worked for me then, let me try now. I just want Diego to follow me with the ropes."

Kabirma offered to help too.

"No, no . . . You should watch, you're the best for that. If they get scared, it could provoke a stampede and alert the people we don't want to run into."

From that moment, Benazir watched her husband with admiration. She saw him walk slow, with such aplomb, stomping through the puddles. When he was close to the first one, he lowered his head like a stallion and threw out his arms with determination. Then he stood by her side, watching her with incredible assurance. The animal looked at him strangely and sniffed at his head without showing much worry, but at that moment, something frightened her and she jumped away from him quickly. Galib repeated his strange walk with another female and was luckier that time. She accepted him submissively after he walked around her twice in a circle and gave her a series of rhythmic claps on her haunches. In a moment, she nodded tamely and began to follow him to where he was going.

Diego learned every gesture of Galib's in order to imitate each afterward. He saw Galib stop at last in front of the mare's head, where he grabbed a handful of her mane and tugged softly. From that moment, the animal stopped resisting, hung her head, and let herself be led. The albéitar passed a rope around her head and knotted it. Diego took hold of it, and Galib did the same with six more of them. Each time he finished, he passed the horse to Kabirma.

"Now you try it, Diego."

Between the two of them, over the course of almost five hours, they collected the animals with extreme care. Everything seemed to be going well.

Benazir watched with nervousness nonetheless, and never stopped looking around. Any noise or movement, no matter how small, attracted her attention and made her remember that they were in an area under the protection of the Imesebelen. In Seville, she had seen them many times around the caliph. She knew perfectly the dark legends that surrounded them, but never before had she felt their threatening presence so close.

Kabirma sighed, on edge; he felt they were taking too much time. A gust of wind changed direction, and when he felt it on his face, it seemed to bear voices, very tenuous and distant. He looked instinctively in that direction. He thought he saw something, some small points on the horizon, dark against the blue sky.

"We need to go now," he recommended to Galib once he had brought over a beautiful male, young, no more than four years of age.

Galib looked at the altitude of the sun.

"It will be dark soon, and we only need two more. We'll spend the night close to here. We need the mares to be calm so that they'll follow us later without any problems; now they're too riled up. I remember there's a beach to the east, close to where we met up. Before you arrive at the sand there is a dense pine forest with a lake in the middle where the horses can drink and rest. The trees will keep us safe from danger—"

"And if they find us?" Fatima interrupted, her face full of dread. "Those men . . . They could track us and finish us off."

"To get to that place, you have to find a steep embankment with a narrow entrance, and it's not easy to see. I don't think they know of it."

Hours later, when they had arrived at the warm sands in front of the sea, Galib breathed in and tried to share his feelings.

"Don't let your senses forgo what this place is harboring for your enjoyment."

He observed the horizon, painted a spectacular range of ochers, oranges, and yellows. True waves of color, flashes of light, and the first hints of night.

"Look at this water now. . . . Breathe in the air that covers it before it changes color and temperature. Absorb the infinite variety of scents that you received from these marshes."

He stopped and waited for the sun to fall in silence, watching it intently, until he saw the last halo of light disappear.

With a spectacular starred sky as a witness, after a frugal bit of food, they rested a while on the sand, taking advantage of the peace that the place offered them. And yet Fatima was worried, looking all around, waiting to see the devilish appearance of those soldiers at any moment.

Galib noticed she was nervous.

"I don't think we'll see them."

"Where does their terrible reputation come from?"

"It is said they don't have souls. I don't know if it's true, but it is a fact that they don't have free will. They are known for their fanaticism and for their decision to carry out one single mission in this life: to protect the caliph and his possessions. They also guard over his women, palaces, and most important properties, this herd among them. In their childhood, the Imesebelen were raised without any kind of care, far from their relatives and their roots, and they don't now the meaning of the words *pity*, *fear*, *understanding*. They only know how to kill. In battle, if things go badly, they are always the last to flee. That is how the Imesebelen are."

None of those present was happy with the thought of spending the night there, close to those people, but the weariness of the day prevented them from doing otherwise.

They had left the horses in the pine forest, on the edge of a lake not too far away, and they lay down in a dry, secure clearing.

After a while they heard the flapping of wings, snoring, and the blowing of the wind through the trees. The three men slept without problems, unlike the women.

"What are you thinking?" Benazir turned and whispered to Fatima.

"I can't stop thinking about those savages. . . . My soul shrinks when I think of them."

Benazir sat up to look at the profile of the sea between the trees.

"Don't worry, we're very far from them." She stroked Fatima's hand to calm her down. "Would you like to walk a little? Maybe it will tire us out and we'll sleep better."

"I don't know . . . If we go too far . . ."

"Easy, we'll just go to the shore, no farther."

They covered themselves with blankets and headed to the beach. The reflection of the moon lit up the shore and allowed them to see for a certain distance, which calmed them down. For the first few steps, they didn't talk. Both knew that Diego's name would come up at any second, but neither wanted to be the first to say it.

"How old are you, Fatima?"

"I turned fifteen last month. And you?"

"Old. . . . Ugh. Thirty-three. . . ."

A long silence accompanied them for several more steps. The tension mounted. Fatima believed there wouldn't be a better opportunity and made up her mind to speak.

"You're too old for him. . . . You've confused him."

"What?" Benazir said, though she knew what the girl was talking about.

"You're married. And you know I am talking about Diego."

"You're judging me before you know anything."

"I do know," the girl replied without compunction.

Benazir felt uncomfortable. She didn't know what Diego could have told Fatima, if he had said anything, but just in that moment she remembered them kissing in the stable. Envy clouded her face and she replied, stung: "You don't have anything to offer him, you know? Nothing but a mere physical relation. But I do. . . ."

Fatima heard those words with pain. And the worst thing was that Benazir might be right; Fatima herself had thought the same thing at other times. With her young age and her lack of experience, she felt incapable of combating the older woman's charms. Benazir had a special gift that overcame everything, a kind of halo of attraction; she was much more beautiful than Fatima and her conversation was cultured and surely more interesting to Diego's ears.

"Maybe you're right." She sighed. "But I know that nothing but suffering awaits him with you. You will pit him against your husband, whom he adores. And I, well . . . Maybe I'm not the person to say it, but you should stop seducing him."

"How dare you tell me that?" Benazir raised her voice.

A sharp, dry whinny, rather strange, came from inside the pine forest. They looked, but they couldn't tell from where.

"It was my horse, Asmerion. Something's happening to him. When he makes that noise, he's scared. Could it be the Imesebelen?"

They walked close together in the direction of the forest, and when they had entered, they stopped again to listen. More horses were making noise. Benazir took Fatima's hand, and together they ran to the camping spot. From there they could see the animals and they seemed calm. They looked at each other without knowing what to do. The men were sleeping so calmly that they felt bad waking them, especially if it was for nothing. They thought better of it. They sharpened their ears and could hear nothing but the occasional snort from the horses.

"I think they're fine, but if you want to feel more relaxed, we'll come closer, carefully. If we see something out of the ordinary, we'll wake them."

Fatima agreed, still feeling as ill at ease as she had before. The darkness, the place, the fear that had assailed her since they had entered into the marshes . . .

"Wouldn't it be better if we went with one of them?"

"I would be the first to say yes if I was actually afraid of anything. I've been around horses my whole life, and they seem relaxed to me."

The two women walked holding hands to the edge of the lakeside forest. They crouched down to look. The horses hadn't moved from where they'd left them. Some were drinking from the lakeside, others seemed asleep, and some turned to the women, hearing them approach.

They scrutinized the area without finding anything strange.

"You go . . . I don't know . . . maybe your horse sensed the presence of some animal, like a fox or something," Benazir affirmed. "I'll wait for you close by."

Fatima walked around the edge of the lake, looking around until she reached the horses and found Asmerion. When she petted him, he was tranquil. She looked in the area where he was standing without seeing anything noteworthy. Only the wind broke the night's silence. She felt calmer when she returned to Benazir, but then she saw in front of her the black outline of an enormous man on horseback. He wore a leather cuirass and had a sword in his belt; there was no doubt, he was an Imesebelen.

He spoke to her in a whisper, but firmly.

"Silence!"

Fatima was paralyzed. Against her will, her tears flowed forth. The man didn't move. He had seen the Arabian mares, and now two women, and close to them, three men who seemed to be asleep. He imagined what they were after and weighed his chances if he decided to neutralize them, while with his ominous manner he manipulated the young girl's will. She remained paralyzed. Slowly, silently, he got off the horse and turned to her.

Benazir, surprised she hadn't yet seen Fatima, finally saw the man as he followed after the young girl. He was right beside her. He was much taller than her, much stronger, much bigger. A wave of panic overcame Benazir and she threw herself to the ground, not knowing whether she'd been seen. She covered herself with the blanket, instinctively, as though inside there she would be protected. But from inside her hiding place, she could hear Fatima scream, and how her scream was choked back instantly, assuredly by the hand of that man who was trying to not alert the others.

Benazir, curled up from fright, listened. She heard the groan with which Fatima took leave of life, her death gargle. Terrified, she imagined the dagger of the man being driven into the girl's heart, and she felt a sharp cramp in her legs; her teeth chattered as she shivered. She squeezed her jaws shut with one hand to stop the noise. She didn't want to think of what he would do to her if he discovered her. She imagined his hand touching her back, taking off the blanket; she almost felt his steel being plunged into her belly. She stopped breathing, swallowed, heard steps around her, someone was coming close. Would it be her Galib, Kabirma, the Imesebelen . . . What had happened to Fatima?

She sobbed hysterically and thought she would die in that very instant.

"Fatima?" It was Kabirma's voice.

Benazir heard other steps running close by. She huddled up tighter in her tiny hiding place. She could make out someone running and then the hooves of a horse escaping at great speed.

"Benazir! Where are you?" Galib looked for her.

She pulled up one corner of the blanket and looked all around. She saw her husband running to her and embraced him, shivering.

"They've killed her!" Kabirma screamed in anguish. "Noooo!" The man from Jerez had found the bundle lying at the edge of the lake. He knelt at her side and touched her back tenderly, giving her a careful nudge, as if to wake her from a deep and terrible dream, but Fatima didn't respond. He pulled her head from the water with great delicacy and took her in his arms, crying with pity. It was then that he saw the death wound in her breast and contracted until all the muscles in his body hurt, and his soul even more.

"My poor girl . . ." He clenched his fists with rage. "Who has stolen away your life?"

Diego approached them with timid steps, afraid to look at her, unable to believe what had just happened. He stopped in front of them, unable to express what he had begun to feel. He stretched out his hand to caress his friend, crippled with pain, and when Kabirma saw him, his eyes pouring tears, he showed her to him, bowled over in death. Her hair covered up half her face; blood covered the other half. Diego remembered those same hairs tickling his cheeks and looked at the lips where he had tasted such pleasure. And he cried, without tears, an intense, deep inner grief. He knelt with them and embraced Kabirma and Fatima.

Galib knew that in that moment a cruel task had befallen him: to get them out of there. The one who had fled would undoubtedly bring other Imesebelen. There was no time for anything, not even for mourning Fatima.

"Kabirma, Diego, that man's already escaped, and . . ." Both looked at him, unwilling to separate from her. "Listen to me, I understand what you are feeling, we are all paralyzed by her horrendous death, but we are running the gravest risk if we don't go. . . . Even if it's in her honor, we should flee. Think about it, they could already be close, maybe the one who killed her wasn't alone. Imagine if they are only a step away from us."

Galib didn't stop moving, looking among the trees, attentive to the least movement of a branch and alert to any strange sound.

Benazir supported her husband.

"We must escape, my husband's right."

"You go!" Kabirma embraced his daughter. "Flee! I won't go. I need to say good-bye, to cry for her, to tell her how much I loved her, to accompany her on her final trip to heaven. After I bury her, I will come to look for you. I'll find you on the way."

"Kabirma, my friend, I know this is hard, the worst thing that could have happened to us, but don't let those bastards rob you of your life as well; they will kill you. Staying here won't help anything. She is already in heaven and she will see you there. Think that she is happy, that what you have in your hands is just a body, it's not her anymore."

"Leave me and go. . . ." He pushed Diego and grasped his daughter with firmness.

Galib understood that he could do nothing and began to give orders. Diego and Benazir ran to gather what they could in their infinite grief. They went without knowing where they were going, dazed, as if living through a horrible nightmare.

Meanwhile, Galib readied the horses and tied four mares to each of them. He left three more with Kabirma, because if they took more, it would slow them down, and they couldn't risk it.

The animals neighed frantically. They had been pushed and buffeted from one place to the other; the men had tied them with strong knots, whistled at them, kicked. The horses breathed in the sharp tension in the atmosphere, smelled the fear, and began to gnash, giving terrible bellows of rage, and bucked in all directions.

Galib armed himself with a long branch and proceeded to flog them to stop the madness, but the animals grew more frantic with his blows and drew face-to-face with him; some even raised their legs to strike him.

Diego mounted Sabba and ordered her over to the group. As frightened as the rest of them, she took a step and began to pull the females that were tied to her. Benazir followed, and Galib got on his horse as well once he saw the group had set off.

He looked at Kabirma and gave him a final salute.

"Don't fail to keep your word. Come back to us."

The last image of Fatima lying over her father preceded a vertiginous rush of the riders over the shore heading north, looking for another egress that would get them out of that hell.

A scandalous chorus of whinnies accompanied their flight. The animals, still wild, resisted following that frenetic gallop, but Sabba's singular energy and determination, as well as those of Galib's and Benazir's horses, made them cede their resistance, little by little, and be taken.

Diego looked behind them. The sand flew up as they passed, the hooves breaking the smooth surface that had been burnished by the water; they were running for life, escaping the horror and the infinite grief caused by another death, that of a friend, almost of a lover. He clutched Sabba's reins, letting himself be carried, racked with consternation.

All of them left a part of themselves behind.

They heard the sound of horses, and after ascending some dunes, not without enormous difficulties, they soon smelled dry land. From there they sought out the riverbed of the Guadiamar to leave the marshes behind— those beautiful, unique, and mortal wetlands.

XXII.

They thought Kabirma had died.

They didn't know anything for weeks. They had arrived in Toledo after a long, sad journey, a journey they would remember forever.

But one good day, he showed up.

His exhausted tone and his aged face called their attention. He was much leaner, and his body showed the effects of fierce battle. His hands and face were furrowed with cuts and scrapes. He didn't know how he had managed to escape those savages—he could barely even talk—but there he was, beaten, half dead, and with the sole satisfaction of having managed to bury his daughter in that pine forest they would never forget.

Yes, he was wounded, but it wasn't his body that bore the worst damage; it was his soul.

A few days after his arrival, Kabirma surprised them with the news that he was leaving the city. He felt incapable of taking back up the life he'd led before without his daughter. Everything reminded him of her. Peace was no longer possible for him, even less so when he was so close to his memories.

"I will sell the horses we got, but I don't want my part. I can't touch that money now."

"You're mad, Kabirma. It's not that you deserve your part, it's that you have the obligation to take it."

"I pledged to make an impossible journey and I put everyone's life in danger. I did it for money. . . . Now I don't want it. I lost Fatima because of it."

Kabirma lowered his head and sank into his grief. He wanted to leave, but Galib wouldn't let him.

"Stop punishing yourself. How will you survive? In Toledo you are someone, and people love you. Sadly, Fatima is no longer here, but you should give yourself a chance, sell those horses, move forward."

"I can't, Galib. I can't," Kabirma whispered between sobs. "I will sell my house, the stables, and with what I make, I will have a fabulous garden built, as beautiful as she was, as innocent as her gaze. I want it to become a living memory of my daughter, where I can leave a bit of my heart amid the jasmines, rosebushes, and honeysuckle. And then I will go."

Galib embraced him, sharing everything that the distance had deprived them of. Without words, he expressed how close Kabirma was to him, his understanding, the enormous affection he felt for him.

Diego, hearing that Kabirma had arrived, ran to see him, wanting news, anxious to see him. And he found him with Galib. No words were necessary. When they saw each other, they hugged, and everything was said, an embrace that spoke of Fatima, a crossing of sad sentiments.

"You know, Diego, she loved you, as more than just a friend. . . ."

That was the only thing Kabirma said after a long silence.

Diego heard those words with great pain, aware that they were true and still with the recent memory of those passionate kisses. He felt deep bitterness in his mouth and also in his soul. He knew something important in his life remained forever inside those two people, but more in the one who had been his only friend, Fatima.

For the following months, Diego and Galib took refuge once again in their work: the construction of the stables, attending to the horses, new patients, the study of illnesses . . .

They hardly spoke. The death of Fatima had clouded their lives and whenever their work progressed, they thought how it had cost them a life.

Galib paid all his debts, and months later he could look at the finished stables.

One afternoon, alone in the library, he counted the money he had left, the money that should have gone to Kabirma, and he felt greedy for having it in his hands. He missed the man from Jerez every Tuesday when he went to the market. He would have liked to show him the new installations, to explain the improvements.

That money had been won at a high price, the life of Fatima. And here, in the shadows in his home, sitting before that pile of coins, he called Diego.

The boy's face had matured and bore the traces of Fatima's disappearance. Master and student sat down to talk.

"What will you do when you become an albéitar? Where would you like to begin?"

That was a question he had never asked before. Diego hesitated. "I still have two years left, no?"

Galib nodded.

"I don't know, maybe I would go back to Malagón to work there, as long as I could . . ."

"Be independent. . . . Of course. . . ."

"Well, that seems logical . . . but I still don't know."

"The beginnings aren't easy. You know the great sacrifices I myself went through until I got the business going in this city. And I didn't start from zero. Thanks to my savings, I could hold out. Listen to me, Diego. In this profession of ours, winning a reputation is everything, that's why you can't begin with limitations. You need to have everything, a proper place to work, books . . ."

He opened the drawer in the table and took out a leather bag full of money. He left it at his side.

"Here are three hundred *sueldos*. They're yours."

Diego's eyes opened wide. He made two *sueldos* a week. That was the equivalent of three full years of work.

"I can't accept this." He pushed the bag away.

"Your gesture is honorable, but I will not deceive you; it's money that Kabirma didn't want to accept for the mares that we took from Las Marismas."

"I don't want it either."

"Wait, Diego, I understand. . . . Everyone is devastated by what happened, but what better use is there for it than establishing a new life, yours. That's why I'm offering it to you, so that you don't have to start from zero. I don't believe there's a better destiny for it."

"I thank you for it, master, but I don't know . . . I can't help it."

"It's fine. Let's do something. I will keep it for you until then. But at least take fifty. With that money you can buy some books and some surgical materials that will be useful for you. . . . Why not?"

Diego remained pensive and finally accepted.

Days later he visited Gerardo de Cremona, the translator, and proudly bought four books from him. In reality, those were his first acquisitions, books that he began to devour at night and that didn't take him long to memorize. Cremona also let Diego read, without buying, a strange book that he had just translated called *Mekhor Chaim*, or *The Source of Life*. It contained the philosophical principles that were the basis of the kabbalah, a science as old as it was surprising, one they had talked about in depth on various occasions, which Cremona claimed to have a great understanding of.

Many days Diego studied those new titles he had been able to buy alongside Galib and heard his explanations of the parts he didn't understand.

It was then that Galib began to devote himself to the study of botany. He went over it almost every day. He would linger on detailed explanations so that he would learn how to select the curative parts of all the plants and where they were found. He taught Diego to prepare hundreds of unguents and potions: one to soften the hooves, others for mange, for the curing of fevers, even to keep away flies . . .

Months after Kabirma had abandoned the city of Toledo and his business, they received a letter saying that he had settled in the kingdom of Portugal, in the city of Coimbra. He was trying to start up a horse business there with the help of a woman; his associate, he said, but he admitted that it could become something more than a merely mercantile relation. The news was celebrated by Benazir and by Galib and Diego as well. It seemed that fatality had decided to leave them alone at last, and that they could go back to being happy.

At the end of that winter, Diego met a number of times with the Calatravan friar he had met in the translator's workshop on his first visit. He liked to talk to him; he was loquacious and very cultured. One day, the friar said that besides translation, one of his tasks was to visit the libraries of all the monasteries built in the various Christian kingdoms. With this work, he was attempting to compile an ambitious record of all their books and writings at the behest of his master.

He spoke with passion about some of those temples of learning, but he confessed that the greatest library of them all, the one that possessed the richest resources, was that of the Cistercian monastery in Fitero, in the north of Castile, almost at the border with Navarre. Only there had he seen truly fabulous works, lone copies sometimes, many unknown by even the greatest scholars.

"I spent two years in that monastery, the cradle of the Calatravan order, and I would go back, I assure you. Moreover, I remember that one of the friars there was an albéitar like yourself. He was remarkably prestigious and I suppose that his knowledge was as well. Those who work in your profession aren't called albéitars in those lands, though their job is similar. Some call them veterinarius, others say *mariscal*, and the rest call them horse healers."

Such was the friar's passion as he revealed the nature and extent of the treasures of that place, that both the monastery and the library began to appear in Diego's dreams with a certain frequency, sometimes in the form of nightmares. Some nights he saw himself running down long dark hallways of stone, followed by a man on horseback hidden under a black garment. It seemed so real that he even felt the hard hooves when they struck him. In other dreams, fortunately nicer ones, he was surrounded by a fabulous crowd of hundreds of books, in a room with an infinite roof and blinding light. There he saw himself enjoying his reading, as well as the feeling of touching the books. They were bound in gold and taffeta, and in his dreams he enjoyed sniffing them, stroking them, as though they'd been bound in the petals of a flower.

The following spring brought with it a torrent of light and color, an explosion of sensations, but also an infinitude of births, almost all with complications.

For a while, Diego came to think that all the mares of Toledo had reached an agreement to foal on the same days. It was so much work, it was almost suffocating.

And thus, during those bustling days, when it seemed impossible to take even another case, Galib passed him a letter from the Laras, an urgent notice.

"For another bleeding?" Diego saw himself again in those stables surrounded by those giant warhorses, half crushed between their ribs and knocked about by their robust necks.

"Don't worry, he's only trying to understand what could be causing a limp in Doña Urraca's walking mare, and afterward, of course, fixing it."

Galib raised his voice, making it sound slightly feminine.

"And bring that handsome young apprentice of yours to help us. . . ." He laughed. "That's what Doña Urraca said to me when I saw her early this morning."

"I remember her well. . . ." Diego reddened. "She was a very nice woman."

"Very pretty, no?"

"You're right, she is."

The mare was standing calmly in the central courtyard of the castle without seeming too affected. To her side stood a boy who brushed her with a currycomb in one hand and a softer bristled brush in the other.

Only a moment after they were announced, she appeared. She was in a green dress and had her hair pulled up in a veil. Her bodice, showing generous cleavage, glimmered with an intricate design of gold. The first person she looked at was Diego.

"I do say, though you've become quite a man, you still have that clean and noble gaze from before. I'm very happy to see you, Diego."

"Your words do me honor, madame. And forgive me for saying so, but I find you much more beautiful than I remembered."

She thanked him for the compliment, asking about his age.

"I'm eighteen now, madame. Imagine, four years have passed since I came to Toledo."

A curly-haired girl, blond and with a roguish gaze, peeped out from behind her mother's skirt.

"This must be little Flora!" Galib stroked her head, impressed by her incredible resemblance to her mother.

"Did you hear her grandfather has remarried?"

Out of pure courtesy, he said he had not, though everyone was informed of the dishonorable episode that Doña Urraca's mother had been involved in; the wife of Don López de Haro, she had fled in the arms of a simple blacksmith from Burgos.

"He's on his way to introduce his new wife to us, Doña Tota Pérez de Azagra. They were married only a month ago. The Azagras are a very influential family in Navarre. They have a title and rights as the lords of Albarracín."

Diego, estranged from the conversation, looked over the mare without finding any injury, mark, or discoloration on her hooves that might awaken any suspicion.

Doña Urraca continued talking with Galib. She began to explain that her husband, Don Álvaro Núñez de Lara, was in Normandy, on orders from the king, to reclaim the lands of Gascony from his English counterpart. According to him, those lands had been established as a dowry of Queen Eleanor of England, the wife of the Castilian monarch and sister of the English King Richard.

Diego used a small hammer to tap each of the hooves in case some difference of sound indicated foot rot. Galib watched him from the side without ignoring the woman. He trusted that Diego would have seen that detail as well, only that one. . . . If he did, he would have a definitive diagnosis.

"I need to have her walk on sand."

The stable boy was the only one who heard Diego. Doña Urraca seemed lost in her thoughts and Galib was at her disposal.

The boy untied the rope and led the mare to a place alongside the courtyard where there was ample river sand. They exercised the horses there regularly to keep them in optimal condition.

"Do you see her limping?"

Galib pulled slowly away from his hostess to come closer to the spot where Diego was, not wanting to miss anything.

"You'll have her trot right in front of me, at least ten or twenty times." The boy obeyed immediately.

Both Diego and Galib concentrated on how she moved her legs in case she showed any abnormal or strange movement, but they saw nothing until the mare stopped, when the exercise was over.

Diego looked at her feet, how she placed one over the other. After forcing her to change her posture three or four times more, the animal still kept the same defect. It left no room for doubt.

"There is a solution, madame." Diego spoke with Galib's permission, after receiving from him a gesture confirming his suspicions.

"As you say, young Diego." Her expression showed great satisfaction.

"The problem is in the rear part of her hooves, in what we call the heels. Luckily it can be repaired with a special horseshoe." He lifted one of her feet and showed her the area he was talking about. "I myself will make them. You'll notice the difference from the first day."

Doña Urraca seemed convinced, even more so after seeing the expression of pride on Galib's face. She praised Diego without restraint, petted her mare's neck, and shared one last surprise before saying good-bye to them.

"By the way, I would like very much to have you both among the invitees to the feast we are holding this Saturday. We are celebrating the presentation of my father's new wife."

"We would be most thankful, madame, but we are not of your class, we might stick out," Galib commented, hardly believing what he had just heard. As a mudéjar, he had never been invited to such an event.

"Be quiet and come with Benazir. We'll be waiting for you!" Doña Urraca made a gesture of leaving, considering the conversation over.

As Diego and Galib returned to their stables, besides remarking on that surprising invitation to the feast, Diego wanted to talk about something that had been eating at him for some time: the impotence he felt at not knowing the origin of many diseases.

"In Doña Urraca's mare, what do you think could have been the source of that pain?"

"I don't actually know," Galib responded. "But as you well know, the normal cause is an imbalance between the different humors."

"Humors . . . Ridiculous!" Diego protested, tired of not finding other reasons more compelling than those of the Greek Hippocrates. "I remember the day you denounced the blacksmiths to me because they thought themselves as capable as the albéitars. A problem, a solution. That's precisely what I heard you say. . . . According to you, they acted blindly, applying remedies they couldn't understand the workings of, for diseases they couldn't understand either. Don't deny it. It's the same thing we're doing!"

Galib remembered that abandoned, skeletal little boy who had come to him years back. Now he had become a man, almost a colleague, capable of arguing and supporting his reasons. He decided to teach him something that could seem very far from the matters of his profession, but before that, he explained what could have made the horse limp.

"I suppose that it's the fault of an erosion of a small bone that has hardly been described in any of the books you've read up to now. That small bone is attached to a tendon that supports flexion throughout the leg."

Hearing that surprising explanation, Diego felt bad. After contradicting him and putting his professional capacities in doubt, Galib had once again overwhelmed him with unexpected perspective.

"Master, why did you speak to me of humors, then?"

"As I just said, it's a supposition. Hippocrates, whose wisdom you've just knocked down several degrees, attributes this kind of a limp to an overabundance of yellow bile. I don't know if he's right, because I haven't yet been able to demonstrate my theory. Do you understand?" Diego agreed and bowed his head in conciliation. "It makes me happy to see you dissatisfied with whatever doesn't seem clear to you. And I beg you, don't ever abandon that attitude. Always try to explain to yourself what has been the reason for a certain pain, lump, fever, or even death." He tousled Diego's hair affectionately. "But you should also learn to be humble when you don't know the answer. In those moments, look to heaven. Your god and mine know all. We are only a smallness at his side. We chase after the truth; he is the truth."

XXIII.

———

D oña Tota Pérez de Azagra was a woman with few blessings.

Still, Diego López de Haro, her husband, possessed one of those gifts that turned its possessor into something special. Maybe it was his grandiose stature, maybe his clear, honest gaze, or perhaps both.

He was a well-formed man, strong, already with gray hairs. His brown eyes shone with intelligence, and his nose, great seriousness. But it was his chin, wide and powerful, that gave him an air of undeniable authority.

Diego looked at them shyly, unable to forget his father. How proud he would have been to see him there, among all these important people. He tightened his belt to cinch the long tunic of green silk that he had bought with the money Galib had saved for him, the first proper clothes he'd had in his life, far from the simplicity of the woolen vests and leather shorts that he usually wore. Under that cloth, he also wore new red breeches and shoes with a lozenge design. For the first time, he felt important. The only thing that made him feel uncomfortable was the tall cap atop his head, since he normally kept it uncovered, but still, he felt happy. . . .

He had never been to a feast, and he marveled at everything. He was surprised by the luxury that blazed in the dresses of the women, some very beautiful, and in the food that was offered. Without any company with whom to take refuge, his best ally in his quest to go unnoticed was dark red in color and had a deep scent of wood: an excellent wine made on the banks of the river Ebro, as the person who served it explained.

Four mugs of that product robbed him of his timidity and pushed him toward some solitary young woman with whom he could talk. While he walked around and studied his possibilities in that regard, he listened to snatches of various conversations. He heard some say that the worst of their enemies had just died: the Almohad caliph Yusuf. And that he had been succeeded by his son Muhammad, whom they called al-Nasir. Others repeated the surprising news about Sancho VII, the king of Navarre, who was in Marrakesh, supposedly wooing a woman from the caliph's court, after repudiating his wife some months back.

"He must be planning to carve up Castile with that Moor, or else he'll be asking him for money, as he's already done on other occasions," a brother of Álvaro Núñez de Lara said loudly. "King or no king, he seems like a mere traitor to me. . . ."

Diego saw that a young woman with dark skin was looking at him from aside. He looked away for a moment until he decided what he was going to do with her, and then Doña Urraca came over, wanting to introduce him to her father. Diego followed her steps until he came to the man who was oozing vitality, although he was around seventy years of age.

"Father, I want you to meet a promising young man who works as an albéitar. A new friend of my family, Diego of Malagón."

"Have I seen you before, young man?"

"I don't believe so, sir."

"Diego is the assistant," his daughter clarified, "who has come with Galib's wife, Benazir."

"I still have not had the chance to greet that good man . . ." He studied Diego from head to foot. "I'm glad to know you're in training to be an albéitar. We need them in Castile, good ones especially. Take advantage of your time; you're in the hands of the best one."

"To work at his side is a privilege, I assure you."

"Young man, you must understand that the cavalry represents our greatest arm to defeat the Saracens. We need healthy horses, vigorous ones, and someone who can act with diligence and a steady hand when they fall victim to some infirmity. That is why your profession is so important, I would even say vital, perhaps more so than a doctor's."

"Father, is it true you're staying in Toledo only a week?"

"Sadly yes, my daughter. The king has called me to Burgos to begin a new campaign, this time against Navarre. His Majesty is trying to open a new path to the sea and unite Castile with her possessions in Gascony, on the other side of the Pyrenees. It is decided that in this quest, he will take Vitoria, San Sebastián, and Fuenterrabía. And he will, believe me, as well as anything else necessary to meet his objectives."

"And what response do you expect from the king of Navarre when he sees his territories attacked? He will declare war against us again. . . ."

"No, my daughter. It appears he is lost in a strange love affair with an Almohad princess. If he is in Marrakesh, as our spies assure us, he will not change our plans." He stopped conversing in an instant when he saw the archbishop of Toledo. He begged their pardon and ran after him.

Doña Urraca accompanied Diego a while more, introducing him to other people. The most influential families in Castile were there: the Azas, the powerful Castros, the Ruiz Giróns, the Laras, of course, and the Haro clan.

Then Diego was alone again and tried to find the girl he had seen before, but he couldn't, and suddenly he found himself captured by friendly hands, those of Benazir, who pushed him to the center of the hall where the dancing was taking place.

"It would be cruel for you to leave a feast like this one without feeling a woman's body beside yours," she whispered in his ear.

Diego reddened immediately. More proof that Benazir had decided to display her seductive charms once again. It wasn't the first time she'd done it in recent weeks. While they were measuring him for his clothes, he could feel how her hands sought him out with renewed desire, and he noted her agitated respiration when she helped him remove his tunic, grazing his skin with her hands, touching him on all sides.

"Don't be alarmed, Diego. We have my husband's permission. And besides, I won't accept the excuse that you've never danced. The steps aren't difficult; I'll teach you."

"I'm all yours," he answered her, without wanting to give her the impression that his words obviously did, judging from her sweet gaze.

Diego looked at the men's posture and imitated it. He passed an arm around her back and they faced each other, waiting for the first notes to sound. He didn't manage to hide his nervous tension.

The first sounds from the clavichord rang out, and all present bowed to their companion. The women bent over graciously, receiving the men afterward with two small leaps. When Benazir did it, Diego looked once again at her lovely body. That night she wore a dress not often seen on Muslim women. The cloth gripped her waist, showing her curves clearly, and opened at the top, showing generous cleavage. She seemed to intuit his thoughts and also saw where his eyes were roaming, and she smiled, showing she was in league with him.

The dance was an authentic martyrdom for Diego, and not because it was unknown to him and difficult, which was also true, but rather for the whirlwind of feelings that he had begun to feel. Benazir's excessive proximity, her perfumed skin, the touch of her body; he fought against his own thoughts and desires, but at the same time, she made him aware of hers. She took advantage of the least contact to make him feel her body. Their cheeks touched several times and were finally touching throughout the last steps, when they spun one around the other.

When that dance was over, she said something in his ear. Diego couldn't hear clearly because the noise of the applause drowned out her voice. He even thought it had been a stupid misunderstanding, but he thought he had heard something as terrible as it was worrying; he thought he heard her say that she wanted him. . . .

From that night forward, Diego avoided Benazir as much as he could.

And yet the echo of those words followed him over the course of the following months like a heavy torment. He knew he was too fragile to decide between duties and desires when it came to her. But he was also conscious of the grave consequences that his lack of strength could lead to if he wasn't capable of holding back that storm of sensuality. He still could. Besides the profound and enormous affection he felt for Galib, he would never offend the man who had given him work. To wound him with such a deception would be like wounding himself.

For that, and for everything, he couldn't betray him.

He stopped his Arabic classes to avoid temptations.

Galib didn't understand, but Diego justified himself by saying that the pace of the work had become exhausting. He tried to avoid Benazir at every moment. He fled from those places where they might run into each other. He also went more frequently to church and tried to busy his mind with more reading to keep from thinking of her.

Amid so many tribulations, the month of December came, with cold and snow as a prelude to the changing of the century.

A few days after the beginning of the year 1200, on a day like any other, Diego arrived at the forge very early. He needed to make a complete set of horseshoes for the horse of a demanding and rich Jewish businessman. He had promised to have them ready before lunch.

He lit pinewood—its resin would keep the fire burning—and he readied enough coal to reach the desired heat. He didn't ask after Galib, because he assumed he was at the market, like every Tuesday, where they needed him to affirm the good health of the animals before people would buy them.

Diego breathed in a mouthful of smoke with pleasure. The scent that came from the furnace had always captivated him. He hummed, enchanted, proud of the work that he had in his hands.

He placed several bars of iron inside to soften them and readied his hammer and a chisel to cut the metal afterward. He also placed a punch close to the anvil. He would use it to perforate the metal, opening holes where the nails would later go. Afterward, he would use another tool to finish the edges of the holes.

He took off his shirt and looked for his thick leather apron. He tied it around his back and checked the heat of the oven.

In that moment, he didn't realize she was there. Benazir had been watching him for some time, in the shadow of a stable wall, sure of what she wanted. Without his noticing, she approached him in silence. Her breathing was agitated, full of excitement.

And at once her hands embraced Diego's nude torso, and then her lips moved over his back, then his shoulders, until they reached his neck.

Diego knew who it was. He felt a temptation so intense, so hard to elude . . . He turned and looked at her, first frightened, and then desirous.

Benazir kissed his mouth, making him feel her silken texture. Diego tried to pull away, to allay his own longing, but she resisted him and kissed him with more ardor. No words had any effect on her.

Diego, in despair, decided she was the most beautiful of all women, and finally gave in to her. He kissed her as though his entire life were in those kisses; he felt the warmth of her skin, her shoulders, her stomach. Benazir twitched, invaded by pleasant feelings, especially when Diego's hands began to move over her, making their presence known on her thighs, her stomach, her breasts. The woman's ardor inflamed the air they both were breathing. Diego took in her perfume like a mouthful of soft sensations and let its aroma suffuse him. She swayed like the desert sands, her hands seemed to melt on his flesh, to penetrate it, and her hair floated over his face, making him feel drunk.

At that moment, Galib entered and saw them. Sajjad was at his side.

"Sajjad say to master . . . Find master for this. Sajjad no lie."

Diego and Benazir separated, and she choked back a shocked scream.

In an explosive succession of thoughts, Diego, confused, nauseated by that horrible tension, tried to speak, to explain himself, but he couldn't find the way. It was horrible. He imagined the pain that his master must feel, seeing himself deceived by the two people he trusted most. Diego hated himself for letting himself be swayed into doing something he should never have done.

The desolate expression on Galib's face said it all. The damage was done. With the sole aim of softening his pain, the only thing that occurred to Diego was to try and salvage Benazir's honor.

"Master, I don't know how to explain it. . . . What . . ."

"How could you. . . ?"

"She has always avoided me, I swear. . . . I confess it, I lost my head. . . ."

"What?" Galib closed his eyes in rage. He ran toward Diego with clenched fists and a furious demeanor.

Benazir, cringing from the situation, covered her mouth, destroyed. Diego was lying for her, assuming a burden that didn't belong to him, but she didn't speak; she preferred silence to the terrible consequences that would come to her if her husband knew the truth.

Diego felt Galib's eyes on him and his disgusted expression, and he knew that his strategy had been the correct one. He kept going.

"I wanted her so much. . . . And today I managed . . ."

Galib couldn't take more and pounced on him, hoping to still his rage by punching him. His head was spinning. He could understand nothing. It seemed so atrocious that he had never imagined it. He had considered Diego a son, his greatest disciple; he loved him. He had just suffered the most dreadful disappointment, seeing them in intimate contact, caressing each other in that way. He felt humiliated, betrayed, offended to the point of wanting to die.

Diego took in his hate without any response. Galib was pounding his body all over, and he wanted to bear the fury of the man he loved like a father, whom he had never wanted to betray. But it was too late to talk; it was too late for anything.

From a corner, Benazir watched them, ashamed. She had decided. She would confirm that supposed abuse if her husband asked her. If she didn't, she would be reputed by her husband as an adulteress, and her life, her name, and her honor would be stained forever.

She pulled away from them crying, but just before she left, she turned back to Diego and saw his gaze, serene, conscientious. With her eyes, she thanked him for his generosity and loyalty, but she only felt more ashamed. She left the stable running, with indescribable bitterness and despair.

Diego packed up his things without knowing how to continue or where to go.

He paid the rent for his room, assuming Toledo would no longer be his residence, and said good-bye to the proprietors, who were frightened at the battered state of his face after Galib's blows.

Furtively, without saying good-bye to anyone else, he left behind Master Galib's stables and house, his school, the place where he had learned almost everything, where he had received the love that others had stolen from him back in Malagón. In the shelter of their walls, he had also grown inside, becoming a man. That house felt like his second home, there he had learned to love an albéitar whom he would never be able to forget.

He left Toledo depressed, tears rolling down his face, carrying on his back the deep disappointment of his master.

He left behind five beautiful years at his side, vanished because of a fleeting instant of sin with a woman he had lusted for too much, and whom he had sworn he respected.

He remembered poor Fatima, strange Sajjad with his false smile, full of triumph, when he saw him enter.

He relived in a mere moment so many of the events that had composed the most gratifying experience of his life. He memorized everyone's face, their voices, and some of their conversations, like the greatest of treasures.

All those names, with their memories, now formed part of his past.

Diego caressed Sabba. She knew they wouldn't return. She turned her neck and nibbled at his cheek, conveying her understanding.

"Good old Sabba, You'll always be with me. . . ."

He scratched the base of her ears and they headed north, to a place still without a name, to a new and unknown future.

PART II

Christian Lands

In the absence of the king of Navarre, Sancho VII, lost in African lands, the city of Vitoria falls to the troops of Alfonso VIII of Castile after a long siege.

Other towns, like San Sebastián and Fuenterrabía, ask to be incorporated into the crown of Castile.

In León, Berenguela, the daughter of the king, recently married with the monarch Alfonso IX, her second uncle, attends the annulment of her marriage by Pope Innocent III, on the grounds of an excessively close blood relation.

The always delicate relations between the neighboring kingdoms of Castile and León suffer yet another crisis.

Meanwhile, the new caliph, al-Nasir, studies how to break the ties among the different Christian kingdoms to the north and also rearms to prepare for their conquest.

Blind to his intentions, they continue to fight among themselves.

I.

Diego was almost frozen.

The snow whirled around him and buffeted his face as he began the descent to the pass of Somosierra on the north face.

The old Roman road that united Toledo with Burgos had disappeared under the intense snow, and a frozen gale hid whatever other reference point might help one trust the route.

He was traveling alone, sunken in deep sadness and repenting everything that had happened in Galib's home. Owing to his rapid flight, he hadn't taken the necessary precautions to face a harsh winter storm. For that reason, faced with that infinite blanket of whiteness stretching out on all sides, he felt doomed, with no other answer than to trust in Sabba's instincts.

He barely opened his eyes to keep them from freezing.

He tried to avoid the effects of the frozen wind on his cheeks, because the water drops it carried were flying like frozen daggers into his skin. He could hardly feel his ears; they hurt like he was going to lose them. And it was only thanks to the heat of his mare that the tips of his fingers stopped throbbing when he wedged them between the saddle and the animal's back.

Diego had left Toledo four days ago without imagining what a difficult journey it would be. He had hardly any warm clothes, a rather thin blanket, and a leather bag with all his savings, just over thirty *sueldos*. Those scant possessions were all he had to face a new life.

He made the decision that would shape his destiny when he was crossing the city walls and had to decide to take one of the two roads that emerged from them.

In that sea of uncertainty there was only one thing clear: He wanted to be an albéitar, but to do it, he had much left to learn. He needed more education, more practice, more study, maybe someone like Galib who could teach him. And it was thus that he remembered that Cistercian monastery that Friar Benito had mentioned so many times, and he came to the conclusion that it could be the best place to learn what he had to know. The idea encouraged him.

He would read in the library, would help to shoe or cure the horses if they let him, and maybe he would find that horse healer among the friars who could be his next master. Together with him, he could learn everything that he still did not know; it wasn't a bad idea.

Absorbed in those thoughts, a steely wind from the north brought back to him the horrible reality of the mountain.

He was entering into a pine forest when Sabba lost her step and fell to the ground, taking him with her. The damp and icy contact with the snow made him fear an unfortunate wound. He inspected Sabba from head to toe, frozen from the cold. Luckily she was unscathed.

Looking around, Diego could identify nothing farther away than two or three feet. From that moment, he thought it would be better to go on foot, so that Sabba could rest until they had made the precarious ascent. But when he stepped onto the soft hill, he saw to his horror that his legs sunk in up to his knees. He continued as best he could, until he began to despair, because of the little distance they had covered and a dreadful weariness that showed itself in sharp shocks all over his body.

He paused and recovered a bit of strength after rubbing his frozen legs together vigorously, but then he looked into the ugly panorama that awaited them.

Even worse for them, the sun had begun to disappear and a thick haze was rising up the hillside and would reach them at the moment that they were approaching a perilous gorge. Almost unable to see, they were obliged to turn back to look for another road, and at that moment, a savage wind burst began to thrash them mercilessly.

Between the sharp sound of the wind and the cracking of the frozen snow, they heard something. Sabba turned her sharp ear to where the source of the noise appeared to be and soon understood what it was. Terrified, she stretched her neck, opened her eyes wide, and began to push at Diego's back.

"What is it, Sabba?"

The mare heard it again. She heard the echo of footsteps on the snow and began to detect a worrisome scent. She filled her lungs and whinnied with incredible energy, trying to drag Diego back to separate him from the danger. She was very upset.

"Something's scaring you, but I don't know what it is. . . ." Without finishing his phrase, Diego looked in the same direction as Sabba and there he saw them. First there was a bluish shimmer, their eyes, then the reflection of fangs, many fangs.

"Wolves!" he shouted in fright.

He heard a pack of barks coming toward them at a hellish speed. Diego mounted Sabba so quickly that he lost the bag that held his money and his three valuable books. He saw them fall heavily on the snow, and when he tried to dismount to grab them, it was too late; he felt a hard and painful bite sinking into his leg. He beat the animal's head with his fists until it let go. The nearness of the other four made him give up any further thought of getting hold of his things.

Two of the beasts leapt at Sabba's neck, trying to reach her jugular, though she escaped from them. She kicked one so forcefully that she launched it into the trunk of a tree.

Diego looked at the ground again and saw his books and savings disappear into the snow under the feet of those animals. With pain and grief he saw there was nothing to do but flee as soon as possible if they didn't want to end up dead.

"Run, Sabba!"

The mare obeyed the order and rushed downhill without knowing where she was even stepping. One of the wolves seemed to fly at her rump and sank his teeth into her. Diego managed to tear off a piece of a tree branch and beat him in the muzzle and the eyes. The animal howled, wounded, and let go. Six more ran very close, not wanting to lose that tasty prey.

"Don't look back. Run. Run faster . . ."

Diego grasped Sabba's neck and felt the warmth of his own blood flowing over his ankle. They crossed a small stand of trees quickly and dangerously, because there was no time to try and avoid the branches that stood in their path. Many scratched Diego or Sabba; others broke off as they passed through.

In a clearing in the forest, the wolves seemed to guess where they were going and two sped up until they were just in front of them. Sabba saw them without time to change direction; to avoid them, she turned her body so fast that she lost balance and tumbled to the ground. Diego was trapped beneath her, frightened at how little time they had before the canines reached them. He saw them arrive with absolute impotence and closed his eyes, waiting to feel their fangs, but to his surprise they remained still, very close, but still. They seemed to smile. They surrounded them, salivating with rage, as though looking for the best spot to attack from. Sabba tried to stand, but the abundant quantity of snow under her kept her from finding soil to support herself.

The wolves panted with agitation and clouds of steam bellowed from their mouths. One of them, darker than the rest, came up to Diego's face, sniffing his nose and then showing its fangs in a menacing growl. Diego smelled its awful breath and shook from pure panic.

He thought it was all over, but soon Sabba had recovered her strength and stood up with incredible speed. Still atop his horse, Diego felt a sharp pain in his leg. He didn't know if it was broken, but it didn't matter; there was hope again.

The wolves, even more furious, if that was possible, leapt at them, looking for a place to bite, but Sabba left them behind, galloping at a spectacular velocity until she lost them from view half a league later.

After a final hill, less precipitous, they reached the flatlands and continued walking until they found a small town. Diego pinched Sabba's neck and scratched her ears in gratitude.

"I remember Galib one time told me your name meant the East Wind, and also that the other horses of your race were made from it. . . ."

Diego recalled that night, when he was returning from the home of Kabirma and Fatima, when Galib recited to him that beautiful poem that spoke of the creation of the horse.

"'Virtue will suffuse your mane and your haunches. You will be my favorite among all the animals because I have made you master and friend. I have conferred upon you the power to fly without wings, whether attacking or retreating. I will sit men upon your haunches and they shall pray, they shall honor me and sing alleluias to my name.'

"Today you've made that poem come true, Sabba."

To the right of the first houses, once they were inside the town, they saw an inn that seemed well heated and comfortable. A pain in his stomach reminded Diego that he hadn't eaten anything since the day before, but he immediately realized that he hardly had money, only a few coins that he had kept in his vest. He thought of his savings lost on the snow and decided to spend as little as possible from that moment on.

He looked for a discreet place to take refuge, and at the end of the frozen village he found a half-ruined stable. They entered and quickly looked around to find the best insulated corner to rest. He found straw and a handful of hay and offered them to Sabba. At least one of them could eat.

"I don't know what we're going to do. . . . What a disaster!" he whispered in the animal's ear. Sabba turned with an understanding expression.

Diego explored the wound in his leg. There were only two small holes that attested to the bite from the first attack. They looked too swollen and he didn't like their color. When he squeezed them with his fingers, he managed to clean them a bit. He immediately knew he would need to open them completely if he didn't want further complications. He took out a small dagger, the only keepsake he had from Galib, and cut his skin with determination. Immediately there flowed out a yellowish liquid and afterward a bit of blood. With a shred of his shirt, he wrapped the wound so that it would close better and felt it without sensing as much pain as before. That seemed like enough. Then he examined Sabba. Except for the bite on her haunches, he found nothing but minor scratches without any apparent importance.

That night Diego ate nothing, nor the second day on the way to Burgos. On the third day, he found a dead hare on the roadside about to be eaten by a wild dog. He threw stones at the beast and jumped down, devouring the animal in mouthfuls. Another traveler whom he shared the route with for a few leagues exchanged him a piece of dried mule meat for a stirrup. It was a bad deal, but that's how hungry he was, and Diego was happy to trade. He ate part with fervor and kept the other part in reserve.

Very poor, thirsty and tired, they finally reached the city of Burgos. Without entering, they walked around it to head toward Nájera, the former capital of the kingdom of Navarre. That was where they had been told to go if they wanted to arrive at Fitero.

Some leagues to the east, they began to ascend another mountain that reminded Diego of the difficult moment with the wolves. It was cold there too, very cold. They had been told that the pass was open and that it wouldn't cost much to cross it.

When they reached the highest point, it was nighttime, and they decided to find shelter. Not far from the road, they found a small cabin for sheepherders protected from the freezing wind by a dense neighboring poplar grove. Since the wood they could find was damp, Diego couldn't manage to make a fire and he had to cover up with the clothes he was carrying. He tried to sleep another night without eating anything. Curled up in a corner of the hut, against its north face, in the silence of the night, shivering and gnashing his teeth, he finally fell into a deep sleep.

Hours later, in the still of the night, a light crunching awoke him. He opened his eyes slightly and saw someone rifling through his things. The person appeared weak. He made sure he was alone. Diego waited to see his back to leap onto him and knock him down by surprise. He did it, and when he had the person on the floor, he looked for his neck, grabbed it with both hands, and managed to completely immobilize him.

The person didn't put up much resistance.

"If you stay still, I'll let you live," Diego threatened him.

He felt around in his leather pouch and took out Galib's dagger. Pressing it into his adversary's throat, he promised to use it if he tried to escape.

"Now you're going to tell me who you are and what you're after."

"My name is Marcos . . ." The light of the moon illuminated his face and Diego tried to see it more clearly. He was somewhat younger than Diego. "I was just looking for a little money, you know . . . to eat with. I wasn't trying to take anything else, I swear."

Diego looked disbelieving.

"Sir, believe me . . . please."

"I'm not a sir, so you can save the good manners. And even if I was, I wouldn't believe you."

The boy begged his pardon and tried to pull away from the steel at his neck, promising he wouldn't try to leave. Diego agreed but kept his eye out for any strange movements.

"All right, I'll be honest. If I could have, I would have fleeced you bare." He kept talking without giving Diego time to respond. "Wouldn't you do the same if hunger was eating away your stomach, or if you didn't remember what the last thing you ate was, or when?"

Diego could see that he was extremely thin. He didn't seem like a bad person. His desolate aspect, almost childlike wrinkles under the filth on his face, and a certain goodness in his gaze inspired an immediate understanding on Diego's part. He wasn't the only person who was hungry.

He looked for that bit of dried meat that he had preserved and gave it to him. The intruder pounced on it, bit it, savored it as though there didn't exist a finer repast in the world.

"You wouldn't have a piece of bread to go with it, no?"

Diego relaxed, seeing him as harmless.

"No, that's everything I have."

Without losing a minute, he finished the meat in silence, and felt around on his clothes in case any scraps of it had fallen and he could eat them.

"I thank you from the bottom of my heart. You seem like a good man. If there's anything I can do for you . . ."

"Yes, you can leave me in peace."

"Don't you want to know who I am, where I come from? I wouldn't mind telling you."

Diego shook his head.

"I just want to sleep. Get out of here."

"It's all right. I'll let you sleep, but tomorrow I'll tell you."

Diego didn't have time to answer him before the boy had left the hovel. He heard his steps falling away in the night and grabbed onto his leather pouch to avoid further surprises. That night it took some time until he was able to fall asleep.

It surprised him not to find the boy near the next morning when he awoke, though he didn't much mind. He picked up everything quickly and mounted Sabba to arrive at the neighboring town of Belorado where he would try to get ahold of something to eat. Before he had gone even half a league, Diego heard noise behind him. When he turned, he saw the boy on a mule.

"Where are you going, sir? Where are you from? Why are you traveling alone? Maybe you have a little of that tasty meat left?" That unending succession of questions bothered Diego.

"None of that should matter to you," he replied drily.

"I'm intrigued. It's obvious you're not a beggar, and yet I know for sure you're traveling without money. Do you believe in predestination? I do. There exist unknown forces that move life, everything . . ." He lowered his voice and adopted a serious tone.

"I'm serious, don't get into my business. Yesterday I felt bad for you, but today is another day. Don't try your luck further."

"Do you have a family?"

"Get out of here." Diego was starting to get mad.

"Fine, fine. Don't be that way."

Without going even twenty steps farther, the boy decided to speak again.

"I'm coming from Burgos, I'm running from . . ."

Diego stopped and stood there staring at him, shocked by his persistence. Once more he was going to command him to go, but Marcos beat him to it.

"I'm leaving. Don't worry. I was just trying to make the journey more agreeable for you, that's all, keep you a little company."

"Bye."

Diego resumed his march. Every once in a while he looked back to confirm that the boy wasn't following, but unfortunately, there was no way to get rid of him.

Passing Belorado in the direction of Nájera he saw him again, this time a quarter league away. Marcos kept his distance, but it was evident that he was following. If Diego stopped, he did the same.

Tired of that stupid situation, Diego took advantage of a long plain to press Sabba to gallop away, imagining that it would be impossible to keep up with him on that mule. He thought that the rest of the day, and the next morning, but unfortunately, the boy showed up again. The sweaty mule seemed to be exhausted, but Marcos looked contented. He even saluted Diego when he saw his gaze from afar.

Diego sped up once more, thinking to leave them behind, and soon they were out of his sight. Since he was close to the city of Nájera, he was excited to enter in order to lose him definitively. He ran through the streets, stopped in a market, and slyly picked up some cast-off fruits and vegetables that had been left behind but weren't in bad shape. He left the city to the east and to his great irritation, not long after, just before he reached the river Ebro, he saw Marcos again. Diego sighed, exhausted, unable to comprehend what motivated the boy's insistence.

He arrived at a crossroads and the lack of waymarks made him hesitate as to where to turn. So he was happy to see that down one of them came three armed bailiffs, although their attitude was far from friendly.

He stepped aside to let them pass with the idea of asking them where to go.

"Stop in the name of justice!" one shouted to his astonishment.

They instantly surrounded him and grabbed hold of his reins.

"What's happening? What do you want with me?"

"You know well . . ." another one with a serious face said.

"I don't understand."

"We don't understand your cruelty either, but luckily we've found you." The one who spoke grabbed him by the hair and twisted it without mercy. The others put manacles on his wrists.

"But . . . I'm only traveling. I'm coming from Toledo. I'm afraid you've got the wrong man."

"I can't remember a single arrest where I didn't hear the same story," the oldest of the three said, laughing in his face. "Stop resisting and come with us. We'll take you to the court and they'll decide what your punishment will be."

"But can I know what the devil this is all about?"

Diego began to worry when he received a resounding slap as the sole answer to his question.

"Watch your mouth and don't be insolent. A witness saw you on that same mare fleeing from the convent of San Diego just after robbing it."

"I've never been in that place in my life!" Diego exclaimed aloud, until he felt an unexpected punch to his ribs.

"Sir, sir!" someone shouted feverishly from afar. "Do us the favor of not delaying! You know your father is waiting for us at the castle. . . ."

All present turned to see who was talking. On his mule, Marcos approached them and took Sabba's reins from one of the bailiffs.

"What are you saying, castle . . .? Who are you?" The one who seemed the head of the group waited impatiently for a response.

"You still don't know who you are talking to?" Marcos confirmed from their faces that they were surprised, as he had wished. "My master Don Diego belongs to a sacred and noble house and has been convened by his father to join the king's troops. If you delay us further, we'll arrive too late."

The three men looked at him in disbelief. If what he said was true, they would be best to free him unless they wanted to receive an extraordinary reprimand.

"What is your last name and where is this castle?"

Diego swallowed. Now he was happy for the presence of that little thief. He followed along.

"Azagra," he answered rapidly. "From the Azagras from Albarracín."

That was the first name that came into his mind, that of the new wife of Don Diego López de Haro, father of Doña Urraca.

The men spoke among themselves in low voices. First they seemed to argue, but at last, the one who led the choir begged their pardon, embarrassed.

"Forgive me, sir," he said, taking the cuffs from Diego's wrists. "We may have committed a terrible error with you."

"No, we're not going to forget this," Marcos rebuked them. "It will be found out."

The men, chastened, said a respectful good-bye as they left, ashamed of their mistake.

A little while later, now far from the crossroads, Diego thanked him for his fortunate help. Marcos dismissed it and began to explain who he was.

"I'm the son of a slattern from Burgos, the best one there is."

"I'm not acquainted with that profession."

"Which one have you heard of, whore, slut, hooker, public woman?"

Diego cleared his throat, taken aback by the boy's lack of shame.

"When I met you, I was fleeing that city on her account, I mean, because I defended her honor against a soldier who had treated her too roughly. I must have hit him too hard that evening when I found him beating her, because the man was severely injured. Later, I found out he was a high official in the court of King Alfonso, and that's why I had to flee Burgos; I was afraid of being arrested."

While he spoke, Diego looked more closely at him. Marcos had chestnut hair, very curly, and expressive eyes. His nose was round but well proportioned and his chin had a divot in the shape of a cross, a peculiarity that gave him an air of class.

"You seem proud of your mother's work."

"I am. She is the second-most-famous woman at the court after the queen herself, and I say it with all due respect. Her name is Lidia. She gained great fame thanks to the generosity of her virtues but especially the ease with which she gave herself to all. She said it was a job like any other, but those who enjoyed her assured that in love, she was like a goddess."

"For a street urchin, you're well-spoken."

"Understand me; I've never wanted for money. My mother took me to the priests. They taught me arithmetic and how to read."

Diego asked him why he was following him.

"He whispered it to me." He looked at the sky and crossed himself. "He wants it to be so. I was brought to you by force. I only obey him . . ." He adopted a solemn expression.

"When you say 'he,' are you referring to . . ."

"Yes, to the very same." He was trying to convince him.

"Right . . ."

Diego was impressed by his resourcefulness. In little time the boy had shown a great variety of aspects. He had been a thief, he was the son of a courtesan, he acted like a swindler, with those lawmen, for example. He wasn't illiterate. And now, to add to the confusion, he added a spiritual angle that seemed as false to Diego as anything else.

"I'm headed to a monastery, the one in Fitero, close to the Navarrese frontier," Diego said in a dissuasive tone. "I don't think it will interest you as a destination. . . . I'm going because I'm trying to study and learn my work better."

"I will come with you." Marcos thought rapidly that the place, distant and isolated, could serve as a refuge to hide from the people who were looking for him. It seemed like the perfect spot to disappear for a certain time.

"He told you that, of course."

"Yes, yes. You hear him too?"

II.

———————

The doors of the monastery remained locked all day. They had been told that by a beggar who was in front of them.

"You will never get in." The man waved his hand, demonstrating how impossible it seemed. "If you don't know one of the friars, they won't attend to you."

"We'll see, we'll see," Marcos promised, cooking up an idea.

Since the affair with the bailiffs, and throughout the days, they had passed through vineyards and rivers, towns and hermitages, rain and fog, before arriving at Fitero.

The monastery, still in the boundaries of Castile, had been raised by the express desire of Alfonso VIII in a provocative corner, the border of the kingdoms of Navarre and Aragon. It belonged to the Cistercian order and was the first monastery founded in a Christian kingdom inside the former Visigoth Hispania.

During their long journey, Diego and Marcos had time to talk and get to know each other better. Marcos's personality was strange, in many cases ambiguous, but interesting. Diego finally accepted his company, thankful for his aid with the bailiffs, without knowing how long it would last.

"You see yourself in a monastery?"

"And why not? Where better to hide? Besides, I get along with the friars. They're easy to get along with and I know what they really like."

Those affirmations, like so many others Diego had heard in the course of their travels, made him see that Marcos, above all else, was a rogue. A clear example of how a person could turn the capacity for trickery into a kind of art. But beyond that, he was rabidly nice, joyful, and dishonest. He lied so much, he didn't seem to be able to know when he was telling the truth.

"You think they'll let us in?" Marcos observed the enormous walled-in structure with the bell tower rising above it.

"I know how to forge horseshoes and I'm skilled as an albéitar. I can read Arabic and Latin, and besides, I know a Calatravan friar, Benito, who can serve me as a recommendation. I think I can manage to get us in to talk to the superior."

Immediately a sharp screak caught their attention. From the entrance to the monastery a tight group of friars in white habits began to emerge, some on horseback, some in carriages, and the rest on foot.

Diego dismounted from Sabba and went up to one, asking where he could find the superior in charge. The man studied him and then replied, with little courtesy.

"If you ride south for twelve days, you will find the castle of Salvatierra, at the border with Al-Andalus. He only shows up there when there is a general assembly, once or twice a year." He goaded his horse and continued on.

Marcos, unused to being beaten by adversity, tried to help him and turned to another of the friars.

"Where are you going?" He grabbed the friar's horse by the bridle, stopping him. The man looked at him indignantly.

"To work on some of the lands of the monastery. Who do you think you are, stopping me like this?"

"You have stables, I suppose?" The monk nodded without knowing what the question was about. Many watched them as they passed by.

"We've been hired by the grand master to assist you with them. We have come from Salvatierra." Diego was stunned by Marco's inventiveness.

"Then speak with Friar Servando; he is in charge of the monastery's stables. You'll find him inside."

Diego reproached the daring boy softly, since he was now obliged to continue in that lie, but remembered that the name he'd just heard was one Friar Benito had referred to several times as the brother who was the horse healer.

"From now on, leave it to me; I don't want more complications."

Marcos responded with resignation.

The friar who guarded the doors of the monastic premises remained firm in his refusal and did not help them get inside. They had to leave him Sabba, Marcos's mule, and everything they had on them with the promise they would leave the monastery once they had spoken with Brother Servando. And in reality, he only did so when he had heard Marcos say that Servando was a family member of his, a cousin.

While they walked through a broad courtyard lined with stones up to the stables, Marcos received a blow to the ribs in return for his most recent lie.

They saw on one side a grand church of peculiar orange-colored stones and a precious rosette at the entrance. Diego enjoyed its stained glass, excited to be so close to that cradle of knowledge, already dreaming of a great and well-nourished library, seeing himself there.

They reached a low structure that seemed to be the one they were looking for. The strong scent coming from inside assured them they had reached their destination. Pushing open a dilapidated door that must have weighed as much as ten men, they listened to the hammering over an anvil. They entered without fear.

That was the first time they saw Friar Servando, and he left a strong impression on both of them. He must have been over fifty, but he still preserved the strength of a twenty-year-old. He stood well over six and a half feet; he was two heads taller than most people, though that may have been the projection of his shadow against the fire making him seem bigger than he was.

When they spoke to him, he paid no attention; he didn't even shout at them. He kept his eyes on his work. His torso was uncovered and his habit was knotted around his waist. When they approached closer, they saw an enormous scar on his stomach in the shape of a smile.

At his side, a boy shook exaggeratedly while being recriminated harshly. He was bending a red-hot horseshoe and seemed unaccustomed to doing so, because each hammer blow was bending it farther out of form.

"Hold it tighter with the pliers! No . . . Don't hit it that way. Don't you see how you're splitting the metal?"

The gigantic individual breathed in and shouted hatefully.

"You must be an idiot. Let me." He pushed the boy brusquely, took the pliers and the beaten piece of iron. He only needed to hit it five times to set it right.

When he was done inspecting it on both sides, he plunged it in a basin of cool water, and at that moment he saw Diego and Marcos amid the dense cloud of steam that rose up when the hot iron was cooled. Though he didn't recognize their faces, he smiled and changed his manners as soon as he'd sent the boy away.

"I have to admit that every day I have less and less patience for the scarce spirit of sacrifice and the lack of nerve in this generation of young people. This one you just saw may be the worst one I can remember." His deep voice echoed like thunder. "What can I do for you two?"

"They have told us you are responsible for the stables, you make the horseshoes, and that you are also a recognized horse healer." As soon as he'd finished the phrase, Diego shot a glance at Marcos to warn him, remembering his previous comment.

"No, they haven't lied to you. . . ." the friar admitted, waiting for further explanation.

"I would like to be able to learn at your side," Diego said at once.

"Learn at my side? What is this about?" Rather disconcerted, the man took off his leather gloves and left them on the anvil. "I don't know who you are. . . . Nor what you're after, and even less who sent you here. But whoever it was, you've made a mistake. I don't teach anyone who hasn't taken vows." He loosed the hammer and scratched the crown of his head, bothered by the time he was wasting with these intruders.

"You wouldn't have to start from zero with me." Diego tried to approach from another angle, despite the setback. "I know how to forge horseshoes, I can manage horses well, and besides that, I have knowledge of the albéitar's work."

That last word provoked a sudden change in attitude in Friar Servando.

"Albéitar?" A grimace of displeasure crossed his face. "That's a Moorish profession. You aren't one of those mudéjars who run rampant in Castile?" He cleaned his hands on his apron and studied him with an unpleasant expression.

Marcos was quiet, waiting for his opportunity.

Diego, somewhat frustrated by the lack of progress, believed it was the moment to mention Friar Benito.

"We are good Christians and I assure you that infidel blood does not run through our veins. I understand my proposal might strike you as strange, but if we have come to you, it is because you were recommended by a Cistercian brother I knew in Toledo. It was he who spoke to me of the library this monastery possesses and the immense riches inside it, but even more, of you. It is from him that I know you are good, the best in your profession."

"Who are you talking of?"

"Friar Benito."

"Good old Friar Benito . . ." His face softened. "And you say you met him in Toledo . . . And he spoke well of me to you?" Undoubtedly, the reference had made him happy. "But I still don't understand how you managed to come to me, if you know we don't accept anyone from outside." He scratched his beard pensively. "I respect that man very much . . . I don't know what he could see in you that would lead him to recommend you to me, but believe me, I'm going to find out."

He took a piece of red-hot iron from the fire, shapeless, and passed the hammer to Diego.

"Show me what you know how to do."

Helping himself to the pliers, Diego held the iron over a gauge and began first to smooth it out and isolate it and then to curve it without overusing the hammer. Once he was happy with it, without losing more time than necessary, he handed it over.

Friar Servando slowly looked over his work without talking.

"What would you give to an eyesick horse?"

"I would make a paste of mastic and put it inside," he responded, almost without thinking.

"And if it was an animal with laminitis, where would you begin?"

"I would bleed it in its hindquarters and then prepare a salve of barley and straw to rub in."

Friar Servando thought of something more difficult.

"What would you use to soften a stubborn callus on the knee of the beast?"

"If it was ulcerous and in bad shape, I would try with a mixture of dry pig manure, salt, and sulfur, all mixed with wine."

"Do you know Latin?"

"I read it well, and Arabic too."

The man began to warm up to the idea of having him by his side, being accustomed to suffering the habitual ignorance of his helpers, many of them unacquainted with the world of horses and the majority of them illiterate.

Diego went on talking.

"I know how to treat some colics, geld a stallion, and also what the best cure is for cramping or against flying pests. I think I can tell when a horse's stomach is bothering it and how to calm it down when it's angry," he said, looking into the monk's eyes. "I know that you harbor great knowledge apart from your experience. I pray you share it with me, please. Until now, what I have learned of this noble office I owe to a wise albéitar I knew in Toledo and to the books I was able to read in those years. Help me to finish my education, even if I am not one of you. In exchange for the trouble, I could take care of those tasks that you find most bothersome. And of course, I would promise to serve you in anything you needed. What do you say?"

Friar Servando kept silent and began to think. He liked the idea, but he still needed to be sure.

"Follow me. . . ."

He turned to a mare tied to the wall.

"Name me the parts of her leg."

Diego approached the animal and touched the various parts as he named them.

The friar lifted a leg and asked him to do the same with the hoof. Diego explained to him where the cleft, the crown, the heel buttress were, and defined the water line, the corner, and the bulb.

"That's good. . . . I see you are very well prepared; till now you've been correct with everything." He knocked at the hoof three times with his knuckles and looked at him. "What would it sound like if she had foot rot?"

"Like an empty barrel."

Marcos listened to them feeling rather stunned. He thought the best thing would be to pass unnoticed.

"If the horse puts its weight on its foot, and the knee goes over the vertical line, what would you call that deformity?"

"It's a lateral fault, buck-kneed, and if the opposite happened, it is calf-kneed," Diego answered, more calmly.

Friar Servando could scarcely conceal the excellent impression the boy was making on him.

"Follow me now down the hall; we are going to see other horses. I want to know if you can figure out what condition they're in."

Diego looked at the first. Just one look in its eyes told him what was happening.

"It's uncomfortable or angry, I don't know which."

Friar Servando admitted it had just been disciplined for leaping over a fence.

The following one had its eyes almost closed. Diego raised his voice and it closed them even more.

"This mare is frightened, and I don't think it's just shyness."

"She's been that way for a few days, it's true," Friar Servando said. "She has a bad eye infection, but you couldn't know that. It's true that if she were very frightened, she would act the same way."

Without finishing the phrase, he pointed out a male that watched them from afar.

"And that one?"

The animal opened its eyes exaggeratedly and its upper eyelids were extremely wrinkled. It whinnied intensely and its nostrils were highly dilated.

"He seems dispirited, like something is worrying him a lot."

"That's enough . . ." He turned back to the forge, picked up a piece of raw iron, and buried it in the coals. "I admit you're capable but I can't tell you anything until I have my superior's approval."

Suddenly Friar Servando fell quiet, realizing that Marcos was there, and turned to him.

"And you?"

"I don't have his learning, but I'm not afraid to work. Give me whatever job, the most pressing one, and you'll discover that I won't give you any problem. I'm a worker with a strong willingness to do things right."

"I like what you're telling me. . . ." Friar Servando looked at his weak arms and legs. "The work I can offer you is hard. Do you dare?"

"Try me," Marcos answered.

"Since I will have to arrange food and lodging for you, and for your animals as well . . ." Those words sounded glorious to them. "I will have to take half your wages. The work begins after morning prayers and ends with the evening prayers, after dinner. Now, go clean the stables, and you"—Diego assumed he meant him—"don't ever call yourself an albéitar again in my presence. Use the Latin term *veterinarius* or if you want, horse healer, it's all the same to me. That is what I will call you from now on. If I manage to speak with my superior, tomorrow you will come with me to visit a client, outside the monastery."

"I thank you for it," Diego said.

"Don't patronize to me. I hate courtesy. I only require loyalty and sincerity. I reject people who try to cover up reality with excuses. If we accept you in this monastery, you will have to follow certain norms and rules that are sacred among us. Don't neglect them."

He arched his enormous brows and adopted a serious tone to stress the importance of their behavior.

"You will only give an opinion when it is asked of you, whether you understand or not. I will not allow you to compare the treatment you receive with that of the friars, nor the food, and you must always respect them. You will be silent throughout the premises and you will not be able to explore them without my permission. You will help in everything I ask of you, and that includes any kind of cleaning or maintenance tasks. And for now, that's all."

"Pardon me, but I have a question. Could I see your famous library?" For Diego, that was a matter too vital to be forgotten.

"Before that, you will have to win my trust. If that happens, maybe after some time, I will tell you that any reading you do will be guided. That is how I think. I will not say that science is bad, but it has do be well dosed so that it doesn't damage the conscience. That will be my job."

He sat down next to the anvil and gave a final warning.

"Don't take any action without consulting me. I expect loyalty from you. And last of all, remember always that if there is one thing I hate, it is people hiding things from me. . . . Ah, and also, I will expect you at Mass every day, and at sexts, nones, and vespers."

In spite of the challenges they would have to survive to live every day, Diego felt happy. Marcos and he had managed to get into the monastery, he was almost accepted as apprentice, and that meant his education could continue. He didn't like the name veterinarius or being called a horse healer—he preferred the term albéitar—but it was far from the most important thing. Although Friar Servando's character seemed the exact opposite of Galib's, Diego wanted to believe that his knowledge was broader.

He thought about the library. Among those stones, caressed by the tranquility of silence, reposed a great part of human wisdom. As though it were a precious treasure, there it was, waiting for him, until the moment when that obstreperous friar blessed him.

Diego closed his eyes and saw himself submerged in thousands of pages, unraveling their theories, absorbing their science . . . an awareness that would improve his diagnoses, would make his hands more skilled when he operated, and would stir his intuition so he would see further than the external signs of illness.

But Marcos, who hadn't seen any special advantage in being in the monastery, didn't care for Friar Servando. Unlike Diego, he started to doubt whether this had been the best decision. Though he was safe from his pursuers, what awaited him seemed discouraging.

Both, from the same moment, and with different thoughts, began to sweep the stable, obeying the friar's first command.

III.

Friar Servando did not call Diego the next morning to accompany him on his visit. Nor did he give any explanation. In fact, for the following week he disappeared from the monastery without anyone knowing where he had gone or why.

Obeying his directions, when they had finished cleaning the stables, Diego and Marcos cleaned out an enormous pit into which the latrines emptied, located in the monastery's cellars. It took them three whole days, and when they finished, they changed to another job that was less arduous but more dangerous.

The new task consisted of unclogging all the gargoyles that bordered the top of the church and cleaning the moss and filth from the roof tiles. To get to those places, they had to climb wood scaffolds and make a crane to raise the containers of water they needed for cleaning the stone. Armed with coarse brushes, some tied to long rods, they did their work, accompanied by an icy wind.

That took them three whole weeks and made Marcos sick.

When Friar Servando was back in the monastery, Diego watched his friend's cold get worse day by day. He began to get really worried when, apart from a fever, Marcos began to blather, remembering his first thefts and cons nostalgically, or reliving the brutal beating that had been the cause of his escape from Burgos.

Diego spoke to Friar Servando, asking him to excuse Marcos from work for at least two days, since the coming days would be colder and windier. But the friar didn't like the idea and wouldn't tell Diego when he thought his apprenticeship would begin either.

"Son, vigor is a virtue for all Christians. . . ." was the first thing he said. "And on occasion, there come hard tests that God presents to measure our strength." He crossed himself. "And now, get back to your work and don't bother me anymore. When you're done with the roof of the church, you'll continue with the cloister. And please, don't be so anxious to accompany me. Everything will come in its proper time. Remember that to be a good healer, you need to exercise patience. You have to practice it a great deal so that one day, it will become a virtue in you."

That same morning Diego had to tell Marcos he had not been relieved of his duties and they went back up on the dome, explored the buttresses, and reached the cupola in the center of the nave, the last area they had to clean. But Diego didn't let him work, not that first day or the following two. Since no one could see them at that height, as soon as they had ascended, Diego covered Marcos with two blankets to protect him from the bad weather and make him sweat out his sickness. Marcos passed hours in this way, curled up and sleeping, leaned against a low wall.

From there, Diego observed the work in the scriptorium, where he saw a group of monks copying books and embellishing them with drawings on the page. They worked behind windows filled with an abundant curtain of light, not far from where Diego was scraping the stones.

The next week, Marcos recovered his health and his good humor.

That improvement coincided with the beginning of the labors inside the cloister and the chapter house beside it. Both agreed that if the first was beautiful, the second was even more so.

The roof supported nine vaults held up by four columns in the center and others built into the walls. The cinnamon-colored stone changed tone when struck by the light, and especially at midday, the effect it produced was incredible, almost magic.

Diego and Marcos had a hard job there but it was more gratifying than the previous ones. They scrubbed the stone floor and the benches until they gleamed, and then they carefully cleaned the columns and walls.

"From what I could hear yesterday, we are right under the library," Diego remarked while he used a chisel to clean a leaf carved into one of the columns.

"You have too much faith in that man." Marcos sighed. "You think he's going to let you go with him to teach you what he knows, and that after he'll open the doors to the scriptorium, but I don't think he'll do either of the two." He had to lower his arms a moment until the blood began to circulate again. He was cleaning the ribs of the vaults and the job required him to keep his arms raised. "As I see it, we're living a farce. He's cheated us like two idiots, you'll see."

Soon they heard steps. When they looked to the cloister, they saw a group of friars in a procession. They were headed to the church to pray the terce, which Diego and Marcos had fortunately been excused from. They respected the monks' silence until they saw them disappear.

"I take a man at his word and Friar Servando promised," Diego responded, without abandoning the previous conversation.

"And I believe in my intuition."

"Intuition, you say? Intuition is a very necessary ability for an albéitar, since our patients don't tend to talk much." He smiled at him.

"It's always worked for me. That's why every time I see Friar Servando, it reaffirms what I just said: He's using us."

"Maybe it's true, but he's the only person who can help me right now. If he wills it, I can finish my education, and he has the power to open the doors to the library for me or to keep them sealed. I don't want to imagine that he's lied to me; I prefer to think it is hard for him to believe us. Sometimes we come to erroneous conclusions early on. That could be what's happening with Friar Servando. For example, take the feeling you get being in a place like this one. . . ." He explored the room with his gaze. "I'm excited by such beauty and grandeur. And you?"

"I just see work. Lots of work."

"You see? We see the same thing but we feel different things. You look to these stones and that's all you see, stones. But if you look at them with other eyes, you can find messages, stories hidden in them. Do you know what I'm referring to?"

"Not really."

"These structures are authentic books in stone, edited by stonemasons. Some wanted to leave the sacred history written for those who didn't know how to read book. Others tried to hide messages enclosed in shapes or symbols, sometimes mysterious ones. Some of these you might have seen in this room. . . . When you see it, you'll say I'm right."

Marcos looked at the walls, columns, and roof and stopped on a rather special design.

"You mean that one?" He pointed to a column on the east wall. Under the capital, there was a curious form sculpted in relief, a braid of three cords. They rose and fell in diagonal, and every twist closed at an angle, both on the upper and lower parts. Small hands held it, as they seemed to hold the column itself.

"Right!" Diego traced that curious figure with his finger. "It attracted my attention the first day, and since then I haven't stopped thinking about why. I think it was placed there to speak to us about the goodwill of the brotherhood, the bonds between them, their unity toward a single destiny. If you think about where you find it, it seems like an appropriate message, given that this is where the monks gather every day to talk about ideas that—"

A deep voice rose from behind him.

"Diego, I want you to come with me right now."

Friar Servando had entered the chapter house in a rush. He seemed to be in a hurry, so much so that he didn't even check on how their work was going.

"And you, Marcos, go to the courtyard and help receive the poor. Today is Friday and the refectory is open to them."

He pushed Diego's back, trying to get him out of the room.

"Go saddle my horse and then yours. We have to go to a neighboring village, to Cascante."

Without understanding why, Diego saw him look at both sides of his hands and ask him to do the same.

"Mine are too thick and I need some that are leaner . . ."

Although Diego's first reaction was to ask why he needed him, the excitement of being needed filled him with optimism.

The small village of Cascante, only three leagues to the southeast of Fitero, had an important Jewish quarter and a populous mudéjar neighborhood. But they were going to the Christian area, to the baker's house. It wasn't difficult for them to find it; they just followed the scent of bread.

When they got there, a woman waited for them at the door with an expression of absolute worry.

"I thought you would never arrive." She looked at them with consternation. "Be fast, please."

They dismounted from their mares and left them tied outside.

"I only have one horse to deliver bread through the rest of the villages. This is a disaster! I had to ask a woman for help to . . . Well, it would be better if you saw with your own eyes."

"How old is the animal?" Friar Servando knew what they were going to find, unlike Diego.

"It's passed eight winters with me, but when I bought it, I believe it had worked previously for a farmer. It could be twelve."

They entered a filthy and narrow stable, poorly lit. As soon as they got used to the poor visibility, the scene they saw left them stunned. The intestines had come out of the horse and were hanging there free, full of flies, with a dark red color, and very swollen.

Beside it was an older woman who seemed determined to put everything back where it had been. Without hearing them arrive, the old woman panted and sweated terribly as a consequence of the enormous effort she was exerting. Between pushing, besides uttering a few blasphemies, she spread her legs to press them better into the floor, and used both hands to begin to push inside, little by little, all that had come out. To her despair, the horse whinnied in pain and at that moment, the little she had managed to push in came out again with surprising ease.

"Don't expect me to work with that ill-spoken old witch doctor. . . ."

Friar Servando looked at the baker and then at the woman. He had seen her three times before, and every time, apart from solving the main problem he had been called for, he'd had to repair the consequences of her errors.

"Well, of course the priest had to come!" the old woman shrieked contemptuously.

"I don't have to put up with her. . . ." The friar stood before his customer and the woman reacted. It was to the detriment of the old woman, and soon she was pushing her out of the stable against her protests.

Once they were alone, Friar Servando and Diego approached the animal to study the situation.

"What would one of those albéitars do faced with a situation like this?" Friar Servando's question was certainly a double-edged one, but Diego answered nonetheless. Besides, he understood why the man needed his hands.

"I would prepare a paste of fish and salt and would mix it with a good bit of oil. Then I would anoint the tissue that's come out with that unguent before trying to put it back where it was."

"I'll leave the cure in your hands. Ask that woman for what you need, but first, I recommend you add a bit of incense to your ointment. You'll see how the swelling goes down faster."

The baker listened to what they needed and brought the ingredients over without being asked. While Diego ground the ingredients in a mortar, Friar Servando took advantage of the wait to question the woman.

"Maria, I've heard things about you that don't make me happy at all." The woman reddened, surely aware of what he was referring to.

"I don't know . . ." She pretended, scratching her nose nervously.

"Yes, you do, and also that he's married."

"Are you questioning my honor?" The woman bit her lip and offered her help to Diego with the mixture, trying to escape from the uncomfortable conversation.

"I'm not the one responsible for your virtue being on everybody's lips," Friar Servando insisted. Recently he had been informed of the adulterous relations the baker was keeping with a farmer who maintained one of the farms belonging to the monastery.

The woman tried to change the theme, asking after the cure for the horse.

"This never happened to him before." She looked at Diego. "What could be the cause of it? You're a horse healer, no?"

Friar Servando saw the moment had come to give the horse a little arnica, and to begin, he tried to answer her question.

"Illness is a penitence that God sends to purge us of our sins, which in your case are many, Maria. What has happened to your horse was provoked by your sinfulness. You are incapable of suppressing your lower instincts, and that is why our Lord continued placing new adversities in your life, so that you will smite the disorder in your soul. . . . Confess as soon as you can and stop seeing that man!" He raised his voice. "If you go on this way, everyone will treat you like a whore, and I will accuse you of it at trial."

Diego had felt uncomfortable at first, but when he heard all that, he was indignant at the humiliating behavior of Friar Servando. He hadn't come there to judge whether the woman's actions had been good or evil. He understood that such a job was the exclusive provenance of God. But it seemed to him despicable and frankly cruel to relate the horse's illness with the behavior of the woman.

When he saw the woman's downcast expression and saw how she shook, he felt compelled to put a stop to it, and there was only one way he knew.

"Don't believe him!" Diego interrupted. "This horse's problem has nothing to do with any sin, and much less with divine retribution. The fact is, it's old, and you probably make it work too hard. It may have been forced to carry loads that were too heavy recently. . . . Don't worry for him; there's a solution for his problem."

Friar Servando didn't react for a moment, but when he did, he was enraged. He couldn't bear to be contradicted, even less in the presence of a woman. He began to insult Diego and to accuse him of being a Moor. Infuriated, he spit on the floor very close to Diego and predicted for him, amid his imprecations, a long bout of cleaning the latrines.

On the way back to the monastery, the monk didn't talk or look at him, though Diego could tell what his thoughts were by his face; Friar Servando was deeply disappointed.

"This is absurd," Marcos protested when he found out what happened. "I don't know what we're doing here. They'll never let you get to those books, and you won't learn anything from him."

"Maybe I was showing a lack of loyalty when I contradicted his words. I admit he's a difficult person, maybe impossible. I know my attitude may seem absurd to you, but I came here to finish my education as an albéitar and to enter into that magnificent library, and I won't leave these walls until I do it."

Marcos didn't try to explain how he would do it, but from that moment he decided to intervene so that Diego's wishes would come true faster. If they respected Friar Servando's rhythms, they could spend years there without managing anything but a shiny polished floor. And he didn't have the patience for that.

For a few days the two friends didn't see each other again since Diego had been sent to the latrines, but Marcos's luck changed suddenly, and only because he heard a conversation.

It was between two monks; the key keeper in charge of the kitchens and another who managed the finances. Marcos was helping the first to empty a wheelbarrow of olive barrels when the other came over to ask a question.

"Have you talked yet with the prior?"

"I did, but he still hasn't offered me anyone. Can you believe it?" He slapped his knees. "Right now I only have one helper, and to top it off, he's sick. My previous employees will be arriving in Salvatierra to help defend that fortress. How am I going to feed two hundred friars, organize all the purchases, store the necessities, and clean everything on my own. Anyone who thinks that's possible is mad. For me it's impossible. . . ."

Marcos saw the opportunity to get out of the stables and away from Friar Servando and do something he liked better.

"Maybe you're not being insistent enough," the friar replied.

"I've already gotten a serious reprimand from the prior. He says I don't show sufficient interest in my job, I don't know how to sacrifice, and I've lost my trust in providence." The man put his hands on his head in desperation. "Providence . . . I don't imagine providence plucking chickens, but that's what I have to do."

"I could help you with that job," Marcos soon interrupted.

"Excuse me?" The man was surprised.

"Since I was very young, I've been working around ovens." He was lying, as was customary. "And I know cooking well enough to let you get a bit of sleep."

The friar, fat, but in excellent health, remembered the prior's words. Could this boy be the fruit of that famed providence?

"Boy, I have no idea how you know I've been suffering from insomnia lately, but I like your proposal. Tell me who's in charge of you and I'll claim you for myself right now. You work in the stables?"

Marcos nodded.

It didn't seem too hard for Friar Jesús, as he was called, to convince Friar Servando, because from that afternoon on, Marcos began to work with him in the kitchens of the monastery, content and more enthusiastic.

But for Diego, those days were not as fortunate as those of his friend, and in fact, a few days after he left the latrines, he became acquainted with Friar Servando's true character, as well as making an already bad situation much worse.

And all because of a horse illness that almost everyone calls "fig."

IV.

Friar Servando, as a horse healer, attended to different cases both inside and outside the monastery.

At last Diego had managed to accompany him a few more times, not many but enough to begin to feel deceived.

He couldn't understand where the monk's reputation came from when his shortcomings were obvious and the consequences to his patients grave. Diego came to think that the friar lacked even a quarter of the knowledge Diego himself had; he had never seen him use any diagnostic technique that Diego didn't already know, and his catalogue of remedies was both limited and often absurd. His limitations were so grave that Diego began to suffer even when he saw him shoe a horse, because he wasn't particularly good at that, either.

Nevertheless, Diego was quiet, preferring not to speak, until that morning when everything went against him.

A stallion belonging to the royal ensign of Navarre arrived at the stables. It was the first time he had been there and he arrived with a squire.

Diego was lighting some kindling to start up the forge when the animal entered in the stable, led by the squire. The stallion was a beautiful specimen, strong, with an enormous frame. Its coat was cream colored with an almost cherry undertone.

When Diego saw it, and especially when he discovered the enormous lump on its hindquarters, he couldn't resist the temptation to come and watch when Friar Servando attended to it.

Diego looked at the color and texture of the tumor. Luckily for the animal, it was red and seemed recent. He had seen those tumors a number of times with Galib, but never as large as this one, which was as big as an orange. He remembered that in the treatise on the albéitar, his first book, the one Benazir gave him, such tumors were described in detail. They called them "figs," and they were classified by color: the black ones were more serious, then the red ones, and finally the white ones.

Without taking even a breath, the stable boy returned with the news that Friar Servando was not in the monastery and that no one knew when he was coming back, whether that morning or even at night.

Given the situation, Diego couldn't resist and decided to treat that malformation. He looked for a piece of leather and made a hole in it equal to the size of the tumor. Then he put it over the horse to isolate it from the rest of the skin.

"It has what's called a fig, sir." The squire said he didn't know what it was. Diego explained it to him and begged pardon for Friar Servando's absence, presenting matters as though he was the assistant as well as a horse healer.

"You know how to cure it?" The man studied Diego. He didn't seem to be sufficiently convinced to leave that valuable horse in unfamiliar hands, but the boy was so secure and firm in his words that he managed to convince him.

Diego began to compound various ointments. One was made of lime and earth. The other, a paste, from dry river herbs and water. And a third, with a repugnant scent, warm chicken feces mashed in a mortar with soap.

With the herb paste, he made little cakes and took them over the forge. He placed the first on a hot iron and afterward pressed it against the horse's lump. When it was cold, he changed it for another. And he worked this way for a while until the tumor began to whiten. Diego explained to the man that this was a way to lower the blood before he cut it with a sharp knife.

All the stable boys left their labors and gathered around to watch him in action.

"I need you to give me a hand holding the horse. It's going to feel a good bit of pain now."

With ropes and cinches, a number of them working together managed to immobilize it. Diego approached with a knife, the tip of which he had heated in the fire, and began to cut the fig down to the base, pressing down the flesh on either side of it. He cut deep, but carefully, not wanting to damage any nerves. It was fast, demonstrating that he had a sure hand and wasn't intimidated by the sharp whinnies of protest on the part of the animal.

"Now he'll bleed a little. That's a good thing."

The knight's eyes were focused on the enormous lump that had been extracted and its enormous size.

Diego dusted the wound with a mix of lime and earth and quickly pulled away from the animal, foreseeing its violent reaction. Then he took a red-hot iron and passed it around the edges of the wound to stop the bleeding. The horse, furious and in pain, wouldn't stop moving.

"Does he have to go through all this?" the squire asked, white from witnessing the terrible pain the animal was suffering.

"Be calm. The next ointment will relieve his pain."

Diego soaked a linen cloth in the blend of feces and soap and laid it over the wound. Last, he prepared an unguent of honey and pentamyron and told the man to apply it warm once a day.

"If it grows back, ask them to make you a thin rope with hairs from a young nag that has never been with a mare. Use that to tie off the fig until it's strangled. You can do it one, two, even three times, as many as necessary until it falls off."

Diego ordered them to untie the animal carefully and he spoke, very low, into its ear, at the same time scratching its breast to gain its trust. The horse began to look at him timidly, but shortly after, it was neighing more calmly.

Diego felt pleased with his work. The silence that had accompanied him while he operated was suddenly broken by spontaneous applause. All present were sincerely impressed.

"You should find the most comfortable place for him inside the stable, keep him away from dampness, and make sure he doesn't lick the wound. If he does, it will complicate the healing process."

The squire was satisfied with his explanations and congratulated him without any criticism. He asked the young man for his name in case he might need him in the future.

"My name's Diego, Diego de Malagón, apprentice albéitar or horse healer, whichever you prefer to call me."

The squire, the horse, and its illness left, as did the rest of the stable boys, still amazed by the abilities of their companion. And yet that satisfaction lasted for too short a time; Friar Servando was not appreciative of Diego's work.

As soon as Diego saw him step into the stables, he saw he'd been informed of what had happened. The monk looked crazed, and his eyes reflected his bottomless rage. At Diego's side, he began to scream and upbraid him as if he'd gone half mad.

"Do you want to explain to me who gave you the right to attend to my clients?" He walked around Diego with his fists clenched. "If you knew who that horse belonged to . . ."

"To the royal ensign of Navarre."

Friar Servando pushed his shoulder violently, offended by his response.

"Don't you have just a bit of shame?" he snorted, exasperated. "Perhaps you think yourself more capable than me?"

"I'm an albéitar," Diego answered proudly.

The man, beside himself, grabbed Diego's tunic and began to pull so furiously that he ended up tearing it.

"You know I hate that name . . ."

Diego decided not to speak, since in that moment anything he said would be taken badly. That reaction enraged the monk even further. Tired of Diego's silence, the friar decided that punishment would be the best thing to put the young man in his place.

"You'll go back to the latrines, but from today on, you'll sleep in them as well. You will eat there, amid the stench, and you won't come out until I say so. I hope that for once this will make you reconsider your actions."

Diego felt tempted to choke him right there or give him a serious kick to the stomach. He also considered abandoning the monastery and forgetting that absurd person once and for all; but instead, he decided to take another approach.

"Fine," he responded, without raising his voice. "Should I consider this penitence or punishment?"

"Well . . . Well," Friar Servando repeated, indignant. "A penitence . . . Your sin is known as disloyalty and vainglory."

"I don't understand."

"You understand very well. I know you still consider the albéitar's a science greater than the one I possess, and you are stubborn besides. You don't like me calling you a horse healer or veterinarius, I can tell, and you are judgmental of every job I perform. I have felt it when you watch me."

Friar Servando swallowed, angered by Diego's tranquil mood.

"If it is a penitence, then, will I be absolved of my sin afterward?"

"Ummmm . . ." It took the friar an eternity to answer and a strong dose of humility. "Yes, I suppose so."

"And once my sin is forgiven, will I be able to go to the scriptorium afterward?"

Friar Servando clenched his fists and looked at Diego with exasperation, but he did not say no.

The third night he spent in his new destination, Diego received an unexpected visit that relieved him. It was Marcos.

He arrived with a piece of stewed meat, a pound of black bread, and the best repast for his soul, a bit of affection.

"How are you?"

Marcos lit up the floor with a torch to make his way through such filth.

"Not as well as you." Diego stared at the contents of the clay pot that Marcos was carrying in his hands.

Marcos left the torch in a crack in the wall and looked for a seat close to Diego. He couldn't hold back an expression of disgust when he perceived the scent.

"I'm coming to give you good news."

"You don't know how welcome it will be." Diego smiled.

"I've made friends with the friar responsible for the library. His name is Friar Tomás. He's a cheerful man, with a dreamy gaze and forgetful face, but he likes to eat as much as I like scheming. Since I spend the whole day in the kitchen, it hasn't been hard for me to satisfy his weakness, and I've been pleading your case with him."

Diego opened his eyes wide. All he wanted was to hear the words that were about to come out of his mouth.

"I spoke to him about you without leaving out any detail. He knows your wishes to learn and that you can read Arabic without difficulty. He also knows what's been happening with Friar Servando. Believe me, he's interested in your case and wants to know what you're looking for."

"And . . . ?"

"I have bad news and good news."

"Start with the bad."

"Friar Servando is lying when he says you can enter the scriptorium or the library with relative freedom. I found out that those who haven't taken vows are not granted admission."

Diego sighed, defeated. That could mean the end of his plans.

"But wait! I haven't told you the good news."

"Can there be anything positive after what you've just told me?"

"If we can't go in, they can still come out. . . ."

"What?"

"Friar Tomás has another weakness aside from eating."

"Tell me."

"Herb brandies." He smiled roguishly. "Two bottles and the promise of a regular supply took care of it, and thanks to that . . ." He took out a package wrapped in cotton cloth. "While you're down here in this filth, you can read the Roman Vegetius. Isn't that one of the writers you were looking for?"

Diego pulled back the wrappings anxiously and found a book with the title *Digestorum artis mulomedicinae*, signed by Publius Flavius Vegetius Renatus, written in the fourth century.

"He also told me that if you're interested," Marcos continued, "he would pass you the book by the author from Cádiz, Lucius Junio Columella, and then two more treatises in Latin, I think he said from Pliny and one from Paladius. Anyway, I don't know any of them."

Diego couldn't contain his emotion and felt a few tears stream down his cheeks. At last he had one of those books in his hands; it didn't matter anymore that he'd had to put up with so many calamities, far more than could be considered reasonable. Now, thanks to this treatise, he could broaden his knowledge in an area little studied among the Arabs, the methodology for diagnosing illnesses.

Vegetius had been a soldier in the Roman army, an expert in war strategy, a defender of the use of cavalry as a weapon when the rest of his colleagues trusted only in the infantry. Perhaps for this reason, he studied and compiled the most extensive collection of knowledge about those animals, even than that of the Greeks. The book's pages contained marvelous descriptions of the most varied illnesses, recommendations for raising the animals, breeding them, and other aspects such as the ideal physical form and an organized system to select the best stallions.

By candlelight, Diego passed night after night reading, learning each one of the paragraphs by heart. At last he felt happy. That compensated for everything.

In the mornings, he washed the large pieces of perforated marble where the monks emptied their waste, or went down in the dark to clear out the frequent clogs in its drains, but it scarcely mattered. Nor was he bothered by the need to carry spadesful of human waste to the carriages where it would be later used as fertilizer.

He even grew used to the horrible odor, with the lone desire to wait for nightfall and feed himself on that delicious and nutritive science of the books, as he called it. He became drunk with the wisdom written in ink, without understanding why it should be hidden from the eyes of the world. He didn't understand what harm could be done to men's souls by knowledge or what reason there was to have to hide between those stones and temples, authentic walls of faith, the sweet effect of knowledge. He would never understand it.

And thus the days and weeks passed until the last night of his punishment.

He didn't go to sleep until very late, absorbed in his reading of a treatise by Hippocrates. From his deep and solid thought he extracted three rules and the wise man defended them as the basic principles of the medical profession.

Diego memorized them and repeated them out loud several times.

"*Primum non nocere*: First do no harm." He savored the meaning of it. "It's better to do nothing than make the situation worse."

He breathed in and remembered the second, the one he agreed with the most.

"One should always go after the cause of the complaint, and fight against the principle that produces it. And last, abstain from acting against incurable illnesses, accepting their inevitability."

V.

———

Sancho VII had fallen so far in love, he was losing his mind.

He had arrived in Marrakesh for a short diplomatic mission, but Princess Najla compelled the king to stay almost two years.

"Bringing him to us has been an excellent decision. . . ."

Caliph al-Nasir ordered his pipes refilled with those herbs that raised his spirits.

"You remember how hard it was for me to convince you? No?" Don Pedro de Mora filled his lungs with a deep mouthful of smoke.

"It's true, but the decision to use my own sister as bait was not easy for me to take. You are right, though; now I have no doubts about it working."

A slave came over on her knees, without looking at them, with a tray full of sweets made of almond, honey, and coconut. They tried them. Al-Nasir lifted her veil, stroked her cheeks, touching a fatty finger across the corner of her lips.

"I don't know you. What's your name?"

"Abeer, sir." She looked into his eyes, taken aback by their intense blue color.

"What does her name mean?" Don Pedro asked, entranced by her beautiful body.

"Fragrance. . . . An insinuation of passion. Doesn't she strike you as beautiful?"

"She's majestic."

Al-Nasir stroked the girl's chin.

"Come back later."

"Thank you for choosing me, sir."

The caliph slapped her with extreme violence.

"Did no one warn you yet that you shouldn't speak to me if I haven't asked you to first?"

The woman lowered her head submissively and left them alone, without turning her back at any moment, as they had explained to her.

The caliph and Mora went out to the terrace to take in some fresh air and saw King Sancho walking with Najla through the palace gardens.

"When I visited him in Navarre, he had just separated," Pedro de Mora remembered. "You were necessary to him for his policy of territorial expansion. . . . And Najla, in her youth, dreamed of being loved by some noble and valiant knight. All I had was to put the two pieces together, and—"

"The accord with his kingdom is good for us, very much so," the caliph interrupted him. "With Navarre on our side, we will break the dangerous unity of the Christian empires that Castile has been seeking so ardently."

"Can you imagine how King Alfonso VIII would see a marriage between Najla and Sancho? Al-Andalus united with Navarre . . ." Don Pedro rubbed his hands together as he thought of it.

"What I don't understand is how he still hasn't asked me for her hand. They've been like this more than a year." The caliph pointed at them. The two lovers looked at each other with absolute commitment, holding hands, Sancho stroking Najla's hair shyly. "What the devil could he be waiting for?"

"Think, my lord, that since Sancho has moved into the vizier's palace, he is too far from your sister, whom you also never let leave here, no matter what the excuse. If you facilitate their intimacy, perhaps they will taste love's essences together and they will thus accelerate your wishes." Don Pedro confirmed that al-Nasir had captured the sense of his words.

"I will think about it. Every day I pray to Allah that he bless their love and make it grow, but also that it be soon. I need to seal this accord once and for all."

That same night, a bundle of nerves, Najla entered the harem looking for Blanca and Estela, anxious to tell them the news.

"They are going to move him. . . ."

The princess didn't even wait to reach the blue chamber where they were normally found. She spoke to them in Arabic, since the sisters had begun to speak it. For some time now they alternated between one language and the other.

"Who? What are you talking to us about?"

"Sancho. I just found out my brother is going to allow him to lodge in this palace."

Blanca winked at Estela. Some months back, the princess had promised to take them to Navarre if she finally managed to get married. They understood that the lovers' being closer to each other could speed up their relationship, and if they announced their wedding at last, the sisters' way out of that hell could be closer.

"He's such a marvelous man. . . ." Najla let her hair down in front of a large mirror. Immediately her hair flooded down over her shoulders and breasts. "Do I look pretty?"

Blanca got behind her.

"You are beautiful and young. You have a gorgeous body and you radiate grace. Any man would get lost in your eyes, as soon as he caressed your silken skin. I assure you that you will drive him mad." She tugged Najla's hair upward, leaving her lithe neck free, and breathed in her scent. "To captivate him, perfume yourself with sandalwood and honey, put on a tight-fitting dress, and ask your slave to draw something beautiful on your breasts."

"I've never been with a man. . . ." The princess grew red, looking at them with an almost childish face. "And there's a lot that I don't know. I don't know how to please him. I imagine you both know very well what I'm talking about."

Estela's face clouded over with a grimace of restrained rage and humiliation. It was still hard for her to swallow that truth. They were nothing more than two concubines, kept alive and well fed for the sole purpose of pleasing the caliph and various of his closest collaborators.

"Don't try to be what you aren't," Blanca went on recommending. "Be natural and let yourself go. When you disrobe, don't be fast, look at him with ardor, and then . . ."

The door opened suddenly and a black guard came in, an Imesebelen.

"They are looking for you, ma'am. Come out from here. You should get back to your bedroom as quickly as possible."

Blanca and Estela were paralyzed, almost shrunken. The vision of his black face took them back in time. The horrendous images of their abduction, the brutal death of their sister, Belinda, the uncertain fate of their father and brother—all those terrible experiences were relived every time one of those men came near them.

"Which of you is named Blanca?"

"Me." She looked back at him with an almost physical fear.

"Right now, they're looking for you as well. Move quickly."

"Thank you for letting us know," Najla interrupted. "Tijmud is my most faithful protector. Don't be afraid of him; he is different from the rest of the Imesebelen who guard me." When she finished this phrase, she took leave of them, and in an instant she disappeared, turning off down the hallway.

The two sisters arrived at their room and lay down as fast as possible, hearing footsteps. Shortly afterward, two men entered. They were servants of the caliph. One of them asked after Blanca from among those present, and when he found her, he came over and touched her shoulder. That was the signal the concubines all knew too well for when they were expected to spend the night with someone. She rose and followed the men.

Unusually, they took the east wing of the palace and walked through other hallways. Blanca couldn't imagine to where.

They reached a beautiful gilded door and opened it for her to pass through. At the moment, she didn't see anyone inside. The soft breeze that greeted her face as soon as she entered came from a window through which the reflections of the moon filtered as well. She walked toward it and looked outside. The night in Marrakesh captivated her. She listened to laughter in the distance, maybe in some plaza or side street, and sighed. She dreamed of being free again, she missed her former life, she wished to escape from that terrible prison.

Soon she heard some footfalls behind her and turned.

Once more it was the individual she hated. To look at his long scar made her relive the most hateful moments in her life. His face reflected a deep and subtle intelligence, but also wickedness.

"You are precious, as always. . . ."

Resigned, she received his first kiss on her lips.

VI.

Horse manure, sweat, and science.

Those three ingredients characterized Diego's life for the following six months, as well as a permanent atmosphere of reproach from Friar Servando. That man had pledged not to forgive a single error on the part of Diego, though he also wouldn't teach the boy any of the little that he knew. Maybe it was for that reason that Diego sought a refuge in books.

A year after arriving at Fitero, the winter had penetrated the walls and Diego continued soaking up knowledge. He needed hours and days to order his learning, assimilate what he was reading, and think about how he could apply it to the future.

On one occasion, without Friar Servando's noticing, he dissected the hoof of a deceased horse before it was buried in quicklime. Thus he could understand how it worked, what forces and pressures were borne by the bones and tendons, how movement was generated. He rooted around inside it, trying to find answers to where the maladies inside it had their origin, the tumors and swellings, impactions and decays.

He also decided to order the illnesses differently in his mind from how he had read and done up till that moment. He would do so according to their anatomical location. This way, it would be easier to distinguish one sickness from another.

One day Marcos found Diego thoughtful, seated on a pile of straw, close to his mare, whom he still visited every night.

"Talk to me about your sisters. . . ."

On that occasion, Marcos had brought him a book written by a Palatine nun, Hildegard of Bingen.

"I already told you what happened. . . . God! It's horrible; it was already six years ago. . . . Can you tell me why you're asking me now?"

"It's something that eats you up . . . and yet, you never talk about it."

Diego pensively stroked the smooth cover of the book and opened it brusquely, with such anxiety that he seemed to be looking for the answer in its pages. Then he closed it and approached Sabba. She shook with pleasure.

"If they're still alive, which I think they are, they could be living as slaves in Marrakesh. Many days I think that I could do something to help them, but I usually end up demoralized. The idea of saving them is so far from my possibilities. For that reason, every time I think it, I come to the conclusion that now I can only prepare myself, gain the sufficient strength and braveness, as well as the money, to be able to travel later."

Marcos stayed there thinking.

A month back, sick of so many restrictions and so much poverty, knowing that at this point, no one was looking for him, he had been tempted to leave the monastery. But he decided not to. For him things had begun to change. His situation in the kitchens was good, no one oppressed him the way Friar Servando had before, and he could leave the monastery whenever he liked. And he did so every two or three days, to one of the neighboring villages, to buy food.

Thanks to this freedom, he no longer felt caged in and he began to stray off, though less frequently than he would have liked, with some nice girl or other he had met.

Diego opened Hildegard's book again and read the first thing he saw.

"Wild lettuce: the best remedy for the stomach pains of donkeys. Nettles for horse fever. Lovage or wild celery for colds."

He closed it again and studied the face of Marcos.

"Easy remedies, certainly. . . . Hildegard, like others before her, investigated many remedies that they wrote down for the good of following generations." He chewed a piece of straw pensively, savoring its bitterness. "The Greeks called albéitars *hippiatros* or horse healers, as Friar Servando likes to say. The Romans said veterinarius. How can I be a good hippiatros, albéitar, horse healer, veterinarius, if I don't know first what this nun, or others much wiser than her, left written down?" He remained pensive, staring at the sky. "Marcos, this library holds the better part of all knowledge, human as well as medical. If I manage to soak it up, I will be able to help many people who have nothing but animals to support them in the future. Do you understand the real reason I'm staying in this monastery?"

"Fine, fine," Marcos answered. "Keep going with your nuns and Greeks, I don't care. But leave the practical things to me." He shook his hand with a disdainful expression. "Because what's practical are the four hundred *sueldos* I've managed to save.

"How?" Diego feared the worst.

"Friar Jesús, my mentor and as sensible a friar as you could find, is the keeper of the keys of the monastery and has placed all his trust in me. And to test me, he puts me in charge of all the monastery's purchases. A good opportunity, believe me." He winked.

"You're not robbing them, are you?"

"It's not that. . . . I've managed to convince the monastery's main suppliers to reserve a bit of money from each order for me. It's good for us."

"You'll never cease to amaze me. You're a scoundrel!"

"By the way, now that I think about it . . . Remember that squire from Navarre and the lump you made disappear from his horse?"

"Of course. That was the root of the worst punishment I've received in my life, almost a year back."

"They tell me he came to see you today. Apparently they gave him some excuse. And besides, from what I understand, this isn't the first time he's tried."

"Why would they have hidden that from me?" Diego felt a deep rage. He remembered the man and his warm praises as well. "What did he want me for?"

Diego didn't get an answer to his question until three months later, at the beginning of the spring of 1202, in the sunny month of April. Diego had just turned twenty-one. Friar Servando now had no choice but to tell him why his presence had been requested.

"Get ready to travel the day after tomorrow," he blurted out sternly, without bothering to justify his words.

"Could you tell me where and why?"

"You'll be away three days, and you'll go alone." He carried a basket of oats on his shoulder and came over to the troughs to spread it out for the horses. The monk didn't seem disposed to give him more information.

Diego observed him, intrigued.

"Where do I have to go?" he insisted, happy as he saw the irritating effect his questions were producing.

The man snorted, cleared his throat two or three times, and finally answered.

"You're trying to make it hard for me, eh?" said the monk. Diego adopted a face of false surprise. "It's fine. . . . There's going to be a tourney or a joust, I don't know, really, in Olite. It's a town close to here that belongs to the kingdom of Navarre and they've asked us to send you."

"Me?"

"You know Gómez Garceiz?"

"The one with the tumor on his horse's rump?"

"That was his squire. The one who's asking for you is his master, Gómez Garceiz, the royal ensign of Navarre."

"And he wants me?"

"I would say so!" he exclaimed even more dryly.

Friar Servando was green with envy.

"And why would they need an albéitar, or better said, the apprentice of a horse healer, at a tourney?" Diego had never seen one, but he had heard fantastic tales of those contests between knights.

"For some absurd reason, he wants you there. I don't know, it might be for your horseshoes; I can't imagine another reason." He swallowed, humiliated. "And that's enough! Don't ask me more."

Diego reckoned on the enormous power that ensign must have to make Friar Servando let him go and swallow his pride as well. If Gómez Garceiz preferred Diego's services over the friar's, who was supposed to be famed throughout the land, that had to be eating him up inside.

"I'll go gladly!" he exclaimed with joy. "Thank you so much for remembering me. . . ." Friar Servando's look couldn't contain more rage. "But I will ask you for one thing more."

"Don't force the situation more."

"I'll need my friend Marcos."

"Agreed." He sighed, resigned. He thought of his prior and how he had forced him to respect the ensign's order.

The two days that passed until they left the monastery felt like an eternity for Diego.

He was excited for many reasons. It would be the first time he would go out of the stronghold in fifteen months. He was going to attend an unknown spectacle and, moreover, for the first time, he had been asked because of his knowledge and not just his skill in pushing a broom.

Once Diego set out on the path north with Marcos, feeling the warmth of his mare beneath his legs and the fragrance of the fields in flower, he thought they were getting back something much more immaterial but deeply pleasing, a little bit of freedom.

VII.

Marcos dreamed of seeing lots of women in Olite.

Beside Diego, he crossed the border of Navarre through the small town of Corella; at midmorning, they arrived at the town of Olite.

It was a populous area, and it was the festival season. There must be lots of women waiting for him. He would talk with them just enough, encouraging them to look for some discreet farmhouse where they could make love. He had spent more than a year and a half walled in among stones and friars and had only come across two nice girls on his brief ventures out, and he had just turned twenty-two—one year older than Diego.

As soon as they crossed the walls, they began to enjoy the incredible bustle of the streets. They saw many children, some who ran up to them holding out their hands for a coin. Others were going around disguised as knights and pretending to fight with swords and shields of wood. Farther on, they stopped to breathe in the various aromas that floated through the air, some sweet and seductive, like burned wood, some like food.

They asked a toothless boy with vivid eyes and a swollen forehead where the tourney was being celebrated. He pointed in the direction but corrected them: It wasn't a tourney, but rather a joust.

"Do you know what the difference is?" Marcos asked Diego a few steps later.

"In a tourney, the knights fight without real arms, as if it were a war, until one team manages to defeat the other. The winner takes the glory and the spoils. In jousts, on the other hand, it is a confrontation between groups of two. They fight with thick armor, with a shield or *adarga* for their defense, and a long wooden lance they use to try and knock down their opponent. The field where they fight is usually divided by a fence that separates each person's path and across which their combat takes place."

"And all this to win the prize of a beautiful woman's heart and graces, I suppose."

Marcos looked among those present for the one whose virtues would identify her as being the mistress of the festivities. He found one, very pretty, blond, and with a kind face. He complimented her when he passed by her.

"Jousts are games of honor and they entertain the knights and help them improve their abilities in wartime," Diego went on explaining. "They are also a test of valor and gallantry."

When they turned a corner, they ran into three men. Two of them seemed to be escorting a third in noble dress. Their faces were hidden under helmets and they pushed through with such violence that Marcos ended up on the ground. Diego, however, managed to avoid them in time.

"Let my master through, you miserable yokels."

"Who do you think you are, speaking to us like that?" Diego stood firm in front of them, indignant. He saw a sword drawn and felt its point at his neck.

"And who are you, you damned fool?" The voice reverberated inside the helmet of steel, but was nonetheless threatening.

"My name is Diego de Malagón, a man unarmed and being threatened by the hand of a coward."

The man they were escorting removed his helmet and looked at Diego with respect. He threw back his hair, scratched his head with evident relief, and told his squire to sheathe his sword.

"What I admire about a man is bravery, and you just demonstrated it, young man." A knot of onlookers gathered around them immediately. "Pardon my squire. My name is Luis. Luis de Azagra. I'm coming to compete in the jousts."

He extended his hand and asked about their reason for being in Olite.

"I've been summoned by the royal ensign Gómez Garceiz."

"And what is your profession?"

They were on a stone street, rather steep, that led down to a broad esplanade. There was the stockade with its steps and track, the tents of the contestants, and all the stables.

"I'm preparing to be an albéitar, well, I mean, a horse healer. . . ."

"Horse healer? I live in Albarracín, but I'm from Navarre. There, the people of your profession are called *mariscal* or veterinarius, though the second term isn't heard so much now. Did you know that?"

They arrived at the square and Diego was surprised by the frenetic activity. Numerous men with hammers in their hands were finishing the stands. Some boys, mounting tall logs, were affixing banners with the shield of the city. And in the place of honor there were women placing floral decorations and beautiful tapestries. On the track, a dozen men were emptying wheelbarrows of fine sand to smooth out any irregularities where the horses would later run.

On the other side was a group of excited boys engaged in a sack race, and others were playing bowls. In front of them, some women were arguing heatedly with a hawker in a makeshift market.

Without abandoning his conversation with the man, Diego tried to find among the tents the flag bearing the arms of his ensign. As they had explained to him, they consisted of a field of gules and an oak with two rampant boars.

Diego left his companion behind, as Don Luis was obliged to greet someone, and they agreed to meet again later. Marcos and Diego continued walking toward the place where the tents were being raised. They counted some twenty of them, lined up along both sides of a long central street, in the shadow of a stand of trees. Around them was a bustle of activity.

In the first tent, they saw two pages polishing a suit of armor, and in the next one, women braiding the mane of a beautiful horse. Farther ahead, they found a sweating young man smoothing out the horseshoes forged by an enormous man. They also noted a green tent where they saw an old man emerge with iron gauntlets and a cotton cloth, burnishing a fabulous helmet.

Halfway along their journey, they saw an extremely beautiful lady step out of a nearby tent. Though she covered her face with a veil, Diego could see her face. Without knowing why, something moved inside him, as if time, life, everything had stopped as that woman passed.

They crossed paths. She seemed thoughtful.

For an instant she looked into his eyes. Diego could make out beneath the tulle a bluish landscape of extraordinary beauty, a fine nose and well-proportioned and attractive features. Her cheeks were firm and rosy and her skin seemed silken and delicate. A long blond mane fell loose over her fine dress of turquoise blue.

"Welcome, Diego the albéitar . . ." A familiar voice awoke Diego from his trance and he had to look straight ahead.

It was the squire of Gómez Garceiz.

Diego extended his hand and introduced Marcos.

"I thank you very much for your kindness, but I am not yet an albéitar, only an apprentice, and I still lack experience and knowledge."

"Don't be so humble. Follow me. I will introduce you to my master."

Diego turned back to see the woman, but she had already disappeared.

They walked to the last tent, and the squire invited them inside. They were received by a well-built man, middle-aged, with a short, thick beard. He sat in a chair and indicated for them to do the same.

"My squire has spoken well of you to me. He says you have a special touch when it comes to healing horses, and that you understand them. Is it true?"

"I spent the better part of my youth with them, watching them. Maybe for that reason, I learned their reactions, how they express themselves when they are alone, and even at times what they are thinking."

The man seemed worried.

"As you know, tomorrow we are holding a joust, and I will be one of the participants. I will be facing García Romeu. Does that name ring a bell for you?"

"I have to say it does not."

"He is a knight from Aragon, an ensign like myself. He is in the employ of King Pedro II, and I serve Sancho VII. For diplomatic reasons, he has been among us these days and when he found out about these festivities, he wanted to test himself against me. And therein lies the problem. . . ."

"I'm sorry, I don't understand."

"Let's go to the stables. Then you will."

They left through the rear of the tent and approached a corral with six horses inside. Assorted pages were trying to get hold of one, a chestnut-colored animal, to fit it with a bridle. It reacted with fury, utterly beside itself.

"Do you remember this one?" He pointed at another: a bay horse with a cherry coat. It had a slight discoloration on its rump.

"The one with the fig, right?"

"He got better, just as you said, and he's never had another, nor did the one he had come back. He's the one I'll compete with tomorrow, though he wasn't the one I had in mind."

He put a thick belt around his cape that was embroidered with his coat of arms. He leapt over the fence spryly, and the young men followed him. Though they were approaching the horse he had operated on, Diego continued to look at the other, the chestnut-colored one.

"What are the necessary virtues for a horse that will compete in a joust?" Diego said as he looked approvingly at the scar that had formed on the horse's rump.

"Physically, it should be very fast, with strong back legs, to achieve a fast and sustained run. But its character is even more important. It has to be a steely, decisive, and firm animal, one that won't hesitate in the middle of a charge. No matter how good the knight is with his lance, if he doesn't feel the horse as a part of himself, if they don't become a single thing, he will certainly be defeated."

Diego studied the expression of the horse. It seemed timid and therefore inappropriate for the battle.

"You said this horse is not the best one. Why are you choosing him, then?"

"I was going to compete with Centurion." He pointed to the chestnut stallion. "A horse born for jousting . . . but he's been crazy for weeks now. That is why I called you. Look at him right now!"

They had just put the bridle on him, and the furious animal was up on two legs and had lifted up two pages with him. The young one, holding on to the reins, seemed to fly from one side to the other as the horse flung his head. As soon as the horse had come down, he began to buck in all directions.

"He was never like that. Before he was forceful but docile. He always reacted reasonably, doing whatever was asked of him. I'd like you to take a look at him."

Diego scratched his chin and sighed, pleased to have such a difficult challenge.

He jumped over the fence and approached the other horses, which didn't seem to be bothered by his presence. He greeted them in his customary way, sniffing at their noses, and began to speak to each one, to get them on his side. The one that seemed most energetic he gave a clap on the rump, while a soft slap to the ribs sufficed to get the rest of them to move. One by one, he tested their obedience, and when the time came for the last one, he already recognized Diego as the leader of the herd.

From that vantage point, he looked at Centurion. He was at the other end of the corral. The horse looked back at him, his head raised and emanating aggression.

Diego decided to use the herd to try and confuse him. He set the most docile horses in motion and got them to surround him, and in an instant, he found himself by Centurion's side without problems. He managed to get the group to walk in step and took them around the corral a few times while watching the stallion. He studied his reactions down to the slightest detail. He saw how he moved his ears, the expression of his eyes, the tension of his lips, the way he stepped, his respiration, his composure, everything. And then he suspected something.

He stopped the march and turned to him, whispering words that sounded like Arabic to everyone present. The horse immediately turned its ears to him. He didn't seem agitated. Diego passed his hand over his neck, slowly, until he was sure of being accepted. He continued stroking him until he came to his head and he explored it as well. And when he was close to the right ear, he noticed the lump. He squeezed it a bit and the horse reacted with pain and fear. He came as close to his ear as he could and heard a slight buzzing. Centurion's breath began to race.

"Bring me a very sharp knife and a pitcher of oil."

Gómez Garceiz transmitted the order to one of his pages.

"What did you find?"

"Flies have laid eggs under his skin."

"Flies? How is that possible?"

"Through a small wound. The blood and fluids attract them and they leave their eggs there. Then, when the wound closes, the larva keep growing until they've reached adulthood and they try to get out wherever they can. In his case, they've chosen his ear."

"That explains his behavior," the ensign Gómez Garceiz concluded.

"The sound of them buzzing ends up driving a horse crazy."

The stable boy approached with the supplies and passed them over to him.

Diego grabbed the horse by the bridle and cut the skin around the lump. Centurion turned away, but Diego managed to calm him down again. He lifted the flap of the wound and found a sac full of fly offspring. He managed to get it out and threw it on the floor. When it broke, a number of them took flight. He confirmed that there were none left in the wound, and no eggs, either. Then he poured oil in its ear to drown the ones that might have managed to get inside, and he scratched Centurion's muzzle.

The horse seemed to improve immediately, although he still shook his head, bothered by the presence of the liquid. His eyes began to shimmer as they had previously.

Gómez Garceiz was enchanted.

He praised Diego in the highest possible terms, and even more so when he found out he could compete with Centurion in the joust.

"I called you here for the good references that I received and because I don't trust horseleeches or anyone else who calls himself an animal healer. I don't have the same opinion of the albéitars. Now I'm happy I summoned you."

Diego jumped over the fence and cleaned his hands in a washbowl.

"We were happy to come as well; we've been shut up too long in that monastery."

"It's too bad you're not more . . ."

"I don't understand."

"While he was in Marrakesh, our king met many albéitars, became convinced of the seriousness of your trade, and realized that you have an understanding far superior to what we are used to in these parts. He was moved by that, and since his return from those distant lands, he has tried to recruit some of your colleagues to care for our cavalries, but it hasn't been easy. The religious tension, almost warlike, that exists between the two cultures proves an almost insurmountable barrier. That's why, when I found out you were an albéitar, I had you come."

Centurion approached his master and sniffed at him. Gómez Garceiz scratched his chin with satisfaction.

"Your friars have been hard to convince. I had already called for you on other occasions, but they prevented it before now. I imagine you don't know this, but I had to have King Sancho II himself sign my petition to get you here. The monastery couldn't hide you anymore, and here you are. Now go. Rest awhile and enjoy the festival. And another thing: this evening we will celebrate a great dinner in honor of our King Sancho. And before, they will proclaim the rules of the joust. I encourage you to attend. You will enjoy it."

"Will the king be at the jousts?"

"He will preside. If you've never seen him, I assure you that you will be impressed."

VIII.

The man shouted with all his strength without losing his dignity.

He was the herald, the figure in charge of protocol during the jousts and tourneys. A clearly recognizable figure, with his flamboyant tabard, an emblazoned garment with long, open sleeves. His mission was to oversee the rules of the game and to register all that happened in writing and, of course, the result of the competitions.

Diego and Marcos listened to him declaim the order of those who were going to participate the next day. He did so from a platform to the right of the tribunal where the religious authorities and nobles sat.

Before, they had witnessed a spectacular demonstration of falconry with six birds.

They marveled at their pirouettes in the air, at the rapid, enchanting flights they took when hunting the various pieces that the assistants threw up for them to catch. The beating of the birds' wings, their sharp shrieks as they attacked their prey, the hurrahs and applause of those present—the mere fact of witnessing it was a true joy for the senses, and another first for the young men who were attending the event.

Night fell. Diego and Marcos walked along the esplanade without overlooking the animated air of their surroundings.

"What is that one dressed as?"

Diego spoke too loudly and the person alluded to heard him. He was wearing a suit covered in colored patches and a hat with various points suspended with jingle bells.

"I'm a fool," he replied in a strident voice.

He skipped three steps toward Diego and saluted him with a feigned comic reverence.

"I make women laugh and men grumble, because the women enjoy me more than they do their husbands." He cackled to himself and garnered the applause of the onlookers.

Marcos tried to escape him, as Diego had already done, but he didn't manage to.

"You're so nice to me, I'll make a prediction for you. . . . May everyone hear!" The little man leapt around incessantly, circling Marcos. In one hand he held a wooden staff with a fool's head like his own at one end. "Years back I signed a secret pact with the fairies, and for that reason, whoever divines my riddles will win a marvelous night of love and joy. But I also signed a pact with a black dwarf of the forest for those who get them wrong . . ."

"And what?" an old, red-cheeked woman asked him with a beaming smile.

"What's the bad thing that will happen to him?" a young girl asked.

"A long stomachache that will last him a whole week." He covered his nose, making exaggerated gesticulations to the laughter of all.

"I'm not playing at that," Marcos protested, but then, from out of the crowd, he picked out the same blond woman who had interested him that morning. The fool, agile as a lynx, knew how to read his thoughts.

"Think it through . . . I am promising a night of passion. Can you imagine?" He winked.

Marcos looked at the girl's eyes and she went all red, flattered by his interest.

"Fine, say it." Those gathered yelled out their support and broke into a round of applause. Diego stood to the side, smiling.

The fool shook his head and made his jingle bells ring out, as though inspiration would come to him better that way.

"My dwelling is not silent, but I make no noise. The Lord commanded us to be together. I am faster than my dwelling, sometimes stronger, but it works harder. At times I rest, but my dwelling never does. I will live there as long as I live; if we are separated, my destiny is death." He opened his arms with a definitive gesture. "What do I speak of?"

Marcos began to think. He had it repeated twice. Then he scratched his head, looked at the floor, and covered his eyes, to shut himself out from his surroundings. He was worried about getting it wrong, and he felt the pressure of the public gathered there. He looked for the girl's gaze and was filled with pleasure when he saw a promising response there. And all of a sudden he thought of a possibility. He ruminated on it before responding. It seemed to work, although the answer could be something else as well.

"It's a fish, a fish in a river. It can't live out of the water, when it wants, it is faster than the current, but the current never tires . . ."

The fool did a somersault and applauded with rabid glee. Marcos looked for the girl and she replied with a generous smile.

"You've won! You did it!" He leapt and frolicked with incredible agility. "The fairies will look for you tonight and they will keep their agreement. Salute, and good luck, young man!"

The fool pushed Marcos, wanting to ask him another, and Diego rescued him, joking and congratulating him for his right answer. He couldn't avoid feeling a certain envy. He had see him playing the fool with that blond girl and wasn't able to do something similar; he always got flustered and was awkward with women, or maybe he was waiting for something different.

A few steps farther on, they stopped again to watch the jugglers show their talent. They were throwing up colored balls while never stopping their acrobatic twists and turns. One climbed under the other's legs and caught the balls he dropped with apparent ease. They changed these out for torches and managed to get six going in the air at a time.

Afterward they walked over to a large fire where large pieces of pork were being roasted, and beside them, on another fire, a dozen ducks crackled over the heat of the coals. Between the one and the other, the boys felt an enormous craving overcome them.

Seeing them wander around, a smiling woman with a thick waist came over to them with six clay jugs in each of her hands.

"How is it that these good boys are still not acquainted with my wine?" She passed them two jugs. "Try them, and tell me if you've had a better brew in your life for the price of a mere cent."

They drank the wine, very bad, incidentally, and turned to an enormous tent of white cloth where the dinner was to be celebrated. At the entrance, two men asked their names and looked for them on a piece of parchment, then let them through without any problems.

Inside, there were four long tables arranged side by side as well as a small one that was undoubtedly being set for the king and his court. Since more than half the benches were already taken, they took their seats at the outer edge of one.

But as soon as he sat down, Diego saw her.

She was two tables away from him. She also realized he was there, but dropped her gaze immediately. For strange and irrational reasons, that woman with blond hair and blue eyes had Diego mesmerized, even though he still didn't know who she was.

Marcos spoke to him, but he didn't listen. He couldn't stop looking at her or hide his interest. He tried not to miss a single gesture or expression, however subtle it was. That got on the nerves of his table companion.

"You're going to force me to change places," Marcos grumbled.

Diego tried to justify himself.

"I understand she's a jewel, but don't limit yourself to just one woman. Look how many there are!" Marcos winked at his blonde. He had just picked her out, not far from them.

"I'd like to know who she is. . . ." Diego leaned his elbow on the table and his gaze got lost again in that beautiful lady.

Then a chorus of trumpets broke out, attracting the attention of all present. And just after, the herald shouted out his announcement of the arrival of the king of Navarre. Everyone stood up to see him. There appeared an ample retinue and Diego recognized in its midst the ensign Gómez Garceiz. Full of interest, he asked his tablemate which one was the king.

"If you look up, you won't have any doubt about it," he said, laughing.

Though at that moment he didn't understand, when he looked again, Diego realized. A gigantic figure stuck out from the group, with his hair in ringlets and a firm and serious face. He must have measured between six and seven feet and was almost two heads higher than everyone there. His vestments were regal, and his red cape had a black eagle in its center, the standard of the kingdom of Navarre.

As soon as they sat down at the table of honor, an orchestra of dulcimers and dulcians began to play. And almost at the very same moment the first plates began to be passed around, with roasted pork and large clay bowls filled with vegetables.

The four jugs of wine Marcos had drunk must have awakened his artistic side, because without warning he got up on the table and began to walk over it, gesticulating and narrating a made-up story to all present. It must have struck them as good fun, for not only did it attract the interest of their fellow diners, it also made them laugh and provoked a long string of humorous commentaries.

Diego decided to step away from the racket and find out more about the woman.

"Are you from around here?" he asked his neighbor on the bench.

"I live in Sangüesa."

"I have a question and I don't know if you . . ."

"You want to know the name of that woman, right?"

Diego felt awkward.

"You haven't stopped looking at her for a second," he explained.

"You're right."

"I know her."

"Then tell me who she is." Diego's anxiety was eating at him.

"Where are you from?"

"Close to Toledo."

"Now I understand. . . ." He slapped the table. "But if you're interested in her, you can get that out of your head. Her name is Mencía Díaz de Azagra, and she's the daughter of one of the most powerful noblemen of Navarre, Don Fernando Ruiz de Azagra, the second lord of Albarracín."

Diego remembered the other Azagra he had crossed paths with as soon as he arrived in Olite and also the wife of Don Diego López de Haro. *A big family*, he thought.

"The Azagras are well known in these parts because they govern not only Albarracín but also the territories of Calatayud, Tudela, and Estella. Their power and wealth go beyond anything you could imagine."

Diego savored that name, Mencía, as though it were manna from heaven. Soon, his tablemate noticed Diego's absentmindedness and grabbed a pork rib in his hands, abandoning himself to it without saying another word.

Diego hardly ate a bite; he only watched her, over and over, so long as the heads of her tablemates made it possible.

In the meanwhile, Marcos had gone over to his blonde, and the laughter and warmth that crossed the girl's face suggested he was telling her something very funny or very piquant.

Once the dinner was over, a troubadour named Giraut de Bornel sang the adventures of King Sancho himself during his wars against France, extolling the aid he had given to his brother-in-law, the king of England, Richard Lionheart, who was married to his sister Berenguela. In Romanic and Latin, the troubadour emphasized Sancho's ferocity in combat, the fear he inspired in all his enemies, and the magnanimity of his heart when he had to pardon his enemies.

"Why did your king spend so long in Marrakesh?"

His neighbor turned his back without responding. He preferred talking to a girl who had been smiling at him to being bothered by the bore seated next to him.

"It was over a skirt. . . ." another said to him, in a very low voice, as though his words warranted great discretion.

"Tell me. I promise I won't repeat it."

"They say he went there to solicit military aid and funds from the caliph, since his treasure chest was decimated after the conflicts from before. He received no soldiers, but he did get a considerable quantity of money.

And it is said that while he resided in the palace something extraordinary occurred. . . ."

The man let them refill his wine and began to chew a golden, crispy duck leg with relish.

"Carry on, please. You've got me on tenterhooks."

He spit out the bone and carried on while he chewed what was left of the bird.

"Someone informed him that the caliph's daughter was madly in love with him. Apparently the woman had heard marvelous things about our king from the lips of an Almohad ambassador who had come to Navarre years before. The princess, who they say is beautiful, had idealized him to the point he'd become a dream for her."

"And he felt the same way?"

The man spoke more closely, into his ear.

"People say they had an intense romance full of passion and sensuality. A few months after he arrived, Caliph Yusuf died. His son, al-Nasir, who is eighteen years old, succeeded him, and he gave his blessing to the relationship as well. Some even state that he offered his sister to him as a bride, because her mother had been Christian and that matrimony could strengthen their ties against Castile, their common enemy. Others say that our King Sancho fell so deeply in love with her that it took him two years to come back to himself."

"Is there anyone who doesn't become vulnerable when face-to-face with a beautiful woman?" With a certain bitterness, he remembered Benazir.

"You speak wisely, but even when he heard the king of Castile was attacking Vitoria, he didn't react, and he carried on with her. Those who have seen the Moorish woman say that her charms are many. Then, because of a severe rebuke from the pope, he had to return, and he did so without her. . . ."

While he listened, Diego realized that Mencía was speaking with someone he knew; the knight Luis de Azagra, he remembered. The latter must have felt his gaze, because he turned his head at that very moment. Diego tried to look away, but he was recognized immediately. When he looked up again, the knight was already at his side.

"Forgive me for bothering you, but when I saw you, I remembered that we had to cut short our conversation this morning, and maybe you would like to continue it over a jug of wine with my friends over at that table." Diego accepted, nervous, imagining himself much closer to the woman.

Before he left, he looked for Marcos, but he didn't see him. He must be away with the blonde.

As he walked, he thought he was living a dream. He had hardly gone twenty steps, but they seemed like two hundred. When he got there, Don Luis presented him the people closest to him first, and then it was her turn.

"This is my cousin Mencía, Mencía Díaz de Azagra."

"It's a pleasure, Diego the albéitar." She offered her fragile hand, and Diego kissed it holding his breath, taking in its sweet aroma.

"Well . . . really, I'm not one yet . . ."

He stopped, quiet, doubtful. She helped him with another conversation.

"Did my cousin show you the horses he'll be competing with tomorrow? What did you think?"

"I don't know." Diego was incapable of articulating words. He began to feel like a fool.

"Come and sit down beside me." Don Luis showed Diego to an empty place, unfortunately far from her. "I have to ask you about something." Diego begged her pardon before he had to pull away.

"I'm sorry, but . . . I hope . . . we'll talk at another . . ." He couldn't even manage to finish a sentence.

"Of course, of course." She smiled at him and when she did, two marvelous dimples appeared in her cheeks.

Diego sat down with the others but he couldn't manage to pay them attention. He decided that was the most beautiful and perfect woman he had seen in his life. And he felt something new, very intense and intimate, a turbulent and frightening sensation.

Could that be love?

IX.

That night, Marcos didn't sleep in the tent. Diego confirmed it when he awoke, very nervous, the memories of the night before still fresh in his mind.

When dinner ended, there had been an exciting torchlight procession, as was the custom on the evenings preceding a joust. At least four hundred people accompanied the knights to the tents were the arms were safeguarded. They were escorted by an intoxicating smoke cloud of burned wood and oil.

That ceremony was the one the town was most desirous of, since there they could see up close the great ladies, their knights, the members of the high clergy, and their governors.

Diego stayed close to Mencía for the whole of the procession. He hadn't been able to speak to her, since her family and her servants followed her, but he could admire her, sense her, smell her, and listen to her.

"Albéitar Diego!" The voice of Gómez Garceiz pulled him from his thoughts and out of the tent.

"Could you look at my horse once more? If he looks good, I'll get him ready for the joust."

"I'm coming right now."

Diego came out of the tent and up to his host, but a stern voice stopped him from behind. They turned to see who it was and when he recognized the person, Gómez Garceiz smiled.

"Wait a moment, you're going to meet my opponent in the joust, García Romeu, the ensign of the king of Aragon."

Diego looked at the man. He had his coat of arms sewn onto his breast, a black eagle over a white background, and from his belt there hung a redoubtable sword. He came up to them and once again saluted his colleague from Navarre, with whom he had shared a table and food the night before. Gómez Garceiz introduced Diego as an albéitar, and Diego praised the man's horse.

"You've got a good eye, young man; it's the most valiant specimen I have." He took off his steel glove and shook his hand. "This is my farrier, Giulio Morigatti, he's from Naples. Since your work is related, maybe you'd like to share your experience with each other."

Giulio came over with a forced smile.

The two ensigns began to speak away from them. With a strong Latin accent, Giulio spoke to Diego. His voice was melodious.

"It seems odd to me to meet an albéitar in Christian territories."

Diego wrinkled his brow, imagining the intention behind these words.

"And it's strange for me to meet a farrier. I thought that job only existed during wartime."

"I detect a certain disdain in your voice. I suppose it's due to your ignorance." He shook his vest. "I practice a kind of medicine that's not for everyone. I'm sure you wouldn't even know where to begin."

"What are you referring to?"

"How to treat, diligently and efficiently, horses that have suffered deep lance wounds, severed tendons, skulls struck with maces, or how to sew up open stomachs . . ." Diego waited for him to finish without speaking. "We farriers have the noble task of caring for the cavalry of armies, like the sacred and ancient calling of the veterinarius that had such prestige among the Roman legions." Diego thought of Friar Servando and his mania for using that name. "To say it in fewer words, we are part of a militia and we have the responsibility of looking after one of the greatest weapons: the horse."

"I don't see them as a weapon."

"They are one. Tell me one of the great horses that are still remembered by history, and you will see how they have taken part in famous battles, at the hands of their owners, who of course were valiant warriors. Like Bucephalus, the horse of Alexander the Great. A specimen from Thessaly, pitch-black, impressive in beauty and strong in battle. And what about Hannibal? Or Strategos, another from Greek Thessaly, with which he crossed the Alps, and that he said was unquiet and aggressive, of enormous stature, and black as well. Or who can forget Aetha, the horse of King Agamemnon in the Battle of Troy, or Julius Caesar's famous Genitor . . ."

"For me, the horse is something more, poetry, loyalty," Diego replied.

"And since I see that you enjoy history . . ." Giulio stood erect, proud, with that bearing so common in military men. "I will give you the example of other horses, also famous, but not for their warlike character. Surely you've heard men talk of Pegasus, the winged horse of Zeus. A cross of breeds from Persia and Thessaly, white. Raised on the very slopes of Olympus, he was said to be was the fastest creature on the earth, because he ran like the wind."

"He never existed. You're talking to me of a legend, a myth."

"And Lazlos. Does that ring a bell?"

"I have never heard that name."

"It was the first horse of the Prophet Muhammad." Giulio's brow wrinkled on hearing that name. "A son of the desert that he journeyed with on his first travels to Mecca, Lazlos was loved and respected as the highest of all earthly beings. It was such a noble specimen that Muhammad affirmed not even the devil would dare to enter a tent inhabited by its race, the Arabian."

The Neapolitan was so offended with the example, for him almost heretical, that his face was inflamed with rage.

"Filthy albéitars! Sons of Islam! I see what you're about, very clearly. Stay with your Moors and pray with them. And while you're at it, ask your Allah to inspire you with a bit of science and not just poetry, if he can."

The voice of García Romeu put an end to their conversation, though the Italian gave Diego a serious warning before leaving.

"I hope I can take your measure one day. And when I do, you'll see how little education you've gotten along with that Moorish apostasy you've taken on."

After inspecting Centurion and making sure of his capabilities, Diego returned to his tent. He set to organizing the material that had been left at his disposal when Marcos appeared with a weak smile. His eyes attested to a long sleepless night.

"You've been inspecting some hayloft . . ." Diego held in his laughter when he smelled the intense female perfume that assailed him on all sides.

"You know the best thing about Bernarda?"

"I suppose you're talking about that blonde . . ."

"She's single, she's sweet as honey itself, and she lives in the village of Corella, only three leagues away from the monastery!" Marcos's eyes shone with excitement, as he knew he could go back to the girl whenever he wanted.

They joked a while about his nocturnal adventure and Diego told him what he had found out about Mencía, sighing with pleasure each time he recounted one of her virtues.

They were only silenced by three loud trumpet blows, the signal that the jousts were commencing. Nervous, Diego gathered together all the tools he would need to attend.

In two small boxes, he counted assorted knives and scalpels of different sizes, some iron files, a bone saw, and a lancet with three spare blades. He saw a wooden clamp used to immobilize the horses. Diego hated that instrument, which twisted the animal's lip, causing intense pain. In another box, he found silk thread and needles for sutures. And last, he took a small hammer and a very sharp adze.

When he was done getting ready, he left Marcos in the tent and went to find Gómez Garceiz. They told Diego the ensign could be found with the horses. When he entered into the makeshift stables, he saw him at Centurion's side. He was speaking softly into its ear, and the animal breathed softly with pure pleasure.

"I heard yesterday that from the six groups of horses, you will be fighting last. Where should I be if you need me?" Diego asked, simply to make himself noticed.

"You'll be standing on the track. You'll see two small blue tents set up for emergency services. You'll be there with the farriers and squires." He took a cuirass in his hands and began to put it on. "Help me tie this, please."

Diego was amazed at its thickness. Under it, the man had on a cotton tunic with the colors of his coat of arms, and on the helmet, two ferocious boars showing their long fangs. Diego left the ensign to finish getting ready and walked to the southern edge of the track. After he passed through the guards, he stood there, impressed by the fantastic spectacle taking place before his eyes.

An enthused public filled the stands completely. He calculated it must have been more than two thousand. In that moment, they were avidly applauding the abilities of three *saltimbanques*, cheering them on to do more risky somersaults and pirouettes. In the center there were stands ornamented with a colored cloth where the spurs of the combatants hung, left there as a proof of their valor until the duels were finished.

A sea of standards bearing the arms of the kingdom of Navarre and the town of Olite waved all around. Diego looked all over with an inexhaustible capacity for surprise.

On stepping onto the lists, the procession waved at the people and sat in their appointed spots. Still, the palfrey and the lady of honor gave one more turn before the applause and turned to the tribunal where they would preside over the joust. A trumpet blasted three times and everyone fell quiet. The king raised his voice.

"Let the jousts begin!"

A thundering shouting drowned out his words. The order allowed the participants to enter.

Each one of the twelve horsemen filed past on horseback, in the company of his pages and squires. All were adorned with the coat of arms of their masters.

Diego watched it all in excitement. He found Marcos among the public, seated beside his conquest, cackling. He also looked for Mencía, without luck. It was strange not to see her; her cousin didn't appear either.

When the opening protocol was finished, a long drum roll prepared for the first joust. The first combatants turned to the judges to get their approval.

"Albéitars . . ."

With that disrespectful tone, the greeting could come from none other.

"Farriers . . ." Diego replied with sufficient eloquence.

Three times the public shouted the name of the woman presiding over the joust, Doña Blanca, the princess of the kingdom of Navarre. Attending to their desires, the woman stood to wave from the tribunal, beautifully decorated with pink flowers and robes, to the judges' left. One of the judges came down to the sand to talk with the contestants. In accordance with the laws of chivalry, he made them show their arms to measure their correct length, apportioned the alternative posts, so that the sun would not unfairly disadvantage any one party, and made them swear to loyalty in combat.

When that was done, he returned to his stand and waited for them to get into position to finally give the signal to charge.

And charge they did.

Diego understood immediately the public's respectful silence. Nothing could be heard but the breathing of the horses, and then the thunderous clashing of their hooves on the soil, the clacking of the spurs, the blinding light of the armor. He saw them speed up and the lances descended until they were in line with the breast of each opponent. Breath held, maximum tension on the sand, not a single ovation for the warriors.

"The black one will win," someone beside him said. Diego didn't turn. He didn't want to miss the encounter.

The lance of that knight stayed firm when he struck, a gnashing sound of broken wood erupted, and the other man fell. The horse, free, trotted off until it was caught by a group of pages.

Diego turned to his unknown neighbor and asked what had signaled the winner.

"He's my cousin." A hood was pulled back and the blond mane and face of Mencía were revealed. He smiled, enchanted to see her.

"You disguise yourself as a page and you understand jousting. . . . You surprise me."

"I enjoy risk. If I could participate in these games . . ." She smiled bewitchingly. Diego felt himself melt at her side. "And to answer your question, my cousin was holding his lance better. Man, weapon, and horse were a single thing. Faced with that much inertia, there is no one who can resist the attack."

"And if they find you out?"

"Better if we don't press our luck and you be quiet. If we keep talking, they'll recognize me." She covered herself again with the hood and observed the following jousters in silence. They weren't as quick as the ones before them, nor were their victories as clean. When one of the combatants didn't fall from his horse in a joust, the judges made their decision by counting the number of lances broken, and three was the minimum number to decide a victor. Mencía explained to him why the public never applauded until they knew the verdict. The rules of jousting mandated that whoever failed to respect the silence have their tongue cut out. The reason was none other than to preserve the honor of both knights until it was known which one had emerged victorious.

And the last duel came. The one that would pit Diego's mentor Gómez Garceiz, clad in red, against García Romeu in white. Two royal ensigns battling on the sand, as if their respective kingdoms were at stake. The black eagle of Romeu against the boars of Garceiz.

A complete silence accompanied their first two sallies. In each one, their lances broke into pieces without knocking anyone down. In the third, they were playing for all. The Aragonese had the advantage.

They began at a run. Maximum tension in the muscles of horse and rider. The wooden tips face-to-face, until they met in a brutal shock. The sound of the blow sliced the air and García Romeu and his animal fell in a mound over the sand. The lance of the Navarrese had knocked against his armor, and from there to the neck of the animal that had made him fall.

The ovation sounded throughout the stands. The Navarrese had won cleanly and would therefore be named winner of the sixth joust. Everyone applauded. Helmet off, smiling, he turned to the seat of Princess Doña Blanca to receive the honors.

But in the meantime, on the sand, things were going badly. García Romeu's horse was still grounded, and blood was spurting from its neck. Giulio Morigatti ran forth with his bag of instruments, and Diego went over to see if he could help as well.

They arrived at almost the same time.

"A sliver of wood is stuck in his neck," García Romeu confirmed, kneeling, watching the copious bleeding.

Giulio, the farrier, examined the damage. He was immediately alarmed, discovering that a pointed piece of wood as thick as a finger had perforated the horse's jugular. Diego came to the same conclusion.

"I'll pull it out as fast as possible, but I'll need the help of two strong men to close the wound right afterward," Giulio said.

Diego thought he was crazy. If he did that, he would open a torrent of blood and the animal would perish in an instant.

"You'll kill him!" Diego's voice, which he had meant for only Giulio to hear, rang out too loud and too clear.

All those present, including Doña Mencía and the ensign García Romeu, heard him. Giulio did also; he looked at Diego with hatred and rage.

"What did you say?" García Romeu interrogated him frantically, wanting to hear his opinion. That horse was his finest specimen.

"It shouldn't be pulled out all at once. It will provoke a collapse and the hemorrhage will be irreparable," Diego responded.

"You're saying nonsense; don't listen to him, master. I know what I'm doing. It's nothing more than one of those battle wounds that I've already dealt with. . . ."

"He'll kill him!" Diego insisted in a stern voice.

The nobleman from Aragon ruminated over his decision. He looked at both of them, regretted having to decide between them, but finally asked Diego to take charge of it. His hypothesis seemed the more realistic one.

"Let the albéitar do it!"

Diego knelt beside the horse and acted with enormous speed and efficiency. He made two pages hold its neck, and with a very sharp lancet, he cleared away the skin on top of the wood. He found the jugular. With a silk thread, he isolated it, tying it tight to seal off the flow. He knew he had little time for that operation. Mencía was at his side. Half hidden under her hood, she watched him, shocked by his abilities. He sliced the skin that surrounded the wood and asked someone to open the edges of the incision. To Diego's surprise, the hands that helped him were those of Mencía. No one recognized her, but he knew. He didn't want to even think about having her so close. . . . In that moment, he had to concentrate on García Romeu's horse.

Diego removed the splinter carefully in order not to tear the vessel, which was no longer bleeding, and sewed the outlines of the puncture, pulling it closed right afterward. Those present admired the speed and accuracy of his hands. No one saw the slightest tremor. Then he loosed the ligature around the jugular and the vein filled with blood, with life, without spilling a single drop.

They hurrahed and applauded him. By then, Gómez Garceiz had appeared as well as many nobles and judges, all impressed by his skill. Even King Sancho VII was informed of the magnificent feat of the young albéitar.

They clapped him on the back, smiled at him. Everyone seemed enthused by his actions, except for one person, Giulio Morigatti. He had hoped for, even wished for, the death of that horse in order to upbraid Diego afterward. He took advantage of a moment of distraction to approach Diego. He spoke very softly in his ear.

"I will never forget this humiliation. You're nothing more than a filthy and vile dog, Diego de Malagón. Sooner or later we'll meet again, and then . . ."

"What are you threatening me with?" Diego raised his voice, attracting the attention of those present. "Say it now, you rogue."

Giulio felt himself surrounded by the gazes of disapproval of all present.

"Filthy Moor!" He spit at the floor, furious.

Diego leapt at him but was held back by two knights.

"Quiet, now!" The order came from García Romeu, now grasping Giulio's tunic. "I've always taken you for a man of integrity and skill, but today you have just demonstrated the contrary. Your attitude has stained the honor of my house and of the very crown of Aragon."

The farrier's expression said it all. Ire, pain. He was clenching his jaw so hard, his face seemed deformed.

"From this moment on, you are no longer at my service. Get out of here! I don't want to see you again."

Giulio did so, protesting between clenched teeth, and disappeared among the tents, swearing vengeance.

Diego heard García Romeu himself beg his pardon once the jousting was over. Still upset by the violent scene, Diego turned back to the tents to leave his instruments in that of the ensign. Mencía was there once more. She had taken off her men's costume and was again dressed as a woman. Diego didn't try to approach her and she could not come closer than what decorum demanded, but when she had a glimmer of opportunity, she didn't waste it and said, as though in a whisper: "I've never seen anyone work like you."

"Thank you so much for the . . . compliment, my lady." Once more he was tongue-tied.

They were almost to the tents when something unexpected happened. A furious shadow rose up at his back. Someone shouted but did not give him time to react. A dagger was seen seeking out the albéitar and striking him straight in the neck.

Diego looked at Mencía and fell right to the ground.

X.

For him, she was more than just another concubine.

Her undulating red mane, the fragility of her gaze, her elegant stride, each of her gestures was adorable, however subtle it seemed. She was pure magic.

"Swim with me, Estela."

The young caliph al-Nasir lived captivated by that woman. Nervously he observed the elegance of her movements, her shyness as she undressed. He longed for her delicate body when he saw it nude.

Estela submerged herself in the warm water of the pool and went toward him. Al-Nasir grabbed her waist and kissed her lips, but he didn't feel passion from her this time either.

"Do you want me to perfume you?" She stretched her hand to a glass jar with floral oils.

"What I really want you won't give me. . . ."

Estela remained silent. He would never get it. How could she love him when he was nothing more than her filthy captor, a jailer she hated with all her soul every time he took possession of her body?

She spread aromatic oil on her hands and looked for his back. When she moved through the water, she felt too cold, and the hair on her body stood on end. She began massaging his shoulders, then his arms. He closed his eyes, trying to feel every last sensation.

"You know I never call any of the others anymore? That you're my favorite?"

"I don't deserve such an honor," she lied.

She oiled her hands again and continued with his neck. She wanted to choke him. She would certainly have done so had she had the strength.

He leaned his head back and looked at her.

"I am the one who doesn't deserve it," he said to her. "I want you so much." Estela offered him a thin, insincere smile. He would never possess her heart, only her body.

She held her hair in her hands and wrapped herself around him, stroking him until she was in front of him. Insane with passion, the man's lips looked for her neck and then descended.

"You are perverse with me."

For the first time since she was in the harem, Estela played along with his intentions. She needed to finish soon, and besides, she knew it would be the last time. . . .

The break between King Sancho and Najla had caused a great uproar in the caliph's court. Sancho had returned to Navarre and she had stayed, heartbroken and disconsolate. That separation had not only broken her dreams, but also those of Estela and Blanca. Their hopes of escaping that hell, of going with her to Navarre, had vanished.

Since that split, Blanca consoled Najla every day. She chose her words to try to heal the girl's wounds and also showed her tenderness and support. And yet, her charitable attitude toward the princess had other motives; she had achieved greater freedom of movement inside the harem, and that was just what she needed to carry out her plan. She had thought it through infinite times until making a decision. It would occur that very afternoon, when her sister returned from being with the caliph.

"You'll find another man, my princess. Don't let this embitter you so much."

"No one will be like him, Blanca." Najla took Blanca's hand and held it between hers. "You're a Christian; do you understand why he left?"

"The pope is the representative of Jesus Christ on earth. The rebuke the king received for your relationship is a very serious matter. Imagine that you had an equivalent figure in your faith and he took you to task. How would you respond?"

"We have one. He is the caliph, my brother, but he blessed our love. . . ." Najla broke into unstoppable tears.

Blanca embraced her and cried as well, though her motives were very different. She imagined the pain her flight would cause. She kissed her forehead and then caught the tears that streamed down her cheeks.

"Be strong, be strong, my dear friend. . . ."

Estela lifted the false bottom of the trunk and took out two dresses, the least conspicuous ones she had in her wardrobe. When she had left the caliph, he was dressing for the reception that afternoon.

She heard the call to prayers.

Everything was going according to plan. She dressed in those garments and waited hidden behind a column until Blanca arrived.

When she no longer heard the potent voice of the muezzin, she discerned steps approaching. Her heart beat so hard it pounded against her ribs. The door pulled open and the hinges creaked.

"Estela, are you there?"

She came out from behind the column.

"Take this and change fast." She looked into her sister's eyes, perplexed. "What's wrong? Why are you crying?"

"It's for Najla . . ." Blanca took off her tunic and put the new one on.

Estela folded the used clothes and hid them behind the trunk.

"There's nothing here that matters enough for me to shed a single tear."

"Let's go now." Blanca pricked up her ears but could hear nothing. "Once we're close to the reception room, we'll blend in with the group that the caliph's receiving. We'll do it when they're leaving. I've heard there are lots of women and for that reason, he won't notice."

They took off their shoes so as not to make noise. Not seeing anyone in the hallway, they ran until they reached the steps. An Imesebelen was guarding the ground floor. They waited for him to disappear to the left and then rushed downstairs as fast as they could. They turned right and stayed close to the wall, never shifting even a moment from that spot, running until they reached an open room. They heard nearby voices but could see no one. They were close to the larger chambers.

Their breathing hurried and their muscles all tensed, they entered the small bedroom that would serve them as a hiding place until the time was right. Blanca confirmed that they were close to the hallway that led out, where the group was going to pass, and she left the door half open.

"We'll make it, Estela."

"God willing. . . ."

A little while after, the doors of the great hall opened and a large group of guests began to file out. The moment had arrived. The sisters covered their heads with niqabs and crossed their fingers. When Blanca made the sign, they rushed out and turned right to reach the group, but in their hurry, they didn't see the Imesebelen. He, however, did see them. He grabbed them by the arms with incredible force. Those hands hurt. The African recognized the expression of panic in their eyes without knowing what they were trying to do.

"You shouldn't be here." He heard the voices of the group and turned back to them. They were shaking with panic. Then he thought of something.

"I will not allow it." He grabbed Blanca by the neck and began to squeeze with terrible might. She was choking. Estela felt his other hand, but she decided to act. She bit him as hard as she could on the wrist, and though he didn't let her go, she managed to drag herself to the side room where they had been hiding. The Imesebelen, holding on to them as best he could, tried to stop Estela, but she managed to pull away, and when he tried to grab her neck again, he felt a sharpened wooden stake plunge into his heart. He tried vainly to pull it out before falling dead to the floor. As fast as they could, they pushed him into a hiding place, cleaned the blood with a rag, and closed the door. They breathed in and out several times to calm their agitated state, and when they were calm, they looked at each other, still filled with fright.

"If we didn't do it, he would have killed us," Estela said in self-justification.

"Let's hope they don't find him soon."

The two sisters then hurriedly looked for the group and mixed in with the guests, trying not to look nervous. For once, they appreciated the obligation to wear the niqab.

They went outside with the rest and crossed the courtyard, looking for the exit of the castle. They looked at the door. It was protected by four well-armed Imesebelen. One of the men in charge came forward to count the women again before they left the palace. Estela and Blanca panicked. They were the only ones who knew why he kept counting them over and over again. They were only ten steps away from freedom.

"We're not going to make it, Blanca," Estela whispered in her ear.

"When we make it through the checkpoint, run with all your strength. We'll hide in the alleys in the city. There's a market today, and they won't find us among so many people."

"I'm scared. . . ."

"Me too, but we're going to make it." Blanca stroked her chin.

"Stop!" the man shouted. "There are two extra. . . ."

Two Imesebelen came over to see what was happening.

Blanca understood this was their only opportunity to escape and shoved Estela violently.

"Now, run, and don't look back!"

The two sisters leapt into the street and managed to penetrate the gate, taking advantage of the guards' temporary confusion.

"Look for the narrowest alleys!" Blanca screamed.

"I'm so scared!"

"Run and don't think!"

The four Imesebelen gave chase, screaming and telling everyone to get out of their way. Whoever didn't obey and had the bad luck to get between them wound up on the ground. They ran a long while. The sisters came to a crossroads and were separated against their will. The guards split up as well. Blanca arrived at the market square. It was full of people, too many to be able to run. She crouched to avoid being seen by her pursuers, but bad luck made her trip against the supports of a stall and when she tried to stand, she knocked over a set of plates, provoking a great racket. Before she could react, the Imesebelen had caught her.

They threw her down and one stepped on her and pressed her ribs into the ground. Blanca thought of Estela. Might she have been luckier? She cried with rage at her failure and imagined the horrors those savages would commit. She began to pray for her sister, but for herself as well.

Al-Nasir was waiting furious on his palace's stairway. He couldn't believe what had happened, and even less that Estela was involved.

He saw his personal guard appear, dragging a red-haired prisoner. Her head was hanging down. The caliph flinched anxiously, not knowing which sister it was. He couldn't stand it anymore and walked forward to meet them. He knelt to look at her and sighed when he recognized Blanca.

The qadi, as the servant of justice, slapped her without pity.

"Do you know how a person pays for what you've done, filthy Christian?"

A trickle of blood slipped out over Blanca's lip. The man had just split it.

"No, sir, but I beg your pardon." When she raised her head, she saw Princess Najla, red with fright. She looked for Estela and was glad not to see her there.

"The law says that all slaves who try to escape shall have their head cut off immediately. Did you know that?" He stretched a hand out so they could pass him a sword. "I will do it myself!"

"Nooo!" Najla couldn't bear it and knelt in front of the qadi, begging his clemency. Her brother interrupted quickly to save her the humiliation and commanded that they carry her off.

"Make all the slaves come," the qadi ordered while he felt the blade of the sword. "I want them to see an example made."

Al-Nasir seemed distant from the dramatic situation. He just looked at the castle gate, full of anxiety, worried about the future of his beloved Estela. He wished to see her, but in the case that they captured her, he knew she would suffer an identical fate.

The first women began to arrive and they were arranged in a circle around Blanca, gripped with fear. Some came close to console her, but at that moment she was remembering other times, when she lived with her father and her brother, Diego. Between tears, she asked herself what would have become of them, and also of Estela.

"We've captured the other!"

All turned to the entrance, including the caliph and Blanca herself.

Estela twisted and turned, held by two Imesebelen, and shouted, enraged. When she saw her sister, Blanca tried to pull away and embrace her, but they stopped her.

Al-Nasir didn't hide his anguish and looked away.

"Your error will be paid for with your life," the qadi yelled in Estela's face. "Now, look at your sister. . . ."

He turned to Blanca and raised the sword over her head. Many of the slaves broke out in screams and closed their eyes, unwilling to bear witness to that dreadful spectacle.

Estela looked for al-Nasir's eyes, imploring him to intervene, but he stayed motionless and silent.

"What . . . are you going to do?" Estela stammered, infuriated with her captors, trying to bite them.

Blanca looked into her eyes, between tears, telling her wordlessly how much she loved her, and Estela shouted, with all her might, refusing to believe in what was about to happen.

The qadi looked at the caliph to get his approval, and al-Nasir lowered his head, conceding it.

The heavy sword whistled as it sliced through the air and separated Blanca's head from her body.

A murmur of fright coursed through the group of slaves when they saw her head roll past.

Estela sobbed, destroyed by the pain of it. She looked away from that horrible spectacle, hating them with all her soul.

"Now it's your turn." The executioner, his sword stained with blood, turned to her to execute her as well.

Estela closed her eyes and asked for help from God.

An Imesebelen held her by the waist while another pulled her hair from her neck to leave it clear. The qadi calculated the force he would need to use if he wanted a clean cut and exhaled as he awaited the order.

He looked at his caliph.

"Stop!"

The man, disconcerted, kept his sword held high.

"Lower it, and don't execute her."

"But, sir . . . Our law . . ."

"I am the caliph and I possess the prerogative to waive any sentence, including death."

"You are right, but the crime is so grave that . . ."

"If you continue to disobey me, you shall be punished! Will you respect my wishes or no?"

The man bowed his head submissively and put his sword away.

Al-Nasir approached Estela.

"You will never try that again," he whispered in her ear.

"Let your qadi kill me. I don't want to live anymore."

Al-Nasir felt broken from pain when he heard her say that, and he wished only to hold her and console her, to cover her in kisses.

"I do want you to live. Get out of here!"

XI.

Diego regained consciousness covered in sweat, disoriented, and trembling.

"You're finally back," he heard from someone at his side.

When he turned his head, he felt a painful tearing in his neck. He tried to see where it came from and discovered a thick bandage. He saw Marcos. Though he looked exhausted, a smile spread across his face.

"I figured you for dead, you lost so much blood."

Diego tried to talk but couldn't. His tongue felt sticky and his mouth dry. A horrendous vision came back to life in his mind, the same that had awakened him from his sweet dream. He felt a dreadful anxiousness. He looked around nervously, unable to figure out where he was, and his pulse sped up. He had to pinch himself to be sure he was awake. It was something terrible. He had seen it. . . .

"Marcos . . . Something dreadful has happened," he managed to babble out. "My sister . . . It was Blanca. . . . I saw her blood. Nooo!"

"But what are you saying?" Marcos checked to see if he still had a fever. "You were wounded. You don't remember?"

The ensign Gómez Garceiz came through the door with another middle-aged man who introduced himself as a doctor. Without getting lost in other considerations, the man took Diego's pulse and checked the state of his eyes and his mouth.

"Blanca is dead." Diego began to sob to the shock of all present.

"He's still delirious." That was how the doctor justified his strange reaction. "It's due to the trauma."

"It's not true," Diego himself replied. "I've seen it. . . ." He was breathing with difficulty. His eyes seemed on the point of exploding from pure pain.

Gómez Garceiz tried to calm him down.

"You've had a bad fever and it's normal for you to have strange visions.

You've been asleep more than two days and we've heard you screaming, cursing, wailing, and even grunting."

Diego tried to sit up, but he felt suddenly nauseated and let himself fall back over the soft bed. Maybe they were right, he thought. Maybe those dreadful images were just a part of his illness. He let that console him.

"What happened?"

"When the joust was over, that cur Giulio Morigatti attacked you, humiliated by your masterful work with García Romeu's horse," Gómez Garceiz answered. "After committing that villainy, he was detained by the troops of the Aragonese."

"And Mencía?" He remembered she'd been by his side. "Did anything happen to her?"

"Relax. She didn't suffer any harm." Diego studied the face of the ensign and his words seemed sincere. "She was asking after you constantly until yesterday, when she returned to Albarracín. Anyway, she left you a note."

He took an envelope sealed with wax from a side table and passed it to him. Diego didn't open it. He preferred to do so alone.

"You'll get better fast, young man," the doctor interrupted. "That dagger passed less than an inch from your jugular." He lifted the bandage and examined the wound. It had a good color and aspect. "That's what I call luck."

The doctor ordered them to continue with the same treatment and remedies he had recommended. He also advised that Diego begin walking a little, even if it was just around the palace, so he would regain his strength. Then he took his things and said good-bye.

Diego began to question Gómez Garceiz again.

"Excuse me, but I'm feeling very confused. Where am I?"

"You're in my house, in Olite. You can stay here as long as you need to recover." Garceiz heard a noise of horses and looked out the window. "Now I have to leave; I see the Almohad ambassador is here and I have to receive him."

Two days later, Marcos helped Diego to stand up to take his first steps inside the palace. There was a beautiful loggia on the third floor that opened onto a courtyard where they took their walk.

Diego went slowly, feeling a painful sensation in his neck with each step. The dagger had opened a long wound and he was afraid he would begin to bleed again, as had already happened once when he'd strained himself.

They left behind a group of smiling maidservants whom Marcos had stopped to compliment, and stopped to listen to a heated argument on the ground floor. They grabbed the banister with curiosity and heard Gómez Garceiz and another man in noble dress who had their backs turned to them. The stranger appeared very angry and moved nonstop. Garceiz shook his head over and over stubbornly.

Marcos thought he knew who the visitor was.

"I think it's that ambassador . . . the one from the Moors." He spoke softly.

"He's still here?"

"I heard he was staying another week."

There was something about that man that awakened a strange interest on Diego's part, but he didn't know what it could be. He appeared Christian and when he heard him speak, the man spoke perfect Romanic, with hardly a trace of an Arabic accent. And yet he represented the Almohads and was negotiating on their behalf. . . . He didn't understand.

"Look at him now." Marcos pointed in his direction.

The two men had just gotten up from their seats and headed toward a fountain in the center. And then, Diego saw him. It was only an instant, but he recognized that scar on his face. Unaware of what was happening just a short distance away, the man lowered his face.

"It's him!"

"What?" Marcos was frightened to see Diego seized up, his eyes pinned to that figure.

"It's the same one who . . ."

Diego spoke too loudly and, without trying, attracted the attention of the ambassador and his host. Though Marcos pulled him away from the banister, it was too late, they had already made eye contact.

"What's going on with you?" Marcos shook Diego until he reacted and chose this moment to cut their walk short.

"That face . . ." Diego's legs shook.

A cold sweat covered the nape of his neck as he remembered the state he found his father in and the wretched consequences of his sisters' kidnapping. The man he had seen that day had a similar scar. . . . He doubted it was anyone else. He had seen him from behind some boulders, from afar, and it had been almost seven years. He looked at him again and his stomach turned as it had then; it was definitely him. Diego writhed with rage and clenched his fists, murmuring between his teeth.

"You act like you've seen the devil."

"I have. I have. . . ."

Back in the bedroom, Diego told Marcos what had happened on that tragic day and in what circumstances he had seen that man, whose similarity to the ambassador was extraordinary.

"You should tell Gómez Garceiz."

"Not without knowing what their relationship is. I'm not sure."

That night, Diego could hardly sleep a wink. He knew that the ambassador had been lodged in a room just above his own. For that reason, feeling him so close, he believed that every noise he heard came from him, and he imagined him there. Hardly able to breathe, he tried to listen close to hear what the man was doing at each moment, until he felt himself obsessed.

He tried to think about something else, but he couldn't. Over and over the image of that man came back into his mind and he couldn't forget his hard, cruel expression, the one he saw on that mountain pass.

The next day, he awoke confused and anxious, with his mouth completely dry, but he decided to ask about the man. He needed to know who he was, where he came from, and what he might know about his sisters.

When he asked about them, he learned that Garceiz had gone out very early in the company of the ambassador.

In the afternoon, Diego went down to the stables to see Sabba. After those days of separation, the mare was glad to see him, sniffing at him contentedly while he stroked her. Diego stayed a long time at her side; he didn't know how long.

"How are you today?"

Diego looked up at the voice of the ensign, Gómez Garceiz. He saw him enter on horseback in front of the ambassador. Both left their animals in the hands of the stable boys and came up to Diego.

"You're still not well." Garceiz noted his pallor.

Diego didn't know what to do. He felt the ambassador's gaze and could barely breathe. His heart raced and even his temples began to ache. He had to answer, but he felt incapable.

The two men found his silence very strange.

"I'm a little nauseated. . . ."

"Pardon me for saying so, but a corpse has more color than you do." The ambassador stretched his hand to Diego.

"Let me introduce you to Pedro de Mora," Gómez Garceiz interrupted. "The ambassador to the great caliph al-Nasir."

When it was Diego's turn, he added his profession of albéitar to his name.

"So you're from Malagón. . . . I understand. Malagón brings back memories for me. . . ." The ambassador scratched his chin and looked at Diego more attentively, pensive. He remembered that town was close to Alarcos. He could see a tense attitude in the young man, and he didn't care for it. "An albéitar at a Christian court . . ." he commented thoughtfully. "Interesting. . . . Your profession is a common one in Arab towns, but I haven't heard of such in lands so far to the north."

"It's not common, no. . . . The truth is . . . but . . ."

Diego felt incapable of talking. His tongue didn't respond, or any other muscle in his body; everything had seized up.

He stared at the ambassador's scar and didn't know what to say. And if he had the wrong person? He looked back at him and his eyelid twitched. He tried to stop it with a finger but had no luck. His face reflected enormous angst, fear, uncertainty. That began to alarm the two men.

"Maybe you should rest a bit," Garceiz proposed. "We'll accompany you to your room."

They did, but after no more than fifteen steps, Diego could no longer resist and vomited in a corner.

Gómez Garceiz came over immediately to look at him. He had seen the discomfort Don Pedro's presence produced, and he decided to figure out what was happening after the ambassador had left.

"You knew him from before, no?"

Diego decided to speak.

"It was the day of the defeat in Alarcos. He was there during the siege. It was terrible. . . ." Diego began to feel an overwhelming grief as his memories emerged, and he fell silent. His eyes expressed terrible anguish.

Gómez Garceiz did what he could to calm him down, and when he did, he asked what had caused him such deep grief. And Diego told him.

That same night, Pedro de Mora was walking through his rooms and could not manage to sleep. He felt perturbed and irritable. For some strange reason, that albéitar had stirred his conscience, stirring up certain memories he thought were forgotten.

The town of Malagón had become the center of his memories. He looked back and saw the raids and pillaging after the victory at Alarcos. He remembered as well that group of Imesebelen he had captained. Thanks to them, they had captured countless slaves, especially women who would later serve to fill the harems. And then he realized that those two red-haired concubines, Estela and Blanca, were among them, that they had been snatched those very days, and close to Malagón as well.

One floor below, Diego heard Pedro de Mora's steps on the wooden floor. He couldn't sleep either. To feel him so close sped up his breathing. He felt his flushed cheeks and his rapid pulse, the effects of acute anxiety.

At one point in the night, Diego was tempted by the idea of going up there with some weapon from his lodgings to pry the truth out of him. He looked around, searching for something suitable, but found nothing. His dagger, a gift from Galib, was with Sabba, hidden in her saddle. It was too late to go looking for it.

He considered what chances he had to get away with his life if he confronted him. The man was strong, maybe stronger than he was, but if he acted fast, he could avoid his reaction. He looked again amid the firewood for a stake that could serve him, but all were about to turn into ash.

Pedro de Mora tried to remember the traits and the eyes of those two concubines, and as he did, he began to see something similar to the albéitar in them. They had something in common, but he didn't know what. . . .

He thought that if they were family, it was possible the boy had seen him during the siege. Given his strange reactions, it was one explanation.

For a moment he felt himself in danger. If it reached the ears of Gómez Garceiz, his situation could be delicate. He had to do something. He should avoid it. After thinking of when and how he would act, he decided to visit the young man before dawn.

Shortly afterward, he left his bedroom stealthily and went down to look for Diego. He was fortunate not to cross paths with anyone before he arrived at his door. He opened it, trying to make the least noise possible. Darkness covered everything. At one end of the room was a fireplace about to go out, casting the room in an orange glow. Using the scant light, Mora made his way to the middle of the room.

"Who's there?" Diego asked, recognizing the ambassador's presence.

Without answering, Pedro de Mora sped toward him, a dagger in his hand.

Diego saw a metallic gleam rushing toward him and he tried to duck it, having no other defense. He knocked down a heavy shelf beside him atop that shadow. The resultant clatter broke the silence of the night without striking Pedro de Mora. The same was not true of the second, which fell on him before toppling over with even more noise. The man escaped quickly from that weight and went after Diego, furious and thirsty for blood. Diego heard the sound of his dagger whistling only an inch away from his face. Frightened, he hurtled toward the door. His aggressor, guessing his intentions, chased him with all his energy. And when Diego got to the door and tried to open it, a hand grabbed him by the neck and he felt the steel point over his breast.

"Scream and I'll run you through."

Diego didn't doubt it; he knew he was serious.

"Where do you know me from?" Pedro de Mora asked.

Diego calculated the odds he had of getting away, but they were minimal. He felt lost.

"Nowhere," he lied.

"Do the names Blanca and Estela mean anything to you?"

Diego reacted furiously.

"Bastard!"

"I see they do." He ran the dagger over his flesh and pressed it until a wound began to open. Diego felt the warmth of his own blood running over his belly. "I know them too, and rather better than you might imagine. . . ."

When he heard that, Diego turned around, filled with rage. He searched for the dagger with his hand and stopped it in time, while dealing his attacker a brutal punch to the chin. He tried to grab the knife but he didn't manage to. Pedro de Mora sliced the air several times, looking for him but not striking.

In that moment, steps could be heard behind the door and Gómez Garceiz entered with Marcos. They had a large torch that lit up the whole of the bedroom.

"What is happening here?" the royal ensign demanded.

The dagger fell to the floor without their knowing whose it was.

"You arrived just in time!" Pedro de Mora pointed at Diego and then at the dagger. "He was trying to kill me with that. . . ."

"Then why are you in my room?"

"Somebody explain this to me," Gómez Garceiz said, his sword in his hand, looking stunned at one of them and then the other.

Without answering, Diego lifted his tunic and showed the wound he had just received in his breast.

"It was him!" he swore. "That man has his hands stained with blood. Innocent blood. He's a murderer, a depraved being who acts without pity. He was responsible for the brutal siege after the Battle of Alarcos, which killed hundreds of Christians, and he oversaw the rape of women and children. He also pillaged and massacred entire populations. He commanded the troops. . . ."

"He lies!" Pedro de Mora shouted.

"I'm afraid he's telling the truth," Diego heard Gómez Garceiz reply, "and it's not the first time I've heard this about you, though I never wanted to believe it. If I could detain you right now, I would, but you're an ambassador and I don't have the jurisdiction." He pointed his sword directly at his chest. "Besides my contempt, from this day forward, I assure you I will be looking for my opportunity to make you pay."

"But I saw him!" Diego exclaimed when he saw Mora would go free. "I could testify before a jury if you asked. . . ." He looked imploringly at Gómez Garceiz.

"This boy is trying to confuse you," Pedro de Mora replied.

"And you dare to say that?" Gómez Garceiz threatened the ambassador's throat with the blade of his sword, "when you are the greatest deceiver I have known? I hold you responsible for my king's absence in Marrakesh. Your manipulation and conduct brought terrible consequences to Navarre."

Without anyone expecting it, Diego found the dagger of Pedro de Mora, picked it up off the floor, and pressed it into his neck.

"What happened to my sisters?"

His eyes blazed with a thirst for vengeance. Both Marcos and Gómez Garceiz were alarmed to see him in such a state.

"Leave him! If you wound him, I'll have to arrest you."

Garceiz turned to Diego to take away the dagger, but stopped when he was warned what would happen if he took another step.

"Do I have to remind you of who I am?" Pedro de Mora turned to the ensign, adding more tension to the atmosphere. "Stop this madman right now!" he continued. "This is unacceptable. An outrage!" He looked furiously at Diego. "If something happens to me, or if this ill-bred cur hurts me and you do nothing to intervene, Ensign Garceiz, you will unleash the wrath of al-Nasir. And you don't want that. . . . You know that. For that reason, I ask you to put a stop to this situation."

"What did you do with them?" Diego pressed the dagger until he made him shake.

"I don't know what you're talking about," Mora blubbered. "I don't even know who your sisters are."

"You lying, filthy snake. I never told you the names of my sisters . . ."

Diego brought the dagger to his face and cut him from the edge of his lips to the middle of his right cheek. The blood flowed generously. He knew it wouldn't kill him, but it would leave him with an ugly face for life, an indelible memory of Diego.

The man brought his hand to his face. He screamed in pain from the cut and began to blaspheme. Gómez Garceiz took this opportunity to grab the dagger before Diego used it again. As soon as he got it, he ordered Marcos to take hold of his friend and he turned to Don Pedro.

"Tomorrow I will inform the king about you and will do everything possible to have you stripped of your ambassadorship. But for now, get out of my house. I don't want to see you here again."

Pedro de Mora looked at Diego, covering the wound with his hand.

"What happened to my sisters?"

"Answer him," Garceiz added.

"I know nothing. . . ." He could barely be understood.

"I know he's lying," Diego assured.

"I'm not lying." His eyes expressed deep rage.

"Get out of this house now!" Garceiz commanded him.

Pedro de Mora left the room, trailing behind him a stream of blood and an infinite hatred for Diego.

His name, that face . . . He swore by the most sacred he would not rest until he saw Diego dead.

XII.

On that night, in her note, Mencía had invited Diego to visit the church of Santa María de Albarracín.

After what had happened with Pedro de Mora, Diego and Marcos left Olite and headed toward Fitero, eight days later than they had previously imagined.

His heart told him to go after Mencía, but above his desires, he knew he had to go back to the monastery and take advantage of the opportunity, maybe his only one, to have in his hands the treatise of Celsus, which he hadn't read, or Cato, whose praises Galib had sung. Later on, once he had exhausted the medical resources available there, he would go to his destiny. Marcos didn't object, since his conquest lived in proximity to the monastery.

Before he left Olite, Diego thanked Gómez Garceiz for his attentions without imagining the surprise he had in store for him.

"It's the surgical instruments you used during the joust. You will get better use out of them."

He offered Diego a leather bag inside which chimed the excellent instruments, made of steel by expert hands. When he took it, Diego was overwhelmed by the kindness and promised to put them to the best possible use.

Nevertheless, their reception in the monastery couldn't have been worse.

Friar Servando had received word of Diego's brilliant performance with that wounded horse, but he threw it in his face as soon as he saw him enter the stables.

"Fortunately, I'm not the only victim of your disloyalties." He spit out a piece of chewed leather without looking in his face.

"I don't understand," Diego answered.

"I've heard it said that in Olite you provoked the wrath of a colleague from Naples, making him look ridiculous in front of everyone. I see you enjoy treading on others' authority, yes . . ." He forked a bundle of hay and spread it over the floor of the stable. "It reminded me very much of what happened with that fig you cured behind my back . . . or when you ignored my diagnosis in front of that baker. . . . And why not mention the many occasions when you have taken the chance to talk ill of me, show me up, almost always in front of the other stable boys. . . ."

"The fact is that I cannot bear injustice," Diego replied sternly. "Even less so when it affects someone weaker, and now I'm not talking about horses."

"You must know as well that the farrier stabbed him in the back and tried to kill him," Marcos added, indignant over the friar's ill humor.

"It must not have been so bad." Servando took up another bundle of straw and split it open without paying much mind. He looked at Diego, complained of seeing him standing there idly, and ordered him to clean the water troughs and then to go for grain.

"Before dinner I want it spread out in all the feeding troughs."

Diego sighed. Again he was faced with the hardest reality, with reading the only nourishment to make up for such misfortune.

While he brought in the first barrow full of oats, he remembered Mencía nostalgically. The wound in his neck still hadn't healed, but now he felt a much deeper pain, that of being far from the most beautiful woman he had ever known.

Luckily, within a few days Marcos was able to reestablish his contact with the friar responsible for the library, and in accordance with his desires, he brought a large copy of the book *De Medicina*, written by the Roman Celsus.

That important treatise fed Diego's nights, thanks to an oil lamp that his friend also provided the fuel for.

From Celsus, he learned another kind of anatomy, that of the interior. His work explored the organization of the tissues and the functions of the different organs. Though all the references were to humans, it worked just as well for Diego, since he understood that the differences from the animals couldn't be so extreme as to make what he was learning irrelevant.

He delved into the descriptions, especially those that studied the inflammation that Celsus analyzed according to four symptoms: inflammation, color, pain, and tumor.

As grand and wise as his science was, the wise Roman spoiled it when he began to explain inflammation itself as an effect of divine punishment, as Friar Servando did. He even read that Celsus defined medicine as the art of speculation.

That provoked his resistance, and how. What would make the gods of the Greeks and Romans, or his God, decide to impose an inflammation on a creature lacking in soul and sin, like a horse? What were they punishing? The more he thought about it, the less charming he found those absurd theories.

For a long time, almost since his first books in Arabic, Diego had been obsessed with finding the true causes of each illness. The classic theory of imbalances in humors had never convinced him. Nor the others that accused malign spirits, as his current master did. And even less the ones that mixed the effects of the seasons and age to justify various pathological processes.

Diego believed in the existence of other types of agents directly responsible for the illnesses, even if he still wasn't able to give them a name. To know them and then fight them was becoming an important and attractive challenge for him.

On one of those long late nights, while he read that manuscript, he enjoyed a bit of counsel from Celsus that seemed almost magical. A thousand years had passed since he'd written it, and yet it still had the same relevance.

It went thus:

"The surgeon should be young, or at least little advanced in age, with a hand nimble, firm, and never trembling; equally dexterous with both hands; vision, sharp and distinct; bold, unmerciful, so that, as he wishes to cure his patient, he may not be moved by his cries to hasten too much, or to cut less than is necessary. In the same way, let him do everything as if he were not affected by the cries of the patient."

As an albéitar Diego disregarded the last part of that reflection, since it was so far from the reality of his patients, but he accepted the logic of it.

He was also interested in the surgical technique Celsus proposed, as well as the remedies employed to cure wounds that were already badly infected, such as alum, cantharides, egg white, or salamander ash. He never imagined that the ashes of lizards, pigeons, and swallows could work for a similar end. He decided to try them as soon as he could.

The following winter in Fitero was much harsher than the ones before. It snowed with such intensity throughout the month of January that no one could leave the monastery.

After being closed in for so long, many of the horses became ill because of the poor ventilation in the stables, and some were even close to death. But as always, no one asked for Diego's advice.

One day, Friar Servando decided to bleed all of them, even Sabba, despite Diego's protests. He said this would lower their interior moisture and stop the constant flow of mucus.

Diego had no faith in bleeding, since he thought that this liquid carried not only diseases, but also the defenses against them. He therefore thought it better to leave things as they were.

Once he knew what Friar Servando's plans were, he decided to treat Sabba secretly every night, making use of his own remedies. He gave her dried lovage as he had read in the book of the nun Hildegard. He also made Sabba inhale an infusion of mint and oak. With a fistful of straw he rubbed her breast to warm it and then covered it with a blanket. Some nights he even was able to sleep leaning against her breast to give her warmth.

After a few days, those remedies did Sabba good and she improved notably, unlike the rest of the horses.

In just a week, four animals had died, two of them very young, and for that reason the worry among the friars grew serious. Diego began to treat a few more animals, in secret, but someone told Friar Servando about his initiative and once again he was sent to the latrines where he was shut up two full weeks.

With that, he began to get fed up.

When that time had passed, he returned to the stables, where he was assigned the usual task, but he was no longer the same and didn't behave as he had before. He had made a number of important decisions.

One of them he set in play three days later, when he decided to sneak into the library one morning and look for the last two books that interested him. If he got them, he could read them and consider his education finished and leave that inhumane prison once and for all.

"Marcos, I'm doing it today!" He looked at him decisively.

"Just like you asked, I got hold of the key to the library. You don't know how hard it was for me to get it, since Friar Tomás sleeps holding on to it, as if it were his mission in life. Please remember I have to give it back before morning prayers."

Diego waited until midnight to enter the cloister and look for the stairway that led to the third floor, where the library was located, just above the chapter house.

While he walked along the archways, he squeezed his fist, feeling the key inside it. Marcos had explained to him that he should look for a long passageway to his right, at the end of which he would find his objective. He also warned him of a danger; along that hallway were the twenty-four cells where the monks slept. If he made the least noise or someone saw him there, the situation for both Diego and Marcos could get very dire.

Diego didn't meet anyone on his way.

Luckily, it was too late for anyone to still be awake. He leaned against the stone banister of the winding staircase. It was cold. Before stepping out onto the floor, he pricked up his ears. Everything seemed quiet.

He headed down the passageway and left the first doors behind him. He didn't hear any strange noises, nothing alarming, just an intense chorus of snores and deep darkness. He continued slowly to the middle of the hallway without problems, but then he heard one of the doors open. He threw himself to the floor and prayed that the person wouldn't bump against him. Diego listened closely to calculate the distance of the footsteps and confirmed with panic that a monk was coming toward him. The hallway was narrow but he pressed himself as close to the wall as possible and therefore the man passed beside him without being aware of his presence. He listened to the monk's steps going dim around the corner and decided to move rapidly so he wouldn't catch him on the way back.

He reached the two thick doors that opened into the scriptorium and the library and opened them with the key. They creaked too loudly.

Once inside, he could smell the intense aroma of oil and calves' leather. It was the material the monks used to make the vellum, a type of soft parchment well suited to copying.

Diego tried to adapt to the scant light that entered from the windows to his right. On a table of large proportions he saw laid out in perfect order the inks and mixes of oil and minerals used to produce the different colors. On a smaller one there was a great well of black ink ready to be used. He counted a dozen desks with half-copied books atop them. He looked at them tenderly, marveling at their delicate drawings and their excellent form, at the perfection of the handwriting.

Then he heard a noise outside the room and stayed still until he was sure he was safe. Afterward, he opened all the doors looking for the one that opened to the library, and at last he found it. When he entered, he was stunned.

The room was as high as ten men and all the walls were lined with books, from the floor to the ceiling. Some were enormous, so much so that one person would be incapable of moving them. They were arranged inside niches carved into the walls over wooden shelves.

In the center were two long reading tables with various mechanical supports where the heaviest books were placed.

He looked toward the ceiling and counted five skylights that let in the light of the moon. Its bluish color, mixed with the fine dust that floated in the air, made the place into a magical, almost ghostly stage.

Diego sat down in ecstasy and regretted not having come before. He stood then and walked down the narrow wooden passage that ran alongside the shelves, only a few feet from the floor, and read a few of the spines.

The wood creaked under his feet.

He identified some of the books, though the majority were unknown to him. At first, he didn't understand how they were arranged, but after he had traced the perimeter, he concluded it was by theme. In the first two rows to the left were the enormous books of canticles. Until the end of that wall, the rest of the space was taken up by religious books, including two enormous bibles with covers embossed with gold.

Farther on, he found some Latin treatises, many of which he already knew, and some Greek ones. They were followed by books of science, mostly of medicine. He touched their spines with a desire to read them all.

At the end of the room he found two old cabinets with their doors locked. Through a grating he managed to see what they held. One of them was *The Curse of Love*, and he also saw a Torah and a strange tome called *Opticorum*. There were many others, almost all with dark spines and an ominous air. He decided they must be books considered impious. He explored them one by one, since it must be there where what he wanted was located, the reason that had brought him there.

He tried to force the lock but there was nothing nearby to help him. He remembered having seen a gauge in the scriptorium, and he went for it. When he returned, he slid it between the two leaves of the cabinet and levered. After a strong crack, the doors gave without further problems and he immediately set to examining the spines of the books until he found what he'd come for.

"Who are you?" he heard behind him.

Diego thought he would die from fright. When he turned, he saw a monk with small, threatening eyes. He was holding an oil lamp. Diego immediately tried to flee but the man was faster and grasped him by the tunic.

"Where do you think you're going?" He saw the jimmied cabinet and then the book Diego had in his hands. It was a copy of *Mekhor Chaim*, an old philosophical treatise on the principles of the kabbalah, written two centuries back by a famous Jewish poet from Malaga, Solomon ibn Gabirol.

The monk took it from Diego's hands and looked him straight in the eyes.

"Aren't you the albéitar?"

Diego nodded his head.

"And you are Friar Tomás. . . ."

"The very same."

Though that man had become his supplier of books, that was the first time they had spoken. The religious scholar never left the library except to go to the rectory to eat, to the temple to pray, or to his cell to sleep, and he was never seen speaking to anyone. That is what Marcos had told him a number of times.

"I hope you have a good reason to justify yourself. I didn't expect this of you."

"Before I explain myself, I have to thank you for your help with all the magnificent books—"

"Yes, fine." The monk cut him off. "But skip the formalities and get to the point."

"Don't worry, I will. . . . Up to now, everything I have asked you for through Marcos I've gotten without any problem. Now then, with this one, I didn't dare." He pointed to the one he was trying to take. "I imagined it in the list of prohibited readings and so I decided to take it without your mediation. I want to read it without compromising you. Do you understand? That is the truth."

"Your sincerity makes me trust you. But tell me: What are you looking for in that book? If it's the truth you want, you won't find it there."

Diego turned to look at the book and then at the friar.

"I only want to know how the great wise men of the past thought. I want to draw conclusions from them that will help me further my profession," he answered, convinced.

"And what do you plan on doing by studying philosophy and the kabbalah?"

"In Toledo I met a wise translator, Gerardo de Cremona, who let me read a small fragment of this same book. He said that through reading it, it was possible to deepen your awareness of being, but not just that; it would also help to understand illness and, in an indirect way, to recommend remedies, though not from the classical point of view. He himself admitted that he had learned a great deal from the *Mekhor Chaim*, some of the great truths of human existence."

"I see you met a man with an open mind, ready to learn from any discipline. I must admit this attitude pleases me, and you can't imagine how much."

Friar Tomás set the lamp on the table and drew three small lines in the dust with his finger.

"What do you see here? Three marks or something more?"

"I don't understand." Diego looked first at the drawing and then at him, rather disconcerted.

"Numbers rule more things than we think. Here you have three, the most perfect number of all. The number of days our Lord Jesus Christ was dead. The basic periods of any life: youth, maturity, and death. The three parts of the Trinity. Do you know anything about that?"

Diego shook his head and the friar went on talking.

"The poet Virgil said that divinity loved odd numbers. I don't think he was wrong, for being indivisible, there is greater immortality in them, unlike the even ones. But look as well, how even the names of our monastic prayers, like the prime, the terce, and the none, are numbers. That book you're trying to study also speaks of numbers, especially about their interpretation," he explained to Diego, who was enchanted by his words.

"I never imagined that numbers were so important."

"Let's make a deal. I won't say anything about your visit if you promise to keep the secret I am going to tell you."

"You have my word." Diego brought his hand to his heart as a sign of his surety. Friar Tomás sighed and decided to speak.

"I adore studying this type of ancient belief, the kabbalah, for example, but also what has come down to us from Egypt and Greece. I have to recognize that I learn something from all of them, and there's nothing worse than closing yourself up inside one single truth."

"Even worse is to defend it with fanaticism."

"You speak well, young man. He who defends his opinions with violence or tries to impose them on others does it because, at bottom, he is not sufficiently sure of them. Sadly, in this very monastery you can find brothers of mine who act this way. I hear that Friar Servando has treated you poorly, undoubtedly because he envies your talent, or because you've made him aware of his own limitations."

"Friar Tomás, it comforts me to know that for you, intransigence is the fruit of ignorance."

"It's true. I live in a monastery that is a treasure trove of knowledge, and yet, because it's something good, instead of spreading it to the four winds, we keep it hidden. We prohibit access to anyone who is not religious or a nobleman, maybe to avoid people from a lower station, commoners, as was your case, beginning to think more than they should." He breathed in deeply and changed his tone of voice, becoming graver. "I am a person of deep religious convictions, and for that reason I wish for a faith more open to all, one that is taught and not forced. And besides, I believe that in every one of these books"—he stretched his hand out, as if trying to reach for them all—"there is God. I look for him inside them and I assure you that I find him there."

Diego thought of the poverty of thought that accompanied the life of

Friar Servando compared with Friar Tomás. If only he had been the one in charge of the stables and Diego's education. Everything would have been much easier for him.

"So can I read this book?" He pointed to *Las Fuentes de la Viva*.

"I encourage you to. It may open new pathways in your thought, and maybe it will help with your work, as you say."

"Do you think I can apply it to one of my cures?"

"Don't dismiss its science until you know how numbers influence our lives and, why not, our illnesses as well. If you make of them your allies, you will see how they will point you toward certain solutions. Try to give three medicines instead of two, or have your treatments given three times a day, or for three days straight . . ."

"Forgive my commentary, it may seem stupid, but that seems more like magic than science."

"The next book I will get to you through your friend will be Cato's. Look at it with other eyes. As an example of what I'm saying, you will find in it a potion recommended for oxen that has to be given for three days and to each ox three times. The recipe has twelve ingredients, a multiple of three. In reality, and this is the most mysterious fact of the matter, it is a philter, a remedy for the conjuring of pain. I know it by heart. It goes:

"'If you fear illness, give your healthy animals three grains of salt, three leaves of laurel, three shoots of leek, three cloves of garlic, three grains of incense, three plants of Sabina, three leaves of rue, three of white bryony, three white beans, three burning coals, three pints of wine, and give this potion to each ox for three days.' What do you think?"

"I just remembered something similar in Columella," Diego interrupted. "To expel the excess humors from an intestinal ailment, he proposed the use of three measures of a certain liquid for three days. And to avoid bleeding, he recommended three ounces of ground garlic with three cups of wine. And all this without letting the animal drink for three days."

"See? Pay attention to me and don't forget to use numbers in your favor when you work as an albéitar. They can help you. . . ."

"For other things, too?" Diego thought of his worst enemy, Pedro de Mora, and his sisters, and last, of winning Mencía's love.

"What are you referring to?"

"I don't know, when I'm praying, for example." Diego hid his true thoughts.

"Yes, my son. Also when you are praying to God."

XIII.

Diego read the strange treatise that conversed about philosophy and the kabbalah and then one by Cato called *De Re Rustica*.

At that time, he met with an unexpected circumstance that led him to deal with the most notorious of the monastery's inhabitants: the prior.

Everything happened one Monday in February, when his best horse began moving its head in a strange way. Instead of calling Friar Servando, as he would have normally, the prior wanted to see Diego.

Without knowing what the problem was, Diego showed up in the stables that very morning. From a first inspection, knowing the terrible prognosis of its particular disease, he decided he wouldn't be the one to administer the cure and recommended they let Friar Servando know. He didn't feel ready to suffer more late nights in that stinking muck heap just because his master felt put down once more.

When Friar Servando learned of this, he was so thankful that he asked him to be present during the observation of the animal.

The prior, present all the while, seemed very worried and was rightly concerned about the animal's awful appearance.

"Has he been very cold?" Friar Servando broke the tension ineptly.

"What kind of stupid question is that?" The prior's cheeks lit up with ire. "Are you not the one person responsible for the stables? Don't you even know what's happening right in front of your blessed nose?"

The man seemed truly upset.

"Forgive me, prior. I was thinking about a cause that, if confirmed, will mean a grave prognosis. Before saying anything to you, I wanted to be sure...."

Diego understood that Friar Servando was right in his diagnosis by the commentary he had just made.

"He had a problem with his lung, maybe a year back." Friar Servando remembered. "Maybe it was in those same days..."

"Yes, it's true. He suffered a high fever, but this is different." The prior motioned to him bitterly, almost ready to lose his patience. "For days now he's been moving his head strangely and lots of liquid is coming out of his nose."

"He has nasal catarrh," Friar Servando explained. "It's a secondary illness related to what was wrong with him last year."

The prior looked at Diego to see if he could find any hint of disagreement on his face. He saw none.

"I will treat him with a very effective remedy and you'll see that his sickness will clear up soon."

Diego's expression became perplexed when he heard him say that, since the disease in question had no cure. He looked at the friar but preferred to say nothing, waiting to see him act.

Friar Servando ordered the stable boys to pass a rope around the animal's head and tie it to the rings in the wall. That way he would keep the horse from bucking its head. Then he opened a cabinet where he kept his cures and took out a box full of silkworm cocoons. He counted them and seemed satisfied.

The prior observed, confused when Friar Servando placed a little pile of them on the floor, just under the horse's head, but even more so when the monk began to burn them, so that, as he said, the horse would inhale the vapors.

"They will enter through his nostrils and go to his brain, where they will dissolve the bad humors that are concentrated there," Friar Servando assured, very confident.

"I hope so!" the prior replied, covering his nose. "That smells like the bowels of hell."

Diego watched Friar Servando and then the horse. He knew the uselessness of this remedy and stepped a bit away, fearful of what could happen.

Still not content with the effects of that pestilential odor, Friar Servando asked a stable boy with a thick stick and a linen cloth to roll it in the ashes. When he had, he took the stick into his hand and began to shove it in the animal's nose without mercy.

The horse opened its eyes wide and stomped at the floor.

"You're hurting him!" the prior complained, already angry.

"Don't think that; I'm just trying to push the humors out of their place, so that they will be better balanced and he'll recover."

At that moment, the horse must have noticed a sharp pain and Diego sensed its reaction. He warned both of them, but there was no time. An impressive quantity of mucus exploded from his nostrils into the face of

Friar Servando and onto the white habit of the prior. Diego and all those present couldn't help but break out in laughter.

Diego had known from the first that the horse wouldn't be cured that way, and he also guessed at the repercussions that would result from his laughter. But he still enjoyed himself like never before.

His punishment consisted of two weeks in his now-familiar and foul-scented latrines, though it was only four days in the end. For the first three, he couldn't stop laughing every time he remembered the scene, but on the fourth things changed. Once more, the person responsible was Friar Servando, and everything was the fault of his regrettable presence.

Diego was pushing a wheelbarrow full of human dung with the idea of scattering it in a field close to the monastery. When he crossed the central courtyard, he saw Friar Servando come out of the stables with a shattered expression. His head was low, he was grumbling, and he seemed absorbed in his thoughts. Soon he was close to the pestilence of the dung, and when he realized who was carting it, he walked up to Diego decisively.

"You knew that the cocoons weren't going to work and you didn't tell me, right?" His face was so close to Diego's that he could feel his breath.

"You are correct," he replied unrestrained.

"I thought so. . . ." The nostrils of the man's nose flared, and his eyes reddened. "Because of it, I have suffered serious consequences. . . . Did you know? And it's your fault!"

"Permit me to disagree with your conclusion, though in reality I care very little about what happens to you from now on."

Diego walked off again without paying attention, tired of the monk's constant bitter treatment.

"Stop!" Servando stood in front of him, blocking his way. "The prior just took away my responsibility for the stables and now he's sending me out to plant the fields, like I was just anyone."

"Well, that sounds like excellent news. Finally you'll leave me in peace."

Without another word, Friar Servando responded to his commentary in an unbelievable way. First he took the wheelbarrow from him and dumped it out in the courtyard with a furious attitude. But Diego was even more confused when he began to stomp on the manure like a madman, kicking and scattering it all around.

Diego looked for someone who might be witnessing his actions, but sadly, he saw no one. Once Friar Servando seemed to consider his work done, and there was no more matter to be spread around, he turned back to Diego, ordering him to clean it up.

"You do it! I refuse!" Diego answered.

The friar, mad with rage, smacked him with all his might and threw him to the ground.

"Insolent little . . ."

That was all he could say, for Diego, more tired than ever of that man, leapt at his stomach and pushed him as hard as he could. The friar's enormous strength was not enough to brake Diego's fury. To the monk's surprise, he found himself floored and on the receiving end of punches to his cheeks, forehead, and mouth. Diego, out of control, managed to break his nose and then began hitting him in the stomach until Friar Servando called for help.

Diego was astonished at himself. He thought he had broken several of the man's ribs as well as his nose, and yet he felt great. He wanted to keep working on the rest of his bones. It was the best relief for all his miseries that he'd ever experienced.

"Have mercy on me," the friar pleaded, almost crying.

"Do you even know what that means? You're asking me for pity?" Diego looked at his fists. They were covered in blood, and he didn't even know which of them it belonged to. "Here's your pity!"

He grabbed Servando's head in both hands and began to beat it against the stones on the ground.

"Let him go, you're going to kill him!" Diego heard someone shouting in his ear. But he didn't want to stop.

It was Marcos and Friar Jesús. They were returning from the market in Corella, where Marcos had visited Bernarda. When they entered the courtyard of the monastery and saw that spectacle, they ran to stop the fight.

"Diego!" His friend grabbed with all his might to keep him from killing the friar. That shout awakened him from his madness and he stopped. He looked at Marcos, shocked, when he helped him to stand back up.

Friar Jesús, in the meanwhile, attended to Servando.

"This man is badly wounded," he said, alarmed. "I'll go tell the prior and the others." He threatened Diego with a raised finger. "And don't you leave until I'm back."

Diego and Marcos immediately understood that their stay in the monastery had come to its end. They ran to the stables to get Sabba and Marcos's mule and galloped away.

PART III

Lands of Refuge

Each of the five Christian kingdoms has signed a peace treaty with the Almohad caliph al-Nasir, although not all with the same motives. Some are weaving murky alliances with him.

The territorial disputes and the infighting among the different kingdoms breed discord. León fights against Castile and Portugal, and Navarre against Aragon and Castile.

Without any accord among them, any attempt at unity aiming for the reconquest of the territories belonging to their Visigoth forebears, the lands now known as Al-Andalus, is doomed to failure.

Even within the kingdoms themselves, relations as solid as those between the ensign Diego López de Haro and his king, Alfonso VIII of Castile, are brought to the breaking point. The tension between them reaches such a high point that the king takes by force the territories of Enkaterri and Biscay and now, with his Leonese counterpart, he has turned, in the spring of 1203, to Estella, where Don Diego has taken refuge with his men. They wish to capture him to avenge their recent losses.

I.

_____

Marcos had to decide: follow Diego to Santa María de Albarracín to look for Mencía or stay in Corella where Bernarda would happily take him in.

If he did the second, he wouldn't want for work, since Bernarda's family had a good deal of land and normally needed people for the harvest.

He remained quiet as they reached a league of distance from the monastery. Diego looked at him from time to time without wanting to influence him. They were crossing an arroyo when Marcos finally spoke.

"Can you imagine me working from sunup to sundown, every day, bent over till my back breaks, soaked in sweat, just to fill up wheelbarrows and carts with cabbages or carrots that will never belong to me?"

"I can, but only as long as she's there to sweeten up your rest."

"Not even then. . . . It's inconceivable!"

Marcos pressured his mule to not be left behind.

For the two leagues that followed, he stayed serious, his head lowered, perhaps weighing his decision, until he began first to smile and then to laugh uncontrollably.

Diego, a little put off at the beginning, began to do the same, without knowing why.

"What is that laughter about?"

"When I lived in Burgos, that monk who taught me how to read and write told me one fine day that there were more than a million of us in Castile." He broke into a cackle that stunned Diego.

"I don't understand . . ."

"If I told you that at least half that million were women?"

"Ah, you rogue . . . Now I follow you. Back to your old self, eh?"

"Does not King Alfonso himself say in his legal code that all Castilians are free men?"

"He does indeed."

Marcos admired the landscape that surrounded them. He was surrounded by gently undulating hills replete with apple and cherry trees. It was a sunny day, warm, with an agreeable breeze that made their travels a real pleasure. He approached one of the trees and took two ripe apples. He threw one to Diego.

"I feel free, and for that reason, I don't want to pledge vassalage to any knight or noble, the way others do in these lands. They say they give themselves up to be protected. They give them their grains, their meat, the milk from their sheep, sometimes even their daughters for the enjoyment of the lords. It's absurd. . . . I say what they actually give up is their freedom."

Diego had never heard him talk that way and was astonished.

"That's why I don't want to stay with Bernarda."

"My father pledged vassalage to the Calatravans almost his whole life, and thanks to that, he was able to run an inn. But he didn't want me to follow in his footsteps. He asked me to fly higher than him, to look for proper work, a master; he urged me to make something of myself, without depending on anyone."

"And did you?"

"I've learned almost everything necessary to pursue my craft, despite the many sacrifices, which you know well. And it's true, I do think I've arrived at the moment to put that knowledge into practice. From now on, I will dedicate myself to it! Fitero was much worse than a prison, but still, I did what I set out to do there."

"It shouldn't be so hard to learn."

"How right you are, Marcos. I don't understand why it has to be that way either. I don't think the monasteries should be all dark and bitter, places where the sternness of some sleeps side by side with the goodness and wisdom of others. In Fitero we saw obtuse personalities like Friar Servando right beside good men like Friar Tomás."

They reached the city of Calatayud, already in the kingdom of Aragon, three days later.

When they tried to enter the town square, they ran into a large group of knights and carters blocking its access. They tried to go around them, but the streets were closed off because of that entourage.

Diego dismounted to talk to a young girl who seemed not to belong to the group.

"What's happening here?"

"They are Castilian nobles. Fugitives, I believe," the girl replied, impressed by his height and good looks.

Diego stood on his tiptoes to look over the crowd. He didn't see any banner or coat of arms that identified them. When he tried to ask again, the girl had gone.

"This is all very strange," he commented to Marcos. "What would Castilians be doing in Aragon, and why would they be fleeing? I'll try to figure it out. You wait for me with the horses in the meanwhile." Marcos took his reins. "I'll be right back."

Diego made a hole in the group until he arrived to the square. The fanfare was such that he could hardly hear the responses of the people he questioned. Finally someone told him everything.

"We are following Don Diego López de Haro."

Diego was stupefied. He didn't understand how the lord of Biscay, whom he knew, could be fleeing Castile, since he was the most loyal servant of the Castilian king. It seemed very odd.

He looked for the center of the square, where there was a large group of knights, and when he arrived there, he questioned them.

"Where have you come from?"

"From Estella," one answered.

Diego knew that city was in Navarre, which made even less sense.

"We had to leave," the man explained when he saw the confused look on Diego's face, "after we suffered a long siege at the hands of Alfonso VIII and his cousin, the king of León. They didn't manage to break us, nor did they capture Don Diego López de Haro, even though that's what they were after, but when they left, we had to as well."

"Diego de Malagón?"

All of a sudden, Diego heard a voice at his back that sounded familiar. When he turned, he recognized its owner: Don Álvaro Núñez de Lara, the husband of Doña Urraca and the son-in-law of the lord of Biscay.

"But what are you doing here?"

"I could ask you the same," Diego answered with a broad smile. He had always liked that man.

"A long story, I assure you. But before I tell it, come with me. When you see my wife, she will be overjoyed. How long has it been since we've heard from you? Two years?"

"Three. I spent them in the monastery in Fitero."

Don Álvaro, perplexed, studied his clothes.

"You don't look like you've adopted the habit. . . ."

"No, no. Nothing could be further from the truth. I was just there for the sake of my education."

On the way to one of the corners of the square, Don Álvaro surprised him by looking several times in a certain direction.

"Are you here with someone?"

"Yes, I'm traveling with a close friend. I have to tell him. Let me know where I can find you and I will come back with him."

After encountering Marcos and telling him what had happened, they headed for the house Don Álvaro had told him about. They were waiting for him there, Álvaro and his wife, Doña Urraca.

The woman ran to Diego and gave him a kiss on the cheek.

"How you've changed!" she exclaimed.

Since Toledo, Diego had grown strong, and he was taller and more attractive. She was as beautiful as he remembered, or maybe even more so.

Diego introduced them to Marcos, and naturally he clung to Doña Urraca's side from the first moment.

"Let's go into the inn," the woman said, pointing into the house. "Are you hungry?"

While they waited to be served, the woman asked Diego in a soft voice whether he'd heard what happened to Galib.

"I don't know what you're referring to. Nothing bad happened to him, did it?" Diego awaited her answer anxiously. He tried to guess from her eyes what it could be about. Was she talking about the turbulent events he had been a part of in the stables? Or was she going to upbraid him for his disloyalty to his master?

"I'm sorry, but I don't know what you're talking about."

Doña Urraca saw he was nervous.

"Shortly after you disappeared, he rejected Benazir."

Diego felt terrible. He had surely been the cause of that disgrace. He regretted it, especially for Galib, whom he loved like a father.

"I didn't know."

"Wagging tongues said you had something to do with it."

Diego turned red. He tried to talk, but he couldn't find the right words. She knew why. She had had a long conversation with Benazir, who confessed everything to her.

"Don't worry. I know you acted nobly and faithfully. She told me."

Diego felt relieved.

"And Benazir . . . is she still in Toledo?"

"No, she went back to Seville. I think she's living with her father, the Persian ambassador."

Diego clenched his fists with rage. In the end, his departure from Galib had been for nothing. If it had been to save Benazir's honor, not only had he failed to do so, but their marriage had actually fallen apart.

His face reflected his deep sorrow.

Don Álvaro purposely changed the conversation.

"If you've been living in a Cistercian monastery so long devoted to prayer and study, which by the way I find very praiseworthy, I wonder what your next destination could be. . . ."

"Santa María de Albarracín," Marcos answered for him. "A woman lives there who's got him up in arms."

The couple looked at each other with expressions of surprise.

"We're going there as well. If you remember, my father-in-law made his second marriage with an Azagra. A name closely tied to our lands—"

"And who is she?" Doña Urraca interrupted her husband to find out from Marcos's lips, full of curiosity. She needed to know what woman could prove so attractive to Diego as to make him chase after her.

"Mencía," he answered, playing along completely.

"You're not referring to Mencía Fernández de Azagra?" Doña Urraca's gaze clouded. If it was her, a relationship with Diego, a commoner, would be as difficult as snowfall in a desert.

"The very same," Diego said.

Doña Urraca turned to her husband with a frustrated glance.

"My wife and Mencía are cousins," Don Álvaro added.

A strange silence overcame the table until the noble Lara resumed speaking, giving a rapid summary of what had happened in their lives during those years, leaving the reference to the girl to the side.

"A little after that feast, I was named ensign to Alfonso VIII, substituting for my father-in-law. But that did not last long. We spent a number of months on the siege of Vitoria, taking advantage of the king of Navarre's absence while he was away in Moorish lands."

Diego indicated that he was aware of the matter.

"But the tensions between the king of Castile and my father-in-law began to be unbearable. In the siege of Vitoria, the king made use of men and resources from Biscay without ever asking my father-in-law's permission. He was furious when he found out, but even more when, months later, he heard that the king, who had always been his proud friend, had taken the side of the Leonese monarch in a claim that the Haro family had against the latter concerning a number of castles."

"I thought they were like brothers," Diego interrupted.

"Certainly, but it changed into hate, so much so that my father-in-law has asked no longer to be a Castilian subject."

"I don't know what that means."

"He's renounced all the privileges, holdings, income, and even his ability to reside in the kingdom. That upset the king so much that we had to leave Toledo as fast as possible. We found our first refuge in Estella, thanks to the Navarrese king, but a few months back we were attacked by troops joined under the banner of Castile and León. The two monarchs, formerly irreconcilable enemies, now brought their forces together to capture Don Diego López de Haro. We holed up in the impregnable castle that they call Zalatambor in the beautiful town of Estella, and there we were able to hold out.

"Tired of making no progress, they finally abandoned the endeavor. But shortly afterward, King Sancho of Navarre expelled us from his lands under pressure from Alfonso VIII. And now, Castile has become a hell for us; the kingdom of Aragon has closed its doors and doesn't want to have us either. That's why we're going to Albarracín. Since it's independent from the other kingdoms, we won't have problems there. And anyway, it's governed by family."

Diego was feeling more attracted by politics, although he didn't always understand it well, and it even seemed like something distant from him. He admired the king of Castile for his firm commitment against the Almohads' fanaticism, for his willingness to protect the lower classes, and for his establishment of a code of law. He admired his intention to unify the different territories of Hispania to defy the Saracen enemy in spite of the difficulties that arose, such as the one he had just heard of with that estimable family.

While he listened to Don Álvaro, Diego looked at him. That man was one of the highest representatives of the nobility of Castile and as such he enjoyed abundant riches and power; however, Diego didn't envy him for what he had, but rather for how he was. Don Álvaro possessed a virtue he wanted for himself: bravery.

Diego understood that without that ingredient, he would never manage to fulfill his obligations or reach the high goals he had set in life. Did he have that virtue? He didn't know.

It was now long ago that he'd disobeyed his father and failed to protect his sisters. . . . And he didn't know how to do it now.

Life went on, time passed, but Diego always lived with the burden of a debt that he owed those who shared his own blood.

II.

To arrive at Santa María de Albarracín, they climbed the Sierra de Balbanera at its easternmost point and then went on southward until they set foot in the first lands of the region. It took them four days.

Diego and Marcos had been invited to travel with the Castilian expedition. It was the thirtieth of May when they set eyes on the magical enclave of the city. High on a twisting rock cliff, it looked like a long tongue licking the riverbanks of the Guadalaviar.

Behind double walls, at one edge, there rose a small church situated a certain distance from the main part of the city. Between them, there was a solid fortress of limestone with a strange reddish cast, in common with the other buildings. Closing the city in and protecting it completely, the walls ascended notably toward the east, along a mountain pass.

A few leagues before arriving at his destination, Diego was overcome by a swell of feelings that affected his stomach as well. Though he longed to see Mencía, he wasn't sure if she would feel the same. Full of emotion, he had held on to the note inviting him to visit her in Albarracín, wanting to see more in it than what its three spare phrases had contained.

Almost at the city gates, Don Diego López de Haro began to converse with his son-in-law Álvaro Núñez de Lara, both close to Marcos and Diego de Malagón.

"As soon as we go in, I will present you to my sister-in-law, Doña Teresa Ibáñez. Since she is the mother and guardian of the young lord of Albarracín, she has become the apparent head of the territory. She is a Castilian to be on guard against, you will see."

"There are lots of us. Will they be able to take us all in?"

"I sent an emissary shortly after leaving Estella and I am almost certain that they will have lodging prepared for all of us, but the first thing is to say our greetings to her."

"How old is the young lord?"

"Only eleven. Until he reaches the age of majority, the territory will be governed by the Order of Santiago."

The north gate of the walls was open, but only a few knights passed through it, and the rest of the carts and the heavy cavalry for war and transport were taken to an esplanade on the outskirts of the town.

The streets of Albarracín were precipitous, sinuous, and narrow, so much so that the travelers were relieved to have left the better part of their companions behind. Some paths were so tight that it was almost impossible for two people to travel side by side.

After a few shortcuts, leaving a busy square behind them, they reached a clear esplanade. To their right, on a great outcropping of stone, they contemplated the grand castle of the Azagras. Under an enormous barred portico they saw the proprietors.

Don Diego López de Haro, together with some of his most loyal knights, dismounted quickly and saluted the widow and her young son, Pedro. Beside them, there was a knight of the military Order of Santiago and two unruly young girls. Some distance away, Marcos and Diego looked at the scene and couldn't find Mencía anywhere.

"Welcome all to Albarracín." Doña Teresa greeted Don Diego and embraced her sister-in-law, Doña Toda. Then she pushed her son by the shoulders to introduce him.

"This must be . . ." Don Diego studied the boy.

"Pedro Fernández de Azagra, third lord of Albarracín and your nephew," the boy answered with a childish but unwavering voice.

At that moment, the two girls escaped running toward the castle's interior, laughing and shrieking, far from any social obligation. When she saw them, the mother adopted a face of utter desperation.

"And those two ragamuffins are Belén and Beatriz, your nieces." She realized she still hadn't introduced Ordoño de Santa Cruz, the man dressed in the uniform of the Order of Santiago. "Forgive me, I forgot to present our administrator to you."

The Castilians saluted stiffly.

"And my niece Mencía?" Doña Toda was surprised by her absence.

"Mencía is in Ayerbe, in Upper Aragon. An important nobleman from that kingdom, Don Fabián Pardo, has been courting her for months and at last has managed to meet her." She winked and continued in a low voice. "I wouldn't mind if this ended up in marriage, but we will see where it goes."

"Is that man not the justice to King Pedro II?" Don Álvaro recognized the name, but at that moment he was thinking of Diego and his impossible mission.

"You are right," Doña Teresa answered. "That is why I am interested in seeing their relationship flower, because his influence in that court is incomparable. But let's go inside; I suppose you'll want to rest a bit before dinner. My servants will take care of your horses and the lodgings for the rest of your men in the city. If you are planning to stay in these lands awhile, the best thing is that you all be as comfortable as possible. I am happy to have you here, really, and don't worry, everything is taken care of."

Diego and Marcos were considered as members of the expedition and therefore assigned a dwelling. It was rather far from the center, in terrible conditions, and completely filthy inside, but at least it had a stable and incomparable views of Santa María de Albarracín.

While they inspected it, Marcos felt disgusted, so much so that he felt in the bag where he had kept the money he saved in Fitero.

"This isn't a house. . . . Let's look for another place where we can breathe." He took out a handful of golden *maravedíes*.

"Let's not waste them. We might need them later. I understand this is pretty bad, but others might have had even worse luck. Try to look at it in a good light; when it's cleaned, it will be better."

They gave it a close looking over to see what the most urgent problems were, and that only made matters worse. The walls were crumbling and the clay floor reeked of dampness and rot. And if that wasn't enough, the house was pervaded by a stench so strong it almost turned their stomachs.

"It smells like a goat!" Marcos protested.

Diego tried to dismiss its importance. The possibility of seeing Mencía compensated for any of those setbacks. Marcos, who knew him well, guessed at what Diego was thinking, but he was still angry. Tired of talking, he kicked a stone against the wall. An enormous chunk flaked off onto the ground and broke into a thousand pieces. Diego had a resigned expression.

They piled up a bit of straw in one of the better-situated corners of the house to spend the first night. They didn't imagine that their harsh bed, besides allowing them a bit of rest, would also bring them unwanted company: dozens of fleas, thirsty for blood.

As soon as dawn came, Diego went into the city to look for Mencía. As soon as he'd crossed the eastern side, he found a large smithy with three forges and five men bending iron. It reminded him of Galib's forge in Toledo. That was where he first asked after her, but no one knew where she was.

He did the same in some of the more central streets, stopping at once place after another.

"She's a good girl," an old woman told him.

He managed to gather a number of other testimonies, like that of the pastor who swore he didn't know of another woman as beautiful as Mencía, or of the fat old woman who assured him she was as sweet as honey pie. But the majority, before they said anything, directed him to the castle, saying he should ask there. En route he stopped a priest to ask him.

"She's not in the city."

"Do you know where she went, or if she'll be back soon?"

"How should I know, if all I dedicate my life to is prayer and contemplation, my son?"

Depressed by the lack of results, Diego continued walking to the town square where he found a market. He bumped into a beaming young woman carrying a large basket, and with her he had more luck, since she was a servant of the Azagras.

"We don't know when she'll be back, but it will be at least a week." The girl asked a hawker if he had pheasants.

"But where did she go?" Diego pressed her.

"Do you know her? I don't have to tell you. Who are you to be asking after her? Did you come with those Castilians?"

Diego replied to all her questions while he followed her from one stand to the other. The girl began to feel uncomfortable with his insistence and even more so when she turned her back on him to look at some lace and then bumped into him again.

"Could you leave me in peace?"

"Please, I beg you . . . I need to know more about her." Diego grabbed her by her blouse so she wouldn't escape, and she tried indignantly to pull away.

"Let me go."

"Until you tell me what I want to know, I won't."

The girl's cheeks swelled, she looked at him with exasperation, and she shouted out for a guard. After a brief silence, people began to murmur and point at him, and some men, with an unfriendly mien, approached him. Before he got into more problems, he took a street onto the main road and got away from them.

Marcos began to look for work throughout the city, not wanting to wait another day, but he had no luck. Without a trade, nobody had much trust in him, and there didn't seem to be an excess of jobs in any case. He convinced Diego to try to work as an albéitar, not knowing it was necessary to have the approval of the Azagras before doing so. When he heard this, Diego looked for Don Álvaro Núñez de Lara to ask for his help, but luck wasn't on his side there, either. They told him Don Álvaro had left the city and no one knew when he was coming back.

"The widow wants to talk to you. Go immediately to the castle!" The man introduced himself as a servant of Doña Teresa. As soon as he'd obtained Diego's agreement, he left as fast as he'd come.

Diego went to the meeting immediately, alone, not knowing what Mencía's mother could want. He crossed the city on foot until he arrived at the entrance to the fortress, and there he presented himself to the guard. He was told to wait outside while his presence was announced. Both of them were surprised when Doña Teresa herself appeared in person to receive him.

"You are the albéitar Diego de Malagón, correct?" The woman, in her forties, looked splendid. "Last night they spoke very well of you to me. That is why I've had you come. I'd like you to look at something."

"As you wish, my lady." Diego was brief, but not from discourtesy; rather, he had discovered Mencía's eyes in her mother's and felt intimidated by them.

Doña Teresa had him follow her to the stables of the castle with a strange expression, as if something worried her. Don Álvaro had talked to her a great deal of Diego, but he had left out something important: his great physical attractiveness. She had thought she'd meet a rough and ordinary young man, as was normal with the commoners, and yet in him she'd seen nothing but a fine appearance and great courtesy.

"A little more than a month ago, our albéitar left us, a Jew with an excellent clinical eye and a great deal of wisdom. He was called by the Almohad governor of Valencia, supposedly for a mere consultation, but he never came back." The woman pushed the stable doors firmly and walked softly down a long passage that opened onto a large and very luminous space. Once there, she continued her conversation. "And the fact of the matter is, it would mean a great deal to us to have a new albéitar to service the city."

"If you are thinking of me, it would obviously be an honor. . . ."

At a certain point in their conversation, Doña Teresa fell quiet, her lips trembled slightly, and then she stood still, watching him. Those eyes . . . "Perhaps . . . Well, the reality is, at present I have a grave problem. . . . Or, better said, I don't have it, my mare does. If you were able to bring her back her joyousness, the job could be yours. What do you think?" A malicious glimmer blossomed in her eyes.

"I would be happy to, but to make a horse happy is not one of the things explained in books. I suppose the animal is suffering from some illness that is making it sad. With that, if I can, I will help you."

"Of course, of course. . . . If she's in pain, it must be her back. It's been swollen with scabs on it for a week. Obviously I can't ride her. But what's hardest for me is seeing her sad, without appetite, without any cheer."

Diego began to think. That was a trivial complaint. If the only test to be taken on as an albéitar was that, she was making it too easy for him. Something wasn't right.

The mare was a precious specimen with a dapple-gray coat and a long mane, and dark and very expressive eyes. But that wasn't what stood out the most; she also had an iron nerve. She shook her tail so hard she made it whistle. Diego knew that was a sign of great irritation.

When he came over to the animal, it snorted threateningly. He put out both his hands for her to smell, but unlike other horses, the mare showed no interest. To the contrary, she reared up aggressively as soon as he approached.

Doña Teresa stayed leaning against a fence waiting for Furia to buck and react. That was her most aggressive and dangerous mare, and everyone feared her. She didn't want to lose her.

Furia was the excuse she used to test anyone who wished to work for her, be it an albéitar or a stable master.

"Do you know if she kicks easy?"

Diego pulled away from the animal seven or eight feet so that she could see him directly in front of her. He had figured out that at close distances, horses didn't focus well unless they turned their heads.

"Well . . . she's a little nervous, but nothing serious," Doña Teresa lied.

The mare didn't react to any of his tricks and soon began to stamp with her hoof, digging at the ground with a frustrated expression. Diego decided to attack without further delay, whispering to her; he pinched her back and then her flanks, avoiding, naturally, the wounded area. He did the same with the base of her tail as well.

That seemed to distract the animal and confused Diego, who didn't predict her next reaction. Furia waited until he was behind her rump to press him into the wall with extraordinary speed and skill.

Diego tensed his muscles to resist the pressure she was applying to him and inhaled a mouthful of air to strengthen his chest. He looked at Doña Teresa, holding his breath, but not concealing his expression of panic. She seemed unmoved by the situation and continued speaking calmly.

"She's a little sly. . . . One time, she managed to stomp on the former albéitar with such good aim that she almost flattened one of his toes. But she's very sharp. When she sees that her victim can't play along with her games, she leaves it aside and tries something else."

Diego gave off a feeble cry, almost inaudible. He begged for the mare to get bored as soon as possible so he could breathe again. And he got lucky.

The animal became interested in a sparrow that had just landed on the watering trough, an apparition Diego considered almost miraculous, and she set him free. He ran to the fence, where Doña Teresa, a malicious smile on her face, waited to see what he would do next. The determination he showed from that moment on would decide whether he was fit for the job. Now the real test began.

"Are you all right?"

Diego's cheeks were so red, they seemed ready to burst. "Yeah, yeah, I'm perfect."

He breathed in deep three times, recovered his strength, and turned to Furia again. That showed he wasn't easy to beat. To the contrary, Diego was the type to grow stronger in the face of adversity. Without his knowing it, that gesture alone had made him pass the test. It was just what Doña Teresa had wanted to see.

Diego explored the scabs on the horse's back. They were obviously caused by sweating and chafing from a saddle that was too tight. Some were open and gave off a terrible-smelling yellow bile. Diego took a lancet out of his bag and cut the dry edges of skin. He knew that wouldn't hurt her. Then he lifted some of the scabs to see how they had evolved.

Doña Teresa, surprised by his able hands, let him work without distracting him, observing each of his movements, and said only one single thing: "From now on, the job is yours."

That produced enormous satisfaction for Diego. In the end, it would be the first opportunity he had to engage in his profession without having to depend on the opinion or the final decision of some master. He felt a shiver of satisfaction and noticed how from that moment, the tension between them dissipated.

"I met your daughter Mencía."

"Ah, yes?"

"In Olite. Three months back, during a joust."

"Now that you say that, I believe I heard something about you."

"Did she tell you?"

"I don't remember."

"She helped me to save a horse that had been wounded in the neck."

"I didn't know."

"Then I was attacked with a dagger and she was by my side."

"Yes. Terrible, I understand. . . ." She answered distractedly. "Do you need anything from me? I have to go to an important meeting now."

Diego turned back to the mare.

"For her cure, I'll need vinegar, fish, sap, sulfur, and a bit of oil. Oh, and an apron!"

"I will be sure they bring you everything." She made as if to leave.

Diego then remembered he wanted to ask her when her daughter would return, but Doña Teresa didn't give him the opportunity.

"I will order them to clean and prepare the albéitar's abode. It's not far from here, and I believe you'll like it. It has an open stable where you can house the horses you need to treat or supervise. The house has its own staff, which will be at your service from this moment forward."

Just before she disappeared, she made a half turn.

"Oh . . . I will pay you a hundred sueldos a week. If you agree, I will announce your nomination tomorrow."

III.

Mencía returned filled with fear.

She entered Santa María de Albarracín with a discreet escort of knights, a couple of servants, and her three ladies-in-waiting.

By her express wishes, she had traveled on horseback in opposition to the desires of her suitor, Fabián Pardo, who had set aside a carriage and an entourage for her protection. So fiercely had she wanted to leave that castle that she didn't want to wait for their arrival from another one of his terrains. In spite of that, the six long days on horseback had left her feeling defeated.

She admitted that Fabián had been charming with her, and that, though he was approaching middle age, he was rather well preserved. His relation to the Royal House of Aragon had gotten him a high social position and abundant lands and fortunes. And he had other virtues besides: he was talented with the spinet, and he liked painting, falconry, and especially reading.

Mencía returned from that voyage with a bitter aftertaste from a maelstrom of contradictory emotions. Since she was a girl, she had always hated others to organize her life. And for that reason alone, she had rejected the man out of hand. Yet she had to recognize that Fabián had done much to redeem himself, and he was skilled in the arts of seduction. He was so dogged that he had managed to provoke a certain interest in her.

Mencía was sure that any other women in her circumstances would have fallen victim to his enchantments. But not her. When she saw him, she knew she would never marry him.

Her arrival at Santa María was highly celebrated. The church bells sounded out gleefully, attracting the attention of all the inhabitants of the town.

"What could all that racket be about?" Diego and Marcos were having lunch in the new house.

"Today is the third of June, but I don't remember there being any celebrations that day." Diego looked out a window from the third floor. "People are saluting and hurrahing for a small retinue, but I can't see who it is."

He sat back down at the table, and before he returned to his steaming plate of green beans he looked at Marcos. His expression was both strange and familiar.

"For a few days now, I've seen you turning something over in your mind . . . and knowing you, it's something to do with women, money, or both. Am I wrong?"

Marcos smiled sincerely.

"Either I'm an open book or you are very smart." He served himself a bit of wine, gave some to Diego, and drank it in one swallow.

"It's not women. I just need to do something," Marcos said honestly. "I've asked around, to one person after the next, where I can find work, and except for three salt mines on the outskirts and what comes from the small shopkeepers and so on, the main business in the city is wool. Well, that and the sale of sheep to neighboring Aragon. You remember we saw lots of flocks just before we got to the city, but it seems there are many more to the southeast, heading toward Valencia."

"Sheepherder wouldn't be a bad job for you, since it would give you time to go chasing after the shepherdesses in the fields." Diego weighed the possibilities of this idea.

"That's the furthest thing from my mind. No, it's not that." Marcos became serious. "But the thing is, I also found out that on the other side of the border, in the kingdom of Valencia, the Saracens adore sheep meat, the way we like mutton or even suckling lamb."

He stood up and began to walk around the table.

"And think about it; they come all the way to Santa María de Albarracín to buy wool . . ."

"I understand. It's occurred to you that they could take the sheep as well," Diego deduced.

"Exactly."

"But I see one problem. I doubt the pastors will sell them. Normally, they let them go only when they are sick or too old."

"You're right, but what if we take those, the oldest ones? Imagine if we could corral them for a few weeks and feed them barley, which is a grain that grows abundant in this area." Marcos leaned both hands on the table.

"I understand. If they're nice and fat, even if they're old, the Saracens will want them and will pay a good price."

"That's the idea. We buy them cheap from the shepherds, we fatten them up in a pen, and then we sell them for double the price."

"It's not a bad idea, but if you don't have a good contact with the Saracens, I doubt it will work."

"His name is Abu Mizrain."

"Are you pulling my leg?" Diego shook his head several times, awestruck. "We've been here for just a week and you've already got one?"

"He's a trader who lives in the south of Valencia and comes to Albarracín every two weeks to buy wool. He did it yesterday, and it was then I managed to talk to him a bit. Though a lot of people have the same business, he has an advantage over the rest of them."

"Have you met the other traders?"

"No, but I've heard things. . . ."

"Don't be so shy and spit it out."

"The rest travel alone."

"And what's the disadvantage in that?"

"Abu Mizrain always goes with his daughter." Marcos sighed, doe-eyed. "She's gorgeous . . . and I think she likes me."

"Now I understand." Diego slapped him on the back of the neck. "And you've got a place to feed them, I suppose."

"Not yet, but I'll try to find one this morning. Will you accompany me?"

A few streets away, at the gates to the castle, Doña Teresa Ibáñez received her daughter Mencía, anxious for news. She scrutinized her face, looking for the least sign of contentment. As usual, Mencía was unreadable.

As soon as she kissed her, unable to take anymore, Doña Teresa asked her openly.

"Mother, don't be a bother. Leave me in peace. Now all I'm dreaming of is a long bath and taking off these dirty clothes." Mencía shook her dress and a cloud of dust emerged. "I'm tired; I'll tell you everything afterward."

"But did you like him? Is he handsome?" Doña Teresa grabbed her arm while they entered the castle and went up to the bedchambers. "I understand he's highly thought of in the court of King Pedro II, and that he's very rich as well . . ." Her questions and comments went on without giving the girl a chance to answer. "What did you think of his castle? I'm sure he treated you like a queen. What color did you say his eyes were? Have you set a wedding date? I suppose King Pedro of Aragon will be coming to the ceremony—"

"Mother!" Mencía had to scream to stop her.

"Fine. . . . Just think that you've been gone for three weeks and that I missed you a lot," she protested. "I've been so worried. You left in such a huff that I was terribly nervous." Her eyes went damp and tears began to fall. "You don't know how a mother suffers when her daughter becomes a woman, when she flies off in search of another life, in your case, with this man."

"That's enough! Stop pestering me with the same issue."

"But how do you expect me to leave you alone when you haven't given me the slightest indication of what your feelings are?"

Mencía sighed, tired, defeated by her insistence. She was standing at the door to the bathroom.

"Listen. Fine. If you want to know what I think, I'll tell you now. I don't think he's the man for me. That's how I see it right now, though I admit I disliked him less than I had thought."

With that dry phrase, she closed the door in her mother's face, but it didn't matter much to Doña Teresa. An enormous smile crossed her face. That was celestial music compared to what she had expected to hear.

Before she got lost down a long hall, she heard the bathroom door open. She looked back and saw Mencía peeping out.

"I have just seen a bunch of knights I don't know. Who are they?"

"Your aunt Toda is here with her new husband, Don Diego López de Haro. You know the problems he had with King Alfonso of Castile. Since he was exiled, the poor man goes from place to place. They just arrived from Estella and I told them they could stay here as long as they wish."

"You're always so kind, Mother."

Mencía turned and closed the door and called one of her ladies-in-waiting to prepare her bath and then help her to undress.

Once she was nude, she stayed still in front of the mirror, waiting for the hot water to come. She studied her reflection. She checked the tension of her skin, her round forms, their whiteness. The face of Fabián Pardo assailed her suddenly, provoking an unexpected shiver. She didn't want that man, nor did she imagine him as the final recipient of her passion.

She heard the tub filled with water and approached it. She put a foot inside and then submerged herself completely. When she came out, she gave off a long, relaxing sigh.

All she had to do was convince her mother to accept her way of seeing things.

"It's going to be hard," she said out loud.

"Do you need anything, ma'am?"

"Nothing, Berta, nothing."

IV.

Diego knew Mencía had arrived in Albarracín, but after two days he still hadn't managed to see her.

He started work very early, since it was at the beginning of the day that his clients became alarmed when they went for their horses and mules to go out into the fields. Any infirmity or illness would make them nervous, and they would come to his house to let him know.

Mencía came out of the castle early as well, to hear Mass, but she hardly walked more than a few yards and never where the fieldworkers lived, so they never saw each other. The rest of the morning she passed inside the fortress with her music, painting, and poetry instructors, and in the afternoons she would travel around the outskirts of the city on horseback.

Nor had Diego seen Marcos those days, because he had left Albarracín to look for sheep that he could fatten up in the pen he had already managed to find: a good-size one, two leagues southeast of the city.

In his absence, Diego couldn't share his loneliness with anyone, as much as he regretted it, especially when he found out the reason Mencía had been in the Aragonese lands. From that moment, everything went downhill. The dream of imagining her in his arms vanished with the same speed as the sharp pain that took possession of his soul.

The day after he found out, desperate, he showed up at the gates of the castle deciding to ask for her directly, tired of not having managed to speak with her yet.

While he waited, he listened without trying to a conversation between two friars, and what he heard made him change plans.

"At midday, the archbishop will bless the work on the future cathedral," one commented. "Are you coming?"

"Who could fail to show up for an event like that?" the other answered. "I'm sure the city will break out in celebration."

Diego thought that Mencía would go to that ceremony and decided to see her then. Back on Sabba, he headed to the southern extreme of the city, to the church of Santa María. There the chaplain's mule was waiting for him, apparently with its guts infested with worms. Diego calculated that however long the cure would take, he would still have time to make it to the blessing.

Only a few hours later, the narrow streets of the city were filled with people. A contagious cheer seemed to impregnate the steep hills, covered with hundreds of boys and girls rampaging about.

With great difficulty, Diego crossed though them until he made it to the town square. He observed once more, enthusiastic, its extraordinary houses. Raised on the same rock, their walls of red plaster were crossed by hard beams of black wood. Also notable were the shapes on their windows and the colorful panels of the window shutters.

Diego left the square behind and stopped at the end of another hilly street where the cathedral was being raised.

For the moment, the construction was no higher than a few men, though every day it could be seen growing. To one side, a wood platform decorated with tapestries, a carving of Christ, and four enormous candles awaited the archbishop's arrival, as well as the other authorities in the city.

Amid pushes and shoves, Diego reached one side of the esplanade and chose the place closest to where the retinue would pass. From there he could observe all the preparations.

"I didn't imagine I'd see the new albéitar of Albarracín here."

Diego recognized the voice of Don Álvaro Núñez de Lara.

"Well, you know . . . I enjoy these religious affairs."

"I don't know whether to believe you or consider other motivations."

"You wouldn't be wrong. I'm actually here to see Mencía."

Don Álvaro didn't know if Diego knew of her relationship with the Aragonese noble, but either way, he decided to tell him.

"I'm sorry to have to give you bad news—"

"Don't bother," Diego cut him off. "I know why she went to Ayerbe."

"Then I suppose you've forgotten about her."

"No. Not yet."

"But, Diego . . ." Don Álvaro grabbed the young man's arm compassionately. "What are you trying to accomplish? Most likely she's forgotten about you."

"I just want to talk, and look into her eyes. I need to know if I mean something in her life or not."

Don Álvaro felt sad, and though he thought Diego would have to face reality on his own, he wanted to do something for him. For Diego to pledge himself to win Mencía's love was absurd—Don Álvaro knew it; that is why he had to forget anything that had to do with her. But at that moment, he had other things that he couldn't put off.

"I'd like to talk to you about it more calmly," Don Álvaro said. Diego found his interest odd. "Every morning I do a little bit of training, you know, a bit of archery, a little swordplay. Why don't you come tomorrow and we'll chat?"

"I'd love to. . . . I've never seen it done, and maybe I could learn a little from you."

"There's no problem on my end. How about first thing in the morning at the river?"

"I'll be there." Diego shook Don Álvaro's hand.

"Good. I have to go, I need to get my sword before the procession begins."

Until the celebration started, Diego distracted himself watching the public that was nearby. Two toothless country people stood beside him, their faces wrinkly as raisins, uglier than anyone he'd ever seen, and they wouldn't stop laughing. No one knew why, but they did it so happily that it ended up spreading to the people around them. And thus, choking from laughter and sucking in breaths, he saw her arrive.

Her face was hidden beneath a blue veil and she walked holding her mother's arm, in a procession behind the young lord of Albarracín.

Diego shouted Mencía's name, but his voice was drowned out by the crowd. He tried waving his hands to attract her attention, but that did nothing either. Only sixty feet stood between him and the place of the ceremony and he tried to make his way in that direction. People stopped him; some protested, others pushed him from side to side, but still, he managed to get a good position, different from the one he had in mind but close to the road where the retinue had passed and would do so again. And there he stayed, behind a wooden fence, in the front row, somewhat farther from the stage but with good visibility.

"How pretty Doña Mencía is!" said an old woman at his side.

He looked at her entranced. She really was gorgeous, so much so that conquering her heart seemed unthinkable. She had two blond braids and a dress of blue velvet, the same color as her eyes; and she looked happy as well.

The archbishop, together with his deacons and assorted other monks, came at last to the stage and immediately the ceremony began. The celebrant intoned a chant in Latin and afterward a litany of prayers that Diego couldn't hear well. His attention was directed solely to the face of his lady, to her eyes.

He tried to make her notice him when she turned to the public, but sadly she only seemed to pay attention to the celebrant. And yet, even though a good deal of time had to pass, finally it happened. When she turned, from among the multitude, she saw him, first surprised, then smiling when she was able to return his greeting.

She turned to her mother, signaling his presence. Diego saw Doña Teresa answer into her daughter's ear. She seemed to be upbraiding her for getting distracted. Mencía only looked at him once more, but she did it with a beaming smile on her lips. Afterward, she took on a devout posture, lowered her head, and continued, attentive to the ceremony.

Diego waited anxiously for the affair to be finished. He carried the note that Mencía had left for him in Olite in his pocket. On it, Diego had written his address so she could find him. He would try to hand it to her when she passed by him.

When the blessing was over, the archbishop intoned the "*Te Deum*" and like a single voice, all present followed him with solemn emotion. Then they left the platform and began to file down the street where Diego was.

Mencía changed her position in the retinue to pass closer to him. They went slowly, too slowly for his patience. She didn't stop looking at him, gleeful. Doña Teresa, walking beside her, did the same.

"Diego! I thought you'd never come," said Mencía.

"How could I reject that invitation?"

Diego was conscious of the little time they had. He stretched to kiss her hand and passed her the paper. She took it and read it quickly. Then she hid it between her sash and her dress.

"I'll come see you."

Diego heard that and almost exploded with excitement. When the streets emptied out, he returned to his dwelling to get Sabba and take a long ride outside the city walls.

They galloped against the wind, in the solitude of those outlands. Diego talked the whole time. He told her what had happened with Mencía and the animal listened.

He needed to share his happiness.

He filled his lungs with fresh air and breathed happily. Sabba did the same.

Diego loved Mencía.

V.

E arly in the morning, it was always cold in Santa María de Albarracín, even in July. Due to its particular situation between the mountains and its altitude, this was only natural.

On the shores of the Guadalaviar River, Diego managed to hold back a sneeze while he waited for the arrival of Don Álvaro Núñez de Lara.

Soon he heard the steps of a horse approaching him.

"Cold tempers your soul, right?"

Don Álvaro dismounted in one leap and shook Diego's hand energetically.

"I saw you talking with Mencía yesterday . . ."

"I hardly had time, but I think she was happy to see me."

"When it comes to a woman, never trust your instinct. It doesn't work, I promise you."

"I suppose you're right."

"Believe me, I am, and especially in your case."

Diego, astonished, asked him why he would say that.

"What I'm going to tell you will sound harsh, but the sooner you understand it, the better for you. Don't dream of her anymore, Diego. She's far, far outside your possibilities. I have never seen a relationship between a commoner and a noble that has worked. Society won't permit it; the cultural differences between you won't either, and I don't even want to think of how her mother will react."

"Do you think I haven't already thought about this before?" Diego hung his head, conscious of the reality. "But still . . . I don't know, I have to hear it from her; I'm sure of her feelings."

Diego showed a stubborn attitude, resistant to all reasoning. Don Álvaro understood that nothing would make him change his mind, only Mencía. He unsheathed his sword and swung it energetically, making it whistle. He decided to change topics.

"During a fight, the defense is more important than the attack. Do you want to know how to fight with a shield?"

"Isn't it more effective to know how to use a sword?"

"No. In combat, you have to know how to be clever on your guard to later be fierce on the offensive. Many times, the effectiveness of your strikes depends on how well you've been able to withstand the ones that have come your way."

Don Álvaro took off his shield and passed it to Diego. It was triangular in shape, rather long, and its edges were rounded. On the surface were painted the arms of the Laras: two cauldrons.

"A good shield is made of wood and then covered with thick and hard leather, able to resist swords and make the steel bounce off. It is carried attached to the neck by a cord, which is called a guige. That way we don't lose it in combat and it doesn't bother us when we need both hands, as is the case in a cavalry attack."

Diego tied it on with another, shorter strap called an enarme and held it close to his body, covering almost his entire flank, from the shoulder to the knee.

"The iron piece you see in the center is called the boss. As you can see, it ends in a point and it's very sharp. When you fight man-to-man, it can help you wound your enemy."

Don Álvaro turned to his horse, took out a sword, and grabbed a morning star in the other hand.

"And my sword?"

"You won't need it," he said curtly. "Now we'll go on to the action. I guess that's what you want, right?"

"What do I have to do?" Diego stood on guard without losing sight of the morning star—an enormous ball with sharp spikes.

In that moment, without giving him time to react, Don Álvaro's sword fell over one of his shoulders. Instinct alone made Diego block with the shield repeatedly, but when he least realized it, the steel grazed his leg.

"Always be on alert, young man. The shield resists a certain type of arms, but not others. Be more careful with the morning star; avoid it however you can. Ah! And you should learn to use your enemy's own movements to destabilize him."

Don Álvaro walked around Diego, the sword in his right hand and the morning star in his left, looking for the young albéitar's weak points, making him turn and follow his steps. The heavy steel ball swung with the cadence of his movements. Diego thought it could end up stuck in his flesh if he wasn't careful. He never stopped looking at it. He held the shield close, pretending it formed part of his body. He believed he could move it at the same speed as his hand.

Don Álvaro approached to his right. That was Diego's least protected flank, and without expecting it, he was surprised by an incredible shout, three blows from the sword in succession, and one from the morning star that he managed to sidestep.

"When you fight against someone holding one of these"—Don Álvaro raised the spiked ball—"you should concentrate on it at all costs and try to avoid it. Try to get him to lose it, by pointing your sword at his hand, for example, or giving him a hard blow with the base of it. Maybe that way he'll drop it, because if you're not careful . . ." With a rapid movement he struck the shield with the morning star, splitting it in two pieces. Diego fell to the ground. "You'll be in serious trouble."

Don Álvaro's sword was raised in the air, just above Diego's neck.

"I'm begging for mercy . . ."

"Today, naturally, you have it, Diego, but never trust anyone. Don't let your enemy bring a sword across your jugular, as I could have done just now. Before that happens, look for his leg, for example—it'll be close—and stick him there with your dagger. In the inner thigh, there is a vein, and if you reach it, he'll die instantly."

Diego stood up, trusting Don Álvaro wouldn't attack him again, but immediately the sword began to strike at him mercilessly, ten, twenty times—it could have even been forty—a rain of steel and fury that the boy tried to withstand until he felt defeated. Now incapable of even holding up what remained of the shield, he was overcome by an unstoppable quivering in his arm when his enemy's sword gave him a definitive strike. As a consequence, Diego wound up stretched out on the ground and defeated.

Don Álvaro looked at him, sweating and panting, his teeth clenched, still grasping his sword. Without words, he pressed him not to give up yet, to go on defending himself until the end. . . .

Diego understood. With the splintered shield, almost breathless and still on the ground, his thoughts turned to the past. He remembered the two Calatravan knights who had pledged their life in his father's defense. In the eyes of Don Álvaro, he recognized that same spirit; he emanated the same strength as them, the kind belonging to a single, exceptional breed of men. Then Diego stood up, pressed on by an unknown force. He tensed the muscles in his legs and chest, breathed deep, and shouted as he never had before. He threw himself at Don Álvaro waving what was left of his shield, and since the latter had no time to foresee the blow or to attack with the morning star, he received a tremendous strike that managed to knock him over. When he fell, he hit his head on a stone, but he came after Diego again with zeal. He was expecting the second movement, but there wasn't enough time. Don Álvaro immediately saw the boss of the shield and its sharp point just above his eyes.

"Surrender!" Diego sighed in triumph.

"I congratulate you. . . ." Núñez de Lara pushed the steel away with his hand. "You learn fast, Diego. Maybe you should put on a bit of muscle, especially in the arms. Try to pick up that stone." He pointed to a large, round boulder. "Do it over and over till you think you're going to die. And repeat that every day with others, at least three times a day."

"I want to be brave."

"Bravery." Don Álvaro cleaned the earth from his tunic. "I suppose you're thinking about your sisters again, no?"

"My soul burns for not going to help them when I could have." Diego lowered his head, entrusting the ensign with his painful secret. "I can't forget it."

"You were only fourteen. How were you going to face a group of men alone, especially those savage Imesebelen? Don't torture yourself anymore. . . ." Don Álvaro clapped Diego on the back gently. "For now, work on your body, strengthen it, and then grow inside, that's what's really important. To do it, you'll have to fight your lower instincts; from now on, think of them as your worst enemies. Fight so that laziness doesn't beat you and battle against comfort. If you manage it, you will feel more capable, more skillful, and you'll see how that bravery you wish for will grow inside you." He breathed in and took a dry branch to draw with it in the sand. "In ancient Greece, it was said that bravery was a virtue only given to the gods. But I think we can all have it, you too. . . ."

That afternoon, Diego found Marcos in the kitchen after he had settled on a first shipment of sheep to his partner, Abu Mizrain. He was counting his earnings on the table.

"Today, he's taken the first twenty and they'd hardly been feeding for two days. For next week, I have thirty more ready." Marcos had decided to invest what he made in buying more livestock.

"Looks like you've got an eye for business. . . ."

They heard someone calling at the door.

Diego sent one of his servants to open it. It could be a message for him.

To his surprise, the servant returned in the company of a mysterious woman with a covered face.

"Who are you?"

"I have a message for you." She turned to Diego.

"Give it to me, then." He imagined something urgent.

"My mistress, Doña Mencía Fernández de Azagra awaits you tomorrow in the church of San Juan before the first Mass. She insists that you be discreet."

"Why so many precautions?"

"Best if you ask her. She will wait for you at the confessionals."

"Thank you very much. To whom do I owe the favor?"

"Forget me. Believe me, it's better that way."

Diego arrived at the church a good deal before Mass, so much so that he found the doors locked. He waited around until they were opened, and when he could, he entered, wrapped in a dark cloak.

When he found the confessionals, he walked toward them and hid behind a thick column to wait for her. From there he could see the door.

The darkness protected him.

A number of people began filing in, but not a trace of Mencía. At one moment he heard steps coming close. He hid better and held his breath, wishing for it to be her. Someone passed by, a priest.

He looked again at the door.

People kept coming in, until finally he saw her. Though she was wearing a veil, he recognized her by her blond hair and her way of walking. She was in the company of two ladies. She wet her fingers in a font of holy water and crossed herself. With a certain slyness she glanced around the interior of the temple and found him. She spoke with one of her ladies and turned to where Diego was with a decisive step.

"Hi," she whispered in greeting.

After making sure no one saw them, she found an empty confessional and pointed it out. Diego understood the message and went in without losing time. On one side of it, a small door gave access to the penitents. Mencía closed it quickly, caught her breath, and knelt in front of the wood grille that separated her from Diego.

"Here we'll be able to talk more peacefully."

"Why do we have to do it in secret?"

"It's my mother. She hasn't let me have dealings with any man since I returned from Ayerbe."

"I heard you were engaged to a nobleman from Aragon."

"That's what they say."

"It's not true then?"

"I am not."

Diego breathed a sigh of relief.

"Lift your veil, I beg you. Let me enjoy your beauty for a moment."

Mencía smiled, flattered.

When she took it off, her beautiful blue eyes appeared. Diego saw them. They were cloudy.

"How lovely you are!"

He surprised himself. It had always been hard for him to express his feelings about women, but with Mencía it was different.

"You'll make me blush if you carry on telling me these things."

"I have to admit the only reason I came to these lands was to see you."

Mencía was quiet, and Diego regretted having been so direct. He saw how her breast moved nervously and heard her sigh. She seemed to be thinking.

"I'm sorry. Perhaps I was too frank. . . ."

"You said what you felt. In that, you're luckier than I am."

"I don't understand."

"You can't always have what you want."

"Sadly, what you say is true."

"I still remember you in Olite, when you were with that horse. Your hands were the lords of its life and death. In that moment, you seemed like a god to me, and I admired you deeply. . . . And then, that bastard hurt you. I was by your side when it happened, and I thought he'd killed you. It was then that I felt something very strange for the first time."

"What do you mean?"

The door of the confessional opened abruptly. Mencía was frightened and looked to see who it was. It was one of her attendants.

"Your mother's coming. You should be seated on a bench, with one of us. . . ."

"Thank you, Braulia."

"Are you going?"

"Every afternoon, before night falls, I go out to walk my horse around the riverbed of the Tuerto. If you can today, look for me."

"I'll be there."

VI.

Sabba trotted along, infected by Diego's joy.

Again he spoke into her ear, as he used to do some time back. Those soft sounds caressed her and sounded glorious. She turned her head to her master and observed him.

As on every afternoon since two weeks ago, she took him to the riverbed to meet with Mencía. The two talked and talked. They recounted their lives, their dreams, all their memories, day after day. The relationship grew and became more vital, more secret; it seemed there was no turning back.

Halfway there, Diego and Sabba descended down a dangerous path that made them focus their attention. When they left it, the sky started to fill with dense, dark storm clouds and a damp wind picked up. As soon as she felt the first effects of it, Sabba reacted unexpectedly. Without knowing why, she pulled off at an explosive gallop, leaping like a young colt in springtime.

"But what's going on?" Diego laughed at the mad reaction of his mare, grabbed the reins, and tightened his knees over her ribs to avoid falling off. She had been more nervous than usual all day, and he supposed it was because she was in heat. She responded with three sharp neighs, as if trying to explain herself, in her own way, after hearing his question.

"You know what I'm saying to you, right?" He scratched her neck and Sabba snorted. "Mencía told me about an abandoned hermitage without letting me know where it was. But it must be around here. . . ." He caressed the mare's face. "Sniff the air. . . . You have to be able to make out the scent of its stones, or the moss that must be growing in its shadows, or if not, the noise of the woodworms inside it. Find her, and take me to her, Sabba!"

The mare dilated her nostrils to the maximum and breathed in a large mouthful of air. Then she turned around a number of times and pricked up her ears. Diego waited attentively, without talking, and let himself be taken north, first at a walk and then a trot, convinced that she knew where she was going.

In the depths of a narrow gorge, damp because of the nearby stream and the walnut grove, they found a construction of rough stone, in bad condition.

When they reached it, on the southern side, they heard a whinny. At that moment, thunder broke loudly over their heads. The sky went from being overcast to blackish in color, and just afterward, the first drops began to fall, heavy and loud. They had to find a place to take shelter fast. Once they walked around the structure, they saw Mencía's horse tied to an old oak.

"Mencía?"

Diego raised up from the saddle and scanned the surroundings without seeing her. Then he dismounted and left Sabba beside the other animal. In spite of the strong rain, that tree was leafy and its branches formed a natural roof.

Diego went up a stony path to the hermitage and looked inside. At that moment, a powerful lightning bolt light up the sky, followed by a quaking thunder.

He called her again but still didn't get an answer. As soon as he entered, he decided to walk to the apse, where there was a bit more light because of three small embrasures.

"Hello, Diego." He heard the soft voice of Mencía at his back. He turned.

"Mencía . . ." He felt trapped by her eyes.

A new thunderbolt rang out with fortitude. The rain began to spatter on the roof so hard, for a moment they feared it would cave in. In just a breath's time they counted more than a dozen places where rivers of water were draining in.

"That chapel looks dry." Diego pointed to his right.

Though they were in summer, the temperature had dropped so much that Mencía felt a sudden shiver. On her way through the hermitage she had tried to avoid the puddles and leaks but her dress had still gotten soaked. Diego embraced her and felt her shivering. That spontaneous reaction kept them together almost without breathing, living that moment with great emotion.

The water beat the walls of the hermitage and the thunder mounted with growing intensity. Between one and the other, they heard Sabba neighing.

"I'm going for them. . . . I feel bad for them."

Diego went out of the temple and untied the horses as fast as he could amid their discomfited whinnying. He managed to get them to the hermitage and convince them to go up to the narrow entrance. Sabba sniffed inside, decided to enter, and immediately sought out a dry corner. The other horse followed her. It seemed calmer.

From the first time they'd met, Mencía felt happy with Diego, though her attraction for him had grown in later encounters. She thought him a fine man, well mannered, someone it was easy to talk to. She was curious about his life, how he had come to practice his profession, what he liked. Mencía wanted to know everything about him. She wasn't very reserved; she wanted to open herself to him as well.

They talked about everything, but about themselves most of all. Mencía confessed her love of music and poetry to him and tried to transmit her passion to him by reciting some of her favorite verses.

Unafraid of anyone, and without calculating about their relationship, Mencía showed him her rich personality, her way with words. Little by little they began to feel the same need to see each other, to want it all the time. They shared the same shortness of breath when they thought about each other, and both of them got goose bumps when they touched. They didn't need much time to understand that what they felt was nothing other than the effects of love.

When Mencía saw Diego appear in the chapel, wet to the bone and his hair in disarray, she looked at him with desire. He brought his lips close to hers and pressed them down, surprised by their suppleness, that taste of heaven, of glory. He couldn't believe it—he loved her. Mencía embraced him and pulled him to her breast; she needed to feel protected.

Diego explored her with more kisses. He looked for her dimples, her cheekbones, then her lips again. She responded quivering, discovering the taste of love.

"I feel like there's something truly great between us," she whispered into his ear.

A violent flash came through the windows and crossed the entire nave. It was followed by an extended, brusque noise, like thousands of stones skipping down a hill.

"I love you." Diego caressed her check and she looked for his other hand. "I don't think I'd even know how to breathe if something happened to you. . . . When I found out you were getting engaged, I thought I would die."

Mencía offered him a passionate kiss, more adoring than ever, but wet with tears. She asked him to hold her tight, and she engraved in her memory all that she was experiencing. She nestled in his arms. She felt small with him, weak, frightened. She was afraid of her mother's reaction when she found out what she really felt. She was nervous about the future.

She felt a caress on her cheeks, the softness of Diego's lips on hers, then on her chin, on her neck. Those sensations finally resolved her thoughts.

"I know what I'm going to do. I will write to him. I don't want that man to go on thinking I'll accept his proposal."

When the afternoon passed into night, and the darkness enveloped everything, Mencía said they should go back to the city. They peeked out of the hermitage and saw that it was still raining. They also confirmed that the water had soaked everything.

"I'm scared. Let's go before it gets worse."

"Wait inside. . . ." Diego responded. "I'll go study the terrain and see how it is."

Mencía stayed in the doorway. She saw him walk away until he vanished from her sight. After a moment, she tried to look for him again through that thick sheet of water, but realized it was an impossible task in such darkness. She let a bit more time pass before she got worried, but when she saw he wasn't coming back, she became afraid. She thought of her mother; she would be hysterical. Surely she had organized a search party.

While she thought of all her problems, Diego was looking for a way to get out of that flooded streambed.

On all sides there were branches and tree trunks torn up by the roots and tangled together from the effects of the violent inundation. He walked a good while under a sheet of rain. He saw huge stones roll and walls of earth slide away whole. Alarmed by the terrible sight, he turned back to the hermitage, deciding they must spend the night there.

When Mencía saw him arrive, she hugged him and rubbed his body vigorously so that his temperature would rise. She took off his tunic and wrung it out so it would dry. Then she ran her warm hands over his chest, his back, his legs, stimulating warmth on his skin.

"There's no way to escape the streambed. I've looked at all the possibilities, and believe me, it's impossible, it would be too dangerous. We'll spend the night here."

"I have to go back. My mother will kill me."

"She'll understand."

"You don't know her. When she knows what's happened, I don't know what she'll do, especially if she hears it's been for you."

"Our first night together . . ."

Diego kissed her on the mouth with passion. She did the same, but she was a bit upset. Diego noticed.

"Don't be afraid."

"Hold me tight."

Diego squeezed Mencía and together they huddled in that corner. Love floated between them, rose with the steam that was coming off their clothes. Mencía hugged him, trying to make him a part of herself, holding him forever.

Amid kisses and caresses, sweet words and whispers, they finally fell asleep, very close to each other.

The first rays of light penetrated through the windows and with them, the announcement of the storm's end. Mencía awoke in a rush. In that overwhelming clarity, a cloud of anguish floated through her soul. The arrival of a new day meant awakening to the harsh reality: facing her mother and mailing that letter to Fabián Pardo.

During the night, she had lived far from those obligations, dedicated only to dreaming with and enjoying her beloved.

When Diego woke up, he found her on the threshold of the door. He went to her back and embraced her from behind, kissing her neck sweetly. He breathed in with pleasure and a strong scent of wet earth reached him, but at the same time, he felt nervous for Mencía.

"Are you thinking of Fabián?"

"Yes, and I feel terrible. . . ."

She exploded into painful sobs. Her relationship with the Aragonese had been almost sealed, and to break it could provoke a territorial conflict. With that matrimony, her mother was trying to soften the king of Aragon's aspirations for the territory of Albarracín. Besides that, Diego's position as a commoner was no help. Her mother would never accept him, nor would the others who were close to her. Mencía was conscious of the consequences that love would have in her life. It would mean she would have to flee, begin a new life elsewhere, maybe with another name.

"I've built up too many expectations." Mencía dried her tears with a handkerchief, not daring to look at his face.

"I don't know if I understand what . . ."

"No, you don't understand anything." She grabbed him by the shoulders. "I'm looking for a solution that probably doesn't exist. . . . But I know I love you, only you. I want you for me, forever, and yet there's him."

"He's noble, rich, and powerful, everything your mother wants for you, but imagine for a moment what your life would be like at the side of someone you don't love. Think about it, it's your only life! Would you waste it being unhappy? I wouldn't. I know there's a lot I don't have, that my blood is humble and my sole inheritance is a mare and a destroyed family. I admit I'm the son of a poor vassal, a simple innkeeper, but I have something more valuable than all the properties that nobleman from Aragon possesses: your heart."

Mencía responded to his words by kissing his lips passionately.

"I don't know what to do to solve this problem."

"Don't let anyone strip from you the most important thing in your life: your freedom. Be yourself. Stand up without fear. Tell them both. Let happen what has to happen. . . . I'll be by your side."

"Don't ever leave me alone, I beg you."

"I won't. Never."

An hour later, Mencía and Diego entered the church of Santa María de Albarracín. Before reaching the castle's esplanade, they split to avoid being seen together. But Doña Teresa had spotted them from the tower, before they even entered the city.

Mother and daughter met at the gate to the fortress.

When Mencía saw how bloodshot her mother's were, she imagined how long and hard her night had been. Doña Teresa didn't wait until they were inside, but began immediately to assail her with questions.

"Are you really fine?" She inspected her arms and legs, looking for a scratch, a wound, some bruise.

"Yes, Mother. Nothing happened."

"Tell me what you've done, where you spent the night. Where, in that infernal storm?"

"In the hermitage of Santa Clara."

"Unless I'm wrong, that's not on your normal route. What was there, then?"

"Nothing, Mother."

"I sent half the city to look for you. I thought you were wounded, alone, that you'd disappeared. It was horrible. There was a time when I thought you were dead."

Doña Teresa felt relieved to see Mencía healthy and unharmed, but she needed answers, and especially wanted to know why her daughter had been with the albéitar.

"Nothing happened."

"I prayed to God for someone to find you last night and be able to help you. You didn't see anyone?"

"No, I was alone the whole time," she lied.

"Are you sure?"

Mencía held her breath, full of doubts. That insistence could only mean her mother knew something. . . . Just in case, she decided to tell the truth.

"Well . . . the truth is . . . I was with the albéitar Diego."

Doña Teresa's eyes opened wide.

"What?"

"Yesterday I saw him on the path, when it was beginning to rain. But don't be afraid; he acted like a gentleman the whole time. He simply stayed with me so I wouldn't be afraid during the storm. It was lucky he found me."

Mencía preferred not to explain to her what Diego really meant to her. She knew her mother well; she would have to space out the bad news.

"I don't like how you've hidden that from me until now. Was it really by chance? You don't have anything else to tell me?"

"I have nothing else to say."

"Are you sure, dear?"

"Of course, Mother. Certain."

Once she was alone in her room, Mencía wrote the letter. She took care not to wound Fabián's honor, but she made it clear that, from that moment, their relationship was broken off.

But that missive never arrived at its destination.

Doña Teresa Ibáñez was able to intercept it thanks to the help of one of her daughter's ladies-in-waiting who was on her side. Instead, Fabián received another message, written by Doña Teresa herself in her daughter's stead. In it, she made him believe her love had grown stronger and that she was urgent to seal their relations. She ended the note with an invitation to meet in Santa María de Albarracín. And to deceive him further, she put a note beneath Mencía's name that read, "Your future wife."

The same lady-in-waiting also told Doña Teresa where her daughter went every afternoon when she walked her horse and who she had been seeing for the last month.

The woman was greatly alarmed. She was well acquainted with the power of the heart and the difficulty of stopping its inclinations in time. For a moment, she imagined them madly in love, and the idea seemed so catastrophic to her that she decided to intervene. She wouldn't allow it, not with her daughter. She had decided that Mencía would have to marry, and certainly not a commoner.

She began to think. There had to be something that would separate them. She didn't know whether to speak about it with her daughter, but then she became convinced that in those circumstances, a prohibition would work against her.

After two days, all Doña Teresa's unhappiness and distress was transformed into hope. Chance and an occurrence at the border suggested an excellent solution. She saw it so clearly that now nothing would stop her.

On a hot sixth of August, the governor of neighboring Valencia, Abu Zayd, sent an urgent letter to the young lord of Albarracín.

That same afternoon, Doña Teresa gathered all the grandees and knights in the city, among them her brother-in-law, Don Álvaro López de Haro.

She told them that the king was looking for military aid to repel an unexpected attack from Pedro II of Aragon in the region of Rubielos de Mora, situated between the Aragonese border and Albarracín. It was a strategic commercial route for the economic development of the three areas.

Albarracín's position was very difficult. It was important to maintain good relations with the Valencian, whose friendship yielded enormous commercial advantages, but Aragon should be kept happy as well, in order to check its shameless desire to annex territories.

"An attack under your flag would not be good for you at all," Don Ordoño noted.

The knight of Santiago and territorial administrator observed Doña Teresa shyly. Rather than the territory itself, he was more worried about the political repercussions for his order if he were forced to fight against other Christian soldiers.

"Better then for us to go with your men, the Knights of Santiago . . ." Doña Teresa looked at him sternly, putting the burden back on him.

"Can you imagine what the pope's response will be?" Don Ordoño gestured in horror.

"This territory was a concession of the Moorish king of Murcia," Doña Teresa spoke again, now in a firm tone. "And the Azagras, with the blessing of the Navarrese crown, has governed it since. For its frontier position with Al-Andalus, it has long been a target of the ambitions of Aragon and Castile. Navarre has clamored for us as well, for if they expanded south, this would be their only border with the Moors."

Doña Teresa knew that it would be difficult to respond to the problem without compromising the future of her lineage. She looked at everyone, disappointed. None of those present seemed to offer any solution. Almost all of them looked down.

"I will go!" Don Diego López de Haro rose and slammed a fist down on the table.

"I as well!" Don Álvaro de Lara followed suit, and then Don Sancho Fernández, his nephew and candidate to the crown of León.

"We can leave when you wish. We are ready," Don Diego reaffirmed, proud of the reaction of his men. "Think it over well, Teresa. Our people will never compromise you. Both the Castilians and the Aragonese would justify our warring spirits after the siege we suffered in Estella and the subsequent refusal of asylum on the part of the king of Aragon. If we come out victorious, you will win the gratitude and the favors of the governor Abu Zayd. And if we don't, he will still consider himself well rewarded. In my case, whatever the result of our intervention, it will have been an honor to have tried to repay your great favor of sheltering us in this city as you have done."

"What do the rest of you think?" Doña Teresa looked at the faces of the collaborators. "Do it then. With this, I consider the matter to be closed. You may leave."

Those congregated there left the armory, each taking leave of their hostess. When Don Diego began to walk out, she asked him to remain a moment. Once they were alone, she had him sit and offered him a mug of wine.

"You have been very generous." She approached him from behind and kissed him tenderly on the cheek. The man found that gesture strange.

"It is the least we can do for you, Teresa. . . ."

"That's not true. You can also satisfy me another way as well," she finished, brusque and mysterious.

"I don't know if you mean . . ."

Don Diego remembered the mad and impassioned encounter they'd had years before. Something they had never talked of since. A fleeting adventure that never had further consequences. He saw her in his arms again, and she, guessing his thoughts, arranged her bodice coquettishly so that her gorgeous bust was pushed further into view.

"It could be . . . Why not . . ." she answered. She pulled out the pins holding up her hair and let her hair fall over her shoulders.

"I suppose you've held me back today for other reasons. What else can I do for you?"

She put her ideas in order and then set to explaining them.

"What I am going to ask of you is urgent, almost indispensable." She tasted the wine and dried her lips with a cloth. "I need you to take the albéitar Diego de Malagón with you."

Her brother-in-law remained silent to see what else the favor consisted of.

"And that is all?"

"See, it's easy!"

"May I ask what reasons have moved you to make me this second request?"

Teresa turned nervously in her seat. She wasn't sure if she should be more explicit.

"I believe I've heard Don Álvaro say the boy is expert in Arabic. He could be very useful in your discussions with Abu Zayd." She knew that argument wouldn't be enough to satisfy her brother-in-law's curiosity, but at least it would win her a bit more time.

"I know you too well, Teresa. Your eyes give you away; you're not telling me everything."

She sighed three times, feeling defeated.

"Do you promise to keep the secret?"

"You have my word." Don Diego López de Haro began to imagine something.

"It's about your niece Mencía. From who knows what whim of fate, it seems she's fallen in love with that Diego de Malagón, something that I neither can nor should allow." Her cheeks reddened from pure rage. "I've decided to break off their relation by putting many leagues of distance between them. If I separate them, his love may cease to grow while that of the person who really will benefit Mencía, Fabián Pardo, will increase. He will protect her welfare, give her an insuperable position and a fitting dowry. I suppose you agree with me. Am I right?"

Don Diego weighed the situation before answering. He couldn't accept that a commoner would try to win the love of a woman of standing either, even less when it came to his niece. The daughters of the nobility had always married men of illustrious background, and that was a sacred tradition that, naturally, he was bound to defend.

"Count on it, Teresa." His sister-in-law smiled, thankful. "Tomorrow we will head east. I will do what I can to erase him from the life and heart of your daughter. Hopefully I manage to do so. . . ."

Teresa's breast swelled, excited at hearing his words. Even then, she didn't want to leave the possibility of a loose end.

"There is only one more thing I need. Don't tell anyone about this, not even your son-in-law Don Álvaro. I understand they have a good relationship."

"I will keep the secret."

She repaid his favor with a sweet kiss on the lips. To both of them, it tasted of forbidden fruit.

VII.

D iego could not even say good-bye to Mencía, because he received his orders shortly before midnight. The note that called him to action was urgent and came to him in the hands of a page of Don López de Haro.

"Forgive the hour, but I bring orders to depart directly from my master."

"Tell them to me, I will listen."

"You should be present tomorrow in his residence before six in the morning to leave immediately on a journey."

"Where? Do you know why?"

"I don't well know, but I believe it is an urgent military expedition."

"War?"

"Forgive me sir, but I don't know anything else. I must leave."

The boy ran to continue his mission and Diego closed the door, worried. Why did they want him if he wasn't a knight and had never fought in war? It didn't seem logical, unless it was for his skills as an albéitar, to attend to the horses if they were wounded.

He looked for Marcos to tell him what had happened but he wasn't home. Diego imagined he was with the daughter of Abu Mizrain, remembering that the latter had been around Albarracín.

Before he went to bed, he packed a bag with some clothes and a case with all his instruments. He also wrote two notes, one for Marcos, and one for Marcos to deliver to Mencía. In both he explained what he was to do, and to Mencía, he pledged his love.

He could hardly sleep. He couldn't understand what was waiting for him and he was tortured by the idea of leaving his beloved for an indefinite time. He got up before the hour, nervous, readied Sabba's saddle, and tried to make her eat some hay before they left.

The sun still hadn't risen when he arrived on the esplanade beside the palace where López de Haro and his people were residing. A hundred knights with their pages and squires were waiting there in silence.

As Diego arrived, the bells in the church of San Juan broke the silence, tolling six times.

They saw Don Diego López de Haro appear punctually, flanked by two men: Don Álvaro Núñez de Lara and his nephew, the prince of León, Don Sancho Fernández. Doña Teresa was there as well, to take leave of them.

They received the blessing from the archbishop of the city, said good-bye to the few people gathered there, and began their march, leaving behind the walls of the city, heading east.

Mencía awoke worried. When she looked for her mother in the castle, they told her she had gone out to say good-bye to her brother-in-law, who was leaving the city. That struck her as strange. No one had told her. She dressed quickly and left the castle to go to the square where the expedition was supposed to depart.

On the way she crossed the path of her mother, but she wouldn't answer her questions clearly and Doña Teresa's irritated face indicated that she was hiding something important.

Mencía sped up until she came to the square, but she didn't see anyone. Puzzled, she looked for Diego's house.

"The gentleman left a while ago," his servant responded, still half asleep.

"But do you know where?"

"He told me he was leaving with the troops of Don Diego López de Haro and that he wouldn't be returning for days or weeks."

Mencía sped over the steep streets of the city to the northern gate, where she imagined they would be leaving from. She needed to see Diego. She didn't understand why he hadn't told her anything, or what reason he had not to tell her good-bye. She lifted the skirts of her dress to go faster and dodged the still-fresh piles of horse manure on the trail, but she didn't meet the riders.

When she crossed the gate in the city walls, she looked east and saw a large contingent of horsemen a half league in the distance. They were too far to hear her, but she cried Diego's name several times as loud as she could.

"Why did you leave me . . ." She knelt, disconsolate, in a shower of tears. "My love . . . My Diego . . ."

At least a league outside the city, Don Álvaro turned back to find Diego. He saw him looking behind them. He had heard a rending cry from the city, but he didn't know where it came from or what it meant.

"I'm happy you're coming with us, Diego. You're going to be a great help."

"I thank you, but I regret that I still don't know why I've been called. I've heard we're going to aid the governor of Valencia, Abu Zayd, and I don't understand why I've been asked . . ."

One of Álvaro's pages reached them with an urgent expression.

"The lord of Biscay requires your presence."

Álvaro looked ahead and saw his father-in-law. He signaled to him and explained, before he left Diego: "You will be the interpreter for the Arab governor."

Between the towns of Mora de Rubielos and Rubielos de Mora, two days away from Albarracín, there was more happening than just the coincidence of their names: it was also the place of a long dispute between the kingdoms of Aragon and Valencia. The first city had been conquered five years back by the Aragonese, and now Pedro II was trying to make off with the second.

Only a half-day's travel separated the two cities, though there were some narrow mountains. When Don Diego's troops reached their sullen contours, they knew they were close to the armies of Pedro II and the governor Abu Zayd.

The troops entered the Saracen camp on the southern side and were greeted with great enthusiasm and fanfare. Diego felt immediately affected. Those Saracen garments, the turbans, the curved swords—everything reminded him of the dramatic moment he had lived through in his father's house.

Without dismounting from Sabba, he was called by Don Diego to accompany him to the governor's tent. Both were impressed by its beauty when they saw it. It was grand, of blue silk, with designs embroidered in gold thread and soft and undulating profiles. Two black panthers protected its entrance along with two brown-skinned soldiers. When they passed by, the fierce beasts growled, showing their ferocious fangs.

"Salaam aleikum!" The voice came from a small man seated on an endless pile of cushions.

"Aleikum as-salaam!" Diego answered.

Abu Zayd greeted them, raising a hand to his turban. He showed them where to sit and had a servant come with a beverage, which he called *sharbat*.

Diego began to translate his first few words.

"I thank you for your assistance and your urgency, which is required, as the king of Aragon is seven leagues away."

"Tell him that everything is thanks to the generosity of Doña Teresa Inbáñez and her son the young lord of Albarracín." Don Diego took a long drink of the refreshing beverage, surprised by the presence of ice inside it, particularly given the heat that month. He asked Diego to inquire as to how they made it.

"He says that in wintertime they bring ice from the mountains of Granada and keep it in deep pits that they bore into the rocks. In this way, it lasts throughout the summer. And as far as its composition, it is an equal blend of orange, lemon, and pomegranate."

"Delicious and refreshing." Don Diego licked his lips.

After those introductory courtesies, Diego began to translate the tactic they had in mind to detain the advance of the Aragonese. Abu Zayd, dark faced but with smooth features, almost Castilian looking, had plans brought over where they could study the distribution and location of the various troops.

"He wants to show you"—Diego turned to the lord of Biscay—"that he has three hundred men on horseback and a thousand infantrymen. He proposes that his horsemen attack from the flanks and rear, while yours face off in a closed formation directly from the front."

Diego listened to the governor again. He pointed to a specific place on the map he assigned enormous importance.

"He's pointing out a streambed just three leagues from here. He says it is the ideal place to defeat them if you can drag the troops from Aragon this far. The north face is high and steep, as are the east and west. Once they're there, they can't escape."

"And how does he propose that we corner them there?"

Diego translated the question.

"He thinks you will figure out how."

"Great. So he's leaving me the easy part." His expression tensed. "Don't translate that please."

"He's asking what you're thinking."

Don Diego paused for a moment. He looked at the map over and over while Abu Zayd waited anxiously for some response.

"There it is! We'll set up tents inside with fires and horses, making it seem like we've camped out there. We'll also set up blankets, branches, and bundles to look like men. From their position, they won't see well and when they notice how hard that position is to defend, they'll strike. . . . The most important thing is to make everything look real, but I believe it will work."

After listening to Diego's translation, Abu Zayd looked satisfied.

"He agrees with this idea and would like to know when the deception will begin."

"Tell him immediately."

"He thanks you again for your help and encourages you to rest awhile to recuperate from the long voyage."

When they were getting up to leave the tent, Don Diego was struck by one last question that he had forgotten to ask.

"How many enemies does he think are with King Pedro?"

"Five hundred cavalry and two thousand infantry, he says."

"It's a lot . . . a lot, by God. . . . Too many."

They took leave of the governor with lowered spirits after hearing what the dimensions of the enemy's army were. They left the governor's tent and went to their own, where they could rest.

"Congratulations, Diego. You've been a good translator." Though the boy was there for other reasons, Don Diego had to admit that he was skilled.

"It was an honor to be able to serve you."

"Have you ever been in war before?" Don Diego asked.

"Never, my lord. I am the son of a modest commoner and I have never taken up arms."

"War is a part of our lives. I don't remember five years going by when I haven't fought in one."

"Pardon if my comment seems inopportune, but it seems incredible to me that you see it as something normal."

"I never will. . . ." He stopped short and looked to the horizon. "How could I, if it's in war that you discover the very worst things about the human condition: hatred, vengeance, avarice, cruelty. In wars, all the mortal sins are combined, but it is true that the highest virtues are present as well. You would be surprised to see people as common as yourself, from the lowest groups, fighting with a valor worthy of heroes. In the heat of battle, generosity, disinterest, and bravery above all spring forth."

The last of these—bravery—pierced Diego's heart. He thought that maybe if he participated in this war, he could cultivate that virtue. For a moment, he was tempted to ask, but when he thought of Mencía, he was afraid of never seeing her again.

A few hours later, the false camp had been set up. Two of Abu Zayd's men, who knew the terrain perfectly, hid close by to watch every movement the enemy made.

Diego used the tense wait to look over the contingents of troops, surprised by their remarkable differences. The Christians were equipped with heavy armor, maces, and swords and rode enormous, powerful, and fearsome horses. But the Valencians rode light coursers, wore thin cuirasses of leather, and colorful, cool clothes, and their animals were smaller and full of energy.

At dawn, they knew that the Aragonese had fallen into the trap. Abu Zayd's soldiers had seen them take the road to the streambed and they returned to the camp at top speed to inform them.

Shortly afterward, they began their march.

The central corps of the expedition was formed by Don Diego and a hundred horsemen. On the flanks, more disordered, were the troops of Abu Zayd.

After two leagues, they reached a broad, barren plain where they stopped. From there they could see the streambed. When they saw the enemy plunge into that hollow, they would attack.

Diego and Álvaro conversed at a distance from the rest of the corps. Neither of them was armed, and they would not participate in the battle.

Don Álvaro would take charge of the ordering of the troops and maintaining the attack plan they had agreed on beforehand. From where he stood, on an elevation, he could scrutinize the scene of combat, predicting any of the enemies' movements.

Diego, at his side, had taken over translating all the changes and new directives that would be issued.

"Doesn't it seem terrible to you, the idea of fighting other Christians?" Diego breathed in an aromatic scent of rosemary.

"We're knights," he responded brusquely.

"So are the Aragonese."

Don Álvaro remembered one of the first laws of chivalry.

"The knight should be loyal in all his pledges." He gave a long sigh on finishing. "That is one of our commandments. That virtue is the mother of all good customs that a man should possess if he wishes to form part of the order of chivalry. Loyalty is what is owed to one's master. Necessary in these moments, however cruel the combat may be, and even more today, when our enemies may be, as you rightly say, our brothers."

With the echo of his words, Diego heard a stern chorus of whinnying. Hundreds of horses, upset, began to smell the intensity, waiting for the orders of their riders. They were loyal to their masters too, and ready to face the unknown, perhaps to receive a lance in their breast or a fatal arrow in the neck, but always obedient. Diego's stomach sank when he thought that something like that could happen to Sabba.

"A knight lives loyally, heroically, for three reasons, Diego." Don Álvaro counted them on his fingers. "The first, because he understands he has been chosen to watch over and defend others. The second, to preserve the honor of his own bloodline, protecting his good name and the memory of his ancestors as well as his descendants. And last, to avoid shame, which is what would come to us were we to falter in the duties we have contracted toward our master."

Diego thought on it with all his good faith, but it remained incomprehensible. No pact of loyalty could require another person's death. He never would understand it.

He stroked Sabba; he could see she was nervous. She seemed to have been affected by the general agitation of all present, men and animals, during the anxious wait. He spoke to her softly, whispering sounds that he knew would calm her down, while Don Álvaro observed him.

When the mare shook her head three times, snorting and grunting three more, Diego imitated her. It seemed as if they shared their own language, different from all others.

Once more Don Álvaro felt admiration for Diego. The boy possessed a brilliant mind, he was responsible and discreet, also humble, but above any other consideration, what most impressed him was the peculiar rapport he had with the horses.

"Horse and horseman," Don Álvaro added, "a beautiful relationship, even more so in wartime. Do you know how you measure a horse's ability for war?"

"I do not."

"The Greeks recommended that the warhorse have three qualities: good color, a big heart, and powerful legs to respond properly to the hard labor. I would add one more: that they have good lineage, like their masters." He stroked his horse, sorrel with a lovely profile and tall stature.

"And in the relation you just mentioned, what does the horseman need to give the horse?"

"A lot. He must reinforce its generous character. He must correct its bad habits, and protect it from illnesses, which, naturally, he has to know."

"According to what you've said, there is a color that will make a horse into a dignified companion to its master. Are there other colors that make them poor ones?"

Don Álvaro was going to answer when a long trumpet blast sounded out. All looked at Abu Zayd and Don Diego López de Haro, awaiting the signal.

The white banner of the governor rose up amid the cavalry and flapped frantically. When they saw it, a few horsemen galloped quickly toward the streambed, followed by the rest of the cavalry of the lord of Biscay. The main part of the Valencian army hung back in reserve. Don Álvaro looked for the highest point on the hill to be able to see the battle lines in their entirety.

Diego went to his side and watched, impressed by the first clash with the Aragonese troops. First the swords sounded, then hundreds of arrows whistled, fired from bows and crossbows. The first men fell to the ground while the horses trotted furiously; some fallen men asked for help, others walked on as if doomed, missing an arm, bearing horrible wounds. He saw one with a mace stuck in his back, trying to extract it without success. Diego gave thanks to God for saving him from that slaughter.

The Castilians, sheltered by the advantage of surprise, had descended down the only usable slope. The first line of them had attacked the Aragonese and the second was on the point of doing so. Each row consisted of twenty-five men on horseback and three reinforcements. Behind them, the infantrymen followed.

At one moment in the struggle, the Aragonese believed they had managed to stop the attacks by breaking their order and surrounding them.

"They just committed a fatal error," Don Álvaro thought out loud while he observed the movements of the various groups.

He looked for the standard bearers of Abu Zayd's troops and found them waving their banner up and down excitedly. That signal called forth another three hundred furious horsemen, bearing down, toward the thick of the Aragonese troops. Suddenly they saw themselves trapped between two forces: on the inside, the Castilians, now greater in number, and on the outside, the Saracens, who were attacking them without mercy.

From there the blood began to stain the steel, the bodies, everything. . . . It even reached the manes of the horses, and the earth welcomed innumerable broken and dead bodies onto its surface.

Don Álvaro pointed to one side of the struggle, where King Pedro II was fighting.

"Watch what happens now. . . ."

They saw Don Diego de Haro come close to the position where the Aragonese king stood. Luck had changed quickly, and the life of the king was in serious danger. Don Álvaro was sure of what his father-in-law would do.

"You're going to be witness to a remarkable rescue. Watch. . . ."

They saw the lord of Biscay with a dozen knights take on the Valencian troops. Once beside the king, they dismounted and began to fight hand to hand at his side, protecting him with their lives. Abu Zayd's warriors, stunned, fought back with greater fury. One touched Don Diego with his weapon but was then pierced by the sword of the king of Aragon.

"Now! Now or never!" Don Álvaro exclaimed.

And then they saw the king mount a horse, along with two other knights, among them his ensign García Romeu, Diego's old acquaintance. Two Castilians opened an escape route, and they all fled at top speed.

"Imagine the anger of Abu Zayd . . ." Diego commented.

"A knight who takes pride in himself would never permit a king to die at the hands of an infidel. That is what we call loyalty. Today, Pedro II of Aragon has been defeated, but who knows whether tomorrow he might not be fighting at our side."

The battle over, Diego and Don Álvaro met back with Don Diego López de Haro. He was wounded, but his face reflected the joy of victory, the satisfaction of a duty well performed.

When he saw him, Diego felt deep pain. While he watched the rescue, he had been thinking of his own situation. He was already an albéitar and was gaining a good reputation, and to that extent, he had obeyed his father's command. But he still wasn't truly at peace. His sisters were still present in his conscience.

He squeezed the neck of his mare and stroked her forehead, and in a low voice, he shared what he felt just then.

"One day I promised it, and you were the only one there. I will free them, however I can, together we will do it. . . ."

VIII.

Estela was disgusted with her life, with her destiny.

Every night, for months now, she would go to the caliph's chambers to sleep in his bed. She hated him.

He would look at her, smell her perfume, feel her close to him in the cool sheets, but he never touched her.

Al-Nasir was utterly in love, lost in her, and wounded by her indifference.

"Estela . . . if you knew the pain my heart feels . . ." He looked in her eyes, in that blue sea, and as always he found them empty, almost frozen.

She sighed. She looked for answers in his as well, for why he had permitted the brutal execution of her sister Blanca. Four months after the terrible occurrence, she hadn't forgotten. She didn't want to.

"I know very well what it is to have pain in your heart; you have given me so much."

Al-Nasir was getting tired of it.

He had humiliated himself too many times asking for forgiveness, though he didn't feel guilty for what he'd done. He was sickened by her scarce gratitude when he had saved her life from the hands of the vizier.

He rose up from the cushioned bed where he was resting and exhaled furiously. He kicked a table with a tray of fruit and it went off flying through the air.

Estela was nervous. He was tense and out of control. He threw a sideboard full of porcelain to the floor and then shattered an enormous glass pitcher. He closed his fists and clenched his teeth, full of rage. He tore his tunic in half and came toward her. She huddled, frightened, thinking he was going to hit her.

"What do I have to do to make you love me?" He spoke so close to her she could feel his hot breath. Estela didn't dare to move. "Ask me for whatever you want. I will give you anything. Do you want to be the queen of this city, or maybe you prefer my kingdom? Jewels, precious garments? Everything will be yours, everything. Just love me one day, one night . . ."

Estela stood up, raising her chest and chin in a gesture of insolence.

"What I truly want you will never give me."

"Prove it."

"My freedom!" she exclaimed, full of despair.

"Is that all you want?"

"No, not only that. I also want to see you dead one day." Now she looked straight at him, not showing an ounce of fear.

"Quiet!" he exclaimed in despair. "For the sake of blessed Allah, what must I do with you? What further proof must I give you? I have respected you since that tragedy. I haven't touched you again. I treat you delicately, and after all that, I receive nothing but hate from you, a deep, savage hate." He walked decisively to a wall where weapons hung. He took down two golden daggers.

"Do you want to see me dead? " He turned back to her. "That is what you want, right?" He handed her the sharpened steel and opened his tunic, showing his chest. "Do it, then, but with your own hands! Fulfill your desire!"

Estela gripped the daggers' pommels, entranced by the blue shimmer of the blades. She pointed one at his stomach and the other at his heart. She looked at his skin and imagined it open and wounded, bleeding until he met his death.

She inhaled a large mouthful of air, but it didn't reach her lungs. Tension squeezed her chest. Suddenly she didn't know if that was truly what she should do. She hated that man, more than anything in the world, but if she killed him, she would be as terrible as he was. She would be a murderer.

"Do it!" the caliph screamed.

Estela looked into his eyes. She could do it, but she didn't want to. She threw the two daggers to the floor and wept. Al-Nasir did not know what to do, though he only wanted to embrace her. If she hadn't attacked him, she must feel something for him, something better than just hate. Whether she didn't do it because she felt a glimmer of compassion or a lack of bravery, he didn't care. Estela had taken his life in her hands and she hadn't disposed of it. He loved her more than ever.

He brought a finger to her cheek to wipe free a tear, and the mere contact with her skin was like a paradise. He followed the trail of another to her lips and brushed it away slowly and sensually.

"I want you. . . ." He pulled a long tress away from her forehead and stroked it between two fingers.

Estela gave him a serious look, tired of him and his insistence.

"Look for another who will enjoy you. You will never have me, and though you think you have rights over my body, it will never be yours."

"I don't understand why I have to take this. You know what? I'm tired of you, your pride, your cruelty!"

He shouted for his personal guard.

"Shut her up in the dungeon tonight!" al-Nasir screamed, beside himself.

The two guardians picked her up from the floor and asked the caliph what punishment he wished for her.

"Whip her in the square tomorrow, first thing, beneath the minaret. That is my will. . . . Twenty-five lashes. . . . No, better fifty. And then leave her chained there for three days, so all may see her."

He went to the window and felt the cool of the night on his burning face. Then he looked for his Koran, the most beautiful of all books of poetry. He wrote something on a leaf of parchment, folded it, and slipped it between the pages. He always did this when something important occurred.

"Wait!" the caliph exclaimed when they were already leaving his chambers.

Al-Nasir approached Estela and looked into her eyes.

"If now you ask me for forgiveness, you can avoid this martyrdom. This is your last opportunity. What is your answer?"

"You may wound my body, stain my skin with blood, but you will never have my heart," she answered without fear.

When he heard that, al-Nasir felt a wound tear open in his heart, worse than if she had stabbed him with the daggers. He had never loved another woman so much, and now nothing could avoid his wrath.

"Get her out of here!"

The next morning, after the first prayers, Estela was dragged to the base of the minaret and tied to a wooden pillar. Five imposing Imesebelen protected her from the public that had begun to gather around her.

One of them was Tijmud. He saw how her legs shook and he was saddened. They bent on their own, beyond the girl's will, and then, when she was about to fall, they would straighten and hold her up a bit longer. Her elbows, arms, all her body was shivering from the terror she seemed to feel.

Estela had decided not to scream and to bear any blow, however hard. She thought of her sisters and decided to sacrifice herself willingly.

"Don't hurt her. She's good. . . ." A sweet and childlike voice attracted her attention.

She raised her head and saw a girl of around eight years old with a clear, sincere gaze. The girl extended her small hand offering her little strength, her support, as if she could help. Her father, seeing the gesture, reprimanded her, saying that Estela was a heretic, a filthy Christian. The girl's eyes welled with tears. Her innocence moved Estela before she lost sight of her, just when the vizier appeared.

"Are you Estela de Malagón?" he shouted.

"I am," her thin voice responded.

"Very well, then we will get started as soon as we can." She heard a murmur of satisfaction from the public. The man turned to the soldiers and signaled Tijmud.

"You shall begin." He passed him the whip.

The guard took the leather and looked at the woman in her tribulation. They had trained him to kill in defense of the caliph, and his pulse had never quickened when he had been given the opportunity, but this was different. The girl was defenseless, and besides, he knew her.

Nonetheless, he understood his obligation and readied to obey the order.

"Begin, and be firm." The vizier tore Estela's tunic in half. "This is the wish of your caliph, whom you owe everything to, even your very life."

Tijmud breathed deep and flicked the whip twice through the air before bringing it down on the girl. A tense silence accompanied the first blow. As the leather cracked over the girl, there was heard a light murmur of pain. The people applauded his action, anxious to see blood. The second lash tore her skin, opening a wound from the base of her neck to the middle of her back.

The vizier ordered him to stop and turned to the prisoner. He grabbed her hair and twisted it, making her look at her observers.

"Look at their faces, whore. See how they enjoy it?"

She didn't answer. She felt the wound in her back and the ache of exposed flesh, but she still felt she could bear it.

"Go on," he said again to Tijmud, "and show no mercy. Find her ribs, and give it all your might."

Tijmud tensed the muscles in his arm and gave her a series of ten lashes without any rest in between. As if it was a knife, the whip opened her flesh, lacerating her, violating the silky texture of her skin. She screamed during the last few, incapable of resisting that terrible pain further. Her back was on fire.

Tijmud cleaned the blood from his hands and approached her to see how she was. Secretly, he spoke into her ear.

"I hate doing this," he whispered. "Forgive me."

Estela looked into his eyes and forgave him between her cries of anguish. There was no need to say it; he saw it, he knew it, and he felt an unknown and unrecognizable feeling. It was like a strange impulse that seemed to push him to protect her from more pain. He still had thirteen lashes left to give. He had never felt anything like it. He thought it must be what others called pity, a feeling he didn't know. He cleaned the tip of the leather, somewhat confused, before he went on. His hands failed him. . . . The vizier shouted in his ear to continue, insulted him, even grabbed one of his hands, cocking it back so he would strike the girl.

Estela filled her lungs with air and squeezed the muscles in her back to receive the final lashes. As the number went up, the public began to get nervous. Some women protested that the penalty was too harsh, others shouted for them to stop the butchery, but the vizier paid attention to none of them. He had precise orders from the caliph and he was determined to carry them out.

Estela, frightened, awaited the whistling sound that preceded the stinging of the whip, but she began to think of other things. She remembered her life in Malagón and her thoughts fled in pursuit of the family's inn. There she saw her siblings, back when they were still happy, and she thought of Diego. What would have happened to him?

A terrible pain shook her thoughts when the whip came around her ribs, and its tip, hard and cutting, scratched one of her breasts.

She clenched her jaws and awaited the arrival of the next lash, looking at Tijmud. She saw compassion toward her in his eyes, and she began to think of him.

Ever since the wicked execution of Blanca, that Imesebelen, guardian of Princess Najla, had approached her a number of times. Though they had hardly spoken, she saw something special in him from the beginning, different from the rest of those wicked guards. And then she saw herself fleeing again, with Blanca, through the streets of the city, in that same square. She remembered a man with a flute, and at his side a basket of serpents, he was playing a beautiful melody when she was captured.

Then she suddenly felt very tired, and only wanted to sleep.

She stopped hearing the blows on her skin and began to feel her head, heavy, very heavy, and let it fall.

The vizier, clearly angered, tried to see if she was just faking, and approached to observe her. He ordered Tijmud to stop once he was sure. He waited a moment for her to regain awareness and then sent for a bucket of water to revive her. He himself threw it over her head, but to no effect.

"Who cares?" he decided. "Finish with the lashes she has coming to her, and then leave her there; maybe the sun will heal her wounds."

Unable to go on, Tijmud passed the whip to another Imesebelen. The new man gave Estela a blow that resounded through the whole of the plaza. Immediately it aroused cries of protest among the people. Some began to insult the guards; others threw fruit and stones, accusing them of being cowards.

That soldier, impervious to what was happening around him, continued hurling the leather once, twice, five more times, until suddenly Estela awoke and opened her eyes in fright. When he saw her, the vizier stopped the whip with his own hands and watched what she was doing.

She clenched her fists, shouted in pain, stood up from the floor with great difficulty, and screamed. She did it with such desperation that it penetrated the consciences of all who were there. Najla heard her from inside the palace. She was with her brother. Both looked at each other horrified, aware of who it was coming from.

"One day you killed my best friend, Blanca. Are you going to let them do the same to her?"

Al-Nasir covered his ears to flee from his own torment, but Estela screamed again, much stronger than before, until the entire city could hear her.

From the place of punishment, Estela looked proudly at the vizier, and far from begging him for clemency, she spit on the floor with contempt, having heard the multitude clamoring for him to take pity on her.

Some of the women who screeched, now emboldened, picked up stones and began to hurl them at the torturers. The vizier took charge and raised his voice so that he could be heard.

"In the name of Allah, the benevolent, the merciful, listen to me . . ." He raised his hands in the air and repeated the same thing three times until he managed to get complete silence. "As you know, our law commands that we publicly flog those who fornicate, who commit adultery, and accuse others of lying." He walked around Estela and placed his hands on her back, staining them with blood. Then he showed it to everyone. "I assure you the blood of this woman was not spilled in vain. You must know that you have here an infidel, a Christian, a deviant who has dared to offend our glorious caliph. Her sin must be punished, and that is what has been done. But I have just seen you pray to Allah for her, begging for mercy, perhaps. And I want you to know Allah has heard you. And in obedience to his will"—he raised his voice higher—"the beating will be suspended."

A clamor of approval coursed through the crowd.

"Free her, then," a boy shouted.

"Free her, free her," a chorus started up.

"I cannot. . . ." the vizier concluded. "She must finish paying for her crime. She will go on tied to this wood for three days, as our caliph has demanded."

The people, murmuring their disapproval, began to scatter through the square known to all of them as Jemaa el Fna, to the stalls where they sold their wares. The vizier, too, after giving his final orders, left the square.

All that remained was a guard of two Imesebelen to prevent the curious from meddling. One of them was Tijmud.

After a while, Estela turned her gaze to him and saw his eyes, as dark as his skin, with scarcely enough strength to bear the pain running through her body.

"Tijmud, I need to drink. . . ."

"My lady, I cannot. . . . You must understand."

"Please, I beg you. I'm dying of thirst."

Tijmud studied his companion's face and understood that he wouldn't approve. He went over to him and whispered into his ear in their language. Then he called a young girl and sent her to bring a pitcher of water. Tijmud himself helped her to drink.

"Thank you again."

"Now rest, and don't speak more. Try to sleep so the pain doesn't sap your energy."

"You're right. . . . I feel very tired and it's hard to speak. . . ."

"I'll try to help you."

"Why are you doing this?"

"I don't know. . . . When I see you suffering, I feel something moving inside me, but I don't know what it is."

Estela gripped the wood and closed her exhausted eyes. Her torment was so great that she didn't know what it was or where it came from. After a while she was defeated by weariness and fell asleep.

When the sun began to rise the next day, a warm light touched her cheeks and stirred her awake. When she opened her eyes, she looked for Tijmud without seeing him. He had been replaced by another soldier who refused to answer her questions. But Tijmud came back that afternoon, and then they were able to talk.

"My back feels like something is tearing at it from all sides," Estela confessed. A hard crust of blood covered it entirely. "There are moments when I can hardly breathe from so much pain. . . ."

In midafternoon, a punishing sun fell like lead over the square, emptying it out. Tijmud took advantage of the circumstances to cool the wounds on her back with fresh water. Using a cotton cloth, he carefully dried them.

"Tell me about your family," Estela said.

"An Imesebelen does not have a family."

"That is impossible."

"No, señora, it isn't. In case you didn't know, as soon as we are born, we are separated from our parents and taken to a special school. There they prepare us so that one day, we will be the faithful guardians of the caliph. In my case, I learned that as a newborn, they left me in a stable where there was only a camel. I will never know how I made it, but it seems the animal raised me on its milk. That is usually the first trial they submit us to so that we become good Imesebelen. He who shows he has sufficient instincts goes for the camel when hunger strikes him. Those who don't, die. Some are not even capable of absorbing the camel's dense milk, and some get stepped on and killed. That is how we are selected. From the first day, there begins a cruel triage that follows an infinitude of harsh tests where those who are too weak are exposed and only the strongest are chosen to finally protect the caliph."

"And the love of a mother, the protection of a father? How can someone live without that?"

"I don't know. I've never known what those things meant. Believe me. We Imesebelen live only for the caliph. He feeds us and we protect him; it is a simple and practical arrangement. During our preparation, those who show the most weakness, try to escape, or do not manage to get through the harsh circumstances of our training meet a harsh destiny."

"I can't imagine."

"They become targets for our exercises."

"What kind of exercises?"

"We learn how to kill in ways you couldn't imagine."

Estela curled up from fright.

"Then you have never known love, or the effect of a caress . . ."

"I was taught in another language, the language of duty, of loyalty, of total sacrifice. I belong to a unique breed, an elect group, and I am proud of it."

"You aren't, believe me. You have missed out on the very best in life. One day I hope to explain it to you."

That night, when he returned to the palace, Tijmud pondered what they had discussed. It had never occurred to him that his parents had been real, and the mere thought of it was causing him a strange disquiet. Might they still be alive?

Once he crossed through the gates of the Alcazaba, he found the ambassador Pedro de Mora. He was walking in the company of the vizier. Though he hadn't seen him for some time, there was something in his face that called his attention, blurring the outlines of his smile.

They looked at each other. The two men were talking.

Tijmud thought he heard something that piqued his interest even more. He hid behind a wall, with his back to it, and inched along it until he could hear them clearly.

"It was a little bastard who did it to me; he said he was the brother of that redheaded whore you just punished, Estela."

"Be careful what you say about her, and to whom . . ." the vizier explained. "I will tell you in confidence, but before, you must swear not to repeat it to anyone."

"You have my word."

"Good. It is about our caliph. He is madly in love with the girl. There is no other woman in the harem who can make him happy, none. He loves her so much, in fact, that no one can understand what happened today."

"Thank you for warning me. What you tell me doesn't surprise me especially, though it's been some time since I've seen them together, nor have I spoken with him of this matter. I will be more careful, but I will also tell you, I will exact my revenge on that woman for the evil her brother has committed. I will take it out on her one day."

IX.

Doña Teresa Ibáñez entered quickly into the music room where Mencía was playing a psalm.

"Run, run. Leave that, and go to the ballroom. A great surprise is waiting for you."

Mencía left her instrument on the bench and got up mistrustfully. The rushing about, the change in her mother's tone of voice, her nervous stomping, all that made her suspect she was covering up something.

"What's it about?"

"Better if you see for yourself, darling. Come, quick."

Mencía crossed the courtyard full of blossoming camellias and turned to the other wing of the castle. Her mother was following her, almost touching her. When she arrived at the sitting room, Mencía found a man with his back to her looking out from one of the balconies. She coughed delicately to make her presence known, and he turned.

"My beloved Mencía . . ." She was petrified when she saw it was Fabián Pardo, especially when he turned to her with an attitude that seemed so at odds with the contents of the letter she had mailed a few weeks back.

The man took her belt and pulled her to him, intending to kiss her on the lips. She avoided him as best she could.

"But why are you here?" Mencía put her hands between them to push away. "You are at war, you should be with your king, Pedro."

"My calling is the law and not arms, and I wanted so much to see you . . ."

Doña Teresa interrupted their conversation.

"You can't imagine the joy your visit has brought us." She moved around them like a sandstorm.

She offered him her hand to receive his greeting and returned the courtesy, kissing him on both cheeks. "Forgive me these confidences, but I almost consider you part of the family already."

Mencía looked at her with horror.

Doña Teresa was receiving the Aragonese as if he were her son-in-law. Though this struck her as already audacious, the worst thing was that Fabián seemed enchanted with the idea.

"You are perfect," he affirmed without warning, turning again to Mencía. "The greatest wife a man could ever dream of."

She was paralyzed. She had rejected him in writing and yet his reactions seemed to indicate the contrary. In her letter, she had left things sufficiently clear, and for that reason, his presence was incomprehensible. She armed herself with her courage and decided to broach the issue, looking for some logical explanation.

"Did you get my letter?"

"Yes, of course I received it." The Aragonese closed his eyes and made an ambiguous face. It could have been excitement, sadness, or even both. "That's why I made the decision to come. It moved me so much inside that I felt compelled to rush here and better understand your decision."

From his words, sadly, Mencía concluded that he hadn't yet given up.

Hanging on their every word, Doña Teresa shook with fear. She needed to sidetrack the conversation immediately, before her ruse was discovered. Tense, but with a forced smile, she grabbed the invitee by his arm and almost dragged him away to show him her rooms.

"You must be exhausted from the journey. We understand you may want to rest a moment . . ." Fabián looked at Mencía with a frustrated expression. "We will dine at eight. You'll have plenty of time to talk at your leisure."

Mencía, once alone, fell nauseated into an armchair without understanding how she would get out of this bind. Fabián was stubborn and known for not stopping until he had gotten what he wanted. If he had read the letter, he already knew her opinion. What more could she say to him but stress that she had meant it?

In her chambers, while she got ready for dinner, Doña Teresa was thinking. She needed to do something to transform her subterfuge into a promise, something that was definitive and could not be questioned. And then it occurred to her. The idea might be wicked, but it was all the same; it was doable, very doable.

She calculated carefully what her steps should be and how she would overcome the difficulties. She turned it over in her mind many times. The idea was good, she was sure of it. It could work.

She took a new parchment, a goose feather quill, an inkwell, and began to write.

Many leagues away, in the highest tower of the castle of Cirat, half a day on horseback from Mora de Rubielos, Diego de Malagón listened with a heavy heart to the new battle plans.

They had managed a first victory, nothing more. Both López de Haro and Abu Zayd knew King Pedro II wouldn't give up so easily.

"If he didn't reach glory this time, he'll ask the grandees of his empire to lend him new cavalry forces and soldiers to form a bigger army." Diego was translating the Valencian governor.

"Besides cursing your behavior for allowing him to flee," Diego went on talking, "he says that, in recompense, he will need you to stay with him another four months, until winter comes."

"Answer him that I just sent a letter to Lady Teresa to inform her of what has happened and to solicit her blessings to achieve victory."

Don Diego López de Haro took a drink of wine spiced with cinnamon poured by a servant with mysterious almond eyes. He hoped the translator would do his job without getting lost in the woman's voluptuous curves.

"He thanks you from the bottom of his heart and says he will be generous with you."

"He already is. It has been some time since I've eaten delicacies such as these and received such attention. . . . Not to mention the beautiful company." He studied the woman while she refilled his glass with that rousing wine.

"He says he will pay you in gold as well."

Diego began to translate worse when, not long afterward, the fourth glass had been drunk.

"Excellent news then, Your Highness . . ." Don Diego's tongue was tied, and from that moment on he spoke rather little.

Diego continued to translate the words of the Valencian into Romanic, though it was now harder to understand him. Maybe it was due to the woman's presence, rare in the past few weeks, but he began to think of Mencía. Four months without seeing her would be hell. He drank another sip and began to feel bad, as if his stomach had been split in two. He heaved, but managed to keep it down. From then he decided to remain very still until the illness had passed.

Though he wanted to think of her, his body was too busy with more primary tasks to concentrate, and that only worsened when the dancers came in.

To the sounds of an animated music, they began a richly sensual dance. They seemed determined to use every one of their muscles. Their bodies, hidden behind fragile veils of color, were intoxicating and seductive, and the aromas they gave off were captivating. Diego let himself be distracted by that atmosphere charged with sensuality, because of the effects of the liquor and the charms of those five women. One of them pulled on him to get him to dance; the others did the same with the governor and Don Diego. That devilish dance required a great deal of skill, and they had to hold on to the women's hips to feel the rhythm and follow along. Amid laughter, blinded by the beauty of their bodies, Diego forgot his misfortunes.

They went on pouring that dangerous brew that confused the mind and gladdened the heart. They drank it until they were almost falling down, laughing boisterously. Diego blathered nonsense words instead of translating, and the governor seemed to have lost his head, since he was trying to dance while he was lain out on the floor, after his third fall, without any apparent desire to stand back up.

After midnight, someone proposed that they go to the bedrooms with the women. Don Diego López de Haro forced the albéitar to pick the most beautiful one. In secret, he offered Buthayna, which was the name of the concubine, fifteen *sueldos* to pass the night with the boy, and a hundred more if she would stay with him from then on. All this was done in the hope that he would forget his niece Mencía.

Buthayna accepted the challenge gladly and turned to Diego with a seductive look, offering him her hand and then taking him down a long hallway that led to the guests' area. Before arriving at the bedroom, she stopped Diego and kissed him ardently, rubbing herself against him, making him feel her body.

Diego's thoughts were focused on Mencía and he tried to reject the dancer, but the woman had great ability in the arts of love and managed to rouse his passion. They stumbled into the bedroom. Buthayna began to undress him amid caresses and whispers. Diego let her. Blood was rushing in his temples and his pulse sped up in time with his desire. When he then undressed her, he admired her body and pushed her down onto the bed.

"Your parents were wise to give you that name, Buthayna. It means woman with a beautiful and giving body, no?"

"Try and see. . . ."

The woman smiled, pulled him to her. Diego took refuge in her body, running his fingers over her warm flesh, feeling its softness. In a sudden reflection he thought again of Mencía—he could almost see her—and then he couldn't continue. This wasn't what he really wanted, nor what he should do. Stunned, he stopped moving his hands.

"Buthayna, you are beautiful and sweet; I like you, but I don't want to keep doing this." She looked at him disturbed. "It's not you, it's my fault. I'm in love with a woman, the most sweet and sensitive being I have known, beautiful outside and in. I feel I owe her loyalty. She is my life, I breathe for her, I can't live without her."

The woman, though she'd been rejected, was moved by his noble reaction and seemed to understand him, though she still inspired pity in Diego.

"Don't suffer for me. I promise you that you are beautiful and very appetizing, but . . ."

"That's not why I'm crying; it's from pure envy. I hope to God someone will one day feel the same for me. You have the correct attitude. . . . I can't help it, you've moved me."

She sat up and looked for her clothing to dress while Diego put on his tunic, both of them seated on the bed.

She looked at him, doubtful, but finally decided.

"I have to ask you a favor."

"I will try to do it."

"Let me sleep here. I won't bother you, I promise. Understand, if they see me come back so soon, they will think I haven't made your night pleasurable enough, and they will throw me out in the street; I'll no longer have this job."

"Of course. You can sleep here."

She lay down on one side of the bed, and after a while, she noticed that Diego was still awake.

"What is the name of this lucky woman?"

"Mencía," he answered.

"A beautiful name."

The woman turned her back to him again and slept between tears of emotion and a little shame.

That same night, Mencía was thinking of Diego as she lay on her bed. The distance between them hurt her even more since she had seen Fabián. The pressure she was suffering from her mother and the indirect approaches of her suitor were in a maddening race to see which one would tire her out first.

She hid under the sheets as though there, nothing could affect her, but she did not manage to get to sleep. Her thoughts flew crazily and she couldn't stop sweating because of the enormous stress that was affecting her. As a consequence of all that, her eyes shot open against her will.

Someone called at the door to her bedroom.

"Mencía?"

"Mother?" She saw her enter.

Doña Teresa's expression showed an acute state of tension. She pulled the sheets and uncovered her daughter. Without giving another explanation, she covered her up again, satisfied.

Doña Teresa began to speak in a serious tone, assuring herself that her daughter understood every word.

"At midnight, he will come into this bedroom and you will let him. . . ."

"What are you talking about, Mother?"

"I am speaking to you of Fabián Pardo. He is surely reading your note right now. . . ." Mencía tried to ask, but her mother wouldn't let her. "Don't talk, and listen!" Her expression was firm. "I imagine that he will come here, because your invitation will excite him, and he will overcome his prudence. When he arrives at your bed, you will give yourself to him, with all the passion you can muster."

Mencía rubbed her eyes and looked back at her, believing she was living a horrible nightmare. But now, there she was still. She couldn't understand how her mother could propose something so monstrous.

"But, Mother, that is . . . I don't know . . . Do you realize what you're doing?"

"Perhaps you will understand it better in time." The mother wrinkled her brows, feeling agitated. "As absurd as it may seem to you, I've thought about it a great deal, my daughter, and I am sure it is what is best for you."

"Don't expect me to let him in!"

"Not only will you do it, you will give yourself to him and you will like it."

"Never!"

Mencía threw off the sheets and leapt from the bed, looking for her clothes. She wanted out of that bedroom, to get on her horse and leave the castle, the city; to flee from here, from this insane world, from her mother. She didn't care where to.

Doña Teresa stopped her. Her look was threatening.

"If you leave through that door, you will be condemning Diego de Malagón to death."

That stopped Mencía in her tracks. She felt her legs tremble and was overcome by a feeling as if she was choking.

"What are you saying about Diego?" she panted nervously.

"I have informed your uncle of this little delusion of yours, and he agrees with me. I have a messenger on hand. If you don't accept the offer I have proposed to you, he will rush off like a lightning bolt in search of your uncle to give him an order."

"And what is that order?"

"Diego will be sent to the front line of the infantry. With his lack of military training, it is most likely he will have a number of problems facing off against the enemy army. . . . So you understand, if my messenger has to leave this castle, something terrible could happen to your friend. It all depends on you."

"But, Mother, how is this possible? That is a foulness so terrible . . . You are, you are . . . cruel and hateful."

She leapt at Doña Teresa to scratch her, disgusted by what she was hearing. Her mother guessed her intentions and was able to avoid her. She shoved her and Mencía fell down on the sheets. She was going to speak, she needed to understand, to ask why she was doing this to her, but her mother cut her off.

"I know what you feel for him." Doña Teresa changed her tone and suddenly became more tender and understanding, almost even maternal. "Believe me, my poor daughter, I understand. You love him, no? You feel yourself dying for him and it seems impossible that anyone could ever replace him."

"You don't know what I feel. And you have no right to decide my life. Do you understand?" she shouted, furious.

"You are the one who understands nothing. I know who deserves you and who doesn't. Forget that nobody and behave like an adult for once; erase that stupid daydream from your mind."

"It's not a daydream." Mencía turned around, exasperated, in her bed.

"I don't care what you call it, but forget him. And stop thinking about it anymore. It's very late and I'm not in the mood to hear more nonsense. Now you will obey me."

She opened a small glass bottle and spilled ten drops into a glass of water.

"Take this. It will help you to forget . . . and it will also awaken your senses."

Mencía couldn't believe what she had just heard.

"You're trying to drug me?"

Doña Teresa pounced on her and made her drink it. Mencía's chin began to quiver. She felt stunned, and she couldn't find a way out. She looked at her mother and saw a stranger. She studied every line in her face, trying to find there the slightest sign of compassion, kindness, or concern, but she only found sternness, coldness, cruelty.

"We've talked enough. The messenger awaits my orders. The life of Diego de Malagón depends on you. If you truly love him, you know now how to show it."

"My uncle doesn't have to listen to you. . . ." Mencía looked for one last solution before surrendering herself to cruel reality.

Her mother gave an insensitive and cruel laugh.

"He agrees about all of this. I insist, don't think about it anymore. Do what I say."

When the bells of the neighboring church of San Juan rang out at midnight, Doña Teresa rushed from the bedroom, prepared for Fabián's imminent arrival.

X.

Amid sheets of ice, stones with sharp edges, and snow up to her flanks, Sabba brought Diego back to Santa María de Albarracín.

They had been away almost five months; it was already December, and there were only two days left till Christmas.

Diego's longing to see Mencía made him pull ahead of the rest of the horses when they were reaching the vicinity of Teruel.

Three hours later, a few leagues from Albarracín, the weather got notably worse; a lashing blizzard struck and the day was darkened by a thick fog, so that orienting oneself became impossible.

"Poor Sabba, you've got ice up to your mane."

Diego took a hand out from his cape to clear it off.

When she exhaled, a thick cloud of steam emerged from her nostrils. Sabba opened her eyes wide, surprised at the effect. She jerked her head several times and whipped her tail from front to back in a signal of danger, a danger much greater than her master seemed to be aware of.

Diego sped up to avoid hitting the storm, though shortly afterward, when he could no longer of the path, he realized he was lost. Sabba looked down, fearful; she didn't know where to step either. At a certain moment, she ceased obeying Diego's orders and stopped. He spoke slowly to calm her down. He assured her that he had it under control, but Sabba refused to advance. She twisted her head from side to side, refusing his directions.

Tired of her behavior, Diego dismounted, took hold of the bridle, and pulled on it. He gave it his all, but she would only budge a few steps. He didn't understand. He doubled the reins around his wrist, tensed them, and clenched his teeth to drag her along, even if just one inch at a time, but then he noticed that she wouldn't step down on one of her feet, that she kept it hanging in the air. He turned, confused, and it was then that he noticed he was on the edge of a dangerous precipice, right there in front of his nose.

Sabba breathed out another cloud of steam and rested her head on his shoulder. Her fear had vanished and she was waiting for her master to reward her for her carefulness.

"You're my guardian angel." He scratched her jaw and got back on her. "Find the path we lost, take it, and get me to Albarracín, please."

Diego's breeches were so stiff, in fact they were frozen, that when he got back on the saddle to look for the way, their folds cut into his skin.

"We should be close, Sabba. At least I hope so."

The mare turned back over her footsteps and began to walk more carefully. Diego was conscious that his responsibilities had grown. Not only did he have to take care of her, but he also had to protect the fragile creature she had in her belly. He still didn't know how it had happened, or when. He thought about the night he spent with Mencía in the hermitage, keeping safe from the rain. . . . Sabba was there with Shadow, but . . . It also could have been any other moment throughout the five months he had spent away. He had been so insensitive and apathetic recently that he hadn't even paid attention to the change in her attitude or, later, in the size of her belly.

But there she was, about to become a mother for the first time. Diego was sure she already felt the stirring of a new life in her womb. He caressed her tenderly and with the warmth of his embrace, he encouraged her to continue on her path.

When they glimpsed the long city walls as they curved around the Guadalaviar, their spirits lifted. Diego pushed onward down the hill until they reached the northern gate, and then passed through the streets in search of his house.

Night was falling, and he scarcely saw anyone on his way; it was too cold to be out in the street. He and Sabba entered the stable and he readied her a bed of straw and gave her a pitchfork of dry grass to eat, and he left her there lying down and resting from the journey.

When he entered the house, he found Marcos sleeping by the fire. He blew air on the coals and put on more logs. Before he sat down, he had a little cheese and a mug of wine. He stretched his legs in the heat and closed his eyes, overjoyed to be back home.

For a while he enjoyed that silence, only broken by the occasional creak or the crackling of the fire. But when he went to get more wood, he accidentally made too much noise and awoke Marcos.

"But look who we have here!" The two men gave each other a sincere embrace.

"Marcos, my dear friend . . . how has your trading gone? You have to tell me everything. But first you have to tell me how Mencía is. By the way, you're looking a little heftier." With each question, Diego tried to make up for the five long months away from the city.

"Relax . . . You're trying to make me talk to you about too many things at once," Marcos protested, perhaps to put off the one bit of news that was actually important.

"The trading couldn't have gone better, but what about you? How was your war experience? And have you been by the castle yet?"

"No, I needed to warm up and change clothes first; I smell like a horse." Diego smiled openly; he looked beaming, anxious to see his beloved. "I have to admit, my experiences in the war helped me to make new decisions. Among them, I'm going to ask Mencía to marry me, and there's another one I'll tell you in a moment, but I need to have some time to think it through."

Marcos's face twisted into a grimace of displeasure.

"I have to tell you something . . ."

"What happened?"

"It's about Mencía." Marcos grabbed a poker and began to jab at a piece of wood to work up the fire.

"What happened to her?" Diego felt a sudden sensation of anxiety. "Is she sick?"

After holding his breath a moment, Marcos finally spoke.

"You won't find her in Santa María de Albarracín. . . ."

"Is she traveling?"

"No, it's not that. . . ." He looked at Diego downcast. "She married that man she met before we arrived, the one from Aragon."

Diego put his head in his hands and felt a sharp pain in his stomach, as though someone had pierced him straight through with a sword. His eyes began to water. He couldn't speak.

"Everything happened after you left. One day this Fabián Pardo showed up and a month later, to everyone's surprise, their marriage was announced. A while later they went to Ayerbe, to live in the castle of the Aragonese."

Marcos, crestfallen, put his hand around Diego's shoulder.

"She swore her love to me. . . ." Diego was defeated, desolate. "She told me she loved me more than anyone. How could she deceive me this way?"

"I should tell you another thing. . . ."

"There's more?"

"She was pregnant when she married." Marcos cleared his throat nervously. "And I didn't know whether to ask you or not, but understand, from the dates when she'll be giving birth . . ."

"I never made her mine, if that's what you want to know. So there can be no doubt about the child's paternity. . . ."

"I'm sorry, Diego. Women . . . They're like that; unpredictable, volatile. That's why I never trust them. They change from one day to the next, and what goes on inside them is a mystery. That's why I enjoy them, I let them love me from time to time, I sample their plump bodies, and nothing more. You should do the same and stop being so romantic. It's not worth suffering so much over them."

"I don't understand, Marcos." Diego had gone pale. "I . . . I thought she loved me, she swore it. I thought she could overcome the barriers that came between my world and hers. . . . But she didn't. How naive I was! Just like others told me, lineage was stronger than love." He brought his hands to his head again, wounded. "I don't know how I thought I would win the heart of a girl who was a daughter of the nobility, when I was a commoner, a miserable son of the earth. I thought I was someone because I was an albéitar, the way I saw Galib was when he walked around with the nobles in Toledo, but it's clear it's not enough. Mencía . . . yes, she gave in. Her surroundings made her choose something else, different for me, and she let their will break her." He pushed the air from his lungs until he thought he would choke. "And what will I do now, Marcos? Die from pain?"

"You have to see it's just how women are. Like I said . . ."

"But she didn't leave you a note for me, something written before she left, nothing?"

Marcos lowered his head without answering. He understood his pain. When he looked at Diego again, his friend was trembling from rage or mourning. Marcos saw him go to the window, the one that opened onto the square. From there, he could see a corner of the Azagras' castle. Diego imagined Mencía in the arms of another, kissed and caressed by another man, and he couldn't take it.

One question, always the same, assailed him over and over. What could have happened to make Mencía break her oath of love and fidelity?

"This city, the streets, the air . . . Everything is making me sick," he confessed to Marcos. "It's all impregnated with betrayal, lies, mocking. I can't go on living here another day, Marcos." He began to pace nervously through the room until he stopped suddenly in front of his friend. "I need to get far away from here."

"What do you mean?" Marcos did not seem convinced.

"Maybe it's time for me to go to Marrakesh and look for my sisters." Diego's eyes explored a spot on the ceiling. "Of course, that's it! Now I can do it; I will cross over again into Al-Andalus."

Marcos frowned. He didn't like that idea at all; Diego had told him about the difficulties he'd had to pass through when he crossed the marshlands, and he thought it was madness to go there again. Besides, it would mean abandoning his trade.

Anticipating what Diego's reaction would be, Marcos had already thought of another solution days before. If he managed to convince Diego of it, the fate Marcos had chosen would be even more profitable than selling sheep to the Valencians. While Marcos tried to find the best words to explain his plan, Diego made it easy for him.

"Wait, no . . ." Diego realized how selfish he was being. "You should stay. I'm sorry, I'm insensitive. You've already put down roots here, and I don't want you to leave behind what you've worked so hard to get. I'll go, but alone. That's what I'll do!"

"I won't allow it."

"I won't allow you to come with me."

"I know you too well not to have guessed what you'd be thinking, Diego. So I already made the contacts I needed to set up somewhere else, and . . ."

"Forget it, I insist. . . . I'll leave tomorrow at dawn."

"Listen to my idea first."

"Fine, tell me."

"First remember this name, Cuéllar."

"I don't know it. Where is it?"

"It's a free village south of the Duero River in Castile. From what I hear, it has an enormous herd of sheep. Two months ago I found out that Abu Mizrain, my intermediary with the buyers in Valencia, had the thought of setting up shop there, but to buy wool and not just meat. Apparently the sheep they raise in the region of Cuéllar have finer coats than those here, and the lamb is tastier, with more fat. I managed to go with him, and I liked it. I have a good contact with one of the largest livestock owners, and he could definitely help us break into that market."

Diego was only half listening. Disappointment and misery were drowning him and nothing tied him to this or any other place. He didn't even have the strength to decide. . . . All he wanted was to be lost to the world, to disappear, to cry out his pain.

"I'm going to Al-Andalus. . . ."

"Why?" Marcos decided to change his strategy and at least make him delay the trip.

"I swore I would do something for my sisters; that is my plan," Diego answered firmly.

"It sounds to me like a very noble decision on your part, but I suppose you also must have thought about how much it will cost you to carry it out. You'll need lots of money and someone to go with you, and it's best if you go armed; and you'll need a good excuse to be down there among the Moors, and lots of bravery above all. I don't deny that you have the courage, but the rest of it you still need." He put a hand on his friend's shoulder. "Listen, Diego, great debts like the one you have aren't paid with weapons and strength. You need brains, intelligence, and especially a good plan. And to make it, you need time and plenty of economic resources. Let's go to Cuéllar, Diego. We'll do business there and we'll make money. We'll figure out afterward what to do with it, I promise. What do you think?"

Diego embraced him. He had never felt so wretched, but he'd also never received such a sincere show of friendship.

They sat in front of the fire and watched the wood burn with a feeling that they were sharing not only heat, but their lives and destinies as well. The tongues of fire twisted around the dry wood, in silence, until another crack opened and they devoured its interior.

Diego was so absorbed in his pain that he couldn't even move. His eyes were prisoners to those flames and couldn't pull away from them. He felt wounded in the deepest part of his being, as if he had been torn in half, from his head to his toes. Without Mencía, life itself had no meaning.

"I've been cheated, humiliated . . ."

He promised himself he would forget it, but he couldn't. He saw her blue eyes again, her beautiful hair, her sweet voice. Mencía had been his only love.

PART IV

Lands of Confusion

At the end of 1203, Pope Innocent III obliged Alfonso VIII of Castile to annul the marriage of his daughter Berenguela with the Leonese King Alfonso IX. The rivalry between the two monarchs grows until their recent accords fall to pieces. Alfonso IX, enraged, calls the enemies of Alfonso VIII to his court.

Don Diego López de Haro returns to León and takes over the lands of Sarria, Toro, Extremadura, and the capital of the kingdom, León.

That same year, a treaty is signed by the kings of Castile, Navarre, and Aragon; each monarch uses it to reinforce his own position. Pedro II, recently married to Maria of Montpellier, fights to broaden his realm to Valencia, and Mallorca falls into the hands of the Almohad caliph al-Nasir.

Alfonso VIII of Castile, wishing to compromise the power of the great nobles, begins to concede charters of freedom to numerous villages and towns that benefit their trade and permit him to make use of their militias without contracting costly obligations later.

Such is the case of Cuéllar, a town with surrounding territories deep in the heart of Castile.

I.

———

In his exile, Diego drowned his lovelessness with wine.

That night, Marcos cursed to himself while he looked for the young albéitar urgently. It wasn't the first time he'd taken the carriage late at night to Matias's inn, on the outskirts of Cuéllar, to retrieve Diego, half drunk. But on this occasion, the news was worrying. Sabba had begun foaling and was having serious problems.

For the five months since they'd arrived in Cuéllar, Diego's bitterness had infected everything. Even the most run-of-the-mill actions, like deciding where to live, became an almost impossible task. Nothing seemed to satisfy him. In every house he found some irreparable defect, some imaginary, others perhaps real.

They had changed their lodgings four times before arriving at the splendid house where they now lived. It leaned against the walls of the fortress, in the very center of the town, just a few steps from the town square. It was noble in appearance and large in size. Though the rent was high, Marcos was making ten times as much as he had with his former business in Albarracín and had money to spare.

Owing to a general lack of knowledge about the care of animals in Cuéllar, Diego became very popular as soon as he began to work as an albéitar, though he practiced with little passion now. He didn't care about learning more or investigating the causes of one illness or the other. Nor did he look, as he had before, for the deeper origins of pain, suppuration, fever. When someone called for him, he went. He tried to fix what was wrong, he prescribed a remedy, and he gave advice as he saw necessary. But he knew he had lost the most important thing he needed for his job: his happiness.

His emotional fiasco had thrown everything in his life into chaos, his job as well. That noble calling he had fought for so much since his days in Toledo no longer filled his life; in fact, he was restless.

Over the months, all Diego did was let himself be dragged along by life. And amid so many upsets, wine became one of his closest allies. It was his ideal companion to drown the nights, to leaven his misery, and to mend, in part, his broken heart.

On the other extreme, for Marcos, Cuéllar was a magnificent opportunity for wealth and success. The wool trade kept him busy all day, and he gave it all his attention and strength. Huge flocks roamed the land; many belonged to the clergy or the nobility, but others, more than a few, were the property of the *pecheros*. That's what they called the free men and women who came from the north of Castile searching for opportunities, which the king would give freely to whoever wished to come repopulate these territories that had been won back from the Moors.

Marcos soon controlled the better part of the wool trade thanks to his friend Abu Mizrain from Valencia. After buying the wool at a good price, Mizrain would leave for the great markets of Egypt, Damascus, and Persia. There they needed more and more and were willing to pay a good price for it.

For this reason, it was easy for Marcos to convince almost all the herdsmen that he was better than their former customers from Flanders.

"Sabba, my Saaaaabbba . . ." Diego began to sing, riled up by the rocking of the cart. "You are the maare of the suuuun and the moooon . . ." he wailed out, his tongue lolling around, in a pathetic state.

Without loosing the reins, his friend turned to look at him and was immediately discouraged.

"Save that music and try to get your head on straight; we need you thinking clearly when you have to look after Sabba."

Marcos had needed the help of two men to get Diego out of the inn, and not even two buckets of water over the head were enough to clear his mind. When they got home, Marcos helped Diego out of the carriage and almost dragged him into the kitchen. He sat him down close to the fire.

"I don't feel very good." Diego leaned his head over a table, feeling on the verge of death, nauseated and covered in a cold sweat.

Marcos heated up a piece of tallow in the fire with castor oil and an infusion of thyme, an infallible remedy on these occasions. He looked for a wooden bucket to hold Diego's vomit and shouted for Veturia, whom he had employed as soon as they moved into the house. Veturia was a single woman, robust and not very smart, though she had a divine talent for cooking. One of her many defects was her rather contradictory character; she could be loving and protective, and yet prickly and cold at the same time.

When she appeared in the kitchen with her hands stained with blood, Marcos decided not to ask. He had left Sabba in her care but had asked her not to touch anything. Judging from her appearance, she had paid him no mind.

"How's it going?" Marcos asked, worried.

"Worse. It's getting very ugly, señor. She's not having contractions anymore."

"All right, all right . . ."

Veturia saw Diego and was filled with compassion.

"The wine again, right?" The women knelt to look into his eyes and clicked her tongue. "Today he's much worse than usual."

Diego, far from worried about his compromised dignity, smiled at her idiotically, grasping her hair in his hands as if he were looking at the woman of his dreams.

"Señora . . . it's such a pribbulege"—he tripped over his words—"to meet a woman as beautiful as yourself." He ended by bowing reverently.

"Good Lord! Like this, we can't hope for any miracles," Veturia concluded.

Marcos approached with a steaming pitcher, and the two of them made him drink it. It didn't take long for it to reach his stomach.

"Now I'll go down to the stables," Marcos explained. "When he's better, send him to me."

Veturia soaked a few cloths in cool water and put one on Diego's forehead and one on his neck. Once he had emptied his stomach, he began to feel a bit better.

"You should go see her fast, sir. Your mare needs you. She's in very bad shape. The poor girl . . ."

Diego went to look for his instruments first and then went down to the stables, still clumsy and a bit sick at his stomach, but when he saw Sabba in her distressed state, he felt a sharp pain in his abdomen.

He coughed, swallowing the rest of the stomach acid, and regretted not being there before. He called her by her name and Sabba responded immediately, turning her head to look for him. A weak gleam shone in her eyes while she blinked, signaling she was calmer now.

"I see . . . You think everything's going to be better now, right?"

Sabba whinnied loudly, showing her agreement.

Diego pushed aside her tail and inspected the birth canal. Part of the placenta was hanging out and had an ugly, almost black color. He soaped his arm to the elbow and looked at Marcos, warning him that this would hurt the mare. He conscientiously explored Sabba's interior, not losing a second, and was filled with fear when he realized what was happening. Now he would have to act fast if he wanted to save the two of them. Her offspring was so twisted that if he wasn't careful, he could tear Sabba's insides. He saw that the sac was broken and the foal on the point of suffocating. That operation would require not only skill, but great concentration, and at that moment, he had neither the one nor the other.

His hands shook, he couldn't feel his fingertips, and his head felt like it would explode, but he set to work and put all his soul into the task.

He turned the foal's neck and pushed it toward him, then felt for its front hooves. He moved them bit by bit when he could, but whenever he managed to get them to the right place, the foal would return to its previous position.

Diego sighed, terrified by the delicacy and difficulty of the work that stood before him. He took the small forelegs again and managed to move them, but they slipped away once more. Sabba began to complain. He tried once more and managed to get the legs. He tied them, and then, now more hopeful, he passed the end of the rope to Marcos so he could hold it tight and keep the foal from reacting.

"Tell me if you feel anything strange. I'm going to start with the hard part."

Now Diego would have to turn the rest of the body with nothing but his fingers, overcoming the foal's resistance. He clenched his teeth and tried with all his might, but it had hardly any effect. He felt weak, he wasn't sure of what he was doing . . . the fact was, he was still too drunk.

Then he felt a heaving, and he left Sabba and ran to a corner to vomit. When he came back, there was a terrible powerlessness in his eyes.

He slid in his hand again and looked for the foal's mouth to get a sense of where things stood. Then he found its neck with his fingers, and when he reached its backbone, he put his weight on it, trying to drag the creature out; but strangely, he felt no reaction from the foal.

He pulled again and felt a small quiver, barely anything, or so it seemed. He couldn't tell, because in that moment he grew sick again, and when he came back, there was nothing he could do. Marcos looked at him with pity. Diego looked for the foal's heart and couldn't feel it beating. It was dead.

If what had happened was already bad, what lay ahead was worse; he would have to cut the creature into small pieces, take everything out, and then clean the mare's interior.

He explained it to Marcos, asking for more hot water and thyme to prevent problems in the wounds, as well as silk thread and needles to sew, and a set of thin iron saws that he himself had forged.

"We have to stand her up; if she's lying down, it'll be impossible to tell if she's completely clean."

"She's too tired. . . ." Marcos warned, trying without success.

Whenever Diego gave her a pat on the rump, Sabba would normally stand. He tried two or three times, but she wouldn't react. He whispered to her and pinched her at the base of her mane, the way she had always liked. Sabba snorted in response, flared her nostrils, and moved her ears a little, her exhaustion evident. When he touched them, they were hot, she had a fever.

A terrible grief overcame Diego at that moment. His eyes went damp, and for a flash he was afraid of being left without his mare. He felt guilty for all that had happened. He hadn't been at her side when she needed him, the way he had always been. If he hadn't been drinking that night, he would have gotten the foal out alive. Diego looked at his arms, his hands, and he saw how they were shaking, and then he looked at his mare.

And then he made the decision to act.

It was then that Marcos saw him work one of those miracles that only Diego knew how to bring about.

He had hunched down over Sabba's back, placed his head against hers, embraced her neck, and kissed her, in a scene full of tenderness. Marcos heard him whisper in her ears, making brief, almost inaudible sounds in Sabba's language, so that she understood.

Soon the animal began to breathe more energetically. Diego spoke to her and she seemed to respond with short whinnies, snorting, hardly perceptible echoes, and soft grunting; it was a strange conversation, intimate and profound, but effective.

At that instant, though with obvious difficulty, Sabba stood up, and remained there still for as long as the extraction of the foal took. Diego sped up the work as much as he could. Several times, he made sure he had left nothing of the placenta inside her, sewed her wounds, and then began to wash her insides with a system he himself had devised. It was a hollow can sewed to a pig intestine that he filled with warm water and a brew of garlic and thyme.

After three cleanings and a last inspection, he considered his work done. Then he helped her lie down and rest on a soft bed of new straw.

Diego watched her, choked with guilt. That foal had died because of his irresponsibility, as a consequence of how slow his hands had moved during the operation, all as a result of the damned wine that had blurred his thinking.

Sabba was anxious. She raised her head and began to look around in all directions, as though she was expecting her little foal to appear at any moment. A thick milk began to flow from her teats and her eyes reflected a sharp pleasure. She whinnied a few times, calling her offspring, without understanding why the creature wouldn't call back.

Tired from receiving no response, she rested her head on the straw, disappointed, though her ears remained attentive.

"I'm going to change, Marcos. When I got to Cuéllar, I made a series of decisions that have turned me into a complete wreck. I took the wrong path, and now I've hurt a creature as innocent as Sabba."

"Will you stop going to the tavern?"

"I will devote myself to working. That is what I'll do. Yes. I'll get back my way of being, my goals, my lust for learning . . ."

Months after her foal had died, Sabba was better physically, although from then on, she seemed sadder.

Diego stopped drinking and took his work much more seriously. He thus reached a degree of fame throughout the region, and without realizing it, he was provoking a growing interest among a number of women. He was an attractive, well-built young man, and single besides, and he soon became the target of their desires.

Over the following months, he turned from one to the other, leaving his old self behind. That definitive, conclusive love he felt for Mencía gave way to other, more fleeting feelings, less vital but still interesting. He decided to imitate Marcos in that game of his, enjoying whatever woman crossed his path.

And thus an entire year passed, until one cold Christmas Eve.

It was then that he came in contact with a person full of mysteries, disgraces, and worse. . . .

Her name was Sancha de Laredo.

II.

Sancha de Laredo was a woman of normal appearance, married, and a mother of two daughters. Her life seemed like that of any other woman in similar family circumstances: working at home, making her living from a small flock of sheep. But in her case, it wasn't that way. . . .

Diego met her by chance, during a thick snowstorm. He was coming back from a neighboring village were he had taken care of a sick cow.

The snow was more than three feet high, and Sabba could hardly walk over the arduous road. For some time, Diego had been looking for refuge to wait out the storm with a roof over his head, but since night had fallen, he had found nothing.

Between the thick curtain of snow, close to a frozen stream, he finally made out a house. He didn't remember ever seeing it before, but it didn't matter. He went there with the hope of getting in, not knowing the house belonged to Sancha.

"Look at that smoke, Sabba. Maybe they'll let us pass the night sheltered there."

He called at the door a number of times without getting a response. He also looked through the window, between the curtains, without seeing anything.

There were some stables beside the house. He thought they wouldn't be closed and he rushed over to them against the vicious wind that was striking him like a lash. When he saw the owners, the next day, he would explain everything.

When he entered the stables, which were small but well cared for, he heard a clamorous chorus of bleats from a pen full of lambs. To one side of them, in another pen, Diego counted no fewer than three hundred sheep. They looked fat and well treated. He looked in his saddlebags for a wool blanket and tied Sabba close to another horse, well built and of an indeterminate breed. The presence of so much livestock would guarantee they would sleep warmly, as long as the sheep would quiet down.

Between the wall and the pen where the sheep were enclosed, there was a narrow passage that Diego walked down, looking for a place to lie down. Halfway along it, he heard a strange sound that came from one of the corners. It could have been a violent dog, so Diego armed himself with a long board he found at his feet.

"Who's there?"

He looked for the corner, step by step, squinting his eyes to see better. And then he discovered two little girls huddled down and holding each other.

"Who are you?" The older one spoke to him, her voice quavering. "This is our house, what are you doing here?"

The girl was around thirteen years old. She had straight hair and a frightened face, peeking up at him as she held on to a long stake.

"Don't be afraid, little girl. My name's Diego and I just want protection from the storm. What are your names?"

"Get out of here!" the younger one yelled. She couldn't have even been six.

"If you want, tell your parents. I'll speak to them so they'll let me spend the night here. Tell them I'll pay."

They looked at each other and began to whisper. Diego couldn't hear them, but he knew they were arguing.

"Don't worry, I'll go to the house to talk to them."

As soon as he turned, the girls screamed at him.

"No, don't go, please."

Diego interrogated them with his stare.

"He's with her right now, and if you bother him, he's going to get mad and then we . . ."

"Are you talking about your father?"

"He's with Mama," the smaller one responded.

"And why aren't you inside the house?" When he saw them from closer up, he was stunned by the fear he saw on their faces.

"So we don't have to hear Mama cry."

"Be quiet, María," the older one said.

"Do you know why she's crying?" Diego began to assume something.

"She does it every night," the girl answered, though her older sister nudged her.

"And you, what did you say before, when you were talking about your father being angry?"

Though he meant his question for the older one, Diego looked at the younger sister. She rubbed her hands together without stopping, and her dress and hair as well. The poor girl was very nervous.

"Nothing. I didn't say anything," said the older girl.

"It's not true. . . . Sometimes he hits us, very hard," the other exclaimed.

"You don't have to explain anything to this man," her sister shrieked. "You'll see; now Papa will find out."

"I don't care."

Diego imagined the father must be intransigent and authoritarian; the girls were probably being punished for some minor misbehavior. But still, with the terrible weather that night and the rough state of their lodgings, he felt bad for them. He heard the older girl call her sister María, and for some reason he remembered Estela. The girl had her same smile and a similar expression in her eyes, and her forehead was as broad as his sister's too.

"How long have you been out here?"

"Two days," María answered innocently. "Papa said we couldn't come out till tomorrow."

When he heard that, Diego was paralyzed. He couldn't understand. If this was some simple trick they'd pulled, it seemed excessive.

"You mean you've been out here for two days without your parents? And what do you eat?"

María rubbed her belly and pointed to a sheep that was suckling a little lamb. She ran to it and grabbed onto one of her free teats. To Diego's astonishment, she put it into her mouth and began to suck. The animal grunted, sniffed at her angrily a few times, but finally accepted it.

Diego looked at the older one, still unable to believe what he had just seen. Rosa confirmed it, nodding her head.

It seemed incredible to him that someone could treat two innocent beings that way, as if they were animals. How could their parents act that way?

In an instant, María ran to Sabba and he followed her. The mare sniffed at her with evident curiosity, and the girl scratched her muzzle.

"What's her name?"

"Sabba."

"She's very pretty." María hardly reached the animal's knee, but she caressed it so sweetly that Sabba snorted with pleasure.

Diego sat her on top of Sabba and the girl, shouting with joy, grabbed onto the mane and pulled, imagining herself galloping, bucking over and over in the saddle.

"Run . . . Fly!"

Diego held her arms tight to keep her from falling.

"Don't touch my sister again!"

That scream from the older sister left him shocked. There was fear, panic, rage in the girl's expression. Diego was disturbed, and a terrible thought came upon him.

"Get out of here, I beg you . . . Please." The first tears sprouted from Rosa's eyes. "If my father finds out you've spent the night here, he'll kill us, and you too. He'll do it to me again . . . no . . ."

Diego got María down from the horse and stood in front of them, upset. On the one hand, he had no right to insert himself in these people's lives. But if he listened to them and left, he would hardly make it far, because of the force of the storm. He understood something strange was happening here and that it wasn't anything good.

María ran to his side and grabbed his leg with a force that was moving. He saw them so fragile and defenseless in those moments that he felt incapable of just doing nothing.

"I'm sorry, I'm not listening. I'm going to go talk to your parents."

"No! Don't do it now." Rosa grabbed his sleeve and pulled on it, begging him.

"But why?"

"Because Mama always says we need a father, and even if he hits her a lot, she can take it, and she's teaching us to do the same."

Diego understood what was happening. That bastard was so wicked, he must be mistreating all of them.

"What is your father's name?"

"Basilio Merino." For some reason, he seemed to recognize that name.

Then they heard a terrifying roar coming from the house. Diego ran out with the girls to see what was happening.

They pushed open the door and went into the house. Crawling along the floor in a nightdress, a young woman was covering her head with her hands.

"Filthy whore! You're a waste!" The man beside her made as if to kick her.

"What are you doing?" Diego ran toward him with clenched fists.

"And who are you?" With olive skin, the man's enormous eyebrows seemed to take up the whole of his face. His eyes showed incredulity and then fury. "You want to tell me what you're doing in my house?"

"It doesn't matter who I am." Diego grabbed the man's shirt and twisted it. "You're a coward. I dare you to touch me and not those poor girls."

The man stood still until, when Diego stopped paying attention, he grabbed a kitchen knife and threatened him.

"Don't butt into issues that don't concern you." He aimed the sharp point at Diego's stomach. "Get out now if you don't want to get sliced from end to end."

"You're not even a man. You should be ashamed of what you're doing with these poor girls."

Basilio called them over with his free arm, as if he needed to protect them from Diego, but Rosa pushed him, escaping him.

"Don't touch me, Father! I hate you!" she shouted.

The man lifted a hand to strike her, and Diego charged him. He stopped, seeing the point of the knife, and then found himself pushed toward the door. The man's face reflected pure madness. Diego could do nothing. The man seemed bent on using the knife, and Diego didn't know how to respond. He looked at the woman. Her face was covered in bruises and her lip was split. She looked back at him, unable to express anything other than desperation.

"I'll tell the authorities about you. . . ." Diego threatened him from outside. "I'll leave, but you should know there will be punishment for this, I swear to you."

"And who is it who's threatening me, if I may know?"

"You'll know when the time comes, and don't worry, it will be soon. And I'll warn you of another thing. You touch them again, and I promise you, I will chase you to the far edges of the world. And when I find you, you'll suffer just the same as they have."

"Look how scared I am," the man said, shaking his hands.

III.

M arcos noticed Diego was furious, beside himself.
   While he told him what had happened, he was so upset that he
wanted nothing more than to return to that house and see what had happened with those three unfortunate girls.

"I'll go see them this very afternoon. Yesterday I couldn't do anything,
but today I'll return better prepared."

"He's not even worthy to be called a man. How can someone be so terrible?" Marcos was deeply disturbed by the story Diego had told.

"If you could have seen that poor woman. . . . She was so wretched! But
in spite of that mask of suffering, she was beautiful."

"And you think he hits the kids as well . . ."

"Yes, and I'm afraid he does even worse with the older one. I don't know,
the girl's face expressed something more than terror when he grabbed her,
while he was trying to throw me out of the house."

Marcos clenched his fist, indignant. That wickedness, wherever it came
from, deserved a severe punishment.

"His name is Basilio Merino and he has a good flock of sheep, maybe
one of the best you can find in the whole community."

Marcos's eyes widened and he sat there stunned.

"You know him?"

"Well, yes . . . Maybe I've heard of him . . ."

He took a mug of wine in his hand and drank slowly, taking his time
and thinking.

Of course he knew Basilio. That man traded wool and meat with him,
and he did a good job, too. Just a week ago they had spoken about a matter
of mutual interest. Marcos had proposed buying his merchandise, since he
had barely been able to fill the orders that were coming in from Valencia.
The deal would benefit both of them; Marcos would be able to give a good

deal to Abu Mizrain, and Basilio would be able to sell ten percent more than he had been to Marcos alone. And the offer had been accepted. For that reason, confronting that man would be a more delicate issue than simply informing the bailiff of his deplorable actions.

"What are you thinking?" Diego took the mug from Marcos's hands and looked into his eyes.

"About Basilio. I remembered a few things about him. . . . He's an influential man, Diego. Maybe too much for us and our reputations."

"What are you saying?"

"He's a trader like me, and I happen to be doing business with him right now. And you know, a problem like this one could—"

"I understand," Diego interrupted him. "When you said *us*, you meant you and your reputation. I get it."

Diego stood up from his chair and began striding around the room, very upset. He tried to restrain his desire to smack Marcos for his pathetic attitude.

"I can guess what you're thinking, but I promise you that if you report him, you're the one who will end up being hurt."

"I don't understand why. But if that was true, I would rather that happen than be responsible for the abuse of those girls, not to mention his wife."

Marcos dried the sweat from his forehead. The situation was disagreeable, but he thought it would be better to talk it through till the end.

"You need to know that Basilio is related to the lord of the villa. That means you'll never get more credence than him if you do report him, unless you have real proof of his crime, and that's not easy. In these cases, the wife usually doesn't testify against her husband, since she depends on him for everything, or else from pure devotion or to keep her children from harm. The most likely thing is you won't have any success."

Diego knew that wasn't the real reason Marcos was dissuading him, that it was his business he was worried about seeing endangered.

He sighed, disappointed, and took on the responsibility alone. He knew he was going to carry on with his plans.

"We'll see, Marcos. . . . We'll see."

Basilio told his wife he would come back soon, just after he had finished with a job.

When they saw him disappear with his cart over the hill, the two girls ran into the house to look for their mother. They found her lying down and drowning in tears.

They got into bed with her and looked for her cheeks to caress and kiss them. They wanted to console her after the brutal beating she had received that morning. They hadn't seen anything, but they could hear their father screaming at Sancha with an unbelievable fury.

"Mother, you need a doctor. . . ." Her older daughter touched her ribs and felt that one was cracked under her fingers. Sancha had one eyebrow split open and her right cheek had an open cut from one of their father's punches.

"I don't need it, honey. It's not so bad," Sancha replied. "You're going to upset her," she said, pointing at María.

The little one had stayed in the stable during the brutal fight. Now, as if in a trance, she played with a long curl from her mother's hair, wrapping it around her fingers. Sancha's inflamed eye caught María's attention, and the girl asked her mother how it had happened.

"My little girl . . ." She stroked one of her cheeks. "Don't worry, dear, I accidentally hit myself on something."

"Be more careful, Mama."

"Of course, my dear. I'll pay attention and be more attentive."

Sancha sat up, a sharp pain in her stomach. One of his kicks had hit her somewhere sensitive, and she had been feeling jabbing sensations for a while now.

"María, go get Mama a little bit of water."

The girl obeyed and skipped away.

Once they were alone, Sancha looked into the eyes of her older daughter.

"Tell me the truth, and don't lie like you did other times to calm me down. Has something happened to you?"

"No, I promise. But if he tries again, I won't do like you. I won't put up with it again, Mother."

"Who was that man you showed up with?"

"His name is Diego, and he told us he was an albéitar. He came to the stable to get protection from the snowstorm. He looked like a good man, but as you saw, he didn't do anything for us. He's just another coward. I hate all men; they're all trash."

"Don't say that, my daughter. He tried, but your father got too violent and he had to flee."

"If he had reacted better, maybe you wouldn't be here now." The girl looked at her mother, so beautiful before, now full of bumps and bruises.

María returned with a pitcher and three glasses. She served the water carefully, but it spilled all over the bed.

"Father will beat me if he sees what I've done." She began to cry.

"See how María reacts over something so unimportant? Imagine the fear she must be suffering inside to say that." Hearing those words from her older daughter, Sancha felt her eyes dampen. "Why don't we leave, Mother?"

"We can't, honey, we can't. Where would we go? He would hunt us down, and it would be worse."

"I've heard you say lots of times you have family in Laredo, close to the sea. Let's go there, Mother. Leave him for once! He's nothing more than a miserable dog. . . ."

"Where are you saying you want to go?" The unexpected voice caught them by surprise and filled all three with an immediate foreboding. He had just entered the bedroom without making a sound. He turned directly to Rosa and grabbed her arm, full of rage.

"You're hurting me," she complained.

"I see how much my daughter loves me, calling me miserable, a dog. You'll learn your lesson now. Come outside with me!"

"Leave her in peace!" the mother screamed, trying to get out of bed. He pushed her violently. "Why are you doing this to us?" she cried, full of misery.

María felt something very bad was going to happen and without thinking twice, she leapt at her father's back, pounding on him with her little fists.

Basilio pushed her away without difficulty and threw her on the bed next to her mother. Rosa, furious, bit his arm with all her strength. Basilio howled, then grabbed her by the neck and lifted her off the floor. He dragged her to the kitchen. She kicked and scratched him amid tears of impotence. She wouldn't allow it, not this time, she thought.

Basilio sat her on the table and looked into her eyes.

"You think it's normal, what you're doing? I come home and I find you encouraging your mother to leave me . . . with all I've done for you . . ."

Rosa wanted to answer, but he squeezed her neck tighter and managed to choke her words.

"Now you'll shut up, little girl."

"Don't touch her." Sancha was at the door, ready to face off against her husband.

"She's my daughter . . . and I can do what I want."

The man looked for her cheek to kiss her, but Rosa took advantage of his nearness to bite his ear. She clenched her teeth so furiously that she managed to pierce it. Basilio began to shriek like a mad dog, but the girl wouldn't let go. The man squeezed her neck harder to choke her and gave her a powerful punch in the chest. Rosa felt asphyxiated, began to cough with pain, and had to let go.

"You act like a beast and I'll treat you like a beast. I'll make you calm down today, you'll see." Touching the wound on his ear, the man went to look for his leather riding crop. When he had gotten it, he brandished it in the air, making it whistle.

He grabbed his daughter by the waist and threw her on the table. Then he tore her shirt, and with her back exposed, he raised the leather to begin her punishment.

Rosa, between tears, waited for the first blow to come down, and when she felt it, it seemed like he was splitting her back in two. Her mother got there in time to stop the second with her hand, though a slap from Basilio made her fall down. When he saw her stretched out and defenseless on the ground, her husband kicked her in the stomach, making her writhe from pain.

Rosa tried to escape but he was holding her down on the table by the nape of her neck.

Then somebody knocked and called at the door.

Basilio told everyone to be quiet, threatening to choke Rosa to death. Whoever it was pounded more fiercely.

"Be quiet or it will be worse. . . ." he warned them

At that moment, little María came out from the bedroom, where she had stayed hidden under the covers. There was fear in her eyes.

Sancha looked at her at the very moment when the person knocked at the door again. The girl knew what she had to do and ran over, opening it.

Diego entered decisively and found the dreadful scene. He looked for his dagger and aimed it at the man.

"Drop that riding crop now!" he shouted, enraged. His gaze radiated dangerous intentions.

"You again?" Basilio replied contemptuously.

Diego looked at the woman, lain out on the floor, with signs of having passed through genuine humiliation, and then at the back of the girl, red and full of marks. He felt a deep hatred for that man, for his wickedness.

"You'll get out of this house right now or else . . ." Basilio flourished the riding crop, hitting at air. "I'm not going to repeat it again! Go!"

Basilio charged Diego like a madman, trying to grasp his dagger, and Diego stabbed him in the thigh in response. Basilio brought his hand to his leg and, before he could do anything, Diego struck him again in the arm.

"I told you to go. . . . Leave her in peace! Do you understand me?"

"You don't know who I am."

"I do indeed. And I also know that if I explain to the abbot what you're doing with your wife and children, and if he knows the terrible sin you've engaged in with them, he will put you on trial, whether or not you have blood relations with the people who run this town. And even if you do get off, your name will be soiled forever. I'll make sure of it, I swear. So get out of here. Leave this place. This is the last chance I'm giving you." Diego pointed the dagger at the man's heart.

"You'll pay for this. One day I'll avenge this insult."

"Get out now." Diego pushed Basilio through the door and followed him out to the stables.

The man saddled his horse and mounted it, shooting a last hateful glance at Diego.

For a few days, Diego stayed with the woman and her daughters in case Merino came back. But when that didn't happen, he returned to the house in Cuéllar, still visiting them every day and taking care of their needs. He felt partly responsible for their future, and he helped them with whatever they lacked. He took care of the sheep, treating their worms and kidney problems, and that spring, they had many new lambs.

After a few months had passed, a great deal changed in that house. The summer brought an abundant harvest of barley, enough to easily sustain their flock. Their income improved and Sancha was flush with money.

She, Rosa, and María worked hard to recoup their joy and peace, their will to live.

With the terrible beatings now nothing more than a memory, the real Sancha appeared, a beautiful woman. At twenty-six years old, she had an almost perfect body; tight hips; firm, large breasts; and very dark eyes. Her lips were fleshy and her voice sweet.

María and Rosa took the various flocks out to pasture in different fields, farther and farther away, and came back at midday. They would make supper with their mother and help her with the rest of the chores.

Sancha tried to carry on with her husband's business, but it was impossible; no one wanted to do business with a woman. Besides, Basilio's disappearance had been looked on suspiciously by nearly everyone, and soon there were voices that criticized Diego's presence in their house. Some even murmured that they had become lovers.

Diego didn't worry too much about those rumors, but Marcos did, since on more than one occasion he'd had to listen to reproaches from some of his clients blaming him for his friend's behavior.

During that time, Diego took care of all the assignments that came to him as an albéitar, though he noticed that they were becoming fewer in number. Marcos had been right. His relationship with Sancha had stirred up all sorts of comments and it was damaging his work. Many asked him about Basilio Merino, as if Diego should know where he was. And there were some who even blamed him for the man's disappearance. But if that wasn't enough, a strange competitor called Efraím had also appeared in the area. Until now, Diego had never seen him, but he knew he was an old Jew who had recently arrived from Granada, and he had a reputation as a talented healer.

For some time, Diego had been finding strange objects the man had left on the farms. They didn't seem to do any harm, but then one morning he saw something truly unsettling.

He was treating some sheep that had ringworm when some stones hanging from different parts of their bodies caught his eye. The owner explained to him:

"They are black snakestones. . . . That's what Efraím calls them."

"I see . . . And what does he say they do?"

The shepherd took one in his hands and showed it to him. It was round, with an irregular hole in its center run through with a cord. This particular one was tied to a sheep's tail.

"This sheep has always had problems giving birth. He told me if I left this hanging here, they would go away."

"And that one?" Diego pointed to another sheep with a stone over one eye.

"That one has always been really mean to her lambs. She pushes them away and I have to pass them off to other sheep. Efraím put that stone there so she would open her eyes and her heart too, that's what he told me."

"And you believe him?"

Diego began to feel discomfited by the man. Without any apparent science or wisdom, the Jew was managing to hoodwink many of Diego's customers. Diego's presence and his counsels had suddenly lost their prestige. First people called the Jew, and if he didn't solve the problem, then they would have Diego come.

"And how could I not listen to him, when he performed an actual miracle for me?"

"Did he hang a stone on you as well?" Diego smiled, imagining one hanging on the man's head to help him with his stupidity.

"Don't make fun. You know as I do that the sheep don't go into heat in the springtime easily, but he told me to rub them down with oil and parsley, on, you know, their parts. . . . And it's like a blessing from a saint. I have more of them pregnant than ever."

"I'm happy to hear that, but I think it might be the result of something else. The land was fertile this year, and the more they eat, the more of them get pregnant."

The pastor looked at him with benevolent disdain. The Jew had powers a mere albéitar couldn't access. It was logical that he'd be jealous, the man decided.

Diego began to be tired of the Jew, of seeing how his followers increased, of his false abilities, of how they worshipped him. . . . Tired, until, during the harsh winter that followed, they met each other.

IV.

Diego helped pull the girl from the ditch and tried to empty the water from her lungs, but she was no longer breathing. Five worried women surrounded her. All thought she was dead.

"Let Efraím try, let him through . . ." one of them said.

Diego looked back and saw the arrival of a man dressed in black from head to toe, with a pointed hood, scowling, with sunken cheeks. A long goatee hung from his chin, and his eyes were small and impenetrable. He seemed quite old.

He made an opening among the women and looked askance at Diego. He pressed his wooden cane into the girl's chest and waited for some reaction. He clicked his tongue twice when she remained there unmoving, and he began to look around on the ground. He found a group of dogs drinking from the river. To the astonishment of all, he walked over to them and rooted around in their feces. For some incomprehensible reason, he selected a pinch of it with a whitish color. He took the girl in his arms and tore open her tunic, exposing her breasts to the air, and rubbed that filth carefully onto her chest.

Diego, like the rest of the spectators, covered his nose with disgust and tried to stop that nonsense, but he had to be quiet. Soon the girl began to cough, and at the same time, water shot from her nose and mouth. When she opened her eyes, she saw the man's emotionless expression. She wrinkled her nose, smelling a repulsive scent, but then she smiled.

The obscure personage turned to the public and looked at them without saying a word, very mysterious. And without even saying good-bye, he turned back to where he'd come from. The women mumbled among themselves, astonished at the miracle, but they didn't dare to call after him, because they were afraid of him.

"Wait!" Diego exclaimed. "Allow me to accompany you."

With his look, the old man gave his approval.

"My name is Diego de Malagón . . ."

"I know that, son, I already know," he responded, his voice grave. "I know much more than you can imagine."

Diego looked at him incredulously and studied his profile. A long nose curved down from his forehead, and his face was furrowed with wrinkles, deep, dry, and branching out in some places.

"In your opinion, what is it in dog feces that manages to cure a drowned person?"

"There is a power that is present in stones, in vegetation, and in matter. It just needs to be recognized by someone with enough sensitivity to be able to apply it at the right time and in the right place." He coughed in a violent, almost forced manner. "You're a healer, I suppose you know what I'm talking about."

"I'm an albéitar. Science is all I know."

"I don't deny its power, but your science isn't good enough for everything."

"What is it not good enough for, in your opinion?"

"To reach the world hidden behind reason. The magic realm."

Diego laughed when he heard that.

"Magic? Magicians? Farces, they're only good for entertaining the gullible at markets and fairs, with tricks and sleight of hand . . ."

"You're a fool," the old man replied drily.

"Why do you say that?"

"One more simpleton. . . . One of those who only believe in what they see. The limit between the real and unreal is very fragile, like the one between science and magic. Don't get me confused; I'm not a wizard or someone juggling at the market. I am acquainted with dimensions of reality you can't even imagine."

"You are speaking with a man schooled in science. I only believe in the tangible; everything else sounds like trickery."

"Science. . . . For you everything is science, yes? You mean, then, that everything outside of reason is false, or a clumsy trick. I see . . . And if I gave you a potion or a remedy that would make you see clearer, that would be helpful to Sancha, so that she would never be bothered by her husband again?"

Diego lost his breath and stopped.

"How do you know about that?" He looked for answers in the depths of his eyes. "She . . . I don't know, she's always kept that a secret, it's impossible."

"I already told you I knew many things."

"But you didn't finish. No one can know what took place in that house. And besides, it's been months since anyone's heard from her husband."

"He'll return, wait and see." The man's face turned somber. "He'll come back full of evil and will sow darkness in the house. He will come back soon. As I told you, I am acquainted with magic, and I know how to guess many more things. . . . Now do you believe me?"

"I admit you've surprised me."

"Magic is everything that confounds reason; sometimes it is words, sometimes deeds. Magic is in the surprise, in enchantment, sometimes in charm. . . . All that, the cause of which is hidden to reason and hard to clarify, is magic."

Diego listened to him with real interest. He thought he had read something similar in *Mekhor Chaim*, the treatise on philosophy and kabbalah that Friar Tomás had lent him. It was explained there that the twenty-two letters of the Hebrew alphabet were spiritual forces that had formed the universe. And it also described the ten Sephirod and the hidden meanings of life and of the realities that surrounded us. But he remembered that it wasn't a book of magic. Diego's mind was open to any sort of knowledge, call it kabbalah or call it magic, but still, even though he had guessed the situation with Sancha and her daughters, the man's way of working clashed with Diego's habitual manner of learning. Diego approached the truth through observation and study, not daydreams or journeys into the ether, as this old man did.

"They call me Efraím. Now I have to go, but if you need that potion I mentioned before, look for me. I'll prepare it so that you can believe me as well."

A few months passed before Diego remembered that potion and that strange magician, until the following spring had come and gone and it had rained nonstop for a week straight. It happened one day when he was visiting Sancha. His last job for the day had been very close to her house.

As soon as she saw Diego, the woman looked very nervous and didn't speak until the two girls were in the stables and they could be alone.

"He was here yesterday. . . ." She was twisting a cotton kerchief in her hands.

"Your husband?"

"Yes, Diego, yes. He wandered around the stables and then he disappeared. Since then, I've been staring out the window imagining him coming to the door. I'm terrified. He's crazy. He painted some strange black figures on the doors of the stable and also on the walls outside. I don't know what he wants. . . . I don't know what he'll try to do to us now. . . ."

Diego embraced her to calm her down and then remembered his conversation with the magician. He had predicted that Basilio would come back to sow darkness in the house. He was sure those had been his words and the worst was that they matched what Sancha had just told him.

"I'll sleep here tonight with you and the girls. If he sees I'm here, he won't dare to come in."

"I thank you from the bottom of my heart, but the terrible thing is, the danger won't end tonight. How will we protect ourselves when you go to work? What will become of us? Nothing and no one will stop him and he'll hit us again. . . . You'll see." Sancha felt her legs giving way and had to sit down. "In the past, there were times when I was tempted to do something so he would never touch us again. Do you understand what I'm saying?" Diego nodded. "But I wasn't able."

Diego thought of Efraím again. He felt confused. Just the idea of asking for his help turned his stomach, but he couldn't stop thinking about his offer of a potion that would prevent Sancha from suffering such humiliation and abuse.

"There may be a way to avoid it." Sancha opened her eyes wide and begged him to explain.

"I still haven't talked to you of Efraím, right?"

She shook her head.

"It's time for you to meet him."

Sancha entered the Jewish quarter of Cuéllar that afternoon, but alone. Diego had thought it was better for them not to be seen together on the street and for that reason he had stayed behind, half a league outside the city walls. Before he said good-bye, he explained how and where she should look for the magician and what his incredible prediction had been.

Once he was alone, Diego dismounted from Sabba and began to walk through the cool, tree-lined path alongside the river. A little while later, he heard the noise of hoofbeats. He made sure it wasn't Basilio, but to his surprise, Marcos had come. Diego didn't call or make himself known since his friend was with the only daughter of the lord of Cuéllar, and he looked very occupied.

"Efraím's house, please?"

A young redhead, with long curly hair and a mischievous face, pointed it out to Sancha. She turned left and took the street that ran on the inner side of the ramparts.

An enormous line of people in front of a small door was the definitive clue that she had found what she was looking for. Some identified her upon her arrival.

"You're Sancha, correct?" The woman at the end of the line was one of her neighbors from the village. "I'm here for my daughter. She can't have children and I heard this man concocts excellent remedies for all types of ills."

"I understand," Sancha said, not wanting to make conversation.

"And you, what do you want from Efraím?" The woman looked at her shamelessly, not respecting her silence.

"I don't really know," she responded softly. Her life didn't matter to anyone.

"You can't come here without a firm reason in mind," the woman went on.

Sancha waved her hands, compelling the woman to talk more quietly.

"Don't tell me, it doesn't matter. . . . You're going to ask him to make your husband come back. Or maybe it's the opposite you want, so that albéitar will take his place. Of course, that's it!" she shouted.

"Leave me in peace, señora," Sancha protested.

The comment bothered her, and she hoped no one else had heard. She observed those who preceded her in the line, and judging from the murmurs she heard and a few sidelong glances, she could see she wasn't correct. And moreover, the woman had turned her back to her, indignant.

"How dare you," Sancha protested in her ear.

"You're a harpy. Look how you take advantage of your husband's absence to shack up with another man. I've never seen such a thing in my life!"

When she heard that, Sancha became enraged and was tempted to choke the woman then and there. She was saved by the opportune appearance of an old man with a hooked nose who peeked out from the door of his shop.

"You, Sancha, come in!" Efraím pointed a finger at her, and she looked back, thinking there might be another person with the same name.

The rest of those present protested, but the old man silenced them with a sharp stare. While she walked to the door, she was surprised by the submissiveness his clients showed. As soon as she entered, she asked him how he knew her name.

"I saw it in the water this morning. I knew you would come."

The man had her pass through to a circular room where there was only a table in the center with a collection of strange figures. He showed her where to sit.

"You don't believe in this, do you?"

"Not very much. I'm coming on Diego's recommendation."

"That's good to hear. You are the proof that finally he has begun to believe. . . . Do you love him?"

"What?" That question not only disconcerted her, but also made her blush brightly. "Are you talking about my husband?"

Efraím looked deep into her eyes, and she felt ashamed.

"I know what you want; that is why I've prepared a potion that will make him disappear from your life." He coughed loudly and wiped his mouth with a black cloth. "Now, it depends on you whether the effect is fatal, definitive, or only temporary." She didn't hesitate to confirm that was what she wanted, though she didn't understand the implications of his commentary.

Efraím picked up some small knucklebones, shook them, and threw them down on the table. He pushed his hair out of his face and looked at how they had landed. Then he sniffed them anxiously and looked at her again.

"When I was talking about your love, I didn't mean him. . . . You have to understand that I see into realms no one else can reach. That is why I know what is moving inside your heart." He closed his eyes. "You like Diego, you feel more and more attracted to him, you want him . . ."

"He's never touched me! From the first day he's respected me, and I have him as well," she protested, though the man was partly right.

"Make him yours, if you love him so much." He lifted a hand to stop her from commenting further. "But now you have to decide about the potion. I have much to do and little time. Do you want it, or no?"

"Yesterday he was wandering around my house. I hate his face, his voice, his breath. I don't want to see him ever again."

"Then you are deciding to have a more definitive effect on your husband, correct?"

"Yes."

"Good. I will not ask any further."

Sancha looked at his sharp fingers and felt disgust when she saw his nails; they were long and painted black.

Efraím read out a fragment of a strange book entitled *Picatrix* that he had picked up from the table.

"'You take a leaf of laurel and tear it with one hand, not letting any of it fall to the floor. It should be placed behind the ear of the person the spell is meant for. Then he is to be given wine. He should take as much as he wants. Then love will disappear from his eyes and it will never return with its erstwhile passion.'"

"Forgive me, but that doesn't seem strong enough," Sancha affirmed.

"Fine. Urgency is a bad companion to wisdom, but let us see what one of the ancient Hindus tells us, something stronger." He turned two more pages of the *Picatrix* and read aloud again: "'The Rowan is a tree contrary to human beings, not by nature, because it kills, but its properties, because it changes hearts . . .'" He raised his eyes and pinned her with his gaze. "This is the one you need," he said, and he slapped the table, convinced, before reading on: "'If a man tries its flower on a full moon, he will no longer be slave to the vice that tormented him, and if he still attempts to engage in it, he will die that very day. No antidote can work against this recipe.'"

Sancha seemed to be more satisfied with this remedy. She still wasn't sure what she was doing there or if it would work, but she could see that the man had something that floated around him, a power she had never seen in anyone. She would try it; she had nothing to lose, however absurd it might seem.

"What tree is this?"

"Relax, you won't have to look for it or wait for next spring to get one of its flowers. Every year I pluck a number of them and dry them out."

He got up from his chair and looked in a clay jar. He took out a handful and showed them to her. Sancha saw that he kept them in branches of six.

"Heat up a tea with two dozen of these and give it to him to drink. It will take effect immediately, and from that moment you will be free of him forever."

Efraím wrapped the flowers in a cloth of white cotton and passed it to Sancha.

"That will be ten *sueldos*."

"Ten?"

"No one said magic was free. You get what you want and I pay my debts."

Sancha took the ten coins from a sack and shook his hand.

"Tell Diego I will look for him in three days, at sundown, at Arroyo Grande."

"Should I tell him anything else?"

"Yes, let him know I will open the doors to other worlds for him."

V.

———————

M encía felt something moving in her stomach.

Her son went on growing inside her without knowing that his mother would never consider him the fruit of love, only of deception.

Full of bitterness and sorrow, Mencía was looking from the window of her bedroom in the castle of Ayerbe, the property of her husband.

This was her second pregnancy. She had lost her first child months before the date of birth arrived. No one knew what the cause of death had been, but she did: that baby had been engendered against her will, against her heart, and her body itself had rejected it from the beginning.

Now, in her sixth month of pregnancy, she had the sense that the same thing was going to pass.

She listened to a loud thunder peal penetrate the castle walls and saw how the water beat against the stone. The storm took her back to another one, that night in the abandoned chapel. She crossed her hands over her breast with an expression of pain and deep grief. Diego had been her only love, a love broken by her mother's ambition, someone erased from her life for the sole reason of maintaining her noble name.

She thought of him every day, remembered his expressions, his words, the sweetness of his kisses. There was not a single night when she went to sleep without saying good night to her beloved Diego. Even when her husband took her, she pretended it was her true love.

Her pain was intimate, fatal, inconfessable.

It was already getting dark when a great bolt of lightning suddenly lit up her bedroom with a cold blue light.

"My lady . . ." Mencía turned away from the window to speak with her lady-in-waiting. "Your messenger has just arrived."

"Let him in, quickly, before my husband comes."

Mencía rubbed her hands together nervously, waiting to see if the news she expected would come.

As soon as he entered, she ran to him anxiously.

"Tell me, what have you found out? And how is he? Have you spoken with him?"

The boy pulled his rain cover from his belt and made ready to answer a series of questions. His throat felt very dry.

"Before I explain, do you have a little water?"

"Blanca, bring him a pitcher, hurry!"

He drank two whole glasses, cleared his throat, and began to speak.

"He's no longer in Albarracín."

"Then you couldn't give him my message?" Mencía clenched her hands in fury.

"No, I didn't manage to. But I found out where he is presently staying . . ."

"Where is he, where?" Mencía's eyes bulged out. "For God's sake, answer me! I'm dying to know everything."

"In the town of Cuéllar, in Castile," he answered, satisfied.

"I don't know that place." Mencía felt a kick in her belly and stretched out in her chair to find a more comfortable posture.

"Between Segovia and Valladolid, halfway. Apparently it's a town rich in pine forests and sheep. I was told this by a trader who had met someone named Marcos. . . ."

"Of course, Marcos is his friend; he's been with him for years," she confirmed.

"Well, his friend chose that area for its excellent commercial possibilities."

"Cuéllar, in Castile . . ." Mencía savored that name aloud, but at just that moment, her husband, Fabián Pardo, entered.

"What's happening in Cuéllar?" He greeted her with a kiss on her lips and stoked her round belly. "My love, has it been a tough day for you?"

"You can go now, young man." Mencía touched her face and felt it burning.

The messenger bowed respectfully and sprinted from the room, faced with the questioning stare of Mencía's husband. She tried to think of an explanation for his question about Cuéllar.

"May I know who that boy you were speaking to was?" Fabián waited until he'd shut the door. "I don't recognize him at all."

"Well . . . I don't think so. In reality, he's . . ." She coughed three times. "I mean he's . . ."

"Leave it, don't continue. You aren't trying to tell me that actually he's your secret lover. Confess it!" He smiled before kissing her on the lips again, with renewed passion. "My God, but how can someone love a woman so much? All day, the only thing I long for is to be by your side."

"Blanca, you can leave. I don't need anything else."

Mencía stood up with difficulty from the chair and walked to the window. It was still raining. Fabián's arms wrapped around her back and met at her breast. He began to kiss her neck and cheeks.

"My love, how I want to feel you again, to recover the passion of our encounters," he said, stroking her belly, "like before . . ."

Mencía fell quiet. To see him so in love with her made her doubly unhappy. She didn't love him; she never had and she never would. Her heart knew only her love for Diego, and he was so far from her. . . .

The tears welled in her eyes and she caught them with her fingers.

"What is it, my darling?"

"Nothing. I'm all excited. . . . It must be for the child." She lied again, as she had done ever since she'd been with him, because her sorrow had another name: Diego de Malagón. Impossible.

Many miles to the south, Sancha took a dish full of boiling water from the fire. Hot on her fingers, she left it on the table and smiled at him.

Basilio Merino, her husband, looked at her without understanding that strange demonstration of affection.

He had come back to the village to stay. Business had been bad since he left Cuéllar, and his family was here anyway. He thought that, if he tried, he could overcome the tensions with Sancha. For all the time he'd been away, he had missed her cooking, the warmth of his home, her body . . .

When he came near his house, he took all the caution necessary to be sure he wouldn't come across that man who had threatened him. Since he didn't see him anywhere, he entered the house without fear, and he was surprised indeed when Sancha welcomed him without problems as soon as she saw him. He had imagined her more bitter, full of rancor, and he found a woman changed, as though she had forgotten all that had happened.

"Sancha, I missed you . . . and the girls, too." He stroked her thigh while she poured the water into a smaller pitcher. "I'm sorry for what I did back then. I've changed, believe me. I'm here to ask you to forgive me."

"You've been away more than a year."

"I didn't dare to come back. I thought you hated me."

"Your sin was great, and not just toward me. But maybe with time, I don't know, maybe we'll forget all that, it could be . . ."

Sancha was disgusted when she felt his hand running over her belly, looking for her breasts. She pulled away in time and placed the steaming pitcher between them, telling him to sit down. Basilio did, though unhappily.

"What is this for? You know I hate these herb drinks. I'd rather have a bit of wine."

Sancha smiled at him but went to a shelf to take down a few clay cups and filled them with hot water. Then she took out a cloth and unfolded it slowly. Basilio watched her, interested.

"What do you have there?" He stretched his neck and saw that they were small white flowers. "I already told you I hate that nonsense. Don't expect me to drink it."

"Are you disrespecting me?" Sancha faced him, her hands on her hips, with a disappointed expression. "Aren't you trying to repair things with me?"

Resigned, the man accepted what she said.

Sancha counted the flowers before dropping them in the cup. Efraím had recommended she use two dozen, but since they were so little, she wasn't sure how many had gone in. It could have been more. Maybe it was.

She poured a bit more in his cup and stirred them with a spoon until she saw the leaves were well steeped. Soon the water was whitish in color and had a sweet and appetizing aroma.

"Try it, you'll like it." She brought the cup over to him and sat on his lap, giving him a suggestive look.

Basilio smelled it and took a sip.

"You didn't put anything strange in it?"

She brought the cup to her lips and pretended to drink.

"The only risk is that I might not let you finish it." She grabbed his chin, kissing him passionately on the lips.

Basilio drank it down in one sip and, hot with lust, grabbed her by the waist. He covered her neck and chest in kisses. Sancha pretended to reject him, waiting for the potion to work. She then let him have her. She deliberately pushed her cup little by little until it fell to the floor and broke in a thousand pieces. That way she wouldn't have to drink it.

Sancha didn't know what effect it would provoke, and so she waited, passive, submissive.

Basilio threw her on the table. Sancha was liking it less and less. He tore at her clothing, and she was beginning to feel increasingly uncomfortable. She had trusted completely in the effects of that remedy, but it didn't seem to be working on her husband. And she couldn't stop his strength. . . .

"Be still! It's been so long that I've lusted for you. . . ."

"Leave me be. . . . I don't want to." She scratched one of his arms, not excessively, as a warning, but he became angry and violent as he had been before, slapping her without consideration.

Sancha shouted and insulted him. And she shouted again when he struck her in the face, when he began to shove her. He had his head over hers and for that reason, she didn't see her come in. Nor could she stop her hand when she drove that enormous knife into his back, and then another, piercing his ribs and driving it into his heart. It was Rosa.

When she heard her mother's cries, the girl had rushed into the kitchen and seen her mother in the hands of that repugnant being. The blood had rushed to her head and, with it, an infinite hatred that pushed her toward him and made her erase him permanently from their lives.

Basilio couldn't speak; the wound had been mortal. He remained fallen over Sancha until she could get away from him, full of disgust. Then she held her daughter, and together, they cried.

When Sancha turned to look at her, she remembered Efraím. He had told her to choose between partial and definitive separation, and she had chosen the latter.

This was the result, though she had never imagined the potion would act in this way.

When Diego arrived that afternoon and found out what had happened, they decided to keep the secret to protect Rosa. He found them calm, without the least flicker of penitence.

They left little María in one of the bedrooms so she wouldn't see anything and Diego dragged the body to one of the stables, where the three of them buried it. Rosa was the first to throw a shovel full of earth atop it. Her and her mother's martyrdom was over, the worst horror they had known in their lives. She felt relieved when she saw her father disappear forever beneath the earth.

Once they were done, Diego left them alone to take the horse of that vile character northward. He decided to sell it at the first fair he saw far enough away so nobody would associate the horse with Cuéllar or its former owner. Days later, once he'd returned to Cuéllar, he saw Efraím.

As always, the old man surprised him.

"How is the widow Sancha?"

VI.

The soft breeze of the desert shook the heavy curtain of Estela's bedroom.

Hidden behind it, a shadow waited for the first light of day to reach the bed in order to act. Its owner breathed heavily, nervous.

Two guards watched over the doors of that bedroom, and that is why he had gone to the patio. It was the only possibility of reaching her.

For a moment, he hesitated. The risk of being discovered was huge. Anyone could easily know who did it. He scratched his forehead and made the decision to try things differently.

He was about to jump to the neighboring patio when he heard her cough and looked back at her. A crescent of orange light had just reached her face and bled over it, blending in with the color of her hair. Her beauty was enchanting, and his intentions toward her were definitive.

He approached in utter silence and brushed against her sheets. Temptation ran through his hands. He could do it right there, at that moment. He observed the rise and fall of her breast while she breathed, sleeping.

He was so close to what he wanted. . . .

Without touching her, his eyes trailed over her cheeks and her fingertips, then her lips, and he longed to feel that thin neck between his hands. He would do it at that moment. . . .

The sudden call for prayer stopped him. When he heard someone coming into the bedroom, he ran and hid. He made it to the curtain in enough time not to be seen, pushed it back, and left Estela's patio, making it to the neighboring one after jumping over a low wall that separated them.

That new bedroom wasn't safe. He immediately thought of a new way to make his plan happen, maybe harder, but he thought he could do it.

He inhaled deeply to recover from the panic he had just felt, and when he walked down the hallway, he found himself faced with one of Estela's servants who was about to enter her room.

He decided to ready everything for after her bath.

Princes Najla sank in the warm waters of the enormous pool inside the private baths of the harem. When she stepped out, she flung her hair back.

"You know that spirits like to live near water? That's why we light candles when we invoke them, so that our presence is pleasing to them."

Najla chose a flat candle and made sure it would float. She pushed it toward Estela and the girl received it with a smile. When she felt her servant's hands on her back, she closed her eyes and tried to relax. The aroma from the rosemary oil the girl was massaging her with rose to her nostrils.

Najla began to sing the praises of the Prophet.

The hammam, or weekly bath, was the best experience in the harem for Estela. There she forgot her misery while being transported by the fantastic sensations that came with the ritual.

"In water there is poetry, purity, and wisdom, because it quenches the thirst of the soul." Najla toyed with the rose petals that floated around her and came over to her friend. She looked at her back. It was covered in scars from her cruel punishment in the square.

"Do they hurt?" She ran her finger over one of them.

"It's not there where I feel the most pain."

Najla felt compassion for her.

"He shouldn't have done it. My brother has been cruel with you." Najla stirred the water to clear her image from its surface. "I know what it feels like when they make you suffer."

Estela imagined she was referring to her break with Sancho of Navarre, which Najla had never gotten over. Estela likewise remembered her brother. She had been thinking of him since Tijmud told her about the conversation between Pedro de Mora and the vizier, when the name Diego had come up and the former had promised to avenge himself.

The gladness that she felt on knowing Diego was alive was immense, though there was little information about him. According to Tijmud, Don Pedro had confronted him. He didn't know where or how it had occurred, but it didn't matter, the news had filled her with hope, but also fear.

The two slaves helped them to leave the water and waited for them to lie down on some hammocks before anointing them on the back with lotions of heather and almond. Afterward, they gave the two women long massages.

"I love you, sister." Najla turned her head to Estela and watched her, bewitched by the beauty of her body. "I don't understand why he makes you suffer. . . . How can you torture a woman you desire?" She sat there a moment in silence. "Even if you're a slave, I understand you deserve respect. I consider you a sister and I understand your pain. More and more, I feel your pain. You are fragile and he is so powerful."

Estela thanked her for her words.

"Anyway, if you wished, my brother would give you everything. You could be the greatest, his favorite. . . . That idea never attracted you?"

"Never, Najla; I only want to be free," she answered, while the slave wiped the excess oil from her stomach with a cloth.

"Free! Do you think I am? No one is. You should realize that for once. Neither you nor I will ever be. Think about it. Our culture prevents us from aspiring for anything except matrimony. We are born and live for men. We are like their limbs, entirely at their service. That's how it is. Before, I too longed for that sense of liberty, when I studied in Seville. I believed I could reach it if I cultivated my intelligence, absorbing the different arts and the science of philosophy. I imagined then that I could teach poetry and ideas to my women, as others had done with me. And once I had enough preparation, I would flee to Christian lands to begin there, without being anyone, my way, without the impositions I suffer now. . . . That was my plan, but none of it happened. Even running away took courage, and I didn't have it. I returned to Marrakesh, I met the king of Navarre, and the rest you already know." She rubbed her hands with rose essence. "Free, you say . . . An impossible dream."

When she sat up, she called for Ardah, the slave who painted her skin with henna. She took two towels and dried herself neatly, wiping away the last traces of oil.

Najla walked naked to a narrow window facing north and felt a pleasant breeze on her body.

"Enjoy the wind. The wind is free."

Estela came over to her, closed her eyes, and was transported to an infinite, relaxed, drunken state by the aromatic traces of oil on her skin, feeling the air caress her body.

"Princess Najla . . ."

When they heard that voice, they turned and saw Ardah. She was carrying a copper tray with two jars of henna paste and two brushes. One was for Estela. The woman was nervous, afraid of making a mistake.

The paste they were tattooed with once per week was made in a special section of the harem, and two women with expert hands were in charge of it. There they mixed leaves of the plant with water, sugar, and lemon.

Afterward they added aromatic oils of acacia, tamarind, and clove. But that day, after they made it, a man showed up, and the women didn't dare to ask any questions. He threatened them with death if they told anyone he had been there. And they said nothing. They let him have one of the jars, because they knew his reputation and didn't doubt the threats he had voiced. He emptied inside a few drops of a brownish, stinking liquid and told them that that jar, only that one, was for the concubine Estela, the Christian with the red hair.

Najla looked at her hands and arms and decided on a new tattoo, less boring than the one she had. Those vegetal forms were always the same. She turned to Ardah and asked her to go for another stencil.

The woman stood up, ready to take the tray and everything she'd brought with her.

"But leave the tray here."

The slave became nervous, cleared her throat, and hesitated, but she didn't dare to touch it and left it where it was. The jar on the right was the one she had to use with Estela. That man had ordered her to do it that way, after paying her for the favor with a generous bag of money. She didn't want to ask anything because she desperately needed that money for her family.

When she returned to where the two women were, she thought she would choke. Princess Najla had one of the jars of henna in her hand and Estela the other. And, laughing, they had begun to paint each other.

"Allow me . . ." she screeched, losing control.

"What is with you, Ardah?" Najla looked at her surprised as she passed her the jar and the brush. "Don't worry, we won't take your job. No one does it better than you."

The woman, trembling, began to draw butterflies on Najla's hand, and then on her back, and on her legs some scorpions, and circular figures on her breasts. She didn't know it, but that paste was the one Pedro de Mora had given her for Estela.

Efraím passed him the book carefully, as though it were the most delicate object in the world.

Diego looked at its outside. The strange drawings and symbols attracted his attention.

"It's *Picatrix*." The man's voice was grave and transcendent. "The greatest treatise ever written about the noble art of magic. The greatest compilation of ancient knowledge. From ancient Greece to Persia, from Damascus to India, without overlooking the mysterious of Egypt. A one-of-a-kind book. It's written in Arabic, and you will be able to understand it. In it you will find another kind of science. I think it will help you open your eyes. Inside, it explains everything from how to destroy a city with a ray of silence to the most sophisticated techniques for influencing people who are far away. But above all, in your case, it will tell you how the stars influence the apparition of certain diseases, disordering mineral, animal, or vegetal elements."

"I remember seeing another copy in the monastery in Fitero."

"How strange. . . . Christians are prohibited from reading it. What use could it be to friars?"

"Maybe someone wanted to know whether magic came from God or the devil."

"And what is your opinion?"

"I prefer to think God has given it his blessing."

They were seated on a log, facing the stream. Efraím threw a large stone in the water and immediately waves circled around it.

"You see them?"

"Are you referring to the rings?"

"Yes. I counted five rings, an uneven number, a good omen."

"If you try with a bigger stone, you'll get more than five. You'll see. Things don't happen because of mysterious causes; they're the fruit of physical causes. A bigger stone pushes away more water around it."

Efraím threw another, larger stone, and there were only three rings.

"A magician can change the logic of the elements, as I just did with the water. It responded not to your logic, but to my will. And if you learn to capture a spirit with a star and then guide it toward matter, you will achieve goals that right now seem impossible."

"Do you think in this way it is possible to cure one of the diseases that albéitars currently consider incurable?"

"Try and see, my friend. Read the *Picatrix* and we will see if it's possible or not."

VII.

E fraím slit the throat of a lamb in Diego's presence to take out its liver shortly after it died.

"When it's warm, you can see much better," he commented as he separated the viscera.

Diego was skeptical.

"Are you going to guess my future with those organs?"

"Have I ever deceived you before?"

Diego watched him. He was aware he was entering into much darker regions of reality, at the hands of someone whose final intentions he didn't understand.

He had to admit that Efraím knew how to locate powers inside the most unbelievable objects, and that was as real as it was disturbing. Every time he asked him how he did it, the Jew attributed it to a conjunction of cosmic forces, material Diego knew nothing about. And yet he had seen him working with stones and firewood and getting utterly incredible responses from them. It was as if, thanks to him, objects discovered they had been made for other reasons. Something unbelievable for a mind like Diego's.

For example, he still couldn't explain what had happened with Basilio, and nothing Efraím would tell him shed any light on that dark circumstance. Though six months had passed since then, he still asked himself if the potion had had any kind of effect on the death of that bastard, given how it occurred.

Though he had serious doubts about the goodness of his magic, Diego was still interested in Efraím. For that reason, he tried to see him every week, on the banks of the Arroyo Grande, far from inopportune gazes and malicious commentaries.

Diego wanted to know whether in any of his books there were descriptions of the diseases that had still not been explained. The Jew assured him there were and gave him, as an example, certain remedies, truly strange ones, that were described in them. According to him, every treatment needed a special touch, depending on which constellation was dominant during the cure, something very difficult to apply.

Diego wanted to apply logic to his strange theories, but that always became an almost impossible task.

One day Efraím initiated Diego into the fundamentals of magic, its key ideas, revealing to him that everything came from the power of the seven stars as they cast their light over the earth. According to the old man, the celestial bodies had the ability to influence the essence of each individual, the same way as they did with minerals and vegetation. In the middle of that strange theory, he defined the concept of a potion as a common tool among magicians, a mix of the three kingdoms present in nature unified to achieve a definite end.

Many times Diego felt incapable of distinguishing when he was talking about the real or the imaginary, for he referred with equal mastery to both worlds.

"The gallbladder is swollen."

Diego abandoned his thoughts when he saw how Efraím was separating the gland from the liver to show it to him.

"This indicates to us something of true importance." He handled it without restraint, and his eyes moved back in his head. "It tells me that one day, you will be a servant to the highest power, and that to him, you will offer your ears, your talent, all your wisdom . . ."

Diego listened to him with skepticism but studied the remains of the liver, seeing three whitish lines on the upper lobes that he didn't remember seeing on healthy livers.

"I don't understand what you're saying to me." He pointed at the marks. "Do you see another message in those lines?"

"Of course; they are another good omen. But now be quiet, I need to concentrate."

He put a finger on each temple and breathed in a forced way, no fewer than five times. When he finished, he spoke again.

"The Sumerians employed a complex technique for seeing the future. Once they had looked at the liver, they burned it to interpret the effects of the flame upon it. I have only tried it three times, but I assure you the result has always surprised me."

"Are you going to burn it?"

"Exactly."

Efraím extracted the liver from the lamb, cleaned it off, and placed it on a bed of dry straw. Then he made a fire and lit a twig. He brought it over to the straw and the liver, and that instant it produced a column of thick gray smoke, sticky, with an unpleasant odor.

"From here forward, Diego, please memorize everything I tell you. Do it, because I will not be able to remember it when I awaken."

Efraím breathed in that smoke until he had filled his lungs and immediately closed his eyes while he pronounced some words with a hollow, rough voice. When he opened his eyes again, he focused his attention on the flames and explored their colors, the forms that evolved as they danced over the remains of the liver, and studied the twists of vapor that formed as it combusted. As if in a dream, he began to listen to the crackling of the fire over the straw. And without any warning, Efraím opened his eyes as wide as possible and a strange tremor possessed his lips, as if he was trying to talk but something prevented him. He sucked in more smoke and seemed to chew it. After all those preparations, he finally began to talk.

"The mountain will weep blood, glory, and love."

Diego shook his hands in front of the man's eyes and confirmed he was in a trance. It seemed useless to him to dive any deeper into that vision.

The magician then brought his hand to his mouth and gave a startling cry.

"A shout in the air . . . A minaret. You flee . . ." After he said that, his legs began shaking violently, and he scratched at himself. Diego looked at him, worried, without knowing what to do. Efraím continued:

"A rope, wood, life, and death. Resist."

As soon as he'd finished speaking, he seemed exhausted, as if done with a long, strenuous job.

Diego memorized the phrases with dedication; he didn't want to forget.

Once it was done, Efraím spit out a disgusting-looking black paste and fell on the ground as if dead. Diego ran to help him and pulled him unconscious from the flames, without understanding what had happened. It took the Jew a while to come to.

"Are you all right?"

"Well . . . more or less . . . I think that . . . it's back . . ." He paused long between his words.

Diego remained astonished. Soon he saw how the man again stared into the flames and heard him recite something that seemed like a prayer. Then he turned, aware of the moment's importance.

"I don't pretend to know what I told you; I just want you to remember it for the rest of your life. Only you will know if those three prophecies finally come true."

And that is what Diego did. He held them in his memory, feeling incapable of deciphering them. A mountain, blood, air, wood, rope . . . They could mean so many things that one day he decided to stop thinking about them and just kept them in the back of his head.

Marcos seemed on the edge of fainting from pure exhaustion. He had just returned from Medina del Campo, where he had spent two straight weeks because of a commercial dispute with a minor noble who had hoped to cheat him on a costly order of wool. He'd had to split hairs repeatedly to get what was coming to him. And though he was satisfied in the end, those maneuvers had left him exhausted.

"You've already taken over the markets of Tordesillas, Peñafiel, and now Medina. And you still want more?" Diego served himself a cup of cherry liquor and put wood on the fire. "What you really need is a woman and to settle down for once."

"I suppose you're telling me because of the great experience you have of it," Marcos replied sarcastically, but Diego didn't take it personally.

"What happened to Lucía, the daughter of the local lord? I've hardly heard you talk about her recently." Diego took another sip of the smooth liquor, a gift from a sheepherder.

"Uhmmm . . ." Marcos licked his lips when he remembered her. "She was a real joy, I assure you. The problem started when she began with the word *marriage*. And you know, I had to get serious."

"Right, but since then I haven't seen you with anyone else. . . . And for you, that's strange."

"I've always said it's better to change, not to stick with just one. I'm not like you."

"You're saying that because of Mencía."

"Not exactly. Now I'm thinking of Sancha, the one you're taking care of."

"As far as what you're thinking, there's nothing there. You know she's a married woman."

"I know, but we all think it's strange that you've been around her all these months without ever once trying her sweet charms, because even you'll admit, she has them." Diego didn't want to give any sign of agreement. "Imagine . . . A lonely woman, no sign of her husband, waiting up for him so long. I don't know. She must really be missing . . ."

Diego stopped him before he said something vulgar.

"I tried to help them, nothing more."

"People are talking."

"What do you mean?"

"They think you're lovers, and some have even suspected you to be wrapped up in Basilio's disappearance. Understand?" Diego looked away to not show his worry. If some time they discovered the body in that stable, they would definitely come after him. "And the worst is that the rumors of your supposed untoward relationship are reaching the highest ecclesiastical authorities."

"Let them worry about their own business."

"I understand, but besides there's that strange Jew. . . . For them, that relationship smells even worse. You know perfectly well that people don't like to see a Christian and a Jew, or a deicide, as they call them, mixing with each other. I don't know what you see in him, but they've told me the man is accused of witchcraft and that elsewhere he was already been tried for demonic practices. Think it through, Diego; that is how the abbot sees it. You must know what you're doing."

"I'm interested in what he knows, that's all."

"That sounds fine, but remember that he's being watched. Be careful where you go and be discreet. And please, stop going to see Sancha. She doesn't need you anymore."

Marcos's worry was not as disinterested as he made it seem. The suspicions people had about Diego could affect him too, and his business as a consequence. And he wasn't about to let that happen.

"I don't know, Marcos. . . . We'll see."

VIII.

People were dying without knowing why.

It wasn't the plague, and it wasn't cholera.

Every day the number of the affected rose and no one knew how to stop the disaster.

The panic ran through the town of Cuéllar and the surrounding villages while their citizens died. The churches were full, and the blessed walked through the streets trying to combat that unknown evil. There were too many bodies, too much pain and fear. Some even affirmed that it was the end of the world.

Seeing the gravity of the situation, Diego presented himself to the town council, but they paid him no attention. On his own, he tried to investigate what could produce those symptoms, examine the lesions, and try to draw a relation between what he saw and things he'd read.

The lord of the town, Rodrigo Bermúdez, asked one person after another what should be done. He felt worried by the gravity of the situation and disappointed at the lack of explanations or easy remedies.

As the first delegate to the king of Castile, Don Rodrigo was the maximum authority in the region. His reach covered not only the town, but also a grand extension of lands conceded by King Alfonso VIII. A total of thirty-six villages made up the community of Cuéllar. Every six of them formed a group that sent a representative to the council. These representatives would meet on occasion to talk about the apportionment of pastureland, the punishment of certain crimes, and other themes of common interest, such as the present epidemic. Each man had a voice and vote at these meetings.

Most of the inhabitants of the region were free men, many arrived from the north of Castile with the dream of gaining land and livestock for their families. In exchange, they assumed the risk of attack by the Saracens, since the reconquest of those lands was recent and they were still close to the frontier. As a recompense, they depended on neither nobles nor clergy, as was more common in the feudal lands to the north.

Rodrigo Bermúdez resided in a preserve at the top of the hill, in a grand fortress, a citadel in the middle of the city. That was where the leaders of the community—the six representatives of the towns, four members of the clergy, and Rodrigo himself—would meet, in a great hall.

That first Friday in April of the year 1208, the matter that had brought them together was the gravest one to ever be discussed around that table. Those present argued heatedly in an atmosphere of great agitation. They were conscious that any of them could be affected.

"I'm telling you, it's witchcraft!" the abbot announced. He was a man of small stature, hunched, with a cold, hard stare.

"Or a divine punishment," the town representative from Navalman-zano said. Among the villages he represented were Sanchonuño, Zarzuela del Pinar, and Navas de Oro. "It's not like anything we've seen before, and it doesn't discriminate based on age, class, or religion. It seems like one of those biblical plagues. . . ."

"And it provokes madness and hallucinations," the representative of the southern villages added. "Just in my case, I saw this very morning one of my neighbors invoking Saint Matthew in a shout, while he rolled around on the ground like a pig in a mud pit."

The lord of the town dried the sweat from his hands on his vest without knowing how to solve that disgrace. The dead were already more than a hundred, and only two weeks had passed since the first victim was struck. The doctors didn't know what caused it and could only fight against the symptoms. Desperation was absolute.

"It's also started affecting the sheep," the representative from Mon-temayor said.

The rest sat there without speaking. The population was most important, but if the livestock was also affected, the disaster was even worse. Sheep were the chief source of income for the area.

The man explained that in the neighboring village of Rapariegos, a flock of sheep had been affected by a very strange illness.

"They were turning in circles as if they'd gone mad, without stopping. Some hung their heads and ran crazily, running into everything and leaping about for no apparent reason. They all seemed possessed by the same devil. The strange symptoms and the terrible lesions they had led the owners to call the albéitar Diego to get his opinion."

"I don't see how they keep giving work to a man who refuses to even hide his relations with that devilish Jew," the abbot said, without letting the other man finish.

"What are you talking of?" Rodrigo asked him.

"It's strange to me you don't know. No one's mentioned to you the albéitar who is frequently in the company of a wizard—or magician, it's all the same—who goes by the name of Efraím?" Rodrigo shook his head. "Well, it's true, and nothing could can come of a person whose job consists in telling fortunes or making strange remedies that confuse our parishioners. Behind his apparent benevolence, I assure you he hides a personality full of unspeakable secrets."

"And what does that have to do with our albéitar?"

"It seems that he too has relied on the Jew's remedies to cure some of his horses. I suspect he may have been contaminated by the black arts."

"Where I'm from, we know him well," the representative of Hontalbilla said. "Diego can often be seen in the home of one of our neighbors, a beautiful woman named Sancha de Laredo who was abandoned by her husband not long ago. At this point, no one doubts he's having relations with her, disregarding the good example the two of them should be setting for the poor daughters from that marriage."

"One more proof that the filthy Jew has got him caught up in his evil magic. . . ." the abbot remarked.

"All right, all right, I see where you are going," Rodrigo Bermúdez interrupted them. "I'm not a person to judge his deeds or who he spends time with. Diego de Malagón is the best at his job, and his opinion could be essential to us in these difficult circumstances." He turned to the man who had mentioned the illness of the sheep.

"The albéitar said it could be worms." They all looked at him, shocked. "Yes, he said worms in their brain. I had never heard of it before either."

"If it's that, it's not related in any way to our problem," Don Rodrigo resolved. "Just today I found out that this week, two women have miscarried and we have another five about to die, eaten up with gangrene." He stood up from his chair and looked nervously at those around him. "Does anyone have a suggestion?"

"We should call more doctors. Maybe they will see something the others haven't," one of the churchmen offered.

"I agree, and I will take care of it myself," Don Rodrigo answered. "I will order all the sick people be confined to one parish." The abbot began to protest, thinking it would be his own, but Don Rodrigo used his authority to silence him. "We will isolate them to prevent more contagion."

Everyone approved of the decision except for the abbot and the other churchmen who were aligned with him.

"I propose we hold prayers tonight and tomorrow, given the ineffectiveness of the measures that have been taken thus far," the abbot spoke again, conscious of the effects his words would have on Don Rodrigo's prestige.

The latter was indignant. Since he had arrived in Cuéllar, he had detested the attitude and personality of that man, though he tried to keep up appearances.

"You pray, and I'll dedicate myself to helping our neighbors in the meantime," he answered viciously.

"I will. Of course I will. . . . When man doesn't find the necessary answers, he has to look for them in God. He will open our eyes." He crossed himself devoutly.

Veturia shook Diego to wake him up. She knew he had gone out the night before to oversee a mare giving birth, but it was already late, almost noon.

"Señor Diego . . . that Jewish gentleman is waiting for you downstairs." The servant cracked the windows.

"He's come with an awful-smelling package."

After washing his face and dressing, Diego went downstairs without losing a second. Efraím's presence at those early hours struck him as odd.

"I've tried almost everything, Diego." His voice quivered and he seemed desperate. "The truth is I don't know what we're up against, or whom."

Diego looked at him, worried. He had never seen the old man in such a state; he was sweating unstoppably and rubbing his hands together nervously. His face, moreover, reflected tremendous weariness and an expression on the edge of panic.

"My two sisters have fallen sick, Diego, and they're going to die. They're shaking terribly, having hallucinations. I saw their eyes roll back in their heads, and they were shouting words that made no sense. I tried three different potions and two talismans, and nothing worked. They have the same sickness that's killed the others."

Diego understood his fear. He saw many people die every day, and he shared the same feeling of powerlessness with Efraím.

"Come to the kitchen. You'll see, we'll come up with a solution."

On one side of the chimney, they saw Veturia stirring a cauldron over the fire.

Diego pointed for Efraím to sit and brought over a pitcher of fresh water. He waited for him to drink, watching him the whole time. Then he asked for a bottle of hot milk and a little bread from his servant. He hadn't had breakfast, and he felt himself on the verge of fainting.

The woman left it on the table and began to knead a mass of dough with butter in the other corner of the kitchen. She appeared to be going about her business, but in fact she was doing something else. She didn't want to lose a single detail of what they spoke of there, and even less if it pertained to that strange character.

"Do you remember that one day I spoke to you of the twenty-eight mansions of the moon, the ones the *Picatrix* refers to? The ones the Hindu wise men talked of?"

"If I understood correctly, you said they were the model for the man-ufacture of talismans for very concrete uses. . . . Wasn't that it?" Diego answered.

Without giving any explanation, Efraím opened the packet he had come with and took out a dead serpent and three balls of soft green paste.

Veturia looked at it sideways, feeling disgusted.

Diego noticed the woman's curious attitude and sent her out of the kitchen. She was stupid but very religious and thought that the oddities they had couldn't reflect the benevolence of God, especially if they were in the hands of a Jew. But she obeyed Diego and went into another room, though she was careful not to shut the door all the way.

"What are you thinking of doing with that?"

Diego pulled away from the table when he saw the package's revolting contents.

"These balls are called *tintas*. They contain the visage of Capricorn and are made with verdigris and fermented resin. They capture the spirit of the dominant star and channel it into a function, a talisman; in this case, over a snake or serpent, because it is a symbol of wisdom. I will need a pot with warm water where I can leave the *tintas* to dissolve little by little. Then, I will drain all the blood of this snake over the liquid and you will read what comes up there. . . ."

Veturia, from the adjoining room, cracked the door wider to hear a little better. What they had said up to that moment had astonished her. She couldn't imagine what strange enterprise could bring that wizard into contact with her master, but it must be something sinister. She was afraid. Her legs began to shiver and she felt choked. If she didn't breathe a bit of fresh air, she would faint. She pushed the door open and turned to Diego.

"Excuse me, but I have to go out for a moment."

"Of course, Veturia. Feel free."

She almost ran out and didn't even look at what they were doing.

Efraím went on explaining.

"You should concentrate on the ripples, and on the forms the blood makes in the water. Then think of whatever it evokes. Let yourself be dragged into the other world. If you're lucky, you'll see what is happening and where it comes from. For some unknown reason, I can't manage to, maybe there's some aura that's preventing me, I don't know . . ."

"What you're proposing seems so strange. I don't think it will do anything, to tell the truth." Diego felt deceived by the ridiculous solution.

"You could save many people, my sisters as well, or even us, if we get sick too," Efraím responded, truly at his wits' end.

Diego stood up to stretch his muscles. It sickened him that this man could believe that the solution to all this drama could lie in a pot full of garbage, when Diego had been working for days on end using all the science and wisdom he had to find an answer.

"I've gone over dozens and dozens of treatises in my mind looking for something similar to this scourge," Diego said, "and not only that, I've also looked over the lesions on more than twenty sheep, to see if I could establish any relation between the deaths of the animals and of their owners shortly afterward." He sat back down for a moment in silence. "And after all that, I don't have an answer."

Efraím scraped the serpent with a sharp knife and squeezed it from one end to the other so that the blood would drain over the greenish water. Besides a swirl in the center, there were various irregular shapes inside.

"Forget it, Efraím. I believe in science, not in auguries or strange predictions like the ones you're trying with me."

"Don't reject it now! Trust me. You still haven't seen the power that resides in matter. Don't think so much of your science and open your eyes to the dark side of reality. Sometimes there is no solution but to cross over."

Diego was uncomfortable. Those last words made him doubt the benevolence of the man's techniques.

"Are you talking about black magic?" Diego stared at him pointedly. "Is that what you did with Sancha's husband?"

Efraím lowered his head and answered reflectively.

"I know it, I admit it. . . . When I saw that the poor family needed a final solution, I took advantage of an old spell that could have, so to say, a dark effect. Yes, that's how it happened."

"You don't sound remorseful."

"Nothing is more satisfying than destroying evil, it is true, and that man's soul was rife with it."

Diego was worried. The answer was not especially convincing, and he failed to see the logic in looking for God knows what information in that colored water.

Efraím had disappointed him. Maybe he had overestimated him.

"Do you think there could be black magic behind the evil that's descended upon us?" Diego asked.

"I have the feeling there is. Some time back, I heard the story of a Prussian colleague who apparently won his reputation with sinister deeds. They say that he once cursed an entire town for refusing him entry, and as vengeance, prepared a concoction that brought great misery to the inhabitants. When he threw it into the well where the people got their drinking water, the effects struck everyone. I memorized the formula, more from curiosity than anything else."

He closed his eyes and modulated his voice as he recited it.

"It went thus: Take fourteen laurel seeds and five mustard seeds, mill them very fine, put them in a clear spring with a mix of calf and sheep rennet, and cover the whole with goat's milk; beat it, and the mix will cause madness to all who drink it, and no one will know the source of the madness."

Efraím stared at Diego, waiting for some commentary.

Diego said, "I don't know. . . . The rennet ferments the milk and I suppose the seeds have some toxic element, and once they're mixed . . . it could be . . . but I still think our problem has a more basic origin, something more accessible to the knowledge we have."

Efraím pushed the cauldron with the mixture of water and blood toward him.

"Then look for it there. . . . And quick!"

Diego felt overwhelmed by his insistence and looked into the colored liquid.

"Clear your mind," Efraím told him.

Diego paid attention and concentrated on what he had seen in the sheep, their symptoms, the miscarriages, the nervous convulsions, their rapid deaths . . . He remembered the inflammation in their livers and the hemorrhages in their intestines when he opened them up.

He also thought of that strange recipe the magician had just told him. He thought it over slowly. None of the ingredients he had mentioned could provoke such a reaction on their own. Something had to happen when the laurel was brought into contact with the rennet, or the mustard with the milk, or all together, to produce such a terrible effect on the mind.

He remembered hearing Efraím say that sometimes, different elements in nature could come together to transform the use of something.

He turned these ideas over in his head repeatedly without coming to any solution. That is what he told Efraím. His plan hadn't worked. He had seen nothing.

The magician left, destroyed, without a single hope of doing anything to prevent his sisters' deaths or those of so many others who would follow on them sooner or later.

For the rest of the day, Diego couldn't stop thinking about it. He felt as if he were stuck in a maze, sensing there was an exit close by but unable to take the right path. For days now, he had the sense that the cause must lie with some food or perhaps the water supply.

That same afternoon, when he was headed to the house of a client, he had to cross a damp pine forest that scarcely anyone ever passed through. The sky was still blanketed with clouds after the day's rainfall, but the temperature was still mild that early autumn afternoon.

Sabba heard the crunching of fallen branches under her hooves as she crossed by the tree trunks. Amid the leaves, Diego saw a great quantity of mushrooms and got down to pick some. He loved them. There were all different shapes and colors, the most delicious ones right alongside those that could kill with just the smallest taste. He found one of the worst, a red one with white spots on its cap, and stomped on it so no one would mistakenly pick it. He remembered reading of its effects in a treatise on botany: blindness, attacks of madness, and fantastic visions, among others. He saw another like it, still bigger than the one he'd destroyed, and went to crush it as well when he stopped, smelled his hands, and realized something that hadn't occurred to him before then. He shouted with joy.

He had just figured out what was killing the people. It had been right under his nose, and neither he nor anyone had figured it out.

He just needed to do one more test to prove it, just one.

IX.

Veturia watched what Diego was doing without knowing what he was after.

The afternoon before, the woman had returned home somewhat calmer; she had decided to forget what she had seen and heard in the presence of the Jew. They always told her she suffered from an excess of imagination, and maybe she had wanted to see things where there was really nothing.

First thing in the morning, she crossed paths with Diego when he was running out to the stables. He disappeared inside and then galloped off shortly afterward on the back of his mare, Sabba. Though she imagined she wouldn't see him until lunchtime, soon he was back. He had a number of bags, some full of rye bread, old and hard looking, and others with seeds of the same grain.

As soon as he'd greeted her, he asked her for ten mugs filled with water and a bigger one with hot water and fennel. Veturia made it for him and left it as he had asked. She decided to stay there, dying with curiosity, to see what he was going to do with all that.

Diego sniffed a few pieces of bread and scraped the moldy parts of the crust with a knife. He made a mound of the worst parts in the center of the table. He seemed happy as he looked at the result. The color was purple, the consistency dusty. He took a pinch of that powder on the tip of a spoon and dropped it in the first cup of water. He did the same with two or three handfuls of damp rye, mashing the seeds before he put them into the cups.

"Sir, pardon my curiosity, but may I ask what you're doing?"

"I'm going to lock horns with this evil," he responded forcefully, his spirits inflamed. "Yes, that's what I'm going to do."

Veturia held her breath and felt much worse than the day before. She thought he had gone completely mad and decided to keep her eye on him.

Diego, unaware of the reaction he had just provoked, took two of the cups and emptied them into another one. He stirred it well and then emptied a teaspoon from one cup into another until he had gotten a very low concentration of the mold in the last one. He shook it up energetically and then drank it in one sip.

"But what are you doing?" Veturia shivered when she saw him swallow that disgusting brew. "That's not going to be good for you."

Triumphantly, Diego stood up, threw the rest of it in a bucket, and answered her.

"Veturia, listen to me. I know how to cause that illness everyone is afraid of!" He paused for a moment. "Now I will be affected by it, too; I may begin to note the effects in a moment. If you see me very sick, tell someone, but most important, make me drink milk, lots of milk."

"But how can you say that? How stupid. How are you going to know how to cause an illness?" The woman was terrified.

Diego sat down and raised his hands to his head when he began to feel the first waves of nausea. His strength was so low that his arms couldn't even support the weight of his skull. Immediately he felt himself floating through the air, above an enormous green prairie. Surprised by his own speed, he looked at his arms and saw two long wings full of black-and-white feathers. He flapped them enthusiastically and at his side there appeared a group of swans with women's faces, beautiful and completely identical. He was going to touch them with his feathers, but then their faces changed to horrendous demons, cold and dark. Diego shouted, afraid he would die.

In the meanwhile, Veturia wiped his chest with a hand towel, horrified at what was happening. A terrible suspicion began to creep into her thoughts.

The day before, she had seen Efraím with that dreadful serpent saying things she couldn't comprehend. And now, she saw her master moving his hands like a madman, his eyes rolled back in his head, and screaming like someone possessed. She felt defeated, nervous, unsure of what was going to happen.

She put a damp cloth on his forehead, asking herself what was happening. A force inside her was telling her to do something, and soon. But what? All that had happened—could it be witchcraft? Or even worse, some dreadful satanic ritual?

Though she was consumed by doubts, she felt an enormous responsibility, being the only person who knew that secret. For a moment, she thought she should call Señor Marcos, but he might not believe her, or maybe he would take his friend's side. She didn't know what to do. . . .

Then, Diego opened his eyes, looked around, confused, as if he'd just woken up from a long dream, and acted as if nothing had happened. He just said, before he left the kitchen, he was going to lie down for a while.

Once she was alone, Veturia was assailed by the same doubts. Though she didn't want to report him, she couldn't keep what she knew to herself.

In that sea of tribulations, she thought she had found the one solution that could clear her conscience. She took off her apron, looked for a clean linen shirt that wouldn't smell as bad as the one she was wearing, and after combing her hair, she left the house as quietly as possible.

She went uphill, and after crossing the arch of Saint Martin, she entered the Church of San Pedro and looked for a confessional. Luckily there was one empty, and even more luckily, she found the abbot there.

When she began to recount her fears and what had produced them, she felt relieved. The soft voice of the abbot, his questions, the promise that things would get better—everything pressed her to go into detail about what had happened. She told him everything Diego had admitted, and about his strange companionship with that Jew. She also talked about the different potions he had prepared, their ingredients, and that grotesque snake.

After she'd been absolved, the abbot thanked her enthusiastically for the information she'd given. Through the wooden screen that separated them, Veturia saw his acid gaze and a strange smile. Her blood froze immediately and she felt filthy inside. Her master had always acted well with her, and yet, she had just betrayed him. Veturia regretted doing it, but she didn't fear any consequence, because she had admitted everything as a matter of confession.

"What penance shall I do, Father?" The abbot had just blessed her and had forgotten it, getting up quickly from his seat.

"None, my daughter. Others will do penance for you, you'll see."

Diego awoke with a sharp pain in his spine. Something was jabbing him there. The sharp edge of a stone. He felt around and identified others, as damp and sharp as the first.

When he opened his eyes, everything was dark except a small grille to his left where a bit of light filtered in. He touched his arms and face. For a moment, he feared he had died.

When he sat up, he felt the presence of another person at the other end of the room. He heard him cough. He turned when he heard steps at his back.

"Who are you?"

"And you?" the voice was deep and scratchy. "Damn! Some company I've managed to get."

Diego saw a person pull away. He looked at the walls, and his eyes stopped at a small window. Standing near it was a man of forty or so years of age, tall, with a gray beard. He looked like a nobleman.

"You were unconscious when you arrived, talking nonsense, with your eyes rolled back in your head as if you were possessed. You slept for at least half a day. I guess you got nice and drunk yesterday and couldn't stand up." The man sat on a bench attached to the wall. "They treated you even worse than me, I don't know what you must have done."

"Where am I?" Diego raised his hands to his head, shocked at how his words echoed.

"In jail."

"I'm a prisoner?"

"Smart conclusion, my friend," he responded sarcastically.

Diego remembered the rye and what he had done before he entered into that spell of unconsciousness. His body was living proof that the strange illness had a name and a cause. He wondered what had happened to make him end up in jail. He remembered flying through imaginary worlds and dreamscapes; he had even floated among the clouds. Could he have done something wicked while in that state?

"What happened to you?" He observed the man's fine clothing and a belt where his sword had hung. "Why are you here?"

The man grumbled something incomprehensible and then began to cough to clear his throat, until he finally regained his voice.

"I drank too much. . . . And when I do that, I lose control."

"You're not from here, are you?"

"That's correct, I'm from Oñate. Though actually I live farther to the south." Another coughing fit overcame him, and it took him a moment to recover. "I was just passing through."

"I never heard of them throwing people in jail for drinking."

"Only when they do it and then strike the most reverent abbot. I did it last night. He insulted me when he saw me stumbling from the tavern, and . . ."

"Now I understand."

Diego began to notice an intense trembling in his hands and a strong urge to vomit. When he understood these were new symptoms of the disease, he had a sudden feeling of anguish. If he was imprisoned and isolated from outside, this was not only bad news for him, it was the worst moment for everyone. He should warn them, tell the authorities what he had found out, and as soon as possible.

"My name is Bruno de Oñate, and you?"

"Diego de Malagón."

When they shook hands, Bruno noticed Diego shaking uncontrollably.

"Is something happening with you?"

"You might see me get worse."

That response disconcerted the man even more.

"What do you mean?"

"I might start having convulsions and hallucinations, even an episode of delirium."

"Can you tell me what's going on?"

Diego felt better for a moment and breathed in and then sighed, relieved. He even felt his hands stop shaking.

"I have given myself an illness, and listen to this closely, for the sole purpose of being sure of its cause. The symptoms I'm showing are more benign than they would be if I was truly affected. I'm speaking to you of something that has killed more than a hundred people in this community in the past few weeks, and their livestock as well."

"I knew nothing of it."

"The worst is that until now, no one's been able to do anything about it because they didn't know the cause. But yesterday I was able to find out. Because of that, I know what to do. I could still save many people."

"And what is this sickness?"

"Have you ever heard anyone speak of Saint Anthony's fire?"

"Never."

"It's a poisoning that comes from eating damp rye or black bread made with that grain. Its consequences are terrible. People begin to suffer frightful hallucinations and all sorts of convulsions, tremors, and nausea. Many end up dying. Sometimes the extremities are struck with gangrene, and if a pregnant woman ingests it, she will miscarry. Cows, sheep, and goats also suffer from it, but it is rare in horses, because they don't usually eat rye. I figured it out almost by chance when I saw a group of poisonous wild mushrooms. That made me think of the sickness that affects men and animals when they eat these mushrooms, and then the rye, because they grow there too, though they're very small."

Diego explained that on his way back from the pinewoods he had remembered a description of the problem in a book written by a nun, Hildegard of Bingen. He said, "The existence of this fungus is due to the poor storage of grain in the presence of excessive humidity and high temperatures."

Bruno de Oñate looked at him, shocked for a number of reasons. If what he said was true, then what he had done was not only generous; it showed a bravery that had to be described as heroic. He was also surprised by Diego's fantastic memory, hearing him recite whole paragraphs from a treatise that he claimed to have read only once, years ago.

"Are you a doctor?"

"No, an albéitar."

"And no one but you has figured this out?"

"No one, I don't think. It's not a common illness in this area. It's better known in climates more humid than ours, since that is where the fungus grows better."

"And if you die? How will your discovery be known?"

"I'm trusting that I didn't make a mistake in the dosage I ingested; at least, that's what I hope. . . ."

"Bruno de Oñate, you have a visitor." The voice of a guard interrupted their conversation. "Come close to the bars." Bruno went to see who it was. It was a Calatravan knight. Over his white tunic, there was a Greek cross with gules and a fleur-de-lis at each end.

Diego could hear nothing they discussed, but the man was looking over at him the whole time. Soon he began to notice a slight burning in his feet and a pinprick feeling. He thought the fungus from the rye must contain some substance that drew blood away from the extremities. That was the reason many of the infected ended up suffering from gangrene. Now he had no doubt. The cause of that massive poisoning in Cuéllar was nothing other than the rye.

He needed the guard to tell the authorities. They couldn't keep making bread with that grain or feeding it to the animals. Why had they locked him up? he asked himself over and over.

He screamed for a guard, but nobody came.

"If someone can hear me, go and tell the authorities," he continued loudly. "They should burn all the rye in the storehouses. Nobody should make cakes or bread with it. . . . It's poisoned! I'm telling the truth."

"Shut it, you imbecile," he heard at the end of the long hallway, on the other side of the bars.

The two men there were frightened when they saw how suddenly the young man suffered a rapid series of convulsions throughout his body.

Diego tried to bend his legs, but his muscles were as rigid as stones and wouldn't obey him. He shouted with pain, trying and failing to get up. For a moment, he feared he had taken too much of the poison, and he imagined a slow, anguished death in jail.

He looked to the light of the small window and its reflection drilled into his head, and he was suddenly tired. Without realizing it, he fainted and fell to the floor, striking himself against a stone.

Bruno ran to his aid.

X.

———————

M arcos couldn't believe what he'd just heard from Veturia's mouth.
"I was just trying to free my soul from the weight of those terrible doubts. How could I know they would arrest him right after?" She justified herself. "Supposedly if I confess to the abbot . . ."

"How could you, Veturia? How could you?" Marcos knew the abbot well. His presence made everything worse.

Marcos had just returned from Valencia, where he was with Abu Mizrain closing on a good deal. He hadn't even been able to sit down before his servant came over to tell him what had happened. She spoke to him nervously, stumbling.

"Poor Master Diego! I feel so guilty for what's happened. But put yourself in my place; what was I to think after what I heard and those strange things he was doing that afternoon with that magician. I imagined terrible things."

"Anyone who would think Diego is responsible for those people dying is an idiot, insane, and doesn't know anything about him. But it looks like someone saw it differently." Marcos came over to her. "And you, tell me, what kind of stupid proofs do you say you have against him?"

"But he said it!" She raised her voice. "I remember his words well. He affirmed that he knew how to make the disease." She explained herself in a tone of protest. "I even saw him make the poison. He did it in front of my eyes, right here." She struck the table with her hands. "And then he took it and I don't know, he started to do strange things with his hands and he was having spasms . . ."

Marcos dried the sweat that ran down his forehead while he listened. His anxiety was killing him.

"I'll see how I can help him . . ."

Mentally, he tried to think of anyone who could intercede with the lord of the town but nobody occurred to him. Of course, Marcos was the very worst person to do so, after leaving the lord's daughter heartbroken.

He thought the accusation against Diego, because it was so grave, would lead to an immediate trial. For that reason, he didn't have much time.

"What can I do? God, I can't think of anything!" he exclaimed.

"You should be careful; maybe they're looking for you, too."

Marcos froze.

"Why do you say that?"

"When I was done confessing, the abbot asked a lot of questions about you. He even made me swear I would tell him when I saw you come back."

That upset Marcos even more. The situation was getting very dangerous, and now it was affecting him as well. He was well acquainted with how the town's trials worked when they supposedly meted out justice. He'd had to settle numerous complaints there and could verify that they were far from aboveboard. He had seen evidence manufactured and witnesses paid off when the trial seemed to go against the interests of the presiding judge.

And if that wasn't worrying enough, it was even worse to have the abbot in the middle of it. Marcos knew that cleric had been after Diego for some time because of his relationship with the Jewish magician, whom he called a wizard, a demon, a deicide, and a long list of other lovely names. He had even spoken to Marcos before, knowing of his friendship with Diego, pressing him to influence Diego to bring that mad influence to an end. He still remembered the fury on the abbot's face, his viciousness, when he talked of how dark and malignant the magician was; a stealer of souls, he called him.

Marcos thought of visiting Friar Gabriel, the abbot's second in command and a person he trusted completely, because he had done business with him for some time, taking care of the purchases of wool and lamb for the church.

Two hours later, returned from speaking with his contact, Marcos felt hemmed in. Friar Gabriel had confirmed the gravity of the charges against Diego as well as the abbot's desire to accuse Marcos of the same. His protests were meaningless, since, according to the authorities, his close relationship with the accused was sufficient to consider him guilty. Nor would it work in his favor that the local lord considered him a lowlife, or that there remained several loose ends in his business dealings with the abbot.

Marcos came to the conclusion that Diego's situation was unfixable and that his own influence would be counterproductive. But what about him? If they arrested him, his luck would be no better, he was sure of it. He had too many enemies, and some would undoubtedly be part of that jury. The risk that he would be found guilty was as real as it was dire. He couldn't, wouldn't, let them capture him.

He thought of a solution, painful, ignoble, horrible, but maybe the only one possible. He looked for Veturia in the kitchen and sounded her out.

"You're not going to tell anyone I've come back. Do you understand?"

The woman imagined he meant the abbot.

"If you command it . . ."

He took out a bag of gold coins from his sash and gave it to her.

"This is for you, in recompense for your silence. With this, you'll be able to have a better life."

She opened it, and when she saw its contents, she paid close attention.

"I'm leaving Cuéllar right now; I'm going to Burgos. If they ask you, tell them I had to leave urgently, but don't tell them where. I know I can do nothing for Diego, and if I stay, I'll end up rotting in prison beside him."

An hour later, Marcos was galloping through a vast pine grove half a league from Cuéllar. When he looked at the tower of the fortress, he imagined Diego inside, and he felt like a dirty traitor.

Such a great pain in his stomach came upon him that he bent over in the saddle and turned to the side to try and relieve it. He also felt his throat burning. His head was about to explode. He felt ashamed, despicable, unworthy of Diego's friendship. In his grief, he could barely swallow. But he kept on. His only consolation was that he could do nothing for him, but save himself.

A cool breeze soothed his pain. Between tears, he tugged at the reins and pressed his knees into his horse's side, forcing it to head north. Before he got lost in the infinitude of trees, he wished Diego luck.

He even prayed for God to send it to him.

"Did I not tell you that I am also a Calatravan, a knight of Salvatierra as we have been called since the fall of Alarcos and almost all our castles with it?"

Bruno de Oñate didn't dare to try the crust of black bread that was the only food they had given him once he'd heard what Diego said.

"No, you didn't say that." Diego looked shrunken. He had just returned from the tribunal and he was utterly desolate.

"What are they accusing you of, then?"

"They say I'm responsible for the death of all these people and more than two thousand sheep. They say they have proof I poisoned them. It's incredible . . ."

"And how will you defend yourself?"

"Tomorrow the trial will continue and if I don't prove the contrary, they'll declare me guilty. It's a complete farce. They're accusing me without any evidence and they won't listen to me. I think they see this accusation as a way to calm the ire of the people, because the administrators have done nothing. I don't know how this will end. . . ."

"Dirty bastards!" Bruno kicked the floor resoundingly. "If only I could help."

"I wish it were possible, but you see how it is."

"But how stupid of them. You're the only person who knows how to solve this grave problem that is devastating you all. Have you told them?"

"Yes, but they don't believe me. I've told them what to do. I even gave them as evidence the fact that horses don't get the disease because they only eat oats. Believe me, I begged them. I shouted for them to burn all the rye, but nothing."

"What evidence do they have against you?"

"The testimony of my servant, Veturia. She heard me say I knew how to make the illness when I was poisoning myself. She must have misunderstood my words, and now I think they're forcing her to come and testify. I saw how the abbot looks at her when she is looking for words or changing the meaning of what she heard. I don't know what strange motives could be behind that priest . . ."

"And you don't have anyone who can testify in your favor?"

"A good friend would do it, but they already suspect her of being my lover and she's married. I could also call the Jewish magician, but I think he's on trial as well, or Marcos, my best friend. He could be my only chance. He knows me better than anyone and he can explain how I've always been, my morals."

"If it was in my hands, I would do it."

"Thank you, Bruno. But what could you do?"

"This morning, I've learned they will set me free in two days. I will try to help you from outside. Three friends I traveled with are waiting for me; we are going south, to Salvatierra."

"The south . . ." Diego sighed. "How I would love to go with you."

Diego explained to him why he said that.

Bruno de Oñate learned what had happened to Diego thirteen years before, when he was a boy. He heard the tale of the murder of his older sister, the kidnapping of the others, and the death of his father, aided by the Calatravan knights. He spoke to him of Sabba, that beautiful mare that he would never separate from, the only memory he had of his family. And then about Toledo, where he had learned Arabic and the albéitar's trade. Diego praised the figure of his master, Galib, without saying why he'd left him. Then he talked about Fitero, the books, and the appearance of his archenemy, Pedro de Mora, after an exciting but dangerous joust in Olite. He told him why he'd met him and why he hated him so deeply.

And last of all, what had happened in Albarracín, the loss of his only love, Mencía. Being abandoned, being wounded by her pregnancy. The overwhelming necessity to leave there, to leave everything behind. And he finished by telling him about those last few years in Cuéllar, the story of Sancha, of the girls.

In fact, he went over his entire life, summing it up in a number of stories.

"I wish you had killed that traitor, Pedro de Mora. . . . For some time now, I've dreamed of avenging his treachery. He's become a terrible nightmare for Castile and for all of us."

"He was the one who took my sisters to Marrakesh."

"They've been looking for him for years. King Alfonso VIII will pay a hundred thousand *maravedíes* to whoever brings him in alive, just to see his disgusting treachery repaid."

That evening, the other Calatravan knights returned to visit Bruno. Diego couldn't hear what they said, but he thought it had to do with him.

XI.

"The accused insists he is innocent. . . ." The prosecutor looked at Diego, keeping a long and deliberate silence.

He was an expert orator and knew how to twist situations to his favor better than anyone.

"We've heard him say," he continued, "that the only thing responsible for our misfortune is a tiny mushroom, and that we should be judging that today and not him." Laughter circulated through the room.

The man walked from one side of the room to the other, pulling on a long curl of his beard. The silence was such that nothing could be heard but the shuffling of his feet across the floor.

"I forgive you for smiling," he continued, "for I understand that his argument can only appear comical." The public murmured in agreement. "But let us return to what is important. For these past few days, more than a hundred of God's souls have been sacrificed."

He stood behind Diego and pointed his finger at him.

"You just heard him. During his testimony, he has tried to convince us of his noble undertaking, but who believes him? When he explained to us how he infected himself to prove the existence of this mysterious mushroom, he nearly made us weep with laughter." Sarcastically, he took a pocket cloth out and pretended to dry his tears. "But let us not forget one thing. What is certain is we have a heartless assassin before us. . . ." He grabbed Diego's tunic and twisted it, spitting these last words in his face. "A man known only for strange behaviors ever since he set foot in this lands, yes, very strange behaviors indeed."

The public was anxious to hear him. He punished them with a long silence.

"Are you asking yourselves what I am referring to?"

"Using witchcraft to cure animals!" a man from the public shouted. The rest turned to see who it was.

"If anyone interrupts again, I will have you all put out," the lord of the town interrupted. "Go on, prosecutor."

"That man was not wrong." The person he referred to smiled, proud. "For the accused has been seen to engage in bizarre practices that he surely learned at the feet of his master, the Jew Efraím. He picks up dead animals and takes out their livers and even burns them, inhaling their fetid vapors. He has also practiced divination, using snakes and strange potions, as his own servant has told us. And besides, we have all heard how he performed strange acts with bread before making a potion which he then drank. . . ." He took another pause. "Is this the normal conduct of an albéitar?"

The masses followed his words with bated breath.

"I doubt whether we are judging an ordinary murderer or if he is not, in reality, a magician of the black arts, sowing terror in our villages, making our women miscarry and decimating our flocks—"

"You are twisting around everything!" Diego suddenly shouted. "Your words bespeak bad faith, and there is no proof that I committed this evil. You should listen to me and destroy the rye in the storehouses. That is the lone cause." He looked around the room, searching for Marcos.

The lord of the town, who was presiding judge of the tribunal, admonished him, and ordered him to be beaten.

One of the bailiffs fulfilled his command so zealously that he split Diego's lip. When he saw the blood, he begged the pardon of the court for not removing his iron glove.

"You say that I lie . . ." the prosecutor continued. "I see . . ."

Another member of the tribunal passed him a paper and he read its contents aloud.

"They have just informed me that the lone witness the accused presents, Marcos de Burgos, not only has failed to show up to this tribunal but has also been seen fleeing Cuéllar."

When he heard that, Diego felt despair for the first time. He couldn't believe Marcos would betray him; it couldn't be true. He was defeated, desolate. If that was the case, then no one would defend him, and he was surely doomed.

The prosecutor continued talking.

"Therefore, there is nothing left but to ask for a sentence from the court."

The crowd began to shout.

"Hang him! He killed my wife," a toothless man yelled, flames dancing in his eyes.

"Let him pay with his life!" an old woman shrieked from the corner.

"Death to the defendant!" the rest of the people screamed.

"You see. . ."—the prosecutor turned now to Diego—"it seems no one believes your mushroom story. . . ."

"Silence! Let the prosecutor speak."

"Thank you, my lord. I shall. And I shall because all this would be funny did the souls of more than a hundred of our neighbors, all friends of ours, not weigh upon this room. I confess that I feel them calling for justice in my heart, for vengeance, they are begging us to make amends for their terrible deaths, indeed, they are shouting at us from their tombs. I hear them, we all hear them. . . ." He circled Diego. "The evidence, the witnesses, what we have heard up to now, all of it incriminates this man, Diego de Malagón, as the culprit of these terrible deaths." He pointed a finger at him and raised his voice for the finale, full of gravity. "He poisoned them! He . . . along with that despicable Jew, Efraím the magician."

The spectators began to murmur Efraím's name. His luck was going the same way as Diego's after he had been dragged before another tribunal.

The prosecutor continued.

"Not a single testimony we have heard has defended his arguments, not one has favored him. Are there any doubts left then?"

The lord of the town stopped him short. He wanted the trial to be brought to an end and a punishment to be decided on. It was best that way. The people needed their leaders to protect them from evildoers, and he needed someone to put all the blame on. He wasn't sure that Diego de Malagón was that person, but he would do it to give the people what they wanted.

"If you believe that the role of the accused has been proven in this case, and I have to confess that the tribunal shares this opinion, what punishment do you demand for him?"

"I ask the tribunal for the penalty of death!"

When they heard it, the public broke out in cheers and applause.

Diego felt knocked down and utterly defeated. He knew everything was lost. He looked at the five judges, seated behind a table, while they all consulted with one another. He saw them ready to impose an exemplary punishment on him. He felt a dreadful nervousness, an atrocious fear.

The notary was called over by the lord of the town. He heard the final sentence from his lips, and then approached Diego, ordering him to rise.

"Diego de Malagón!"

"Yes, sir . . ."

"This court, after hearing the testimony of the witnesses and studying each piece of evidence, accuses you of responsibility for the death of more than a hundred citizens of this community as well as an infinitude of animals. And for that, it sentences you to death by hanging."

The room exploded in applause once more. Diego turned to those seated, not knowing where their hatred could have come from.

"Moreover," the notary continued, "you must know that it is our will that the punishment be enacted tomorrow morning, before midday." He looked into his eyes before finishing: "May God forgive you."

Diego collapsed into his seat, nauseated and depressed. Two bailiffs had to drag him off, because he was incapable of standing, and thus he was taken off to the dungeons. In his cell, they pushed him so rudely that he fell onto the floor. There he could hear the laughter and insults of the two men.

"Sweet dreams, murderer. Tomorrow you'll go to bed in hell."

Bruno de Oñate ran to his aid, imagining the very worst. Diego's breathing was frantic; he was sweating, and he looked like a corpse. He needed time to be able to speak.

"I . . . I . . ." He sighed, destroyed. "They're going to . . . hang me . . . it'll be tomorrow . . ."

"I'm truly sorry."

"It's fine, what can I do? This is the end."

"I don't know what to tell you."

"Leave me. . . . I need to think."

"No, speak to me, believe me, tell me everything you're thinking. . . . I will help you."

Diego felt all the muscles in his body cramp. He stretched out to relax and breathed slowly until he felt a bit calmer.

"Bruno," Diego said bitterly, "I'm only twenty-seven and my whole life is ahead of me. It has taken so much effort to get here, so much work, so many dreams. I left so much of myself behind on the way, and I had to abandon people I loved with all my heart, and I did it to be able to keep my promises. That's why I still don't want to die. . . . I still have work to do."

Bruno was thinking of nothing but how to help him. The situation was so critical that any possibility that occurred to him would have to be considered. And one thing did.

Diego went on opening his heart to him.

"But, all in all, what hurts the most is knowing that if I die, everything I've done has been for nothing, that I'll have hardly given back anything for all that's been put in my hands, all my understanding."

Bruno answered him immediately with a deep voice, full of consideration.

"Death is a liberation. Be hopeful; maybe it's nothing but a path to a greater destiny."

"Is that how you're trying to console me?"

"Yes, I think that's how I have to do it. Don't think more, Diego; trust in my words, and from now on, let things happen. Years ago, a man I considered my greatest master told me something that has been useful to me many times. He said that nothing is what it seems, that behind everything that happens there is always a meaning, though sometimes it's hidden. Maybe the same is happening with your death," he concluded.

Diego's expression could not have been more incredulous.

"I never imagined you'd be so harsh . . ."

Bruno put his hand on his shoulder.

"Don't think I don't have feelings. Just listen to what I have to say. Maybe that harshness will become something peaceful."

Diego heard him and prayed to God with all his might that the man was right, and that all wasn't what it seemed.

XII.

The gallows was built over four thick pillars of wood, with a trapdoor in the center that opened when the bailiff gave the order for the sentence to be carried out. The hangman pushed a lever, and the accused hung in the air till he choked to death.

Bruno was released from the cell some time before Diego and promised to be in the square to accompany him on his final journey.

People crowded the place where the sentence was to be carried out. In this case, the person convicted was known by everyone, and everyone had heard he was guilty of the worst nightmare Cuéllar had ever lived through.

When Diego appeared, escorted by two soldiers, the people greeted him with insults. They spat at him and cursed his name as he passed. He saw hate in their stares, lust for vengeance, and they seemed happy to witness his martyrdom.

Diego bore it all with resignation. Some of the ones now cursing him had sung his praises when he'd cared for their animals. Maybe they didn't really feel what they were saying; maybe it was just that insane atmosphere contaminating them.

He was struggling for breath. The unbearable pressure of their gazes weighed heavily on him. He was innocent and his face reflected worry and fatalism.

When he looked at the scaffold, he saw another man already hanging, swinging from a cord that would soon be wrapped around his Diego's neck. It was his friend Efraím, he saw sorrowfully when he came closer. While he climbed the steps to the platform, he looked into those swollen, lifeless eyes, which seemed to stare back at him. Efraím's neck was twisted, and his face showed the marks of his long agony. Diego had heard that some hanged men took longer than normal to die and that seemed to be the case with the Jew. At that moment, Diego prayed for his soul and out of respect, he continued to look at him until they took him down, without the least consideration. His body fell, striking the wood, but no one seemed to care. A man, hunchbacked and filthy, approached the body and pulled it by the wrists to drag it to the edge of the platform where an open wagon was waiting to cart it off. He failed in his first attempt, and the crowd laughed when the corpse plunged to the ground. As if it was a dog, the man stomped on the body, angry, and threw it over his shoulder to dump it into the wagon. Diego swallowed, feeling the hole that had been carved inside him. At that moment, he remembered the prophecies Efraím had made to him. "A rope, wood, life and death. Resist." Now he understood what it meant. Resist. But how would he resist his own death?

When he stepped onto the platform, the people clapped enthusiastically. Some avoided his gaze, perhaps ashamed, while Diego tried to understand their thoughts, not knowing where their bottomless rancor could come from. He was shocked by that enormous thirst for collective revenge.

At one end of the square, he could see Bruno de Oñate wave at him. That was the only thing that calmed him even slightly.

Beside him he found Sancha, completely destroyed by sorrow, with her daughter Rosa. He caught her eyes. Diego smiled at her tenderly and she said good-bye silently amid tears, thankful for all he had done for her and her daughters. In her eyes he saw friendship, love, the longing for one last kiss.

The hangman examined the knot and passed the noose over Diego's neck, tightening it until it scratched his skin.

"Please forgive me." Clear blue eyes could be seen through his hood.

"I do. . . ."

The bailiff asked him if he wanted his head covered. Diego said yes, so no one would see him. From then on, each word he heard seemed worse than the lashing of a whip. There were few, just enough to spell out the death sentence.

"Are you ready, then, to receive your punishment?"

Diego nodded his head and tightened his muscles, all of his body, waiting to hear the last words.

"Any final requests?"

"The blessing of a priest."

The bailiff made a sign for a man of God to step up to the platform.

Diego lowered his head when the priest put his hands over the cloth and made the sign of the cross on his head, reciting a prayer in a soft voice. When he finished, the accused thanked him for his words.

"Soon you will be free, like all of God's sons," the priest said in parting.

"God bless you, Father. . . ."

"Everything is ready to carry out the sentence."

The bailiff made a signal to the hangman and he grabbed the lever that pulled the trapdoor.

Then some women broke into shouts, begging for clemency. Others drowned out their shouts, asking for vengeance and death. They seemed soulless beings, hungry for agony, for blood.

Diego couldn't see them under the cloth, but he could smell the scent of a wish for punishment in the air, and with it, his own panic. He waited to hear the bailiff's fateful words, and when that happened, he felt himself fall into the void until the rope around his neck stopped him with incredible, fatal brusqueness.

The people shouted, impressed when they saw him kicking, those last attempts to hold on to life. Others applauded joyously. They were comforted, for once more justice had managed to uproot evil and that thought eased their conscience.

"Rot in hell," a woman shouted.

The echo sounded out across the plaza; maybe Diego heard it too.

And then there was silence.

The hangman shoved his body to be sure it wasn't moving. He untied the rope and Diego fell to the ground. They all saw him, Bruno de Oñate too.

He shoved through the crowd to escape that horrendous square as soon as possible, with a tense expression.

Before he got on his horse to leave through the city's gates, he said aloud: "Diego de Malagón, you just did your part, now it's our turn to do ours."

PART V

Lands of Danger

In 1208, the Navarrese Rodrigo Ximénez de Rada is named archbishop of Toledo. Thenceforward he becomes the main counselor to King Alfonso VIII of Castile and the chronicler of the incredible events that take place in the borderlands.

Ximénez de Rada establishes, as objectives for his mandate, convincing the pope to consider the reconquest of Al-Andalus a Holy Crusade, and attempting to restore the primacy of the bishopric of Toledo.

Once the treaties with al-Nasir are broken, the campaigns of siege and conquest against the Saracens begin, such as the one led by Alfonso VIII to retake Jaén and Baeza, and the Calatravans' battle for Andújar in 1209.

Encouraged by his counselors, the Almohad caliph decides to move to Seville to organize a definitive strike against the Christian kingdoms of the north. In his citadel, not far from the Aljama or Great Mosque, in the shadow of its towering minaret, an exact replica of the one in Marrakesh, a transcendental battle begins.

I.

_____

There are secrets that stay buried with their possessor and never come to light. In fact, they die with that person.

But that wasn't Diego's case.

"Officially, I'm dead," he roundly affirmed.

"That's right, Diego. That is what we're saying." Bruno de Oñate patted his back to knock off the bits of straw and filth that still clung to him. He was pleased by his plan's success.

"In theory, you no longer exist."

Diego had just appeared in the company of his hangman, who was none other than one of the Calatravan knights who had come with Bruno de Oñate.

Not long before, they had left the cemetery in Cuéllar after spending the night hidden inside a storeroom on the cemetery grounds. A generous quantity of money had been enough to distract the warden there for a few hours, so that no one would witness how a sack of dirt had been placed in the tomb instead of one that should have harbored the body of Diego de Malagón.

The unfamiliarity of the place and the tension he had lived through over the past few weeks kept Diego from sleeping all through the night, and he had time to think through his life, not without some bitterness. He thought of how he had lost all the people he had loved and how that must have been his fate: his family, Galib, Marcos . . . Through that endless night, over and over, he saw himself on the gallows, hanging by the neck, apparently dead, and he sweated from the anxiety.

First thing in the morning, his false hangman, Tomás Ramírez appeared to pick him up and to leave the place. Luckily no one saw them, not even when they galloped to the spot they had agreed on, an abandoned grazing field half a league from the town of Carbonero, on the edge of the Eresma River.

When he got off his horse, the first thing Diego asked was for them to take off that thick leather collar, thanks to which he had managed to resist the rope without dying. On its front was an enormous Greek cross engraved with fire, and on the back, Diego felt a solid eyelet, also of leather, well hidden, where the hangman had looped the rope to prevent him from being choked.

"We had to get it ready fast and almost without any tools." While he talked, one of the knights took the collar from his hands and tested its strength. Then he shook Diego's hand energetically. "My name is Pinardo Márquez and I am the one who made this device."

"When I felt the rope around my neck, I had my doubts, believe me. Now I have to thank you."

"We didn't have time to organize it . . ." the last knight added, the one Diego had still not met. "My name is Otón, Otón de Frías." He brought his hands together devoutly and falsified his voice.

"Find peace in Christ, my son. . . . Do you recognize me now?"

Diego immediately knew who it was.

"The old priest who received me on the gallows . . . the same one who put the collar on me 'to feel Christ's cross closer to my heart and relieve me of my sin.' Isn't that what you said?"

"Exactly. It seemed like the only way we could manage to get it on you."

"And if the bailiff had prevented it or had seen the eyelet in the leather?"

Diego felt goose bumps when he thought of it and almost preferred not to hear the answer.

"We usually have a second plan," Pinardo interrupted, not sounding convincing.

"Don't tell me what it was; we'll leave it as it is. The first one worked out fine."

Bruno interrupted them, looking nervous.

"We can't lose more time in these parts; let's leave now. It's a long road to Salvatierra."

Diego looked around and saw no other horses than those of the four men. He felt profound grief for abandoning Sabba, but he understood it was impossible to go back for her and it would be insane to propose it. In Cuéllar everyone thought he was dead and buried.

Then he heard a whinny coming from nearby and his face lit up. He ran to look, and there he saw her. It was Sabba. The mare came over with her head lowered and a chorus of snorts and neighs expressing her joy.

"I figured you wouldn't want to leave her behind," Bruno de Oñate said as he came over. "Believe me, it wasn't easy getting her." He showed a bite mark on his arm, and Otón a large bruise on his leg.

Diego caressed her head and mounted Sabba blissfully.

"Now we can go. . . ."

For three days, they galloped without rest until they reached the outskirts of Guadalajara, where they made a longer stop. There Bruno needed to meet with someone.

They chose an inn close to the city walls and without stopping to rest, he asked Diego to come with him into the center so they could talk a while on their own. Diego kept up with Bruno despite his enormous strides.

"You'll have to adapt to a way of doing things very different from what you've known before. So it's reasonable if you feel confused for a while, but I want you to know we have chosen you for your abilities. For some time, we've been looking for someone who spoke Arabic and who could pass for a Saracen. When I met you in that cell and I heard your misfortunes, the route your life had taken, your experience and your merits, I saw you could be the right man. That's why I chose you."

Diego tried to listen attentively. He was still stunned by the sharp turn his life had taken in such short time; one day he was afraid for his life and the next he was riding alongside knights.

Of all that had happened in those anguished hours, it was what Marcos had done that provoked the most bitterness. Diego felt deeply deceived, wounded, cheated by someone he had considered more than just a friend. He couldn't understand what might have happened to make him betray him at his darkest hour. It made his soul bleed, almost as intensely as when he lost Mencía. He felt alone. He was still alive thanks to those knights, but he was dead inside, with no hopes and no dreams. And moreover, he didn't know what they wanted with him.

"What can a mere albéitar do for you?"

"When we get to Salvatierra, you'll understand. It is like an island in the middle of enemy territory, just six leagues from the border with Castile. We live surrounded by Muslims, ready to kill us at any second. Its strategic importance is related to its location, because it's right at the foot of the Muradal Pass, the most frequent route for traffic between Al-Andalus and Castile. Our main objective consists of knowing what our enemy is doing at every moment, their plans, where they're going, what are their weaknesses and strengths." They arrived at the door to a building and Bruno introduced himself to one of the guards. "But anyway, I'll explain better once we're there."

They entered a palace next to a beautiful church. They left behind them a rectangular courtyard with a fountain in its center and climbed a set of stairs till they'd reached the third floor. Going right, they passed through an open gallery and arrived at a door flanked by two soldiers. Diego noticed they wore the arms of Castile on their tunics.

One of them let Bruno through.

"You stay outside," he said to Diego. "I won't be long."

Once he entered, Bruno went to a man of modest stature who was reading beneath the light of a broad window. He saluted him.

"Most Reverend . . ."

"I'm very happy to see you, Bruno, but leave aside the formalities and listen. I have direct orders from King Alfonso for you, and I assure you they are of great importance."

"How is the king?"

"He is more excited than ever and wants to see the Almohads defeated, just as I do. The truce with al-Nasir is about to expire, and our king has no desire to renew it. From now on, the strategy will change. We have an idea that, if it works, will completely turn the situation around."

"What are you referring to?"

"As your responsibility is for the maintenance of our intelligence services, I suppose it's not necessary to remind you that our conversation must be absolutely secret." Bruno nodded his head. "Good, then I shall explain. We are trying to get the pope to declare our war against the Saracens to be a Holy Crusade. As the archbishop of Toledo, I will go to ask him in person. If I manage it, I will pass through the neighboring countries to preach it."

"Of course. . . . That way the reconquest of Al-Andalus will become a collective enterprise. Then no one can see it as simply the ambitions of Castile, and if it is not carried out, it will bring direct sanctions from the pope, correct?"

"Excommunication. A very serious penalty for any of our monarchs who still have not united their forces with Castile, such as León, Navarre, and Portugal. I shall not speak of Aragon, since they have been on our side for some time now."

Bruno had known the recently crowned archbishop of Toledo and counsel to the king, Rodrigo Ximénez de Rada, whom he was speaking with now in the palace, since childhood. He admired his talent and ability, as well as his demonstrated loyalty toward the Castilian king. The archbishop spoke several languages perfectly, Arabic among them, and had been educated in Bologna and Paris. Their families were friends, though not neighbors: Bruno was from Oñate and Ximénez de Rada from Navarre.

"Do you think we'll need the Ultramontanes to defeat them? I don't."

"Bruno," Don Rodrigo answered him, "think it over. Strength is not what we most need. What we are trying to break, once and for all, is the idea that our conflict with the Saracens is a matter of borders, of neighbors who don't get along, who want to recover long-lost territories, as it has been for the last four hundred years." He looked into his eyes sagely. "Now it's not about that. This war has to involve more global intentions. We want to force a grand battle, a definitive one; to face off, without half measures, one religion against the other, so that the supremacy of the Catholic faith will be imposed in all the territories that once belonged to the Visigoth kingdom."

"When I hear you speak, my spirit grows. What can I do to help in this cause?"

"We know the efforts you're making to get men to the south of Salvatierra, and the information they have gathered is valuable, but from now on we must think on a much larger scale. It's urgent that you infiltrate deeper, get more men into Seville, the capital, where the military actions against us are decided. I understand the difficulties this request involves, but at this moment, it is vital that we be informed before we put any other plan in place. Therefore, you should rethink all your priorities and dedicate yourself to this task. Everyone's success depends on yours."

"You may tell Your Majesty he can count on it," Bruno affirmed without a flicker of doubt. "We will plunge into their very entrails, and from now on, nothing that happens in Seville will escape our attention."

At the inn, Otón and Pinardo were waiting for Bruno and Diego with two jugs of wine emptied and a third one started. Only Tomás, the false hangman, was missing. They explained that he had just left with a bit of bread and milk to feed the dove he always traveled with.

On the way back from that mysterious interview, Diego had tried to wheedle some detail out of Bruno about what his future job would be. But once more he'd been told that he would know in due time, when they reached their destination.

Over the two days following, the group covered the fifty leagues that separated them from the fortress of Salvatierra. Diego knew that the last six would be inside Muslim territory, where they couldn't stop for an instant and would have to press their horses on to the maximum.

It was then when he understood the usefulness of that dove that Tomás fed and cared for with such attention. The false hangman wrote a tiny letter and tied it tight to one of its feet.

"This is one of the best ways we have to pass information back and forth. In Salvatierra we live isolated and surrounded by the enemy. Thanks to these doves, we know what's happening to the north and south of our positions. I will show you my dovecote soon."

"Is it certain they will arrive at their destination, the castle, I suppose?"

"Of course. They never fail." He had the dove in his hands. He scratched its head and said something before letting it loose. The dove looked at him nervously and took flight right after, circling a few times before heading south as fast as possible.

"Well done, girl." Tomás watched the bird until he'd lost sight of it.

"What information does she have?"

"I let our brothers and the knights know we will be there soon. They will get ready to receive us. You'll see . . ." he answered in a mysterious tone.

Once they had set foot in Al-Andalus, just four leagues from Salvatierra. Bruno ordered his men to surround Diego and to speed their horses up. They had a long esplanade ahead of them, open, with no forest to protect them or ravine to take cover in. For that reason, they needed to get through there quickly. Only that way would they reach the walls of the fortress.

None of the five men wanted to talk at that moment. They kept watch in front of them, to the sides, behind. They knew that at any moment, an encounter with the enemy, with death, could be waiting for them.

"Otón, to the right!" Bruno shouted.

Two Almohad warriors had just spotted them and came toward them on horseback. Otón took out a bow and aimed at one. He tensed the cord until his fingertips hurt and shot a first arrow, missing. He tried with a second and felled the rider's horse. Tomás rode over to him and together they subdued the second.

"Nobody relax. This moment is critical. It's do or die now. We will face the greatest danger when we top this next hill, where they usually wait for us."

"Sir, if we travel so close together, we'll be easy prey to their arrows. We should separate. . . . That way we'll disperse them and we may run fewer risks."

"That's not a good idea, Pinardo," Bruno answered. "We need to protect Diego, understand?"

The three knights obeyed him without any objection.

When they passed over that hill, they could see the magnificent fortress a half league in the distance. But they also saw, to their left, a large group of Saracens, and as soon as they looked back, they began to shout and ran for their horses. The first arrows weren't long in coming.

Diego watched Tomás take out a long horn from his saddle. He brought it to his lips and blew three times, very hard, so that it resounded across the esplanade. An arrow struck his thigh just as he blew the last one. After an initial jolt of pain, without thinking twice, he broke the wood in half and threw it away with a curse. In fury, he grabbed his bow and fired arrows all around. Diego counted five enemies who fell by his hands.

"To the right! Protect yourself with your shields! Now!" Otón shouted.

Almost without time to react, a hellish rain of arrows fell upon them from a neighboring hill. They were Turkish archers. Luckily they weren't mounted and soon they'd been left behind.

Diego looked behind him and saw with a tremor that they were being tailed by no less than fifty soldiers. He was taken back in time to his flight from the inn, not so far from where he was now. He stroked Sabba. She was sweating as she never had before, just like the rest of the horses, which were all showing immense effort.

"The doors are opening!" Pinardo yelled to them.

"Look now," Bruno said to Diego.

When he looked in that direction, they saw coming from inside the walls a hundred armed horsemen who formed a long passageway to cover their entrance. Others flanked the first group, and then they began a rapid cavalcade to catch up with them. They had their lances pointed at the enemy and approached screaming and shouting.

Diego felt great emotion when they met. The men wore Calatravan insignia, powerful weapons, brave faces. As soon as Diego and the others were in their midst, they closed ranks behind them to cover their entrance into the fortress.

When Diego was inside, relieved by the protection of those solid walls, he sighed, unable to believe what he'd just lived through.

Bruno de Oñate approached him and clapped him hard on the back.

"Welcome to the castle of Salvatierra!"

II.

A sharp whistling interrupted his sleep.
Diego jumped from the bed and ran to the courtyard of the fortress as the rest of the knights were doing.

The noise came from outside the walls but was coming closer. He looked up, instinctively, and somebody shouted: "Catapult! Take cover!"

Diego ran, without knowing to where.

A second creaking sound came, and then a third, almost at the same time. An enormous stone came over the double walls and fell over a shack where the water vessels were kept. In an instant, everything was thrown into the air. Another one struck the walls of the tower, and a third, judging from the tremors it produced and the thunderous sound with which it struck, must have landed on the walls of one of the terraces.

They were followed by many more that seemed to do minimal damage to the walls or other structures, thanks to the fortress's solid construction. But the upper levels, were the masonry work was more shoddy, did not resist as well, and crumbled in places.

"It's been a few days with not much action," one of the knights commented. When he saw Diego doing nothing, he asked, "Can you tell me what you're doing standing there and not helping? Come with me to the battlements and shoot at anything that's moving down there below." He passed him a crossbow and a quiver full of arrows.

They mounted a wooden stairway up to a long passageway that covered the perimeter of the outer wall. Diego looked out and saw a group of Saracens, some manning the four catapults and a few more with other siege machines. They were in the company of at least a hundred soldiers on horseback and twice as many infantry.

He dodged an arrow, saw who had shot it, and without hesitation he began to fire off his.

"Get used to this, you'll see it's pretty common. . . ." That voice could only belong to Bruno de Oñate.

"Is this how you wake up in Salvatierra?"

"What better way than with a little bit of action?" He laughed. "Now leave this for the others and follow me. We have lots to do and little time."

Bruno went down to the courtyard, followed by Diego.

"Take cover!" someone shouted from the battlements.

They both looked at the sky and saw a projectile pass over their heads. They followed its trail until they saw it land on a carriage, destroying it. To Diego's surprise, Bruno showed little worry about all that was happening, while he himself continued to look into the sky nervously, fearing he would be crushed by one of those tremendous boulders.

"We'll train you. . . ." Bruna affirmed before he opened a trapdoor on the ground level on a side wing of the main building.

He crawled down into that narrow hole, watching his head, and told Diego to follow. They descended down a steep stairway until they arrived at a passageway beneath the fortress. Bruno took a torch from the wall.

"Train me for what?" Diego asked, imagining he meant fighting and strategy.

"To combat those fanatics, but not with arms, as a spy," Bruno answered.

"Did I hear you right?"

"That's correct. That will be your task from now on."

At the end of a long hallway there was a door. Bruno knocked three times.

"Password?" was heard from the other side.

"Sancho has not returned," Bruno answered.

They heard the shifting of a lock and the door opened.

"Enter, sir." The man looked at Diego. "And you are?"

"Diego de Malagón," he said, offering his hand.

"My name is Teobaldo de Córdoba; come on in."

The man was extraordinarily robust in appearance and stern in his expression. He accompanied them to a circular room lit by two skylights in the ceiling. In the center was a large round table with a symbol painted on it in black, two kestrels flying low over a Calatravan cross. Seated around the table were Otón de Frías, Tomás Ramírez, and Pinardo Márquez, as well as six other men, making twelve total. They greeted one another informally and then all sat.

Bruno looked everyone in the face, making himself the center of attention. As if all were one man, they raised their hands to their breasts and shouted their motto at the same time: "Faith and blood; God and valor!"

Bruno began to speak.

"Before entering into a matter as grave as the one I shall bring before you today, I want to present to you someone I would like to add to our group." All looked at Diego. "Though some of you already know him, his name is Diego de Malagón."

He greeted them without knowing well what he was doing there. Bruno went on talking.

"As we know from our own experience, the boy has a long period of apprenticeship before him, and I trust in your aid to get him through it as fast as possible. We have important missions to take care of in the coming months and we will need all the assistance possible. Diego speaks Arabic with ease and has as many reasons to hate our enemy as we do." He looked at Otón and pointed to him. "From now on, you will be in charge of his training."

"We will begin today," he answered.

"Good, then let's move on to something else. As you know, some of us have gone to Provence in search of a better way to conceal our communications, and luckily, we have found it. It's a set of machines; one makes messages with letters and symbols, and the others are necessary to decode them. I will show you."

He looked in his tunic and pulled out a bag of red cloth. Inside there was a small metal cylinder made of twelve discs that spun independently. Each disc had a series of letters and symbols that added up to seventy in total, Bruno said. The knights passed it around from hand to hand until it had made it back to Bruno.

"It's simple to use; I will give you an example." He stood up to look for an inkpot and a white parchment. "First you must memorize a sequence of equivalencies that relates each symbol with a word. Then I will pass it to you. Keeping them in mind, to write a message you move the twelve wheels selecting the necessary symbols until you have a complete row." He squeezed a lever that stopped the wheels from moving. "Once it is set, as it is now, you put ink on the surface and roll it on the parchment." He passed it only once. "As you see, the result is a rectangle formed of twelve lines by five, seventy figures in total, completely illegible for anyone who doesn't have a second device."

Bruno passed the parchment to his right for all to see.

"If you receive a message like this, you have to order the discs on your machine according to the sequence in the first line. Afterward, when you print the message on your parchment, it will show you a box of symbols that you will be able to understand."

A murmur of approval moved through the room.

Bruno didn't want to give more details about that instrument and asked Diego to leave the room; later they would speak in private about one further issue that they needed to discuss.

Diego took leave of them and climbed the stairs, anxious to be back outside. He had never liked enclosed spaces, and that room was terribly damp and dark.

The siege of the fortress had stopped and he could walk across the broad courtyard and meditate with a certain calm about all that he had just lived through.

He had always considered himself a simple son of the soil, a commoner who had made his way through hard work, overcoming all sorts of obstacles to reach an uncommon degree of knowledge and skill for a person of his position. He had the profession of albéitar, the most noble of all of them, and saw himself serving others by caring for their animals. Maybe for that reason, it seemed unbelievable that they would now propose that he become a spy.

The incredible events that had happened during his last hours in Cuéllar had upset him, and he still wasn't able to react logically. He felt insecure and weak willed and had begun to distrust people since he had been betrayed, first by Mencía, then by Marcos.

Far from Diego's thoughts, the meeting in the underground room followed its course.

"Let us speak about a project that could become the most important one entrusted to us up to now." Bruno paused and felt the tension in the air. He filled his lungs with air and continued. "The mission comes from the king himself and is part of a complex plan that we will all take part in." He took a sip of water. "For the moment, I can only tell you that a grand battle is being planned, the most decisive one that has occurred to this date. We have been asked to prepare for it by stepping up our spying in Seville, where we unfortunately only have two men at present."

"The others have been arrested," Otón reminded them. "We haven't made any progress there since the Almohads have had their new man in charge of spying. We know nothing of him except that he has improved their information services and the efficiency of their people. We also believe he has managed to infiltrate our empire with a number of agents. If only I could get a hold of them . . ." Otón closed his hand around the imaginary neck of a Saracen.

"I know we are talking about a very difficult task, but we have shown we can work in worse conditions. Remember that it is a direct order of the king, and we have no choice but to carry it out."

All, in unison, pledged their complete obedience to the mission.

"From now on, we will work in groups on different tasks until we have managed to better our position in his territories. We have to be better trained and ready to go anywhere we are asked. I will bring you up to date on the rest of the plans as soon as the dates are confirmed."

Otón left the room first, as soon as the meeting was over, to look for Diego.

"Do you want to meet some nice girls?"

"There are women in Salvatierra?"

"You can tell me when you meet them. . . . Now follow me, we're going up into the tower."

Diego had thought it over several times and couldn't bear not to ask it any longer.

"Otón, I would like to be in charge of the stables. Do you think Bruno would let me?"

"For that job, we already have a farrier and he's very good at what he does. Regardless, I will mention it. I don't think he'll be opposed to it, given your profession as albéitar."

They rose to the final floor of the tower on a circular stairway that Diego thought would never end. Once they'd arrived, Otón placed a large key inside a lock, and before he opened, he told Diego to enter slowly and not to speak.

He pushed the door little by little and suddenly they were inside an enormous cage with hundreds of doves. When they saw them, some flew noisily to the other side of the room. An infinity of black, vivacious eyes looked at them in fear.

"Here you have our friends. . . . You thought it would be something else, right?" he cackled, placing both hands on his fat belly.

"Why do you have so many?" Diego had never cared much for birds and even less for their strong odor.

"They're the best messengers. They are trained to fly to certain points where our men are hidden and then to return home, to this castle. Their instinct for orientation is incredible, they are never wrong."

"And to transport the message, do you tie it to their legs, the way I saw Tomás do?" A dove posted on his shoulder and looked at him with curiosity. Diego didn't hesitate to scare it off.

"That's what we did until recently, but those damned Turkish archers are so good they manage to knock them out of the air and neutralize our sensitive messages." He took a dove and lifted a wing, digging about underneath. Not satisfied, he looked for another and then a third, until he'd found one to his liking. He showed it to him.

The bird's skin was tattooed, hidden under the feathers, with disordered, apparently meaningless letters.

"Take every fifth one and then put them together."

Diego did it and suddenly a name, Jaén, appeared.

"This one arrived today, first thing in the morning, just before our meeting. It brought this message for one of our men, telling him his next destination. So it's no use to us anymore." He twisted its neck until it snapped. "For now this system is more secure than parchment, but it's costlier." He lifted one finger, then another. "For now, each mission costs us a pigeon."

The sharp sound of a cornet reverberated in the dovecote. All at once, the birds began to fly madly around its interior, beating against the metallic mesh. Diego and Otón ran out and took a small flight of stairs until they arrived at a watch post. Otón peeked out from an embrasure to see what was happening.

"One of our men is arriving."

He stepped back so that Diego could see the approach of a man on horseback, galloping furiously, chased by a group of Saracens. He calculated that he was less than half a league away from the entrance to the fortress.

"Why doesn't anyone go out to help him?" Diego turned to Otón, not understanding their passivity.

"Did you not notice the catapults? We're surrounded. To open the gates now and bring out the cavalry would be to put the fortress right into their hands. Unfortunately we can't do anything today. We have to trust in fate and in the protection of God, of course."

Diego turned to look through the embrasure. The man was in the worst possible situation, with two of his pursuers about to catch him. He didn't have much farther to reach the fortress, but a length of rope landed on his horse's neck and stopped him. He defended himself as best he could, wounding one of his attackers, but he didn't see the other coming at his back with a sharp sword.

Diego turned away at the moment when the Saracen, after running him through and slicing off his head, stuck it on the tip of his lance to brandish it with pride before the onlookers in the castle.

That night, the pressure from the Muslims would not let up, though they did change their munitions used. From their catapults, they launched nets full of sticks and stones covered in flaming pitch. When they reached the straw or wood roofs, the consequences were fatal. Their nonstop shooting and the ruinous effects turned that night into a living hell.

Inside the fortress, they were working without respite. The walls had to be defended against the onslaught of those who tried to scale them, raining down stones, burning tar, and arrows upon them. Groups of men ran from one end to the other with water to put out the fires, and others carted up more arrows from the armory, lances, darts for the crossbows, so that no one on the battlements lacked for ammunition.

Diego didn't sleep the whole night through and helped in whatever was asked of him.

Almost at dawn, when the attack had begun to die down, he was fortunate to find Bruno and take the opportunity to speak with him about those matters that were upsetting him.

"There are still those who believe wars are won by those who possess the best means, horses, weapons, the greatest number of combatants," Bruno explained. "And they don't know how wrong they are."

The Calatravan tried personally to assess the damages suffered by the troops and the buildings and asked Diego to come with him while they spoke.

"Wars are won by the side that has the best information about its opposition. The one capable of guessing the movements and tactics of the other, who can upset the enemy's strategy and emerge triumphant. With information, the weakest can overthrow the strongest, disarming him. Diego, that is our work in Salvatierra: knowing what the enemy is planning, figuring out his movements, knowing where and when he plans to attack, and with what means. Our monarch, Alfonso, knows very well how battles are lost when no information about the enemy is at hand. That is what happened in Alarcos. It won't happen to him again."

They were looking out over the battlements to the north, watching their assailants' movements, far from the reach of their arrows. Bruno went on leading the conversation.

"Before you asked me why you were among us. Do you feel ready to hear it? If so, listen to me now."

Diego swallowed and listened attentively.

"Before all else, I want you to know I feel a great respect for you. Don't expect to hear me say it again in the future, because that's not my way."

Diego was stunned.

"You are the very example of a kind of bravery that's not easy to find in our day. I'm referring to your ability to rise above and the spirit of sacrifice you seem to have. Look, Diego, I'm a knight of noble origin. I come from an old family and my acts must continue to do honor to them. Many of the Calatravans you have met in this fortress are also sons of the nobility like me." He stopped to give an order to some men who were transporting an enormous cauldron of boiling water to spill over the side of the walls. He told them to save it for another occasion. "Life has forced you to survive. An unexpected destiny separated you very early from your people, and yet that misfortune made you grow. Since then you've fought to be someone, you tried to learn more, to broaden your knowledge, to be a better man. And with that goal, you found a master who taught you a trade."

"I suppose anyone would do that in my situation . . ."

"That is not so certain, no. When I listened to you in that cell, I recognized two clear virtues in you: great ability and a strong character. I saw you had a gift that not everyone has, I assure you. You learn faster than anyone else, and you can memorize any text you set your mind to quickly. You should feel proud of all that, Diego, because you have transcended your humble origins as the son of a poor innkeeper to become the greatest albéitar in Castile. And in addition, you've garnered a prestige very few could dream of, and the trust of very powerful people. Do you need me to go on?"

"I'm overwhelmed by what you say. Now, pardon my boldness, but you still haven't told me what you want me for."

Bruno sighed. He had decided to tell him everything.

"There's no one else in my command who has the talent you have. That's why I want you here. I need you to put your intelligence at our service, for you to let us make use of your knowledge. I began by telling you that wars were won with the mind, not the arm or the sword. I saved your life when I took you down from the gallows, and now I need your mind, your knowledge. You will help me to make decisions, tactics, plans. That is why I need you! Do you understand now?"

Diego was floored, but he no longer needed to know more. He would obey that man, whatever he asked.

"You will have a period of initial training that may take six months. After, you will take part in a smaller mission with your colleagues; that will steel your bravery and put your apprenticeship into practice. We will teach you to live in hostile environments and we may charge you as well with some more difficult missions, when you are more ready. At all times, your abilities, your knowledge, your instincts, will be put to the test. If you work well and do everything that is asked of you, we can help you resolve those matters that are most worrisome to you."

"What do you mean?"

"Rescuing your sisters. Your mission will become ours, all of ours, and we will go with you to look for them."

"Really?"

"You have my word."

Diego became excited. For the first time in years, someone had proposed rescuing Estela and Blanca. Though it was still a long way away, he was filled with great joy and inner peace.

"Where do I begin?"

"You already have. From today forward, we will teach you the abilities you'll need to become a good spy. You will learn the most refined techniques of observation, you will be taught how to master disguise, you will have to memorize writings, documents, maps, codes; and you will do it without making a single mistake. We will train you to exercise the mental discipline you'll need to adopt different personalities and how to react when faced with extreme situations. You will have to improve your decision making, adapting it to situations where the tension is high. All that, with the help of your own virtues, will lead you to achieve any goal you set yourself in life."

"It sounds like an attractive and exciting challenge," Diego interrupted.

Bruno cut him off, adding a few last considerations.

"Remember from today on that there exists between us a mandate that must reign over any other you might receive in the future; you will always help your comrades, when they ask you to and even when they don't; you will give your life for them if it's required and you will never betray them, and you will care for their wives and orphans should they ever die."

Diego felt the weight of an enormous responsibility, but also the praise of all that had been said about him.

"Count on me. I will do whatever you ask," he affirmed, fully aware of what that meant.

"There is only one thing left to warn you. You have hard months ahead of you. You will sweat like you never have, you will ache to your very bones, and you will dream of being able to rest . . ."

"I shall."

"You will need to strengthen your muscles to brandish a sword or a mace, and your physical training will include concentration techniques to withstand torture and stare death in the face."

"I have already done that. . . ."

Bruno looked into his eyes.

"Are you still interested in the job?"

III.

Another miscarriage left Mencía even more alone. Her husband, seeing how her pregnancies ended, decided to find another woman who would leave him descendants, even if they were bastards.

For that reason, Mencía barely saw him, and the love that he had once pledged to her seemed to have been snuffed out.

Apart from that, she knew he had been courting a lady from a neighboring county and was already bedding her. In fact, he only came to Ayerbe one day a month to settle accounts with his employees and vassals.

She would go out to ride her horse every afternoon through the extensive woodlands surrounding the castle, remembering her walks with Diego.

What can have happened to him? she asked herself every day.

Five years had passed since the wedding in Albarracín and four since she'd last heard he was residing in Cuéllar, in Castile. A long time not to find another woman, enough time even to have his own descendants.

"My lady, my lady . . ." Her lady-in-waiting rushed into the music room. Mencía was playing a difficult piece on the clavichord.

"What is it?" She was alarmed when she saw her so upset.

"The master . . . The master . . . Dear God . . ." The woman brought her hands to her head.

"But it's only the middle of the month. . . The poor vassals don't have to pay him yet. Or is he in one of his ill humors and he's decided to see me?" she asked sarcastically.

"No, it's not that, no . . . The master has had a terrible accident."

"What are you saying?" She grabbed her shoulders, imploring more information.

"His page just arrived, my lady. He will tell you himself."

"Show him in then, quickly!"

The boy came in, pale, and approached her with urgency. He kissed her hand and begged her pardon for his appearance.

"Do not worry about that and tell me, what has happened?"

"A bad fall from a horse, my lady. I'm sorry . . ." He breathed in to calm himself down. "He was close to the castle of Monzón when a tree branch knocked him to the ground and he broke his neck. It killed him."

Mencía remained calm. She made sure he knew he was dead and sent away her servants so she could be alone. They imagined she would weep from grief in her solitude, but that was not the case. She regretted Fabián's death, to be sure. Her pain was the same she would have felt for anyone close to her, but nothing more. Of course it was her husband, but only by dint of force and subterfuge. That is why she had never managed to love him.

He had been a good man and had always respected her. Though recently he had looked for the warmth of another woman, Mencía hadn't held it against him. It was even something of a relief to know that in the beds of others he had found the kisses and caresses she had denied him, and of course, the descendants she couldn't provide for him.

Mencía dressed in black for the well-attended funeral that was held two days later. A long veil hid her from the better part of the gazes that tried to divine her inner state from her expression. And yet it was everyone's opinion that Mencía showed great restraint and self-possession, virtues appropriate to a well-raised woman like herself, at all times.

Despite the recent nature of the occurrence, many figures from the kingdom of Aragon attended, including Queen María de Montpellier and the bishop of Lerida, requiring Mencía to pay great attention and feign a sorrow that in fact she didn't feel.

During the reception, people were astonished at her beauty, which many had heard of but had never actually seen. The rumors about the infidelities of the deceased were told and retold among the attendees. Some even affirmed that, contrary to what had been told, he had died in the bed of a woman who might even be attending his funeral. It was hard for them to understand what could have provoked those marital betrayals when a woman sweeter and more beautiful than his wife was unthinkable.

When the interment was over and the body of her husband was in the tomb, all eyes turned to Mencía as the moment came for her to approach in silence and give her last good-bye. Aware that she was the center of attention in that moment, Mencía knelt beside the pit, sighed heavily, and took a handful of earth to scatter over the dead man. After, a chorus of choked-back tears erupted from the women when, in a gesture charged with emotion, she took the gloves from her hand, kissed them sorrowfully, and left them over her husband's breast.

For all, it was a beautiful gesture, but for Mencía it was the last moment of a marriage she had never wanted, the freedom to act as she wished from then on, and, why not, to dream of finally meeting her true love again.

She was moved, of course that was true, but a light of hope glimmered inside her. The death of her husband changed everything, affected her future, opened new possibilities, like being able to make her own decisions or finally following the dictates of her heart.

With the coolness of the air on her cheeks and her heart fluttering, there amid the people watching her, she felt alone, and made her first decision, thinking of nothing else. She would wait for her inheritance, then take a long journey to Castile, a journey with no turning back.

In just two weeks, Mencía had managed to arrange all the formalities that followed the funeral and the testament was read. From then on, Fabián's grand fortune would be in her name. She was named an administrator with power to decide the ends to which his lands would be used, and she ordered the sale of a palace that he possessed in the village of Jaca, to raise money for her purposes.

The day after she received the payment, she concluded a couple of minor matters, took off her mourning clothes, and mounted one of her best horses.

It was the last morning of that long autumn when she was last seen leaving the castle in the company of her lady-in-waiting. No one but her minister knew where she was headed.

Mencía reached the city of Cuéllar on the tenth day of her travels, full of excitement to see Diego. She needed to discharge the enormous debt she owed him, explain to him the true reason she had left him and why she had gotten pregnant. Even if he was engaged to another woman, it would only be right to let him know the conditions that had been imposed on her by her mother if Mencía had given in to her love for him.

It was possible that for Diego all that was now in the distant past, but not for her. She needed to explain it to him, regardless of what would happen, even if she didn't have any hope of bringing about a new relationship with him.

When she crossed the walls of the town, Mencía felt deep emotion and the tears welled in her eyes. She wanted to see him so much . . . to hold him.

As soon as she took the first street she stopped an older man and asked him if he knew where to find the albéitar Diego de Malagón. To her astonishment, the man ran away from her without responding, gesturing like a madman, as if they had mentioned the devil.

"Señora . . ." Mencía got down from her horse and stopped a woman with a child. "Could you tell us where the albéitar Diego de Malagón lives?"

"Lord Jesus!" She crossed herself twice and did not stop walking. "What sort of question is that!"

Mencía looked at her lady-in-waiting without understanding what was happening to these people and why they weren't answering. A young man came toward them dragging a mule by its bit and Mencía guessed that he must have known Diego.

"Boy, excuse me, boy . . ." When he turned, the boy saw a beautiful woman, blond with incredibly blue eyes, who took his breath away.

"Señora," he said, and coughed involuntarily. "What can I do for you?"

"We've come from afar looking for Diego de Malagón, and . . ." The boy put his hand to his mouth in fright. "What is it?" Mencía grabbed him by the shirt, ready to get the information from him however necessary.

"You don't know anything of what happened?"

"What are you talking about?"

"Are you from his family?"

"I'm simply a friend he hasn't seen in a long time."

"A terrible tragedy happened."

Mencía was choked by a terrible fear.

"Explain yourself, please."

"He was accused of poisoning the people, and many of our neighbors died . . ."

"What nonsense!"

"It's not nonsense, Señora. More than a hundred of us died and so they put him on trial. And then . . ."

The boy lowered his head, distressed at having to recount his terrible end.

"And . . . what happened after?"

"Well . . . what happened is . . . they hanged him." The boy studied the woman's reaction. "I'm sorry to say it like that. I regret having to tell you, but unfortunately that's what happened. It was several months back."

Mencía heard the news like a blow from a club. She leaned against her horse, and, almost fainting, she looked at the boy with a destroyed expression, feeling utterly helpless, dying with anguish. She breathed deep to recuperate a bit of strength but she couldn't speak; her voice failed her. Her servant, seeing her in that state, spoke for her.

"Do you know where he lived? Could we speak with someone who had contact with him before he died?"

"They were in a house close to the town square, right against the walls of the citadel. Ask around there."

"Who else are you referring to who lived with him?"

"A trader named Marcos. He disappeared just before your friend's trial."

"Can you come with us?" Mencía regained her speech and placed a gold coin in his hand.

After finding out that the house where Diego lived was now occupied by another family, the boy went with them to where Veturia, his former servant lived.

Mencía paid him another five coins for his service, before saying good-bye to him at the door of a house that was excessive for a woman of the servant's stature.

"You're Veturia, correct?"

As soon as she opened the door, the two women came in without being invited.

"But . . . Who are you, and what do you want?" Veturia was shocked by their boldness.

Mencía explained to her the scantest details and began asking about what had happened with her former masters. Of Marcos, Veturia would only say he had gone to Burgos shortly before the execution, taking all his possessions with him. But when she spoke of Diego, her face flushed and her voice began to falter.

"I'm sorry, señora. Without meaning to, I was partly guilty for what happened to Diego." Mencía didn't wish to tell her that she was talking about the love of her life. "I just confessed to alleviate my conscience about a series of events he'd been at the center of, and then, everything happened so fast. . . . I saw him die myself, hanging from that terrible rope."

Veturia began to cry while Mencía observed her, boiling over with sorrow and rage. She felt powerless and disgraced. Her illusions of seeing him again were shattered in a thousand pieces. A sharp pain pierced her soul. And she cried without consolation, as no woman had ever cried before. She was drowning in her own tears.

A few hours later, in the cemetery, Mencía found Diego's tomb, topped with a rough cross of wood, half rotten and painted with his name and the date of his death.

She knelt and caressed that mound beneath which her beloved was resting.

Her lady-in-waiting looked at her mistress full of anguish, lain out on the ground, and embraced her, covering her with tears. The pain she exuded was so great it filled the air and the grass growing around her. And she listened amid whispers as Mencía told Diego how she had loved him, promising him her eternal affection, broken beneath the pain of never again seeing his eyes, feeling his arms or lips.

Mencía began to kiss the earth with grief-filled passion, looking for his soul inside it. Though her servant tried to drag her away, she took pity on her and could not manage to do so. She begged her aloud, pulled at her belt, insisted, and maybe for that reason, neither of them heard the arrival of the person behind them.

"Who are you?" the person exclaimed.

When they turned, the two women shouted. They were tense and frightened by the man's strange looks until they found out what he wanted.

"I saw you down there on the ground hugging the earth like you'd been the lover of the person buried there, but I don't know you. I didn't see you during the trial or after. Who are you?" Mencía stood and looked into his eyes.

"My name is Mencía Fernández de Azagra. I loved this man with all my soul and one day I abandoned him, without ever telling him why. To my great dismay, I couldn't live at his side, and believe me, I wished to dreadfully. . . ." Though her tears mixed with the traces of dirt on her face, the man could see sincerity and purity in her eyes, and he felt a deep sorrow for her.

"I'm the gravedigger, señora." Mencía pinned him in her blue gaze. "I think you should know something."

"Speak, I pray you."

"That day, when they hanged him, everything was very strange. Weird stuff was happening. That night, some men gave me money, they did . . ."

"I still don't understand . . ."

Mencía clenched her fists until her nails dug into her hand.

"They paid me not to bury him and asked me to leave the cemetery for a few hours." He looked at Diego's tomb. "So I couldn't see anything, and since then I've had the suspicion that they didn't ever put him in the earth."

"What?" Mencía choked when she heard him. "You think there's nobody there?" She pointed to the place where Diego was supposed to be.

"That's what I believe."

"Where do you have a shovel?"

Days later, a smiling woman, accompanied by her lady-in-waiting, waited for someone to open the door to a house in the center of Burgos. She called twice, until a man of undefined age answered the door.

"Could you please tell Marcos de Burgos that Mencía Fernández de Azagra is here to see him?"

IV.

A year after his arrival at Salvatierra, Diego was preparing for his first mission.

On a table sat a number of creams, wigs, paints that would darken his eyes, and a paste that would wrinkle his skin until he looked like an old man. Pinardo explained how to use them and what each one of them was for.

To the techniques of disguise was added an extensive training in bettering Diego's sense of orientation. Hundreds of times he had traveled blindfolded through the entire fortress, his hands tied behind his back, following the odors he smelled and being guided by the sounds and the feel of his feet over the floor. He had also learned to handle every sort of weapon and to camouflage his face. He mastered forging documents and making invisible ink and had recently learned a complex sign language that the knights sometimes used to communicate.

Before being with Pinardo, Diego had worked with Otón. As a test, he'd been forced to memorize a difficult text in under an hour. It was written in Arabic, a poem with complicated rhymes. With a first quick reading and a later, slower one, Diego had managed to recite it without wasting time and without a single error.

"This one will defeat you," Otón said, choosing one in Latin and throwing it on the table almost offended, since he himself had needed at least a week for it.

Diego took it in his hands and read it in a low voice. It was a treatise entitled *Origin of the False and the True* and it was written by Saint Augustine. For a while he shut himself off from all else, concentrating on those reflections. Then he closed the book and began to recite the first paragraph.

"'Noli foras ire, in teipsum redi; in interiore homine habitat veritas . . .'"

"That's fine. . . . There's no fooling you. Come tomorrow so we can go over the maps of the cities of Seville, Córdoba, and Granada."

~

Diego told Pinardo what had happened with Otón while Pinardo was disguising his face.

At midday, when his transformation was complete, they went to the courtyard of the fortress to see how it had turned out. Diego attracted so much attention that people came from all areas of the fortress to see him, astounded at his appearance.

"I'm almost scared to pat you on the back." Bruno stared into the false wrinkles around his eyes, impressed by the magnificent results. "You look like a fragile old man."

Diego was stooped over, walking with a cane and wearing a long white cotton tunic like the ones common among the Saracens. He was employing a fragile, hollow voice, pretending to lose his breath as he spoke.

"Excellent work, Pinardo," Bruno said, looking over at him. "And good acting, too, Diego. I hope everything functions according to plan. Now, follow me to the meeting room and I will tell you the next steps before we put everything in motion."

Diego stood up and smiled at those present before disappearing into the subterranean tunnels. He was accompanied by Otón, Pinardo, and Tomás, as well as six other knights who frequently attended their meetings.

Bruno was already seated at the center of the large table, and as the knights filed in, they all sat as well, not losing any time. He raised his voice to call their attention.

"Our informers assure us that the enemy courier left Seville with the message three days ago," Bruno said, bringing them up to date. "He's also been seen passing through Jaén and Écija, which means that if he keeps up that pace, he'll arrive at the Muradal Pass tonight around midnight. The idea is to place Diego near its end, before he enters the plateau, on the edge of the road. For everything to turn out the way we want, we need to take care of a number of issues before nightfall. While Pinardo finishes with his makeup, Otón will organize a party to distract the enemy, pulling them away and leaving the path open for Diego. Use twenty horsemen!" Otón showed his agreement. "The more they are, the more troops they'll devote to chasing you down. The key in this mission is to get Diego's disguise to provoke pity," Bruno continued, turning now to Diego. "What do you do then?"

"He'll believe I've been wounded and when he comes close, I'll stab him in the neck with my dagger." He breathed nervously, not yet resigned to that difficult task. "So he doesn't shout, I'll have to do it fast, and the cut needs to be deep. Then I'll take the message and hide his body in one of the small caves that run along the slopes of the gulley."

"Exactly. The only difficulty is that you will have to act in complete solitude, Diego. The pass is very narrow and it's impossible to hide even a single horse. If we did it earlier, where the trail is broader, there would be too much risk of being seen."

"And how will he know if it's the right man?" Otón asked curiously.

"They have told us he's traveling alone on a black horse. He also has a long goatee, a thin moustache, and his skin is very dark."

"If he wears a turban, those details will hardly be visible." Otón was trying to help Diego so that he would not make a mistake.

"His horse's forehead has a strange, cream-colored swatch shaped like a figure of eight. Regardless, I don't think many people will be traveling on that pass at night. Our agent in Seville has assured us that the message he is transporting is of dire importance. Just think, it may be our only opportunity, because once he's through the mountains and onto the plain, he'll have more chance to escape."

Bruno, still harboring certain doubts inside, looked at Diego. Though he had been the one to decide to put Diego in charge of the mission, it was going to take great bravery and ability to react. If things went poorly, the peculiarities of that terrain would make it impossible to hide, and he would be in great danger. He would have to deceive the courier, prevent him from fleeing, and kill him, all that without being noticed. It was a serious challenge for a first mission.

When their talk was ended, Diego returned to the room where Pinardo had left all his tools so that they could finish with his disguise. As he walked, he thought silently about what lay ahead of him and he was surprised by his determination. Until that moment, he had never killed anyone, though he would have liked to slay Pedro de Mora, and in a fit of rage he had almost done away with Friar Servando. For him, life was a gift too precious to destroy without good reason.

And yet, in the past few months, things had changed, and his impressions as well. He began to see himself as part of an ambitious project: to strike back at and annihilate the Almohad Empire. He understood it was a task of colossal proportions, but necessary to preserve the civilization he knew. And maybe it was the mere fact of participating in such an enterprise that filled his heart with peace.

Every day, he was learning more from his comrades, and he valued them like no one he had ever known before. They were brave and committed, a special breed, able to practice the highest principles and values without boasting about it: duty, selflessness, loyalty, devotion. At their side, he understood that the tasks that they were entrusted with might bring difficult consequences, just like the one he would carry out tonight. But that was reality: To keep their civilization alive, their beliefs and their principles, to put a stop to the hate and extremism of the Almohads, a heavy price would have to be paid.

While he waded through these thoughts, he felt his stomach shrink from nervous tension. He went to the kitchen and swallowed some food to take his mind off it.

Then Pinardo finished painting his face, leaving what looked like a long scratch on his cheek, tore his tunic at his belly, and splashed lamb's blood around another wound he had painted. The look was very convincing.

Just a few hours later, Diego was lain out on the ground waiting for the messenger to appear. The silence was almost absolute. Nothing could be heard but the occasional flight of some nocturnal bird giving chase to its prey.

From his uncomfortable position, assailed by his frantic nerves, his only relief was a gust of wind that crossed from the north end of the pass to its south.

Before long, he heard something. It was a soft echo that soon became the clear sound of clacking horse hooves. The moment appeared to have come.

"Help . . ." Diego writhed in the middle of the path, covered in dust, looking wounded. "Please . . ."

The man heard his cry and went for his sword.

"Who is it?" His rough voice resounded off the sides of the gully, growing louder.

"Help . . . save me." Diego's voice seemed to come from a person on the edge of death.

The man dismounted a few yards away from him and threatened to strike with his sword if Diego made any strange movements. The light of the moon left no shadows to cover them. The courier realized that was a good spot to be ambushed. He looked at his surroundings and saw to his relief that there was no vegetation around them where an enemy might hide.

He thought he saw something moving in the distance and threw a stone. A frightened rat ran from its hovel.

He kept walking toward the man lying in the middle of the road, unsure of whether to help him or carry on. His orders were strict; he should take the message to a young translator from Toledo without stopping for anything.

"I need help, in the name of Allah . . ." Diego continued to moan and forced a dry, sharp cough.

The horseman took pity on him and came over.

When he pulled back the cloth from his face, he revealed eyes of steel. He seemed self-assured and very strong. His long goatee and pointed moustache were unmistakable: he was definitely the courier. Diego kept his eyes on his sword.

"What's happened to you?" The voice was steady and the face unmoving. At all moments, he kept a safe distance from Diego.

"Praised be Allah the most merciful for guiding you here to me. . . ." Diego raised his head and turned so the man would see the scratches on his face and the blood staining his clothes. "They robbed me. . . . Curse them." In a gesture of impotence, he squeezed a handful of soil in his fist.

"Who are you talking of, my good man?"

"A group of bandits. They fell on me, took what I had, and then dragged me along the ground, kicking me like a dog."

The courier contemplated the old man, still mistrustful, and asked him where he was from and where he was going.

"I was returning to Úbeda with merchandise for my store when they attacked me. I'm from there. . . ." He howled opportunely and twisted on the ground, holding his stomach.

That last deception worked, and the man put away his sword and came over to help. When he knelt, Diego made use of their proximity, taking a sharp dagger he had hidden beneath his clothes and plunging it into the man's neck with no hesitation, while he covered the messenger's mouth with his other hand to muffle his screams. He struggled powerfully, but Diego had been lucky enough to pierce his jugular. He began to count to ten before letting the man go, but at five the man slumped down beside him.

Diego threw the dagger away and looked at the man, filled with grief. He was panting, drowning in his own blood, his eyes wide open and fear in his pupils. He was still conscious, though a cloud of death began to shadow his gaze. Diego felt bad for what he had done and stayed there to watch him die. Then he felt in his clothes and found a leather belt with a small wooden box embedded with copper and a false safe conduct for travel through Castile. When he opened the box, he removed a small parchment with minuscule letters. He slipped it into a leather bag that he hung around his neck.

Shortly afterward, Diego found the entrance to the Black Cave, as it was called, and dragged the cadaver there. It was exhausting, especially at the end, because the opening was uphill from the pass. Once the body was inside, he covered the entrance with branches and then turned to look at the result. Satisfied, he took the man's horse and returned to the fortress, careful not to be discovered, and weighed upon by his conscience because of what he'd done.

"Congratulations, Diego. You did your job perfectly." Bruno could imagine what he was feeling. "Sometimes, our work makes us get our hands dirty, and it may even affect your principles, as I told you already. But don't think that you've sinned because of the blood you've spilled; don't let it affect you. See it as something necessary on the way to a much nobler end."

"A noble end, you say. . . . I doubt that killing is one."

"We are at war, don't forget it. Kill or die; many times there is no third option. We are living in dark times, in dangerous lands. Here there's no room for feelings like the ones that are tormenting you. You have to be harder." Bruno became more serious. "The death of that man will save many others. With your action, you have given them life. That is how you need to see it, the only way you need to see it."

Bruno served Diego a generous glass of wine and then made him drink.

"Forget what happened. God will judge that man, just as he will judge you when your time comes. We all have our time to live and our time to die."

V.

Mencía's arrival in Burgos loosed a veritable whirlwind of emotions in Marcos, all swirling around Diego. The mere mention of him reopened the wound of his disloyalty.

When she told him what had happened to his friend in Cuéllar, he shrank with dread, though he felt relieved immediately at the news that his tomb had been empty.

Mencía had come to him convinced that she would find Diego, but she had been wrong. How could she have known that Marcos would have no idea what had happened, and worse, that he had disappeared from his side at the most critical moment?

Of course Marcos knew why he had done what he had done. Once he'd managed to think through the negative consequences that would arise once he set foot into the courtroom, he had been filled with a terror so overwhelming, it had made him fear for his very life. He thought that he would end up thrown into a cell with Diego. And how could he have helped then? Not at all. Cuéllar needed a sacrificial lamb and they had found one. A poor man like him could do nothing to change the verdict that he was sure they would impose upon his friend.

"Let's go look for him together," she encouraged him. "I'm sure we'll find him."

"I don't think it will be easy, Mencía. I don't know, I think we should calculate better and try to figure out where to start. And remember, I still have responsibilities here and . . ."

Mencía fell quiet. She was wounded by the lack of interest this alleged friend was showing, and it was clear he wasn't telling her everything. Something bad must have happened between them on those fateful days to justify that silence.

Though she felt disappointed, she decided to carry on and look for

Diego on her own. But to begin, she needed a clue to follow, and worst of all, she didn't know where to find one. It occurred to her that there in Burgos, the capital of Castile, there had to be some kind of register where the documents compiled throughout the kingdom were kept, and that evidence of what had happened in Cuéllar must be there.

Marcos told her there was such an archive and where she could find it. Mencía saw a gleam of hope. Maybe among those papers she could find something that would tell her what had really happened during the trial and especially in the days just before his execution.

To reconstruct the facts she only had two clues: the fake burial in the cemetery in Cuéllar and the mysterious existence of those men who had paid off the gravedigger to keep silent. She determined she would begin with the registrations of the prisoners and then look at the trial records, studying everything to the last detail.

Marcos promised her he would help her get access to the documentation through his contacts in the city government.

She would give it time and persistence; there was no need for anything else.

For the next couple of years, her efforts were as disappointing as they were slow. But Mencía was still able to discover something, thanks to a contact of Marcos's: the chief registrar for Castile, García Rodríguez Barba.

The institution the man represented had great influence in the royal court. He was the first among the king's functionaries, and one of the few who oversaw every royal document and edict. As justice of the court, he was charged with leading investigations as well as prosecuting those guilty of high crimes against the crown. And though Diego's case had been outside his jurisdiction, the story of that terrible poisoning in the town of Cuéllar had been much talked about even there.

Mencía went to see him two or three times a week. He worked in one of the outbuildings of the convent of Santa María la Real de las Huelgas, close to the royal palace and built at the express wish of King Alfonso VIII and his wife, Leonor. That beautiful building had been raised as a monument to the crown of Castile and was the most important of the Cistercian convents in the land. Its grand prestige meant that it was soon chosen as a retreat for the daughters of the nobility.

Thanks to its extensive archives and the help of the registrar, Mencía was able to begin tying up loose ends and figuring out a good deal of what had happened.

~

"Marcos, I think I finally know who helped him."

One afternoon in the spring of 1211, Mencía entered the main room of his house like a whirlwind, kissed his cheek, and sat on a stone bench beside the window with a splendid smile on her face.

"What?"

Marcos closed a thick book where he made note of his accounting and looked at her expectantly. She was wearing a dress of lilac and white, with gemstones trailing down her collar and a translucent veil. She seemed more beautiful than ever. She had been in Burgos for four months now.

Mencía looked out into the garden and inhaled the sweet scent given off by the honeysuckle in the hours before night fell.

"The Calatravans!" she exclaimed immediately.

"You mean that ill-famed military order?"

Mencía was shocked. The news could not be better, and yet Marcos had added a disagreeable note to his commentary.

"Do you have something against them?"

"Not at all," Marcos said, hiding the tension he felt when the subject of Diego arose.

"I don't know, I feel like you're not happy about what I've just said." Mencía got up, feeling nervous. "I just had in my hands, finally, the register of entries and exits from the jail in Cuéllar for those days, and all thanks to your friend the registrar. The poor man has no idea what my interest is, though I explained to him already the nature of my friendship with Diego."

"And what have you figured out for certain?"

"A Calatravan by the name of Bruno was held there for a minor crime those days. . . . offenses against authority, I believe. The coincidence of the dates makes me think he may have met and possibly spoken with Diego inside the dungeons. The list has other names of prisoners along-side their crimes: a highwayman, two Moors who hadn't paid their taxes, and a Jew described as 'the magician.' None fit the description the gravedigger gave me."

"Efraím!" Marcos commented sharply. "That magician you just mentioned was friends with Diego; he had shared his secrets with him. I remember he was a strange, shadowy man."

Mencía served herself a glass of water and offered one to Marcos. He preferred wine.

"I've asked everyone about the Calatravan, but no one seems to know anything about him. As if he was a ghost!" She gathered her skirts in her hand and sat down again. "Nor do I understand why people grimace when I mention that order. Can you tell me what's going on?"

Marcos wasn't knowledgeable about political matters except for those that pertained to his business, but this was an exception, as he had heard the story more than once.

"When a castle is under siege by an enemy, its defenders can fight to the death or else turn it over intact and save their own lives. The Calatravans tend to do the second, especially since the defeat at Alarcos. That is the bad reputation they have gained."

Mencía listened without wanting to give an opinion. She just wanted to know how to find the man. Then she remembered something.

"Isn't the monastery of Fitero the place the Calatravan order was founded?"

Marcos nodded.

"Give me a name, quickly!" Her face lit up. "Right now I will write and ask for help. There they will know how to find Bruno de Oñate."

"Friar Jesús, the cook. He knows the order well."

Hundreds of leagues to the south, another woman was also thinking about Diego. It was his sister.

For the first time in sixteen years, Estela was leaving Africa behind, to travel to Seville with the majestic fleet of the Caliph al-Nasir. It was March of 1211 and sixteen years had passed since her imprisonment. Sixteen long years . . .

After two heat-racked days journeying overland, they had arrived at the port of El Jadida, to the northeast of Marrakesh, and five days later they were entering into the mouth of the Guadalquivir River to follow it upstream to the port at the capital city of Al-Andalus.

When Estela saw the city from the deck of the ship, the bustle, the scent, the grand shipyards next to the port and its contrasting vivid colors, she fell in love immediately.

Almost thirty now, she has resigned herself to her concubinage and for months now had been taking advantage of her position as al-Nasir's favorite.

The caliph's sister, Najla, journeyed at her side, dressed in a dark niqab. For some time now, she had been wearing the niqab, to avoid men's gazes but also to hide the scars that had been left on her by a poisoned henna. Her skin had been left a taut and dry mask, changing her expression completely and inalterably.

The person responsible for it hadn't been found out. The slave who painted the princess was found dead, as well as the two women whose task had been to mix the henna. Her brother al-Nasir had ordered an investigation into the events without any success, and as time passed, everything remained hidden under a cloak of mystery, forgotten by almost everyone but Najla, who had to see her own face daily and whose life had been converted into bitterness.

"You know why we're coming to Seville?" Estela asked the princess. Her blue eyes shimmered beneath her black niqab like two stars. While she waited for her answer, she saw that the Imesebelen Tijmud was approaching.

"My brother wants war," Najla answered drily.

"My ladies . . ." Tijmud interrupted. "I have very bad news."

"Tell us, quickly, what is it about," Estela ordered.

"I have just found out from one of the slaves that—"

A high-pitched whistling cut his words short. The sound announced the arrival of the governor of Seville, the brother of al-Nasir and of Najla. The two women saw a young man jump onto the deck from another ship. He quickly came over to Tijmud and the ladies and discreetly pulled them apart.

The man who had just arrived looked a great deal like Najla. His features were softer than those of his brother the caliph, and they reflected a calmer and more cheerful character. He kissed his sister without lifting her veil and introduced himself to Estela as al-Nasir arrived. The two brothers embraced and, after looking at each other, joked at the growing size of their respective bellies.

After those courtesies, the host encouraged them to take a look at the city's magical outline against the sky, with its palm trees and minarets, before they docked.

"Our grandfather transformed this city into the capital of our empire. He paid for the walls that protect it from the river, made of pebble and limestone and crafted by the most skilled hands. He also had an aqueduct raised, a new bridge, and the Great Mosque. You will see the beautiful citadel and the gate of Yahwar, which are also among his works."

He turned to the women with emotion in his face.

"I came to love Seville like a favorite woman. . . ." He turned his gaze to Estela, approving his brother's taste. She lowered her head timidly.

Najla looked at the stepped paths on the edges of the river where thousands of people had congregated to greet them. Never had such a consort of ships as this been seen in Seville, nor such pomp in the caliph's court.

When al-Nasir had embarked, he was accompanied by thirty ships transporting fifty horses, two hundred Imesebelen, his retinue, sixty concubines and fifty other slaves, as well as his porcelain and silver and all he would need to remain away a long time without yearning for Marrakesh.

A sudden breeze from the west swelled their sails as they arrived, bringing the coolness of the distant ocean. When she breathed in, Estela broke into tears. After so many years of confinement and humiliation, for the first time, she felt a little freer. Seville was not so far from her land, from her people. It made her feel closer to home.

When Estela saw the various palaces forming the citadel, she couldn't imagine anything more beautiful. There were more than a dozen buildings surrounding a number of cross-shaped courtyards connected by curving underground passageways. Each had distinct vegetation and its own aroma. One abounded in scents of jasmine, another of iris, a third of basil. Each of the buildings also had distinctive decorations on the floors, walls, and arches. Al-Nasir's father had been responsible for those changes to the Umayyad buildings that they referred to as Al-Mubarak. Above them rose that fantastic residence.

Estela was lodged in an outbuilding close to Princess Najla and, of course, the caliph's rooms. Following the advice of his sister, Estela had gone back to al-Nasir's bed, and since that time she let him love her, although she found no pleasure in the act.

For the first few days in Seville, she enjoyed the gardens passionately. She tried to feel their plenitude, excited to be in some place that wasn't the harem in Marrakesh. She listened to the fountains and saw herself reflected in the ponds, amid the chants of finches and swallows.

On one of her walks during her second week there, she received a secret visit. It was Tijmud, who had managed to slip out of his quarters to warn her.

"Señora . . ." he called to her, protecting himself behind an enormous sheet of honeysuckle under the shadow of a wall.

She turned without knowing who he was.

"Here! Behind you."

Estela saw the Imesebelen and walked toward him cautiously.

"What is it, Tijmud?"

"Come closer. I have to tell you something important; the thing I couldn't tell you on the ship. . . . Remember?"

Soon they heard voices coming toward the courtyard and Estela became very nervous. She feared being discovered with the guard, and to avoid it, she pushed him quickly into the vegetation, and then entered behind him. They gazed carefully between the branches, and to their shock they saw the caliph appear together with Pedro de Mora.

"Either we do it next spring, or you will have serious problems with some of your governors, believe me," Don Pedro explained to him. "I have learned that many are making pacts with the Christian kings, even paying them not to be attacked. As you see, the situation is critical and it is beginning to seem more and more like the one that existed before the glorious Almohad conquest, when other governors named themselves kings of their small territories."

"The king of Aragon is attacking us in Valencia," al-Nasir said. He had just received notices from the east. "And the worst thing is it appears he is conquering territory. To our misfortune, he seems to have forgotten the terrible punishment we inflicted on him last year in Barcelona. And the king of Castile, surely in league with him, has managed to steal from us a number of frontier towns and their castles." He looked at the sky, certain that Allah was the one guiding him. "The time has come to attack them, Pedro. Let us get ready to deal them a definitive blow. A few days ago I had a vision. I was inspired by the Prophet . . ." Pedro de Mora looked in his eyes. The crystalline blue of his gaze was like an open window into his most intimate thoughts. Al-Nasir went on revealing what he'd seen.

"I've been given a sacred mission from him: to sweep the entire peninsula clean of Christians, to eliminate the infidel from the land that was also Al-Andalus to our predecessors. And he ordered me afterward to cross the Pyrenees and turn to Rome. The strength of Allah will force the pope to hand over his city. The Eternally Benevolent, the Grandiose One has made me see it." He brought together his hands on his chest and raised his eyes to the sky. "Pedro, I have a noble lineage behind me and I will not stop until I see Christianity defeated by my hands, forever."

He raised his arms and shook them, enthused by his own words. Afterward, he smoothed out his tunic and seemed to return to a calmer state.

"Therefore, we must consider a long campaign and you will play a decisive role in it." Pedro de Mora wondered what he was thinking. "You must drive a wedge between the kingdoms of the north, stoke up their quarrels, break their ties the way you did in the past with Navarre. If they pulled together, we could never defeat them. But defeat them we shall, and they will taste the dust of defeat if they continue on their own."

"I will go to the kingdom of León. The monarch thinks well of me and I know he will continue in his grievance with his cousin Alfonso of Castile. I will try to make my way into his court, undermine his already damaged relations, try to bring things to a head . . ."

Pedro de Mora was unconcerned with matters of religion; he didn't understand them, he didn't even believe in God. His only faith consisted of chasing the enormous pot of money he would get if al-Nasir managed to see through his plans. He would never have made it so far staying on the side of the Christians. He dreamed of Alfonso VIII, defeated by the Almohad troops, kissing his feet, kneeling before him, absolutely humiliated.

Al-Nasir greeted his idea of going to León with approval.

"Your plan agrees with me. A great deal. In any case, try to return before September. I will need you to support the first of the attacks. That one, as I have foreseen, will hurt a great deal, because we will hit them in the depths of their soul, I assure you."

They went on walking to the next courtyard, and Estela took advantage of their solitude to leave her hiding place with Tijmud. Both were conscious of the risk they would run if they didn't separate soon. The guard spoke to her without losing time.

"It was him . . . Pedro de Mora." He took her hands to prevent her from interrupting him. "A slave saw him tampering with the henna that day. The woman has said nothing since; she was terrified, because she was afraid he would come after her as he had with the other three women. But a few days ago, I gained her confidence and she told me everything that had happened."

"The bastard." Estela wrinkled her brow. "I can't understand why he would want to kill Princess Najla. . . . It's terrible."

"Don't be mistaken. It was for you, not the princess."

"Are you sure?"

"And he will try again."

Estela shivered.

"Be careful and stay on your guard. I will try to be close to you, to protect you, but never take your eyes off him."

VI.

During that same summer, that of 1211, rumors spread all around that there would be war between the north and south. Once more, you could hear words like *reconquest, holy war, faith,* and *crusade.*

When the fields were plowed and the first September rains arrived, some said with relief and others with worry that the battle would take place the following spring, when the new pasture had grown in.

Indeed, the two armies began to prepare themselves.

Amid copious rains that rendered the land almost impassable, the fortress of Salvatierra, on its high hill, was in a ferment throughout that autumn. With reason, it was said that its denizens never slept.

The orders that arrived from Toledo were definitive. They should rally against the enemy, striking out at his positions, burning his fields and granaries, destroying his orchards and robbing his livestock. That mission was given the name "wasteland" and it continued pushing on through the south with very little resistance on the part of the Saracens. No one understood why the Moors had put up so little energy into defending their redoubts.

At the end of September, in Salvatierra, they had a remarkable visitor. It was a surprise for Diego and the cause of his next and most astonishing mission.

"I want to see Diego de Malagón," the recent arrival ordered after speaking with Bruno de Oñate. He had appeared with an escort of twenty well-armed horsemen.

"I will show you where he is," the castle's bailiff said, though confused by the man's behavior, and directed him to descend down what seemed to be an endless set of stairs.

Amid the shadows, at the end of a poorly lit passage, they came to a worn wooden door that creaked as if it hadn't been opened in years. Inside, the atmosphere was suffocating. A great spray of light came down from a skylight in the ceiling. With their back to the door, three men were writing painstaking messages on sheets of parchment no larger than a cherry. One of them was Diego. The recent arrival approached him and touched him on the shoulder.

"Whoever you are, wait. I have to finish a phrase and I can't leave off in the middle."

Without turning to see who it was, Diego wet the tip of a very thin swallow feather in the inkpot and wrote three words and two symbols on that tiny sheet. He did so under the attentive gaze of the newcomer, in a language he didn't know. When he finished, he took off a large lens he'd strapped to his face to expand his field of vision and turned to see who'd come for him.

"I can't believe it!" Diego shook his hand, charmed to see him again.

"Me neither! I imagine everyone thinks you're still dead. . . . Well, not everyone; I've been following you since they hanged you from that gallows."

"Don Álvaro Núñez de Lara in Salvatierra. . . . What a pleasure it is to see you."

Diego encouraged him to sit and asked after his wife, Doña Urraca, as well as his children and his father-in-law, the lord of Biscay.

"Everyone is well, thank you. I'm still grateful for what you did. . . ."

"What are you talking about? I don't remember . . ."

"The message you intercepted. Do you know what I'm talking about now?"

Diego's thoughts turned back to the mountain pass of Muradal, when he had slain that Saracen courier. He still felt the man's agony and the bitter memory of what had happened.

"Yes, yes . . . of course."

"Thanks to your work, we were able to destroy the most important spy network that al-Nasir had planted in Castile and Aragon. That message was impossible to decipher because it was made with new codes and symbols. We only recognized a name and a city: Arévalo. From that, we were able to figure out where the first spy was located, and once we had him, the rest of them fell. Just a little while back, we caught the last one in Valladolid." He paused a moment. "It's been the best operation in memory in Castile. The only thing left to do is find their new leader, and we still don't know his name, let alone where he lives. It's a real nightmare."

"One day he'll slip up and we'll capture him. . . . You'll see," Diego commented. "And by the way, you haven't told me what the motive is for your visit."

"The position of ensign of Castile makes me directly responsible for this fortress as well as its missions. Let's just say I act as a liaison between all of you here and the king. Bruno de Oñate informs me of what happens here, and the king and I study what our next actions should be. Did you know that?"

Diego said he didn't.

"Then listen. Our next mission will be the most decisive one we have undertaken up to now, and that's why I'm here. You'll know what I'm talking about when I have discussed with your superior what your role in it is to be, but I can already anticipate it will be an essential one. Then we'll talk to you."

Two hours later, Diego asked for permission to enter a small room beside one of the armories, a discreet place where Bruno de Oñate and Álvaro Núñez de Lara were waiting for him.

"Close the door and sit down," Bruno ordered.

"Do you know Seville?" Don Álvaro laid a map across the table.

"I was never there, but I've memorized this map down to the last details, the same with Córdoba and Granada. I know the names of the streets, the plazas, the mosques, where the main buildings are located . . ."

"Excellent, Diego. Now you'll have to learn the extensive network of underground pipes." He unfurled another one with a complex system of forking passages that was superimposed on the map below. "You'll need to in order to penetrate al-Nasir's palace. We know he's living in Seville now, and this is the best opportunity."

"Pardon me, I don't know if I heard correctly. . . . You're telling me that I'll have to break into the chambers of the caliph himself?"

"Exactly," Bruno interrupted. "You have heard right. Your mission will consist of making off with his precious Koran."

"A Koran?"

Don Álvaro passed Diego a drawing showing a book with a cover adorned with arabesques and an infinity of geometric shapes. In its center was an enormous green stone.

"Not just any Koran . . . you have to find this one! The most beloved of al-Nasir, his favorite. It is the only copy of its kind."

"And I'm expected to risk my life to steal a book?"

"You won't steal it. If you did, you would give us away and our final objective would be compromised. I'll explain it to you better. We know that al-Nasir is used to hiding a great number of his secrets and strategies in its pages. Some time ago, our ambassador saw him do it and found out from others that it was where he hid his most important documents, as if in a lockbox. They say it's for some mystical reason, maybe so Allah blesses his plans, we don't know.

"Once you take it, you will look for all the documents it contains, one by one. And that is where your participation is essential, because we need you to memorize them. . . ." Don Álvaro added. "Your exceptional ability to remember what you read has made you the chosen one for this plan."

Bruno de Oñate took the floor, explaining more details of the operation.

"We know there is a pipe that opens into one of the courtyards in the castle, the one closest to the caliph's residence. That will be where you enter. You'll be in disguise, and you'll be able to move around the precincts once you're out."

Diego seemed worried about the difficulties of that mission.

"I don't know if I'll be able . . ."

"You've been training for three years, you've participated in many operations, and you've always behaved properly, with the necessary temperament," Bruno said, encouraging him. "You can do it."

"I believe so, too," Don Álvaro added.

"You'll have a week from today to organize everything. We will study the operation, every step you have to take, and we will practice it with you as many times as necessary. In Seville, you will be assisted by one of our best men. Don't worry, everything has been thought of. You won't have any difficulties."

Diego rubbed his hands together nervously. He was assailed by a multitude of questions, though he understood it wasn't the right moment to ask them. Except for one.

"Do we know where the book is kept?"

The two men looked at each other, waiting for the other to respond. Their faces said it all.

"Don't tell me, I have to find it myself, right?"

VII.

Diego spoke softly to Sabba, in the language they shared. He begged her to be calm from that moment on. She understood and snorted discreetly.

They were on the banks of the Tagarete River, where it intersected the Guadalquivir as well as the gates of Seville. His first contact was waiting for him there.

Diego, distracted, watched the incredible effect of the sun on the four copper spheres that crowned the mosque's minaret. It looked like a lighthouse, its glimmer visible from two leagues away.

He had traveled through Al-Andalus with a dozen enormous Flemish mares, posing as a horse trader. It hadn't been too difficult apart from his voyage through the Muradal Pass, where a group of Calatravans had to help him through after an initial operation to clear the area out.

Diego looked at a nearby sundial on a tower close to the river and was surprised to see it was still midday, the hour agreed upon, and he still hadn't seen any visitor.

"Oranges are bitter this season . . ." The voice surprised him. It belonged to a man in a turban and blue tunic.

"I prefer the winter ones as well."

With that answer, each knew who the other was.

"I'll take you to my house, but first you need to know the location of the three great conduits that open onto the river." The man pointed to a place very close to where they were. "You see the first one there? The other one, the next one, used to be named for Saint Bernard. And the third of those old pipes that still bring water to the city is called the cat's cradle."

"I'll use the first one to leave, it's the closest one to the castle. Now let's go; we're too exposed and besides, I'm hungry as a wolf."

"Then follow me. My code name is Blue Heron."

~

In the neighboring village of Coria, on the left bank of the Guadalquivir, the man had possession of a mill and a villa with large stables. They left their horses in there and ate while they discussed their next steps.

"I am only acting as an intermediary," the Blue Heron explained. "The next thing you'll do is look for Wild Fox inside Seville. I can't help you any more. For security reasons, I don't know where he lives. That way we avoid getting each other caught if one of us happens to get arrested."

"Don't worry, I know where to find him. He has to help me with the plans for the castle. Something else: I've noticed a lot of troops gathered on the outskirts of the city. Do you know what might be going on?"

"There are rumors of an imminent attack against Castile. Wild Fox is in charge of confirming that information and then alerting Salvatierra if necessary. Ask him; I don't know anything else."

During lunch, they discussed what Blue Heron had found out about the Almohad's head of espionage; they believed he was of Castilian origin, but no one knew anything about him. Diego devoured the flavorful fish with cabbage and carrots without knowing when he might eat hot food again. The fragrant wine that accompanied it helped to draw out their midafternoon rest.

Shortly after he'd left Blue Heron's villa behind, Diego saw the skyline of Seville and was conscious that from then on, the most dangerous part of the plan was in motion. He would finally be taking action.

He rearranged the disguise he would employ to get in and followed the riverbank until he arrived at the city, then crossed over a new bridge with the idea of entering through the Gate of Water.

He walked without fear of being recognized. The niqab hid his head entirely, save for the small slit he saw through. Under a long tunic, he wore a closer-fitting shirt that he had stuffed with cotton to give the appearance of a woman's breasts. From outside, no one could doubt that he was a woman, and the donkey that accompanied him, loaded down with containers of water, also left no doubt as to her profession.

"Where are you going, woman?" A soldier stopped Diego before he made it to the gate.

Diego raised his hand to his throat, implying that he was mute.

"You can't speak, I understand. . . . Let me see what you have here." He uncovered the containers and bent over to see what was inside them. Once he saw it was water, he let Diego through. "You may go ahead."

He crossed through the archway and promptly turned down an alley to the left. Before it ran into a wall, he took another, circuitous one that went right and then diagonally, crossing a small square that was known throughout the city for its famous baths. Only two streets away, to the right, once he had crossed through another, smaller square, he should find a dead end and just before that, the house of the Wild Fox.

An old man stopped him short while he was trying to cross through the second of these squares and tried to buy a pitcher of water.

"Some water bearer you are. . . . If you don't shout, how are you going to sell?"

Diego once more made the gesture suggesting he was mute while he filled up the man's pitcher. He drank it in one swig.

"Water bearer and mute, what luck." He spit on the ground and asked for another. He looked for two coins and gave them to Diego, who began to feel uncomfortable under the pressure of the man's gaze. He lowered his head so he wouldn't look him in the eyes, praying for him to leave as soon as possible, which he did.

Shortly after that, he was inside the home of his contact, in his courtyard. The Calatravan received him with a nervous gesture, but Diego was relieved to find himself safe. His face seemed familiar.

"It's urgent that they know!" He shook Diego as if his life depended on it. "It's a disaster!"

"But what's happening?" Diego took off the niqab and helped the man to calm down.

"I just found out the caliph is going to attack Salvatierra, and the worst thing is, they're already on their way."

"How can that be? I haven't crossed paths with any army except in the fields here on the outskirts of the city."

"Those are the last of them. The rest have taken another route, I think through Jaén, where they will be joined by troops coming from Africa."

Diego asked him if he had sent a message in warning.

"I was just about to do it. Come with me, fast."

Diego left the donkey in the courtyard and lifted his tunic to be able to run up the stairs to the roof of the buildings. On one end, he saw a small dovecote with no more than a dozen birds.

Before he took one, the man remembered that he hadn't given him the plans to the caliph's palace.

"Take this before I forget. You'll find three of his rooms marked with a blue cross; the book you're looking for could be in any of them. The red crosses indicate the places where the caliph's personal guard is housed. Stay away from them. I risked a great deal to get this information, but I trust it will help you. And one last thing, I must remind you that to leave Seville, you'll need to return to this house. I will furnish you with a new identity and the proper clothes."

"Yes, of course. Count on it."

Diego hid the plans in the inner pocket of his tunic and watched what the man did with the doves. Amid the rush and the scrambled nerves, the man let one escape; another one almost did the same, but he caught it by the neck.

He looked for the strongest one and began to wrap a small fragment of parchment around its leg while he repeated over and over what a disaster awaited them if it didn't arrive at Salvatierra in time. The matter was so urgent that there was no time to use their more secure systems like the cylinders Diego had seen before. With the dove, the information would hopefully beat the enemy there.

Diego looked at their surroundings from the roof. When he found a small raised spot, he got an excellent view of the city. They weren't far from the minaret, and therefore from the castle, and they could see a few of its battlements and outer walls.

The sky was beginning to turn pink and orange as the sun escaped behind the horizon, when Diego heard voices. Below them, in the square, he saw a group of men singing and women applauding them. Everything seemed normal.

He turned to Wild Fox. He had just tied the cord around the dove's foot and was about to set it free for the first leg of its critical flight.

"Go, little one," he whispered into its ear. "Travel swift as the wind, let it carry you. Duck the headwinds, escape the storms, and reach your destination soon."

He let it go, and the bird winged away with zeal. It rose and made a couple of circles over the house. The two of them followed it, waiting for it to find its direction and finally fly toward the north. But at that moment, a shadow appeared, large in size and ragingly fast, threatening the dove in its flight.

"What is that?" Diego asked.

"No . . . It's a hawk!" The Calatravan choked as he said it. "That means they've found us. We have to flee!" he screamed.

They saw the brutal collision of the hawk with the dove; a cloud of feathers left a sign of the hunt, and the dove beat its wings once more in the clutches of the sharp claws. Diego watched it until he saw with fright that its flight ended in the main square. There was a detachment of soldiers there, and he saw one catch the hawk on his leather glove.

Their eyes crossed. Now there was no room for doubt. The situation was desperate.

He heard a high-pitched whistle pass by his cheek. Out of instinct, he ducked. It had been an arrow.

"Where can we flee to?" he asked Wild Fox.

When he turned, he had to hold out his arms to keep from falling. He saw that the arrow had entered in one of the man's eyes and was lodged in his brain. The poor man was already dead.

Diego left him stretched out on the ground and heard a chorus of voices underneath the house. He looked around, clueless as to how he would escape. No one had foreseen this situation, but there was no time to regret that and even less time to hesitate.

He ran to one edge of the roof and studied the situation. Close to the building, there was another, a bit lower, but it seemed too far to jump. Before deciding, Diego looked to see if there was any other way. Then he lifted his tunic to his waist, tied it in a knot, hid the niqab inside, and gave himself a running start.

While he was in the air, he thought he wouldn't make it, regardless of the enormous force of his leap. He felt all the blood in his body accumulate in his legs when he took off. A few feet from the edge, his temples began throbbing from clenching his jaws. Without breathing, harnessing all his might, he made it to the other roof, rolling across it and feeling a shower of arrows coming down around him. He ran, avoiding them as best he could, and jumped onto a lower sloping roof. When he looked back, he saw two soldiers on his trail. One had just jumped onto the roof of the first building. The second, snagged on a ledge, recovered and ran after him as well, screaming something incomprehensible.

Diego guessed at the distance between himself and the street and jumped, seeing no one else close by. Once on the ground, he began to run through a confused network of streets that seemed to lead to nowhere. It was getting late, and in the darkness, everything blended together, but Diego was still able to follow the path he had memorized without the least hesitation.

When he could tell the soldiers were getting closer, he thought about his alternatives. To turn back to the gate where he'd entered the city was suicide, because the guards would already be notified of his flight and would have sealed the exits. He thought of the tunnels, which didn't seem a bad idea, but he had just left the closest one behind and couldn't turn back. With few other options, he concentrated on gaining speed to at least get as far as possible from his pursuers.

After recognizing a small mosque in one of the alleyways, he thought of the other buildings that he would be coming up on, in case any could serve as a temporary hiding place. When he went over them one by one, he suddenly thought of a brilliant solution.

He calculated that only three streets away he would come upon the palace of the Persian ambassador, and he remembered Benazir. Years ago he had heard she'd gone back to Seville after her separation from Galib. Though it was true that many years had passed, whether she was there or not, that was his only hope of salvation.

He covered his head with the niqab and ran as fast as he could until he arrived at the palace gates. He pounded for them to open, looking behind himself the whole time. No one answered. He tried again, this time with an enormous knocker shaped like a panther's head. He waited, panting, all his muscles tensed. No one would open. He looked for somewhere to hide and found two large barrels against a wall. He ran to them and hid himself. Soon afterward, he could see the same men who had followed him and after them at least a dozen more. All overlooked him, and Diego seized the moment to return to the door and knock again.

At last someone opened it a bit. A woman stuck out her head and asked the purpose of his visit.

"I need to speak to Benazir, it's urgent." Diego disguised his voice to not sound too masculine. The woman could tell there was something strange there. She began to close the door when someone spoke from inside.

"Who is it?"

"Who are you?" the woman at the door asked him.

"Please, I pray you, tell her it is one of Galib's sisters." Diego thought that would provoke her immediate interest. He needed them to open up the gates, to enter as soon as possible, or else he would be discovered.

The door opened a bit and Benazir appeared there, more mature but still as beautiful as he remembered. She looked askance at that woman hidden under the niqab, curious as to why she would have mentioned that name.

Had it not been for the presence of the servant, Diego would have taken off his head covering at that moment, revealing his identity. But if he did, she might take fright and call the guards. He decided to keep up the subterfuge.

"He sends me. . . . You must listen to me, it is a matter of extreme importance to all, especially for you."

Benazir recognized something familiar in that voice, though it was distorted by the presence of that thick cloth.

"Come in and tell me." She let him through, finally, and Diego rushed in, causing both women to feel nervous.

"May we speak in private?"

Benazir was unsure whether it wouldn't be prudent to remain with her servant. That woman, her hurried appearance, the time, the strangeness of the situation . . . She was going to tell him no.

Diego could guess her thoughts, and knowing he could be thrown out, he tried another strategy.

"I'm from Malagón; do you remember me?"

Benazir brought her hands to her lips, stunned. She hadn't heard word of that place since she lived in Toledo. And now the voice was a little deeper, more masculine. *It couldn't be*, she thought.

"Ishamadi, you can go now. If my father looks for me, I'll be in the reading room."

She tried to recall whom those eyes beneath the niqab could belong to and finally she recognized him.

"And you come with me . . ." Before she finished the phrase, she made sure her servant could no longer hear. "Diego de Malagón."

VIII.

I n scarcely an hour, Diego had recounted all his ups and downs from the time of his escape from Toledo until he had appeared at that door, dressed as a woman, with half the city chasing him.

Benazir listened to him nervously, because his presence, besides joy, stirred up bad memories.

"How could I make that mistake?" she mourned. "Believe me, I've thought of it so many times. To lose my head that way, when you were only a boy . . ."

A sharp pain, very deep, was reflected in her wounded, fleeting stare.

"Maybe it's better to leave all that behind us . . ."

"I never could, Diego. I've thought about it many times, maybe in an attempt to clear my conscience, or else to just understand myself. And I've realized that throughout my life, I've only known how to waste everything good that's been given to me. In Toledo, I was always obsessed with appearing to be something I wasn't; I tried to be a desirable, charming, seductive woman, forgetting what I really cared about: my husband. I looked down on his work, his responsibilities; I began to hate how even-tempered he was. I acted without maturity, spitefully; I was foolish . . . or just stupid, to be more exact." She caught a tear that was streaming down her cheek. "I came to Toledo and to married life without ever learning how to be myself. Though the years had passed, I was still a girl, I couldn't take on the role life had chosen for me, be a responsible woman, faithful, a loving wife . . . I did everything wrong, Diego, terribly—"

"Maybe you're being too hard on yourself," Diego interrupted.

"Hard? Hard, you say?" Her chin trembled and her nervous hands flew from her lap to her chin and then to her dress. "Can you imagine what it feels like when you take stock of your whole life and you don't find anything important in it? Does it not seem incredible to you that a person can be marked forever by one tragic mistake, just one, however unimportant it was?"

Diego was filled with compassion and felt the need to embrace her. Despite that terrible occurrence, Benazir had been an essential part of his path in those early years of his youth, so full of doubts. At her side he had learned to speak Arabic and discovered the universe of translation in Toledo. She was the one who gave him his first book; he still remembered it, and he remembered, too, that ill-fated trip through the marshes of Guadalquivir. But more than anything, she had been a fascination for Diego, the object of his passions, a savage temptation, awakening his sensuality.

And he realized he still adored her.

He stroked her hair in silence while he remembered those deep conversations with Galib, when he defined her as unique, irreplaceable, a precious essence, the inheritor of the desert, indomitable, indefinable, shifting as the sands. He could still see his master with his eyes inflamed and his hands quivering with emotion when he uttered each of those words.

"From what you say, you have achieved almost everything you set out to do." Benazir admired him with her warm, honey-colored eyes. "When I saw you for the first time in Toledo, you were no one, just a young commoner, son of a poor innkeeper. At fourteen you were already full of ambition and the will to be someone."

"You're right. At that moment I wasn't just running from the Saracens, I was trying to achieve a dream forbidden to people of my class: to learn, to acquire the necessary experience, to brush up against the wisdom hidden in books, absorb the principles of science, master the knowledge of things. How innocent I was; I didn't imagine then that knowledge went hand in hand with power, and that only the nobles or the priests could have it. It wasn't there for a poor son of the earth like myself."

"Your merit is much greater," she interrupted him. "You've made yourself into a famed albéitar, and all that thanks to the iron will you relied on to make it. But beyond that, you've tasted monastic life, you've experienced war, you know the bitter taste of treason and disappointment, and the sweetness of true love . . ." She paused to order her ideas. "My dear Diego, you should be proud of all that. Your life has consisted of so many sensations and adventures; you even knew death up close from a young age."

"I was reborn that day. I've done everything thanks to a combination of luck and fate. You could do it, too, if you would leave the past behind, Benazir."

"You came to life without remorse hunting you down, as it does me."

"Even the worst evil can be atoned for."

"Maybe you're right." She stood up, uncomfortable, and went to retrieve two apples from a large platter. He took one and bit into it hungrily.

"Inside my heart, I feel an enormous debt to you." Benazir sighed heavily. "Tell me what I can do for you, I beg you."

"For now, hide me, that's already a great deal. I can't explain much more because it could put you in serious danger."

Benazir thought of where to hide him and nothing occurred to her better than the storehouse hidden in her father's basement.

"I suppose you know al-Nasir is in Seville."

"Of course," he answered without entering into the theme.

"Might your mission have to do with him?"

"Maybe . . ."

"I understand. . . . You're looking for information for Castile. It's that, no?"

"You could assume that."

"You can't risk it now, you'd be recognized immediately. . . . But I could." Benazir's face turned conspiratorial.

"Don't joke around. I would never put you in any danger."

"I often visit his sister, Princess Najla. We are good friends and I have no problems moving around her quarters. She's an excellent poet and we spend hours together reciting one stanza after another. I know the caliph well, I know his wife, even his favorite concubine, a beautiful redhead who . . ."

Diego choked when he heard that. A redhead, in the court of al-Nasir? It couldn't be. . . . His face lit up and his eyes seemed to be on the point of exploding. Benazir noticed it without knowing why.

"What did I say to upset you so bad?"

"The redhead." His voice cracked. "Do you know her name?"

Diego pulled off his disguise, as if those garments wouldn't let him breathe or had suddenly gotten in his way.

"Wait, I remember . . . I don't know . . . I think her name is Falak."

"Falak in Arabic means star—Estela!" Diego screamed without worrying about his safety.

"Please don't speak so loud. What is it?"

"It's my sister, the younger one. Don't you remember what happened in Malagón before I left for Toledo? Blanca must be there, too."

"I never heard that name, only Falak, or Estela as you call her."

Diego stood up and looked straight at Benazir with an unhinged expression, anxious to act.

"I have to go find them, right now. . . . I must free them from their prison, take them away." He paced around nervously. "I still don't know what to do, but I need to take action now!"

"Don't even think they'll let you enter the castle. Those African fanatics protect it. They'll kill you without thinking."

"I'll go through the tunnels underground. I know how to get to the courtyards. That was my original plan; enter into the caliph's lodgings from one of the conduits that leads into the river."

Diego walked mentally through the underground areas of the city. From the embassy, the best entrance to the courtyards was near the Great Mosque. He took out the parchment of the Wild Fox with the plan of the grounds and unfolded it so Benazir could tell him where he might find Estela. At the same time, he remembered his mission.

"Have you ever seen a Koran with a large gem on its cover in the palace?"

"Of course, al-Nasir always has it with him. The stone you mentioned is actually an enormous emerald, as big as a cherry. Are you looking for it?"

"Do you know where he might keep it?"

She pointed to a place that was very likely.

"I admit that using the underground tunnels might be a good idea, maybe the only option to get to the castle," Benazir commented. "This house has an entrance as well."

"I know, but those passages don't lead to the palace. They won't work for me."

Benazir was shocked by the change Diego had undergone. When she looked at him, she saw a valiant man, cultivated and handsome. She knew he had good reason to go to the palace and that nothing could prevent him, but still, she feared for him. She wanted to help. . . . The presence of his sister Estela had upset him, made him too nervous; he was anxious to do something, and soon. In that state, he might not be controlled enough to act without committing some error.

"I'll go with you." She stood up, decided, and covered Diego's mouth as soon as he began to protest. "I don't care what you say, I need it. . . . I can't stay here. I have to do something, I don't know, at least watch the entrance to the tunnel you have to use."

IX.

Diego waited for Benazir in the basement of the Persian embassy. In addition to countless other feelings, he felt an enormous responsibility weighing down on him, remembering that the enemy was advancing on Salvatierra.

He couldn't linger long in his attempt to rescue his sisters or in finding that Koran. It was vital to make it back to the fortress before the Almohads, so he had to leave Seville as soon as possible.

Benazir appeared with a dark cloth over her head.

"Let's go. . . ."

They went out to the street and walked cautiously to the city center. They followed a number of alleys until they hit a plaza they needed to cross; in the middle of it, under some orange trees, they saw a group of soldiers talking.

Diego tried to remember an alternative route, but none existed. To reach the north face of the Great Mosque, they would have to either cross the plaza or go along its edge. He explained it softly to Benazir.

"They'll see us," Diego lamented.

"Follow me and let me handle it." Benazir took his hand and pulled him toward the men. Diego, made nervous by her determination, felt his heartbeat in his temples. Once they were close to the soldiers, Benazir threw herself in Diego's arms and kissed him on the lips, as ardently as a lover.

"I love you so much," she whispered in a voice loud enough for the others to hear.

The soldiers looked at each other and laughed, though they couldn't see their faces. They were looking for a woman in a niqab, young and agile, supposedly, and not a couple of hot-blooded lovers.

Benazir and Diego continued on their way, their kisses sweet and warm, and left the men behind. Neither of them realized that Diego had dropped a piece of parchment on the ground, the map of the castle; but the soldiers did.

"Wait!" one shouted, his intention only to tell them so. "Stop. . . ."

They ran away, thinking they'd been discovered. The soldiers gave chase, surprised by their reaction. One of them picked up the object and saw it was a map. Then he understood it could be spies.

"When we arrive at the next fork, a long street open to the right. We'll take it," Benazir recommended, gasping because she was unused to running so fast. "In the middle there's a big fountain that's often empty. . . . We'll hide there. Since it's night, they won't see us."

The soldiers ran after them through the neighboring streets, talking to each other without understanding how the couple could have vanished. They decided to split up to better cover the area, and after a moment, Diego and Benazir couldn't hear them.

"Should we leave?" Benazir whispered.

Diego peeked out and then emerged.

"Go home, Benazir. It's too risky with me. It's absurd for you to follow me."

"Don't tell me what to do. I was useful to you in the plaza and you might need me again."

Diego gave up, took her hand, and together they retraced their footsteps. They crossed two more streets and stopped at the entrance to a broad esplanade that angled toward the mosque.

On one of the walls of that temple, there had to be a trapdoor or something similar that connected to the tunnels. Diego looked over the entire wall without seeing anything special. He was awed by the magnificent minaret rising up from the building's center.

"I have to get closer, from here I can't see well." He pointed at the mosque. "You stay here. If you see me disappear, that's a good sign. In that case, don't wait for me."

"You're asking me to do something very difficult." Benazir grabbed him, desolate. For a moment she thought it might be the last time she ever saw him. "How will I know if you're safe?" She stroked his cheek.

"If they capture me, it will be announced. But don't worry, I'll manage. I'll rescue my sisters, get the Koran, and we'll flee through the undergrounds of the city that ends up at the Guadalquivir. I'll escape with them to the north."

Benazir understood she couldn't delay him anymore.

"Go, and God protect you. . . ." She kissed him tenderly and said goodbye to him in tears.

Diego took off running and crossed the esplanade, reaching the wall of the mosque unnoticed. With the darkness as his ally, he passed along the east wall, looking over every inch, but he couldn't find the entrance. It began to disturb him. He looked for Benazir. She was hidden behind the column of a building watching him.

Then something called Diego's attention. He thought he saw a man amid the shadows behind Benazir. He wanted to be wrong, but he wasn't. He could see unequivocally a soldier walking in their direction. He was going to see her. Diego had to help. He shouted with all his might to attract the man's attention; the man ran in his direction. Diego looked around. The esplanade was too big to escape without being seen, and there was nowhere to hide. Looking at the minaret, he saw a small door at its base. Like a fleeting image, he suddenly remembered Efraím's prophecy. He spoke of a minaret, shouting, escape . . . It coincided with what was happening now, but what else did it mean? Without thinking twice, he ran to the tower, and when he arrived, he knocked off the hinges with a strong kick.

Though he could hardly see anything in the interior, he found a ramp that rose at a slight angle toward the top. He filled his lungs with air, listened to the steps of the soldier behind him, and ran upward with all the energy his legs could muster. Every time he reached another level, he looked for places to hide, some door that led to another room, any answer to get away from his pursuer, but everything was locked.

When he finally arrived at the ninth floor, he thought he was going to faint—he had no energy left—and at that moment he heard a metallic sound, like a sword, not far from him, just one floor below. All he could do was run to the highest spot. Once there, he would see . . .

On the ninth floor, the ramp stopped, and there was a more narrow stairway winding around the tower's center. The steps were short and very tall, which meant his legs were working twice as hard. By the time he'd reached the second landing, they were cramping and he felt a sharp pain in his belly.

"You won't escape!"

The threat of that soldier, out of breath and stuttering, echoed through the minaret. It reached Diego's ears just as he made it to the fourth landing. To his right, at last, he saw a door open partway and he pushed it the rest of the way. He felt a soft breeze. He was on a small, very narrow terrace with a short stone balustrade. It wouldn't be easy to escape.

He thought of what he could do to defend himself against the man. He was unarmed, tired, and couldn't get a handle on his breathing. At that moment, he felt all the blood in his body pounding through his head.

He hid in a corner and fearfully awaited the soldier's arrival.

He heard the door. First he tried to calm his breathing, then he heard the panting of his pursuer approaching to the left. He clenched his fists when he saw the tip of a sword appear, and with incredible determination he jumped at the man, pushing him as hard as he could. Surprising the soldier, Diego dragged him almost without resistance to the edge of the balustrade. The soldier was young and his eyes were bulging out: He couldn't believe what was happening. He felt Diego's hands throwing him over the stone barrier into the air.

The boy screamed so intensely that it tore through the evening silence. That, too, recalled Efraím's prophecy: a scream in the air was what he had said. And he had just lived it. Diego looked over the edge and saw the soldier's body lying on the ground.

He ran downstairs and took the ramps, coming outside just as Benazir approached. She had been waiting with dread on the other side of the plaza until she heard the terrible scream and saw the man falling from the heights. She crossed the plaza to find out what had happened, terrified, thinking it was Diego. And when she saw him, she embraced him.

"For a moment I was afraid . . ."

They heard noises. They were standing in front of the main entrance to the castle, though some distance still lay before them. They saw a platoon of soldiers emerge, at their head a man wearing Christian garments.

Diego turned to Benazir with an expression of deep disappointment. That meant his mission was over, and that he couldn't save the sisters he'd been separated from for sixteen years, even though he'd never been so close. . . . He felt a dreadful grief, a cruel impotence, seeing all his plans crumble.

The men were approaching. They were going to capture them.

"Run!"

Benazir pushed him to awaken him from his trance. Diego looked at his persecutors and suddenly recognized who was leading them; the man recognized him as well. It was Pedro de Mora.

"Capture that man!" the Castilian shouted in fury. "I want the head of that bastard, kill him if you have to. . . ."

"Let's go to your palace . . ." Diego yelled to Benazir as soon as they had taken off.

"And when we get there?" she asked, frightened. She didn't understand how he had recognized that man.

"It's Persian territory, I don't think they'll dare enter."

Diego was thinking of the tunnels as his final solution. It was an enormous network of passageways, dead ends, and offshoots, a place impossible to navigate for someone who didn't know it well.

He looked back and saw that the soldiers were gaining ground. Benazir couldn't run any faster; her dress was too tight. Diego knew they had little left to go, but he also realized they would be caught if they couldn't go faster. Stumbling, but without stopping, he grabbed the edge of Benazir's tunic and tore it, leaving a long tear up her side. For the moment, that solved their problems and soon they had reached the door of the Persian embassy. They pushed it open and ran to the courtyard, hoping they were safe, but it wasn't so. The soldiers didn't hesitate to follow them, with Pedro de Mora behind them.

"They're going to trap us, Diego. . . ." Benazir saw them so close that she thought all hope was lost.

"No, you'll see. . . . Inside the tunnels we'll lose them."

"I don't know."

They crossed a long passageway and emerged at another courtyard where the trapdoor that led down into the tunnels was located. When he reached it, Diego pulled on its iron handle as firmly as he could, but years of disuse had sealed it shut. He pressed his feet into the floor and pulled with all his might. This time his luck was better. The hatch creaked open and a terrible odor emerged from inside.

"Get in, Benazir!"

"I won't go," she answered.

"Are you mad? Now is not the time. . . . For God's sake, I can hear them coming."

"Go! I'll lie to them, I'll say you kidnapped me. If I follow you, I'll be a burden. You go alone."

Diego didn't know what to do. Stay? Flee?

Benazir, seeing his doubts, kissed him on the cheek and ran to meet the men.

Diego entered the conduit, and while his torso was still outside, he saw Benazir rush toward the men, screaming. And then he saw a sword come out and it was plunged into her stomach. She gave a long cry and turned back to him with a tranquil expression, full of peace, convinced that at that moment, after all those years, she had atoned for her sin.

Diego closed the trapdoor and slid down a slippery stairway deep into the ground, weeping and destroyed. As soon as he touched flat ground, he ran. He took a passage to his right, and then another when he heard voices coming after him. They were trying to give chase, but he didn't fear for his life; there was not so much danger now. They wouldn't catch him. He went through one narrow passageway after another, climbed and descended stairways, and even waded through one tunnel with water up to his waist. But he managed to leave them behind.

Not long afterward, he came out at the river, outside the city's walls, and plunged into its cool waters. He followed it as fast as he could until he arrived at the Guadalquivir. Once there, he dove in, hiding himself, and made his way discreetly away from Seville to the east. He should reach the village of Coria and then get Sabba. Then he would gallop without stopping to Salvatierra.

He had failed in his mission, he hadn't seen the Koran or his sisters; the only thing he could do, Diego thought, was arrive in time to help his friends before the ferocious attack of the Almohads came down on them.

Two days later, saddled atop Sabba and flying down over paths far away from the main roads, Diego thought of Benazir with pride. There was no braver or more generous act than the one she had performed.

He cried, remembering it.

That woman had shown that she carried the blood of the daughters of the desert in her veins, the braveness of its storms and the contrast of its nights. Benazir possessed a pure soul.

He would remember her forever.

After five days' travel, Diego reached the Muradal Pass. Once he'd crossed it, he saw the fortress of Salvatierra on the hill, dominating the plains below it.

An enormous cloud of dust rose from inside the walls and around it. Hundreds of horsemen surrounded it, growing in number as victory approached.

From afar he could hear bloodcurdling screams, the sound of clashing swords, drums, Moorish trumpets accompanying the attack.

He looked at the tower and saw with sorrow that the flags flown there no longer belonged to the Calatravans or to Castile. Now there was a white one, with no decoration, belonging to the Almohads and another from the Andalusian army.

He had arrived too late; Salvatierra had fallen into their hands.

"I failed them. Dear God, what can have happened to them all?"

The mare snorted nervously, smelling death nearby, and kicked at the soil.

"Where can I go now?"

Sabba turned her head and looked at him. She whinnied and tore off at a furious gallop.

Diego didn't try to change her mind.

PART VI

Lands of Heroes

The news of the fall of Salvatierra moves the entire Christian world of Europe with such intensity that they unite en masse, initiating the crusade that Pope Innocent III convokes against the Muslims.

All the roads of Europe are filled with combatants heading toward Toledo. Once there, they will submit to the orders of the great patron of this movement, Alfonso VIII of Castile. An enormous army gathers at the gates of the former Visigoth capital.

The Castilian monarch has sent an order to all the provinces demanding a halt to the construction of walls and any other such labors so that all effort may be devoted to the war, and he commands knights and pages to be outfitted with arms and horses. . . .

The crusade will oblige the remaining Christian empires to collaborate in this enterprise. Aragon takes Castile's side from the first moment. Navarre is hesitant, but finally agrees. Only the kings of Portugal and León will avoid the war.

On the other front, Caliph al-Nasir has called up a grand army in Seville composed of Turks, Arabs, Egyptians, Berbers, and the normal Andalusian troops.

The offensive will be a definitive confrontation between the two religions and their two gods.

History will know this showdown as the Battle of the Navas de Tolosa.

I.

———————

Sabba didn't take him to Toledo.

Though that was the destination Diego had chosen, on the road, not long before reaching the walls, he heard that some Calatravans had managed to escape from Salvatierra and had taken refuge in the second-most-important fortress the order possessed in Castile, Zorita de los Canes, at the base of the Tagus River, only two days from Toledo on horseback.

From that moment he felt a pressing need to know what had happened to Bruno de Oñate, Otón, and Pinardo, and all the rest of those men he owed his life to, who had been his only real family.

The castle of Zorita rose up over a plateau surrounded by a winding but solid stone wall. To reach the main gate, Diego had to go up a small hill blocked in the middle by a powerful wall.

"I'm looking for Bruno de Oñate . . ." Diego stopped a man coming down the path with an entire side of beef on his back.

"And you're telling me this?" he grumbled, spitting to one side. "Ask up there; I won't have anything else to do with those monks, or soldiers, or whatever they are. They owe me for four months and I can't trust them another day. God damn the hour I decided to sell to them!"

"Eat your own damned meat!" someone shouted at him from inside the grounds.

Diego entered the castle without needing to identify himself; there was no one manning the gate. He crossed the first courtyard, where nobody seemed to find his presence remarkable, and turned toward a drawbridge that led to a wooden portal guarded by two soldiers. They stopped him.

"My name is Diego de Malagón and I am looking for some knights who fought at Salvatierra . . ."

"Step aside!" One of them pushed him out of the way.

"What's happening?"

"Make way for the archbishop!"

Diego saw four groups of Calatravans passing through with at least a dozen churchmen. Among them was one middle-aged man, dressed in a gray habit with a red cape. His head was shaved, with only a thin line of hair trailing around the back of his head, from ear to ear. In spite of his fat face, wild eyes, and almost vulgar appearance, he exuded dignity.

When the man was close to Diego, he stared at him with an absolute lack of compunction, even though he was talking to another man. His look was so inquisitive and insistent that Diego felt uncomfortable; the man was looking him over from head to toe. It was true that his clothing was filthy and his hair oily and unkempt. And he smelled like a herd of swine. He felt ashamed, thinking the priest must have noticed all this as well.

"How do you know the Archbishop Ximénez de Rada?" one of the guards asked him, surprised by the holy man's evident interest.

"I . . . nothing . . . It's the first time I've seen him. . . ." Diego answered without attaching importance to the matter. Coming back to what he had come for, he said, "But I do know Bruno de Oñate. Could you tell me if he resides in this castle and if so, where I can find him?"

To Diego's joy, they told him how to find him. That meant he had survived, and they let him through, though he had to leave Sabba behind with a stable keeper as a guarantee.

Diego dismounted from his mare and passed the reins to the boy.

"Give her a bit to drink. She's probably very thirsty and a little nervous."

"Don't worry; she'll be in good hands." The boy smiled at him kindly.

His face reminded him of Marcos. What could have happened to him? Where might he be now? The time that had passed since Diego was in Cuéllar was still not enough to forget his indignation.

While he walked along thinking it over, he crossed a paved courtyard full of people. When he came to the building where they told him he would find Bruno de Oñate, Diego stopped a moment to study it. He saw a small door with a lancet arch, and since it was open, he went through without hesitation, arriving at an enormous rectangular hall full of people. He moved among them, almost shoving, trying to find someone he knew, but he had no luck. Somewhat desperate, he carried on through the hall, moving from one end to the other, convinced that his lack of success meant that no one had survived the Muslim assault on Salvatierra besides Bruno.

An agreeable aroma of burned wood spread through the room from one of the corners. When he approached it, he saw three men in heated conversation. As he got closer, he thought he recognized one.

"Bruno . . ." Diego raised his vice to make himself heard.

The Calatravan turned when he heard his name.

"Diego?" His eyes bulged. "But what joy it is to see you!" They shook hands and Bruno stared at him in disbelief. "You know we assumed you were dead."

He took leave of his companions to hear what had happened in Seville.

"Then you managed to get a glimpse of the Koran?" He was speaking rapidly. "Tell me what was in it. . . . Tell me everything, fast."

"It was almost impossible to find you," Diego said, trying to change the subject. "When I arrived at Salvatierra, it had already been taken, and then I fled to Toledo, where I heard I could find you in this fortress. I didn't know what could have happened to you . . ."

"As you see, I'm here. We managed to escape that hell at the last minute, but let's leave that aside and . . ." Bruno thought he saw a shadow of remorse on the young man's face, and feared the worst. "Tell me about the Koran."

"I couldn't even get close."

"You mean that you failed in your mission then, right?" He made an ugly grimace.

"As soon as I entered Seville, I went to the house of Wild Fox, and we were discovered as he tried to send a message relating the imminent attack on Salvatierra. They killed him right there, and I had to run with half the city at my back. Luckily, someone I knew from years before managed to help me out."

"You were conscious of the importance of your mission, no?" Bruno's face was cold and his question wounding.

"Of course. . . . Of course I knew, but I'm telling you, there were problems and escaping was the best solution. . . . I came across Pedro de Mora and he recognized me. It was then that I found out he was the one at the head of the Almohads' spying." Diego was stumbling, nervous. Bruno's expression could not have been icier.

"We put great hopes in you . . ." He paused deliberately, for too long, it seemed to Diego. "I feel deeply disappointed and not just because you failed to complete your mission, but also because you revealed your face to the enemy and now we can't use you for another mission. We are on the verge of a great war; this is not the time for spying, but for action. That means, Diego, that your time with us is at an end. . . . From now on, you are free to do as you wish." Bruno's gaze was as cold as steel.

"I don't understand. . . . I risked my life and I did exactly what you asked of me. I don't think I deserve this lack of respect. I'm more sorry than anyone that I couldn't do what I'd been asked, but I also lost a great deal on the way." He was thinking of Benazir.

Bruno showed no interest in his explanations and made as if to leave, but Diego grabbed his arm and stopped him.

"I still think your judgment is unjust, but I won't bother you more. You don't want me to form any part of your plans, and that's fine; though I have a hard time accepting it, I will. But now, I want to remind you of a promise you made me. Remember when you said you would help me rescue my sisters? Well, they're in Seville . . ."

The Calatravan seemed to have no interest in what he was saying.

"Forget it, for now there's nothing to be done." Bruno began to walk toward the exit.

"And when will there be? Can you tell me?" Diego followed him.

"Maybe never!"

"So your words have no honor." Diego raised his voice. "And you're the one who feels deceived. . . . You lied to me!"

Bruno turned and punched him in the chin then walked off, spitting and cursing. Diego felt better in spite of the blow, because he had said exactly what he wanted to say.

Not long afterward, he was taking the exit, with Sabba as his only company and the words of Bruno echoing in his head. He crossed through the last gate, with the bitter sensation of reliving what he had already been through in Toledo, Fitero, Albarracín, Cuéllar. . . . The hardest thing was to admit that all that sacrifice, all he'd endured, his determination over the course of those past three years in Salvatierra had done nothing but make him a pariah.

He turned away from the creek bed and followed the banks of the Tagus, telling Sabba to get him away from there fast. She must have felt his sorrow, and she began to gallop angrily, wanting to see Diego's spirits restored. She snorted loudly, shook her head from side to side, and raised her ears before turning east.

Diego held on to her, felt her power, and with it, his pains subsided a bit. Sabba was the one who was most loyal, least selfish, his only memory of his family, and without a doubt the best gift he had ever received.

He closed his eyes and tried to erase from his memory the bitterness of all that had just occurred. He wanted to recall the positive parts of his experience with the Calatravans. With them he had learned to be part of a group, to participate with admiration in the heroic labors of men ready to give their lives for a great cause, people whose only dream was to give back the freedom of the people yoked under the tyranny of the Almohads.

He inhaled a mouthful of air and stroked Sabba before deciding to go to Toledo to look for Galib. That was where everything had begun. There he would decide his future.

II.

———————

"It's you . . . . Sajjad surprised to see you. Galib has client right now."
Old Sajjad couldn't believe that Diego was back in that house again.
He looked at him resentfully, unbelieving.

Once the castle of the Calatravans was behind him, Diego had crossed the final leagues separating him from Toledo. Thinking of meeting Galib again loosed a torrent of intense feelings. All he could imagine was embracing him again, talking calmly, revealing so many experiences lived through, mourning Benazir's death, sharing their lives.

"You look the same as always," he said to Sajjad and smiled.

"Galib be different . . . very changed, sir. . . . Me also very old."

Sajjad was proceeding calmly. Years ago, he had accused Diego many times of going after his master's wife, and that morning, with Galib, he had surprised the two of them. He must still hold it against him, Sajjad thought, looking at Diego. Just in case, he moved away from him, and he didn't stop looking at him for a moment.

"You seem more like gentleman now. . . . You want lemon . . . nice, cool lemonade?"

"Thank you, Sajjad, with pleasure."

Diego stayed alone in that room where twelve years before he had spent hours and hours studying. Once more his eyes roamed the shelves and enjoyed recognizing one title after another. But he found one apart from the others that he didn't recognize at first. He felt excited as he took it in his hands. He touched the embossed title on the cover with his fingertips: *Mulomedicina Chironis*. He couldn't believe he was looking at that treasure of the science of horse medicine that had been thought to be lost forever. He opened a page at random and began to read. It was written in Latin.

"That book cost me a fortune."

Diego was stunned. That voice . . .

Galib was behind him, older, hunched over, his hair now completely gray.

"I imagine, dear master . . ."

Their eyes met during a long silence full of intense and vivid emotions and the weight of remembered bitterness.

"I . . ." Diego mumbled. "I have to ask your forgiveness for all that . . ."

"Don't go on, Diego. I know what happened." Galib came to him with arms open, embracing Diego with complete affection and sincerity.

"I . . . I don't know where . . . how to tell you . . ." The joy of seeing his master again, someone he had considered his second father, was such that he couldn't utter a complete phrase.

"Let's begin where we left off, and don't treat me with such formalities, not any more. We're colleagues. Sit down, please, and tell me everything."

"Something's happened, something you should know, before anything else." A shadow of anguish crossed Diego's face. Galib began imagining what it could be.

"Something to do with her, no?"

Diego felt his throat tighten, and he could hardly breathe. He had to say it without looking into his eyes; he owed him the truth.

"I saw her die in Seville, less than a month ago. . . ."

Galib's heart broke when he heard that. A few weeks before, he'd had a bad dream in which Benazir was suffering terrible pains, but he never imagined it could be real. He grabbed his head and crossed his arms over his chest, crying bitterly, in the depths of pain, deep, wounding, definitive . . .

Diego watched him dumbstruck, respecting his need to suffer in silence. But then he couldn't bear it, and he embraced his old master to help share his grief.

Once he had recovered, Galib was able to put words to the thoughts and feelings that had overcome him.

"Nothing can stop the desert winds; they have a free soul, like hers. My error was to want her for myself alone, Diego, when that wasn't possible. I loved her to the end, that's why I was dying with jealousy when I found out she had gone after you, lusted for you . . ."

"I . . . didn't know how to remain faithful to—"

"Don't torment yourself more," Galib interrupted. "Benazir was turbulent, passionate, unpredictable . . . A few days later, she herself confessed to me what she had done, and I couldn't endure it. It was a terrible blow to our relationship; I was always doubting her, and I imagined her with other men. I couldn't trust in her kisses. Everything had changed. . . . Our trust was broken into a million pieces, like fine crystal. It affected me so much, so much . . . that I finally rejected her." He studied Diego's face amid his grief. "Your response to what happened was exemplary. To take all the responsibility and free her of any blame showed me how loyal you really were. Benazir was fleeting; like water running between your fingers, she was impossible to restrain. For a while she loved you the way she had loved me in my day. In reality, I never knew how to accept her as she was; I only loved her my way."

Diego told him of the circumstances of her death and the reasons he had gone to Seville. While he did, he relived those last hours with the same intensity he had felt at the time.

Galib listened to him, destroyed, almost without strength, recriminating himself, as he had done so many other times, for pushing her away when living with her, for her, was all he had ever known how to do.

Without worrying about the late hour, he wanted to talk about his wife as he never had before, to open his heart completely, to reveal everything he remembered about her. It would be his homage to a woman he had loved to the very limits of his ability.

Diego listened to him in silence. He remembered the passion he himself had felt for her. Then it had seemed to him that the woman was everything, that nothing good could exist outside her. But when Mencía appeared, years later, he understood what it really meant to love a woman.

With the fresh taste of that memory, Diego wanted to share with Galib all the experiences he'd had since he left Toledo. He mentioned all the places he'd been, the people who had marked him, Mencía and Marcos above all.

"I've had everything, and I've lost everything, Galib. I managed to become respected as an albéitar. I could put into practice all I'd learned at your side, and all I'd read in the monastery at Fitero and all I'd learned in the course of my work. But above all, I thought I was loved by the only woman who has ever really captured my heart. Then everything collapsed; Marcos betrayed me and Mencía married another man."

"Everything is never lost, the way you say. There are moments that are better and worse. . . . Remember you still have much to give to others, many years to live, and that the job you have is an art. Albéitars are useful wherever we go because we have the virtue of healing; we are healers of horses. I would like to call myself that, a horse healer. The power to restore health is a talent Allah has placed in our hands and in our eyes. To you in particular he has given great intelligence, and now, after hearing about your adventures with the Calatravans, it seems he's given you bravery, too."

Diego took the *Mulomedicine Chironis* in his hands and remembered how long it had been since he'd studied.

"I remember one day someone called me horse healer and I didn't like it then, but when I hear you now, I have to recognize it's a beautiful name for our profession. . . . It's been too long since I've practiced it. I stopped studying, reading; in reality I haven't done that work very much these past few years. I miss it."

"I am happy to see you still need the nourishment of science and that, though in these past few years you have learned other skills, your curiosity is still begging for answers."

While they spoke, Galib took two large logs and lit a fire. Then he looked for glasses and filled them with a sweet cherry liquor.

"So many years have passed." Galib swished the liquor in his mouth, savoring it. "I'm surprised by the number of experiences you've had, but . . . would you say you've accomplished what you set out to do?"

"When I came to Toledo, just a boy, I was a commoner, the offspring of the sweat, misery, and effort of my father, who fought against everything, even his own physical limitations, to provide for his family. I swore to that ill-starred blacksmith, innkeeper, shepherd—because he'd been a little bit of everything—that I would become somebody dignified. He wanted me to learn a profession that would be fitting for my abilities." Diego stopped to breathe a moment. "And now you ask me if I've accomplished what I set out to do. . . . I don't know." He hesitated. "In this sense, I may have come farther that what I dreamed of then."

"I'm happy to hear you say that."

"I should be, too, but in reality I'm not. I feel that I left something more important behind on the way; love, friendship, trust in the people I've cared for the most, you among them. . . . I don't know, everything has passed through my life so fast."

"Life is a long pilgrimage on the path to perfection. We try to reach the end and we don't realize how much important there is on the way. I have known many who believed they were unhappy for not accomplishing their dreams. Their ambitions blinded them so much that they couldn't see the goodness offered by the road itself."

"I understand you, but I have to say that I haven't seen so much goodness, maybe because I've had to take too many roads, almost always treacherous and full of obstacles and setbacks. Being a commoner closed so many doors, Galib, some important, like access to knowledge. If I managed to get access to it in Fitero, believe me, it was thanks to lies and tricks and buying off more than one person's indulgence. . . . I also had to learn not to aspire to win the heart of a noblewoman. Just because their blood is different! I tasted the terrors of war and exile because of this love. But if I think of our profession, even there I haven't encountered colleagues remotely as noble as you. One of them, a *menescal* from Naples, was so wounded by envy, just because I saved a horse's life, that he tried to murder me. And to top it off, I suffered misunderstanding and a death sentence for discovering the origins of a plague that was afflicting many of my neighbors."

Galib pushed one of the logs so that the others would set it alight.

"The ability to grow in the face of adversity lies at the root of greatness, and overcoming it is a healthy stimulus for the heart. To learn from your errors makes you noble, and to be humble, in a world full of pride, is the key to happiness, I promise you. Diego, everything you just shared with me, all that is a few steps on the long road of your life. You need to understand that happiness lies not in grandiose goals. Those challenges are what made you grow, and if you think about it, you'll see that each of them has a meaning."

Diego looked at him with the same admiration as before. Galib wasn't only the best albéitar in Toledo, but also a wise man and a philosopher; the man had reminded him of so many things. . . . Paying attention to his words, Diego began to recollect some of the moments he had lived through, and he was shocked to see how they fit together like clockwork. Just as Galib had said, they had all given him something; some maybe in a hidden way, though most otherwise.

"What is missing then?" Galib asked.

"It's been some time now that I've needed to do something."

"What are you thinking?"

"I still haven't lived very much. . . . My father asked me to take care of my sisters and I wasn't able to protect them when they needed me, and in Salvatierra I met some men whose only task was to overthrow the fanatical Almohads. They counted on me, they gave me a mission, but I failed them."

Galib ran a finger around the rim of the wineglass, thinking of how to help him. After a brief silence, he spoke from his heart.

"When Allah wanted to make the horse, he spoke to the south wind: from you I shall make a creature that will be the honor of my legacy, the humiliation of my enemies, and my defense against those who attack me. And the south wind responded: Lord, do it according to your desire. Then Allah took a handful of wind and with it, he made the horse. . . ."

Diego looked at him, astonished. That fable still affected him as much as it had the first time he heard it.

"Do you know what else I told you then?"

"You talked about my future."

"True, and I linked it to you mare, Sabba, as your inseparable companion. I told you she would take you to incredible places, and also that those noble animals would guide your path to greatness and to prominence. With them, you would do good. Remember?"

"Of course, but what could all that mean right now?"

"It means you shouldn't abandon the science you worked so hard to learn. When your father spoke to you as he did, he didn't want to push you to take up arms, though now you burn with longing to punish those infidels, which they are for me just as much as for you. You have to trust in your destiny, and maybe one day soon it will show you how to achieve both realities. Open your eyes wide and listen to your heart; it is free. And then be brave enough to listen to what it tells you."

A bell tolled six times and Galib was exhausted. He would need to rest before dawn.

"I need to sleep awhile, Diego. Tomorrow I have to be fresh; I have a visitor. Would you like to join me?"

"That means we could work together again." Diego was overjoyed with the idea.

"How would you feel about starting with one of the king's horses?"

Hours later, when the sun was about to rise, Sajjad looked for them everywhere in the house before finding the two albéitars at the stables. Diego was speaking with Sabba in a language Sajjad couldn't understand, and Galib was breathing on her nostrils. They were getting ready to ride to the stables in the royal palace.

Sabba whinnied cheerfully, recognizing the man she hadn't seen for so long, feeling his hands stroking her head.

"Welcome back to my home, dear Sabba. . . ."

III.

Diego was happy. It had been years since he had gotten up at dawn and galloped alongside his master, sharing his worries and all that he had learned. Galib, in spite of his age, had continued prospering in his profession. He was always close to the upper nobility and to the wealthy Muslims and Jews, but recently his fame had spread in Toledo and he was now the preferred albéitar of the king.

As Galib told Diego, Alfonso VIII had tried to convince him to work for him alone, and even to accompany him on his travels, but Galib never wanted to abandon his home or his independence.

They arrived at a magnificent palace on the outskirts of the city at the edge of the Tagus River. The building had been constructed by the final Muslim king in the days before Toledo's recapture by the Christians, and it was surrounded by an immense garden with a variety of trees, flowers, and bushes. At one time, it was meant to be a representation of paradise.

Diego felt overwhelmed. He had been in many noble houses, but this place was truly beautiful, or maybe he just felt awed because he was back with Galib in the stables of Alfonso VIII, whom he had heard so much about.

Once they were inside, the royal stable keeper awaited them with a gatekeeper and a steward. They were immediately taken to a sick horse.

"Diego, I'll let you do the honors." Galib pointed out the animal.

The patient was a precious Arabian mare, white, lying on a bed of hay and looking listless.

Diego approached, talking to her softly. The mare met his eyes and tried to whinny but couldn't; she was too weak.

Her ears were cool to the touch.

"Until yesterday she had a high fever," the stable keeper mentioned, "and last night, she peed blood."

When he observed her, Diego could see something strange in her gaze; it seemed more clouded than normal. He knelt to feel her eyelids. The mere touch of his hands made her jerk uncomfortably. Her conjunctiva were yellow and he found a small sac with cloudy liquid inside it.

"Bring me a candle."

Galib knelt and looked in her eyes while Diego examined the rest of her body.

"Muscular pain." He pressed on her neck, and the mare pulled away. "Inflammation of the eyes."

Galib had an idea of what was causing it but waited for Diego to speak.

The steward arrived with a lit lamp and a round mirror to reflect the light. Diego brought it close to one of the animal's eyes and she turned away, closed her eyelids, and kicked, showing her agitation.

"She has an illness of the veins . . ."

Galib looked at him, surprised. He had never heard such a sickness mentioned before.

"What do you mean?"

"It's something I saw in Albarracín. I still don't know what it's actually called. It's not written about it any books, though I suspect it's produced by a parasite, probably something too small to be seen. I studied it in depth and I suspect it enters the animal through an open wound and then migrates to another spot, and it causes all sorts of disturbances as it progresses. It shows up first as fever, which is the organism's defense reaction. If the kidneys are affected, there will be blood in the urine, and an attack on the liver will show in the yellowish color of the mucus. If they finally lose their sight, it's because of an inflammation of the inside of the eyes."

"Do you know how to treat it?"

"Nothing has ever worked. She will go blind and then she'll die. We can alleviate her pain, but that's all. But that's not the worst thing." He sighed, discomfited. "In this state, the animal is a danger, because this illness can be easily passed to man."

"What?" The stable keeper became worried; one of his workers was suffering from fevers and a stomachache.

"You need to isolate her immediately," Diego said, pointing to the mare. "Her disease could reach anyone who comes in contact with her, including the king himself."

A sudden presence interrupted their conversation.

"How is my mare?"

That voice could only belong to one person. King Alfonso appeared in the company of a man of enormous stature.

"Your Majesty . . ." Galib gave a long, low bow. "It seems we have bad news."

"Explain. . . ."

"Better if my former pupil, and now colleague, Diego de Malagón tells you."

Alfonso VIII looked at Diego with little interest. The king was wearing a long garment of red and white with two golden castles embroidered on the breast. His mane was long and gray, his beard thick, his skin dark, leathery, and wrinkled. Diego saw immovable authority reflected in his gaze and felt proud to be so close to someone he admired so deeply. He knelt and caressed the neck of the animal affectionately.

His companion talked the whole time. He was explaining the difficulties they would have in improving the public militias and maintaining the Ultramontanes that were now in Córdoba after the declaration of the crusade. He insisted on the necessity of providing them with good horses, shields, and swords. The person speaking was the first sergeant to the royal master-at-arms, who was responsible for feeding and arming the troops during the campaign. Given the magnitude of the battle that was coming, he was getting more anxious by the day.

"You shouldn't touch her, Your Majesty!" Diego exclaimed.

"Would you mind explaining to me why?"

Diego detailed the nature of the illness the mare was suffering and the danger of contagion that was present. He was surprised by the monarch's good manners, his simplicity, and how comfortable it was to talk to him.

"Give her whatever cures as necessary to ease her pains," King Alfonso concluded. "She has been a good and faithful mare. She has seen me through difficult times. You can no longer find animals of this breed . . ."

"Do you mean her Arabian blood?"

"That, yes. She's a unique specimen, a gift from the former governor of the *taifa* of Valencia. Her name is Faiza. According to what they told me, she descends from one of the five mares of Habdah, the originals. There is a legend that attributes the origin of the most beautiful race of horses, the Arabian, to those five. Do you know that story?" He looked at Galib. "Surely you do. . . ."

"Our Prophet named the others Obayah, Kuhaylah, Saqlauiyah, Hamdaniyah," Galib said. "One day, Muhammad had a hundred mares chosen from among all those of his army and closed them in a corral next to a freshwater stream. He kept them there in the heat of the sun, without access to that vital liquid for days, and then had the gates opened. The mares, called by their thirst, galloped toward the water like mad. But at that moment, he had the horn blown to call them to his side. All ignored it but five that came to him without drinking. Their obedience transcended their instincts. Since then those became his favorite animals and they never left his side."

"Faiza has been as great as they were," the king continued. "I regret her loss like she was a member of my family. . . ." His gaze fell on Diego, and then he remembered where he had heard of him, from his own ensign, Álvaro Núñez de Lara. "Weren't you involved in that failed mission when we tried to take the Koran from Muhammad al-Nasir?"

"Yes, my lord." Diego lowered his head, humiliated.

"In Don Álvaro you have a great ally, for he has spoken well of you to me despite that failure, and even stated you were blameless for that mission's lack of success. In any case, you must know your debt to the crown of Castile is great and has yet to be paid."

"I shall do what you ask of me."

"For now, make sure she doesn't suffer." He said, pointing at his mare.

"I can alleviate her pain, but I must tell you that sooner or later, she will die."

"Galib, do you agree with this diagnosis?"

"Diego is as skilled as I am, maybe more. Sometimes things don't go as we would wish, Your Majesty."

"But this mare . . . cannot die!"

"We will treat her with a number of compounds, but you have to be ready to see her suffer, and soon die."

The monarch was sad and disappointed. If those two albéitars, certainly the best in all the kingdom, could not heal his animal, then certainly there was no cure, however much it hurt him to say so. He approached her. He didn't want to touch her in case she might try to get up, but tremendous grief ran through his body.

"Are you certain?"

"Yes," Diego replied.

"Do what you can for her. I beg you."

On their way back to Galib's house, they talked about the case of the mare.

"I will never get used to the feeling of impotence when I come on a problem I can't cure."

"Me neither," Diego said, "and I am still asking myself what the true causes of illness are. I now reject completely the humoral theory of Hippocrates, and of course the other one relating illnesses to the mood of the gods. But I have discovered some writings of the Persian doctor Avicenna that have captivated me. His words are glimmering with truth. After reading them, I've come to the conclusion that in horses, other than the outward complaints, the causes and signs of which are already visible to us, the internal diseases arise from the effects of two essential principles. One of them is in the malfunction of the essential organs, like the liver, heart, and brain. And the other I attribute to the intervention of certain determinant agents, invisible but real, that produce disorders within these organs."

Galib had also read Avicenna and, being partial to him as an Arab, also believed his theories. In fact, in one of his discoveries, concerning the contagious nature of tuberculosis, he could see reference to the idea Diego just mentioned of certain external agents that caused disease.

"Sometimes I have thought the same thing, but I don't know. . . . That type of explanation seems to bring us closer to the world of magic than of science. Small creatures . . . invisible ones, or particles causing illnesses, call them what you want . . . to my mind, if we embrace this theory, we give more credit to those who interpret diseases as the manifestation of malignant beings, which they call demons or monsters or even wicked gods, and that is the furthest thing from my thoughts."

Diego argued his opinion more vehemently and gave as an example the illness of King Alfonso's horse.

"That inflammation of the veins could be produced by nothing but an external agent, and as I said, I think it's a parasite. I wasn't able to localize it when I opened some of its victims while I was staying in Albarracín, but I know it was there. . . . It takes advantage of the animal's weakness to pass through its vital organs and ends up in the eyes, in that sac we could see from outside. Before I came to that conclusion, I followed the classical thinking. In fact, because they had blood in their urine, I thought they might have an excess of that humor, and I bled them. The result was null. The old remedies were useless."

Galib was content as he listened to him. Perhaps he didn't share Diego's ideas, but once again, he was astonished by his talent. "Therefore, there's nothing we can do to treat the mare the king loves so much."

"I'm afraid not. She's going to die soon, and as he said, I will go on owing him for my failure on that mission."

"What does the one thing have to do with the other?"

"When I offered to pay my debt to him, he told me I could do so by curing her."

"What else would he say, if horses are what you know about?"

When he uttered those words, Diego stopped, silent. An incredible idea had just burst into his head.

"And if we offered him three or four thousand horses of the Arabian race?"

"What do you mean? Have you gone mad?"

"If we go back to the Marismas?"

"Diego, are you running a fever? To go back to that place after what happened. . . . Do you not remember?"

"After hearing the assistant to the master-at-arms, I think it could be a great help. They need many horses for their troops and where better than—"

"What you say is true, but you don't have to risk your own life doing it."

"Think about it, Galib, it is my way of helping the kingdom through the one thing that has always been present in my life: horses."

Galib remembered his own prophecy. Horses would be what would finally show Diego his way.

"And how do you think you'll manage to steal thousands of horses from the very heart of Al-Andalus and transport them more than a hundred leagues back to Toledo?"

"I'll ask the king to put the best knights he has at my service, and for time to organize the mission well."

"It would be a wonderful endeavor, and there's no one better than you to carry it out. It brings together your two great aspirations: to strike a blow at the Almohads and take advantage of your experience and knowledge. But you have to prepare for it carefully. Know that for al-Nasir, that loss would mean not only great pain but also a serious humiliation. To fail to keep safe that inheritance from his ancestors, and on his own territory, would cause him a dishonor he would never escape."

"You'll have to help me. . . ."

"Don't ask me for that. I swore never to return to the Marismas, and I still remember everything that happened. If I did it, I would see Benazir everywhere I looked, and I also don't want to relive poor Fatima's death. No, I'll never return. I'm old now, Diego, but you must go. Those Almohads must be punished. They've proclaimed a holy war against the Christians to return the territories Al-Andalus lost centuries back. They will fight to uproot not only the Christian faith from the kingdoms of the north, but also from any Muslim who refuses their stern practices." Diego had never heard Galib speak so seriously. "If they achieve their objective, we will be submitted to their way of life, and they'll impose their diabolical version of Islam. They will destroy your culture until not a trace of it is left, they will burn the churches and turn them into mosques and madrassas, they will destroy whatever book they consider impious and enslave whoever doesn't want to embrace their doctrines. Don't doubt it, they will only allow one religion and one kind of society; that's why we have to stop them."

Listening to Galib, Diego had the feeling inside that everything was about to fall together. Galib was a Muslim, but his mind was open and his heart was big. He had just put into words what Diego had been longing for. He had transformed his desires into something tangible, and the new task seemed as necessary to him as it was urgent. Now he felt sure. To put a stop to the madness of the Almohads was everyone's job. That plague, born in the north of Africa, threatened to extend to all sides and demolish the world he had always known. He wouldn't allow it. Above all, Diego, hated intransigence and the imposition of ideas by force.

"I will devote all my strength to frustrating their intentions, first by stealing their horses, and afterward however I can."

"Dedicate your intelligence to it; you're not a soldier. And when you finish, go back to your work. You've been well trained for it, and you should exercise your office with all the mastery you've acquired. That is how you can best help the people. Listen to me. The horses will show you the way. . . . Remember that is what I told you?"

"Of course."

"Horses have always been by your side. I still remember your exceptional ability to understand them and the hard days you spent as an apprentice, the first sicknesses and treatments we worked on together."

"I'm a mere follower of your wisdom."

"You do me much praise saying that. But I know that for this labor, what's necessary is not just science, but also an inexhaustible spirit and great courage. And you have both."

Diego stopped Sabba and looked back, full of anxiety.

"I have to go back to the palace and tell them my plan."

"It can't wait until tomorrow?"

"I need to repay my debt as quickly as possible. I owe it to my king and to Castile for failing to get al-Nasir's Koran."

Galib stayed there watching how Diego, retracing his footsteps, galloped onward to his new destiny. In him he saw much more than a disciple, and of course a colleague. He was the son Galib hadn't been able to have. He would have liked to be like him. He was the very image of triumph over adversity, of loyalty, and he had the look of an honest man.

IV.

King Alfonso VIII of Castile decided that a hundred of his best men would accompany the albéitar Diego on the frightening mission to the Marismas.

The horses wouldn't be necessary until the arrival of the volunteer crusaders and the militias that were coming from the villages and municipal councils, and none of them would arrive before the end of May, so the action was postponed until then.

Don Álvaro and Diego planned it conscientiously, prepared the strategies, studied and compared the different routes, and chose the best methods to be sure it would be a success.

The group, captained by Don Álvaro Núñez de Lara, left Toledo the first day of May in the year 1212 and traveled some ways without encountering any serious altercation.

Once they arrived at the Marismas, the first part of their mission consisted of localizing the fifteen observation points where the Imesebelen would be scattered. Afterward, they had to wait for a signal to act in unison against the Africans and avoid their escape however possible.

With their faces painted black and their heads wrapped in dark cloths, as soon as they heard the order they sank down in the waters of the swamp. The darkness of the night and the marshlands and their abundant vegetation hid them from their enemies. The cool water also relieved their flushed faces.

Submerged up to his cheeks. Sancho Fernández, the heir to the throne of León and Diego's escort, still seemed to be listening to the speech Don Álvaro had given before they'd all sunk down in those marshes.

"Don't forget," he had told them, "those Imesebelen are well trained. They've been taught not to fear death, and they are extremely violent. We will only manage this if we catch them by surprise, so we must act quickly, and all at once. And above all, keep in mind that no enemy may live. Be sure they are dead, and keep at them if you're unsure."

They split up in pairs, moving forward with extreme caution. The light of the moon helped them to see their enemies and the water hid them until it was time to strike. Sometimes they passed so close to the horses that some neighed nervously, noticing their presence, but not loudly enough to alert their guards.

"Sancho, to your right." Almost in a whisper, Diego indicated a promontory with two soldiers. One seemed to be asleep. The other was seated and looking off in the opposite direction.

"I'll leave the sleeping one to you and I'll attack the other one," Sancho proposed.

Trying not to disturb the water excessively, they moved forward one foot at a time, hiding behind reeds, not far from the Africans. They unsheathed their daggers and held them under the water, their muscles tensed, ears attentive, waiting for the signal.

It seemed like an eternity. The dampness was wrinkling their skin and causing their bones to ache. They calculated that they had been there nearly an hour when something unexpected happened, forcing them to make a split-second decision.

The man who seemed to be sleeping sat up, and after talking to the other, he threw a sack over his shoulder and went to mount his horse.

Sancho signaled that he would go after him. They stepped from the water at the same time and Diego reached his man just before he turned to see who was behind him. Without any time to react, all he could do was feel the dagger slice him from one side of his neck to the other.

The other saw Sancho coming and jumped on his horse, pressing his knees into its ribs but not getting an immediate response from the animal. He turned to see how far the stranger was from him and decided he was too close. His horse, for some reason, wouldn't react. He felt a sudden jab just beneath his arm, though he managed to duck the next one, and then finally got the animal to trot away. He prodded the horse just enough so he could turn around and see how much distance he had from his assailant.

But after not even a dozen yards he noticed something warm running down his side and then a sharp pain in his stomach. When he looked for the wound, he was frightened by how serious it was. The man had reached a vein, and he was gushing blood. He felt a sudden rush of cold, the solitude of his imminent death, and with a choked cry, he fell down into the water.

Sancho ran over and finished him off.

Just as he turned to find Diego, they heard the signal: three owl-like chirps. From different points in the swamp, all the knights rushed to attack the Africans' positions with incredible determination, surprising them, though their advantage was not definitive.

When they heard the signal again, they met at the assigned spot and saw that ten of the men were missing. Another ten were wounded, some gravely.

"Tell me, have you eliminated all of them?"

Don Álvaro gathered them in a circle, still feeling the tension of what they'd just lived through. One by one, he asked them how each of their assignments had turned out, and once he was done, he ordered them to begin the second stage of the plan as quickly as possible, discreetly, to avoid any complications.

"Listen to Diego now. . . . He will explain what we have to do to get the greatest number of animals."

Diego took over and told them to look at a group of animals pasturing not far away, on the edge of a lake.

"In the wild, mares live in herds and they respond as a group. There are usually one or two adult females at the head and they are in charge of moving the rest. We're going to try to get control of those mares and then get them to influence the others; we'll tie them to our harnesses and, if nothing complicates things, when we leave with them, a great number of animals will follow. That is the only way to do it. But we have to proceed carefully and not frighten them."

"And what do we do to get hold of those special mares, as you said?" one of the knights, a Sorian with a thin mustache and bitter expression asked.

"I know how they think, what to do to get them to trust me, and what they're afraid of. I know how to interpret their reactions and what to do to convince them to follow me. I'll take advantage of the stillness of the night to walk up close to them and win their confidence. Once I figure out which mares command the others, I'll ask you for help in getting hold of them. Try to hurt them as little as possible."

Another of the men asked how much time they would need. Diego guessed around three hours.

"This job won't be the most dangerous one of the mission, but it will be the most delicate." Diego tried to encourage them. "Your work is essential for us to succeed. If they stampede, then we're lost. Daylight will come and I don't think a second attempt will succeed. Therefore, take every possible precaution, do your best not to make them nervous, and follow your instincts. I've always believed that horses are able to intuit men's thoughts. I ask you to make sure yours don't frighten them."

Diego left the better part of the group behind on the edge of an enormous lake where there were as many as a thousand animals. He remembered that Galib had told him, the first time he'd come there, that the Marismas were formed by hundreds of lakes on a broad plain to the north of the mouth of the Guadalquivir and that it took a half day on horseback to take in their expanse. He dismounted from Sabba and walked into the marshes, and water rose up to his ankles. In the shelter of the darkness, hardly making any noise, he went in search of the first mares.

He stopped to study the behavior of the group just ahead of him. Among them he observed the mares that stood apart, and soon he found one with a white coat that seemed to direct the herd behind her and away from him. He heard her whinny in a strange manner and saw how the rest of them submissively lowered their ears and followed. Diego went after her, making a number of sounds and movements that seemed to pacify her fears, because she received him calmly. He breathed on her nostrils and showed her a rope that he would pass over her head and knot around her neck. He passed the end of it to one of the men with him and asked him to stay there until he heard the signal that they were leaving. He headed off in search of other leaders.

He found another group nearby, quite a bit bigger, perhaps four hundred animals or more, and soon he found three older mares and an old stallion that led the others around. Diego walked toward the stallion.

"Why is it not the males that are in charge of the group?" This seemed strange to Sancho Fernández, the friend of Don Álvaro and nephew of the lord of Biscay.

"The stallions fight among themselves or against anyone who tries to go after their females, and they also have to protect them from predators. But for other tasks, like looking for new pastures, finding water, or less important labors, the mares with more age and experience take over."

"Then why are you going up to him?"

"If I get hold of him, there won't be a problem. Some fight with the mares when they don't want to move."

He gave a snortlike sound, and immediately the male looked over at him. Diego stayed there waiting for the stallion to take the initiative. It came over with great authority and sniffed at his head and shoulders. It chewed at his clothing and then sighed, accepting him. Diego pinched its neck and passed a rope around its neck while he whispered in its ear.

After grabbing the stallion, he had no difficulty with the three mares that followed him.

For the moment, everything seemed to be working.

For the next two hours, he managed to get hold of more than fifty guide animals, until he heard a short, sharp whistle, the sign that it was time to leave. Each man tied one of those mares to his saddle, and each mare was followed by between twenty and fifty animals.

At first, many of them resisted, and they even had to let the most nervous ones go to avoid further problems. The rest, with lots of care and not too much pressure, they managed to move toward the north in the direction of the mouth of the Guadalquivir River, where soon all of the knights met back up.

Once they'd crossed the next valley, between the basin of that river and the sierra of Seville, they had made it through one of the worst stages of the journey back. They hoped to make it to the highlands before dawn to avoid being seen, since the image of more than three thousand horses escaping from the marshes would undoubtedly attract attention.

As the horsemen and their herds arrived, Don Álvaro congratulated each of them, happy to have made it through that first stage. He looked for Diego to talk about what they should do from that moment forward.

"Before daylight comes, more than a thousand Christian soldiers will have left Córdoba headed in the direction of Carmona. They left Toledo with the sole idea of serving as our reinforcement. Their attack will attract the better part of the Almohad forces, and if they respond the way we've planned, it should leave the road back clear for us." He observed the enormous group of mares gathered behind them and then looked into the sky. "We only have two hours until dawn. Let's not delay anymore."

"On the other side of the sierra, on the banks of the Huéznar River, I remember having seen a long esplanade where we can rest the horses," Diego suggested.

Don Álvaro, thinking of their incredible expedition, felt overwhelmed with bittersweetness. He had never imagined anything like this, so much beauty in one place, a mission so complex and impassioned. With the pain of his recent dead companions weighing on him and unsure about the future, he prayed in silence and set off.

The second day, while they were crossing the wastelands of La Serena, they decided to speed up. They raised up a thick cloud of dust, but they would arrive faster that way to the north, to a humid zone where they could slake their desperate thirst. The tremendous heat was asphyxiating the herd and making the crossing almost unbearable. Many of the mares were roaring with anger, looking for any opportunity to flee their captors. The riders were doing everything they could to keep them from getting away, but they slowed down the whole group in the process.

Once they'd left the steppes behind them and begun to climb the first hills of the sierra, they had to chase after a Saracen patrol that had spotted them. They killed almost everyone, but a single person did manage to escape.

"That's going to cause problems, you'll see. . . ."

Seeing the risk they were now running, Don Álvaro decided the moment had arrived to make some decisions. He brought everyone together and explained the situation.

"From now on, we have to be able to steer the herd with half as many men. The rest will form five circles of protection around us, at different distances away."

He named five leaders and gave strict orders for them to do everything necessary to keep the enemy at bay.

"Attack them, destroy them, chase them down, and kill them!" Don Álvaro gestured wildly. "You're free to decide how to do it, but I do not want to see a single turban come within ten leagues of those animals. Understood?"

The different groups took off and no one heard from them until four days later, when they reached the area of the Guadiana River where there was a pass leading to the Castilian border, their last hurdle before entering friendly territory.

When they were a few leagues from the riverbank, they saw the arrival of a furious cavalcade: two of the other four patrols. According to what they said, as soon as they reached their positions, they were attacked by an army of no fewer than three hundred Saracens who were not far away now.

Don Álvaro said they would be punished severely once back in Castile for not maintaining the enemy at the distance he had specified. Their impudence had brought the enemy upon them, and now everyone was exposed.

He called Sancho Fernández.

"A few leagues north of the river, there is a castle of Calatravans. Call them to come to our aid. Push your horse as hard as it can go and make it gallop till it dies of exhaustion. As if you were chasing down the devil himself." He slapped the rump of the Leonese's mare and it shot off like an arrow, speeding away until it could no longer be seen.

Don Álvaro had everyone come over and apprised them all of the situation. Seated on his horse, he transmitted bravery and poise as he explained to them what he expected.

"Now there's no time for long discourses, so I will be short and precise. We have to get these animals across the river safe and sound. That means that from now on, you have to form an iron rearguard that will prevent the Moors from reaching them. If they try to reach the herd, make a wall, kill their horses, I don't care. . . . Do you understand?"

A single voice rose up in agreement, sounding with the fury of war.

Don Álvaro encouraged his men to get into position as quickly as possible and encouraged them with a few last words.

"These animals represent the freedom of our people, the possibility of defeating the enemy. They form part of our last cry for victory if we can manage to get them to Toledo. . . . Help them across the river, and you will help our brothers in the faith."

They began to hear the first cries of the Saracens, and Don Álvaro called for them to spur on the mares, pushing them to race north, as they did.

Seated on Sabba at a rapid gallop, Diego looked back and saw how the group that had gathered in the rear was assailed by enemies.

The animals sweated and ran, terrified by the blows the horsemen were giving them, stunned by the screaming surrounding them. They were less than half a league from the banks of the river. If they made it, they would cross through a shallow zone that Diego had recommended. He approached Don Álvaro and observed him. He rode with his eyes narrowed and his jaws clenched. The tension in his muscles and the courage he exuded made him seem like one of those Greek statues Diego had seen in the portals of the buildings in Toledo.

"I have to get to the head of the herd," Diego screamed in his ear. "We need to be sure the herd doesn't disperse before we get into the water; if that happens, they'll never go through the riverbed, and it will be a complete disaster."

"Good, that sounds good. . . . Go on ahead, there's not much more." The first arrows could now be heard. Some horses, frightened by the noise, ran even faster, pushing the ones at the head of the group. When he saw that, Don Álvaro had an idea and fell back to explain it to his guards.

Diego knew, like the rest of the horsemen, that life lay on one side of the river and death on the other if they didn't make it and fell into the hands of the Saracens. The horses would go back to the Marismas, but the men would saturate the ground with their blood.

Diego spoke in Sabba's ear.

"Show everyone you're a daughter of the wind. Show them the greatness of your blood, your name, your breed that was born to fly. Run! Run faster than you ever have, tear through the air!"

Sabba responded with renewed vigor and took the lead of that powerful herd, pointing them toward the best place to cross the river. At her back there was a deafening roar of horses, a dry thumping of thousands of hooves breaking the earth, making stones fly off in all directions.

Diego studied the riverbanks and decided to go through a clearing among the trees that ended in a patch of sand on the river's edge.

Following on the heels of the herd, some of the riders armed with swords jabbed at the rumps of the mares, and their panic rose. The animals ran in fear and the emotion spread to the other horses, which sprinted to keep up with them.

When the first horde of Saracens reached them, the Christian swords gleamed in the air, carrying out the death sentences of their enemies. Without halting their gallop, the knights pushed them away with such bravery that nothing was left in their path but a long line of dead and wounded men, and only two of the Christians fell.

They caught sight of the river and prayed to reach it soon, because the second wave of the enemy attack was about to descend on them, and it could be thirty times larger than the previous one.

A new cloud of arrows slew a number of horses and wounded others, and the dread among the animals mounted. They all sped up further as the swords of the Saracens clashed with those of the Christians. In just an instant, the situation had gotten so bad that some thought all was lost.

Diego made it through the trees, and Sabba's hooves felt the soft earth and then the coolness of the water. He looked around anxiously, wondering where the help from the Calatravans could be, and he saw no one; but just then, over the crest of a gently rising hill, he saw pennants waving in the wind, and then lance tips and an immense group of knights in their suits of armor, full of bellicose fury.

"Hold out!" he shouted to his men, turning around. "They've come to help us!"

In just a few seconds, the river was filled with thousands of horses kicking their legs amid waves of foaming water. A great sea of manes and heads beat the surface, a sea storm of sheer bravery. Don Álvaro, almost at the shore, was being chased by three enemies who had come very close. One took his bow and tensed it to fire an arrow at him when another man stabbed the enemy in the neck, killing him at once. Don Álvaro was filled with hope when he saw more than a hundred Calatravan knights on the other bank of the river. While some were clearing a path for the enormous herd of mares, others crossed the water to repel the enemy's advance, and the rest, atop a hill, fired a ceaseless hail of arrows on the Saracens unlucky enough to have fallen behind.

Once on the other side, Diego stopped and took in the astonishing scene. The waters had been dyed red with blood and were stirred up by the passage of that enormous group of animals. Hundreds of horses crossed onto the shore and walked by him, shaking off water and mud. He didn't care, he was happy to see them make it. He heard the final clashes of swords on the other side of the river and the final call to retreat from the enemy army.

The Yeguada de las Marismas, the dream of Abderrahman III and plaything of the later Muslim caliphs, the most beautiful union of Arabian blood ever brought together, was now in Christian hands.

And in that moment, Diego burst into tears and embraced Sabba.

His joy was immense.

V.

The Christian world had been commanded to meet in Toledo for the sake of a crusade on the twentieth of May of the year 1212.

The response could begin to be seen days before, as the first caravans of Ultramontanes arrived from Gascony, Provence, and Languedoc. These were followed by others, less numerous, from the faraway lands of Pomerania, Bohemia, and Germania.

In only ten days, more than three thousand knights had amassed on the banks of the Tagus, with ten thousand cavalry troops and fifty thousand others, including pages, squires, women, and all other sorts of companions.

King Alfonso VIII of Castile received everyone with great attention, as he had promised he would for any crusader who came to fight at his side, offering twenty *sueldos* daily to each knight and five to each page. In addition, each morning they distributed biscuits, salted meat, cheese, garlic, and water to maintain the men. It was an impressive outlay, knowing it was all being funded by the king's treasury.

"Your Majesty, tonight they have come into the ghetto again," the Jewish representative said, taking off his hat and wrinkling it in his hands, enraged. "They raped . . . they raped more than two hundred of our girls, and . . . they also took three of our businessmen from the neighborhood, dragged them along like beasts, you hear, and then . . . they skinned them alive, jeering at them and insulting them the whole time." The man was sweating and his teeth were chattering from pure impotence. "During the day they laugh at us and throw stones—"

"I imagine you're talking to me of the Ultramontanes," the king interrupted. "Have you identified any of them in particular?"

"They wear hoods, but we suspect by the accent they're the ones from Poitou." He took out two bags full of gold coins. "You know we've responded generously to the requests you've made of us to help financing the new war, and we've never complained, but if we don't have the least security for our-selves and our businesses, understand that we can't go on supporting you."

The archbishop of Toledo, Don Rodrigo Ximénez de Rada, entered the meeting room with a worried face.

"Your Majesty . . . I've just seen fighting in the street."

"Explain yourself better, Your Eminency." The monarch rose from his chair.

"Urban militias have organized, commoners and farm people, and they're putting the sword to any Ultramontane they come across. They're tired of their outrages, of the horror they produce wherever they go, and the violence they practice against your Jewish subjects; they're trying to protect them." He gave a compassionate look to the treasurer, who had just lent more than eighteen thousand *maravedíes* to the cause against the Almohads.

King Alfonso clenched his fists with rage. There were still three weeks until the troops arrived from Aragon and the volunteers from Portugal and León. He was also waiting for the archbishop of Narbonne, Arnault Amalric, who was bringing a number of knights from Lyon, Vienne, and Valentinois. He was anxious to have the churchman by his side, because he was the only one who could rein in the excesses of his countrymen, and he was also sup-posed to arrive with news about King Sancho VII. Arnault had planned on stopping in Navarre on his way down to convince the king to participate, and the Castilian still knew nothing about what had been decided.

"I will order the Ultramontanes to leave the city immediately. I will have enough tents set up for them outside the walls, and I'll get them vict-uals and hay for their horses. From now on, the gates of Toledo will remain closed from midnight till dawn."

Alfonso had them call his friend Don Diego López de Haro and give him the necessary instructions. Somewhat relieved, the treasurer left the king alone with the archbishop.

"You look too tense, Your Majesty."

"How could I not be, Rodrigo? . . . We aren't aware of the magnitude of the undertaking ahead of us."

"You should already be proud of it. In recent centuries, you are the only one who has managed to pull together all the Hispanic kingdoms in a single army—those inheritors of the noble empire of the Visigoths." The archbishop drank a cup of water in one gulp.

"I still don't know what my cousin Alfonso of León is going to do, or King Sancho of Navarre. Portugal is only sending a small group of knights . . ."

"Whether they come or not, you are going to bring together a huge and powerful army. Two thousand Ultramontane knights, three thousand from Aragon, another three thousand of yours, as well as the Navarrese if they come, and the Portuguese. And you have to add the pages, the squires, and the local militias sent by Segovia, Avila, Cuéllar, Madrid, and the rest of the towns in your kingdom. If the knights are ten thousand, you can count another twenty thousand infantry who will join you in this battle. Imagine, thirty thousand souls pledging to make your dream a reality, thirty thousand men taking back those lands that once belonged to our ancestors."

The king calculated how much would be necessary to maintain that force. He had contracted the obligation of supporting their expenses once they arrived in Toledo, and the numbers were now double what he had estimated. The financing of the venture fell entirely on his shoulders and was coming close to wiping out his treasury. In spite of that, it would mean little if he triumphed. His lust for victory was such that he would have gladly lent ten thousand *maravedíes* to the Navarrese king to bring him and his army to Toledo—he knew that kingdom had been left poor by its long campaigns against al-Nasir in the east and in Mallorca.

"Calculate that each knight brings his four mounts," he said, sharing his thoughts with the bishop. "A warhorse, a palfrey for traveling, another for the squire, and a mule for transporting arms and the rest of their necessities. That makes forty thousand animals we have to feed each day, in addition to the three thousand we took from the Almohads and those that the militias bring. I doubt it will be fewer than fifty thousand in all."

Don Rodrigo was impressed by the number.

"A warhorse needs twenty pounds of hay per day and half as much oats, as well as thirty liters of water. And every ten men will require another twenty pounds of food."

"I don't know if you're more worried by the amount of money you'll need to finance all this or how to make sure no one wants for anything."

"Both things worry me. This very morning I calculated the number of carts we would need to transport the food once the campaign begins, and leaving aside the hay, which I hope to substitute with pastureland. Give me a number."

"Two hundred carts . . ."

"Just for the horses we'll need five hundred cartloads of grain each day . . . And another hundred to feed the men."

"Good Lord!" the priest exclaimed.

"Now do you want to talk about how we'll pay for all this?"

The king had just minted a new gold coin after having imposed a special tax on his subjects to subsidize the war, but he himself was still bearing the better part of the expenses.

"In a few days, I'll demand the contribution from the Church of Castile for this Holy Crusade." The archbishop hadn't thought of giving it yet, but he could see the situation was dire. "I've decided finally that it shall be half our income over the course of one year, but paid up front."

The king was astonished.

"Excellent, Rodrigo . . . Excellent. You've just pleasantly surprised me. That is a great deal of money, and a great relief to me in my present state. And by the way, have you seen the excellent herd of mares we took from the Almohads?"

"Not yet, my lord."

"Then let's go see them." He turned to a corner of the room and crossed through a stone arch, entering into a semicircular tower that opened onto a balcony on the eastern side of the castle.

On a swatch of pastureland by the riverside, thousands of mares and stallions were spread out after their long journey from the marshlands of Guadalquivir. For a week now, more than a hundred knights, stable keepers, and squires had been training them for battle.

"Seeing them, I think our lord must have had a special zeal when he created that beautiful breed." Don Rodrigo, impressed, observed their carriage, their noble strut, their vitality.

"As I've heard, the Prophet Muhammad loved horses so much that he commanded his followers to respect and care for them even at the cost of their lives. With this herd, we've not only robbed them of a powerful weapon, which could have been a terrifying blow against us, but we've also wounded their honor."

"I never imagined it could happen. . . . Never."

"Nor I," Alfonso VIII recognized. "That albéitar has shown excellent courage and a strong mind."

"I met him in Zorita de los Canes and even then, I thought I saw something in him, though I still don't know what. Later I found out he wasn't a knight or a nobleman, that he had learned everything at the hands of Muslims, but his knowledge of medicine and his mind were still remarkable. He has something special, maybe the soul of a hero, I don't know. Try to keep him close to you in battle. His intelligence could serve you well." Don Rodrigo heard bells ringing and knew that he would need to be leaving.

"I want to leave Toledo around the twentieth of this month," the king interrupted. "If we wait more, the heat will come upon us and the pastureland will dry up. Those who delay past this date will have to meet us on the road." He looked at the horizon with a deep, serious expression. "It will be the most important battle ever seen on Christian lands. Not even in the Holy Land was such an army ever gathered. . . . From today, my good friend, you will be named the chronicler of this war. You will be the one to tell future generations what happened in the year of our Lord 1212."

In Seville, another great army had gathered on the outskirts of the city, awaiting the orders of Muhammad al-Nasir.

On the back of his beautiful Berber stallion, the powerful Almohad leader considered the different positions of his army while he conferred with the lord of the recovered fortress of Salvatierra, the Andalusian Ibn Qadis, a leader with a reputation for nobility and bravery among the troops.

"Andalusians don't understand jihad," he said to his caliph. "And they're not anxious to regain the territory our Christian enemies have reconquered. They are a peaceful people and they only want to work the land and live without problems."

"You could say it to me that way or with softer words," al-Nasir replied. "But as I see it, what you are describing to me is a society of cowards." He passed by a detachment that had recently arrived from Africa, Zanatas or Gomaras they were called, fierce Berbers from another tribe of Almohads. "So much so that I've had to contract fighters from as far away as Arabia to get the troops I need. Believe me, it is embarrassing to explain that I have to do it because my people do not care for arms."

He saluted the head of the Agzaz, a group of able Turkish fighters who were the greatest archers on horseback the world had ever seen. Even galloping at full speed, they were able to shoot in any direction without slipping from the saddle.

Behind them was the fabulous Arabic army. He had been told that they added up to ten thousand, arrived there a week ago from the faraway land of the Prophet. Their behavior in battle was irregular, but they were good lancers and they used a sword like no one else. They had come with their women and children and were the loudest and most animated group of all. When al-Nasir walked by the cavalry, he remembered with deep pain the theft he had suffered. The Yeguada de las Marismas . . . The lone heirs to the horses of Ishmael, son of the Prophet Abraham, had been reduced by two-thirds by the enemies of Islam. As an affront, it had been the worst news he could imagine after the death of his son Yahia a few days before. He had been the favorite of his children, the one who would become the next caliph. His death had disturbed him so much that he said the same thing to everyone: he would dedicate a victory over the Christians to him, as an homage, and bring him the head of the Christian monarch.

"Besides the regular soldiers from Al-Andalus," al-Nasir continued, "and the Agzaz and the Arabs we have seen, there are the Masmidi Berbers and a multitude of Almohad brothers here from Marrakesh. Of course, we have more Imesebelen and around five thousand volunteers from other places. And last of all, there are three thousand Andalusians and a group of mercenary Christians who take orders from Pedro de Mora; they are few, but very brave."

"How large, then, will your army be?"

"In person, I will command a corps of twenty thousand horsemen and sixty thousand soldiers. Eighty thousand souls ready to knock down the cross, to kill for Allah if this is what he desires."

"Would you allow me a comment, which should not be taken in any way as disrespecting your mission?"

"Tell me, my loyal Ibn Qadis."

"How will you manage to get such a varied army to fight as one? You know the Arabs have come by force, as penance for their rebellious attitude with the Almohads, whom they have never accepted. The Andalusians, my brothers, are only fighting, as I've said, for the money you pay them."

"It's true that the pay is all that matters to them," al-Nasir replied. "But of all of them, they are the ones who know the Christian cavalry the best, and they act the same in combat."

"You are not wrong, sir, but as I say, the motivations held by the groups are too different. And if not, think of the Berbers; they have come here solely in order to defend the Almohad creed, above all else, but if we think of why the other volunteers have done so?" He pointed at one of the detachments that seemed less orderly than the others. "Apart from being almost ungovernable, you can see they have only one ambition: to die in a holy war and gain access to paradise."

"I have one great motive that will unify them all." The caliph looked at the outline of Seville reflected over the waters of the Guadalquivir.

"Would you share it with me, sir?"

"Saladin drove his men to conquer Jerusalem and managed to regain that holy place for our faith. I will do the same." His breast swelled until it was almost touching his chin. "I will drive them on to Rome. We will lay siege to that city, the most sacred one for the infidels, and will deal a mortal wound to their pride. And my name for all of them," he said, signaling the troops gathered there, "will be forever united to that act, as Saladin and his men are to the sack of Jerusalem."

VI.

Mencía entered, screaming at Marcos, very agitated. She had finally received word of that knight, Bruno de Oñate.

"A new message has come to me from Fitero." She showed him the wrinkled letter in her hands. "They say that, after the loss of Salvatierra, he went to another castle, called Zorita de los Canes."

"Relax! Breathe . . . I can hardly understand you." Marcos imagined what Mencía's desires would be and was thinking about whether to accompany her.

Only a month before, she had received a card signed by Don Álvaro Núñez de Lara telling her of Diego's death. Despite the source, she had never believed it, because, apart from what her heart was telling her, she had already seen Diego's tomb empty once.

"Where is Zorita?"

"In Trasierra, to the south of Guadalajara." Mencía pulled a long veil from her hair. "If Bruno de Oñate is in that fortress, maybe Diego is too. Will you come with me to look for him?"

"Well . . . Yes, of course . . ." Marcos thought about which of his affairs could wait and which couldn't. "But I do need a few days to arrange some things."

"Days? I don't think I can wait so long. . . . I'm not as doubtful as you are. We need to leave this very afternoon!"

Mencía knew that if she traveled with Marcos, things would be easier, but he wasn't absolutely necessary. No one and nothing would hold her back.

"Just give me three more days, and I'll go with you." Marcos looked her directly in the eyes to convince her, but he didn't manage to change her attitude.

"You don't want to go. Am I right?"

He lowered his head.

"I have things I have to do here. . . . And a war is coming. I'm not a knight, I don't know how to hold a weapon. I understand you want to see him again, but for me . . ."

"I've calculated it will take me a week to reach the fortress. I don't need you, I'll go alone."

"Why don't you wait for some caravan traveling in that direction? Think about it; ever since the rumors about the war began, there's been far less traffic on the roads, and it's become more dangerous to travel."

Marcos was right, but Mencía was driven more by anxiousness than prudence. Don Álvaro's letter had been a terrible blow to her hopes, and her need for further information trumped her sense of reason. She thought that if she traveled disguised as a man, she would avoid a number of problems.

"Isn't everyone going to war? I'll cut my hair and I'll hide it under a hat. I'll bind my torso and hide my womanhood. That's what I'll do."

Marcos knew that nothing would dissuade her. Feeling guilty, he said good-bye to her, wishing her luck and asking her to send his regards to Diego when she found him.

"I pray you send me news, and more than anything, be very careful."

In the meanwhile, one hot sixteenth of June, only four days from the agreed upon date for the crusading army's departure, King Pedro II of Aragon arrived in Toledo at the head of a numerous army.

All the city ran out to greet him amid applause and acclamation. When they saw them crossing the Alcántara Bridge, his soldiers breathed a sigh of confidence. With their help, they would surely defeat the enemy.

Diego attended the festivities with Don Álvaro Núñez de Lara, close to King Alfonso VIII of Castile. He recognized the king of Aragon's companion, the royal ensign García Romeu, whom he had met in Olite. He rode to the right of the king, holding the standard of the crown of Aragon. Behind them there flapped hundreds of flags attesting to the noble families that accompanied them.

"The viscount of Cardona is coming," Don Álvaro said, recognizing many of the people. "You'll see him under that red banner with a yellow cardoon at its center. And my friend Guillem de Cervera. The design on his shield is a red deer on a white background. I also see Ximeno de Cornell and Dalmau de Creixel, and the counts of Tarragona and Ampurias. Look at that one with the yellow standard with a red stripe, that is Aznar Pardo, the royal butler." Don Álvaro saw them all with real emotion. "They're all here. This is the greatest concentration of Aragonese nobles that has ever been seen in these parts."

With the third blast of the trumpet, all present fell silent.

King Alfonso and his wife, Leonor, in their finest dress, awaited the arrival of Pedro II with great ceremony. He galloped forward on his splendid courser, and before all, he embraced the king of Castile with sincere affection.

"With his arrival, the long wait is over, we are reunited," Don Álvaro said to Diego. "The Ultramontanes have been in Toledo for a month, and Sancho VII of Navarre has finally agreed to come, though he will not meet us until after we've set off. The kings of León and Portugal will not, but we have a strong group of knights who have come from those territories. And you, have you decided yet?"

Diego had been informed two days before that the king had requested his presence.

"I feel flattered, but do you know why he has asked for me to come?"

"Wars are won by the person who acts most intelligently. He knows that, and he's trying to have at his side as much talent as he can pull together. He saw how you handled the mission to the Marismas, he knows about your training in Salvatierra, and he has faith in your abilities."

Diego settled into his saddle and scratched Sabba's forehead.

"I've thought it through, and yes, I'll go."

"I am glad for it, believe me. Your presence will be very useful to us, I'm sure. What finally convinced you?"

"I want to avoid an Almohad victory. I can't even imagine what the loss of our freedom would mean for us. I am pledged to combat their fanaticism, and I feel it is my job to spoil their plans to turn us into their slaves and subjects. We have to confront their single-minded vision. If we don't stop them now, they will demolish our principles and our traditions. . . . For all those reasons, I want to go, but I also have such great respect for the figure of our king, whom I've admired for so long. He has shown great faith in his people by signing charters of freedom for many of his towns and villages. Thanks to his work, thousands of people from the land, men and women with origins as humble as my own, have been able to prosper and reach a degree of comfort unthinkable in other periods when the nobles were in charge of everything."

"You speak well, Diego. This won't be just another war. Here we have a confrontation of two cultures and two religions. Because of my position, I owe a debt of loyalty to the king, but I assure you, even if it weren't so, I would also be here to recover the lands that belonged to our ancestors and expel the invaders for all time. They dream of spreading their faith across

Europe and we are the only ones who can keep that from becoming a reality. Depending on how the wind blows in the battle, we will remain free men or will be subjected to the Almohads' will."

Three more blasts from the trumpet alerted those united there. The king of Castile was ready to speak. He climbed a tower and raised his voice as much as he could.

"Friends . . . Christians! The Moors entered our land by force and laid us low. Only a few Christians remained in the mountains to the north and they struck out against them, killing our enemies and dying themselves. For years, they battled them wherever they could . . . taking their lands until we arrived at the situation we find ourselves in today."

Many applauded his words and praised his name until he began to speak again.

"As sons of the various and noble kingdoms of Hispania, and as brothers in the faith of Jesus Christ, I ask you to join your voices to mine and ask for God's counsel and for success in our mission. And to seal our agreement, and as an offering to our Lord, I encourage you to say along with me: Only for Thee, All for Thee . . . Only for Thee, All for Thee . . ."

In an enormous show of jubilation, those present raised their voices to heaven and repeated his words over and over, enthused to feel part of that formidable undertaking. A great collective feeling spread to all. The mere fact of having reunited people of such different backgrounds and cultures made what they were doing something unprecedented.

In that moment, many of the soldiers thought they were invincible, and some even saw themselves as the hammer of God.

With their souls exalted, their arms prepared, and the crusading spirit instilled in them, the group set off for the south on June 20 to battle their sworn enemy.

They were thirty thousand souls, ten thousand knights, and fifty thousand horses. The Yeguada de las Marismas was reserved for those free citizens who had formed part of the civil militias. To that enormous troop had been added at the last minute more than five hundred knights from the Orders of Calatrava, Santiago, and the Templars.

The motley colors of their standards and uniforms, the clanking of the steel, the beating of the hooves against the road, the immensity of the corps . . . Wherever they went, people rushed to meet them, infected by their ambition, the dream of victory reflected on their faces. Some even joined their ranks.

Don Diego López de Haro, captaining his knights from Biscay, had left for the south three days earlier. He had taken along the Ultramontane troops to indulge their lust for combating the enemy and avoid the conflicts they might cause with the Castilians and Aragonese.

Don Diego had fixed a place to pass each night to be certain there was enough water, pastureland, and firewood. He had been helped by the foragers who went ahead before nightfall to scout for the zones with the best sources of water and most extensive plains.

Four days after leaving Toledo, this first group caught a glimpse of the castle of the village of Malagón, taken by the Moors years before. The fortress wasn't large; it had only one central tower and four more at the corners. It was of stone and cement and its defenses were rather modest.

When the occupants saw the army of Ultramontanes and Biscayans appear, they immediately sent an emissary prepared to hand over the castle so long as the lives of its inhabitants were spared. Don Diego accepted the terms, as that was the common practice in such struggles, but the Ultramontanes, mad with crusading zeal, threw themselves upon the Saracens once inside, putting all of them to the knife while Don Diego and the others stood by impotently.

After that butchery, many of the foreigners were satisfied, though their hands were stained with Saracen blood that they had scattered without concern for age, rank, or sex. Drunk on its effects, they decided to wait in the castle for the rest of the crusaders to arrive.

The better part of the main force arrived in Malagón at midmorning on the twenty-seventh of June, and Diego was with them. When he saw the battlements of the fortress and the Christian flags on its towers, he ran ahead with Sabba to reexperience his memories in that place that had once been everything for him.

He ran to the lake and saw the inn, now in ruins. Beside it, the stables were completely destroyed. There his past was distilled, the drama of the most painful moments of his life, and the death of his family. His father and his older sister dwelt in the waters of the lake, along with those Calatravan knights who had come to their aid. So many memories beat against the walls of his head, so much pain, that he wanted nothing more than to embrace the earth there and let his tears fall upon it.

Inside the fortress and out, the Ultramontanes were complaining rowdily of the lack of victuals.

The carts with the provisions arrived late and were insufficient. The surrounding fields lacked the necessary pasture to feed the horses, and the sweltering heat was unbearable for those from cooler countries. Nor did their thick garments help, as they were ill-suited to that climate.

When the two kings contemplated the blood the foreigners had shed, they called their leaders, among them the archbishops of Bordeaux and Narbonne. They were warned that such a thing would not be permitted again, but that irritated the men who had come from so far at the pope's behest to eradicate the Almohad presence on Iberian lands. They couldn't understand letting the enemy run free to fight again. For many, that even seemed an act of cowardice and a betrayal of Christian ideals.

"Your Majesty, my men have come to see the blood of the heretics flow, the way our brothers did long ago in Jerusalem. They don't understand why anyone would prefer to negotiate the relinquishment of fortresses instead of burning the enemies alive inside them," said a leader from Gascony, presenting the complaints of the Ultramontanes to Alfonso VIII. "They say that if it continues thus, they will abandon the crusade and return to their homelands."

King Alfonso, worried that such a conflict had arisen so early in the campaign, tried to convince them as best he could.

"Tell them I will pay them double. Tell them we can't afford to level the fortresses because afterward we will have to rebuild them to defend the positions we've conquered. Our war against the Almohads won't be over forever in one battle, however grand such a thing might be. We have to retake the land little by little, until we push them into the sea and they return to their own lands, which they never should have left. We therefore need to conquer many more fortresses so that, from more solid positions, we can go on taking territories farther to the south."

"I understand, Your Majesty, but please understand us as well. My men have come to this crusade after hearing of the deeds of their forebears in the Holy Land, and they want to show the same degree of valor. . . . Don't restrain them. Don't despise their combative spirit or they will leave. Think it over well."

The king contemplated the disastrous effect it would have on his men if the foreigners abandoned them and stated his agreement.

"Only two leagues from here is the fortified town of Calatrava, on the other shore of the Guadiana. It is an almost unbreachable defensive redoubt. Built on stone and surrounded by a deep moat, one of its slopes goes down into the riverbed." He took out his sword and brandished it in the air. "Let us take it by force! We will fight together, sword by sword, against its defenders. We will show our warrior spirit and make a conquest worthy of those heroes of the past."

"I will try to convince them, Your Majesty. We will help you, but afterward, leave us to our will . . ."

To reach Calatrava, they had to cross the Guadiana River. There they suffered the first setback of the journey. The Saracens had spread thousands of spikes that penetrated the horse's hooves as soon as they'd stepped into the water.

Diego took one of the objects in his hand, shocked by the wickedness that could come up with such an invention. It was a piece of iron in a pyramidal shape with sharpened points that would enter the foot of a man or an animal that stepped on them.

A dozen watchmen and explorers reconnoitered a broad stretch of the river and picked up as many as they could find, opening a secure pass for the troops. That took some time, and the Ultramontanes used it to complain about the hot midday sun and the lack of food.

A few hours later, they reached the outskirts of the fortress of Calatrava, alarmed at the new defenses that had been put up. There was a thick new wall around it, lined with embrasures and reinforced gates. It was also surrounded by a much deeper moat than the previous one that covered the entire perimeter save one section that bordered the river, where a steep hillside provided scant and difficult access.

Along the walls there could be seen many armed men and a hundred Andalusian knights ready to defend the castle to the death.

Don Álvaro Núñez de Lara approached to speak with the two kings.

"If we come together to plan, we can figure out how to lay siege to it. We know that Abulhachah Ibn Qadis is the head of defenses; he's a famous Andalusian knight, born in Cádiz, and has the reputation of being a great warrior."

"It seems impossible," Pedro of Aragon commented. "We need catapults that we don't have and heavy bores to penetrate the walls."

"We will pitch our tents at a distance," the Castilian monarch decided. "Advise the other ensigns, leaders, and village lords who have come with their militias. We will discuss what strategy to follow. And send spies to the south. We have to know what our enemy is up to. And make one of them that albéitar Diego. I want to know his thoughts."

Twenty leagues or so to the north, a beautiful woman disguised as a man had stopped a moment at a well to cool off and water her horse.

Three days before, she had left the castle of Zorita de los Canes behind her, learning that Bruno de Oñate had left to wage war against Caliph al-Nasir. They explained to her that the Calatravan had left two weeks before, joining a hundred other knights.

Unfortunately, those she asked swore to know nothing of the Diego de Malagón she was looking for. Without losing hope, she decided to go in search of that group of warriors, convinced that finding Bruno would lead her to Diego.

She pulled on the cord and with a great deal of strength managed to pull up a wooden bucket full of fresh water. First, she let her horse drink, and while it did, she looked around cautiously. She was close to a ramshackle farmhouse and had made sure no one lived there. She took off her hat and delighted in the feeling of the cool breeze blowing through her hair. It was fearfully hot that day.

She lowered the bucket into the well again until she heard it splash against the water. She pulled it up again and leaned it on the well's edge. She untied the cord of her tunic and rolled it up to cool off a bit.

A noise behind her alarmed her, but when she turned, there was no one there. But for some time a man behind one of the farmhouse walls had been watching her. When he was passing by, he thought he heard someone wandering around there, and out of curiosity, he looked to see who it was. He was even more surprised to see it was a woman dressed as a man and to see the beautiful shape of her body beneath her clothes. The solitude of the place made him begin to dream of having her. It was so long since he'd been with a woman.

Mencía decided to soak her tunic with the idea of traveling more coolly that way, and she took it off, standing there in her underwear. Behind her, a filthy and rustic-looking man approached without making a noise. Unworried, Mencía dunked her head in the bucket, immediately relieved by the cooling waters. But when she took it out, she heard a twig snap, and she turned to see what was happening. Before she would react, she felt hands clutching her shoulders. Terrified, she tried to escape, and since the man's face was the first thing she saw, she clawed at it with fury.

"Filthy whore!" the man responded, feeling her nails close to his eyes. He struck her so forcefully that he split her lip and without looking, he put his hands around her neck and pulled her to the ground.

Mencía twisted, feeling herself choked, and kicked him, hoping to get away. But the man was too strong, he sat on her stomach and with one hand, he held her wrists to the ground.

"If you don't quiet down, I'll kill you here and now."

"Bastard . . . let me go now!" She scratched one of his arms. "I'm not alone," she lied. "My companions will kill you."

He smiled cynically.

"Just thinking about it makes me shiver."

He tried to kiss her lips but he wasn't quick enough, and she bit him on the cheek. He hit her again and opened a cut on her chin.

"Be quiet now."

Those rough hands moved toward her breasts and squeezed them. Mencía screamed with all her heart to attract help, but when she looked back at the man, she lost all hope. She could do nothing to him, and no one would come to her aid.

She remembered Marcos and his advice. He had told her to travel with a caravan to avoid danger, but now it was too late. She rolled around, crying tears of rage, shrieking, full of fear, but managed to do nothing more than provoke another punch to the nose.

"Let her go now!" The tip of a sword threatened the aggressor's back.

Mencía knocked him off her and looked at who was speaking. Two armed knights stared back at her.

"We heard you screaming and came to your aid, my lady." In spite of her strange dress, Mencía couldn't hide her noble roots.

"Thank God. . . ." She stood up and ran to protect herself behind their backs.

"It's not what you think," the aggressor justified himself. "The woman provoked me and . . ."

"He's lying!" she shouted, enraged.

"You're lucky we don't have time to take you before the court," one answered. "You deserve to die right here, but we can't delay now. Listen to what we say and get out of here now, before we change our minds."

The man obeyed without hesitation, running without looking back, leaving a cloud of dust behind him.

"And you, señora, where are you going in that disguise?"

"To the war . . ." she answered firmly, not realizing the effects of her words. They burst into laughter.

"It's clear you're not a commoner. You should speak with our lord. Follow us . . . Oh, and I beg your pardon. My name is Iñigo de Zuñiga."

Mencía arranged her clothes, hid her hair again beneath her hat, and mounted her mare to follow them.

Half a mile from the river, they arrived at a makeshift camp where they found no fewer than five hundred knights with their pages and squires around a tent bearing the arms of Navarre.

Mencía was taken to the opening where various of the men were talking. Two of them she recognized immediately. As soon as she dismounted, she loosed her beautiful blond hair to the astonishment of all present.

"Forgive me, señora, but I believe I know you . . ." It was Gómez Garceiz, the ensign to the Navarrese king, whom she met in Olite after Diego was injured.

"And I know you," she smiled.

"Mencía Fernández de Azagra . . . correct?"

She nodded her head and bowed respectfully to the king, who was the second person she had recognized.

"A Fernández de Azagra . . ." The voice of the gigantic monarch resounded like an echo in a quarry. "A daughter of my lands, then, just like the rest of your family. . . ." He saw her split lip and the wound on her chin. "What happened to you?"

She explained without entering into details and told them why she had undertaken such a risky trip.

"I apologize, señora, I do not wish to be vulgar," Gómez Garceiz interrupted, "but it seems unbelievable to me that a noblewoman like yourself would want to be present for such a bloody scene. What is your motivation?"

"I am looking for Diego de Malagón."

Gómez Garceiz arched his brows, remembering that name.

"You already were doing so years back, in Olite. I remember it well. Is there something you need from him?"

"I need to tell him that I love him. . . ." Her marvelous blue eyes became moist as she declared her love publicly. "And I am ready to risk everything to do so: my life, my honor, whatever it takes. I will fight anyone who stands in my way, and I will travel over half the world to make him know what I feel for him."

The men admired her passionate declaration, and far from considering it a joke, they envied the recipient of that grand love she felt.

"Come with us, Mencía," Gómez Garceiz said, kissing her hand with deep and sincere respect. "From now on, you will be protected until we reach the front. Once there, you will look for your love; and we, for war and hardship."

VII.

The troops of the Aragonese king and a group of Templars and Ultra-montanes reached the castle of Calatrava at its eastern face, the one nearest the river, and took control of two of its thirty towers.

Shortly after, to the surprise of all, the governor Ibn Qadis signaled his surrender of the fortress. Alfonso VIII accepted, although that decision provoked the ire of the Ultramontanes. In accordance with the pact the man from Cádiz had offered, the fortress would be passed over to the king's hands without the need for a fight. The conditions of his generous offer were that the lives of the occupants be respected: half the defenders would leave on horseback and the other half could be enslaved by the Christians.

"My lord, we can't allow it," Archbishop Rodrigo Ximénez de Rada said, criticizing the king's agreement with reference to the motivations of the church. He reminded him as well of the possible response of the foreigners.

"Rodrigo, wait and listen to me." Alfonso stretched out his hand, asking for silence. "I still don't understand how they've given up so soon, without any resistance to speak of, but it's happened. We've only conquered two of the thirty towers so far. If we'd had to fight for each one, we would have needed no less than a week, and we could have lost many men. And imagine if, in the midst of it, al-Nasir had attacked us from the rear." The archbishop nodded his head, realizing the truth of what the king was saying. "We also have to think about the supply problems we're having, which have gotten worse since we left Toledo. This fortress boasts abundant provisions. That alone makes it worth it, and it might help placate tensions with the Ultramontanes."

From the first day of July, the flags of Castile and Aragon flew over the fabulous fortress, alongside that of Calatrava, the beneficiaries of that enormous walled city.

The success of that conquest encouraged many of the Spaniards, but it disappointed the Ultramontanes, who had not had the chance to slay the infidels, something that was incomprehensible to them. Once more, they could not respect the decision. That and the unbearable heat of the following days combined with their increasingly violent arguments with the Castilians and the Aragonese led to a great number of wounded on both sides and the foreigners' desire to abandon the enterprise definitively. If they couldn't kill the Moors and avenge the blood spilled by their brothers who had died defending Jerusalem, it wasn't worth carrying on. They weren't just there to enrich Castile with the capture of fortresses and castles. For that reason, on the third of July, they met with Alfonso VIII and announced their irrevocable decision to return to their countries.

A total of two thousand knights and nearly six thousand pages headed north that same day to the surprise and disgust of the rest of the crusaders. Only the archbishop of Narbonne, Arnault Amalric, a native of the Catalan territories, decided to stay with a hundred and thirty knights from regions of Valence and Vienne.

The next day, Alfonso VIII headed toward Alarcos with his men and a portion of the Aragonese troops. The remainder waited with Pedro II in Calatrava for the arrival of Sancho VII with his group of Catalan knights.

When they went, they crossed paths with the spies who had been sent to the south, Diego de Malagón among them.

Don Álvaro Núñez de Lara was the first to hear the news of al-Nasir's plans, and he asked Diego and two others to come with him to communicate them to the king.

"According to the route the caliph has taken, we believe that he will reach the south end of the Muradal Pass on the fourteenth of this month, Your Majesty," one of the spies said, basing his guess on the size of the army, the difficulty of the terrain, and the distance still to go.

"We were also able to capture one of their spies attempting to send a message to our troops from the caliph. We suspect he may have managed to infiltrate our forces already, Your Majesty," Diego interrupted.

"And what was this message about?" Don Álvaro asked.

"He promised to give a thousand *maravedíes* to anyone who would desert the Christian army and join with him."

The three Castilians were stunned by the enormous quantity of money that would imply.

"We're lucky the Ultramontanes didn't hear about this offer," the archbishop declared.

"We found out something more, which in this case might be more important for our interests," the third man added. "It seems that, after you set the governor Ibn Qadis free, the caliph, infuriated at the loss of Calatrava, had him executed in public, accusing him of treachery, desertion, and cowardice."

"Excellent news!" the king affirmed. "What I still don't understand is how you managed to get this information from the spy . . ."

"It may be better if we don't go into details, but you may want to know what the last thing he said to us was before he set off on his journey to heaven. . . ."

"What do you mean?" King Alfonso began to feel nervous and harried. He preferred them to speak more directly.

"It seems the Andalusian troops thought of Ibn Qadis as a hero," Diego responded. "When al-Nasir had him beheaded in their presence, he didn't count on the rejection he would suffer from those men, and they have sworn they'll make him pay. It seems it's not the first time al-Nasir has insulted the Andalusians, often simply because they were born on Iberian lands and not in the noble Atlas Mountains."

While he listened, the king thought of a plan.

"The desertion of the Ultramontanes has been a blow to our troops' morale. Many think that the spirit of the Holy Crusade has departed with them, and now they feel it's just another battle, one of the many that have sparked off between Christians and Muslims. With fewer troops, the success of our campaign has been compromised, but I see that a new opportunity has opened up, as long as we are able to take advantage of it." He turned to the three spies. "I have to ask for your help again, though this time it may be riskier. . . ."

The king explained his plan and asked Don Álvaro to take care of the preparations before Bruno de Oñate took over the mission as head of the Calatravans' espionage. Then he called for no fewer than fifty knights to accompany them.

Diego felt discomfited by the news. Since they had spoken in the castle of Zorita de los Canes, he and Oñate hadn't met again. It was a bad memory, being pushed out of the Calatravans by Bruno, though Diego couldn't forget that he was only alive thanks to him. Diego had more reasons to thank him than reproach him, but still, the idea of sharing a mission wasn't a pleasant one.

"While you are getting close to al-Nasir, we will go to Alarcos," the king continued. "I have a great debt to pay off there, and the other kings are to meet me there as well."

"Your Majesty . . . We have one more thing to say; the size of his army . . ." A Sorian with a gaunt face was speaking, looking at the ground daunted and almost ashamed.

"Yes!" the king exclaimed. "I know they left Seville two days after us, the twenty-second of June, but I don't know how many there were."

They looked at one another, trying to decide who would speak. Both Don Álvaro and the king pressed them to get on with it.

"Between seventy and eighty thousand . . ."

"Good God . . . That is incredible," Don Rodrigo Ximénez de Rada said, looking at the monarch's face, but not finding the slightest sign of worry.

"Prepare the mission I have just charged you with. The three of you speak Arabic, yes?"

"Diego is the one who does best," the other two assured him. Alfonso VIII stared at him from his deep eyes.

"Diego de Malagón . . ." His air turned solemn. "Again you bear a great responsibility on your shoulders. I trust in your commitment and your bravery, and I expect a success equal to the one you brought us before. The outcome of the battle could depend on your skill here."

"I promise it, Your Majesty," Diego affirmed resolutely.

Even if he would have to share his fate with Bruno de Oñate, whom he still had his doubts about, he was proud to take part in an action that would help to put an end to the Almohads' ambitions.

King Alfonso captured Alarcos the next day without great difficulty. It seemed that word of what had happened in Malagón and the later surrender of Calatrava had spread through the Saracen ranks and that, from fear, they were giving in quickly.

From there, the royal army moved on to Salvatierra, that emblematic post whose loss had provoked such pain in the Christian world that it was compared with the fall of Jerusalem at the hands of Saladin.

Unlike the previous fortresses, this one was well defended and the difficulties of laying siege seemed impossible to overcome.

The Castilian king decided to camp nearby and await the arrival of the allied monarchs. Together they would decide what to do, attack or continue on.

The Aragonese troops, together with five hundred Navarrese knights led by King Sancho, arrived at Salvatierra on the eighth of July. Alfonso VIII greeted Sancho like a brother, proud to have him there, and immediately organized a meeting to be attended by the royal ensigns. In one tent there were six men who together represented the better part of the territories of Visigoth Hispania.

The meeting didn't go on long before they all came to the same conclusion: they would leave the sack of the fortress for later, knowing that al-Nasir was only six leagues away, on the other side of the sierra.

In the meanwhile, the Christian camp was filled with tension and anxiety; some readied themselves to attack Salvatierra while others sharpened their lances and swords and repaired the suits of armor that had been damaged in the previous clash. Among them, a blond woman, of noble aspect and forlorn face, tried to find Don Álvaro Núñez de Lara to figure out what he knew about Diego de Malagón.

"He just left the king's tent a second ago," a solider said, pointing to where the meeting had just been held. "He'll probably be in that one over there now."

Mencía didn't understand why she'd had such bad luck since her departure from Burgos. When she arrived at Calatrava, the Castilians had left for Alarcos not long before, and with them the knights led by Bruno de Oñate. After that, in Alarcos, she also found they had left, that time heading for the fortress of Salvatierra, and now that she was there, no one could tell her where Bruno was, let alone Diego.

"Mencía?" Don Álvaro doubted whether the woman he found outside his tent could possibly be who he thought she was. Her hair was shorter and she looked different from how he remembered. "Can you tell me what you're doing here?"

"I'm looking for Diego." She answered without mincing words. "Do you know where he is . . . ? I never believed in your letter."

Don Álvaro held his silence while he tried to decide what to tell her. The surprise of seeing her there, her hope-filled face, and the fact that he had lied to her in that letter pained him greatly. She wanted to know the truth, but if he explained it without being careful, it could be a terrible blow to her.

"I didn't know you had lost your husband, I'm sorry. I found out from others." Don Álvaro tried to buy a little time.

"It was three years ago. He suffered a fatal accident and died as a consequence. It was very sad. But, Álvaro, don't avoid my real reason for coming here to speak with you." She grabbed him by the wrists and looked at him, letting him know she would not accept any further evasiveness.

"I suppose there were many other things you should have explained in that letter . . ."

"It may be. . . . At the moment, though, I don't consider it necessary; my only goal is to find the love of my life, Diego. I've traveled from Burgos and faced all types of dangers to arrive here today. I followed the trail of a

Calatravan, Bruno de Oñate, all the way to this encampment. Álvaro . . ." She looked into his eyes. "I've risked a great deal and I believe I've suffered enough along the way. No one seems to know anything about him. And believe me, I've asked everyone. I don't understand; I've looked in the stables, in the tents, and no one seems to have seen him. I don't know what else to do." Desperate tears filled her eyes. "Inside, I know he's alive, but nobody gives me any reason to go on believing it. Please, speak to me, don't hold back what you have to say."

"All right . . . at the time I deceived you when I told you Diego was dead. I did it to protect you, and with your interests at heart, because no one had told me about what happened to Fabián." Mencía's face lit up when her suspicions were confirmed. "Diego was very lucky to land in jail with the Calatravan you're following, Bruno de Oñate, who saved him from the gallows and then brought him here." He pointed to the magnificent outline of Salvatierra. "He sheltered him here, taking advantage of its remote location and its independence. At that time, we were looking for a man with his abilities, and we knew this was the best place to keep him safe from the courts."

Don Álvaro told her another detail or two about Diego's activities in those years and finished by informing her that he had departed the encampment the day before to carry out a delicate mission.

"What could be more delicate than this war?" she asked him, full of anxiety.

Don Álvaro looked around, asked her to lower her voice, and invited her into his tent.

"I can't tell you. His mission may be decisive for all of us. Don't treat my discretion like a lack of confidence in you. We've learned that al-Nasir has placed spies among our troops. Do you understand? If by some indiscretion our plans reached his ears, he would kill Diego with his own hands. I have to keep his safety in mind."

"From what I've just heard, I presume you're trying to infiltrate the Saracens." Mencía brought her hand to her mouth, terrified, and her eyes filled with tears. So many years searching for him, so much effort to be with him, and now the risk of losing him was greater than ever. Overwhelmed by the gravity of the situation, she could no longer hold out, and she cried in Álvaro's arms.

"I never knew you loved him so much."

"More than anyone or anything in the world," she responded, sobbing. "What will happen to him now?"

VIII.

_____

Al-Nasir himself wanted to meet in person with the alleged Christian deserters who had just been captured by his troops on the La Losa trail at the feet of the Muradal Pass.

On catching sight of that numerous group, the Saracen soldiers hadn't trusted their intentions and had tied their hands and led them to the vizier to allow him to decide their fate. Once they were in the Almohad encampment, they were lined up and surrounded by thirty Berber soldiers with hostile faces.

"Which of you speaks Arabic?" a man with olive skin and a long beard asked.

Everyone looked at Diego.

"Apparently it's you." He pulled him from the line and forced him to kneel. Then, he had his men do the same and threatened with death anyone who dared look up in the presence of the caliph.

"No one shall look into his eyes, nor speak to him unless questioned first. I advise you to listen."

All obeyed.

Diego heard some steps and a man whose shoes attracted his gaze, because they were threaded with gold and adorned with gemstones, stopped in front of him. His heart pounded when he thought of the possibility that one of the two soldiers with the caliph could be Pedro de Mora. Diego was aware of the risk he was running after what had happened in Seville. Though not many had seen him before he ran, the Castilian traitor had been one of them.

His desire to arrest the intentions of the Almohad horde had weighed heavier than any other consideration, even his own safety. He also had to overcome the objections of Bruno de Oñate when he found out Diego had been chosen for the mission. The power of Don Álvaro Núñez de Lara had been more important in this case than the opinion of the Calatravan.

"What do you want from Allah's troops?"

"Our gold, sir. We've heard you will pay a thousand *maravedíes* to anyone who fights with you."

"How can you guarantee me that you don't have different intentions? That you aren't spies?"

"We can tell you the present position of the troops, how much cavalry they possess, what their armaments are . . ." Diego knew he was risking everything. "Did you know the Ultramontanes just abandoned them? Or that their power has been reduced by half, or that morale has collapsed?"

Without answering, al-Nasir called over the vizier and spoke to him quietly.

"I think they're lying," the caliph said.

"I advise you to wait for Pedro de Mora. He is the one responsible for our spies and he can confirm whether the news of the Ultramontanes is true. He will also know better how to measure the sincerity of their intentions. He will arrive tomorrow afternoon, and in the meantime, we should exercise caution."

"Even still, I will use my own methods to test their honesty. . . . Look at it as a way of gaining time." Al-Nasir pulled Diego's hair and screamed into his ear.

"Tell them I won't pay a thousand, but ten thousand, three good horses, two female slaves, and a guarantee of freedom to the first one who tells me the truth."

Diego tried to justify himself before translating.

"Sir, we were hired by the king as mercenaries. For us, war is just money. For now we've only made half, because the other part has been reserved until the conflict is over. The rations were scarce, and we've had one calamity after another since leaving Toledo. When the foreigners left and we received notice of the size of your forces, we knew the war was over. Add to this that the king has only pledged to pay us three hundred *maravedíes*, and you promise three times as much, and victory seems already to be in your hands. Do you not understand our decision? The motives of your fighting don't interest us, be they religious or territorial; we just want wealth. . . ."

"Translate for your men what I will pay and be quiet!" Al-Nasir slapped him across the cheek.

"Does anyone want to say anything?" he exclaimed aloud. Diego repeated it in Romanic. No one moved or opened their lips.

"I see . . . You don't want to talk." With a finger, he signaled one of the Berber soldiers to come close and take out his sword. He asked for the first man in line, the one next to Bruno de Oñate, to be brought forward, and forced him to kneel. Al-Nasir stood back precisely when a sharp blade sliced off the knight's head in one swoop, once the caliph had given the order to one of his men.

"Since I see you have still not understood, I will repeat it for you. The person who tells me the truth will receive three horses, two female slaves, and ten thousand gold *maravedíes*. It's not a bad deal. Think about it."

Diego translated it again, emboldened by the victim's silence. If anyone spoke, it would mean death for all of them. Al-Nasir waited awhile, but no one said anything.

"Now it's your turn. . . ." He personally approached the Christians and selected Bruno de Oñate, tugging at his tunic.

"We are telling the truth. You won't get anything by killing us." Diego repeated in Arabic what Bruno had said and saw the bravery shining in his eyes.

"Kill him!" the caliph responded coldly.

The steel whistled again and Bruno's head flew off through the air.

Diego closed his eyes and felt wounded inside. That senseless death, of a man he owed his life to, was as cruel as it was pointless. That immeasurable violence, that hatred so deep that seemed to reside in their dark hearts, was exactly what he wanted to fight against and the reason he was here. He regretted not repairing his disagreement with Bruno when he found out they would be sharing a mission, not showing sufficient gratitude for all he owed him or his admiration for Bruno's work at Salvatierra. The short journey from the Christian encampment to the Saracens' had not been enough to melt the frozen feelings that divided them.

Bruno's death was followed by twelve others, but no one opened his mouth. Diego watched in dread as the heads of his companions rolled away only a few feet from him, and he prayed for it to finally be over.

"Now let's try with the translator, to finish off . . ." Diego's breathing stopped. His eyes lowered, he saw the caliph's shoes again, now splattered with blood.

Someone close to the caliph spoke.

"You possess a firm hand and wisdom in your heart, but listen a moment to what your humbler counselor has to tell you."

"Speak . . ."

"I believe they are telling the truth. I've never seen anyone resist so much. If you go on killing them, they won't serve us for anything, and none will make it into Pedro de Mora's hands."

"Prepare the sword." Al-Nasir ignored his words.

The soldier raised his arm, trembling, exhausted by the effort. When he saw this, the caliph himself took the sword from his hands and raised it decisively. Diego, unflinching, fearless, thought that everything was finished for him. He commended his soul to God and waited for the end to come, his breath halting and his pulse racing.

But then they heard an intense shouting and saw a group of soldiers galloping toward the encampment. They had just spotted enemy troops on the other side of the mountain, ready to enter the pass.

Al-Nasir looked at Diego's neck, then the saber, and was tempted. Dust from the cloud kicked up by those soldiers made it into his lungs and caused him to cough. Angry, he lowered the weapon and turned to the recent arrivals to see what they had to say. Once he'd heard them, he sent his vizier to his tent to talk, and ordered that the deserters be kept under watch until Pedro de Mora arrived.

Diego sighed, relieved, though he knew that worse awaited him when he was seen by Pedro de Mora.

They lifted him from the ground and tied him with the rest of them in a long line that they then led to one end of the encampment.

On the way they passed by numerous tents where the troops were resting, and of all of them, the one that caught their attention was huge and decorated with hundreds of beautiful woven rugs. Not only was it huge, but it was protected by a palisade of thick logs wrapped in chains and a numerous contingent of armed Imesebelen. It was undoubtedly the tent of the caliph himself.

They advanced through a crowd of soldiers of different origin and appearance. Some wore turbans; others, like the Turks, had darker skin and darker eyes. There were also women with them, numbering in the thousands. The esplanade where the encampment lay was a half league long and equally as wide and had a small hill at its center where the caliph's tent was placed. They were taken to its southern edge, where there were fewer but larger tents that were used for storage.

Of the fifty men who had begun the mission with Diego, only thirty-six were left.

As soon as they left the colorful tents behind them, they saw two women come out of them and walk in the same direction. Diego was at the front of the line and he looked at the taller one. She was in a black tunic and a niqab from which a curl of red hair emerged. When she was closer, he looked at her more closely, searching out her eyes, which were hardly visible through the slit. She felt the insistence with which Diego was looking at her and curiosity made her turn back toward him. Her eyes were large and of a blue as familiar as it was magical. Diego knew it could be none other. A lash of emotion buckled his body. He would have liked to shout, to tell her who he was, but fear of what might happen made him hush, and he just smiled sweetly. Estela took a moment to recognize him, but then she realized that the man with the black hair and dark eyes, the olive skin and warm smile, was her brother, Diego. He had changed a great deal, but it was him. She brought her hand to her mouth, feeling tempted to run and greet him, to squeeze him in her arms. Diego could tell, and when they were close, he made a sign for her to be calm. Estela felt the brush of her brother's hand as he passed by her. And when she turned afterward, she saw his gaze full of love and joy.

Estela stopped for a moment to see where the group was being taken and asked her companion, Princess Najla, who they were.

"I don't know what you're asking me."

"Those men we just saw."

"I don't know, but if it interests you so much, let's ask. Soldier!" She shouted to the man following in the rear of the group.

"Who are you escorting?" Najla was brusque.

"Christian deserters who are trying to pass over to our side."

Estela was shocked. She couldn't imagine what Diego was after, but she was sure that wasn't why he was there.

"Where are you taking them?" Estela was calm, concealing the anxiety she felt.

The soldier found her interest strange, but he answered.

"They'll be watched in the big tent where we keep the grain for the horses. That last one." He pointed at a long tent away from the rest of them.

Najla said good-bye to the soldier and took Estela's arm, asking her why she cared about those deserters. Estela hesitated for a moment but then was convinced that without Najla's help, she could do nothing, and so she decided to be sincere.

"I saw my brother among them," she whispered in her ear.

"Are you sure? Many years have passed since you were separated."

"It's him. There is no doubt."

"What could he be doing here?" That question provoked a certain confusion in Estela.

Najla observed her friend and envied her. She was sure her brother would never do something like that for her. On the other hand, at that moment, her situation was somewhat burdensome: She felt the duty to tell the caliph of what she had just learned. She thought about it in silence. She was sure the man was there for military reasons, not personal ones; it

wasn't reasonable to imagine an expedition of that scale for the mere purpose of saving one woman. Najla also thought, horrified, that they might
have come to assassinate the caliph, her brother. At that moment, her chin
trembled, and Estela seemed to guess what she was thinking.

"Najla, I need you. . . . My brother, Diego, is the most important person
left in my life. I only want to talk to him. We've spent many years together
and I've come to love you like a sister. I've never asked you for anything,
but this time . . . you know I can't get to him without your help."

"And if he's here with other intentions . . . how will I forgive myself
after?"

"What can thirty men do against the eight thousand that form this
army?"

Estela took her hands, begging for her help.

"Not much, that's certain . . . but I don't know . . ."

Najla felt doubts though she knew how happy it would make her if she
said yes. . . . She thought of Estela, and then of how hard it had been for she
herself to know in her own life the meaning of that word, *happiness*. When
she lost her only love, King Sancho of Navarre, she didn't imagine how
she could live without his sweet presence. And then, years later, when she
had suffered that terrible crime that almost turned her into a monster, she
realized that the feeling was gone forever. She had never understood what
motives could lead someone to destroy her face, nor the lack of interest
her brother had shown in finding the person responsible. She would never
forgive him for that. Her desperation had been so fierce that for months
she refused to see anyone. She forsook all contact with the world and didn't
even want to see Estela. For that time, her hatred encompassed everything,
including the people around her.

"What do you say?" Estela, more nervous than ever, awaited her
response.

Najla needed to ruminate on her decision.

"We'll see. Let me think . . ."

"No. . . . Promise me you will be silent, I beg you." Tears welled in her
eyes. "I lost my sisters, I lost my father. . . . I don't want to lose him, too.
Help me, I'm begging you."

Najla sighed, saddened, and finally told Estela what she wished so
much to hear.

"Tonight you will speak with him."

On the other side of the mountains, to the north, the Christian armies
already knew where al-Nasir's encampment was located, where they would

need to descend to arrive at the plains, and the enormous difficulties they would face crossing through the narrow pass at La Losa.

Alfonso III's second in command, Don Diego López de Haro, had led a quick expedition in the company of his son, his nephew the prince of León, Sancho Fernández, and ten other men to the high point of Muradal Pass. There they had faced the first bands of Saracens and recognized the enormous difficulty they would run into when it was time to begin their descent. To reach the flatlands to the south, they'd had to pass through a narrow defile, one man at a time, without any protection. All the while, a multitude of archers spread out at different heights along the walls rained arrows on them; they could annihilate half an army and barely budge from their locations.

When they'd returned, they met in the tent where the three kings and their ranking men had spoken before. Archbishop Rodrigo Ximénez de Rada was also there, and the archbishop of Narbonne, as well as three commanders of the military orders.

"Your Majesty, we can try Muradal Pass, but I warn you the descent could be hell on earth. The first part won't be too problematic, until we arrive at a fortified tower halfway through. There we can arrange our positions. But somewhat farther down, the road narrows, and there's a gorge where only one horse at a time can pass through. And there, they can massacre us. I assure you that place could provoke a terrible bloodbath if they come after us with arrows. We were able to see a good number of archers hiding out there."

"Al-Nasir doesn't want to cross the mountains. That way he risks little, keeps his rearguard well covered, and his territories intact," the archbishop of Narbonne commented.

King Pedro II proposed crossing over through another route.

"Let's try first to send a hundred men through the Muradal and see what happens, and we'll decide after." Sancho VII of Navarre thought they should try it, since no one could think of a better place.

The king of Castile had just found out that his cousin Alfonso IX of León had taken advantage of his absence to attack a number of Castile's positions.

"I don't see a clear solution . . ." Alfonso VIII intervened. "As my second in command says, in La Losa we'll be fodder to their arrows. I propose we wait here and provoke them into coming after us. Or maybe we can delay the action and prepare ourselves better, or look for another place. . . . In the meantime, I would like to punish my ungrateful cousin."

"I understand your anger," Pedro of Aragon replied, "and I share your desire, and it is true that he deserves a vigorous response to his villainy, but we should concentrate our anger on the caliph. He's fewer than two leagues away, and we have never gathered an army such as this. Maybe we never will again."

The archbishop said the Aragonese was right and gave his support to a solution in between: some would look for another pass while another detachment would try to get through La Losa. They all agreed with the tactic and immediately set to work.

But half a day later something unexpected occurred. The troops that had gone to see the viability of the pass returned decimated and with their morale wrecked. And those who had explored the terrain looking for another route returned crestfallen as well, completely unsuccessful.

But then there appeared an old pastor from the area who wished to speak with the king. He assured them he knew of another way, a safer one that he would only show them if the king himself asked for it.

The man, very humble in his manners and sparing in his words, explained drily where another route could be found. It was to the west, he said, three leagues away, and he swore there was no one watching over it, as he had been there with his goats that very morning.

"Will you show it to my second in command, Don Diego López de Haro?" the king asked.

"I will do it with pleasure, sire, if you ask it."

"Then make it so!"

IX.

They embraced until it hurt.

Estela cried onto his breast, mad with emotion, and Diego did the same, though he was laid low by the news of Blanca's death years ago.

Najla watched them with envy.

"My dear Diego . . ." Estela caressed his face, trying to memorize it with her fingers, as if that way, she could read his memories.

"How many years since I've seen you, how many things I have to tell you . . ."

"You don't have much time," Najla warned them, for though she had paid the soldiers generously, she knew that she and Estela couldn't be there much longer. "Today the guard changes before midnight."

"Thank you, señora, for your . . ." Diego couldn't finish the phrase because the woman had already walked out of the tent.

"During all those years, I never forgot you." Estela grabbed Diego's hands and invited him to sit on some wooden boxes. His face changed when she told him all she'd been obliged to do since her capture. "I've achieved a good position at the court for the sole reason that I'm the caliph's favorite concubine. You can't imagine how many times I wanted to die . . ." Diego kissed her forehead, understanding her pain. "They have abused my body however they've seen fit, and not only the caliph and his father before him, but also that Castilian who was in charge of our capture, Pedro de Mora; how I hate him in the deepest part of my soul."

Diego clenched his fists with infinite rage when he imagined the torment she'd suffered through.

"I almost killed him . . ."

"I found out from someone else. That was the only time I heard anything about you. And I remember how relieved I felt."

Diego caught one tear on his finger and told her of his life during those seventeen long years.

"You're out of time." Najla peeked through the tent after a moment, giving them their last warning.

"I heard them say Pedro de Mora is coming tomorrow," Diego told her before they separated. "And al-Nasir will send him to speak with us. Estela, you have to understand, that man cannot see me. If he does, he will kill me straightaway. I need to see him in private, and with a weapon."

"I though perhaps you could use these . . ." She raised her skirt and he saw the two sharp daggers hidden inside.

"Perfect, Estela! Now listen close, because what I have to say is very important. Could you convince Najla to get me out of this tent, with any kind of excuse, before Pedro de Mora comes to visit it?"

"I will try . . ."

"I know you will. . . . Ah, wait," he said, grabbing her elbow. "I will also need a preparation of herbs, they're not hard to find, as you'll see." He passed her a scrap of cloth where he had written down the ingredients. "And I need to talk to some of the leaders of the troops from Andalusia. Can you manage all that?"

Estela promised to do everything she could before she left.

"When will you get me out of here?" For the first time she felt confidence in her fate. "Why not tonight, Diego?"

"We will do it, don't worry, but first I have to complete a mission I agreed to carry out. Then we'll leave this hell, I promise you, Estela. Trust me."

"I never stopped. . . . Never."

No one saw the pastor again, but he was right: There was a lone path to the west that ended in a broad plateau facing the enemy positions and was perfect for setting up camp. Some thought the man had been sent by God and others even affirmed it was Saint Isidore himself. For Diego López de Haro and García Romeu, his help was providential. They thanked him for his enormous favor before returning to the Christian positions euphorically, and at the best possible moment, given the sorry state of the soldiers who had returned and the calls from some to abandon the entire enterprise.

When they decided to try that new pass, the Christians' front lines had to pull back from positions they had taken before. The Saracens interpreted this as fleeing. But only a few hours later they saw the other crusaders coming down from a route they knew nothing of. There were thousands of them and they came so quickly that the Saracens couldn't react in time. Even so, al-Nasir's army launched a severe attack with its best archers and a detachment of Arabs. Still, the Christians managed to repel them without great difficulties and improve their position.

The Almohads burned the grass and bushes they found in their path, trying to confuse their enemies with the smoke and keep them from taking the plateau, but a fortunate change of wind sent the smoke cloud over the Saracen camp.

Once the place was in their hands, the Christians decided to rest two days there to recuperate. The men and the animals were both hungry and exhausted by the arduousness of the expedition and the effects of the intense heat.

It was Saturday, the fourteenth of July, when the three kings crossed the sierra and descended to what would be their final encampment, on a broad plain between two riverbeds. The place could not have been better, thanks to the abundance of water for the horses and the men.

Just outside their tents, the three kings observed the Muslim encampment atop a hill in front of them, with another plain at its base. They were separated by a long esplanade bordered by the two rivers. That would be the battlefield, the *Navas*, as those flatlands were called, that would attest to the definitive showdown between Christian and Muslim. History would bear witness to this grand encounter between the troops of Alfonso VIII of Castile and those of al-Nasir, but for now, the protagonists were content with studying which would be the best strategy.

For the following hours, they met to discuss the mobilization, the location of the different troops, and who would form the front line and the rearguard.

While they discussed tactics, inside the camp a tense silence reigned. Soldiers, squires, and knights—all were readying their weapons. Some polished their helmets and sharpened their swords and lances. Others covered their maces in nettle sap and marked their arrows with Christian crosses, hoping that the symbol of their faith would pierce the flesh of the infidels.

Mencía walked among the tents observing everything, trying to comprehend the sentiments of those men who seemed to have fallen mute, though they were sure of the cause they were fighting for.

She asked a horse groom if he knew where the chapel and the hospital had been set up, and he pointed to the middle of the encampment. According to his words, when she saw a long trail of soldiers waiting for confession or a group of women caring for the wounded, she would know, because they were located close together.

When she passed by an area of more modest tents, she heard someone grieving inside one of them. She wanted to know who the sounds were coming from, and looked inside, finding a boy of no more than sixteen huddled under a cloth.

"What's happened to you, boy?" Mencía lifted the cloth to see him better.

The boy, embarrassed, lifted his head and when he saw the woman, he hid again, letting out a loud hiccup.

"I'm scared, señora . . ."

"That's natural, but you must know you are part of a mission that will free your sons when you have them one day, and your friends and family as well." Mencía pulled down a bit of her sleeve to help dry his tears.

"Where are you from?"

Mencía took pity on the boy, who could only be called a man because of his size.

"I belong to the militia of Medina and my parents couldn't pay the tax to keep me from going to war."

Mencía tried to comfort him.

"I will pray for God to protect you from the enemy's swords." She kissed his forehead. "But you have to promise me one thing." The boy nodded. "You will not let fear make a coward of you. Do it for me!"

The boy saw her leave his side, believing he had spoken with an angel.

Mencía headed to the makeshift chapel, and close by, she saw women wrapping the handles of swords and lances so the men wouldn't blister their hands. Others reinforced the seams of the leather on the shields and waxed their surfaces to deflect the enemy's weapons. She also saw a woman hammering sharp iron spikes in the center of a shield, so that it would serve for more than mere defense.

Beside her she found a larger tent that a soldier had just set foot into. Inside she saw boys cleaning the wounds of a dozen soldiers with oil and cotton cloths. They were the first victims of the Saracen raids.

When they saw her, they asked for her help. Without hesitating, Mencía rushed to the aid of a middle-aged man who had an arrow stuck in his shoulder. His whines became wails as the doctor tried to extract the tip. She took his hand in hers and looked at him tenderly. That seemed to comfort him, because his protests ceased just before he lost consciousness.

When they were finished with that one, she helped another soldier, writhing in pain from colic, and then a group of women trying to repair a boy's dislocated shoulder.

She promised she would come back the next day when the first arrivals from the front showed up, and then she continued walking through the camp.

There was a general atmosphere of unease.

Mencía had her own pain inside, when she imagined the terrible dangers her beloved Diego would be facing at that moment.

She saw a long line of penitents and awaited her turn to confess just as they were. When she could, she opened her heart absolutely to that man of God, and he gave her absolution and with it, peace.

Before she entered her tent, she stopped five more times to console other terrified boys as well as some older men.

One of the things that most impressed her was seeing how many of the men embraced their wives, promised them eternal love, undoubtedly thinking that those might be their last caresses and kisses.

She wished she could be one of them.

She also witnessed how some soldiers called the scribes to write out their wills, many of them crying as they did so. And she could hear others swearing to take care of each other's family's if someone should fall.

Amid such emotion, Mencía entered her tent, and she burst into tears, unable to hold back another moment, grieving for the enormous built-up tension. Despite her mourning, she heard a strange clanging sound close by. Someone was repairing his suit of armor, that vest woven with rings of steel, useful to stop a sword but pointless against a lance or a crossbow.

"Diego, you can come out from under the tent," Estela whispered. "The guard knows and he won't do anything."

It was nighttime.

Estela was hidden beneath a dark dress and a matching niqab. She took his hand, and together they ran behind the tents, hiding as best they could. They came to one where she had hidden what he needed, and they entered carefully. Estela looked through a pile of straw and took out a long black cloth and other objects wrapped in fabric.

"It's the first time I've ever put a turban on someone . . ."

Diego lowered his head and Estela wrapped it, knotting the cloth firmly. After she opened a flask full of dark cream and spread it on his face to cover his skin. She did the same with his neck, arms, and hands, and then had him put on a blue tunic and boots.

"With this disguise, we shouldn't have too many problems moving freely through the camp. When we get out, I'll take you to one of the main leaders of the Andalusians, someone you can talk to without problems. But we have very little time. Therefore I have to ask you to be brief and get right to what interests you. Then we'll go toward the twelve tents that surround the caliph's. Pedro de Mora sleeps in one of them. I hear he's just arrived from Jaén."

"I'm proud of you, Estela."

"I owe everything to Najla. Without her, it would have been impossible."

"Do you know why she's doing it? Isn't she al-Nasir's sister?"

"She is, and I imagine she's doing it out of spite. Without being a fanatic herself, she's had to witness terrible decisions made by her brother. Years back, al-Nasir ordered them to whip me for punishment for something I'd said. When I returned to the palace and she saw me wounded and half dead, Najla was incredibly angry with her brother. She insulted him and scratched him. . . . I still remember it. Sometimes Najla seems like those birds that live all their lives in a cage and lose their ability to sing along with their freedom. The love she professes for poetry is nothing more than the listlessness of a person who has lived without liberty and tries to find it in rhymes and feelings."

"I see she's someone very special to you."

"She is; without my asking she's bribed one of our best spies, a person she's dealt with frequently, to convince her brother your intentions are good, and it appears that it worked."

"It couldn't be better!" Diego smiled, enchanted. "Now let's go find this man."

The conversation with the Andalusian was brief; very quickly, they came to an agreement. As they had imagined, the feeling of ill will after the death of Ibn Qadis ran very deep. His compatriots wanted to make them pay, both the vizier and the arrogant Almohads, for the endless humiliations they had been subject to for years.

Both knew what could happen that night, but neither of them wanted to say it. Diego and Estela just wanted it to be over with and to repay the debt they owed their family. They wanted to avenge the blood of their people, spilled so many times by the Almohads.

As they climbed the southern slope of the hill where al-Nasir's red tent was located, they could see the fires of the Christian camp, less than a half league away. The coolness of the night brought aromas of burned firewood, but also of incense. Despite the distance, they could hear occasional notes of the Christians' religious chants.

In both camps, their respective gods were sleeping, but soon they would see how their sons would face off until the last drop of blood was spilled.

"It's that one in front of us, the one with the light inside."

Estela squeezed him when she saw a patrol of soldiers close to the entrance.

Diego weighed his chances and decided to do it no matter what. He knew that any error could bring with it fatal consequences, and that Pedro de Mora would alert the guards at the least sign of danger. It wouldn't be easy, but nothing was going to stop him.

He took a deep breath and blew out slowly until he felt relaxed enough, then he looked for the two daggers in his belt. He looked at his sister and said good-bye to her.

"For God's sake, Diego, be very careful and come back soon. I can't bear to lose you now. . . . I'll be waiting for you." In that moment, Estela's eyes expressed a tumult of emotions. She blessed him for what he was about to do, but at the same time, she felt a terrible fear. She would have liked to help him with her own hands, to breathe in the last breath that man expelled, to steal his life away . . .

Diego stroked her cheek and promised to return.

He shuffled over, kneeling down, until he was close to the tent, and then dragged himself along the ground to approach it from the end opposite where the soldiers stood. He lifted the fabric cautiously and looked inside. Amid carpets and silks, in an atmosphere of luxury, there was Pedro de Mora, seated and looking over some papers. Diego saw the rogue from the side. He thought that if he entered quickly and without making noise, he could even go unobserved. He inhaled, clenched his teeth, and walked silently into the tent. He felt the blood coursing in his veins and thought the beating of his heart would give him away, but Don Pedro remained absorbed in his papers. The key to his success was speed.

Pedro de Mora snorted brusquely and Diego jumped. To his great regret, he couldn't cut Mora's throat, however much that was what he wanted, because if he was discovered in the act, the alarm would sound over the encampment and his mission would be compromised.

He decided to act according to plan.

Now was the moment.

He hunched down on the ground and walked up behind him. He felt the scent of the man's hair gather in his nostrils as he passed his arm over his face, covering his mouth. Making use of his other hand and his knowledge of anatomy, he pulled his head backward until he heard a soft crack in his neck. He let him go and made sure he couldn't move. From that moment on, the man would be paralyzed but would remain conscious.

Diego looked into his eyes and exhaled, satisfied; Don Pedro's expression showed he recognized him. He tried to speak, but he couldn't. To avoid unnecessary risks, Diego put a kerchief in his mouth and then looked for the bag with the concoction that Estela had prepared. Don Pedro's pupils contracted, first from surprise, then from fear, imagining his fatal destiny in the hands of the albéitar. He wanted to escape, but incomprehensibly, he couldn't move a single muscle.

Diego came close to his ear and whispered softly.

"Now you'll taste this death potion. I'll give you something to drink that will burn through your entrails and organs one by one. You will feel yourself burning alive, but without fire." Don Pedro de Mora's eyes swelled with panic. "That's how you'll pay for the evil you've done to my family."

Diego found a pitcher of wine and a glass. He filled it and dropped in the powder, stirring it with precision. The mixture began to produce an acrid smoke. Then he pulled back the man's head, took the cloth from his mouth, and opened it as wide as he could. He held it open with his fingers and made him drink the foul liquid. That poison would leave no sign of a violent death. The next morning they would find him dead, and no one would relate it to the presence of the Christian deserters.

Diego cleaned the saliva that had begun to flow from his mouth and watched how the drug's effects were progressing. De Mora's eyes were popping from his head and his mouth grimaced with pain.

Before he left the tent, Diego, thinking of the crippling pains the man must be feeling in his insides just then, wished him a happy stay in hell. He made sure there was no one around and then ran after Estela.

They embraced intensely and then separated for the night.

"Estela, I saw it. . . . I felt how his life drained away in my hands, and then I remembered father, Blanca, and Belinda. And you, too. . . . At last that monster has paid for the terrible harm he did us."

"From now on, our dead will rest in heaven."

X.

———

The air became thick and the wind hardly moved over the hillsides as the sun rose on the sixteenth of July of 1212.

A closed silence accompanied the Christian army while the soldiers took their positions on the broad meadow that separated the Christian camp from that of the Saracens.

On that damp stretch of land, there were nine large groups, each one consisting of two thousand men. Three battalions were at the head, three in the middle, three more in the rear. The first line was composed of heavy cavalry, split into three groups of a hundred horsemen with three behind them.

During the long, tense wait, a flock of swallows flew over the soldiers in their formations, screeching their strange calls. The horses seemed to wish to chant along, for at that moment, there rose up a timid chorus of neighs that grew until it drowned out all else, a deafening concert of grunts and whinnies. The animals were extremely nervous. They could foresee something terrible. They kicked at the ground, their ears pricked up at the smallest sound as they stood there, weighed down by their riders in their heavy suits of armor, holding their swords.

A cool breeze rose up and everyone felt relieved, because the heat of the day was already vexing them.

Amid so many thousands of men, an anonymous rider from the militia in Frías looked around, terrified. He was on the front line and was about to live through the most dangerous experience of his life. The panic made him shake in his saddle.

At his side, a Navarrese knight attempted to comfort him.

"Always watch your right flank. Their attacks will be fast and they will come after that side. When you see them, protect yourself with your shield right away, because the arrows will be coming at you with incredible speed." With his sword, he pointed at a group of soldiers just in front of them, only a quarter league away. "Those are Arab horsemen, and beside them are the Turkish archers. Those coursers they ride can almost fly. You'll see them coming and going and changing direction with a speed that you won't be able to believe."

"I'll try to keep my eye on them, señor," the young man said in a choked voice. He tried to straighten his helmet, but just then it fell off; it was too big for him.

"How old are you, boy?" The Navarrese knight felt compassion for him and decided to try and protect him.

"Sixteen, señor."

"Is this the first time you've seen war?"

"The first, yes."

The man was afraid for him, knowing his inexperience. He was on a beautiful Arabian mare, but his arms were shoddy and inadequate. An old leather cuirass barely covered him, and his sword was too short. Nor was he outfitted with a lance.

"What are your defenses?"

He showed him a battered shield.

"I also took Communion and listened to Mass this morning, and God will protect me. . . ."

"Don't ever abandon your faith, son, but God's protection won't be enough today. Take my sword," he said, exchanging his for the boy's. "It's long and heavy, but it will serve you better when you strike at an enemy's chest. It's sharp and it will open deep mortal wounds. The one you have is only good for fighting on the ground."

"And you?" The boy was surprised by his generous act. "How will you defend yourself?"

The nobleman pointed to another, bigger sword, and to his lance.

"We are the front lines of this great army, the right flank. We are fighting side by side with the knights and family of Don Diego López de Haro there in the center and with the Aragonese, headed by their ensign, who are over there on the left. When we see the standard of the lord of Biscay waving, the one with the two black wolves on the white background, we will attack. We'll be the first to do so. When that happens, push the side of your horse close to mine, and do the same with the man to your left. We'll form a strong and unbreachable wall that will break apart their formations. Once that's happened, and we're through the first few rows of men, swing your sword with all your might and keep pushing. Cut and stab and don't think about them being men like us. If you do, you've lost, and they'll kill you first."

"I understand, señor. . . . I won't flinch," he affirmed, now more convinced.

"That is what our three kings expect of us. Never before have those three joined hands in battle. Look at them, they're behind you making up the three rearguard formations. Each one bears the standard of his kingdom. Mine, Navarre, is to the right. In the middle is Alfonso VIII of Castile, and to the left Pedro II of Aragon. Today, young man, we're making history."

"What is your name?" the boy from Frías asked, looking at him with an almost filial respect.

"Iñigo de Zúñiga."

Behind them, the grand master of the Order of Santiago rallied his men, reminding them of their duties in battle.

"The soldiers of Christ never retreat!" he shouted, enraged. "Do you hear me?" The man rode around his followers, observing their expressions.

In unison, those men, with their stern faces and gravelly voices, pledged their unshakable commitment. Their huge horses stamped at the ground energetically.

"Then listen to me and let these words be engraved in your hearts." He looked at the men gathered closest to him. "We have come here to win freedom for the sons of God." He was shouting now. "And in the defense of our faith, we will use the weapons and the courage that can only belong to those who bear the truth."

He stopped to examine their faces. In those glances there was fearlessness, willingness to give all, and lust to water the ground with the blood of infidels.

"Let no one strike fear in you!" He raised his powerful voice. "You have been selected for this holy mission. And if you feel they are defeating you, look up into the sky. God will help you to go on swinging your weapon against the enemy."

"War, war, war . . ." they all chanted, pointing their swords in the air.

Behind them, King Sancho VII rode an enormous Neapolitan horse, looking for Alfonso VIII's position. He found him beneath a standard different from the one he normally flew: the emblem was a yellow castle under an image of the Virgin Mary. The Aragonese was answering the call of the Castilian, along with the archbishop of Narbonne and the archbishop of Toledo.

"Together we have agreed as to what our tactic will be. We know that God is on our side and we have been blessed at a solemn Mass before coming here. We possess the greatest army our enemy has ever faced . . ."

Alfonso VIII looked over the battlefield and stopped at al-Nasir's tent. Vivid red in color, it was surrounded by a rectangular palisade of grand proportions guarded by no fewer than five hundred men. "Therefore, gentlemen, this is the day and hour of the truth."

"Today, the troops of Jesus Christ shall win!" the archbishop of Narbonne added, shouting.

The Ultramontane's comment was cheered on by a half-dozen bishops from Castile and Aragon, who were riding into battle like any other soldier.

Don Álvaro Núñez de Lara approached the three kings and requested their attention.

"The cavalry is already prepared for the first sally. It will charge straight ahead in a tight formation. The two hills on each side of the plain will help us, for there is barely space for the enemy to try and slip by our flanks, as happened at Alarcos." Alfonso VIII remembered what had happened just as he was at the point of breaching the enemy's front, when they had been surrounded by the light cavalry and their forces were annihilated.

"How are their troops arranged?" Archbishop Rodrigo Ximénez de Rada asked Don Álvaro.

"They have placed the volunteers in the middle and on the front line. They are foreigners, fanatics who have come to war without any fear of dying. They are normally wild and don't fight particularly well. Beside them are the light cavalry—they are deadly. By my estimation, there are no fewer than five thousand Arabs among them, professional soldiers from the various tribes in the empire. With them, we have to be on our guard, we've seen what skilled riders they are and they are rightly famed for their violence. They will try to disperse us and break our ranks." He pointed to the next group. "In the second row there is a dense group of Andalusian knights." He thought of Diego, wishing he had been successful in his mission. "And behind, in front of the caliph's tent, are his best troops; thousands of fierce Almohad warriors and perhaps ten thousand Turkish archers."

"Is there anything new concerning what we spoke of yesterday?" King Alfonso intervened.

"The local militias are our worst-trained and worst-armed fighters," Pedro of Aragon said. "We need to mix them in with our knights. That way they can protect one another. That will be important when they fight side by side."

"Agreed," Sancho said, speaking for the rest of them, and commanded his ensign, Gómez Garceiz, to transmit this order to the men.

Then a number of troops were rearranged, and everything was ready.

The signal was given.

Don Diego López de Haro began the first charge, speeding up as they descended a slight hill. The Christian troops were silent, but the Saracens banged their drums, hundreds or even thousands of them, and the entire Arab contingent shouted infernally.

The terrain separating them was irregular, full of brush and large stones that forced the densely packed cavalry to open up a bit.

From the Saracen side, the Muslim volunteers, seeing that wall of men approach them, recited sutras from the Koran. The enormous horses panted furiously, picking up speed as their hooves pounded against the dry earth.

The echo of the drums grew in intensity, its rhythm matched by the galloping of the horses. Hundreds of Arab riders pushed ahead, launching arrows and trying without success to surround the enemy.

Just before Don Diego and his Biscayan soldiers reached the enemy's front lines, the drums and the shouting fell silent. Even their breathing stopped. All that could be heard was the galloping and the roaring of the horses. Fewer than ten yards away, Don Diego gave the order to aim their lances.

With the first clash, the Muslim advance was stopped and their troops dispersed with almost no defense. The men under the lord of Biscay were able to penetrate to the second line, where the Andalusians stood ready. Among them was Diego de Malagón and the rest of his alleged deserters.

Suddenly something happened that none of them expected. To the surprise of the Saracens, the Andalusian horsemen, heavily armed and with horses as fearsome as their own, lowered their arms and turned, abandoning the front. That was their way of returning the insults they had suffered from their Almohad masters and avenging the death of Ibn Qadis, one of their most beloved leaders.

The night before, Diego de Malagón convinced them, saying they would be considered brothers of the Castilians, sharing their destiny with the people of the north. He said that he was speaking in the name of Alfonso VIII and that this promise came directly from him. If they were victorious together, they would share the spoils together and their erstwhile disagreements would be forgotten.

"It worked, Álvaro," King Alfonso VIII shouted euphorically when he saw the war was turning in his favor despite the numerical inferiority of the Castilians. "That retreat has just undone our enemy's strategy. Now we'll see what the caliph can do against us."

Inside the Almohad palisade, al-Nasir had just ordered his sister, two of his wives, and his favorite concubine to leave him in peace to think. They went to a second tent and he remained on the ground praying to Allah.

He felt he was blessed, just like Saladin, who had toppled Jerusalem, defeating the crusaders and retuning it to the faith of Islam. Like him, al-Nasir would receive help from heaven to win the war against the forces of evil.

"God spoke the truth and the demon lied . . ." he repeated over and over, repeating the words of that storied leader when he found himself at the gates of the Holy City.

Seated on his shield, he opened the most elegant of his Korans and recited several verses, shortly after ordering the Turks to chase down and kill the Andalusian traitors. He also gave the signal for the first counterattack.

Helped along by the slope, thousands of Almohads rushed toward the Christian advance and soon managed to break it apart. The Christians kept fighting, separated and exhausted, stopped short on the land and trying futilely to progress uphill. In that unfortunate position, they were easy targets for the archers, and they began to fall by the hundreds beneath their arrows.

The second Christian attack, with the Templars and Calatravans at its head, reached the positions held by Don Diego López de Haro and came to his aid, though soon they were pushed back as well by the Almohads' skilled cavalry and the effects of a new rain of arrows. Some, alarmed by their poor progress, began to retreat to lower ground, where they could take better positions, but from the Christians' rearguard, King Alfonso VIII saw this as a retreat. He even thought it could be the lord of Biscay himself.

He understood it was time for him to act. He made a sign to the other kings and leapt into the melee, followed by the monarchs of Navarre and Aragon.

At his side was Archbishop Rodrigo Ximénez de Rada.

"Archbishop, you and I will die here if we don't triumph!" The priest had unsheathed his sword and looked toward the enemy front with eyes bursting with bravery. Though some might have given up the battle, he preferred death to turning back with a humiliating defeat.

"We have to break through the final line of soldiers and reach the palisade," Sancho VII shouted, coming up on Alfonso from his right flank. "If we strike him there, it will be a mortal wound."

Diego observed the course of the attack headed by the kings, for he himself was already close to the palisade, where Estela was located. He tried to make his way up there, slaying anyone who got in his way.

Al-Nasir had protected himself behind a solid defensive barrier: an enormous wooden fence reinforced with thick chains. Behind it there was a second army formed by nearly five hundred Imesebelen: the caliph's personal guards. They were bound together at the knees and some were even buried up to their thighs. Packed closely together, they completely surrounded the place where their master waited.

In this way, if the Christians managed to break through the first wooden obstacle, they would then meet another one made of men, more vicious, and ready to die in their caliph's defense.

Sabba went up the hill, panting, trying to reach the top at the same time as the Christian monarchs and bleeding from a lance wound she's received in the thigh. Diego hadn't seen it and was spurring her on, driving his heels into her ribs to make her run faster.

The mare looked at her wound and saw that apart from the pain, it was bleeding severely. When she saw her master Diego, she clenched her jaws and pulled the last bit of strength from her heart to take him to where he'd asked.

The first monarch to arrive at the palisade was the king of Navarre. He saw the impossibility of leaping over the barrier and had his horse turn around, having it kick against the wood with its hind legs. After just three attempts, he managed to break the chains and knock down several posts. Inside, a human mass of raging Africans awaited them, swords in hands.

Apart from the king, three hundred knights burst in as well. There, a ferocious hand-to-hand skirmish broke out. Because the archers didn't have the necessary distance to fire accurately, they now had to face the Christians' swords. The Almohad troops, without the support of the Turks, began to fall at the hands of the crusaders' excellent weaponry.

A group of Calatravans also plunged into the interior of the palisade just before Diego. Many dismounted to engage with the black-skinned troops who were immobilized over the terrain.

Diego managed to glimpse al-Nasir seated on his shield, holding to his breast the Koran that Diego had hoped to get hold of in Seville. In anguish, Diego thought of the fate of his sister, whom he had previously seen peek from the caliph's tent. If the Christians mistook her for a Moor, they could kill her.

The only way to protect her, he thought, was to punch through those bloodthirsty guards and make it to the tent first. Without dismounting, he pressed his knees into Sabba and took his sword in one hand and his lance in the other. He shouted with immeasurable fury and charged at the men, striking them with his weapons until he knew they were dead. He pushed on as he could while Sabba bore the fury of their weapons. Some sliced her skin, others wounded her forelegs, and one stabbed her viciously in the top of a hoof. The same happened to the horses of the other crusaders who tried to reach the caliph from different angles.

At a certain moment, when the king of Navarre found himself close to al-Nasir, an Arab soldier approached his leader on a young mare and seemed to lift him on it in an instant, leaving his sacred book on the ground. That providential soldier prodded his animal to flee to the rear-guard inside the palisade. Many others followed suit.

Diego saw a number of crusaders make it to the center of the caliph's encampment and head toward the tent. The infernal racket around them prevented them from hearing him when he shouted not to touch the women.

He saw that only four more soldiers stood between him and the center, and he pushed ahead, stabbing at them with his weapons without compassion. When there was just one left, he didn't see that the man wasn't buried to his thighs like the others, but rather kneeling.

Once he reached him, the Imesebelen leapt upward and faced Diego. Trying to avoid him, Sabba bucked quickly to one side. Diego fell to the ground. The guard aimed a long dagger at his heart and ran at him so he wouldn't have time to react. From inside al-Nasir's tent, Estela saw Tijmud and her brother and tried to stop them, but neither could hear.

The African's weapon was aimed to kill and he moved as fast as lightning. Diego saw it and knew instantly there was no time to react. But then, he saw Sabba's body suddenly come between him and the warrior, absorbing the mortal strike. The man's strength was such that the steel plunged straight into her heart. The loyal animal fell between them, looking at her master, her friend, and her only regret was that she couldn't protect him until the end of his days.

The Imesebelen was stunned at what had happened. Diego took advantage of that moment to pounce on him and slice his neck from one side to the other in a single agile movement.

"Nooo . . ." A sharp, painful cry called his attention. It was Estela, running to them with a completely broken expression.

"Tijmud!" To Diego's astonishment, she embraced that man, who had begun to drown in his own blood. "He wasn't like the others."

Diego, without understanding, immediately approached Sabba. He looked at the wound in her side and understood, racked with dread, that it was fatal. His eyes filled immediately with tears.

She made a last effort to whinny; her face was happy. Diego spoke slowly to her, knowing this was a special moment, and he spoke to her with respect. He promised to remember her forever and caressed her as she'd always liked.

Leaning on her neck, he kissed her, and his kisses were laced with his own tears. The mare coughed blood and Diego understood that soon, it would be their last good-bye.

"Nothing has made these last years of my life happier. . . . You have been my tie to the past, the memory of my home, the greatest gift of my father." The mare closed her eyes and sighed, with little strength left. Her expression was peaceful, and Diego understood. Sabba was happy because she had given herself completely to her master one more time, the last one.

The animal turned her head a bit to bring her nostrils to Diego's face and smell his breath so she wouldn't forget it on that long journey she was about to begin.

"We will ride together again, Sabba, I promise you. We will ride on the blue sands of heaven, leaping over the white clouds as if they were dunes, and we will feel the south wind at our backs, forever. . . ."

And Sabba died.

XI.

———

The wounded returned to the encampment by the hundreds.

Mencía, together with twenty other women, took them in, though often they had no idea how to treat their wounds.

One of them, very young, she recognized as soon as she'd begun to treat him. It was that boy she had met the night before hidden in his tent. He had a deep wound in his belly, and parts of his entrails were sticking out. Mencía knew he would die.

The boy recognized her and raised a trembling hand.

"You are my angel . . ." He coughed a mouthful of blood.

"You fought like a man."

"Will I die?" His eyes begged her for sincerity.

She paused, not knowing what words to choose.

"Your silence answers my question." A powerful jab of pain made the boy bend over the blanket that separated him from the ground.

Mencía cleaned his face with a cloth and stroked his cheek while the boy felt his soul drain from his body. His gaze clouded over, but then it glimmered again.

"I beg you, don't leave me alone."

"I will not." She kissed his forehead and prayed for him.

The boy felt like he was drowning, and in that last moment, he looked into Mencía's eyes. In their blue, he thought he saw the gates of heaven, and he died with a smile.

Mencía let him go and covered him with a blanket.

She looked around, frightened by so much pain. The worst face of war surrounded her, the senselessness of so much hate.

And then suddenly she heard something like a song sounding in the distance. At first nobody understood the words the soldiers were chanting, but then someone shouted "Victory!" with all his might, and the echo of that joy reverberated through the hospital tent. Some women ran out to see what was happening and immediately returned, overjoyed.

"They're singing the 'Te Deum,'" one shouted. "We've won the war."

Full of excitement, they listened in complete silence to the throats of thousands of men in the distance intoning that solemn chant of thanksgiving in a single chorus. Their voices rose to heaven from a tract of earth soaked with blood. Across the plains lay thousands of corpses, and with them all their hopes and dreams, now dead.

Mencía went out as well, overwhelmed. Her gaze ran over the battlefield first and then the neighboring mountains. Even they seemed to echo the collective joy and relief.

From the Christian encampment she saw a number of women running to a place where their husbands stood, still living, or else lay on the ground, already the heroes of legends. With the same impulse and intentions, Mencía followed.

She had to dodge men and horses, the wounded and the dead, until she reached the hill where she saw a large group of combatants reunited.

"Diego!" she began to shout, losing her breath as she mounted the slope. "Diego!"

Some soldiers turned when she approached them. In their faces was a mix of pain and joy, of deep grief blended with the sweet taste of glory. Many looked among the dead, trying to find some friend or companion, but no one could tell her how to find the person she was seeking.

"Dear God, please lead me to him. . . ."

Mencía rolled up her skirts and continued climbing until she reached what looked like a half-destroyed palisade. There, terrible human bloodshed had taken place. Mountains of corpses with no one to grieve for them. Alone.

"Diego!" she shouted again, horrified by all that she saw.

Suddenly she could make out a man crouching over a horse beside a woman who appeared to be Arab. Both turned to her. Mencía looked at him, and he at her. Diego stood up with an astonished expression and walked toward her, slow at first, then running to fall into her open arms.

"Mencía . . ." He embraced her fiercely, grasping her body without understanding why she was there. They spun over the earth, feeling immensely happy, though all around them, there was nothing but death and disaster. They couldn't help it.

Diego looked again, unable to believe it was her, his beloved Mencía.

"I only came here to find you, my love. . . ." She kissed his cheeks, his forehead, then his lips, passionately, infinitely, sunken in a sea of tears and feelings.

"Do you still love me?" Mencía sought his eyes.

"I never stopped. But . . . your husband?" He pushed her away, though that was the last thing he wanted, and listened with great relief to her tell him she was now a widow. Then he kissed her lips ardently, unrushed, savoring them forever.

Estela watched them, moved, though she still felt sad for Tijmud. Without knowing what brought them together, Estela embraced Mencía when Diego introduced them. And she saw Mencía's brilliant smile and her warm gaze. In her face she saw the traces of other sufferings, maybe similar to the ones she herself had undergone. Her brother was with her, at last, and no one and nothing could tear them apart. She embraced him again and cried out all her pain, feeling the warm throb of the blood that had united them forever, despite the long separation. And Mencía held them as well, now a member of that small family that had been so much larger long ago.

Diego felt his father's soul close to them, and the souls of Belinda and Blanca, of his beloved mother and also of Sabba. They were present there too, happy to the end, bound together by destiny, forever.

And beneath his feet, Diego felt the damp soil. When he looked, he saw it was blood, all that the mountain had been unable to absorb. And then he remembered those ominous words of the Jewish sorcerer:

". . . And the mountain shall sweat blood, glory, and love."

Hours later, Diego was called to a meeting in the tent behind the Almohads' palisade. He found it strange that the request should be so urgent.

In the company of Mencía and Estela, he walked to the outside of the tent that had belonged to the caliph and saw the three royal ensigns.

"Congratulations, Diego. . . ." The Aragonese García Romeu shook his hand and pulled him aside to make room for the Navarrese, Gómez Garceiz. His friend Álvaro Núñez de Lara also embraced him, then pushed him inside the tent. Without understanding anything, he went in and was instantly paralyzed.

Inside he was awaited by King Alfonso VIII of Castile, King Sancho VII of Navarre, and King Pedro II of Aragon. Diego knelt before them and looked to both sides to see who else was there.

"What is it that brings us here?" he whispered to Don Álvaro, who remained at his side.

"A small matter . . ."

"And what is it?"

"Diego de Malagón!" King Alfonso of Castile shouted.

Diego stood at attention.

"Despite your humble origins, throughout this glorious campaign you have accumulated more than sufficient merits to deserve the high honor of being named a knight. What do you respond? Will you accept the honorable but heavy responsibility that this title brings with it?"

"I . . . A knight?" Diego looked at Mencía and then at Estela. Though all seemed elated, he couldn't believe it. "Your words, Your Majesty, fill me with honor, but I don't know. . . . The truth is that what I love above all is my profession, and now that the war is over, I would like to practice it forever. To be a knight brings other obligations and I wouldn't want—"

"Wait, do not say more. We are still not finished," King Pedro II of Aragon now spoke. "We understand that your case is not like others, and for that reason, we have decided to name a new title for your profession. Therefore, from today forward, you will be known all over as Knight Albéitar to the Three Kingdoms."

Diego was overwhelmed upon hearing that and immediately accepted the honor.

"Dress him now with the tunic!" the gigantic Navarrese bellowed. Gómez Garceiz helped Diego don a white garment open at both sides. "This cloth represents the purity of soul your calling demands," he explained.

García Romeu laid a red cape over his shoulders.

"The color red symbolizes that blood you will be pledged to spill henceforward for God and your king."

And his friend Don Álvaro Núñez de Lara brought over a pair of brown shoes and told him to put them on.

"With these you shall touch the earth, to which all of us will return. They represent your willingness to die."

Finally they put a belt around him and handed him a sword.

At that moment, the three monarchs unsheathed their weapons and dubbed him on the shoulder.

"I, Alfonso VIII, king of Castile, Toledo, and Trasierra, dub you, Diego de Malagón, a knight albéitar of Castile."

"And I, Sancho VII, second him, as king of Navarre."

"And I, Pedro II, do the same in my capacity as king of Aragon."

Mencía and Estela hugged each other, proud of what was taking place.

With his head still bowed and bursting with emotion, Diego remembered his father lying on the verge of death on his bedstead.

He was transplanted to the inn, years before.

For a few moments, those words of congratulations and the wishes for good fortune that everyone offered were far away from him, and he only heard again the voice of his father when years back, he had made him swear he would seek out a better destiny:

"Dream high and fly like the eagles. That's what you should do, to reach life's highest peaks. Look for wise people, learn from them. Cleave to your ambitions, so long as you hurt no one. Always do your work well, never give anyone reason to rebuke you. And whatever the contest, play to win. Don't let anybody make you their vassal, and even if you were born into a humble home, don't think you're any less dignified for it. If you fight with valor, you will achieve whatever you go after. And last of all, take care of your sisters, protect them, your blood runs in their veins. . . . My son, never forget you had a father who loved you more than anything in the world, and who will one day look down on you from heaven full of pride."

In front of everyone, Diego stood up, raised his eyes to heaven, and exclaimed:

"Father, it is all for you. . . . I owed it to you!"

The History

The historical background I make use of in novelizing the life of the albéitar Diego de Malagón is not at all by mere chance. The narration begins in
1195, at the defeat of Castile in Alarcos, and ends in 1212 with the Battle of
the Navas of Tolosa. Seventeen years that, besides signifying an important
chapter in the life of a person, reflect, in this case, episodes with their own
particular charm and with enormous importance for the history of Spain.

The Battle of the Navas of Tolosa marked the before and after in the
conquest of Al-Andalus. It was one of the first pitched battles in an age
when complex military formations were unusual, and raids and skirmishes
were more common.

At the dawn of the thirteenth century, the map of Spain was divided
into six territories: the five Christian kingdoms of Aragon, Navarre, Castile, León, and Portugal, and to the south, in constant combat, Al-Andalus
under the control of the Almohads.

Of all the Christian kings, it was the personality of Alfonso VIII of Castile that most inspired me when I delved into his biography. Over a reign
of more than fifty years, he enacted the dream long cherished by his ancestors, the reconquest of Al-Andalus, and he was thereby the first to achieve
the unification of all the northern Christian kingdoms. Alfonso VIII was a
great strategist and brought significant economic benefits to the territories
under his control. He knew how to surround himself with men of enormous talent who helped to achieve a powerful Castile: a kingdom of free
men and a land of opportunity for all those who were not of noble birth.

The historical context of the novel has helped me to reflect on the circumstances and events that made the dream of the Castilian king a reality.
All the events that accompany the life and journeys of Diego of Malagón
are historical, as well as the places where the various subplots play out.

In some cases it was not easy to document the lives of some of the persons who appear in the novel; this was the case with the king of Navarre,
for example. With him, I experienced great difficulties in reconstructing his
trajectory, and there were moments when it seemed to me that history had
wished to forget him. His anomalous relationship with the Almohad princess and his long residence in African lands coincided with his loss of the city

of Vitoria and the territory of Guipúzcoa, an absence that must have been misunderstood at the time by his subjects and by historians later on.

Another similar case was the exceptional life of the fifth lord of Biscay, Don Diego López de Haro. His story was exceptional. He went from royal ensign, and thus the firmest supporter the Castilian monarch had, to his worst nightmare. Due to family problems and difficulties in his territories, Don Diego asked to renounce his Castilian subjecthood, and King Alfonso chased him over half of Spain until he found him holed up in the spectacular fortress of the city of Estella-Lizarra. According to contemporary chronicles, the thickness of its walls and the height of its defenses were so impressive that the building was impenetrable, as well as being the most beautiful that had been constructed in the Christian kingdoms that make up present-day Spain. The king of Castile laid siege for months outside its walls, together with the monarch from León, but never managed to exact defeat and eventually abandoned this enterprise. Sadly there remain only vestiges of this magnificent structure, but the ruins can be visited today.

Years later, the episode in which Diego López de Haro facilitates the flight from the battlefront of King Pedro II of Aragon did indeed take place. Afterward, the lord of Biscay joined the court of León, at that time opposed to Castile, and reaped great privileges therefrom. Later he would return to the Castilian court, their former disagreements forgiven, and would help combat the caliph al-Nasir in the Battle of the Navas. In his testament, King Alfonso VIII honors his name and recognizes his services to the crown, naming his the most loyal of all his men.

There existed a Castilian traitor, a sworn enemy of Alfonso VIII, who allied himself with the Almohad caliphs to fight against the Christians, though his name was not Pedro de Mora. He was known as "the Castilian" and his name was Pedro Fernández de Castro, son of one of the most noble bloodlines of Castile and León, the Castros, a family with exceptional territorial sway and enormous influence with the court. Though I admit his personality inspired me to create Don Pedro de Mora, I have tried not to confuse fact and fiction and have added a particular little touch of wickedness to my character.

With my modest contribution, I have introduced real names into the plot to make the events and actions in which these men participated more comprehensible and also to render homage to the bravery and commitment they showed to the noble ideals of the Reconquest. For the sake of truth, however, I have also tried to reflect the disagreements that divided the different kingdoms, the territorial struggles that brought them into conflict, and the clashes and failures that came one after the other until at last their forces were united in that monumental fight that came to be called the Battle of the Navas of Tolosa.

To re-create the events that took place around that famous battle, I have relied on numerous relatively recent works, but especially on the writings of one of its participants: the archbishop of Toledo, Rodrigo Ximénez de Rada, in his Latin chronicle of the kings of Castile.

The Profession of Veterinarian
in the Middle Ages

With far more passion than any other objective, I have tried to make this book into an homage to my own profession, to the thousands and thousands of men and women who practiced it across the centuries, who were called by numerous names: *hippiatrus, veterinarius, albéitar, farrier, horseleech,* and now, *veterinarian.* I honestly believe that, besides being the most beautiful of professions, it constitutes a professional corps that has always lived in service of the common good, by concerning itself with the care of animals.

Though for many modern readers, their only relation with the veterinarian profession concerns the care provided for our pets, it is in fact an ancient profession, of enormous importance given the vital role that work animals, and especially horses, played in men's lives.

The first document that mentions the work of the veterinarian and, specifically, the prices charged for the extraction of a tooth and other services appears in Babylon, in the famous code of Hammurabi (around 1800 b.c.). In the biblical city of Ugarit, there have also been discovered tablets bearing fragments of a long treatise laying out the assorted ways of curing certain illnesses of horses, and it attributes its authority to a stable master of the king of Ugarit.

In ancient Egypt, priests possessed great knowledge of the healing of animals, and wisdom was considered to possess great sacred value, given the importance of animal figures in the Egyptian religious system. In the Ebers Papyrus (1500 b.c.), treatments and remedies for the cure of oral abscesses and gingivitis in horses are discussed.

In the ancient culture of China, there also exist references to this profession. In the very old book of Zuo Zhuan, the manner of determining the age and health of horses by an examination of their teeth is described. There are also written references to the benefits of acupuncture in horses, by General Bo Le in the year 659 b.c.

The greatest step forward in the discipline is to be found in ancient Greece. Hippocrates, Pelagonius, Aristotle, and other wise men compiled the better part of antique wisdom in their books, and their own experience as well, to identify and resolve certain infirmities that plagued animals and, above all, horses. In Greece, those who possessed the necessary knowledge were called *hippiatros* (horse doctor) or *ktiniatros* (cattle doctor).

The veterinary profession gained military importance in the Roman Empire, when the *veterinarii* were entrusted with the care of horses in the *veterinaria*: spaces reserved especially for them on the Roman battlefields.

Cavalry was then, and has continued to be, an essential part of armies' battle strategy, and therefore the wisdom of veterinarians became, for some civilizations, a matter of state policy.

Throughout this novel, there are countless occasions when the term *albéitar* is employed. From the first inspiration I had as to how the life of Diego de Malagón would unfold, I knew I wanted him to be an albéitar. With that decision, I have attempted to give due recognition to the importance of that figure in the history of veterinary medicine not only in Spain, but throughout the world.

The diffusion of the term *albéitar* throughout the Christian kingdoms of medieval Europe is an outgrowth of Spain's influence and has an obvious Arabian origin. It arises with Al-Andalus and was in common use until well into the nineteenth century. The term is common throughout all the kingdoms of Visigoth Hispania in the Middle Ages and became a source of great prestige as a result of the skillful techniques the albéitars possessed and the effectiveness of their interventions. The term reached as far as the Basque country, though it only later penetrated Catalonia and Aragon, where functions similar to those of the albéitar were practiced by what were then known as *menescales* in Catalonia and as *mariscales* in the rest of the empire. They soon formed guilds and brotherhoods in Catalonia and Aragon to teach the profession; those of Barcelona were of particular note.

This profession has its roots as well in the blacksmiths' forges, as blacksmiths also often performed some of the common jobs of albéitars and were the forebears of a more ordered and broader discipline.

The rapid diffusion of the albéitar's art during the medieval era is owed to the admiration felt by the monarchs and noblemen of Christendom for Arabian culture, which had been nourished by the wisdom of Byzantium, the repository of Greek wisdom. An example of this can be found in the *Partidas* of Alfonso X, the Wise.

There is no doubt whatsoever that the origin of the word *albéitar* is Arabic. In fact, today countries where that language is spoken today refer to the veterinarian as "al-baitar" and to his profession of "baitara."

Horses

I love horses. I consider them the animals that have served man most loyally throughout the course of history. In *The Horse Healer*, they have a special role, particularly in the case of the mare Sabba. Her breed, the Arabian, carries the bloodline found in the majority of the horses living in the world today. The Spanish and Lusitano, the purebred English, and the quarter horse all owe the better part of their genes to the Arabian. It is undoubtedly one of the most beautiful breeds that exists today.

The importance and great value horses had in the Middle Ages meant that the greater part of the efforts and research of the veterinary profession was devoted to them. The exercise of veterinary science was divided into two rather different activities, which could almost be called specialties: the military branch, largely the responsibility of the aforementioned *mariscales* and *menescales*, and the civilian, which was largely the domain of the albéitars. Moving forward to the twelfth or thirteenth century, it is necessary to recall that not all people had the means to own a horse, and that it was an extremely valuable asset. They were used for work in the fields, were for many the sole means of transport, and served as a weapon in an age when there were very few periods of peace.

One of the oldest books I have been able to consult on the albéitar's craft is *Lo libre dels cavayls*, a Catalan version of another manuscript written in the twelfth century, by an unknown author considered to be of Castilian origin. Many of the technical references that pop up in the novel have their origin in this work, as well as in others that were published in the fourteenth and fifteenth centuries, somewhat later than the adventures of Diego de Malagón.

There were many books in that era that dealt with the illnesses of horses, many in the context of treatises on agronomy. One shouldn't forget that manuals of chivalry also included references on the cures for various common horse illnesses as well as simple recommendations for how horses should be kept. From the fifteenth century on, the treatises on the albéitar's art begin to multiply and to be found in universities throughout Europe. Apprenticeship becomes institutionalized and there comes to be an official exam for those who wish to practice the profession in the age of the Catholic monarchs, when they instituted the Royal Tribunal of Protoalbeitarato.

The Yeguada de Las Marismas existed just as I have referred to it in the novel; for its size, and for the quality of animals it contained, it must have been a marvel. I have tried to express in words the feelings I imagine a person might have had, confronting a spectacle of such proportions in that day and age. Even today a few specimens can still be seen running free in the marshlands close to the lovely village of El Rocío, a temple to the glory of the horse and a unique place for these animals that have lent such great and disinterested service to humanity.

Relations between Characters, by Order of Appearance

Diego de Malagón: Young albéitar's apprentice.

Pedro de Mora: Traitor to the king of Castile, ambassador and collaborator of the Almohad caliphs.

Kabirma: Horse trader in Toledo.

Fatima: Daughter of Kabirma.

Sajjad: Galib's stable keeper.

Galib: Albéitar in Toledo, exiled from Al-Andalus by the Almohads.

Benazir: Wife of Galib and daughter of the Persian ambassador in Seville.

Najla: Daughter of Caliph Yusuf and sister of al-Nasir.

Marcos de Burgos: Friend of Diego.

Friar Servando: Cistercian monk in the monastery of Fitero and horse healer.

Tijmud: Imesebelen. Guard to Princess Najla.

Mencía Fernández de Azagra: Daughter of the esteemed Navarrese nobleman Fernando Ruiz de Azagra, second lord of Albarracín, and Doña Teresa.

Giulio Morigatti: Neapolitan horseleech employed by García Romeu and enemy of Diego. "Horseleech" is an approximate English equivalent to the term "meniscal," which was widely used in Catalonia. They were quite often foreigners.

Fabián Pardo: Aragonese knight and chief justice of King Pedro II of Aragon.

Veturia: Diego and Marcos's servant in Cuéllar.

Sancha de Laredo: Abused woman protected by Diego.

Efraím: Jewish mage in the town of Cuéllar.

Bruno de Oñate: Calatravan knight, in charge of the Calatravan fortress of Salvatierra.

Glossary of Historical Figures, in Alphabetical Order

Abu Zayd: Last Almohad governor of the taifa of Valencia. Friend of the Azagra family of Albarracín.

Alfonso IX: King of León between 1188 and 1230. In his kingdom he was known as Alfonso VIII, but because of the name's coincidence with that of the Castilian king, he changed his numeration to IX.

Alfonso VIII: King of Castile, Najera, Extremadura, and Asturias from 1158 to 1214. Responsible for the Battle of the Navas of Tolosa. Great strategist and defender of the unity of Iberians peoples against the Almohads. Advocated the concession of charters and privileges to numerous cities and villages in Castile, against the wishes of their nobles.

Álvaro Núñez de Lara: Ensign to Alfonso VIII from 1199 to 1201 and later between 1208 and 1217. Son-in-law to Diego López de Haro. Married to Urraca López de Haro.

Diego López de Haro: Lord of Biscay and ensign to King Alfonso during three periods: 1183–1187, 1188–1199, and 1206–1208. In this position, he participated in the Battle of Alarcos in 1195 and in the Battle of the Navas of Tolosa in 1212. Married to Toda López de Azagra, of Navarrese extraction.

García Romeu: Ensign to King Pedro II of Aragon.

Gerardo de Cremona: Translator from Toledo.

Gómez Garceiz: Ensign to King Sancho of Navarre.

Ibn Qadis: Cadi from Andalusia, lord of recovered fortress of Salvatierra, and last governor of the fortress of Calatrava before it fell to the troops of Alfonso VIII in 1212. His death, ordered by al-Nasir himself, who was indignant over that humiliation, provoked an enormous outcry among the Andalusian troops, a key factor in the Almohad defeat in the Battle of the Navas.

Muhammad al-Nasir: Son of al-Mansur, caliph. Lost the battle of the Navas of Tolosa. Builder of the Giralda in Seville, the capital of the caliphate. An identical copy was also raised in Marrakesh. Died of poisoning one year after the Battle of the Navas.

Muhammad ben Mardanis: Also known as "the Wolf King." Commanded the taifa of Valencia and ceded Albarracín to the Azagras in 1170.

Pedro II: King of the crown of Aragon from 1196. Cousin of Alfonso VIII of Castile. After his heroic participation in the Battle of the Navas, died in Muret defending his Cathar subjects.

Rodrigo Ximénez de Rada: Archbishop of Toledo, highly cultured historian and author of *De rebus Hispanie*, a chronicle labeled a *Gothic history*. Advocate and funder of the crusading army that reached the Navas of Tolosa. Loyal collaborator of King Alfonso VIII, he was highly praised in the chronicles. Obtained the declaration that sparked off the crusade from the pope and spread its message beyond the Pyrenees.

Sancho Fernández: Son of King Fernando II of León and Urraca López de Haro, sister of the lord of Biscay. Heir to the throne of León and step-brother to King Alfonso IX. Though Leonese by birth, he always fought on the side of Castile.

Sancho VII: King of Navarre from 1194, known as Sancho the Strong. Between six and seven feet in height, wealthy, ill-famed for his negligence of his territories and his untoward love affair with an Almohad princess. After the Battle of the Navas of Tolosa, in memory of the latter, he placed the chains of a stockade on the arms of Navarre, and in the center, an emerald, symbol of the Koran left behind by al-Nasir.

Yusuf al-Mansur: Almohad caliph, winner of the Battle of Alarcos in 1195, married to the Christian Zaida. Father of Caliph al-Nasir.

Glossary of Locations Where the Action of the Novel Takes Place

Albarracín: During the Middle Ages, it was known as Santa María de Albarracín, a small taifa led by a Berber family with the last name al-Banu-Razin, from whom it derives its name. Later conquered by Muhammad ben Mardanis, "the Wolf King," and passed on to a Navarrese family, the Azagras, becoming thenceforth an independent territory. In 1284 it was incorporated into the crown of Aragon.

Cuéllar: After its conquest by the Saracens by King Alfonse VI of Castile, it was repopulated and shortly afterward granted a charter. The Castilian monarchy did not wish for the reconquered territories to be governed by the nobility or the church, as happened in the former feudal regions of the north, and therefore ceded them to residents arrived from Castile and Navarre, who would pay tribute, thereby guaranteeing support in times of war and compromising the power of institutions not loyal to the crown. In the twelfth and thirteenth centuries, Cuéllar was important for its sheep herds, the wool trade, and its wood. During those two centuries, numerous churches were raised that now constitute an important part of Spain's architectural heritage.

Fitero: Site of the first Cistercian monastery in Spain. Belonged to Castile in the twelfth century and became a strategic enclave due to its common border with Navarre and Aragon. Important treaties between the three Christian empires were signed in its vicinity.

Fortress of Salvatierra: To the south of Ciudad Real, on the Muradal road that connected Castile to Andalusia, there lies this fantastic fortress, much fought over by both Christians and Muslims due to its strategic location. During the reign of Alfonso VIII, it was governed by the military order of the Calatravans, before being conquered by the troops of the Almohad caliph al-Nasir toward the end of 1211. That event provoked such an outcry in Christendom that many compared it with the fall of Jerusalem, and it incited the pope to convoke a Holy Crusade against the Almohads in Spain.

Marrakesh: Capital of the Almohad Empire. In Arabic, its name means "city of God." In the twelfth century, it supported an important cultural and commercial life. The Alcazaba, or Royal Palace, is located close to the Aljama, or mosque, whose minaret is identical to the Giralda, the tower of the Cathedral in Seville, which marks the former location of the Almohad mosque.

Navas de Tolosa: To the south of the pass of Muradal and the east of Despeñaperros, close to the present-day town of Santa Elena, is the scene of what was probably the most crucial battle in the history of medieval Spain. "Nava" is a term describing a humid plain or wetland. Tradition attributed the naming of the famous battle, which took place on July 16, 1212, to the archbishop of Narbonne, because the "navas" in question were located near a fortress that was named for the nearby French city of Tolosa.

Author's Note

The difficult personal circumstances that have accompanied the writing of this novel compelled me, at times, to abandon it, but other times I would cling to it like salve and consolation for my pain. The long death struggle my father experienced in all that time was present in the better part of its pages, and maybe also in the background of the story I was trying to tell.

As Diego de Malagón dedicates all his achievements to his father, I would like to do the same.

It is all for you, Father. . . .

Acknowledgments

I don't want to finish these last few lines without thanking the enormous editing work performed at my side by dear friend Antonio Quintanilla, an expert in listening to stories and plot twists, with whom I've shared many hours and long conversations.

I must also recognize the incalculable assistance of Emeritus Professor Miguel Cordero del Campillo, an illustrious man and a source of pride for the veterinary profession, as well as, in my case, the provider of a good deal of the documentary materials I have made use of to get a sense of the history of this beautiful profession that I love so much, that of veterinarian. With even greater affection, I would like to acknowledge the hard work done by my mother, who translated for me, with inexhaustible patience and great ability, many of the remedies that appear in this novel, which come from an old tract on the albéitar's art written in the fifteenth century in the Latin dialect of the era.

Thank you, once again, to my editor, Raquel Gisbert, the soul of this project and the person responsible, of late, for pushing me to write.

And of course, I would like to recognize my family, particularly my wife, Pilar, for the uncommon patience she has shown in bearing with this project, which has grown to over 550 pages. As many as they are, I have just as many reasons to thank and cherish you. . . .

Thanks to all.

Grupo Planeta

OPEN ROAD

INTEGRATED MEDIA

Open Road Integrated Media is a digital publisher and multimedia content company. Open Road creates connections between authors and their audiences by marketing its ebooks through a new proprietary online platform, which uses premium video content and social media.

Videos, Archival Documents, and New Releases

Sign up for the Open Road Media newsletter and get news delivered straight to your inbox.

Sign up now at
www.openroadmedia.com/newsletters

FIND OUT MORE AT
WWW.OPENROADMEDIA.COM

FOLLOW US:
@openroadmedia and
Facebook.com/OpenRoadMedia